THE TREE
OF LIFE

In memory of my parents
Sima and Abraham Rosenfarb

THE TREE OF LIFE

(A Trilogy of Life in the Lodz Ghetto)

Book 1: On the Brink of the Precipice, 1939

Chava Rosenfarb

translated from the Yiddish by the author
in collaboration with Goldie Morgentaler

The University of Wisconsin Press
Terrace Books

The University of Wisconsin Press
1930 Monroe Street
Madison, Wisconsin 53711

www.wisc.edu/wisconsinpress/
3 Henrietta Street
London WC2E 8LU, England

Library of Congress Cataloging-in-Publication Data

Rosenfarb, Chawa, 1923–
[Boym fun lebn. English]
The tree of life: a trilogy of life in the Lodz Ghetto / Chava Rosenfarb; translated from the
Yiddish by the author in collaboration with Goldie Morgentaler.
p. cm.—(Library of world fiction)
Reprint. Originally published: Melbourne, Australia: Scribe, c1985.
Contents: Bk. 1. On the brink of the precipice.
ISBN 0-299-20454-5 (pbk.: alk. paper)
1. Holocaust, Jewish (1939–1945)—Fiction. I. Title. II. Series.
PJ5129.R597B613   2004
839'.134—dc22   2004053592

Terrace Books, a division of the University of Wisconsin Press, takes its name from the
Memorial Union Terrace, located at the University of Wisconsin–Madison. Since its in-
ception in 1907, the Wisconsin Union has provided a venue for students, faculty, staff,
and alumni to debate art, music, politics, and the issues of the day. It is a place where the-
ater, music, drama, dance, outdoor activities, and major speakers are made available to the
campus and the community. To learn more about the Union, visit www.union.wisc.edu.

Acknowledgements

Many people assisted me in preparing this book for publication. I thank them all full-heartedly. But I especially want to thank my daughter, Dr. Goldie Morgentaler, for her love, for her selfless hard work, her dedication and devotion to me in all my literary endeavors.

Ch. R.

"Love thy brother as thyself."

Rabbi Hillel

"Die Erstellung des Ghettos ist selbstverständlich nur eine Übergangsmassnahme. Zu welchen Zeitpunkten und mit welchen Mitteln das Ghetto und damit die Stadt Lodz von Juden gesäubert wird, behalte ich mir vor. Endziel muss jedenfalls sein, dass wir diese Pestbeule restlos ausbrennen.

Der Regierungspräsident
gez. Uebelhor.
Lodz, am 10 Dezember 1939"

("It is self-evident that the establishment of the Ghetto is only a transitory measure. I reserve my judgment on the point in time and the means by which the Ghetto, and with it the city of Lodz, should be cleared of Jews. In any case, the final goal should be to relentlessly burn out this pestilent boil.")

Contents

		Page
1.	BOOK I: *THE YEAR 1939*	1
2.	BOOK II: *THE YEARS 1940–1942*	311
3.	BOOK III: *THE YEARS 1942–1944*	705
4.	GLOSSARY	1077

BOOK I

The Year 1939

Chapter One

SAMUEL ZUCKERMAN was born in Lodz. His great-grandfather Shmuel Ichaskel Zuckerman had been among the first Jews to leave the Ghetto and settle downtown. He had been one of the pioneers who had laid the foundations for the Jewish cotton trade and textile industry in town, and it was he who in the year 1836 had moved into the massive brick house at No. 17 Novomieyska Street, where Samuel had lived until recently, and where his two daughters were born.

The family archives were filled with piles of documents reflecting not only the growth of the Zuckerman clan, but also that of the Jewish community in Lodz. And while still a *gymnasium* student, Samuel had liked to sneak into the cellar and browse among the dusty papers; he was drawn to them not so much by their content as by the breath of generations gone by that reached him through them. At that time, however, he had been too busy with his own growth, with his own pulsating young life, to summon patience for a serious study of his origins. Then he had been merely proud to be so deeply rooted in his city, and it was sufficient for him to know that he could prove the fact at any time.

Samuel studied at the town's most respected *gymnasium* where there was a *numerus clausus* against Jews; a Jew being permitted to enter only after rigorous examination, or through the back door, by handing over a swollen envelope. (In Samuel's case, the application of both these methods brought about the desired result.) He quickly rose to become first in his class, and the teachers 'justly' appraised his erudition, by seeing to it that he always stood second on the class rosters. The gold medal after the *matura* examinations was bestowed on a blue-eyed, flaxen-haired young man, since it was not fitting that a Jew should be acknowledged to know more than a whole class of pure-bred Slavs.

Samuel did not study worldly subjects only. His father, who had discarded traditional attire for more modern clothing, provided Samuel with a private tutor — an enlightened Jew and the best Hebrew scholar in town — and three times a week, summer and winter, year in and year out, Samuel would go to the tutor's house to enrich his knowledge of what it meant to be a Jew.

Samuel's father was an energetic, stocky man whose body betrayed not a trace of flab or weakness. He looked as if he had been constructed according to a strict geometrical design. Even his hard muscular face, framed by black *Junker* sideburns, looked like a symmetrical rectangle in which two black dots had been imbedded: a pair of eyes whose gaze spoke the language of stubbornness and determination. He knew precisely what kind of person Samuel was to become, and following the blueprint he had in his mind, he shaped — with a strictness allowing no room for resistance — the character of his son, who was

3

one day to inherit the textile factory and the cotton business and to carry on with pride the family's eminent name into the future.

Samuel allowed himself to be guided by his father, for the latter was God's ambassador on earth and to resist him would have meant forsaking the Creator of All Being Himself. Even during his adolescence, the years of rebellion, Samuel had lived his days in equanimity and without incident. If, during those years, the pedestal of authority began to crumble in his heart, it was rather the authority of God, and not the authority of his father, that was in question. His piety had weakened during that time; his belief in God as a moral law-maker was gradually replaced by a more abstract, more philosophical conception. But for Samuel, who from childhood on had been accustomed to subordinating himself to rules, there had to be someone who kept order, who knew the difference between good and evil. Therefore his father grew in stature in his eyes in direct proportion to the loss of his faith in God.

In general, Samuel developed no habit of questioning anything. He was quite satisfied with the way of life his father had imposed on him. His worldly studies never conflicted with the piety and strict observance of religious laws at home. His doubts in God as a moral law-maker and his belief in his father complemented each other, and everything else fell into place, creating somehow a sufficiently harmonious pattern. He was not the one to search for any defect in it. Life was easy and comfortable in its daily ordered rhythm. True, there was no place in it for any particular family warmth, for spontaneous explosions of emotions, for great experiences of joy or sorrow, but there was instead a feeling of solidity and reassurance that everything was right with the world, with his family, and also with him, the maturing young man.

Samuel's mother resembled her husband in stature. She was a tall strong woman, full-bosomed and rounded, wrapped in countless skirts, crinolines and slips. She possessed a pair of lively, almost mischievous eyes — which Samuel had inherited — whose fire she was evidently unable to smother. Yet she never laughed or smiled. It seemed as if her large body were hiding a treasure of joy and laughter imprisoned in a multitude of corset strings and belts, like a bursting barrel secured by metal hoops to prevent it from exploding.

As a child, Samuel used to hunger for his mother's openness, for her free laughter; a hunger that was never satisfied. She had no time for him. From morning until night she was kept busy managing the big household, checking, calculating, commanding the army of servants and receiving guests or merchants from out of town. Instead of her laughter, he would hear the sound of her harsh voice to the accompaniment of the keys dangling from a ring at her belt, jingling, as a warning of how senseless it was to approach her. However, at rare moments, when in a surge of motherly love she would gather little Samuel into her arms, or allow him to embrace her legs and to submerge his head in her whispering secret skirts, which gave off a sharp sweet smell — his eyes would fill with tears, as if he were burying his head between the leaves of a big onion. These happy embraces were followed by a discomfort of an awakened but unsatisfied craving. Samuel was left with his mother's distinctive odour in his nostrils, with the echo of the keys in his ears, and with an unbearable frightening loneliness during which he hated his mother as much as he loved her. As he grew older, however, Samuel gradually forgot these childhood moods and impressions.

In the twenty-first year of his life, he found himself under the wedding canopy with his bride, Matilda Auerbach, whose father was a wealthy merchant from Leipzig. The young couple was installed in the family home on Novomieyska Street, and among the items purchased for the newlyweds was a piano, a piece of furniture which had never before adorned the abode of the Zuckermans. Indeed, as soon as Matilda began to feel herself secure as mistress of the house, she began to organize concerts in the spacious salon, inviting the best musicians in town to participate. They brought along their flutes and clarinets, their violins and cellos, while Matilda, a transported smile on her face, accompanied them faithfully on the piano, carrying them along into lofty realms.

At first Samuel was repulsed by the noise of the musical sounds filling his home. Irritated, uncomfortable, he would wander like a stranger from one room to another, oppressed by the feeling that the big building had suddenly lost its solidity and was rocking on its foundations, that the vibrating walls would collapse at any moment. He stumbled over the large open instrument cases chaotically strewn about the floor; his clothes caught on the music stands, and he collided with the musicians themselves who seemed to him like invaders from another planet. He did not know what to say to them and felt self-conscious and miserable.

But gradually the chaos in the tunes seemed to subside and, instead, Samuel grew to appreciate their harmony, at first only with his ears, then with his heart as well. More than once, almost against his will, he found himself glued to the armchair near the huge oven, letting the music penetrate deeper and deeper into his soul and take him more and more thoroughly apart. And so it happened that along with the music he discovered Matilda. He was unable to take his eyes off her, as her fingers caressed the keyboard, as she languorously moved her full white arms, her head and body swaying in time to the rhythm of the musical waves; she became a part of the sea of sounds that inundated the entire salon. And the more dreamy and unearthly the music became, the more awakened Matilda seemed; as if in that very dreaminess she were most alive and liberated, all her charms and desires set free.

He was in love with her, convinced that it was she for whom he had been waiting all his life. It even seemed to him that he remembered her from some distant past, from another life. Sometimes, as she sat at the piano, he would instead of her, or perhaps in her, see his own mother, transformed into one who undid the many strings of her corsets, releasing her laughter and gaiety to pour forth into the melancholy sweetness of the melodies.

There were moments when he felt something soft, something acutely sensitive vibrating within him. He, who until now had been a 'surface' person, who had been able to call everything by its name with so much self-assurance, and who had had such a concrete sense of reality, began to feel uncertain and vague, to experience a bitter-sweet indeterminate craving, as if something crippled yet trembling with life was desperately trying to break through the thick icy core inside him, crying to come out.

He never understood how it was that Matilda's concerts had such an impact on him. Later on, he explained it to himself by saying that at that time he had been ready for a change anyway, that her music was only like a finger touching the proper chord, to the tone of which his whole being responded. At other times, he explained this state of mind as a presentiment, a preparation of his soul for the tragedies which were to follow: the death of his parents.

His father died suddenly of a heart attack; the mother followed him a year later. It seemed that her sturdiness and strength had been supported solely by her husband. Once he was gone, she shrank and collapsed like a building which had lost its foundations. She expired with an obvious tragic submissiveness. Similarly, Samuel's mourning for her became incorporated into his enormous grief at the loss of his father.

He himself almost collapsed under the weight of his heavy heart. For many long weeks he wandered, sick and apathetic, around the big house, feeding on his pain, driven by the longing for the familiar strong face, the well-known harsh voice, the wise sharp gaze of the dark eyes and the self-assured commanding gestures. It seemed that his father, after he had left the world, had become even stricter and more God-like in Samuel's tormented memory, and yet, at the same time more human than ever before. Samuel was ashamed to admit to himself that it was precisely in his sorrow that he discovered his father's weaknesses, that he began to weigh the latter's good and bad deeds. Beneath his pain, he was amazed to discover a feeling of relief that he had been freed of the bonds that had cramped him for so long. Indeed, the world had crashed down over his head, but from under the ruins a restlessness, an impatience for the future and a new beginning were rising.

Thus it happened that after those critical weeks, Samuel took over his father's factory and cotton business, with a clear head and a new self-confidence. He was twenty-seven years old, the father of two daughters, and it was high time to become a man.

Samuel's father had seen to it that his son should be well-prepared for his new role. Moreover, his death opened up some locked cells in Samuel's own mind, out of which an abundance of ideas, plans and projects began to pour. In one year he reconstructed and renovated the factory. The good name of the family allowed him credit everywhere, providing him with an opportunity to implement his innovations without any afterthought or fear. For the first time in his life he was driven by an impetus; the days were too short for him, the weeks were passing too quickly. He no longer had time for Matilda's concerts. He saw neither her nor his two daughters with whom he had been used to play every day. Success beckoned to him. With meteoric speed his fame flashed across the industrial sky of his hometown. He found himself in the company of the greatest business brains in Lodz, and a still greater future was forecast for him.

But Samuel, like many a man, was unable to continue with the same exuberance. Gradually his enthusiasm cooled. His plans realized, his spontaneous ambitions satisfied, he felt hollow and washed out. His work acquired the tediousness of labour, and once it lost the taste of creativity, it became routine. Boredom set in.

This was the time when Samuel inaugurated the 'Saturday Nights' in his spacious salon. After all the years of preoccupation with dry down-to-earth problems — which had only recently seemed truly dry and down-to-earth — he felt hungry for another kind of nourishment for his mind. He wanted to be with people who were far from the business world, who could bring back the moods he had used to experience at Matilda's concerts. But he knew that music alone would not satisfy him at this time. He was too much involved in the present which restlessly bubbled and boiled like a stormy sea around him; he was too much attuned to what was happening in the world, in his country, in his town, to be able to remove himself from it completely. His insatiable curiosity was like a sensitive apparatus endowed with countless antennae stretching in all directions, eagerly snatching at bits of information, facts, happenings from everywhere, to feed his greedy mind. Therefore, more than anything else, he craved for an exchange of thoughts and for the kind of pleasure which only serious profound conversation can give a man.

Matilda greeted Samuel's 'Saturday Nights' project enthusiastically. She still devoted a few hours a day to her piano, but not as fervently as before and rather out of a sense of boredom and depression than out of pleasure. She was unhappy. The years of Samuel's active creative life were bitter ones for her. She had no idea of the substance of her husband's days, since the two of them never confided in each other, and if there was any intimacy between them, it was a sensual one, without words. If Matilda had reached a certain level of maturity at this time, she demonstrated it by her ability to carry her torment and heavy heart with a proudly raised head. But she still moved about in a dreamlike world, in lofty spheres where factories, machines, the daily talk of business and prosaic facts were of no significance.

Samuel's project of weekly social gatherings in their home was for Matilda a sign of his return to her, and she began, with a vivaciousness uncommon to her, to assist in the realization of his wish. She displayed taste and inventiveness in creating the proper atmosphere and invited some of her musician friends to appear with her. And although she found the topics of conversation rather unfamiliar and uninteresting, the warm twinkle in Samuel's eyes was sufficient encouragement and reward for her.

The most prominent intellectuals in town were among the guests participating in the 'Saturday Nights'. Most of them were social activists, philanthropists, Zionist leaders as well as writers and journalists. Sipping cup after cup of strong tea with lemon and munching cookies baked by Reisel, the cook, especially for the occasion, the eloquent visitors discussed all kinds of topics, beginning with music and ending with the problems of present-day Zionism.

Samuel considered himself a Zionist. "I am a salon Zionist," he would say jokingly, and as a matter of fact he had his own conception of Zionism. He thought that a Jewish homeland would be of great advantage to the poor Jewish masses of the Diaspora; but he himself was too deeply rooted in the country where he lived, in the city his grandfathers had helped to build, to be able to call any other place home. He loved Lodz, the ugly dusty Polish Manchester. He felt the words of the city's poet, Julian Tuwim, in his veins and quoted him enthusiastically, "Let Sorrento, Ganges and Crimea fight for the crown of glorious beauty, but give *me* Lodz. Its dirt and smoke are much dearer to my heart . . ." When Samuel noticed a new building going up in the city, a new shop opening on Piotrkowska, the main street, a newly-paved road or a bit of greenery planted in an empty lot, his heart would swell with pride: his city was growing, expanding! If he happened to spend a few weeks abroad, he missed the particular smell of his smoky dirty hometown. His attachment to it extended to embrace the entire country. He was a devout Polish patriot.

The 'Saturday Nights' were carried on in an elegant Polish, interspersed with expressions or quotations from French, Russian or Hebrew. The discussions often grew heated; they resembled a fire into which, to keep it lively, the guests threw arguments and counter-arguments, came to conclusions, and concluded nothing. Nevertheless, it was exciting to throw one's thoughts onto the heap of other thoughts, to test them and see what was left.

Most of all, the guests' attitudes towards the divergent loyalties of Jew and citizen were ventilated. Were the Jews good citizens of Poland, the disputants asked themselves, if they led lives of isolation, shunning any contact with Polish national life and culture? Samuel's guests defined and redefined the term 'nation', questioning whether the Jews were a nation at all, and if so, how could they be good Polish patriots, if they considered themselves good Jews? And what if the interests of the Jewish nation collided with those of the Polish nation — what would a Jew choose to protect, the shirt on his body, or his own skin? And how was a Jew supposed to behave if he became a soldier and had to fight against another Jew, a citizen of an enemy country? If the Jews were indeed a nation, then the result would be, that two people belonging to the same nation might have to kill each other, while defending the interests of two alien nations. Then how could one reconcile the fact that Jews might be very good citizens and patriots of the countries they lived in, and yet feel closer to the Jews of other countries than to the people with whom they shared the same soil?

Samuel himself was not sure what stand to take. At times he thought that Jewish interests should be tied more to the people among whom the Jews lived, than to the Jews of a foreign country; and since wars were fought in defence of those interests — a Jew of one country must consider a Jew of another country as that country's citizen, and not as a member of his own tribe. At other times, this thought was unbearable to him. He felt that the Jews of the world were united by something more powerful than all outside interests, by something sacred, and it was a sin that Jews should fight and destroy each other for any reason whatsoever.

The 'Saturday Nights' became a great success. Yet at the very moment of the 'salon's' greatest popularity, Samuel found himself losing interest in the whole idea. It was not that he was bored with the discussions, it was that the topics had become increasingly depressing. More and more often the theme of anti-Semitism came up and, after these 'Nights', Samuel felt a bitterness and fatigue that disturbed his sleep. At the same time he felt overfed with talk. Indeed, this was the rhythm that his life had acquired: his hunger for intellectual gratification and his desire for action rotated like the seasons of the year. First there had been Matilda's concerts, then the reconstruction of his factory and business, then the 'Saturday Nights'. Now, suddenly, he felt the need to build himself a new house.

The project had scarcely had time to ripen in his head before his enthusiasm for it was kindled with the same intensity as on similar occasions. He himself drew up the plans, worked on the blueprints, searched for the materials; and as long as the house was in the process of being built, he did not let a day go by without going over to see how it was coming along.

He had not expected, however, that it would be so difficult for him to move out from the house at No. 17 Novomieyska, where he had lived for nearly forty years. It suddenly occurred to him that if his forefathers lived on in him, then, in a sense, he must have lived in them too — even before his birth; that in a way he had come over to the old house from the ghetto, along with his great grandfather. As a result, he began to notice objects he had never noticed before in the old building, trying to guess who had brought in this or that item. He could not make up his mind about what to do with these cherished yet useless antiques, and finally decided that the cellar of his new house would be the most appropriate place to store them. This in turn nourished his guilt feelings for showing disrespect to those whom he revered and respected. So, he tried to convince himself that the tradition he seemed to be breaking would remain with him anyway; that where he lived, or what he did with the remnants of the old house was only meaningful insofar as these things helped him to hold on, only superficially, to the thread of past generations. But he knew too that he would never be able to part with all these relics until he could find a more tangible, a more meaningful and lasting proof that indeed the past lived on with him. And that was when he decided to write a book.

As soon as this idea took shape in his mind, he abandoned himself to its realization with his habitual excitement. He neglected his business. For hours on end he sat among piles of rotting papers, of creased yellow documents reeking of foulness, until his eyes, red with exhaustion, refused to serve him and he was forced to stop. He never questioned for a moment whether he had the qualities to make a writer, or whether the work he had set himself to do would be of any value. He did it for himself first of all, for his own peace of mind. But the more he submerged himself in his material, the more clearly he realized that what he was going to write would have to be much more than a family chronicle. His ancestors were so much a part of the city and its growth, that it was impossible to separate their story from that of the city. Consequently, after a time, Samuel stopped thinking of his work as a purely personal matter. He set out to chronicle the history of the Jews in the city of Lodz.

✦ ✦ ✦

It was the last day of the year 1938. Samuel was sitting in the office of his factory when the telephone rang. Immersed in a pile of papers, he absent-mindedly lifted the receiver and heard the fast hoarse voice of Professor Hager, "Zuckerman? I have something for you! A *Telefunken!* For your celebration tonight . . . of New Year . . . the occasion of your housewarming! You hear, Zuckerman? Paris, Amsterdam at the tip of your fingers!"

"But Professor," Samuel mumbled, despite the fact that he felt like leaving everything and rushing to take a look at the gift. "I'm against . . . as a matter of principle . . ."

The professor laughed, "Principle? Against what? Taking gifts? And this you're telling *me?*"

"I'm coming over to take it!" Samuel exclaimed. But as soon as he had hung up, he remembered that old Mr. Rumkowski was sitting outside in the waiting room. Old Mr. Rumkowski was a prominent social figure, an enthusiastic charity collector for Jewish causes as well as the founder and director of the orphanage in Helenovek, and not to receive him was impossible. So Samuel opened the door, calling in an apologetic yet slightly impatient tone, "Mr. Rumkowski! I've kept you waiting!" He stretched out both his hands to greet the visitor.

The elderly man rose abruptly from his chair, seeming taller than he really was. His face was splendidly expressive, strong and vivid, in spite of its marks of old age. He coughed, threw his dark creased hat on the seat behind him and adjusted his heavy winter coat which hung loosely on his drooping shoulders.

Hurriedly, with one hand, he combed his dishevelled silver hair, fixed his glasses on his nose with the other, and approached Samuel briskly. He shook one of the latter's outstretched hands, with the tip of his fingers. "Never mind. I'm used to waiting," he grumbled and, leaving Samuel behind, entered the office and strode over to the desk. He leaned on it with his hands, as if preparing to deliver a speech, while his sharp eyes inspected everything with spy-like curiosity. Then he turned to Samuel and looked him over with the same searching eyes.

Smiling, Samuel approached him. He had a weakness for the old man who possessed a strange charismatic hold over him. Was it the charm of a person who did not care only about himself? Was it his tireless energy, his readiness to act and his contempt for futile talk? Or was it his ability to forgo his own pride, to stand humiliation and abuse for the sake of a higher cause? Or was it simply that the old man's whole appearance was fatherly and patriarchal, that he radiated an imposing strength from his figure, his silver hair, the thick white eyebrows, the prominent nose, and the tight agitated mouth? Samuel was not really sure. But at this moment he was impatient and sighed with relief when he noticed Rumkowski pulling out a long slim receipt book from his pocket.

"I came to wish you a happy New Year." The old man waved the booklet and wrinkled his forehead as if to pull up the glasses that had slid to the tip of his nose. He peered at Samuel over the rims with a severe demanding look and bent his head like a bull about to charge.

"A happy New Year to you too!" Samuel answered courteously, reaching into his breast pocket. "How much do I owe you?"

The visitor straightened himself, raised his head and loosened his tight lips into a grimace that resembled a smile. His eyes glared at Samuel with prophetic strength, "Me, you owe nothing. You owe the Jewish community. You owe the Jewish orphans."

Samuel waved his pocketbook in the same way that Rumkowski was waving his receipt book, "Yes, yes . . . but how much?"

The offended visitor pouted. "Give me two, three hundred now, and we shall see about the rest after New Year." Samuel quickly counted the bills into Rumkowski's open palm. The old man's gray head shook rhythmically to the beat of Samuel's loud counting. Then his fingers, like the springs of a trap, snapped shut over the money, and with a gesture of triumph he made it vanish into the depth of his coat pocket. He filled out a receipt in his illegible writing and turned to Samuel, his face now smooth and mild. "I wish we had more Jews like you, my son." Samuel reached for his coat. "Where are you off to?" the old man asked, following him to the door. "A belly full of secrets, eh? Are you taking a droshky? Can you give me a lift?" Rumkowski noticed Samuel's hesitation. "Well, never mind. I'm used to running on foot from house to house, rain or shine."

In the street, on an impulse of guilt and enthusiasm, Samuel grabbed Rumkowski's hand. "You know what, Mr. Rumkowski? Tonight . . . come to my house. I invite you. A sort of celebration, and we shall drink to wet my new home." He bent over to the old man, blinking his eyes rouguishly at him. "Rosenberg will be there, and some other pocketbooks . . . Over a glass of schnapps . . . you know . . ."

Rumkowski wrinkled his forehead in order to catch the glasses that were again on the tip of his nose. "Rosenberg, you said? Bless you!"

"Will you come?"

"Can I refuse you, my son?" Rumkowski put up his collar, waved his hand and with the gait of one whose inner energy is struggling with the physical weakness of an old body, he marched away.

Samuel began to run through the windy street, looking for a droshky. One hand in his pocket, the other swinging his hat, his body bent forward; the head, richly covered with thick black hair, was exposed to the wind, and he left behind stretches of sidewalk with every leap of his long nimble legs, as if he were gliding, almost flying over its surface. His prominent nose now red from the frost trembled in lively animation, exhaling columns of steam. He felt light and strangely nervous. He would never have bought a radio, he assured himself. As a matter of principle he was against radios. But he could not refuse a gift, nor could he offend such dear friends as the Hagers.

Half an hour later he was on his way home, rocking happily in a droshky, the huge package containing the radio, on the seat beside him. Unexpectedly, the thought of his father entered his mind, making him realize that he had behaved ridiculously ever since the professor had called him up and told him about the radio. Perhaps his father had something to do with his silly joy over such a simple thing . . . such a childish thing?

A heavy snow had begun to powder the streets in a hurry to beautify the city for the approaching New Year. Gaiety hovered in the air, winding about the houses, reflecting on the faces of the passers-by and in the lights of the shops and restaurants. There was merriment in the rhythmical beat of horse hooves on the softened white pavement, and exuberance in the screams of the playing youngsters, in the calls of the newspaper boys and the bagel vendors on the corners.

Samuel stood in front of his new house on Narutowicz Street, the huge package at his side. He pressed his lips tightly together, trying to repress the gay sounds bubbling in his throat; instead, they escaped through his nostrils, in a panting tune broken up by the rhythm of his heavy breath. He entered the house and looked around. The vestibule was empty. A shaft of light like a path in the red of the carpet led to the half-opened door of the salon. Through it, he could see the back of Wojciech, the servant, who was polishing the floor. Besides the noise of the polisher, he could hear the hoarse voice of Reisel, the cook, giving orders to Renia, the nanny, and scolding Barbara, the cat, with a "Get away, you witch!" From the upper floor came the sound of open water faucets and the reedy voice of Junia, his younger daughter, singing the hit tune "I Shall Meet her at Nine O'clock."

Under cover of all these sounds, Samuel, the heavy load in his hands, sneaked unnoticed into his studio, shutting the door with his leg. He sank into the sofa. As he slowly pushed the parcel off to his side, his hat fell from his head. Too lazy to pick it up, he stretched his legs and played with it with the tips of his shoes, while he let his tired strained arms rest on his lap. He hated hats and wore them only on leaving or entering the house, so as not to displease Matilda who thought that a man should be as correctly dressed as a lady, and that it was not becoming to walk around with an unbuttoned coat, hands without gloves, and a head without a hat.

He shut his eyes and again wondered what was happening to him. Of course, he was relieved that the grim bitter year of 1938 was over. It had been a year of war scares, of Jewish troubles in Germany; a year when thousands of frightened

Jews with Polish citizenship were thrown out of the Third Reich and dumped on the other side of the Polish border, in Zbonshyn; a year during which the Polish government had circulated leaflets stating that the Jews were the enemies of Poland and should be made to leave the country. The old year had been so bad that the new one could not be worse, and therefore had to be better. It seemed to him that he was in a good mood because of tonight's ball which would celebrate the New Year as well and the new house. But he knew well enough that although all these reasons were true, his boyish frivolity, his inner light-heartedness stemmed from another source as well; a source that introduced a kind of mischievous delight into his mood, as if he had successfully played a trick on someone.

He stood up, shook off his coat, picked up his hat, rubbed his hands together and fell upon the gift like a bird of prey swooping down on its victim. After a few minutes, a mahogany box with big white knobs emerged from the wrapping paper. Eagerly he looked into the little window, his eyes scanning the black dots, at every dot the name of a city. He sighed wistfully. No, he did not want to run away from the world, he wanted to run towards it. Indeed, what he had thought about his father while riding in the droshky was true. His father had disliked the world, disliked modern appliances, new machines, new houses — betrayal. Samuel wondered what other preposterous things he might do on account of the memory of his father and came to the conclusion that the book he was about to write had to be written and done with as soon as possible.

He inserted the plug into the socket and turned the white knobs. The indicator inside the little window reached the mark with the word 'Paris'. Suddenly, a female voice burst out of the box, penetrating Samuel's ears with a loud yet agreeable intimacy, "J'attendrai . . . Le jour et la nuit . . . J'attendrai toujours . . ." Solemnly, he rubbed his hands together and threw himself upon the sofa. He felt a sweet melancholy and a longing.

Before long, the door thumped open and two young quivering bodies were pressing against him; soft moist lips covered his face with kisses. "Papa! Papa!" exultant screams mingled with the singing, filling the room with a confusion of noises. Then Matilda came in. She was wearing a bathrobe and her hair was covered with a thick towel in the shape of a turban. She did not look her best in this pre-ball outfit, and somehow Samuel felt deeply offended. She should not have appeared before him like that. Not now. She should have radiated a festive attractiveness; should have harmonized with the alluring voice coming from the radio, harmonized with his mood of romantic elation. He looked at the girls. They too were wearing their bathrobes and turbans on their heads: strings of wet hair clung to their moist foreheads. The sweet heavy smell of steam and soap invading his nostrils sobered him up completely. He stood up and placed himself opposite Matilda, legs spread apart, hands in his pockets. "A gift from the Hagers," he explained matter-of-factly.

Matilda's sensuous lips aimed at his, but landed on his chin instead, because she was wearing low-heeled slippers and he did not feel like bending down to her. "What a beautiful gift," she whispered, then added in a soft caressing voice, "You brought in so much mud with your galoshes . . ." That was not what she wanted to say; she was overcome by the kind of longing she usually felt for him in his presence. He winced nervously, and as he left the room, she followed him. "Samuel," she started again, but then she caught sight of herself in the vestibule mirror. Appalled, she turned her head away, adjusted the turban, rearranged her bathrobe and headed towards the stairs.

The door bell rang. Samuel let in a girl in a *gymnasium* coat. Clean white patches of snow lay on her dishevelled hair which escaped from underneath her beret. "Is Bella home?" she asked.

Samuel turned towards his studio and called his daughter, trying to raise his voice over the blare of the radio. Matilda's eyes fell on the mud puddle forming on the freshly polished floor around the visitor's shoes. "No rubbers!" she exclaimed indignantly, then called with despair in her voice, "Renia, bring a few newspapers, quick!"

The girl withdrew to the door as if she were ready to run away. But then Renia appeared, spread a few papers over the floor and invited the visitor to step on them. Bella had by now appeared as well. In her bathrobe, with the towel on her head, she looked as plump as Matilda. But there was also an air of heaviness about her which Matilda did not have. Her mouth, like her mother's, was sensuous; her eyes, although lively now, were usually nebulous and dreamy. Only her nose, long and slightly bumpy, was inherited from Samuel. Her features did not harmonize and she was not pretty. "This is Rachel Eibushitz," she introduced the girl to her parents.

"I came to borrow your books," Rachel said, and as soon as Bella vanished into her room, she fixed her eyes on the paper at her feet, as if to hide from the inquisitive attention of Matilda and Samuel. Samuel followed her gaze. Fat black headlines caught his eyes: "BENESH RETREATING ... HITLER DEMANDING..." The girl's muddy shoes covered the rest. Bella reappeared, pressing a heavy pile of books to her chest. She arranged them in Rachel's arms. "Thanks," Rachel said, allowing her face to relax. "My boy friend is waiting outside with a briefcase. Good night! I mean, Happy New Year!" she grinned and left.

Matilda turned to Bella. "Who was that?" she asked.

"I told you, Mama, a classmate of mine. She can't afford to buy books of her own."

"But she could afford better manners, couldn't she? She did not even greet us properly." Matilda turned to Samuel, " She said she had a boy friend waiting for her outside. At her age! And she did not even wipe the snow off her shoes. What an upbringing! I wonder what the girl's father does for a living."

"He's a barber," Bella replied, hurt.

Matilda waved her short chubby finger in Samuel's direction. "There, you see? With barber's daughters ..." She sighed. How tired she was of all the preparations for the ball, how much she needed Samuel's affection right now! And she remembered that he had not even stooped down to her a while ago, when she had kissed him. Irritated, she climbed the stairs.

Samuel followed her with his eyes. Her small full figure looked funny from his position at the bottom of the stairs. But he did not feel like laughing. "How heavy she is!" he thought with repulsion. He could not bear the sight of her. She had spoiled his mood, his pleasure in the radio, his anticipation of the ball. Her blue slippers touched the carpeted stairs quickly, softly, jumping up and down against her pink heels. Their rosy roundness touched him somehow. Against his will, his anger faded. "Madziu!" he called warmly, then hurried after her and folded her into his arms. "What's the matter? Are you mad?" he asked, looking into her misty eyes. He did not like her to be mad at him. He felt guilty towards her and did not know why.

She yielded to his embrace and smiled sadly, "I don't feel well when I'm not dressed, and you ... You don't like to see me like this, do you?"

He laughed, relieved, "Aren't you my wife, you silly girl?"

This was wrong again. "It's getting late," she said, and tore herself from his arms.

He undid his tie, loosened the button of his collar and went to take a bath. As he sat in the tub, he heard the muffled blare of the radio, the gay little voice of Junia, Matilda's shouts and the orders of Reisel, the cook. The door bell rang incessantly; messenger boys were arriving with flowers and gifts. Gradually, the pre-ball bustle and excitement took over the house. Samuel soaped himself energetically, as if trying to wash off all previous unpleasantness. He remembered the French song he had heard on the radio and rubbing the white soapy foam over his chest, he hummed in a low baritone, "*J'attendrai . . .*"

✦ ✦ ✦

The ball was in full swing. All the lights were on in the salon and the lustrous glitter of the crystal chandeliers and candelabras made everything sparkle with a glow of its own. The new mahogany buffet tables, a creation of Woodke, a German and the best carpenter in town, were crowded with vases out of which luscious flowers poked their heads through thin green ferns, so delicate that they looked like the filigree work of a meticulous artist. There was also an arrangement of potted plants the size of miniature trees filling the niche of the bay window like a screen of greenery, creating the illusion of a garden. The design of tangled broad-fingered leaves seemed to compete in beauty with the silvery design of the screen created by the frost on the window panes.

In that festive play of light, flowers and greenery, the guests whirled to the tune of the Viennese Waltz. The stiffness and formality of the early evening having faded, the atmosphere was becoming increasingly carefree and frivolous. Bella, dressed in her white tulle dress, her long brown tresses unbraided and spread out over her arms and back, was sitting at the piano, accompanying the dancers. Her fingers with their short nails, which she had the habit of biting to the quick so that she often had to bandage them, now ran whimsically over the keyboard. Her eyes, which followed the dancers, reflected her gaiety as well as the green sparkle of the emerald in the heart-shaped pendant adorning her neck. She forgot that she was the ugly duckling of the family. Now she felt beautiful and romantic. Close to her, leaning against the piano, waited the young doctor, Michal Levine, to whom she had been introduced a while ago. Slim, pale, with an earnest intense face and brooding eyes, he looked like a revolutionary, like one of the fighters against the tsar, ready to go to Siberia or to the gallows for his ideals. He did not really fit in here, yet it suited the two of them to become friendly, even though Bella's heart was hopelessly occupied by someone else.

The dancers passed by her in a faster, increasingly vertiginous swirl. She noticed her sister Junia in the arms of the athletically built painter, Mr. Guttman, another of the guests whom she was seeing for the first time. Junia, scarcely touching the floor with her feet, seemed to be hanging almost completely on the strong arms of her partner. She laughed richly, throwing back her head, as was her habit, and shaking her short pitch black hair.

The pair was followed by Mrs. Hager, the professor's wife, on Samuel's arms. Mrs. Hager giggled as she pleaded, "Enough, Mr. Zuckerman, I can't go on!" Her small feet stumbled between Samuel's big ones, as if they were looking for a place to put themselves down.

Then Bella saw the 'Millionaire', Mr. Adam Rosenberg with his bony wife Yadwiga. They gave the impression of a couple of love birds, caressing each other and kissing discreetly, then looking around proudly, in the hope that someone had noticed. Mr. Rosenberg's bald head glistened under the light of the chandeliers. Every now and then, he removed his hand from his wife's waist, to investigate the few long hairs that grew above one of his ears, checking if they were properly spread out over the middle of his skull. Puffing and panting, he pressed his immense belly to the frame of his skeletal wife who wore a long purple dress with a low back. On that back, her protruding shoulder blades moved in and out, up and down, like the parts of a machine. Her husband constantly stepped on the train of her dress, and she constantly rescued it from under his shoes. Bella could not look at the couple without a pang. She disliked them, and was so much, so hopelessly in love with their son, Mietek.

Bella rivetted her eyes to her mother, who whirled by in her taffeta décolleté dress. Matilda's chestnut hair had a reddish sheen and was arranged in a smooth Greek style which gave her face a classical look. In her black suede pumps, she seemed taller and slimmer than she actually was. She wore a new corset and only her large bosom, emerging slightly from her décolleté, bore witness to the fullness of her body. There was something statuesque about her. Only her eyes seemed alive. Sadly, languorously, they wandered from the face of her partner, Dr. Harkavi, to the faces of the other guests, as if she were looking for someone. Dr. Harkavi, Samuel's classmate and friend, hovered over her like a tall bent tree with two outstretched branches hugging a short stem.

Then Bella noticed Professor Hager and Mrs. Feiner dancing. Mrs. Feiner, the only woman at the ball who did not wear any jewellery or make-up, was the directress of a Jewish *gymnasium* attended by the daughters of rather poor but slightly progressive Jewish parents. Her gray hair, cut in the fashion of the twenties, was gathered at the back of her neck by a big brown comb. Her dress was simple, black, buttoned up to her chin, a corsage was pinned to the left of her flat bosom; it looked like the dress she wore to work at the *gymnasium*. Her shoes were low-heeled and her step was neither light nor feminine, rather it was soldierly; yet Bella sensed a kind of feminine charisma in her manner. Professor Hager waltzed with her hurriedly, clumsily, but it was obvious that they were enjoying themselves.

Close by, danced Mr. Rumkowski. Bella was amazed to see how nicely he led Mrs. Harkavi by the waist, led her against all the accepted rules of dancing, and yet somehow harmoniously. Neither Mr. Rumkowski nor Mrs. Harkavi uttered a word. His face was serious and concentrated, hers was expressionless and dull. He held his head much too close to her cheek. Their eyes were motionless; his, hot and staring, aimed, over the rims of the glasses on the tip of his nose, at the blue of hers; and hers, indifferent, gazed at the floor. Bella had the impression that Mr. Rumkowski was holding a big rubber doll which, according to his whim, moved either left or right.

Behind them, in the other part of the spacious salon, danced the younger and better dancers. There, trains of dresses flew up in the air, shoes stamped, faces flashed by in a circular whirl; laughter and cheers mingled with the applause and bravos of those who took their pleasure in watching from chairs along the walls.

Bella lingered on the Viennese Waltz, repeating it a few times. The Viennese

Waltz was the most appropriate for the moment about to come: the twelfth hour. Young Dr. Levine, who leaned against the piano, looked at his wrist watch. Bella's heart pounded solemnly, impatiently. Levine lifted a finger . . . still another minute . . . another second. She made herself ready and drew in her breath. Finally she fell upon the keyboard with both hands, fingers spread apart. The piano burst out with a thunder of heavy vibrating chords. The lights went out.

For a moment it was very dark and very quiet in the salon. But soon cheers and cries of good wishes and blessings filled the air. Bella climbed onto the piano stool and shouted into the darkness, "Happy New Year, Papa! Happy New Year, Mama!" But her own voice frightened her. She wanted to get off the chair and run to kiss her parents, to embrace old Miss Diamand, her literature teacher who had been invited at her request. She wanted to shake the hand of Dr. Levine. But she was afraid to move. For a while she stood there, completely lost, trying to discern the silhouettes of the guests, to recognize all those who a while ago had pirouetted by in lively dance. But all she could see was the white reflection of faces, hands and necks. They looked like bodyless demons. And now she felt as though something had unexpectedly entered the room and remained hovering over their heads: a sudden, incomprehensible, stupendous fright.

The lights went on again. Wojciech, the servant, dressed in his Sunday best and no longer completely sober, came in with a tray loaded with glasses and wine bottles which clinked lightly in his unsteady hands, as if they too were kissing and wishing each other a happy New Year. Behind Wojciech followed Reisel dressed in her Sabbath best. She wore a silken dress which hung unevenly from her hips; a dress which, the girls said, still remembered King Sobieski's times. She carried two trays with canapés. Swiftly and with servile coquetry, she jumped from one guest to another, offering her fare along with an abundant blessing, pronounced in her juicy Yiddish, "Have a good New Year, people! Have a good New Year, Madams!" She addressed everyone in the plural, as if each of them had the value of more than one person.

Samuel gathered the members of his family and embraced and kissed them with great fervour. Then he jumped onto a chair in the middle of the salon and, with a glass of wine in one hand and a canapé in the other, made a witty toast in honour of the New Year. The crowd drank *lechaim*, so that Samuel's good wishes would come true, then drank again, to make doubly sure — and then a third glass, so that there would be no doubt . . .

Chairs shuffled as the guests sat down in loose disorder. Samuel on one side of the room, Matilda on the other, walked around, making certain that everyone had his hands occupied with food and his mind, with conversation. Once in a while Matilda and Samuel exchanged glances across the room. The wine travelling through their bodies made their heads swim; they were aware of each other with a strange acute clarity, while the distance created between them by the presence of the guests caused them to feel more attached to each other than ever. Samuel wished that Matilda might always look as she looked tonight: her face fresh, her figure full but not flabby, and her eyes so strange in their secret shine, so tempting. He thought that she was the prettiest woman in the room and the only desirable one. All his limbs sang praise to her, his delicate, sensitive loved one, whose yielding body often made him whisper, "You must love me for ever and ever. Because I cannot live without your love."

But another Samuel, also awakened deep inside him by the power of the wine, the Samuel who was somewhat detached from the gaiety around him, knew clearly all the while he was recalling these images of his wife, that Matilda was in truth no more than a marginal note on the big full page of his every-day life; that the page itself, filled with plans, with work, was dry, loveless and full of longing for her whose name was not Matilda, who was nameless. Now he dared to admit to himself that sometimes in the evenings he did not feel like going home, not even in order to work on his book, but felt an urge to run after the other one, the passionate one, the powerful and submissive one, who would submerge him in a bottomless sea of sublime pleasure. He wanted to look for her everywhere, even among the cabaret dancers or the girls in his factory, even among the loose women and prostitutes. Yet at the same time, he was also aware of his inability to deceive Matilda; a disconcerting awareness which embittered him slightly and kindled a whimsical impulse in him — to punish Matilda who was so attractive, so alluringly beautiful tonight. Feeling her eyes on him, he purposely exaggerated the innocent flirtation he had been carrying on with the charming porcelain beauty, Mrs. Harkavi.

Matilda noticed his every move. It seemed to her that she heard every word, every compliment coming out of his mouth, so close to the ear of the young lady. She could not bear his way of talking to women. He befriended them and gained their confidence so easily. He amused them with his carefree boyish charm, handing out abundant smiles and looks which should have been only for her. In fact, she was jealous of his companionship with people in general. She would shrink with shame when they went out on the Sabbath, for a walk, and Samuel would stop to chat with the janitors at the gates, with the Jews in long traditional overcoats, on their way from the synagogue, or with the groups of sloppily-dressed young men gathered in front of the library. Sometimes he completely forgot about her, letting her stand at the side, unheeded and alone. She hated him for this and knew that she hated him because she loved him so powerfully and helplessly. Her soul, calm in its essence, so rich and beautiful, was like a restless insecure bird longing for a solid branch to stand on, to lean against; because she was not sure of her husband. Even at the moments when he said "I love you," — and how much she wanted to believe him! — her being could not sense that love; it was a word without a backing. Therefore she was always yearning for him, even in his arms, even during the moments of their greatest intimacy.

Miss Diamand, a tiny gray-haired elderly lady with a pale almost transparent face and a pair of childlike watery-blue eyes, was sitting in front of the bay window among the leafy plants. Wrapped in a mauve shawl, a big glass of soda water cupped in her bony fingers, she sipped a few drops at a time, like a bird, raising her head after each sip. She was Bella's beloved literature teacher, her personal invitée, and Bella, who had scarcely been able to exchange a word with her through the entire evening, was now navigating in her direction through the clusters of eating, talking and jesting guests.

She was stopped mid-way by her sister. "Come with me!" Junia exclaimed, pulling Bella along. Junia's black bangs hung like curtain fringes over her sparkling eyes. Laughing, she threw her arm around Bella's neck and whispered in her ear, "To Guttman!" Bella tried to free herself, but Junia would not let go. "Come, you'll talk to a real man!" She winked in the direction of the buffet where the painter Guttman was standing, absorbed in a conversation with Dr. Levine. She giggled, "Two satellites of two big stars have met. Editor Mazur doesn't take a step without his protegé artist, and Dr. Harkavi doesn't move without his assistant. Bella love," she tickled her sister, "don't you see that those two are meant for us? But please, no illusions. Guttman is mine!" The two young men, busy with each other, did not notice the approaching girls. Junia grabbed Guttman's arm without ceremony and exclaimed, "We've come to disturb your very interesting conversation!"

Guttman pinched Junia's cheek, "The gipsy girl is here!" he smiled.

"You treat me like a child," Junia pouted, and immediately pushed herself through to the buffet and its trays of food. She speared two chopped liver canapés onto a fork and lifted them to Guttman's mouth. The painter willingly took a bite and she started to repeat the procedure with Dr. Levine. But before she had time to carry the canapés to his mouth, the young man pushed her hand away. "It's kosher," she assured him. "Don't you like meat?" He shook his head and she looked with dismay into his eyes, "I can see it in your face. You look . . . You know like who? Like Gandhi. Gandhi to the smallest detail! And perhaps you are a . . . How do they call it? A vegetarian?"

"Right," he answered.

"A real one?" She opened her eyes so wide that their whites seemed to twinkle. "Impossible! You probably eat meat when no one is looking. A chicken leg? A roast? No?" She put her free hand on his chest. "Let me at least touch such a creature! Full of grass inside, eh? But if it is so, then how can you be a . . . a man?" With a spiteful gesture she shoved the two rejected canapés into her own mouth.

Embarrassed by her sister's arrogance, Bella felt like hiding somewhere and biting her nails. She edged away from Junia and the two young men. All of a sudden, the anxiety of the previous moment, when she had stood on the piano stool in the dark room, took hold of her again. It seemed to her that she was taking part in a kind of demonic gathering, which she was simultaneously seeing from the outside, and wondering who or what had driven out the familiar intimate atmosphere of her home. Then she noticed Miss Diamand in the vestibule. The old lady was taking leave of Matilda and Samuel. Wojciech, clad in his winter jacket, wearing a tall hat with ear muffs, stood nearby, ready to take the guest home.

Fragile Miss Diamand clumsily buttoned her coat and wound her mauve shawl around her head and neck; the mauve frame made her small pale face appear even smaller and paler. She blinked at Bella with watery eyes. "Thank you, child," She whispered softly, "for inviting me."

"You did not enjoy yourself, Miss Diamand," Bella mumbled.

The teacher's parched hand stroked her cheek. "On the contrary, child. Thanks to you I didn't spend the evening alone." And to reassure Bella, she became even more confidential. "We have a tradition, my roommate and I, of spending New Year's together. But this year she had to visit relatives." Saying this, she planted her lips on Bella's forehead, turned and left, followed by the muffled-up Wojciech.

Bella had scarcely re-entered the salon, when she felt a pair of warm hands cover her eyes. Too distracted to guess who it was, she freed herself and turned around. "Mr. Mazur!" She cried out.

"Come, let's find your father," the editor proposed, and holding hands they made their way through the chaos of scattered chairs, passing groups of chattering guests. Here and there they were stopped. Editor Mazur had something to say to everyone: a proverb, an anecdote, a parable. Bella listened to his talk, savouring her regained calm and festive mood. She liked Mazur and was as captivated by his quaint charm as everyone else. He did not have a very imposing figure and there was little in his demeanour to justify his attraction. He was of middle height and half bald; his colourless and sagging face should have escaped notice, yet it arrested and hypnotized. And Bella loved his loquacity. There was no finesse or smoothness in it, but rather something passionate and Hasidic; his enthusiasms were sharp, his bitterness salty. Bella found him stimulating; he led her mind onto unknown roads. He was a good listener as well, the only person frequenting the house who paid real attention to her.

Samuel was animatedly conversing with some pretty young ladies who surrounded him in a colourful lively circle, when he noticed Mazur and Bella approaching. He disengaged himself and looked around for Wojciech, who had returned from seeing Miss Diamand home, and was now walking among the guests with a bottle wrapped in a white towel. "Let's drink to more festivities and to peace in the world!" Samuel cried out, as Wojciech filled their glasses with champagne.

"And to us Jews. May we have some rest!" Mazur added.

"I want to make a toast too!" Bella raised her glass. "I drink," she gave a giddy little laugh, "to our new radio! May it play nice music and broadcast good news!"

"Bravo!" Mazur applauded and clinked his glass with hers. "And what, for instance, would you consider good news, Bella?"

Junia suddenly jumped forward from behind Samuel's back, "Do you know what I would consider good news?" She called out.

"Of course I know," Samuel interrupted her. "Not to have to go to school and to be able to skate all day long."

"Exactly!" Junia winked at Mazur roguishly. "School is the grave of youth, Mr. Editor, if you'll permit the expression." Her attention was diverted by Professor Hager. She rushed towards him with open arms. She brought him over, and they were followed by Matilda who was leaning on Mr. Rosenberg's arm. All three held glasses of champagne in their hands.

"All the best to you!" Mr. Rosenberg lifted his glass first to Mazur, then to Samuel, while his free hand was checking whether his few side hairs were properly spread over his bald head. He opened a mouth filled with a treasure of gold teeth, poured in the champagne, wiped his thick lips and embraced Samuel. However, he had scarcely taken his hands off Samuel's shoulders when his shining face grew overcast. He had noticed the majestic head of Mr. Rumkowski hovering over a gathering of prominient philanthropists. "Why did you let that beggar in?" he groaned.

Samuel could not restrain a smile. "Did you promise him something?"

Mr. Rosenberg glanced sideways at the editor. "Don't you know that I never try to extricate myself from my social obligations?" He waited for a laudatory remark from Mazur, but since the latter, usually so loquacious, did not utter a word, he went on, "Well, look. Does it make sense, at a ball, to investigate people's pockets?"

Matilda agreed with him. Neither Mr. Rumkowski nor a few of the other guests were to her taste. But she was used to the kind of invitations Samuel extended on his own, and now she undertook to change the subject and mend the spoiled mood. She gave a short uncertain glance at Samuel and said as if apropos, "I have good news, my friends. Samuel is writing a book about Lodz."

Resentment and disapproval flashed across Samuel's face. Only he had the right to let people know about his great project. And yet, in spite of his discomfort, he was pleased. It was the proper time and the proper place, since he had recently been feeling a great need to discuss his work.

Mr. Rosenberg's mood changed. He guffawed, showing his mouthful of golden teeth. "You're writing a novel?" he asked Samuel.

Samuel, somewhat intimidated, shook his head. "Heaven forbid. What I want is to put something down on paper about my ancestors, Lodz, the Jews . . ."

He wanted to say more, but Junia interrupted him with the exclamation, "look, Ma! The cat!"

They turned their heads to the piano where Barbara, the cat, was walking over the keys, obviously enchanted with the sounds she drew forth from beneath her paws. Another time Matilda would have felt ashamed of the cook's negligence in letting the cat into the salon. But now, with the alcohol travelling through her body, she found it easy to laugh. The cat on the piano was undoubtedly funny. Together, she and Junia made their way towards the piano, followed by Mr. Rosenberg who was not burning with curiosity to hear about Samuel's book. The cat was replaced by Matilda at the piano. A circle of tipsy guests surrounded her and began, in honour of the cat, to sing the popular hit 'Barbara, my Girl'. With the cat in her arms, Junia waltzed into another corner of the salon, twirling to a wild rhythm of her own, her black hair rising in the air like the thin wires of an umbrella. Her hilarity and exuberance were contagious. The chairs were pushed aside and a circle was formed. Holding hands, the guests, with Junia in the centre, galloped around the room, singing all the hits that were popular in town.

Dr. Levine approached Bella. "Shall we?" he asked, taking her by the hand. They joined the circle of dancers.

Samuel was left with Professor Hager and Editor Mazur. "Our Lodz is a youngster among European cities," he said as if in an afterthought. "According to the census the Prussians took in 1793, Lodz was then a village of one hundred and ninety citizens, amongst them only eleven Jews."

Mazur beamed, "And now we have a community of more than two hundred thousand, bless them. And what Jews! The Jew of Lodz doesn't have an equal anywhere else in the world. Look at the factories we have built, the trade we have fostered and the artists we have produced. Take our writers for instance. They have élan, youthfulness!"

"That's what I call local chauvinism!" Professor Hager, amused, pointed his finger upwards. "What writers are you talking about? What do you call a Jewish writer?"

"Why, clear as day. Those who write in Yiddish or Hebrew."

"Are there such in our town?"

"Shame on you, Professor."

"I'm no expert on Jewishness, Editor. The only Jewish writer I know is Julian Tuwim. But he writes in Polish."

"Tuwim is not a Jewish writer."

"Why? Because he writes in Polish?"

"Yes and no," Mazur turned his thumb up and down. "He might talk about minced onions, but they have no Jewish flavour. Even his anti-anti-Semitic poems are goyish. True, he is not ashamed of his origin. Then again, perhaps he is, but he is smart enough not to betray himself, which puts a nice face on an ugly game."

Samuel had to interrupt him. "But he is as Jewish as, let's say, Heine."

"Right!" Mazur exclaimed. "You know what is Jewish in him? His rebellion, his hutzpah!"

Mrs. Feiner, the *gymnasium* directress who had been standing nearby, listening, crossed her fisted hand over her chest, like someone about to make an oath, and said smiling meaningfully, "If Tuwim were a painter, you wouldn't be able to recognize his assimilation, would you, Mr. Mazur?"

"I would, Madam, I would," Mazur had his answer ready. "True, language betrays itself more easily than colour and form. However, even in painting, yes . . . Take, for instance, Samuel Hirshenberg," he pointed to a painting hanging over the buffet. "The son of a Jewish weaver from Lodz, a Jew through and through. And that's why he is so great. Because he had ground under his feet. Because the artist must be nourished and supported by the creative genius of his people. By blocking those channels, he condemns himself to facelessness and mediocrity. And it is the truly great artist, the one who absorbs the beauty and wisdom of his people, who grows to become truly universal. Take a look at it," he pointed again to the painting on the wall. "It's deeply human, eh? You know why? Because it is deeply Jewish." The painting represented a young *yeshiva* scholar bent over an open volume of the Talmud.

"And I," said Mrs. Feiner, stroking her flat bosom with her fist, "don't see anything in that painting, apart from the subject matter, that would distinguish it from paintings by non-Jews."

"Let's forget about the subject matter," Mazur went on, defending his point. "Let's talk about the interpretation . . ." He halted, caught the eye of his protégé, the painter Guttman, and called him over. "Here we have a specialist!" he proudly exclaimed. "Come on, Guttman, tell them about the purely Jewish character of this painting, tell them about the realism and the symbolism . . . the struggle between the two and the marriage of the two. And isn't this precisely the character of the Jew of Lodz, who has both feet on the ground and his head in the clouds?"

Guttman listened patiently to Mazur's deliberations, his fingers rolling a white piece of paper. At length he intervened, saying, "You'll excuse me, Editor, but as far as I am concerned, your approach is too literary. There is something, no doubt, in what you say. There are indeed artists who make you feel their national or regional background. But the artist depends more, I would say, on the spiritual winds blowing during his times. And even that is related only to external matters, to the dressing up. If you like, Rembrandt actually created purely Jewish paintings. Is he therefore a Jewish painter? And since Gauguin painted the colours and the people of Tahiti, did he become a Tahitian painter? Or Picasso, is he Spanish or French? As far as I am concerned, the only element of importance is the artist's personality."

Saying this, Guttman turned his head to the circle of merry dancers in the middle of the salon. Mazur understood. He knew that Guttman was a painter who did not like to philosophize about art.

Mazur and the professor followed Guttman's gaze towards the noisy crowd.

Samuel himself realized how detached he had become from all the gaiety, although he had intended to let himself go tonight and laugh off the heaviness of the year that had passed. He actually felt a little hurt that the guests managed so well without him. He had always been the centre of all parties. Tonight Matilda seemed to have taken the lead. Indeed, this had turned into a strange day for him. Just as he had felt younger than his age this morning, so he now felt older. He reached for a box of cigars and offered them to the bystanders. "Let's move to my studio," he proposed, "It's impossible to have a decent conversation here."

A few cigar-smoking guests were standing around the studio. On the sofa sat Dr. Harkavi, flipping through the pages of a small notebook. He was talking to Dr. Levine who had just come from dancing and was wiping the sweat from his forehead.

"Here is the radio!" the professor exclaimed upon entering. "Turn it on, Zuckerman!"

But Mazur caught Samuel's arm, "Don't disturb the doctors. Can't you see they are busy concocting a cure for sick humanity?"

Dr. Harkavi immediately closed his notebook. "Déformation professionelle," he sighed and stretched his long legs. "Never mind. We must learn to rest from sick humanity at least one night a year."

Mazur grinned at the professor, "You hear? One night a year one may take a rest."

"I just wanted to hear the sound," the professor said apologetically.

"Precisely! I'm afraid of the sound!" Mazur exclaimed.

The professor pulled Mazur down on the sofa, at Dr. Harkavi's side. "Here is a patient for you, Doctor. Editor Mazur is suffering from soundophobia."

Mazur coughed and extinguished his cigar, pressing it fiercely into the ashtray, as if determined to pierce a hole in the ceramic. "That's it!" he burst out. "I'll tell you more. Sometimes, during the most beautiful concerts, a fear comes over me that the music will suddenly stop and a cold voice will be heard announcing some terrible news."

"An anxiety complex!" the professor diagnosed with pretended seriousness. "And what does Freud say about this, Doctor? We shall have to find out where Mazur's angst comes from. Let's stretch him out on the sofa and take a peek into his subconscious."

Mazur contorted his face. "Pick up a newspaper and you'll find out where it comes from."

"That also depends on the subconscious." The professor would not relinquish his jocular tone. "The very manner in which you read the news, my friend, depends on the experiences of your childhood, on your libido and on the Oedipus complex. A neurotic person reads the papers differently than let's say, a normal one."

"A normal person should read them with fright!" Mazur exclaimed. "With healthy fright, you hear? If you want to know, you should put all humanity on your couch, the whole world that is so afraid to look the truth in the eye and will not move a finger to defend itself." Here he noticed that Dr. Levine was glaring at him with burning eyes. He stopped himself and guiltily rubbed his forehead, "Good heavens, I was afraid of the radio, and here I am myself an announcer of horrible tidings. Really, Doctor, what's wrong with me?"

An uncomfortable silence filled the room. They puffed on their cigars, energetically exhaling the smoke as if to blow away their collective unease. Finally, the professor turned his goateed face towards Samuel. "And tell me, Zuckerman, how did Lodz come to develop so fast? I mean, apropos of what you said before . . . It's geographical position leaves a lot to be desired, after all. We are near no waterway, nor close to any great crossroads or international markets; Lodz is not even in the centre of Poland."

Samuel was grateful to the professor for changing the subject and for touching upon a theme he wanted to introduce into the conversation: to talk a bit about the material he had collected for his book. "True," he agreed, resuming a relaxed position. "But Lodz is close to the German border. After the Vienna Peace Congress, in 1815, when the Polish Kingdom was established as an autonomous territory in the Russian Empire, the government worked out a plan to industrialize the country. Then Lodz, because it was close to Germany, was designated as a textile centre. German weavers were brought over and it was they who built our city. In one hundred years, the population increased six hundred times."

"And the Jews?" Mazur was growing interested. "The Jews accomplished nothing?"

"I did not say that." Samuel smiled. "But the Jews came into the picture later. First, because the Germans, coming from their *Junkerheimat*, were already eaten up by Jew-hatred, which they were the first to call by the fancy name of anti-Semitism, and they took to themselves the exclusive right to live in the new sections of the town, while the Jews remained in the old ones. Second, the Jews themselves were at that time against the weavers' trade. German weavers ate a lot of pork. The Jews called them, in fact, 'pig-eaters', and they were afraid that if a Jewish boy worked with a German weaver, he too would start eating unkosher food. But with time . . ."

"With time," the professor concluded for Samuel, "the Jews became weavers and began to eat pork!"

"Yes, the first Jew," Samuel continued, "who secretly learned the trade from a German was banished from the Jewish community. But soon Jewish weavers and master weavers sprang up like mushrooms from the ground. Almost overnight a Jewish proletariat arose and along with it came hosiery-makers, knitters and all kinds of needleworkers. The first Jewish merchants and industrialists appeared and the Jewish community grew and expanded. But bear in mind, all this was happening in the old part of the city, with repressions and restrictions following one after the other. German sentiments towards the Jews were in perfect accord with the tsar's, and as a matter of fact, at the request of the Germans of Lodz, in the year 1825, the Jewish Ghetto came into existence."

Mr. Rumkowski appeared in the door of the studio, a fresh rose tucked into the lapel of his shabby jacket; he was crumpling another rose between his fingers. He turned to Mazur, "Is this a meeting of your editorial board, Editor? What are you chattering about so thickly?" The old gentleman pronounced the word "Editor" with obvious antipathy. He considered Mazur a do-nothing who busied himself writing verbose articles in the newspaper. Rumkowski thought it unjust that with only words Mazur could sometimes achieve more than he, the tireless man of action. In particular, he could not forgive Mazur his position in the Zionist movement, a position acquired without the slightest effort on his, Mazur's part.

"We are talking about the ghetto which existed in our town a hundred years ago," Mazur informed him in a tone that left no doubt that the antipathy between the two men was mutual.

Rumkowski nodded contemptuously. "Of course, what else do Jews talk about? Not enough troubles in the present, they have to search for some a hundred years old. Even a celebration can't pass without a bit of lamenting."

Samuel, somewhat annoyed by the interruption, went on, "At the beginning, the Jews stayed in the ghetto. But later on some of them broke out, winning privileges as merchants, physicians and learned men. Others came out through struggle, like my great grandfather, for instance. But as soon as the first Jews appeared in the new districts, the Germans raised a storm against the Jewish flood. Complaints swamped the city administration and finally the approaches from the ghetto to the city were blocked. It became difficult to supply food, wood and merchandise to the ghetto, while the Jewish population inside grew and the district became overpopulated."

"I should have been there!" Rumkowski cried out, his eyes sparkling behind their tipsy fog.

He wanted to say more, but Samuel seized him by the arm and stopped him. "Listen, Mr. Rumkowski. Then something interesting happened. The Jews found a way out from the packed ghetto thanks to two men, Blawatt and Birencwajg. They bought the bordering village Baluty from Prince Zawisha, and there they built an industrial centre of their own."

"You hear, Professor?" Mazur beamed. "Now you see what I mean when I talk about the Jews of Lodz?"

Samuel did not let Mazur finish either. "Overnight Baluty was transformed into a little town," he continued. "Around the market place houses rose hurriedly, one close to the other, because people were afraid of the Germans. And the Germans certainly did not give them much rest. They ran to the mayor, to the governor, warning them against the great Jewish danger. And the administration agreed with them. The ghetto would have lost all its meaning once the Jews started to spread out, even if it were in a direction away from the city. Soon Cossacks arrived to stop the construction of the houses and to prevent the Jews from moving into those already built. Whips swished, arrests were made, but Blawatt and Birencwajg did not give up. And before the World War, you know, there were already a hundred thousand Jews living in Baluty." Samuel chuckled. "Because of the hurry, the houses were constructed and placed chaotically, without a plan; no sanitary facilities, the streets unpaved, the buildings without light, and I don't have to tell you about the crowding. It hasn't changed much since."

Rumkowski could no longer restrain himself. "I will cure Baluty!" he burst out. "Rely on me!" For a second he paused for breath, then began to pace the room. "It's about time that we organized a committee! Let's write a petition to the mayor!" He moved towards Samuel almost threateningly. "What do you say, Zuckerman?" He turned to the editor, "And you, Mazur? Why don't you write a series of articles in your paper? And you, Doctor? You could organize a sanitary commission and send a report to the administration. We could raise money too. As far as the support of the Jewish Council is concerned, leave it to me!" Now he stood at Samuel's desk, leaning on it with a clenched fist. His hot drunken eyes wandered off into the distance. Carried away by his own rhetoric, he talked increasingly louder and faster, as if he saw himself addressing a crowd of thousands of people, all looking at him. The crushed rose petals filtered down from his half-opened fist; and, as he stood there, his magnificent head raised high, the silver hair dishevelled, the bushy eyebrows pointed, he looked like a high priest blessing his people with the blood-red dust of flowers.

Then Matilda appeared in the studio. Samuel read reproach in her eyes. Doubtless, he was being a bad host tonight. She announced, "Tea is served in the dining room, my friends."

Rumkowski's forehead rippled with anger. But when he realized who the intruder was and saw her leave on Guttman's arm, he gasped for breath and went on with his discourse.

Guttman was grateful to Matilda for liberating him from Rumkowski's drunken babble and for having chosen him to accompany her. He found her the most interesting woman at the ball.

It was two months since he had returned from Spain and he did not have a groschen to his name. The only way to put himself back on his feet was either by selling a few "pre-revolutionary" paintings, as he called the work he had done before his participation in the Spanish Civil War, or by getting a few orders for portraits. And for that he had to meet the right people. Editor Mazur, knowing his plight, had prevailed on him to come here. And indeed he had profited by the visit, although not materially. Dr Michal Levine, the young man with the pale serious face, possessed eyes of stunning depth, in which there seemed to burn a demonic fire. He, Guttman, had talked to him in banalities; a conventional exchange of platitudes between two people meeting for the first time, who had clung to each other because both felt slightly uncomfortable in the surroundings. But inwardly, he felt that the personality of the stranger had conquered him for more than this one evening, and he looked forward to a friendship which, even though yet unborn, seemed to be announcing its conception. Besides Levine, there was also this woman now holding his arm — a woman dressed with such simple exquisite elegance, a creature so mysterious! Physically she reminded him of the female figures of both Rubens and Renoir. He had even made a little sketch of her sitting at the piano; he rolled it up and carried it around with him all evening.

However, Matilda had always been awkward and shy with strangers, especially those who were not dressed properly and came from a different social class. It was only because she knew that Guttman was a painter, that she found enough courage to take his arm. In her present good humour, she even forgave him for coming uninvited. She wanted to start a conversation with him, but she was unable to utter more than a few polite words. Her discomfort increased when all of a sudden he lifted her hand to his lips.

As he did so, the painter felt himself blushing, and in order to regain his composure, he held his lips on Matilda's hand much longer than he had intended. The taste of this kiss was new and different from all the other kisses he had ever given. There was no desire in it, no passion, just admiration and an ecstasy that came from afar and did not reach too close — and yet it was an act of understanding between a man and a woman, between warm lips and soft skin.

Matilda, so used to people kissing her hand that she would mechanically lift it to a guest's mouth, this time felt completely at a loss. She felt ashamed in front of the people streaming into the dining room, and finally, saying, "Excuse me," she pulled her hand away from his lips and turned away abruptly.

Meanwhile, in Samuel's studio, Rumkowski was still giving his speech, still making plans to cure the slums of Baluty. Those present were already happily conversing among themselves; or they listened to him with only one ear, or looked at him with only one eye, expressing the boredom and impatience shown a child who tells an overly long story. Usually sensitive, Rumkowski, who hated speechmaking, was now so drunk with wine and his sudden vision, that he did not notice what was going on around him. He slurred and swallowed his words and pounded his clenched fist against the table.

Samuel did not want Matilda to be angry with him. It was high time to join the others. So he at length put a friendly hand on Rumkowski's shoulder. "You have touched on a painful subject, Mr. Rumkowski," he said respectfully. "We must come back to it. But now let's go and have a glass of tea." On their way out, Samuel stopped in front of a carved bookcase which was leaning against the wall. "I have an old Passover *haggadah*," he remarked. "It belonged to my great grandfather. He also made this bookcase to order. You see the embossed glass doors?" He patted the top of the bookcase. "Renia keeps the key up here."

"It's a beauty of a bookcase!" Professor Hager admired the old piece of furniture.

Mazur grabbed his arm, "Now do you admit that there is such a thing as Jewish art? You can't tell me that a goy would carve a bookcase like this."

Samuel, unable to find the key, suddenly remembered something. "When I was a boy, I used to push a pencil in between the doors to unlock them." For a moment he manipulated a pencil in the crack between the doors, until they gave in and opened. He wanted to cry out, happy with his achievement, when one of the doors suddenly swung free, broke off its hinges, and fell, first against Samuel's shoulder, and then to the floor. He bent down to pick it up, but one of his feet accidentally stepped on the carved frame and the crack of broken wood, followed by a sound of splintering glass, filled the room.

Matilda came running in, her face lit with a triumph she had trouble concealing. "I begged him not to take this into the house!" she cried out.

"It's a nice bookcase," the professor said, taking Samuel's side.

"Yes, nice . . . for a museum!" She lifted her head proudly. "I knew this would happen. I was always afraid it might fall on one of the children. I will send in Wojciech. Come to the table, please."

As they left the studio, Mazur stopped Samuel. "Don't throw out the bookcase, heaven forbid."

Samuel could not restrain his agitation. "Matilda is right. It doesn't fit in here. Good for a museum. I have a stupid habit of attaching myself to old worthless things."

"This is not a worthless thing. Don't be silly, Zuckerman, fix it."

Samuel stepped away from Mazur. "All right. I'll tell Wojciech not to throw out the pieces of wood. I'll call the German, Woodke. He's the best carpenter in town."

Mazur shook his head, "This needs a pair of Jewish hands. I have someone for you, a carpenter from Baluty. Golden hands. If you want me to, I can find out where he lives."

Samuel agreed.

✦   ✦   ✦

In the dining room the tables were covered with white tablecloths. The gilded candlesticks, carrying slim tall candles, stood out against the whiteness and reflected on the gold-trimmed dishes, on the silverware and the crystal vases. Splendid, masterfully created cakes and tarts garnished with marzipan flowers were set out on crystal platters. Crystal imitations of intricately plaited baskets displayed all sorts of fruit in colourful disarray; the blue and black grapes, luscious and juicy, hung over the basket rims, teasing the eyes and palates of the guests.

Levine and Guttman were sitting together, both pleasantly intoxicated; the mutual strangeness that had at first intimidated them had disappeared. Now they kept intimately silent. Finally, Levine said dreamily, "She is in Paris. Last year of Medicine. I urged her to leave. A masochistic sort of urging." Then his face lit up, his gaze drowned in a candle's flame. "Now she has torn herself away from there, just as I have torn myself away from here, and we met in that flame. Happy New Year, Mira!" he laughed softly, and with sudden warmth threw his arm around Guttman's shoulder. "Meet a friend."

Guttman did not reply; there was no need for it. It seemed that the pregnant silence between Levine and himself had spread through the entire room that was in reality so full of talk and the clatter of dishes — a silence in which two solitudes were woven together by threads of affection. He recalled the heavy snow that had fallen on the city, and blinked. The white tablecloth seemed to be made of snow, and on it he saw the lush ripeness of summer; he saw fruit on snow. For a second he beheld this image; then the snow disappeared and only colour and juicy fullness remained, along with the memory of the singular sweet fragrance emitted by ripe fruit.

He spoke, "It was after the government was transferred from Valencia to Barcelona. We returned from a fierce battle, one we had lost. We marched . . . high rocks and winding sandy roads; sand between our teeth and on our tongues; faces smeared with dust and sweat . . . with blood. Then we rested. Margot, a French girl from the Red Cross, was with us. Her face was black with dust and fatigue. It was sunset. I lay in the shadow of a rock. Above me I saw a green sky with black stars. A vineyard. I sprang to my feet and began to climb the stony terraces. I picked the big clusters of grapes and filled my *casque* with them. Coming down, I found Margot resting, her eyes shut, the medicine box under her head like a pillow. I pushed a grape between her lips. Her eyes opened and I saw two grapes smiling at me. I was daring then with people, with women. I knew no Spanish nor French, but I knew the slogan 'No pasarán!' That was all I ever said to my comrades. I felt close to those strangers with whom I couldn't exchange a word. And here, at this table, how well I understand the language and how . . ." Someone's heavy hand fell on his shoulder.

"Tell me," Mr. Rosenberg, who was sitting on Guttman's other side, moved in his chair. "Are you indeed as good a painter as Editor Mazur has been telling us? Anyway, come to my factory. I'll try to steal a little time away from the hustle and bustle. I heard you were abroad; Italy, the Riviera, Spain — a paradise for artists. So I don't have to tell you about the fashion in portraiture." He pulled out a calling card from his pocket and threw it on the table in front of Guttman. His chair screeched. He rose, stuffing a cigar into his mouth, which he lit with a nearby candle and then moved on to another table.

Guttman dropped the sheet of paper he had been rolling and unrolling, and looked at the card. Coming here, he thought, had been profitable for him from every point of view. He turned his head back to Levine, but at that moment he became aware of Matilda's presence. "How is it that your plates are empty, gentlemen?" she asked, and sitting down in the chair Mr. Rosenberg had just vacated, she began to serve them the pastries that were laid out on the table. She casually reached for the roll of paper, unrolled it slowly and looked at the drawing. "You caught her expression very well," she smiled. "She is not . . . a beauty, but there is something beautiful about her." She added with motherly authority, "Bella is at an age when woman and child meet . . ." She was excited. As she had sat listening to Editor Mazur praising Guttman, she had had a sudden wish to have a portrait of Samuel hanging in their new house. But she could not imagine Samuel agreeing to sit quietly before a painter's canvas, and she wanted to ask Guttman how he thought one could approach a man as restless and as lively as her husband.

Guttman turned to her while glancing nervously at a tiny hole in his shirt. "That is not a sketch of your daughter, Madam," he said. "There are mature women with expressions like that."

Her thoughts were elsewhere. "Tell me, Mr. Guttman," her tone changed to an uncertain whisper. "Do you believe that a painter is really capable of bringing out the inner . . . face of a person?"

Guttman slowly regained mastery of himself. "That is the purpose of the artist, Madam. But it only happens rarely. Because for that you need three things: first, a painter who is capable of looking at a face and seeing through it; second, a model ready to open his or her face and let you look into it; and third, an onlooker, a recipient, capable of understanding what he sees." Realizing the symbolic potential of the situation, with Levine on one side of him and Matilda on the other, Guttman readied himself for the kind of conversation that would break the sealed doors of the soul and reach to its very foundations. "There are mature women," he added, looking at the sketch in her hand. "Mature, in the sense of age, but their inner beings have not bloomed, not awakened or opened fully. Sometimes they die like that, eternal virgins in their feelings and silver-haired grandmothers at the same time. In general, I think the face of a person expresses a mixture of both physical age and the age of that person's soul."

Matilda now understood that the sketch was of her. She wanted to tell Guttman something he perhaps did not know; that the measure of awakening in a woman depended on the kind of love she received. But she said nothing. She thought him fresh and arrogant, talking to her in that way. Slowly she tore up his drawing, destroying in her mind the portrait of Samuel she had not ordered. She left the torn fragments on the table, rose, and smiling regally at the other guests, she began giving orders to Reisel and the other servants who were making the rounds of the tables with slender porcelain tea pots, pouring hot amber tea into the waiting glasses. The room was filled with a strong refreshing aroma.

The Zuckerman girls had already taken their leave, curtsying and wishing everyone a happy New Year; but they were not yet asleep. Junia was displaying her acrobatic skills in the vestibule, while Bella, longing for bed, was waiting for her on the stairs. Then the door bell rang and Junia opened the door to admit a sturdy broad-shouldered young man. His face was red and frost-bitten;

snow-covered strings of hair dangled from beneath the Turkish paper hat on his head. He was all covered with confetti. Hastily, he took off his galoshes, turned down his collar and smiled at Junia, "*Servus*, little one, are my old people still here?" he asked. Junia, offended, wrinkled her nose, made a face and did not immediately answer. But Renia, the nanny, shuffled up to the young man and informed the "cavalier" that yes, Mr & Mrs Rosenberg were still here, and that he should go into the dining room where tea was being served. The young man swiftly shook off his coat and removed the green paper hat from his head. "Do you want it, little one?" he offered it to Junia.

She was standing, both hands locked behind her back, observing him expertly. "I'm not a little one," she declared finally. "I am fifteen years old and the tallest in my class."

"Oh, forgive me!" His face tightened with pretended seriousness. "No offence intended. I call all the girls that — word of honour! Even the eighteen-year-olds." He drew near her and put the paper hat on her head. She did not protest. He pleased her and so did the hat. He inclined himself towards her ear. "I even call my mother Little One, and believe you me, she likes it." He fixed his tie and took her by the arm. "Come, you will be my lady at the table."

She puckered her forehead. "I have to go to bed." She noticed him staring at Bella who was standing on the stairs, motionless, leaning against the rails as if she had grown into them. "That's my sister Bella. She is going to bed too. She is only a year and a half older than I am," Junia informed him.

The young man took a few uncertain steps in the direction of the dining room. Then he turned abruptly back to the stairs, and in another second he was standing in front of the perplexed Bella. "*Servus*," he shook her loose hand. "We know each other, do we not?"

Bella felt her legs giving way under her. Her heart, which had been beating so hard that she could hear it in her throat, stopped suddenly. The skin under her eyes grew hot and prickly and she could feel a chill stream down to her limbs which had become completely numb. She was absolutely unable to move, to open her mouth, or to nod. She saw him through a fog, as in a dream — Mietek, the boy with whom she had carried on endless conversations in her mind. She was afraid that he would disappear at any moment, as if in a dream.

Junia came up the stairs and caught his arm. "Come, sit with us for a while," she said, pulling both him and Bella down with her. The three of them sat down on the upper stair, pressed together, arm to arm. "So tell us about your ball," she turned to him with curiosity.

Mietek shrugged his shoulders. "A ball is not a movie or a story. You have fun, that's all. Right?" As he turned to Bella, he suddenly took her hand in his.

"How should she know whether it's right or not?" Junia exclaimed disenchanted. "She only goes to Papa's balls, just like I do."

Bella felt Mietek's fingers winding around her own. Now she was almost certain that she was dreaming, because only in a dream could one feel one's own body and soul and all one's senses become so small, that they fit into the palm of another's hand. "It's true, I don't go to balls," she stammered. Mietek's hand was now gliding over her unbraided tresses, along her spine, up higher; each one of his fingers burnt her neck like a part of a flaming ring.

Junia grinned. "Yeah, she is Papa's girl, doing everything she is told. That's why I have to suffer too!" She hit her knees with both her fists. "But I fight for my freedom!"

Mietek turned his drowsy eyes to her. "What freedom do you mean?"

"What do you mean, what freedom do I mean? I don't want to be a doll, a puppet. Papa's and Mama's little girl. They think that I am their property."

"What, for instance, would you do that you are unable to do?" He was growing more interested.

"I want to be free like you are."

He chuckled. "If you only knew how dangerous freedom can be. Better you don't know, little one!"

Junia looked at him suspiciously. "You're drunk!" she called out. She felt abused and made fun of. The young man was disgusting. She did not want to have anything more to do with him. She sprang to her feet, raced down the stairs and disappeared into the kitchen.

"You are not in need of freedom as much as your sister, are you?" Mietek leaned his head towards Bella.

"I am free," she stammered, happy and frightened to remain with him alone.

"I mean real freedom — to do, not to dream. Sometimes, you know . . . I am afraid of myself." His mouth was over her ear; she could smell the alcohol on his breath. He pressed her against his chest, burying his nose in her hair. Her face was in his hands. "When you are free," he went on, "you realize how enslaved you are to the master inside you, and that you don't always know what he wants. You follow? You remind me . . . do you know of whom? Of a nun. My word. And, you know, I am attracted to nuns. Sometimes when I see them passing by on the street, I feel desire . . . They are covered, pure . . ."

She was caught in his arms and felt estranged from herself. She shivered with cold. All of a sudden she noticed her own hand on his chest. "You have a nice tie on . . ."

He passed the tip of his nose over her neck. "Let's meet somewhere in town. Tomorrow."

"I'm busy . . ."

His mouth, red and moist, was near hers. "Then after tomorrow."

"Tomorrow night. Wait for me at the gate of Stashitz Park." She tore herself away from him and, stumbling to her feet, ran up to her room.

Through the window of the dining room a pale new day was peeking in. The ladies were already longing for their beds. They had long ceased to follow the conversation at the tables. The yawning into batiste handkerchiefs became contagious. The plates on the white tablecloths, full of fruit peelings, waited in vain for Reisel, or one of her helpers, to come and clear them away. Reisel was sitting exhausted, in the kitchen, near the dying fire, Barbara, the cat, napping in her lap. Renia was dozing on the stairs, while Wojciech sat on a chair in the vestibule, snoring, the last remaining tooth in his mouth like an exclamation mark pointing to the ceiling.

The only people in the dining room who betrayed no sign of fatigue were Guttman and Levine, at one table, and Samuel and Editor Mazur, at another. The two young new friends were exchanging confessions interspersed with long silences, each of them awake, renewed by the miracle of having found the other. The two old friends, Samuel and Mazur, were sitting knee to knee, incessantly refilling their glasses with cold tea and conversing with animation. Samuel had just finished telling the detailed story of his great-grandfather, Shmuel Ichaskel Zuckerman, who had been among the first Jews to break out of the ghetto. He told how his ancestor had fought for the right to live in the house on Novomieyska Street which Samuel and his family had just left. "And I, my friend," Samuel concluded, "his great-grandchild, do not possess even a fraction of my grandfather's fighting spirit."

Mazur did not agree with him. "And the factory you have expanded, and the trade you are fostering, that's nothing? If you want to know, building, developing, conquering difficulties and working towards a goal are possibly the only justified forms of fighting."

"I don't mean that," Samuel interrupted him. "I mean something you call fighting for an ideal. I have no ideal to tie my life to, personally. True, I am for a Jewish country and consider myself a Zionist, but I have no desire to become a pioneer in Palestine. My great-grandfather was a pioneer."

Mazur shook his head energetically. "Perhaps your great-grandfather had no ideal either, only a desire to improve his conditions. Maybe Zionism is also not an ideal, just the desire of a people to improve its conditions; and socialism too . . . If you like, there are no ideals, and on the other hand, all these aims we call ideals. Even the construction of this new house of yours is the realization of an ideal."

"But I have in mind something that would involve others besides myself, that would not be only for my own good."

"All right. So we may say that there are ideals of different calibres. True, the feeling of having ideals in common with other people gives more elation, it's good for the conscience and for one's own morale. But the fight of the individual for his personal goals is not to be minimized. Do you think that your grandfather saw himself in the same light as you see him? The same goes for you. You don't realize that by fulfilling your private ambitions, you play an important part in the life of the community as well. Of course I wouldn't mind if you cared for the Zionist cause more than you do. But who am I to preach to you?"

The first one to rise from the table was Mrs. Harkavi who seemed scarcely capable of carrying her handsome head on her shoulders. Then the other ladies began to wink at their husbands and pull them discreetly by the sleeve. In a moment, everyone was standing. Wojciech woke up and helped Samuel get the coats of the guests. Matilda lifted her hand to be kissed. Again and again they all wished each other a happy New Year and with sleep in their limbs, the guests poured out into the wet cold morning.

Samuel threw his coat over his shoulders and went out to accompany the guests. Some of them left on foot, for the rest Samuel had to stop one droshky after another. He kissed the ladies' hands and helped them with the trains of their dresses as they climbed into the carriages. He tucked them comfortably into the soft seats under the hoods of the vehicles and covered their legs with warm blankets. Then he exchanged a few friendly words, a few last good wishes, until the coachmen snapped their whips and the wheels rolled away on the white snowy road.

In the freshly fallen snow, the many footprints between the sidewalk and the entrance of the house looked like uneven tears in a smooth white blanket. Samuel felt the need to exercise his limbs. He took hold of Wojciech's shovel and began straightening the path, throwing the snow to the side. He was wide awake and restless. The image of his great-grandfather, who in his mind had acquired the features of his own father, disturbed him. Again and again he asked himself whether he possessed some of his forebears' strength and perseverance.

The street lights which swayed with the wind over the middle of the road went out one by one. The first day of the year 1939 had begun.

✦   ✦ ✦

The first day of the year 1939 was an unlucky one for Bella. Sick with anticipation, she ran that very evening to Stashitz Park, to meet Mietek. There, nothing but a frosty white silence awaited her. The beautiful snow-covered park imprinted itself on her memory as the place of her first great disappointment.

The first day of the year 1939 was an unfortunate one for Samuel as well. Someone had broken the big front pane of his office window, and on the wall, by the entrance to his factory, was printed in thick black paint: JEW — TO PALESTINE!

Chapter Two

LUTOMIERSKA STREET was called Hockel Street by the Jews of Baluty. Firstly because this name was much easier to pronounce; secondly, because the name itself carried an obvious mark of distinction. It bore witness to the fact that the street, although belonging to the slums of Baluty, had once had the glory and importance of a downtown artery, the proof being that there had once stood a hotel on it. Where the hotel was located and what had happened to it, no one seemed to know, but there was not the slightest doubt that it had once existed. The proof? The name Hockel Street was in reality nothing but a misspelling of Hotel Street.

Hockel Street was indeed one of the principal streets in the slums of Baluty. From noisy Zgierska, it stretched awkwardly, to one side only, like a left arm, because on the right it was blocked by the red brick church of the Holiest Virgin Mary. The church hovered over the low-roofed houses of Baluty like a mother hen over her chicks, and in particular held the nearby Hockel Street under her protective wing. From the shallow niche in the church's wall a blue virgin looked down on the bustling inhabitants of the street, as if to assure them, with her glass eyes and praying hands, of her blessings, as well as of her particular attention and care.

And indeed, the inhabitants and passers-by in the street were blessed with the privilege of always knowing what time it was. The church's steeple looked down onto the street with its round wise eye: a clock with forged-iron hands which never missed their regular rounds and marked the full hour with a loud, rather awesome tolling of bells. Thus the merchants in the bazaar and fish market on Hockel Street, as well as the horse thieves at the gates and the streetwalkers who plied their trade in front of the gates, as well as the kosher matrons buying groceries, and the pious Jews going to synagogue, and the hosiery workers, the knitters, the school children and the beggars knew what time it was better than all the other inhabitants of Baluty.

Hockel Street started off as a narrow street, wide enough for only two or three people to pass. But as soon as it reached the bazaar, it widened, and from there it stretched onward broadly and comfortably, overhung with the rich leaves of the chestnut trees growing along the sidewalks. (There were no trees in the rest of Baluty, except in the churchyard.) In this way, it continued until the paved sidewalks turned into sandy paths which vanished into the fields surrounding the town.

The majority of the houses on Hockel Street were old wooden cottages, as were most of the houses in Baluty. Here and there stood a fading stucco building with several storeys, constructed in the style of the city. These houses had deep arched entrances leading into dingy backyards walled in by three or four-storeyed apartment boxes. Each of the latter had its own murky entrance with a crooked staircase leading to the upper floors. Each floor had its own dark corridor, and each corridor was filled with the strong smells which escaped from beneath the countless doors.

In one of these stucco houses lived Itche Mayer the Carpenter with his wife Sheyne Pessele and their four sons: Israel, Mottle, Yossi and Shalom. In a sense, Itche Mayer's dwelling in the house on Hockel Street was privileged. It was not necessary to climb any stairs or to pass through long dark corridors, to find it. The apartment had a separate entrance right in the arched gate, across from the janitor's door. And the few steps that led to it went down, not up, since Itche Mayer occupied the front cellar unit of the tenement, right under the bakery of Blind Henech who was Itche Mayer's uncle. The little window of the cellar looked out from under the stairs leading to the bakery. And since the house stood in the liveliest part of Hockel Street, where the hustle and bustle of the bazaar and fish market overflowed into the nearby backyards, Uncle Henech and his wife Pearl and their cat Perelka did not lack business, and Itche Mayer and his family did not lack mud in winter and dust in summer.

Once, many years ago, when Sheyne Pessele had decided she could no longer stand the air in the cellar and had fled for a few days to her home *shtetl*, Konska Vola, she returned with two things: the first, a cherry tree sapling which had since grown into a large tree and stood in the backyard near the landlord's 'palace'; and the second, with an ultimatum for her husband: either he plant potatoes in a window box, or she would go "where her eyes might lead her". Since then, potatoes had grown every summer on the window sill. When the time came to dig them up, they were eaten at a single special meal, for which Sheyne Pessele always prepared six glasses of sour milk. However the potato box could not protect the cellar from the dust in summer and the mud in winter. It only helped to rid the apartment of some more daylight which was useless anyway, since an electric bulb had to shine in the cellar all day, if there was to be any decent light at all.

The cellar itself differed little from any of the other cellars in Baluty, except that the ceiling was not too low. Yossi, the tallest of the sons, had to stand on tiptoe in order to reach it, which he rarely did, as there was always the danger that he would be left with a piece of plaster in his hand. Pieces of plaster fell from the ceiling even when no one touched it; for the main problem with the cellar was that it was damp, or it might be more correct to say: it was wet.

From the walls shaded with a multitude of coloured splotches, water trickled down in streams and rivulets, reminiscent of rivers crossing a fertile plain; while those spots where the water had removed pieces of plaster, leaving white holes, looked like multiform lakes. To further complete the picture, the fungus growing between the 'rivers' and 'lakes' played the part of forests without which every landscape appears uninteresting and dull. It helped little that Itche Mayer and his sons whitewashed the walls before every Passover and covered the holes with a putty product of his own invention. Before long, the 'maps' reappeared with their previous topography intact and new fungus forests resumed their former locales.

The same was true of the floor. Twenty-seven years ago, when Itche Mayer had arrived in Lodz from Konska Vola and had not had a roof over his head — nor over that of his wife and first-born son, Israel, who was still a baby — Uncle

Henech, the baker, had said to him: "You're a carpenter, Itche Mayer, right? Then why don't you take my cellar, cut yourself out a window, lay yourself out a floor, and move in?" This Itche Mayer did. He cut himself out a window, laid himself out a floor, and moved in. And since then Itche Mayer had laid on this floor a few other floors, after which he had taken them all apart and laid a brand new one, and on that brand new one, he had superimposed a few other new ones. But it helped like "cupping glasses might help a corpse". As soon as anyone stepped heavily on a board, slimy mud oozed up through the cracks with a strange squeak, disappearing as soon as the foot was removed, but leaving a dirty stain on the board, as a warning that it would, with God's help, come up again.

On top of that, mice and rats had once inhabited the cellar along with the family. They were boarders at the expense of Sheyne Pessele who, even without them, had difficulties making ends meet. But as soon as Mottle, the second son, began going to school, he considered it his sacred duty to rid the house of the freeloaders. He had his own account to settle with the rats. When he was a baby, a rat had jumped into his crib and bitten off such a large piece of his finger, that he still had a hole in it. No one ever knew whether Mottle's reason for action was his desire for vengeance, or whether he just did it for the sake of hygiene, having learned at school that rats and mice are carriers of disease. Whatever the reason, since the time Mottle had started his crusade, the enemy was rarely seen, except once in a while, in winter, when the garbage in the backyard froze over and a little frightened mouse, running to find a bit of warmth and food near Uncle Henech's bakery oven, would, at the same time, pay a visit to the cellar of his nephew, Itche Mayer.

The cellar, in spite of the fact that it was not too big, was well laid out. Near the door stood the tile oven where Sheyne Pessele cooked her meals, and near that, stood the cupboard where she kept her dishes. On its top shelf she kept the family's skimpy food supply — and she could never decide whether, in this way, she was protecting the food from the mice, or from the greedy hands of her perpetually hungry sons. Side by side with the cupboard stood the water bench with two pails of water. It was adjacent to the shelves where Sheyne Pessele kept her 'heads', that is, the wooden models on which she made wigs for pious Jewish women, for she had been a wig-maker since childhood. When Sheyne Pessele's boys were still small, these were the only heads that turned to them, and to which they could speak; they even included them in their games. But at night the heads turned into monsters, and sometimes one of the children would wake up in the middle of the night and, faced with their wooden eyeless stares, would run into his mother's bed with a frightened scream.

By the other wall stood Itche Mayer's workshop consisting of a few long boards nailed to two saw horses. During the daytime, Itche Mayer and his sons did their carpentry work on it; at night it was converted into a bed for the boys. On holidays the workshop table was covered with a clean sheet and served as a feast table.

Slightly removed from the third wall stood Itche Mayer and Sheyne Pessele's iron beds, and nearby, obliquely placed against the corner, stood the bookcase. It stood obliquely not for decoration, but to protect it from the wetness of the wall. On the four shelves of the bookcase the boys kept their 'literature'. Until the marriage of Israel, the first-born, every son had his own shelf. Israel, a member of the Jewish Socialist Bund, kept the 'History of Socialism', the works of August Bebel and the swollen volumes of Marx's "Das Kapital" on his shelf. The second son, Mottle, the communist, kept on his shelf some innocuous-looking books which hid between their pages the "real stuff": illegal publications, proclamations and party bulletins, written on tissue paper. The third son, Yossi, the Zionist, who had never been a decent reader, had a few illustrated anniversary publications of his sports club *Hakoah* on his shelf, and on top of them, the framed photograph of the founder of Zionism, Dr. Herzl. Nearby lay his football shoes, as well as some copper trophies he had won at various contests as the best dancer in the dance hall on Hockel Street. Shalom, the youngest of the sons and a member of the Bundist youth organisation, the *Zukunft*, used his shelf to store enormous piles of the *Folks-Zeitung* and the periodical *Youth Waker*. On top of all this lay his brass trumpet, since he was a member of the wind orchestra of the Culture League.

After the marriage of Israel, Itche Mayer was finally able to have a shelf of his own too, and he decided to fill it with distinguished works of Yiddish literature. For, in his opinion, these sons, who supposedly read so much, did not really take a decent book into their hands. One day, he had paid a visit to the bookseller who owned a store on Baluty Square, and came home with a full set of the works of Peretz and Sholom Aleichem, to be paid off at fifty groschen a week. As a bonus, he received the biography of the Bundist Leader, Beinish Michalevitch.

Because of the addition of this last volume, the political equilibrium of the bookcase became precarious. Mottle, the communist, suddenly realized that the Bund was spreading its influence too far over the shelves and that it was a scandal that it should grab two shelves for itself, while the other parties had only one each. But he could do nothing about it. After all, the bookcase faithfully mirrored the political predilections of the family members.

Itche Mayer never officially belonged to the Bund, but he considered himself a Bundist and was sorry that he had clung so long to religion before coming to his senses. True, he did not regret the fact that he had sent his eldest, Israel, to the *heder* and the *yeshiva*, and was proud that his son's erudition included the Scriptures as well as the difficult chapters of Marx's "Das Kapital". But his other sons had not been sent to the *heder*. They went to public schools and to the Socialist Children's Organisation, the *Skif*. He wanted them, so to speak, to suck in Bundism with their mother's milk.

It happened however that Mottle, the second son, remained a *Skifist* only until he began to earn a few zlotys for himself, at which time he asserted his political as well as his financial independence, and looked around for a new ideology. And since he had always been resentful of his parents and his brothers, he decided to become a communist, a fearlesss stormer of the existing order. For this reason, the family fights in Itche Mayer's house were very easily carried over onto a political plane. More than once the eternally dusty window of the cellar vibrated with the shouts of political arguments, spiced with epithets, the most popular of which were: "Social Fascist!", "Social Traitor!", "Red Idiot!", and "Stalin's Bootlicker!". The Popular Front never materialised in Itche Mayer's cellar.

As for Itche Mayer's third son, Yossi, he too had decided to get out of going to the *Skif* meetings. He hated all teaching, and just as he did not know what they wanted from him at school, so he did not understand what they were boring him about at the *Skif* meetings. He liked to have fun, to clown around, to do sport, or dance a *horah*. In Zionism there was nothing to study; it seemed as simple as adding two and two. Indeed he could not grasp why his brothers, who worked so hard reading mountains of newspapers and journals, who threw about incomprehensible highbrow words, could not understand the simple fact that the oppressed Jew must have his own country.

The soil in which Itche Mayer's educational theories took root best was his youngest son, Shalom. From the start, Shalom had treated the *Skif* as his second home. Every *Skifist* was a brother for whom he was ready to walk through fire. And when he sang the *Skif* anthem, "We Children, all Equal", he felt a lump in his throat and a heat in his eyes. For he was not equal to others. He had crooked rickety legs and was a frightened shy boy. The *Skif* freed him of the shame and self-consciousness he felt about his legs. On the contrary, he was made to feel a certain pride in them, because they were a wound inflicted on him by social injustice. The *Skif* also taught him about suffering humanity and about a tomorrow of happiness for everyone, which was soon to come. And the *Skif* taught him how to use a toothbrush.

To return to the cellar, it had of course a fourth wall too. In its corner stood a box containing the slop bucket, and beside it, stood the finest piece of furniture in the room: a little mahogany table with carved legs, a jewel of a table, the pride of the family. And no wonder. It had come down to the cellar from nowhere else but the palace of the magnate Adam Rosenberg himself!

It might seem that the road the table took from Rosenberg's palace to Itche Mayer's cellar was complicated and circuitous, but in reality it was quite simple: Uncle Henech, the baker, had a brother-in-law whose wife's niece married Moshe Itzel, the driver of the funeral hearse which took rich corpses to the cemetery. And the magnate Rosenberg was Moshe Itzel's distant cousin's uncle. So, when Uncle Rosenberg treated himself to a new table which was even nicer and more mahogany than the old one, he offered Moshe Itzel the old one as a wedding present. But since Moshe Itzel was a man of aspirations, he said to himself that it did not suit for the man, who took the richest corpses to the cemetery, to have a hand-me-down table, even if it were made of gold, and that he could afford to buy himself an apartment full of new furniture, even if it were made of cardboard. But since he was sorry to throw out such a rare piece of furniture, he offered it with great pomp to Itche Mayer who was the ideal person to appreciate such a gift, firstly, because he was a pauper, and secondly, because he was the best connoisseur of good carpentry in the entire city of Lodz. In this way, the expensive piece of furniture descended into a cellar in Baluty, to decorate and honour it with a spark of capitalist elegance.

Although the mahogany table stood near the slop bucket, it lost nothing of its distinction. It was not, heaven forbid, used for anything; its main function was beauty. On it were displayed a few important family photographs, and its shelf held the family albums and the individual albums of each son. The family had a weakness for photographs.

Near the distinguished table, stood another table of rough planks on which the family took its meals on weekdays and on ordinary Sabbaths. Adjacent to it stood the last important piece of furniture in the cellar: the wardrobe, actually a huge wooden box which held the family's clothes. Itche Mayer promised himself that one day, fortune and health permitting, he would take apart that 'coffin', as he called it, and build a new wardrobe the like of which had never been seen in Lodz before nor would be after. For he considered it a shame that there should be standing in his home a monster such as the one presently standing there. But somehow — as if to prove the proverb that all shoemakers go barefoot — no one had ever had a chance to see this new wardrobe, except for Itche Mayer, who saw it in his imagination.

To conclude the foregoing, it is clear that the cellar had a magical layout since, in spite of all the things mentioned above, there was still room enough left to move around.

✦   ✦   ✦

This Sabbath evening there was a great commotion in Itche Mayer's cellar. It had begun in the morning, and as the day proceeded, it grew worse. Itche Mayer did not spend this afternoon relaxing on his bed with the *Folks-Zeitung*, nor did he take a nap. Instead, he passed the whole day running around Baluty, trying to borrow a fancy-dress suit for himself. It should not have been too difficult a thing to do, since the meat dealers and horse traders who lived in the backyard all had elegant evening suits and even the burglar, Lame King, had coat-tails. But the trouble was that Itche Mayer was middle-sized, or rather on the smallish side, whereas the others were a hefty lot of large men. At length, Yossi had the idea of running across to the dance master Tzinele, who was more or less Itche Mayer's size and possibly even a little smaller, to borrow the suit Tzinele wore at the dance lessons, and perhaps even his top hat.

Tzinele's suit, black, shiny and worn, could not be compared with the elegant tuxedos the guys in the backyard wore to their parties. But Itche Mayer had long ago learned that there was truth in the saying: "If you cannot get what you want, then you must want what you can get." And now Itche Mayer, sleepy and nervous, was busy pulling up Tzinele's too-tight pants. In spite of their tightness, they might have fit, if it were not for one button in the front which would not close. Even when Itche Mayer held his breath and pulled in his 'potato' belly, he felt as if his stomach were encased in an iron ring, so that there were two possibilities: either he would choke, or the button would burst open and he would lose the pants. Itche Mayer looked around to see if anyone had noticed his predicament and could offer help. But they were all too busy with themselves, and he, the forlorn head of the family, could get as much of their attention as a speck of dust on the left sidelock would get from a scholar absorbed in a difficult passage of the Talmud.

Mottle stood half-dressed, a towel around his neck, shaving in front of the broken mirror which hung above the water bench. Itche Mayer could see half of Mottle's soapy cheek reflected in the mirror, as well as his mouth turned sideways against the razor, and one of his protruding eyes which seemed to be looking right at him, in such a way that it was impossible to tell whether Mottle saw his father's problem and was ignoring it, or whether he was so preoccupied with what he was doing, that he had simply forgotten that he had a father at all.

Carefree Yossi, on the other hand, was outside, in the corridor, polishing his patent leather shoes. Going to a wedding was one of Yossi's greatest pleasures. He was singing his favourite song *Hava Nagila*, and when he came to the end of the lyrics, he whistled the tune until he started the song all over again. Yossi's singing got on Itche Mayer's nerves. "He has a light heart," Itche Mayer said to himself. "Provided his father with an elegant outfit and considers his obligations at an end. I could crack my head against the wall before he would notice anything amiss."

Even Shalom, the most devoted son of all, who supposedly could understand his father at a glance — what was on his mind now? In all the uproar and confusion, he lay on the workshop table, his face covered with a *Youth Waker*, engaged in a quarrel with his mother.

And to her, to Sheyne Pessele, the supposedly devoted wife, it was simply impossible to utter a word. She was patching her black Sabbath dress which was falling apart, and crying, as was her habit, with dry tears, sniffling through a wet nose. Of course Itche Mayer knew what was going on in her heart. She was tired and frustrated. Early in the morning, she had gone with her sons to the dance hall, to help prepare the celebration, and although there was a hellish frost outside, she had returned drenched with sweat. She had hardly had time to eat some of the Sabbath *cholent* which was cold and tasteless, before she had to run upstairs, to Uncle Henech's, to help him pack the fish and meat, the tarts and cakes which he was to transport immediately to the dance hall. And now she was sitting, mending her festive dress which should have long ago been exchanged for a new one, arguing with that good-for-nothing, Shalom, who stubbornly refused to go to Gretta's wedding.

Gretta was Uncle Henech's niece. She had lived with her mother and sister at his place since the three of them had arrived from Zbonshyn, where they had been chased by the Germans, across the border, from Germany. Ever since they had arrived in Baluty, the two young ladies, Gretta and Flora, had found themselves surrounded by swarms of young men who looked at them with the reverence and admiration due to such genteel ladies from *Deutschland*. The girls were called the *Fräuleins* and the young men tried to behave towards them in as educated a manner as possible, twisting out of shape their Yiddish mother tongue in its Baluty dialect, in order to make it sound more German than German itself. But it was to no avail. Gretta fell in love with a bookkeeper from downtown, who spoke only Polish and was not such a millionaire either, and it was with him that she was supposed to stand under the marriage canopy tonight. Her sister, Flora, on the other hand, might perhaps have permitted her admirers from Baluty to come a little closer, were it not for the fact that from the first day that she had set foot in Uncle Henech's house, she had felt drawn downwards, to the cellar — by Shalom's big black eyes. And since she was a girl of many charms and the possessor of a strong will, it was not long before the people of Baluty were talking about Flora and Shalom as if they were a pair. The young men of Baluty did not immediately stop courting her, but they soon gave up their big ambitions. No one thought to take away Shalom's future bride.

But today Shalom refused to go to Gretta's wedding. First he said he had a sore throat, then he said that there was to be an important meeting of the Bund, where delegates to the Warsaw conference on anti-Semitism were to be elected, and he would not miss such a meeting for anything in the world. And since he allowed no one to examine his throat, but insisted on doing his share in helping his brothers set up the tables and benches in the dance hall, it was perfectly clear to Sheyne Pessele that it was not so much his throat that prevented him from going to the wedding — as it was the Bund.

She was not in the habit of quarrelling with her sons, as was Itche Mayer. Depending on her mood, she either tried to reason with them, or she gave them a going over with the broom. But how could she talk reason to Shalom, if it was more important for him to go to the Bund than to the wedding of his 'cousin' Gretta who was, after all, the honest-to-goodness sister of his own fiancée? Indeed, Sheyne Pessele felt an impulse to grab the broom and favour her son with a few good bangs. But she was too tired, and besides, she knew it would do no good. And this enraged her even more. Had she ever forbidden him to run every night to his club, or to go on his excursion? Had she herself not sewn the blue blouse and red scarf that made up his uniform? Had she not given him her last groschen so that he could go to their camps? Why should he not do her this favour? Why should he shame Flora (whose engagement to Shalom did not really please her, but this had nothing to do with the problem at hand)? And more than anything else, Sheyne Pessele was hurt by the fact that Shalom was not stubborn by nature; he was generally quite manageable and she considered him a good son. But as soon as something came up which conflicted with his Bund, he was transformed into an unmovable piece of iron. So she cursed the Bund fiercely, and the more she cursed, the more bitterly she cried her dry tears and sniffled through her wet nose.

Itche Mayer's patience was hanging by a hair. Not only was no one paying the slightest attention to him, but on top of it all, he had to look at Sheyne Pessele's sniffling, a thing which always made him feel badly. Hardly able to control his anger, he unbuttoned the pants and, keeping them up with both hands, approached Shalom, saying to him in a hiss, "Don't you see, Mother is crying?"

Shalom knew perfectly well that she was crying. It seemed to him that she was crying so loudly on purpose, to make sure that he would hear her and feel guilty; she knew exactly which chord to strike. But he did not care. His eyes burned, his throat stung as if pricked by needles and his heart was bitter. He could scarcely remember the few words he had prepared to say at the meeting, and they were so important: the fight with the Polish fascists and the question of expanding the Bundist youth guard.

"To hell with Mother, as long as the Bund is all right!" Mottle said, rubbing his smoothly shaven cheeks, obviously pleased with himself.

Shalom tore the *Youth Waker* from his face. How could Mottle, the cold-blooded scoundrel, reproach him with such a thing? "If I were you," he burst out, waving a finger at his brother, "I'd keep my mouth shut!" He was ready to unload all his bitterness on Mottle, when Yossi, balancing two shiny shoes on his hands, came into the room.

"For heaven's sake, what's going on here? We'll be late for the wedding!" Yossi exclaimed, a roguish smile on his face. He put the shoes down, hurried to the wardrobe and flung it open. His *Hava Nagila* burst out in such a deafening baritone that it excluded any possibility of further quarrelling. He put on the shirt which Sheyne Pessele had newly ironed, his tie and his festive suit. His eyes fell on Itche Mayer. "I'm not waiting for anyone!" he said to him laughing.

"Go in good health!" Itche Mayer replied bitterly, and before Yossi had time to blink his eyes, he threw Tzinele's jacket straight into his face. "You can take it back where it came from!"

Yossi slowly removed the jacket from his head, folded it carefully and looked at his father, "What's wrong with the suit?"

"Who said anything was wrong? It's just right — for the devil!" Then, consoled somewhat by the attention he was getting from his son, Itche Mayer complained, pointing to his stomach, "The button."

Yossi began tugging at the top of the pants around Itche Mayer's belly. Itche Mayer held his breath until the button finally went through the hole. Having accomplished this, Yossi triumphantly glided his hand down his father's leg, "It fits like a glove."

"My enemies should have such a fitting!" Itche Mayer groaned. "I can't even catch my breath."

Sheyne Pessele bit off the thread she was sewing with, wiped her nose on her sleeve, and got up. She went over to her husband, grabbed the pants by the belt, and shook them with such violence over his waist that they might have been a tight sack which refused to let go of its blocked contents. Finally, she unbuttoned them. Itche Mayer ballooned his stomach freely and felt much better. Once Sheyne Pessele took him in hand, there was nothing more to worry about. He sighed comfortably, "I built myself a house of wisdom, now it's inhabited by fools, everyone stepping on everyone else's corns." He looked affectionately at Sheyne Pessele's unkempt hair. "So what do you say, Sheyne Pessele?" She said nothing, but took a pair of scissors and before Itche Mayer realized what she was doing, the button was cut off. Then he understood. "I see you're going to move the button over and after the wedding, you'll move it back!" He was delighted with her wisdom.

She went to thread the needle. On her way, she stopped in front of Shalom. "For the last time, I'm asking you with patience," she snorted. "Will you let me have a look in your throat, yes or no?"

This time Shalom surrendered. He sat up slowly, moved his legs off the workshop table, and tottering on his feet as if he were drunk, he sank into the chair Sheyne Pessele had placed behind him. Itche Mayer, holding his pants up with his hands, went for a spoon. He positioned himself behind his wife and stuck his head out over her shoulder, so that he too might look into the depth of Shalom's throat.

For a long time Sheyne Pessele pressed down on Shalom's tongue with the spoon, turning his head in all directions, so that the meager light of the electric bulb would fall directly on his tonsils. At length she removed the spoon, and wiped it on her apron. "He has sonsilitis," she said matter-of-factly.

Mottle, who had been following the movements of his own fingers in the mirror as they strove to knot his tie, stopped and turned his head to her, "Good heavens, Ma, when will you learn? It's tonsilitis, ton-si-litis, not sonsilitis!"

"What do you want from her?" asked Yossi, adjusting his tie with a silver pin. "So she doesn't know as well as you how to pronounce the names of diseases. But she knows how to cure them and you don't."

Sheyne Pessele fixed her bed and ordered Shalom to climb into it. As she was going for the camphor oil, someone pounded three times on the ceiling. "Uncle Henech!" the two spruced-up young men cried out simultaneously. Quickly they filled their cigarette cases with homemade cigarettes and turned to their sick brother. "Take care!" Yossi waved his hand.

"Don't worry about Flora," Mottle added. "I'll take care of her as if she were my own bride!"

They left and Sheyne Pessele, who had completely stopped crying, put a compress of camphor oil around Shalom's neck. On top of it, she put a few layers of stiff parchment paper, then a towel, all of which she covered with a woollen shawl, to "keep in the heat". She energetically tucked Shalom in under the featherbed and threw a woollen plaid over it. "Come here with the pants," she finally ordered her husband. Soon the button was sewn on in a more convenient place.

Itche Mayer put on Tzinele's jacket which did not fit very well either and there could be no talk of buttoning it. But here Itche Mayer did not insist. After all, the problem of buttoning a jacket was not as serious as the problem of buttoning a pair of pants; the sky would not fall if the jacket remained unbuttoned.

As Sheyne Pessele was beginning to change, the pounding could once more be heard coming from the ceiling. "Go, Itche Mayer, I'll follow you soon," she said almost affectionately to him.

"Never mind, I'll wait for you," he replied. He wanted to go with his wife and appear serene and dignified, as was appropriate on such an occasion.

Sheyne Pessele's festive dress was not in much better condition than the one she usually wore around the house. However Itche Mayer thought it more becoming on her. From the drawer in the mahogany table she took out some powder wrapped in a piece of paper and, dipping the edge of a towel into it, she smeared it over her face. She bit her pale lips to bring some redness to them, while she undid the grayish braid of her bun. In a minute, the bun, combed and smooth, was back on her neck. Then she took out the pair of earrings which she had received as a gift from Itche Mayer when she had been his bride, and put them on. That moment, Itche Mayer recognised in his wife the distant reflection of that Sheyne Pessele whom he had once led to the wedding canopy.

He reached for Tzinele's top hat, put it on his head with great ceremony and glanced at himself in the mirror. He admired his height, but then he waved his hand with an air of self-mockery, and approached Shalom. "Don't be upset," he patted the pillow. "A sick Bundist is a bad Bundist anyway. First of all you have to be able to stand on your own two feet."

Shalom shut his eyes. He wanted to be left alone. But Sheyne Pessele had not finished with him yet. She prepared a jug of salt water for him to gargle and a cachet for him to swallow, which was supposed to make the temperature go down. Finally, when everything was ready, she left with Itche Mayer for the wedding.

✦   ✦   ✦

Shalom lay in his mother's bed, covered up to his ears, his head stiff in the cast of the compress. His temples throbbed and his eyes burned. He tried to sleep but could not. He imagined how beautiful Flora would look tonight, and how all evening she would be dancing with Yossi who was the best dancer in Baluty. Yet, he felt bitterly pleased that she did not know of his illness and that he did not have to go to the wedding. He hated weddings and, as a matter of principle, was against all kinds of fashionable ballroom dancing. He tried not to think of the meeting which he would most certainly not attend. Anyway, he had forgotten his little speech. Instead, his mind began repeating other words, actually one word: a name — shaped in the form of a girl's face. It was not Flora's. He recognized it and wondered that it should appear before him, like that, out of nowhere.

Esther. He saw her as she had looked when she was a child, her head covered with wild red curls and her eyes turning into two green slivers when she laughed. What power she had once had over him! As soon as he saw her, he would stand still, his mouth open, holding his breath. He himself had been a child at that time. For many years he had known nothing more about her than her name and that she was an orphan living with her Uncle, Chaim the Hosiery-Maker, by the left entrance of the backyard. During all the years of his childhood he had not exchanged one word with her, although he had seen her often when she came down to the Garden, to the cherry tree, where he was playing ragball with the boys; or when she walked into the stables in the yard where the horse dealers wrestled and lifted weights. Sometimes he waited in the bakery until he saw her passing by on her way to school. Then he would grab his books and follow her. His heart began to pound like a thief's whenever he heard her voice or the sound of her laughter.

On the Sabbath, he would not miss helping Uncle Henech pull out from the oven the pots of *cholent* which were brought in on Friday, so that people might have a hot meal on the next day. He knew she would be coming with her cousins to fetch their pot, all dressed up in her Sabbath dress, with a blue ribbon in her curly red hair. Then he would be able to see her close up and fill his eyes with her mysterious beauty. He would even get a chance to look into the green of her eyes. He noticed the thin blue vein, barely visible, on the left side of her forehead and took this as a particular mark of her charm. He had considered himself fortunate that she had never noticed him or paid any attention to him. He did not know what might have happened to him if she had given him so much as a glance.

The older he became, the more eagerly he tried to find out what she was doing and where she was every single hour of the day. He told himself that it was only a game he was playing, all the while knowing that his life was tied to hers by the hidden hand of destiny. He had long conversations with her in his mind, showing off his agility and cleverness, in his imagination. Once he had even made a sled for her, his first piece of carpentry. He had used it himself the whole winter, all the while trying to figure out how to give it to her. But for that he had had no courage.

When he began attending the *Skif* meetings, his life had changed a great deal. However, his secret did not change. Now he followed Esther less and talked to her less frequently in his imagination, but as soon as he noticed her, the sight of her beauty would gnaw away at his heart, depriving him of the strength in his legs. It was at this point that he started dreaming of her at night.

When he was in the last grade of public school, Esther suddenly disappeared. One day, he overheard Sheyne Pessele mention that her uncle had placed her in an orphanage. With time, he would perhaps have forgotten her completely, were it not for the few times she came to visit the hosiery-maker's family. She had grown to become a thin nimble young lady with a face no longer rosy, but rather pale, almost transparent. Her hair was long, brushed tightly away from her forehead and gathered at the back of her head with a large pin; from there it fell over her shoulders and back in long wavy spirals resembling tongues of flame. To him she seemed a character out of a fascinating novel. He had a secret, particularly tender name that he called her, which was not even a word, but rather a sound, a tone, the clearest and the softest — the one he dreamed of being able to bring out some day on his trumpet, which at that time he was learning to play.

A few years later, Esther disappeared completely. For a time Shalom went on living with her image in his mind. But gradually it began to fade and eventually he forgot her. After all, he was not a dreamer by nature. Besides, there was no time for dreaming. From morning until night he was busy in the workshop where he helped his father. That was in good times. In bad times, he had to run the length and breadth of the city in search of work. And his evenings were devoted to the party, the union or the club; lately he had even begun neglecting his trumpet practice with the orchestra at the Culture League. Flora reproached him constantly, saying that he was neglecting her for his organization.

Shalom felt the sweat sliding behind his ears and prickling his skin. Fatigue picked at his eyes and he kept them shut. He imagined the doorknob moving, the door opening, and Esther coming in slowly, the green of her eyes preceding her image; she looked as she had when he had seen her for the last time. She sat down on the edge of the bed and placed her cool soft hand on his forehead. Her touch made him feel so good that the fever seemed to have left his body. He stopped perspiring and felt completely cured. Esther did not talk to him nor did he talk to her. They looked at each other, and with his eyes he called her by the secret, trumpeting, lofty name which was not even a word. In her presence, he did not feel the usual restlessness inside him. On the contrary, he was calm. His heartbeat was regular, measured. He felt like touching her hand and did so.

When he awoke from sleep, he could still feel the soothing coolness on his forehead. It seemed strange to him that after so many years he should have dreamed of Esther again. He asked himself if this were not a betrayal of Flora and the thought was unpleasant to him.

He pulled out today's *Folks-Zeitung* from a bunch of papers on the chair beside his bed. His eyes fell above the headline, on the white margin. He blinked. Was it possible? He had mixed up his dates! Yes, just like his father, he had a weakness for confusing dates. The important meeting was tomorrow, Sunday. He sighed loudly, with relief. It was good to be sick, wonderful to lie abed in the quiet warm cellar. Again Esther tempted him to concentrate his thoughts on her, but he controlled himself. His eyes began to skim an article in the paper, about the Soviet Union. In the face of the events going on in the world, of the situation in Poland itself, the correct attitude towards the Soviet Union was an issue of the utmost importance in the party these days. It was of particular importance to him, who had a communist brother, to know clearly where he stood on the matter.

It was of no avail. He was still tangled up in his dream and unable to extricate himself completely from its web. He calculated that it was ten years that he had been carrying Esther's image around inside him. The calculation surprised him. An infatuation like that was fitting only for a member of the bourgeosie. Not for him to live with the unreality of a girl who had never exchanged a word with him. He was angry with himself and wondered why he had never fallen in love with a girl in the youth movement. Why did he not long for any of them the way he longed for Esther, nor feel for them what he felt for Flora? He asked himself if this was not a kind of betrayal of the movement and this thought too was unpleasant to him.

A faint rattle, a thin squeaking and squirming coming from beneath the workshop table cut through the stillness of the cellar. The trap had caught a mouse. Shalom let this fact penetrate his mind. Mice were becoming a rarity in the cellar. They could be heard scratching in the walls, running to and fro above the ceiling and on the bakery floor, and Shalom did not mind that; but the panicky flutter of a mouse in the trap was unbearable.

He climbed out of bed with difficulty; his knees were trembling. He was not yet as well as he had thought. Swaying on his feet, he approached the workshop and picked up the trap with its victim. He opened the door and with a hoarse "Go!" released the mouse, which still held in its mouth the crust of bread that had lured it into the prison. He felt relieved. What he had done was a socialist deed and a step forward in the fight with communism. He had avenged himself on his brother Mottle. To give freedom to a living creature was a tremendous thing. Not that he, Shalom, liked mice, but he did not want to have their blood on his hands. And what was most repugnant to him was to lure them into a trap and to their deaths, with a crust of bread. That was Mottle's doing, not his.

He was about to return to his mother's bed when his eyes fell on the mahogany table with the photo albums. He recalled that when he had been sick as a child and was forced to lie in bed, his mother used to give him her album to keep him occupied, so that he would not bother her or get bored. He reached out for it, as well as for his own album.

It was quiet in the cellar. The fire in the stove hissed pleasantly as it flickered through the burners. Through the frozen window came the subdued sound of a far-off horse's hooves and droshky wheels softly cutting into the snow. The hooves clopped louder and clearer, rhythmically, like a clock's pendulum, in the silence of the street.

Shalom opened Sheyne Pessele's album and smiled to himself. On the first page was a picture of his grandparents. He thought he noticed some freckles on his grandfather's nose, but he could not be sure, since the whole picture seemed dotted and feeckled. However, Shalom knew from his father's accounts that his grandfather's freckles could be seen even through his wispy beard. "You say I am freckled," Itche Mayer used to chide his sons good-humouredly. "You should have seen your grandfather. He had as many freckles as there are stars in the sky and grains of sand on the earth." In reality, Itche Mayer resembled his father very much. Both of them had the same kind of eyes, with no eyelashes, and the same blond bushy eyebrows, the same low neck, short figure and strong stubby hands. The hands were freckled too and looked as if they had been dipped in a sack of brown sugar.

Shalom listened. The horse's hooves outside had clopped to a stop. There was a noise in front of the window; someone talking. Then the door of the cellar banged open and a man appeared in it. He was wearing a dark coat, leather gloves on his hands, but no hat on his dark head. His face was brown and frostbitten. A pair of black curious eyes fell on Shalom. "Itche Mayer the carpenter?" the man asked.

Shalom moved up on his pillow. "He isn't home. I'm his son."

The man halted undecidedly. "They told me your father is capable of doing some fine carpentry work."

"Sure he is capable. What is it about?"

The stranger smiled somewhat disconcerted. "It's about a bookcase, an antique, carved." He drew a pen with a gold nib out of his breast pocket, corrected something on a card and approached the bed. "This is my new address."

On the card, Samuel Zuckerman's name was printed in silvery letters. Shalom stared at them while a memory of long, long ago came back to him. His brothers had taken him along, downtown, to the square, and he, a child of four or five, had wandered off by himself and came to a roaring structure, a shaking monster of red bricks, which had cast a spell on him and so weakened his rickety legs with fright that he could not run away. Yossi had led him back to the square. "At Zuckerman's factory, I found him," he had told his brothers. And since then it had remained indelibly in Shalom's memory: the name, the fear, and later on, a hatred was added to it. Now he felt paralyzed again, unable to remove his eyes from the card and look up at the stranger. "I'll tell Father," he muttered, praying for the visitor to vanish.

Samuel, however, was in no hurry. He had rarely had a chance to visit a cellar where people lived. He was curious and felt as if he were visiting an odd museum. His eyes fell on the workshop table covered with the bedding of Shalom's previous resting place. Underneath stood two open tool boxes, a wooden washtub and washing board, and an open sack of potatoes. His eyes wandered over the shelves with Sheyne Pessele's bewigged and wigless heads, then over the water bench with the rusty water buckets. Underneath the bench lay a mouse trap. It occurred to him that he had never held such a gadget in his hand. He thought of his book. Was he really qualified to write it? He, in his ignorance? Could papers and documents alone illustrate life? Perhaps all the things they omitted — petty, dull, uneventful details — were precisely the most characteristic and significant of all?

Shalom mustered his courage and lifted his head, casting a furtive sullen glance at the stranger. He could not understand what the man was waiting for. Was he a bailiff come to take inventory of the furniture? How could he have so much hutzpah and stare at everything with such unabashed curiosity? For that, Shalom had only one name: the arrogance of money. He became increasingly nervous and moved abruptly, drawing up his knees. As he did so, the album shook, sliding off the bed cover to the floor, followed by a rain of loose photographs. Samuel helped him retrieve them.

"What's the matter with you?" he asked, glancing at the album he had picked up "Are you sick?" Shalom nodded, anger boiling inside him. He could not abide the elegant coat in front of him, with the leather gloves tucked so stylishly into its pocket, with the white shirt cuffs with silver cuff-links rimming the sleeves underneath. But most of all he could not abide the hands sticking out from the cuffs: smooth, veinless aristocratic hands, with clean well-tended nails, without so much as a speck of dirt under them. Were it not for his fear of losing his father the job, he would not have hesitated to tell the fancy lord straight to his face what the heart of a proletarian felt towards him. "Your parents were born in Lodz?" Samuel inquired, opening the album. "And you, yourself, were you born here?"

"Yes, here in Baluty!" Shalom burst out. "Here in this cellar!"

Samuel faced the hostile youth, "Is something hurting you?"

"You are hurting me!" Shalom was about to exclaim, but he bit his lips and reached out for the album.

Samuel did not give up. He had a way with the common people. He accepted them as they were — different, strange sometimes, but in a way honest and spontaneous. He did not feel repulsed by them. On the contrary. He admired them — the admiration of the inexperienced for those who had been tried by fate. Long before he had decided to write his book, in his youth, there had been in him a curiosity about the exotic reality of people living in cellars or with no roofs over their heads, about how they spent their existence. More than once had he had the feeling that, in spite of his activities and achievements, he had not really experienced life; that to live really meant to hit one's head against a hard wall and yet survive, just as a hungry man survives the day, or as a youth — like the one before him — survived a childhood in a cellar. He turned the album on Shalom's lap towards himself. "Who is that? Your grandparents?" He smiled. "Have you ever noticed that all grandparents look alike? Have you ever heard of my grandfather?"

"I've heard of you!" Shalom burst out, unable to control himself. The order for work for his father was in grave danger.

Samuel wrinkled his eyebrows. "What have you heard of me?"

Now Shalom felt nothing but fiery revolutionary zeal. "What everyone has heard. That you are filthy rich and an exploiter on top of it! That you hire five Polish workmen for one Jewish one!"

Samuel shrugged his shoulders. "I'm not an exploiter. I pay wages, there are rates, there is a union. And who told you that I hire five Polish workers for one Jewish one? In my office you won't find even one goy." It was, however, true that he preferred to hire Polish workers rather than Jewish ones for his factory. The Poles gave less trouble; they did not threaten to strike every Monday and Thursday. With Jews, the fact that he, their boss, was one of them made for inconvenience and complicated the situation; sooner or later they gave him a headache.

"Don't worry, Mr. Zuckerman!" Shalom, heated by passion, exclaimed. "A day will come when you will have to give account! Don't you worry!" He felt his temples hammering. He was feverish again.

Samuel did not mind Shalom's outburst. He did not feel guilty. All he felt at the moment was this sudden capricious desire to find out about things unknown to him. "My grandfather was Shmuel Ichaskel Zuckerman. You really haven't heard of him?" he asked composedly.

"My grandfather was Israel the dyer. Have you heard something about him?"

"You see, my grandfather was, in a certain sense, a revolutionary too."

"And with us it's just the opposite, Mr. Zuckerman. My grandfather was a reactionary, and we, his grandchildren, are revolutionaries."

"There are all kinds of revolutionaries, of course." Samuel unbuttoned his coat. "But my grandfather was fighting for justice too. He got out of the pale, defied the Germans and the police and moved into a house on Novomieyska Street. A few times they threw him out onto the street; they threatened jail, but he broke open the sealed door every time and moved in. Later on he bought a few neighbouring lots and built his own houses on them. Then they allowed him to lay down an entire street; for many years it was called Zuckerman Street; then they changed the name to a more Polish one and called it Zuckrova. So if one day your children ask you why Zuckrova Street is called that name, you'll be able to give them the proper answer. You still wonder why I'm telling you all this, don't you?"

"Yeah ... haven't you got anything better to do?"

Samuel's eyes lit up with a mischievous sparkle. "Don't you know that the rich do nothing without getting a profit out of it?"

"What kind of profit could you get out of me?"

"I want to have a look at your albums."

Shalom could not believe his ears. No doubt there was something seriously wrong with the rich Zuckerman. Shalom had to smile. As he did so, his revolutionary zeal cooled. "What's there to see in them?" he asked cautiously, embarrassed and amazed by his sudden change of mood.

Samuel drew the album close to himself. "So where did you say your grandparents lived?"

"In Konska Vola. Grandfather was a dyer and Grandmother had an orchard." To his own surprise, Shalom felt almost ready to imagine the strange man in front of him as someone who had nothing to do with Zuckerman, the filthy rich class enemy, if only for the chance to tell him about his grandparents. "Perhaps . . . Do you want to sit down, Mr. Zuckerman?" He quickly removed the papers and the jug of salt water from the chair at the bedside.

Samuel did not wait for him to repeat the invitation; in a minute he was sitting close to Shalom, the open album between them.

"You see, " Shalom lowered his eyes to the picture shyly. "My grandfather was a widower with one son, and Grandmother was a widow with one daughter. My parents are step-sister and step-brother." He pointed to the picture; his embarrassment was fading. "Some grandmother I had! My father called her 'Aunty', and I could never understand how he could add a 'ty' to such an aunt. Father says that her voice was just as heavy as her build. You should hear my father talk about the orchard. Your mouth would water."

Shalom turned the page and pointed to a picture of a dark-haired little girl with thin braids, wearing a dress which reached her ankles; a shaggy dog stood by her side.

"That's how Mother looked when she was small. And you see the trees? This is the orchard. Mother used to run around barefooted in it. The shoes you see her wearing she put on only for the picture. You see the tent in the back? Father used to sleep there at night, during the summer, to guard the orchard. Mother used to climb out to him through the window. Sometimes he played tricks on her, tying her to a tree by her braids. Then she avenged herself on him by upsetting all the baskets of apples he had picked for sale at the market. But their fun didn't last very long, Mr. Zuckerman. Grandfather was displeased with Father's goyish way of life in the orchard. He decided that if father didn't want to become a rabbi, he should learn a trade. Father was eleven when Grandmother took him to the train and sent him off to Warsaw to become a mentsch. Without a groschen to his name, she put him in the compartment, assuring him that he had no need for a train ticket since the women on the train would hide him if necessary. And so they did; they covered him with their long skirts. But this did not prevent him from being pulled out from under the seats, from getting a few kicks in the behind, and from being thrown off the train. Mind you, Mr. Zuckerman, my father had never travelled in a train before, but he was smart enough to understand that if they threw him out of one train, there was nothing to do but to climb onto another one. To cut a long story short, he reached Warsaw and, with God's help, he became a mentsch, a carpenter that is. Because, Mr. Zuckerman, my father always liked to play with wood. When he taught me the trade, he always used to say, 'If you want a piece of work to come out just right, you have to give it not only your brain, but a big piece of your heart as well!' Before he starts working on something, he first strokes the boards as if they were living things, then he smells them, and after that, he begins working. What do you think, Mr. Zuckerman, they gave you my father's address for nothing? There is nobody else like him in Lodz. Mind you, I don't say it because he is my father. But until he became a carpenter, did they ever give him hay to smell!"

"Really? Let's hear . . ." Samuel encouraged him.

Shalom, perspiring, absorbed in his story, moved up on his pillow. "In Warsaw he became an apprentice to a carpenter, and the first thing he learned was to set up the cots for the night, for the master's assistants, since they all lived in the place. Next thing he learned was to peel potatoes for the mistress and to pluck the chickens for her every Friday; he had no chance to see how the chickens looked after they were cooked, of course. The third thing he learned was to take the master's children to the latrine in the backyard every evening. The fourth thing he learned was to receive the master's and his wife's slaps and kicks in good faith, without even blinking an eye. And the only thing that bothered him was the fact that he walked around looking like a girl, with long yellow hair. It went so far, that the master's wife, who did not have a heart of stone, after all, took him to the barber's for a haircut. She promised the barber that she would be back in the blink of an eye, to pay for the job, and she vanished. Half a day Father sat at the barber's, waiting for his mistress to come back with the money. Finally, they gave him a few fiery kicks in his behind, and he found himself stretched out in the gutter. But Father returned to his master's place, the happiest man in the world. He didn't look like a girl anymore. In this picture you see here, he is already the master's assistant, with pay. He asked to be taken, you see how far down? To the waist. He still didn't have enough money for a new pair of pants, and on his feet he wore two left shoes like Charlie Chaplin. And here, you see, Mr. Zuckerman," Shalom turned a page in the album. "Here they are already engaged, Mother and Father."

"They look a little scared," Samuel remarked with a chuckle.

"Scared or not scared, those weren't good times for them." Shalom explained: "Father was back in Konska Vola. Grandfather was sick and the juice in Grandmother's cheeks was gone too. The orchard didn't belong to her anymore. On the other hand, my mother, who was combing wigs at a hairdresser's, was a pretty young lady, and this was when Father fell in love with her for good. Grandmother had smelled it out right away. 'Love is like a swollen nose, you cannot hide it,' she told them. But there was still a long way to the wedding canopy, Mr. Zuckerman. Father had to go to war first, and that was when he took mother to the photographer's. To me, this is the first picture where I recognize my parents. So, they conscripted Father and sent him to the Japanese Front with the infantry. The Russians boasted that they would catch the little Japs like one catches butterflies, with their hats; but they got a good licking from them instead. Father, before he even managed to take a gun in his hands, was hit by a bullet and sent back to Petersburg, to a hospital. Then he went home. He ordered a pair of boots for himself, and my parents went to the wedding canopy. But Father couldn't be content with a hick town like Konska Vola any more, now that he had seen the world. So he decided to move to Lodz, the Polish Manchester."

"That is how the history of your family in Lodz began?"

"Yes, sir. In this cellar. Did you notice the bakery in front of the house? It's my uncle's. He took in my parents and my oldest brother. Wait, I'll show Uncle's picture."

Shalom flipped through the pages of the album, halting at the picture of a tall thin man with spindly legs, a pointed goatee and a pair of half-shut eyes behind thickly rimmed glasses. At his side stood a short chubby woman with a bird-like face and a tightly knotted mouth.

"Here they are!" Shalom exclaimed. "Uncle Henech is almost blind. But if Aunt Pearl wants to know whether a customer has handed her a false banknote, she goes to Uncle Henech. He carries some head on his shoulders, my uncle! And believe you me, I don't say it because he is my uncle. Everyone comes to him for advice, or just for a chat. He likes talking, my uncle. On the other hand, my Aunt Pearl, may she live in good health, is just the opposite. Have a look, Mr. Zuckerman, as much as he is tall, she is small. As much as he likes talking, she likes to keep mum. Uncle likes children, but she can't stand the sight of a child. Uncle has a loose hand. If he has a few groschen, he gives them away; but she doesn't even know the meaning of the word 'charity'. Wouldn't you think, with all that, that she is the one who wears the pants in the household? Surely one would think so. But Uncle, with all his blindness, is capable of tricking her into a sack in full daylight."

Shalom, engrossed in his story, licked his lips, wiped his mouth and went on. "When my folks moved in here, I wasn't born yet. Then Mother began combing wigs and Father had the great idea of working for himself instead of slaving away for someone else. He made a trip to the rabbi of Pabianice, to beg him for a blessing, so that he would succeed in his enterprise. The rabbi of Pabianice did not have any learned followers, but he had what they call blind followers. The rabbi listened to Father's request and said, 'Take me in as a partner in your business and you'll profit in my honour too.' Father returned home, excited and happy, as if he were walking on the clouds of the seventh heaven, and told Mother of the great turn of events. She, on the other hand, was not so enthusiastic about the partnership. She didn't think much of the rabbi and thought even less of his proposition. But Father didn't let her clip his wings. All night, in his bed, he lay calculating and scheming, and in the morning, he woke up feeling like a rich man. He took the few zlotys Mother had saved and set up his workshop here in the cellar. And what do you think, Mr. Zuckerman? The rabbi's honour helped him indeed. That same winter Mother gave birth to my second brother, Mottle. The workshop itself had no luck. Every Friday father made a trip to the rabbi, to give him his profit, until he gave him the last few zlotys and thus ended the partnership."

"And he did not visit the rabbi any more?" Samuel asked, amused.

"No, Mr. Zuckerman. He stopped being a blind Hasid. In one day he took off the kapote, cut his beard and stopped going to the synagogue to pray. He said to Mother, 'Up to now I was for God and for people, but from now on, only for people.' So Mother answered him that if one is for people, one is for God anyway. She personally had no time to be pious; she didn't even mind that Father cut his beard off. Mind you, she had more important things to worry about. She had to work, to make up for the time when she would no longer be able to. She was pregnant again, with my brother Yossi."

"So your father became a freethinker?"

Shalom put his hand behind the stiff compress on his neck and unglued it from the sweaty itching skin, as he went on, "Yes. But father has to believe in something. So he provided himself with a new rabbi: Beinish Michalevitch. Have you ever heard of Michalevitch, Mr. Zuckerman?" Samuel shook his head. Shalom gave him a haughty glance. "Beinish Michalevitch was the leader of the Bund. His hair turned gray overnight when they dragged him to Siberia. And not only was he educated, but he had a heart of pure gold. So Father saw in him the entire Bund. Had he become disillusioned with Michalevitch, he would have stopped being a Bundist altogether."

Samuel pointed to a picture of four boys, each smaller than the other. "Is that you?" he indicated the smallest of the boys.

"Yeah,"Shalom grimaced. "All the pictures they took of me are in a sitting position. Hm . . . my legs were crooked . . . couldn't walk. At that time Mother took me along to Konska Vola. I don't remember a thing about the trip, but from all that I've been told about it, I feel as if I know Konska Vola like my own pocket. Mother brought back the bud of a cherry tree, and even before she took off her coat, she forced father and uncle Henech to go out with her to the backyard, to find a good place to plant it. Everyone made fun of her: how would a cherry tree from green Konska Vola be able to adjust to the dirt and dust of Baluty? But she said, 'Rely on me.' And you should see that tree now, Mr. Zuckerman. Summertime, the girls go there for a suntan and the old women lie in the shade. They even began taking care of the grass, and now this place is called The Garden. Such a person is my mother. She has, as they say, a character of iron. Believe you me, I don't say it because she is my mother."

"A fine mother," Samuel agreed.

But Shalom felt like talking some more about his beloved uncle Henech. He came back to the latter's picture. "This uncle of mine does all his good deeds with the greatest secrecy, so that Aunt Pearl won't find out. For instance, during the holiday of Purim he acts like a real conspirator, the way he sends gifts. He kneads some paper money into a few loaves of bread and sends them with me to the relatives, telling me with a wink, 'Tell them to be careful cutting the bread.' He always carries a wad of money for charity in his shirt sleeve, rolled up over his elbow. I say to him as a joke, 'Uncle, you're wearing a very dear shirt today.' My uncle likes to turn the coal bucket upside down, sit down on it, lean his feet against another bucket and busy himself with his corns. When he is really tired, after a night of kneading and shovelling the bread into the oven, he stretches himself out on the bakery threshold, puts a sack of flour under his head and snores away just like that. But no thief, even barefoot, could get into the bakery unnoticed. Mostly, Mr. Zuckerman, I used to enjoy when uncle's cronies came to visit him."

Shalom turned the pages of the album, stopping at one of them."You see this one here?" he pointed to a picture. "That is Moshe Itzel who drives the hearse for the rich Jews. He is not the best of friends with my Auntie Pearl. Because once, during the World War, she sent him to smuggle a few sacks of flour into the city for her, in his hearse, and didn't reward him even with a pittance for the effort. When he quarrels with her, he says to her, 'You Pearl, my love, may you live forever, you I'll take free of charge to be buried in the cemetery.' Moshe Itzel likes to say that he doesn't carry just anyone in his hearse, that he has his regular customers. One of his good qualities is that he can't stand injustice. Whenever there is a skirmish in Baluty, he is on the spot with his black chariot right away. And you should also know, Mr. Zuckerman, that Moshe Itzel is an excellent clarinet player and, thanks to him, I've developed my ear for music. So this is Moshe Itzel. Aside from him, Uncle has another regular crony, Lame King."

Shalom turned a page and pointed to a picture. "He is one of the two greatest burglars in Poland. Golden Arm from Warsaw is number one, and our Lame King comes right after him. He personally never goes to steal in a private home. His specialty is safes. He got lame when he jumped out of a third storey window after a theft. But he never touches a thing in Uncle's house. Uncle calls him Lame Cripple and he calls uncle Blind Bat. Lame King used to pinch my cheeks so hard that I saw stars in front of my eyes. As soon as he met me, he used to ask if I wanted him to teach me how to become a *mentsch*. He has a school for thieves in his apartment. And now, Mr. Zuckerman, you have a better idea, I suppose, of the kind of company I grew up in."

Samuel did not feel sorry for him. He listened to Shalom's stories with a strange eagerness. Certainly he had heard of similar characters, but they had seemed much uglier, much more repulsive than now, when he heard about them from this youth. There was something strangely attractive and tempting in the roughness of this kind of life. "And who else comes to visit your uncle?" he asked.

Shalom smiled meaningfully, as if he were reading his thoughts. "You like the company?"

"It's interesting."

"Yeah, interesting to hear about, but not to live with." Shalom pointed to another picture. "This one here is Rudolf Valentino. They call him that because he is handsome. He is the prince of the riff-raff of Baluty. He transports meat in a wagon with a tin lid, and has his own stable in the backyard. There, the hoodlums and the smart guys gather to lift weights and try their strength. Thanks to them I have a pair of strong hands too. When I was little, the Polish boys used to attack me, so the guys decided to educate me physically, so to speak. The smart guys are the best of friends with us, but this is out of respect, not of comradeship. They would jump into fire for my father. They call him *Vittisher*, an honest man, in their thief language. So, getting back to Valentino . . . He likes the outdoors, to be free as a bird. That was how, riding about town in his tin wagon, he found himself a wife. He bought her for money, mind you. There is a house of pleasure on Zawadzka Street, if you noticed, Mr. Zuckerman; and in front of it, one of the girls wrapped in a beaver coat had her spot, and there Valentino spotted her. He paid two thousand zlotys for her and she began working for him. She still does, part-time that is, and she is also his wife. Her name is Sheindle. At the same time, Mr. Zuckerman, you should keep in mind that Valentino is actually the 'ristocrat of the underworld. He doesn't insult people for nothing, and normally you'll hear no dirty words from him, except, of course, when he gets into a rage. He goes to the theatre and although he can hardly read well enough to make it through the headlines in the newspaper, he buys one every day. Like Moshe Itzel, he is capable of killing a man for justice, but will never raise a hand if he realises that justice is not on his side. He has his morality, mind you. The thing is that it is not the same as mine. You see, Mr. Zuckerman, you have no reason to pride yourself that you haven't grown up a thief. But I have. Think about my childhood for a moment. My best meal was a chunk of bread with butter and tea with sugar. But most of the time there was no butter for the bread, nor sugar for the tea, or there was no tea either. Then Mother used to colour the water with chicory, and we called it chicory tea. And when there was meat for dinner, it was always dumplings, because you can put all kinds of things into them to make them more economical. Of course, since we have grown up and started working, things have changed. But how much have they changed, do you think?"

Samuel felt uneasy. The youth's anger a while ago had not disturbed him as much as did his quiet words now. "And this is your brother?" he lowered his face to the album, trying to divert Shalom from his thoughts.

"Yes, that is Yossi."

"What are those medals on his lapel?"

"Medals? Oh, yes, for dancing, at dance competitions. You hear, once he came home with the idea of making a dance hall here, in this cellar, a sort of dancing school. During the daytime there was Father's workshop and Mother's hairdressing salon, and at night, a dance hall. He hired the dance master, Tzinele, a funny little man, but a specialist in his field. Moshe Itzel played on his clarinet and Tzinele and Yossi were the teachers. Tzinele sang to the music, 'Tha-ra-ra, forward to the slop pail, back to the wardrobe; tha-ra-ra, up to the wardrobe, back to the slop pail!' But Yossi fooled around so much, that after a while there was no one left for him to give lessons to."

Shalom grew thoughtful, obviously weighing something in his mind. He lowered his eyes, smiling shyly as he spoke. "And now, Mr. Zuckerman, since you already know all my family, I'll show you my fiancée too." He took the other album whose cover was made of nicely carved wood worked by Shalom himself. He opened it and pointed to a picture of a girl with a head of thick wavy hair. From under her eyebrows peeked out a pair of mischievous coquettish eyes.

"A beauty!" Samuel exclaimed.

"Yes, but my parents say that she is not the right one for me. And I am too involved with her to break up."

"Why should you break up with her?"

"Oh, I was just talking . . ." Shalom's face turned a fiery red; his glassy eyes shone. The thread of his talk was broken. Samuel, so as not to make him feel more embarrassed, glanced at his watch. Shalom noticed it and smiled somewhat regretfully. "How do you like that, Mr. Zuckerman? It started with photography, and ended with biography."

Samuel rose and buttoned his coat. Shalom's stories were turning in his head. The evening spent at the young fellow's bedside was not a complete loss, he was sure of that. Now he knew that collecting materials for his work was only the beginning. Matilda came to his mind. He asked himself what she would have said if she had seen him here, spending the hours of his Sabbath evening in a cellar in Baluty, instead of being with her. He blinked at Shalom mischievously. "Tell me, young man, if you were to meet me one day in the heat of a real class fight, would you remember that you told me your . . . your biography tonight?"

Shalom looked at him, disconcerted. "What's worth remembering, one remembers always, don't worry, Mr. Zuckerman."

"Yes, but if it were to come to revolution, let's say, would you be able to kill me in cold blood?"

"I don't know. I've never killed anyone in cold blood or any other way."

"But you are a revolutionary and revolutions aren't fought without bloodshed."

"Sure, Mr. Zuckerman. But revolution is not my goal. It is just a means to achieve a better life. I am ready to make sacrifices for that, even to shedding blood, not only someone else's but my own too." With an air of condescension, he added, "One thing I am not clear about, Mr. Zuckerman, and that is you . . ."

Samuel guffawed. "You imagined me with horns, eh? You thought I had a fat face and a heavy belly." He lowered his face to Shalom. "You cannot artificially divide all people into two categories and put them one against the other. Everyone has his faults and his good qualities; and apart from that, life makes the man, as it made you and your uncle with all his cronies. The same way it made me too."

"But everyone is responsible for his deeds, and so are you."

"What deeds? Why do you see so much wrong in me? I serve society in my own way. I contribute to the growth of industry, I help to build our city, I give employment to many workers. After all, it is the individual who fosters progress, not the masses."

"And whom is your progress serving, Mr. Zuckerman? Progress you call it? Such progress is not worth the price paid by millions of enslaved people."

"So their fates must be improved."

"Aha! You said it yourself!" Shalom was triumphant. "And no one can improve their fates but the slaves themselves." He sat up, again ready to begin a heated debate.

But Samuel would not let him go on. "If you want to know my opinion, young man, I don't consider your predicament to be so grave at all. I mean, it's true you have no money, but instead you have something else of which the rich are in great want."

Shalom fell back on his pillow, looking at the visitor in wide-eyed astonishment. Rich Zuckerman was a real riddle to him. He took Samuel's outstretched hand in his, and shook it hesitantly, reluctant to let go. "To be fair," he mumbled, "It is now your turn to tell me about your father, about your life, Mr. Zuckerman."

"Yes, but since there is no justice in this world, I won't tell you."

"Why not?"

"My father never told me about himself, nor did my mother. All I know about my family comes from reading dead papers and documents, and that is not the same."

"It almost looks as if you could envy me!" Shalom exclaimed, completely confused.

Samuel put on his leather gloves. "You think so? Well, I don't know. I'm sure of one thing though. I would never change places with you." He waved his gloved hand at Shalom. "Don't forget to tell your father to come and see me tomorrow, about the bookcase. Good night and get well." He gave a last quick glance around the cellar and left.

✦ ✦ ✦

Itche Mayer and his family returned from Gretta's wedding in the small hours of the morning. Shalom did not hear them come in. Exhausted, perspiring, he slept through the night and when he woke up the next morning, life in the cellar had resumed its usual rhythm. Itche Mayer and Yossi were busy at the workshop. Sheyne Pessele was combing her wigs and Mottle had already left for work. Shalom's eyes fell on the frozen window, on the dirty electric light bulb and on the stove where a pot was quacking monotonously, steam rising from under its lid towards the damp shiny ceiling. From there it was transformed into hazy rings which spiralled towards the window and the door.

Shalom moved his limbs with difficulty. They felt as though they were not his own. His joints ached and his throat was parched. He called Sheyne Pessele. She left her heads, hurried to the stove, then approached the bed with a bowl of kasha in her hands. The mere sight of the bowl and the smell coming from it made Shalom feel nauseous. Sheyne Pessele touched his forehead. "He's boiling!" she called out to Itche Mayer.

Itche Mayer left his plane and, all covered with sawdust and wood shavings, approached the bed. His rough hand rubbed Shalom's cheek. "Yeah, he is boiling," he agreed and looked at her questioningly, as if expecting something from her.

She twisted her tired wrinkled face. "Don't stand there like a telegraph pole. Move him up on the pillow." The steam rising from the bowl attacked Shalom's face. He shut his eyes. Sheyene Pessele grew impatient. "Open your mouth!" she ordered in a tone which made resistance impossible.

Shalom opened his mouth and swallowed with difficulty a spoonful of soup. "Zuckerman was here yesterday," he said to her after she had finished feeding him.

She looked at him as if he were delirious. "Who is this Zuckerman now out of the blue?"

"The great Zuckerman, Mother, the factory owner himself. He needs Father." He wanted to tell with pride that the great Zuckerman had sat there last night, at his bedside, talking to him as an equal. But he checked himself, preferring to keep the experience to himself, at least for a while.

As soon as Itche Mayer heard of Zuckerman's order, he stopped his work, took his tool box and left for the rich man's house. He returned with parts of the broken bookcase door and set himself to work with great diligence. Fixing such an antique piece of furniture was a job made just for him. During the meal, he told his family about the splendid house of which he had managed to see only the vestibule and the studio. Sheyne Pessele's face lit up wistfully when she heard about the floors which were like mirrors, so smooth and clean that one could sit down on them in the nicest dress and not dirty it. Shalom listened enraptured; his conversation of the day before seemed like a dream.

After lunch, he felt much better. His temperature went down. He had finally finished reading the interesting article in the *Folks-Zeitung* and was mentally rehearsing the short speech he would deliver that evening at the meeting which he would most surely attend. But when evening came and he asked Sheyne Pessele for his clothes, she shook her head emphatically, "Not on your life!" They quarrelled for over an hour, in Flora's presence. His voice grew hoarse, which gave Sheyne Pessele an additional reason not to let him go.

The family went to sleep early. All were tired after the previous sleepless night and the long day of work. As soon as the light was turned off, a chorus of snores filled the darkness. Only Shalom, upset, lay awake in his mother's bed — while she slept in Itche Mayer's, the latter having joined Yossi and Mottle on the workshop table.

Shalom's eyes were glued to the gray frozen window pane as he became aware of a shadow moving across it. After a while he heard a light tapping on the glass. Outside, someone was calling his name. He climbed out of bed. The sound of steps and an almost inaudible laughter reached his ears from the corridor. He opened the door and immediately recognised his comrades, David and Rachel, whose faces shone in front of him in the dark. Feeling sure that something unusual had happened, he was unable to say a word. Then he realized that he was standing in front of them in his underwear. His teeth chattering, his legs shaking, he hurried back to find his coat. Soon he reappeared before the pair, wrapped in Yossi's coat. "I'm sick," he informed them. He felt the cold of the clay floor creeping up his legs and reaching his heart. He was unable to control his shaking.

The pair expressed their regrets. The girl said, "We've come from the meeting. They assigned us to tell you that you're elected to be our delegate to the conference in Warsaw. But since you're sick . . ."

Shalom grabbed them by the arms. "I'm going to Warsaw, comrades!" he burst out. "I'm going!"

"You would have to be at the train station tomorrow at six in the morning," said David.

"Comrades, I'm going!" He shook their arms vigorously. They said something, but he was no longer listening to them. He said good-bye quickly and returned to the cellar, feeling as if he were going mad and were about to explode with pride. Confused, exhilarated, he turned in circles on his shaky legs, not knowing what to do first. The snoring of his family irritated him. He wanted to put on the light, to turn the night into day. He wanted to talk, to shout, to make an uproar. Finally, he could stand it no longer and bent over Itche Mayer who was sleeping on the edge of the workshop table. He shook him. "Father !" he cried out with the voice of a croaking rooster. "Father, I was elected a delegate!" Itche Mayer let himself be shaken for a while, then, still asleep, he shrugged Shalom's hand off his shoulder and turned to the other side. "Father, I am going to Warsaw!" Shalom shouted with all his strength.

This time both Sheyne Pessele and Itche Mayer lifted their heads from their pillows. Sheyne Pessele was the first to catch the sense of Shalom's breathless words. She sat up and rocked the upper part of her body, the mattress springs accompanying her every move with a rusty squeak. "A black year on my enemies," she crooned in a singsong. "The boy is out of his mind! You have sonsilitis, you're sick like a bear, what do you knock on my head in the middle of the night for?"

But Itche Mayer, as soon as the news reached his brain, could no longer rest. He hung both his legs down from the table and sat up, to let the news penetrate him completely. Small thing! His son was elected a delegate to Warsaw! Fully awake, he rubbed his hands against his knees.

Shalom knelt down beside Sheyne Pessele's bedside, imploring her, "Look at me, Mother. See if I'm not completely cured!" He grabbed her hand and pressed it against his forehead. "So, what do you say? I'm healthy, eh?"

"Sure, sure! It's black magic!" She shook her head and went on rocking. But gradually the same feeling overcame her as had overcome Itche Mayer. Her pride awoke. A crowd of people had elected her son to go to a conference in Warsaw! She had not slaved her life away for nothing! She climbed out of bed and turned on the light. Shalom sat down submissively on the chair under the electric bulb and let Sheyne Pessele investigate the depths of his throat. "If I were to say that it isn't red," she concluded, "I would be a liar." She scrutinised Shalom with eyes that were unable to disguise her pride and pleasure. "With such a head of hair you want to go to Warsaw?"

Shalom exclaimed, "Rachel's father! He would cut it!"

Itche Mayer got down from the table and dressed hurriedly. "Right!" he said energetically."Let's go to Comrade Eibushitz for a haircut!"

Sheyne Pessele began to throw pieces of clothing to Shalom: a few undershirts, underwear, long johns and two sweaters. Then she sat down to mend the hole in the elbow of Shalom's jacket sleeve.

Itche Mayer and Shalom rushed into town to Comrade Eibushitz, the barber, pulled him out of bed and instructed him to give Shalom a haircut and shave suitable for a delegate to a conference in Warsaw, the metropolis of Poland. Only when they had returned home and everything was ready for the trip, did it occur to them that there was not enough money in the house for a train ticket. Sheyne Pessele opened up all her hidden knots and Itche Mayer investigated his pockets, but it was no use. The situation was what it was. Shalom felt sorry that he had no savings of his own. Had he asked his father to pay him at least a part of what he had earned, he would not have to break his head now, on such an occasion; it was obvious that he had put all his earnings into a sack of holes.

First they woke up Yossi. But sleepy Yossi shrugged his shoulders. How would he come to have a groschen to his soul? So, there was nothing left to do but to wake Mottle who, they all knew, kept his quite substantial savings tucked away somewhere. But Mottle, although sleepy, knew how to answer them. He said that he would certainly not support the enterprise of a bunch of "social traitors", and he turned to the wall and went back to sleep.

The final thing left to do was to wake up Uncle Henech. And Itche Mayer, Sheyne Pessele and Shalom set out for the bakery. Blind Henech did not have to be woken too vigorously. A touch on the door knob was enough — and he appeared before them in his underwear, his pointed goatee cutting a dark shadow on the white of his flannel undershirt. He hastened to fetch his "dear" shirt, unrolled the "dear" sleeve, and took out a wad of paper money. He counted out the sum for the train ticket into Itche Mayer's palm — and so he remained in their memory for a long time: a white angel with a dark pointed beard who, although practically blind, could count money in the dark.

The town was still steeped in heavy shadows when Shalom left for the train station. His neck was protected by a long woollen scarf, tied firmly over a rolled-up old sweater. However, on his way to the train, Shalom freed himself of the scarf as well as of the sweater. He considered it undignified; it did not look revolutionary at all. A Youth-Guard member and a delegate to an important conference in Warsaw was not supposed to be afraid of such trifles as the stupid inflammation of a pair of tonsils in his throat.

Chapter Three

THIS PARTICULAR MORNING in the month of March, Mr. Adam Rosenberg was in high spirits. His exercises had left him refreshed and, besides that, the frost was finally beginning to thaw and the day promised to be clear and sunny. As soon as he stepped out of his house, Adam breathed in the cool air deeply and felt delighted. He heard the urgent scratching of his dog on the other side of the door. She whined weakly, as if begging for another pat from her master before being separated from him for the rest of the day. So Adam let her out, embraced her muzzle and ran his fingers over her ears which were delicate and as smooth as silk. "You see, Sutchka," he whispered, "spring is coming. Soon we'll go deer hunting." The dog, her tongue drooping from her open mouth, panted happily; her intelligent brown eyes looked lovingly through those of her master, straight into his heart. He pushed her away gently. "Go to the fence, go . . ." A row of sparrows perched on the fence posts like dark knobs on white sticks tore themselves from their perches as the dog drew near, and circled over the roof, waiting for her to fulfil her master's command, so that they could return to their favourite resting place.

At length, Adam could hear the rumbling of a motor and right after, his chauffeur, Marian, appeared on the path. Marian grabbed his cap with the shiny visor off his head. Seeing his boss lose his smile and wrinkle his eyebrows, he stammered out humbly, "The motor wouldn't start, Mr. Rosenberg."

"For such a good-for-nothing as you, nothing would start," Adam replied, looking around for the dog. With one leap she was beside him. He patted her neck, "Go in, Sutchka. It's still too cold for you outside." He opened the door and the dog slipped agilely through the opening.

At that moment, a robust youth appeared on the threshold in an unbuttoned *gymnasium* uniform, his brown hair dishevelled. In his hand he held a bulky school bag and a navy blue cap with a pinned-on silver eagle. Engaged in chewing on his last bite of breakfast, he almost fell over Adam. "I'm coming along, Pa!" he called out, darting after Marian. Adam chased after them. Marian, half bent, cap in hand, opened the car door and waited for his master to squeeze in the bulk of his heavy body.

The sun was still too low in the sky to shine on the sidewalks which were crowded with people. It was just starting to fringe the tips of the snow-covered roofs and no more than a thin strip of golden light could be seen from below. Adam observed the passers-by: the workers, their faces still covered with sleep, lunch bags under their arms and bottles of coffee sticking out of their pockets, the dreamy school children with their dangling school bags getting caught between their legs, and the office workers, flat briefcases under their arms, with their well-polished shoes and dull yellow faces which suggested the coming of fall rather than of spring. The grayness of the people, wagons and cars, along with the grayness of the buildings, of the cobblestones, of the glassy frozen mud on the sidewalks began to weigh on Adam's good mood.

He glanced at his sleepy unkempt son and drew a comb out of his pocket. The youth passed the comb carelessly through his curly hair. "When did you come home yesterday?" Adam asked, regarding his son's healthy head of hair with envy. The boy yawned instead of replying and looked out the window. "There is one thing I want of you, Mietek . . ." Adam was sorry that his good mood had vanished so quickly. "I don't want you to fool around these last few weeks before your matriculation exams."

Mietek turned around to him. "Don't worry," he said and stretched out his hand, palm up. "I haven't got a penny to my name, Pa."

Adam put a ten zloty note in Mietek's hand, "But remember . . ."

"You want just one thing from me," Mietek laughed. "Give me another five . . ."

Adam again reached for his pocketbook. "Another five, another ten. You're like a sack full of holes."

"I like it when you give me money. It shows that you love me."

"You need that kind of proof? You wouldn't know otherwise?"

"Sure, and you need it too. You know very well that you like to give me money."

"You're an idiot."

"In economics, money is a symbol of capital in the state's treasury. Money needs backing, collateral. But with us, it's a replacement for something which is missing from our family treasury."

"You are insulting me," Adam snorted at him. "Tell me, is it possible to satisfy you, ever?"

Mietek shrugged his shoulders. "I am satisfied, as long as there is a jingling in my pocket."

Marian turned onto Piotrkowska Street and skilfully made his way between the noisy crowded streetcars. In the window of one of them, Adam noticed the face of a woman with a small velvet hat on her dark hair. Her rouged lips smiled and something sang out consolingly in Adam's heart. Her smile was meant for him; a smile suggesting a body ready to offer itself. He winked at her meaningfully; she answered with a small nod of her head and a wave of her white gloved hand. He decided to follow the tram and find out where the charming creature got off. In his mind, he stripped her of her blue coat and of all that lay underneath it. She displayed two rows of bright little teeth that made the street, Mietek and the grayness of his mood vanish.

Marian stopped the car. "Good-bye, Pa!" Adam heard his son's voice but did not turn his head. He waved his hand, half to Mietek, half to the lady in the streetcar window.

Marian drove on for a while and stopped again. "The newsstand, Mr. Rosenberg," he said and stepped out of the car. Adam looked after the vanishing streetcar, his heart shrinking with regret. Nervously, he followed Marian with his eyes; he felt capable of tearing him into little pieces.

Marian returned with the Morning Voice, holding the newspaper flat on both hands as if it were an exquisite cake. He tried, with exaggerated care, to place it in Adam's hands, but the latter grabbed it impatiently. "Let's go!" he commanded. He opened the paper and grumbling to himself, began reading the thick print of the headlines: CHAMBERLAIN DISILLUSIONED ... FOREIGN MINISTER BECK GOES TO LONDON ... HACHA ENTRUSTS THE DESTINY OF THE CZECH PEOPLE TO THE FÜHRER ... GERMAN TROOPS CROSS THE BORDERS FIXED IN MÜNCHEN ... THE PROTECTORATE OF BOHEMIA AND MORAVIA BECOMES FACT ... THE FÜHRER PROMISES PROTECTION FOR INDEPENDENT SLOVAKIA ... THE FÜHRER PRONOUNCES MEMEL A GERMAN CITY ... "The Führer here and the Führer there," Adam shook the paper disgruntledly and pulled out the financial page. The car hurried through the poorly paved side streets, jolting Adam up and down on his seat. The numbers jumped before his eyes. He tried to connect them in his mind, but that brought him no satisfaction; he feared the truth of the organized numbers. He crumpled the paper into a ball, threw it to the other side of the seat and looked out the window as the limousine glided into the empty factory yard. He quickly tapped the bald spot on his head, to check whether it was properly covered by the strings of hair growing above one of his ears. Marian helped him manoeuvre himself out of the car. Straightening up, Adam listened for a while to the rhythmic roar of the machines and the light glassy tinkling of the window panes, which were winking at him with the first rays of the sun like countless glittering eyes. He liked his factory. It was equipped with the most modern machinery, which required a minimum of manual control. He dreamed of a time when he would be able to do away with workers completely; but for the time being, what he had was the closest to his goal.

Once again in good spirits, he entered the office.

✦   ✦   ✦

At the sight of their boss, the office workers rose from their desks. "Good morning, Mr. Rosenberg!" they respectfully sang out their greeting.

Adam stole a furtive glance at his bespectacled bookkeeper. He could not stand him, nor could he stand his bespectacled secretary, Miss Zosia. The general manager claimed that she was the best stenographer in the city and that it was lucky for Adam and for the factory that she deigned to work there. But somehow Adam was unable to appreciate his good fortune and to acknowledge the great advantage of having her. If she had had at least a fraction of feminine charm, so that a man might have a little pleasure in working in his own office, in his own factory. But feminine charm was precisely what she was lacking. "Everything okay, Wiseman?" Adam asked the bookkeeper.

"Yes Mr. Rosenberg," the bookkeeper servilely bent his entire fragile torso. "Nice weather, we're having," he said in an uncertain voice, trying to modulate it with a tone of familiarity, so that he might better disguise the nervousness he felt in his boss' presence.

With distaste, Adam let his gaze fall on his secretary's flat chest and ordered, "Come into my office in fifteen minutes, Miss Zosia." Her eyelids were lowered and through the little sliver of eye remaining open behind the heavily rimmed glasses, she concentrated her attention on the tip of her nose. She had been working for him for the past five years, but Adam often wondered if she had any idea what he, her boss, looked like.

Upon entering his office, he hastened to the window where there winked at him, gaily and refreshingly, the grassy underwater life of his tropical aquarium. He crumpled the food for his precious fish between his fingers, and sprinkled it on the water. The fish, trembling excitedly, began to race past the tiny porcelain palaces and through the grassy weeds, for their first bite. Adam gazed into the green world of the aquarium and panted contentedly. He tapped the glass with his soft fleshy finger, calling each fish by its own exotic name; names which sounded so musical that he wanted to repeat them again and again. He checked the temperature of the water and passed on to his chess table where the ivory pieces were in the same position as he had left them the day before, when he had neglected to finish a game with himself. He bent over the table. The steady rumbling of the aquarium motor helped him organize his thoughts clearly and in an orderly fashion. He made a move with a black pawn and straightened up. He took in the room at a glance, avoiding the wall against which there leaned his unfinished portrait which was covered with a cloth stained with brightly coloured blotches.

He shook off his heavy winter coat, carelessly threw it on an armchair and let the full weight of his body sink into the soft seat of his desk chair. He leaned his head on his hands and suddenly felt sleepy. He yawned, his gaping mouth revealing a set of gold-capped teeth. Then he wiped his palms over the top of the desk, until one of them encountered a pile of papers. His fist rested on them like a heavy down-pressing weight. The papers smelled of boredom. He noticed a dusty ray of sunlight reflected on the shiny table top and recalled the woman in the velvet hat. She was like youth itself, like spring. He felt in her disappearance, in the fact that she was unattainable — that the joy of life had flashed him by, that spring had become for him something merely to be admired from afar, no longer to be experienced and lived through. He began to file his nails. Long nails bothered him, the sight of the dirt underneath them was repulsive to him and reminded him of the rusty tin heaps in his father's junkyard.

He was meticulously clean by nature; an idiosyncrasy which had played a major part at the most critical moment of his life: his failing the bar examinations. Even then he had believed in *mens sana in corpore sano*, and he had been so anxious to do well in the exams, so much had depended on it, that he had run off to the bathhouse that fateful first morning, and arrived half an hour late at the university. He did not have enough time to finish his paper. As a result, he had been so tense and so anxious during the oral exam that he had mixed up the answers. And his career as a lawyer was over.

But thanks to that failure had come his future success. From his present height, he could look down on his youthful ambition to become a lawyer with a sufficient amount of disdain. The numerous lawyers with whom he had had to deal in later life had looked up to him like lackeys, while the professors who had instructed him in his youth were no more than worthless pawns discarded forever from the chess board of his life. Once, so many people had held him in their power, thinking themselves to be the masters of his fate. And today? What were they, compared to him, the former failure?

"If only life were not so dull and boring," Adam sighed. However, in spite of his regret, he was aware that things were good as they were; that he did not, in fact, want them to be different. Of course, life had been more interesting when he was starting out to make his way; there had been no lack of excitement then, nor for that matter, lack of worry. Now, on the other hand, his heart was calm.

And now he, Adam, was an honest man, not a swindler or a crook like his father, the sloppy junk dealer, had been. Now police officers respected him. They saluted as for a general when they noticed him passing in his shiny limousine. And now he had his kingdom, his gigantic factory, which exported merchandise as far as South America. Now he was the master of an army of workers and clerks whose fate was in his hands. Wasn't that the highest reward life could offer? Indeed his boredom was worthwhile. He knew he was not the only one experiencing such inner emptiness. All great people felt that way once they reached their goal.

A light tapping at the door was followed by the appearance of Miss Zosia. She was carrying a silver tray, which contained some crescent rolls and a cup of coffee topped with a froth of fluffy cream. Eyes lowered, she approached the desk and placed his second breakfast before Adam. "It's fifteen minutes, Mr. Rosenberg," she said, crossing her long-fingered hands over her small rounded belly. "You wanted to dictate a letter, sir."

"Come back in fifteen minutes," Adam dismissed her, pulling the tray towards him. The cream floating on the coffee was soft and clear as snow. Eagerly, he dipped his tongue in it and took a sip. An unpleasant sting burnt his palate, making him think of Miss Zosia. With all her submissiveness and shyness, there was a certain resistance and spitefulness in her demeanour; as if by lowering her eyelids she were trying to escape him; as if she were hiding something in the depths of her eyes. He felt a cold desire to meet her gaze once and for all, and wondered why he had never ordered her to look at him when he talked to her.

The telephone rang and Adam reached for the receiver. A familiar voice sang out in his ear, "You forgot to take your scarf, darling. Don't you know how capricious March can be? Shall I bring it to you?"

"What an idea, Yadwiga, my kitten!" He too sweetened his voice, while his impatient fingers reached for a crescent roll. "It's spring outside. Go back to bed."

"Why don't you let me do a little thing like that for you?" the voice purred.

"Because I love you." He could not restrain himself any longer and bit into the soft dough of the crescent. With renewed interest he asked, "How is Sutchka?"

"Oh, Sutchka!" the voice began to laugh jarringly. "She's lying here at my feet."

"I envy you," he said, but checked himself immediately. "I envy her. I too would love to lie at your feet and play with the pompoms on your slippers, instead of sitting in this dull office among piles of boring papers."

"Then I shall come to you. *Ich liebe dich. Mich reizt deine schöne Gestalt,*" the voice whispered in melting German and broke off. Adam gulped down the coffee, pushed aside the tray and rang for Miss Zosia.

Miss Zosia was wearing a dark-grey sweater with a row of tiny black buttons reaching up to her neck. Adam could not stand the sweater nor the long black skirt which hung loosely on her bony hips, blown out around her small protruding belly. He looked at her face. It seemed strange that her thin neck was capable of carrying such a full head of hair which surrounded her puffed face; her cheeks were of a deep unhealthy red. Her hair, parted in the middle, was smooth and black, and so tightly knotted into a large bun, that it appeared to be all of one pitch black piece and not some thousands of separate hairs. As usual, Adam saw only her heavy lowered eyelids through her glasses; lids fringed with strikingly long eyelashes which cast a shadow over her entire face. With an awkward movement, she removed the tray from the table and sat down stiffly, ready to take his dictation.

"To Mr. Rumkowski, Director of the Helenovek Orphanage," Adam began. "My very dear Mr. Rumkowski," Adam stopped. "Cross out 'my very dear', 'Dear' is more than enough." He rubbed his forehead and proceeded. "Because of urgently pressing work, I had no time to answer your many ... Cross out 'many', write 'countless' petitions regarding financial support for your institution. However, I acceded to your request and forwarded ..." Adam looked at the secretary. He could not understand how he had been able to bear her daily presence in his office; nor could he understand what the general manager, Mr. Zaidenfeld, saw in her. Were there no pretty girls in town capable of doing the same work? He knotted his hands in front of his chest, rested his elbows on the table and inclined his head towards her. "Miss Zosia ..." With difficulty he forced his lips into a crooked smile. "I would like to ask you something ..."

Miss Zosia tensed her shoulders, stubbornly keeping her eyes fixed on the notebook in her lap. "Yes, Mr. Rosenberg?" she whispered.

"Tell me ... Couldn't you come to work dressed a little more appropriately? I mean ... a little nicer? You've been working for me for so many years ..." ("And I don't even know the colour of your eyes!" he almost added.) She did not move. He felt as if a lifeless mummy were sitting in front of him and his desire to penetrate her rigidity grew. For a moment he imagined that he saw tears pour down from her eyes, wash her face and run down to her neck, disappearing under the collar of her buttoned sweater. He imagined her rising abruptly from her chair, falling to his feet and kissing his hands. He saw himself pouncing on her, his fingers tangled in the countless buttons of her sweater. Unable to control himself any longer, he cried out, "You look like a block of wood, Miss Zosia! For heaven's sake, you might at least wear a decent bra, Miss Zosia!"

Then it happened. Her eyes opened. He saw a pair of enormous dark pupils, doubly deep and large through her eyeglasses. Her burning gaze penetrated him deeply. He had to turn his head aside, frightened that she might consume him entirely. Her gaze remained stuck inside him. Was it hatred? Yes, but also something worse, something unbearable: disgust, multiplied by disdain, elevated to the highest power by the force of her eyeglasses. "I'll fire her!" he decided. It was no use. He could no longer go on in the presence of those eyes.

He realized that she was reading his letter to him from her notebook. He tried to detect a tremor of humiliation in her voice, but it sounded as monotonous and colourless as usual. Once again he saw himself lying on top of her, his hands around her neck, over her face, his fingers groping for her eyes, ready to scratch them out, to extinguish the gaze which lay imbedded in him like an arrow. He forced his voice to remain calm, not to betray him as he resumed the dictation. "Since then," he went on, "I have received neither a note of thanks nor a receipt for the hundred zlotys I sent you. Perhaps I do not deserve the former, but I have a right to expect the latter, that is, a receipt for my contribution." He pointed to the door, "You can go, Miss Zosia."

After she left, Adam felt exhausted as if he were at the end of a day of hard labour. He got up and approached the aquarium; he tapped at the glass with his finger, peering into the carefree fish world. He felt envious of the gay graceful forms gliding among the weeds and the tiny porcelain palaces. He wished he were a fish. Before long, he was sitting bent over the chess board, lost in the complicated calculation of eliminating a bishop. Fatigue left him. Now he felt like a fish, but not the kind that swam in the aquarium. He shed his skin and, liberated, dived into the clear waters of thought — the only kind of fish he could ever become. However, it was not an easy task to win a bishop from himself, since the opposing self who played against him was not an opponent to be shrugged off easily. The fight grew bitter. At length he won the bishop, but at the expense of having his castle ruined and his king exposed in all his naked helplessness — by his opposing self.

As he got up, his eyes unwillingly fell on the wall against which his unfinished portrait leaned. Sitting for the painter, Guttman, had become an irksome chore. It reminded him of his unpleasant visits to the dentist. But even if he had wanted to, he could not put an end to the project. He had both a morbid curiosity about it, and a fear of encountering his own self in the portrait. This was the opposite kind of encounter with himself than the one at the chessboard, but it was just as absorbing. And whenever he noticed the curtained portrait, he was compelled to approach and uncover it, as he did now — like the game played by Dorian Gray — and the mere thought of the similarity chilled his heart. He was not Dorian Gray. He was in the hands of a vulgar uneducated painter who held him captive by the black magic of his brush, so that he might earn a few zlotys. It was obvious that he, Adam, was looking at a caricature of himself. Guttman was making fun of him. How could he, Adam, be the ugly creature he saw before him? Granted, his features were irregular and his body was badly proportioned, but he was an imposing figure nevertheless. He had class, dignity and aristocratic bearing, qualities which Guttman surely envied and therefore distorted. For the hundredth time Adam decided to fire the painter and get rid of his disgusting work. And as he was dwelling on the subject of firing, Miss Zosia re-entered his mind. Her fate too was decided.

He covered the painting and reached into the drawer for a candy. Sucking it, he listened to the rumbling of the machines reaching his ears with their muffled rhythm. Somewhere, on one of the many floors of the building, his general manager, Mr. Zaidenfeld, was busily rushing about. As much as Adam loved his factory, he could not abide Zaidenfeld. How sorry he was that he had transmitted all his responsibilities to the man, so that now he could not get along without him. "I'll fire him too, along with Zosia," Adam mumbled to himself. But an inner voice teased him, telling him mockingly, "You won't do that!" Indeed, he was paying a price for the good life — a part of his power; but he knew that it was worth it. He sighed. Life might have been so good!

He approached the window. The factory yard was empty. The sun shone on the pavement, its light slicing out a part of the opposite wall, so that it acquired the colour of French cheese. Adam noticed the janitor opening the gate for two trucks loaded with raw materials. A few workers in dark overalls helped the drivers unload the gigantic rolls. They called gaily to each other, familiarly patting one another on the back. Adam did not know which he envied more, their agility or their comradeship. One of them distributed cigarettes from his pack. They glanced up at Adam's window and he hid behind the curtain, so as not to be noticed. They laughed and he knew they were laughing at him. The laughter got on his nerves. He pressed his stomach with his hand, on the side of the liver. His doctor, the most eminent specialist in town, had assured him that he was in good health, but as far as his own organism was concerned, Adam considered himself a greater authority than the best specialists in the world. For quite a while he had suspected that something was wrong with his liver.

While examining his belly, he allowed his eyes to wander over the many jingling window panes in the opposite wall. "All this is mine!" he consoled himself. Of what importance was a worker's laughter, or Miss Zosia's burning gaze, he reflected. Of what importance was Zaidenfeld? Were they not his slaves? This was a fact of life: a master needed his slaves and their only advantage over him was their knowledge of this fact. So they champed the bit now and then, they kicked a little here and there. But in the final analysis they were forever stuck in the mire, while their master's fortune grew and expanded. And this was the only thing that mattered, that gave meaning to life. "I must not give in to negative thoughts," Adam decided. "Life is short, most of it is gone already. I must enjoy what is left, relish it."

A taxi slipped in through the gate. Adam recognised the wide-brimmed hat of his wife. He hurried to the desk, took out some files and papers and spread them over the table top. He sat down in his armchair, assuming the expression of a very busy man.

Yadwiga was much younger than Adam. Her face still carried the traces of her fading beauty. Her hair, dyed a flaxen yellow, was curled in a page-boy style around her neck and cheeks, which added a certain girlishness to her looks. A thick layer of powder and rouge covered her face, faintly revealing the fine lines on her forehead and around her eyes. Her eyebrows were plucked and outlined with a thick black pencil; her lips were painted with perfect precision. On her small shapely nose she wore gold-rimmed sunglasses which she removed after a while with a graceful gesture of her gloved hand.

Clicking her high heels against the floor and swinging her slender body which was clad in a cherry-coloured winter suit, she approached Adam's desk and landed gracefully in his unprepared lap. Enveloped in the fragrance of her perfume, he, in turn, enveloped her in his arms. Her thinness brought his mind back to Miss Zosia. The truth of the matter was that lately he had come to dislike scrawny women; he was unable to stand their protruding hip bones, their dry meatless buttocks, and their arms that betrayed bone at the slightest touch. But more than anything, he was repulsed by their flat bosoms. At night, he usually dreamed of full female bodies, round buttocks and large pendulous breasts, and on his visits to the best brothels in town, he usually chose a female resembling those he saw in his dreams.

He kissed his wife's gloved hand. "You look as fresh as the day, my kitten. Take off your jacket," he proposed without great enthusiasm.

She shook her head gracefully. "I just dropped in for a moment, although you didn't want your scarf. But I saw a hat, Adam . . ."

He put a wad of bills between her fingers, gently pushed her off his lap and stood up. She made a gesture as if to embrace him, but he had already placed his hand on her shoulder, pushing her ever so affectionately towards the door. His face lit up with sudden curiosity. "How is Sutchka?"

"She was eating her kasha when I left." There was a slight hint of mockery in Yadwiga's voice. She gave him an unpleasant smile and left.

Yadwiga's mocking attitude was a thing Adam had grown accustomed to. Not that he did not mind it, but this too was the price he had to pay for the good life.

He thought of the many years they had played at being sweet to each other and about what experts they had become at the art of disguise. How well they knew their lines and how rarely they replaced the artificial words with spontaneous real ones!

He was quite satisfied with Yadwiga. Life with her was easy. They never quarrelled, and she never asked for anything more than money to spend on herself. She never criticised him, never complained, nor had he ever seen her crying. The undertone of mockery in her voice was so sweetened that he sometimes thought he was imagining that she was ridiculing him. Even the fact that she was deceiving him with every man that came her way and that she had a weakness for alcohol did not bother him too much. After all, she had a right to get some pleasure out of life too.

Adam removed the papers he had spread on his desk in honour of Yadwiga's visit, and put another candy into his mouth. He thought back to the time when he had first met Yadwiga and had fallen in love with her. She had been beautiful then. Their love affair was short and tiresome, as were all his love affairs; but this one had come at the moment of his life's greatest despair, when he had failed his exams, and it had seemed that he would be condemned to stay forever with his grimy father in the dirty junk yard, to rot along with the rusty junk, to become involved in his father's secret swindles and small thefts and to live in eternal fear of the police.

Yadwiga had brought him luck. The first card game he had won had been played in her presence. He had bid a valuable pair of his mother's earrings which she never wore, since she wanted to spare them, because she was a miser just like his father. Of course they had moved heaven and earth in order to educate their sons; this was the only thing for which they had spared no expense. But him, Adam, they considered a schlemiel. "Nothing good will ever come of you," they had constantly harped at him. They were proven right when he had failed his exams, and they had wailed over the money wasted on him. So he had avenged himself on them by stealing some valuables which they had kept hidden.

Because of the good luck Yadwiga had brought him, he loved her even more. Certainly he had known from the very beginning that she had married him because she wanted to be rid of her own parents, that when she said, "I love you," she meant, "I hate them." And how well he had understood her! He felt an affinity with her, saw a similarity in their fates, and because of that he had loved her still more. Adam smiled to himself sentimentally.

What a playful kitten she had always been! And so she had remained. The only thing he could reproach her with was her attitude towards Mietek. She did not take her motherhood seriously. When Mietek was small, she had treated him like a toy; when he grew up, he was her playmate with whom she fooled around and dismissed when he became a nuisance. But how could he, Adam, of all people, condemn her? Was he a better father? And yet, in spite of all, Mietek had grown up to become a handsome healthy fellow with a good mind, although, like his mother, he was a little too light-hearted and careless. So, perhaps Adam and Yadwiga's method of bringing up their son had been a good one, after all: to let him grow freely — like a plant, like an animal — so that nature might not be disturbed in its natural course by crippling discipline and false laws invented by devious human brains?

After all, Mietek had had ideal conditions for his development: a roomful of toys and books, expensive summer camps and complete freedom. Adam had never forbidden him to go anywhere or with anyone. He had never inquired who his friends were, nor had he ever beaten him or punished him. Of course, he and Yadwiga were not terribly interested in their son's world, in his boyish way of thinking, but where was it written that parents must take an interest in their children's affairs? The main thing was to love them. And Adam never doubted his love for Mietek. That was why Mietek's words this morning, in the car, had so enraged and hurt him. But he had already forgiven him. Mietek was going through bad times, the years of adolescence and, as a modern father, Adam took this into consideration.

As Adam, satisfied with the analysis of his family life, lit his cigar, he heard the door open in the neighbouring office and he rang for his manager. It took quite a while before the latter entered Adam's room. He came in with his eyes buried in a handful of papers. Adam looked enviously at Zaindenfeld's slim figure with no trace of a belly, at his blond crop of hair in which, Adam noted with satisfaction, there were already streaks of grey near the temples and the neck. Adam had not yet discovered a single grey hair in the strands of hair that still remained to him on his own head. "How is production going?" he asked with the dignity of one in command.

The manager, still reading, reached into a pocket swollen with rulers and assorted papers, deftly pulled out a creased handkerchief and blew his nose. He looked up at his boss. "Production? Quite well. Only six idle machines. The flu. Six labourers and twelve machinists are sick. Some fifty others have fever. Four are in the infirmary. Fell sick at work."

"Good-for-nothings!" Adam shook his head so that his goitre swung from side to side. "Send them in to me."

The manager was surprised. It had been quite a while since Mr. Rosenberg had asked to see any of the workers in his office. "I wouldn't advise you . . ."

"Do as I say!" Adam burst out, fully aware that his anger stemmed from the fact that he did not have the courage to tell Zaidenfeld about Zosia. "And look at me when I talk to you!"

Zaidenfeld looked at him with the patience of a parent waiting for a stubborn child to behave. "Do you want to catch the flu, Mr. Rosenberg?" he asked, and Adam no longer felt so certain that he wanted to see the sick workers. Zaidenfeld put the letter he had been reading in front of Adam. "Another circular," he said. "Do you see what they want? You have to take off the sign in front of the entrance and add the name of the owner."

"So take it off and add the name," Adam shoved aside the letter without even looking at it.

"Do you understand, Mr. Rosenberg? This is a new chicanery."

Adam's face contorted. "You see chicanery in everything."

"They ask it only of Jewish firms."

Adam sent the manager away. He took a candy, all of a sudden feeling hot and cramped in his room. He consulted his watch. It was almost time to go for lunch and he reached for his coat.

The sun shone mildly on the street, caressing Adam's face softly. Zaidenfeld had the bad habit of instilling worry in him; he always had some unpleasant stories to tell. But Adam easily shook off his forebodings. He would not let his life be poisoned. That business with the sign was, after all, no more than a trifle which Zaidenfeld, who saw anti-Semitism everywhere, had blown up out of all proportion. After all, why should his, Adam's name not be on the sign in front of the factory? Did he not deserve it? On the contrary, the government was only correcting what he himself had neglected to do.

He walked with a strong robust gait, the candy dancing lightly between his teeth. Such a small bit of sweetness, and yet it had the power to calm his nerves. Candies were his eternal weakness, and the fact that they were forbidden fruit made them all the more tasty. He had always been inclined to fatness. In his childhood, before he had begun exercising, he had had a heavy flabby body which he could hardly support on his legs. Children made fun of him, calling him "bulldog". Polish boys threw stones at him, spat on him. Even his own brothers and his own parents had looked at him with disgust as if he were a monster. He was always alone, hiding in a dark corner, so that no one could see him. With what passion he had thrown himself on the candies he had purchased with the few groschen his mother would give him! Tears would fill his eyes as the soothing mildness dissolved inside him. How passionately he had chewed and sucked on them, kissing the balming juices which flowed straight into his childish heart! The weakness had remained with him, although he now needed them less than he had used to. After all, he had overcome all his enemies and was a man now. Now he smoked cigars. But still, in a moment of tension, or lack of companionship, there was no better remedy than a candy between his teeth.

Adam walked along Piotrkowska Street, his face towards the sun, feeling it warm his bald head. When his appetite had ripened to the proper degree, he turned his steps towards Feldman's Kosher Restaurant.

✦ ✦ ✦

The March days that followed were bright and spring-like. Adam very much wanted to enjoy them. He loved nature and the outdoors and longed for some warmth after the dreary winter. He planned his vacation, looking forward to the days when he could be alone with Sutchka in the forest, under the open sky.

However, he could not fully enjoy the arrival of spring. Although Zaidenfeld, with all his dark prophecies, had a hand in Adam's sense of foreboding, there could be no doubt that the government was beginning a course closely resembling the one followed by Hitler in Germany. Adam had no interest in politics. He would not have cared about what went on on the other side of the border or, for that matter, on this side of the border, if it had not begun to affect him personally.

Until now, anti-Semitism had been just another word for him, nothing else. It had nothing to do with him, since, after all, he was no great lover of Jews himself. When a few years ago, some Jewish financiers were sent to the correction camp at Kartuz Bereza, he did not doubt the official story that they had been caught in some crooked deals. Nor did he pay much attention when General Skladkowski had coined the slogan, "POGROMS ON JEWS — NO. BUT ERADICATE THEIR ECONOMIC INFLUENCE — BY ALL MEANS!" Economic influence was an abstraction which could not affect Adam, at all. He had even tried to ignore the government's appointment of commissioners to the large textile enterprises. But now, that they had begun appointing government officials to sit on the boards of the companies, and now, that the largest companies were almost taken over, he began to worry. He felt that it would soon be his turn.

He tried very hard to fight his worries and was sorry for each wasted day. Now, when the world was so young and fresh in its spring awakening, he did not want to give himself over to destructive fears. However they, the destructive fears, gave themselves over to him. He could not extricate himself from their shackles. They followed him everywhere, waiting to ambush him in a dark corner and grab him by the throat. If during the day he somehow managed to deal with them, he lost all his defences at night, exposed to the ghastly insistent visions. He shortened his nights as much as he could, in brothels, with a drink, and in endless chess games with himself. His morning exercises became increasingly harder to do, and he was nervous and impatient at the office where he unloaded his irritability on Miss Zosia. The warmer and brighter the weather became, the more her presence became unbearable to him. Now that he knew what was hidden under her lowered eyelids, he was glad she kept them lowered. But when his ear caught the laughter of an office girl or he noticed a smile on the face of a worker, he thought of her. The world laughed at him behind his back.

On days when total distress and loneliness overpowered him, he would bring his dog along to the office — and would have no one but Miss Zosia, who had a kind of atavistic morbid fear of dogs, take care of Sutchka. He watched Zosia's twisted face, her tensed contracted figure as she approached the animal, and he guffawed, clapping his hands like a child. He would encourage the huge bitch to jump on the quaking secretary, and tears of delight rolled down his cheeks as he watched Sutchka licking the girl's red-cheeked face. Although aware that these were vicarious perverse caprices of his tired mind, he could not rid himself of their accompanying fantasies, and so he laughed even harder. Until one day Zosia kicked the dog with her pointed black shoe and Sutchka recoiled, howling in pain. That was the last straw.

Adam was having his second breakfast of coffee topped with cream, and crescent rolls, when Zaidenfeld entered with his quick step. Now was the ideal moment to put an end to the Zosia question. But before Adam had time to speak, the manager said, "I forgot to tell you, Mr. Rosenberg. Someone has been waiting for you outside for quite a while."

The food stuck in Adam's throat as a secret worry passed through his mind. "Who?" he asked.

"I don't know. He refuses to tell me his name or what he wants. I told him you don't receive visitors, but he insists."

Adam pushed away the tray. "Let him in." Mr. Zaidenfeld looked as if he had expected just the opposite order, but he said nothing and left.

The visitor entered. He wore a black coat sporting a woman's fur collar; a round Hasidic cap sat on his head, tufts of hair sticking out around it. From his pale youthful face a pair of near-sighted blinking eyes peered at Adam from behind heavily rimmed glasses. Adam sighed with relief and almost burst out laughing, struck by the humour of the situation. But the next moment he was overcome by anger at Zaidenfeld who had frightened him and tricked him into letting this beggar in. "What do you want?" Adam shouted at the intruder who had stopped in the middle of the room.

"Work," the young man stammered, pulling a piece of paper out of his pocket. With quick heavy steps he approached the desk. "I have experience."

Adam's surprise and rage increased. "Why didn't you tell the manager?"

"I have a note to you, Mr. Rosenberg." The young man put the scrap of paper on the desk. "They fired all the Jews in my factory. I have a wife and child."

With disgust Adam picked up the creased note, glanced at it and threw it back on the table. "I don't know anyone of that name."

The young man blinked confusedly. "Guttman, the painter."

"Guttman, the painter! Where does he get the gall to send people to me?"

"I am a Yiddish writer, Mr. Rosenberg."

"You are a what?"

"A Yiddish writer. My name is Berkovitch."

"I have no need for writers in my factory."

"I can work any number of machines."

Adam pointed to the door. "Go in good health!" The visitor did not move. He suddenly seemed taller and his pallid face seemed more proud and mature. The small eyes behind the glasses were wide open. Adam caught the familiar unpleasant gaze which so often attacked him from people's eyes; but this time it was a questioning gaze, shamelessly penetrating his soul and illuminating it like a searchlight. It was unbearable. "Out!" he exploded. The young man left. Adam nervously pulled his breakfast tray back and gulped down his coffee. He ate decisively and when he finished, he had put an end to both his meal and his vacillation. He would teach Zaidenfeld a lesson that he would remember forever! And moreover, he would fire Zosia right away.

But Zaidenfeld was busy elsewhere in the factory, and the messenger boy was unable to find him. In Zaidenfeld's stead, appeared the painter, Guttman. It was the day and the hour of Adam's sitting.

They never greeted each other, but this time Adam felt he had to give Guttman a piece of his mind, and he jumped at him, ready to explode with reproaches. "I would like to know how long this portrait business is going to drag on?" He looked Guttman up and down with a hostile glance. The painter always looked different in reality than in Adam's imagination. In his mind, Adam saw him as small and dirty, but in fact he was taller than Adam and was more athletic than he. He wore a pair of cheap clean slacks and a neat pullover. Now he removed the cloth from the painting and turned the canvas to his model. At the sight of his exposed likeness, Adam felt so uneasy that he had to gasp for breath. "I have no patience for it these days," he groaned. The painter paid no attention and continued with his preparations. He pulled out Adam's armchair and motioned him to sit down. Adam touched his head to check if his pate was properly covered by the hair growing at its side, then sat down, assuming his usual pose. Now, instead of his own image, he saw Guttman's agile figure, his concentrated face, the intense eyes and the sinewy arm holding the palette. "You know what?" Adam was surprised at the calm in his own voice when everything inside him was boiling. "I think you're doing a caricature of me, not a portrait. If you exaggerate the traits of even the most handsome person, the end result is a caricature. Why should you do this to me? Don't I pay you enough?"

The painter did not stop working. "It has nothing to do with money."

"Well, what then? You're supposed to be an artist."

"That's why I have to be true to myself."

"But why don't you use your imagination a little? Take, for instance, my baldness. It wouldn't hurt you to add some hair, would it?"

"Is that what is bothering you?"

Guttman was right. That was not what disturbed Adam. "I mean . . ." he became philosophical, "an artist should be sympathetically inclined towards his model."

The ironic smile playing on Guttman's lips turned into an obvious grimace of disdain. "Perhaps you should find another painter and have him paint the portrait you desire. Because if you look at it after today's sitting, Mr. Rosenberg, you'll like yourself even less. You threw out a friend of mine. Berkovitch is a young poet, a rising talent about whom the whole world will hear some day. He got fired and for a week now he hasn't had a penny to his name. Do you know how it feels to be unable to bring home a bit of bread to your child?"

Adam realized the full extent of Guttman's arrogance. "For your information, young man," he said haughtily, "I give out more charity in one week than you have given in your whole life."

"He didn't come to you for charity."

"I don't need any new hands in my factory, and in particular no protégés sent by you." But to his own amazement, Adam, instead of further unburdening his rage against Guttman, mobilized all his oratorical gifts to tell him about the great philanthropic work he was doing, about the amount of time he spent corresponding with needy institutions. Every now and then he stopped, hoping that the painter would show some consideration and say something. Guttman however remained silent, which made Adam realize that his attempt to make the latter see his humanity and influence his brush to bring out all that was positive in him, in Adam, was in vain. Finally, he could stand Guttman's silence no longer and burst out, "All right. Send him in tomorrow, your . . . your protégé."

After Guttman left, Adam sent for Zaidenfeld again. The moment the manager appeared before him, Adam came directly to the point. "I want Zosia to leave," he said firmly.

Zaidenfeld showed no surprise. He reached into his pocket and pulled out a pack of papers, as if what Adam had said was of no great importance. He asked as if *en passant*, "Do you want my resignation?"

Adam bit his tongue. This on top of all his other troubles! He saw in his mind the coming days without Zaidenfeld: the mess, the worries, the search for a new general manager, a new secretary — in these hard times, in the instability, with the steadily approaching danger. He had to be patient for a while longer, he decided, postpone firing them until he felt more sure of himself. He tried to see the situation in a more positive light. "Zaidenfeld is thinking of the good of the factory, my factory," he said to himself. Then he asked aloud in his normal voice, as if nothing had happened, "How is production going?"

He did not listen to Zaidenfeld's report, unable to stay in the room a minute longer. It had been a bad day, worse than ever. It was becoming increasingly harder to enjoy life, almost impossible.

✦   ✦   ✦

Feldman's Kosher Restaurant did not look out on Piotrkowska Street, as did the other elegant places, but was situated in the depth of a huge backyard full of small shops, large warehouses and noise. From early morning until late at night the yard swarmed with dirty children, with vendors, beggars and a variety of entertainers. A street singer gave concerts here a few times a day. Acrobats and magicians made guest appearances, not to mention the street musicians who often performed simultaneously from different parts of the yard, each trying to drown out the other with the cacophony of their squeaky violins, clarinets and trumpets hoarse with rust. On top of all this, the organ grinder, a one-legged cripple who had a habitual place right at the entrance, played continuously. As soon as a well-dressed person appeared in the gate, he was immediately set upon by the beggars who came running from every nook and cranny, attacking him like locusts, each one chanting a different story, bewailing his bitter fate and waving his outstretched hand in the stranger's face.

Adam felt nauseated by the sight of the filthy creatures, but he remembered his philsophical motto that there was a price to pay for the Good Life, and he found an easy way to get rid of the beggars. Before he entered the yard, he prepared a fistful of groschen which he threw into the beggarly hands, thereby freeing both his conscience and the path to the restaurant.

Wide wooden stairs led to the restaurant, and even before he reached its door, Adam could smell the aroma of the delicious spicy dishes. Inside, on small, spotlessly white tables, stood flower vases with single blooms leaning against fern branches. The flowers too spoke of spotless cleanliness. The waiters, middle-aged men in white jackets, with small white towels hanging from their arms, made their way among the tables. Adam preferred these dignified waiters to the coquettish waitresses of the other restaurants for two reasons: Firstly, because when he ate, he was immune to feminine charms; he believed in enjoying each pleasure separately. Secondly, the waiters in Feldman's Restaurant were experts at their jobs. They could recommend a new dish and describe it in all its minute details; they could discuss various qualities of taste, and in general, talk with professional erudition about all aspects of the culinary art.

The waiters appreciated Adam's refined requirements and their attitude towards him was both amiable and respectful. And Adam paid them back in kind. It never occurred to him to talk to them the way he talked to his servants. If he ordered them around, expecting them to come running every time he clinked his spoon against the glass, it was not in order to exploit them, but out of a desire to transform the consumption of his meal into a truly artistic ceremony.

The restaurant was truly kosher; the waiters wore skull caps. Its owner, Mr. Feldman, had a long partriarchal beard and wore the traditional Jewish garb. He did not interfere in the affairs of the restaurant, which were managed by his son. Young Mr. Feldman had a short black beard and instead of the traditional outfit, wore a three-quarter length jacket and a white skull cap on his dark well-groomed head. But he possessed the same dignified bearing as his father. Just as the father resembled a Jewish king, so the son, with his pale intelligent face and big brooding eyes resembled a Jewish prince in exile. The presence of both father and son added a certain spiritual coloration to the entire ritual of eating. This was one asset Adam could find nowhere else. Of course he did not care too much about the *kashrut*, which meant that he had to sacrifice the comfort of eating without a hat even in summertime; but he cared a great deal for the atmosphere and the beauty of the place.

Adam arrived at the restaurant early; the tablecloths were still spotless and the air was clear. (He did not mind the smoke of his own cigar, but could not stand the smoke of someone else's.) His usual table was free. It stood near a stained glass window which prevented him from seeing what was going on in the yard, but offered a lot of light, and on this splendid March day it made the tablecloth look as if it were made of sunshine. The cutlery was freckled with specks of gold; the crystal flower vase, pierced by the sun, gave off rainbow-coloured sparks. And all this soothed Adam's mind and excited his appetite.

Adam lifted his hat as if greeting someone, to smooth the side hair over his pate, and smiled at Max, the waiter, who stood half-bent over the table, taking the pencil from behind his ear. "So what's new, Max?" Adam brushed his hands against the tablecloth as if to clean it of invisible crumbs.

The waiter flipped the pages of his note pad. "What should there be new, Mr. Rosenberg? Politics you probably prefer not to discuss before the meal."

"No, anything but politics, before or after."

"Entrée?" Max prepared to write.

"What do you suggest?"

"A head. Carp. With congealed sauce. Melts in your mouth." Max kissed the tips of his fingers.

Adam accepted the suggestion and contentedly rubbed his hands together. His glance fell on the newspaper lying on the window sill. An unpleasant feeling swept through his heart, making him turn his head the other way, towards the buffet table where young Mr. Feldman stood leaning against the cash register, humming a melancholy tune. Adam knew that young Mr. Feldman carried a wound in his heart. His only son, a boy of nine, had fallen sick with polio last year. Adam knew that it was proper to ask Mr. Feldman how the boy was, but until now he had never asked. It was better that way, since if he asked once, he would be obliged to do so every day. And he disliked talking about sickness, especially during a meal.

The kitchen door swung open and Max, balancing a silver tray on his palm held high above his head, solemnly approached the table. He gave Adam a quick smile and put down a basket containing breads and rolls and little plates of assorted appetizers; then, with a sweeping gesture, he set down a gold-rimmed plate on which a head of carp lay covered by congealed sauce. "Give me a vermouth, *Nouilly Pratt!*" Adam commanded, tucking the corners of his napkin behind his stiff collar. He set to work with his fork and knife, his mouth watering with impatience. As soon as Max appeared with a large glass of wine, Adam grabbed it from him, brought it to his mouth and sucked it through eager thirsty lips. His head grew light, freed of all dark thoughts; all his limbs were singing praise: "good-good-good!" The front door was now in constant motion, letting in patrons, the merchants and store owners of Piotrkowska Street. Every time the door opened, Adam mechanically lifted his head, but in reality he saw no one.

He had already finished three quarters of his piece of fish, when the music inside him stopped and the bite he was about to swallow stuck in his throat. Although he had noticed no one in particular, he suddenly recognised among the incoming patrons — old Mr. Rumkowski, who was dressed as if for summer, in a loose jacket, his head negligently covered with a creased hat, strands of silver-white hair peeking out from underneath.

Rumkowski cleaned his glasses and, with the quick limp of an old man whose inner energy was struggling with a weakening body, went over to young Mr. Feldman, who showed no surprise at his visit. He shook Rumkowski's fingertips; they exchanged a few whispered words, and Mr. Feldman opened the drawer of the cash register. The old man moved closer to him, wrinkled his nose and lowering his eyes under his glasses, followed the movements of Mr. Feldman's hands in the drawer. He took out a pencil and a receipt book and, leaning against the cash register, quickly filled out a receipt. He gave it to Mr. Feldman and received a few banknotes in return, which he stuffed into his pocket along with the pencil and receipt book. He shook Mr. Feldman's hand again and turned away.

"Beggar," Adam grumbled to himself, bending his face to his plate so that Rumkowski would not recognise him.

His effort was in vain. Rumkowski had seen him and a second later he was standing at Adam's table. "Good that I met you, Rosenberg!" he exclaimed in his hoarse voice. "I owe you a receipt for a hundred zlotys, eh?" Unceremoniously, he pulled out a chair from the opposite table, turned it towards Adam, and sat down. "And tell me one thing, Rosenberg," he went on. "You had no strength to give more? I mean, Jewish orphans aren't worth more than that to you?"

Adam's ears were on fire. He sat aghast at Rumkowski's arrogance. "What gives you the right to talk to me like that?" he hissed through his gold teeth spotted with food particles.

Rumkowski wrote out a receipt in a crooked illegible hand and spoke placidly. "What gives me the right? Hundreds of orphans, that's what."

"You think you're doing them a favour with your hutzpah?"

"I'm the one who has hutzpah? To throw me only a hundred out of your swollen pocketbook, that is hutzpah! And when did you do it? Only after I sent you letter after letter pleading for money."

"If it were not for Zuckerman, you wouldn't have gotten that either. He has such a high opinion of you and your charitable works, that I thought you were a respectable person, not a *grober yung*. But you're not going to get another penny out of me. To me, Mr. Rumkowski, one speaks differently."

Rumkowski checked himself immediately. "It's not me you're giving the money to," he said, "whether or not you like me." He patted Adam's arm cordially. "How often do you want to pay?"

"Never!" Adam said firmly, clinking his spoon against a glass. Max appeared at the table. "Matzo balls!" Adam commanded.

Rumkowski's eyes lit up to a bright gray. "Are you too impatient to wait for Passover with the matzo balls?" Adam tapped his fingers on the table, waiting for Rumkowski to vanish. But the latter was in no hurry. His eyes fell on the newspaper lying on the window ledge. "Have you heard? Hitler has taken Memel." Adam pretended not to hear him. "And they've assigned four government people to the Manufacturers of Vidzev, did you hear that?"

"Perhaps you'll go your beggarly way and leave me alone?" Adam burst out.

Old Rumkowski, who had reached his hand out for the paper, pulled it back as if he had been burned. He jumped up from his chair, his eyes fiery. He chewed his lips, then waved his finger in Adam's face, "I expect your contribution every month!" He straightened himself, lifted his patriarchal head and left the table, kneading curses between his lips.

Max arrived with a plate of matzo balls. Adam flared his nostrils to catch the aroma, like a person about to faint trying to revive himself with smelling salts. He sipped the broth quickly, but it did not have its usual taste; he could not sip himself into tranquillity. Instead of ordering other courses, he lit a cigar. Half-satiated and dissatisfied, he left the restaurant, falling into the hands of the beggars outside. He got rid of them as fast as he could and ran out onto the street.

The shouts of the street vendors, the clamour of the streetcars and wagons penetrated his brain, not through his ears, but through the pores of his entire body. He felt the noises sifting themselves through him, as if squeaky saws were cutting through his flesh and bones. The surging sweating mass of people carried him along. The sun was boiling hot and the passers-by, unprepared for its heat, carried their heavy winter coats over their arms. Women fanned themselves with their multi-coloured scarves, while the men waved their hats in front of their shiny red faces.

Adam took off his coat and carried it over his arm. The windows of the houses attacked his eyes with glaring light. The sky, peering through openings in the eternal factory smog hanging over the town, was almost white. White clouds like balls of loose wool rolled apart and came together above the net of grayness high above the roofs. Adam longed for the forest. He counted the days to his vacation, wishing he could start it immediately.

The fronts of the shop windows on Piotrkowska were mobbed by chattering school girls. "Life is so beautiful," Adam whispered to himself, looking at them. They reminded him of Mietek. He had a premonition that Mietek would fail his exams. The premonition was too dark, his anxiety too strong, to have a bearing only on Mietek's failure — and he chased the thought away. "Life might be so good . . ." he whispered to himself.

He found himself in front of a movie house and stopped to look at the pictures framing the entrance. As he moved over to the wicket, he noticed a lady pretending to look at the photos. Her figure and the way it was wrapped in her coat betrayed the fact that she was wearing very little underneath. She winked at him invitingly and he put the wallet back into his pocket.

It was night-time when Adam arrived home. Overhead the silvery moon shone like a brooch on the breast of a gigantic Negress. He looked up at it with tired sleepy eyes.

Before he managed to open the door, he heard Sutchka scratching behind it. He fell to his knees and embraced her lovingly. "Little darling," he whispered, encircling her neck with his arms. He caressed her ears and let her lick his face and hands. The dog nuzzled the hat off his head and licked his pate. "Here, I brought you something." He pulled a little bag of delicacies out of his pocket and threw them one after another into her mouth. "Eat, Sutchka, eat," he patted her neck tenderly. "Soon it will be summer, little Sutchka. Soon we shall leave for the forest to shoot birds, rabbits and deer." Sutchka swallowed her last sweet and listened to her master, her long wet tongue drooping from her mouth. Wagging her tail excitedly, she followed Adam to his bedroom.

During the night, clouds appeared from afar; they swallowed the moon and covered the sky. The March rains had begun.

Chapter Four

Dr. Michal Levine,
City Hospital, Lodz,
April 19, 1939

My Dearest Mira,

I have the fullest respect for your tactics of answering my letters *en gros*; firstly, because you are saving money on stamps; secondly, because you save yourself precious time. I certainly envy you but am unable to follow your example. What should I do? As soon as I sit down at the table and have a spare minute, your name appears before me, my hands begin searching for a pen and I start scribbling. If love is a mental disease, this behaviour of mine is one of its symptoms.

Words . . . words . . . words. How can they help me? I need you here, with me. I want words to become superfluous, and here I am, left only with them. Our love has turned into a paper affair.

You are curious, you write in your matter-of-fact tone, to know if I have remained faithful to you. How nice of you to display the generosity of your great heart with the assurance that you would forgive me if I consoled myself with one of the nurses. Really? And here I thought that a woman is capable of forgetting and forgiving a lot, but never when *Das evig Weibliche* in her is hurt. Thank you anyway. My problem is only that as long as I carry your image within me, I am immune to all the other women in the world. It is as if you were the only one of your sex walking around on God's earth. And if you catch me by the expression "as long", I can quote to you the saying of a wise old man, that separation extinguishes small passion, but great ones it inflames even more.

It was sheer madness on my part to have let you leave. Why did I agree to it? Did I really want it only for your sake, so that during this last year of your studies you would not have to go through what I went through in Warsaw before receiving my diploma? Did I want you to avoid the bitter experience of the "Bench Ghettos" in the university, the beatings from the hoodlums, the aching feet while standing during lectures as a demonstration of protest? Did I want you to avoid the whole dirty business of studying medicine in a Polish university? Did I want, if not by myself, then with your eyes to see Paris, to listen with your ears to polite words, to move with you in amiable dignified surroundings and be treated like a human being, not an underdog? Did I want, at least with your feet, to walk the famous boulevards of the City of Light and Freedom, to breathe its air with your nostrils, to savour beauty, to delight in adventure, in discovery? Was this the real reason why I was so excited by your voyage, so involved in your plans? Or did I simply want, with this separation of a year, to test our love? Or was I just afraid to say no, because I knew you would not listen to me anyway? Or perhaps I wanted to please you with my collaboration (which was so enthusiastically masochistic) and make you love me more?

I carry within me the ideal of a woman — a builder and guardian of her home, a person who willingly submits herself to the collective being of her family; an Earth Mother; a woman who is the life force itself, serene and free from the restlessness of those who search for answers to nonexistent questions; a woman who is rootedness and rest, to whom man, like the giant Antaeus, returns time and again to suck strength from her powerful breast. And you, although you are, in a way, wise and earthy and more practical than I am, are at the same time restless and impatient yourself, always hungry for the unknown and full of contradictory "illogicalities". Then why do I love you?

Sometimes I doubt if we will ever be happy with each other. When my longing for you fills me with bitterness, I am almost sure that we won't. I want to have children by you. I want a mother for them; a mother radiating warmth and tenderness. And you, how much warmth will you have left, if you deal it out daily to strangers? How much goodness will I find in you, when, after a day of wrestling with the Angel of Death, I come to find consolation in your lap? What will you be able to give, if you yourself return home to receive and not to give?

But when my longing for you is sweet and warm, I think differently altogether. I think that we, the two of us, should be measured by other standards; that the flame burning within us, which holds us together, would suffice not only to bring warmth into the world around us, but also to build a warm shelter for ourselves. Perhaps I am a silly idealist, but after all, for whom was the world created if not for idealists? Only they are able of perceiving the fullness of life. Perhaps it will be given to us, Mira, to fulfil at least part of the dreams we have envisioned for ourselves.

I could write to you all night, honestly. The thread of ink unwinding from under my pen seems to unwind all the stitches of tension within me.

I am sitting in the duty room at the hospital. Three o'clock in the morning. From the nearby labour room I can hear the moaning of a patient about to be delivered. First baby; won't come so soon. She is only seventeen. Perhaps she is beautiful. But now her face is puffed up and with her enormous belly, she looks like an inflated balloon of pain. It is strange to observe spring outside blooming so easily and so free of care, so painlessly, and at the same time to listen to the moans, to the sound of human renewal heralding its arrival with so much hurt and blood. Are we cursed in that way, as the Bible tells us, or are we blessed? Does it all make sense? If this is the price we pay for being creatures on a higher level of evolution, is it worthwhile to pay it? (This is, of course, only a rhetorical question. Our Maker seeketh not our opinion.) But if He were to ask me, the silly idealist, I would say that it is worthwhile, or it ought to be. Because pain leading to birth, to growth, is actually the highest, most beautiful outcry affirming our existence. Suffering which makes sense is worthwhile. On the other hand, suffering which makes no sense and has no purpose — is the antithesis of life itself.

I have just opened the window. It's cold outside, but splendid. The sky is of a deep navy blue, but through the boughs in the garden, I can discern a light blue, an almost white fringe of the horizon. Soon another day will awaken without you being here. Against the background of navy blue sky I can see the white jasmine bush and the blooming acacias. Their tiny white flowers make me think of scraps of a torn letter, full of secrets no one will ever learn. As I think of white, I think of the white veil you will wear one day . . . Or is it the white of your medical jacket I am seeing, the one you will wear when we go out for a walk in the garden after a long night's work? How will your hair smell then, like the jasmine or like the acacia?

Ay, dreams . . . dreams. How do the French say? "*La vie est brève; un peu de rêve, un peu d'espoir, et puis . . . bonsoir.*"

But please don't think that I always have my head in the clouds. I only take pleasure trips to them. Otherwise I stay on the earth, which is a jealous mother and won't let you fly away too far. It seems to me, dearest, that our earth is heading towards a *soir* which won't be *bon* at all. How do they interpret the world situation in France? What do they say about Hitler's demands on Poland? It's clear as day that he is after something more than just Danzig and the Corridor. This time it seems that England and France have decided to resist him. But will they manage to ward off the devil?

Just as I rarely looked into a newspaper before, so now I devour them with a fierce curiosity. Who knows? Perhaps I and people like me are to be blamed for the world having come to its present state. There are too many indifferent people around, proclaiming that they don't care for politics — and they let politics take care of them, allowing irresponsible adventurers take over the world's housekeeping. Is this not one of the great sins of the German people?

I used to reproach Father for devoting his life to such an ugly business as politics. Now I can see how right he was to insist that politics is life, and that to run away from politics means to run away from life. There are times when human fate becomes dependent on politics. But this we realize when it is late, sometimes too late. Yes, I do reproach myself a great deal for my passivity. True, all these political parties have never appealed to me. I hated their devious tactical games, the throwing about of clichés, their cheap stale phraseology. I abhorred the bombastic speeches of their leaders who are primarily out to foster their own petty ambitions. And yet I should have made up my mind where to stand, whom to support, in spite of everything. We physicians have overcome our disgust at disease and the ugly sight of a sick human body and, thanks to this, we are able to help our patients. The same goes for the social organism. In spite of the dirt accumulating around political parties and the politicians, one ought to get into their nests, to join the side appearing to be the closest to our own principles, and try to do something when the necessity arises.

To be honest, Mira, I am attracted to a party which doesn't exist. I am looking for some universal movement of people of good will, who have one thing in common: respect for life. Sometimes I feel that a movement like this will soon spring up, that a great inspiring idea will embrace us all, and that the wheels of history will turn onto the proper road. The only discipline uniting my party would be the struggle against the powers tending to suppress and cripple the human personality.

I don't support the Christian apotheosis of a love superhuman and impossible. But I am very much for a healthy wise love for thy neighbour. We do have a tremendous need for love; it manifests itself right from our birth; it builds and shapes our psyche. If you are left with that need unanswered, you grow up with a crippled soul, in an eternal search for a substitute, and you find it in money, in power over others, and — in hatred. Hatred is, I think, the outcry of despair of the love-hungry, a symptom of undernourishment of the soul. Take, for instance, the dictators; they are the hungriest of the hungry. In their emotional greed, they force their subordinates to love them, holding a sword over their heads.

As you can see, your naive Michal wants nothing more nor less than to start Genesis all over again. Your naive Michal himself preaches pompous clichés, talking about such banalities as love! (It should rhyme with "Laugh!")

And yet — night after night I witness the first breath and the first cry of a newborn baby; very normal routine moments, and yet, what sacred ones! Sometimes, hands covered with blood and excrement, I feel like praying, praising, singing Hallelujah! How can I accept death dealt out by a human hand — death through hatred? Every time a patient dies before my eyes, even if he is a man of ninety, a shiver runs down my spine; I see myself in front of an abyss, unable to cross it, to bridge it. Yet I feel no revolt, rather a helplessness mixed with awe, which enables me to continue with my duties and make peace with fate. But when I see someone murdered by a human hand, I feel like screaming. Just a short while before, there had existed a healthy heart, good lungs, muscles loaded with energy; there were eyes which could have taken in so much more beauty, ears which could have heard so many more sounds, a mouth which could have talked, kissed, delighted in food. When I see all that destroyed, my heart weeps in frustration, like that of an art lover who sees a masterpiece desecrated by vandals.

What strange creatures we are, we humans! What miserable unharmonious beings! Of what use are our wonderful brains, if there is still so much of the animal within us?

Which brings me willy-nilly to the subject of my vegetarianism. I was about eleven when Mother took me one day to the Green Market, to buy a chicken for the Sabbath. There I saw the wooden chicken crates stacked one on top of the other, and all of a sudden they made me think of houses overflowing with people. Some chickens poked their little heads and feathery necks out through the wire nets of the boxes, like people looking out of windows in premonition of a danger approaching from the outside, but uncertain wherefrom. They turned their outstretched heads in every direction. Other chickens inside the cage were clucking, quarrelling over a grain of wheat or a sip of water from the tin can. Their legs tangled, they flapped their wings; they jumped on top of each other; they plucked each other's feathers, filling the air around the crates with a feathery red-and-white snow.

Meanwhile a trap opened in the wire-ceiling above their heads and a hand passed through it, poking around inside the cage; a human hand — about to determine the chickens' fate. The hand belonged to my soft-hearted mother who nearly fainted whenever she saw a drop of blood on my finger. Her soft white hand matter-of-factly searched and poked around inside the cage until it pulled out a fluttering hen by the wings. She blew away the fuzz on its behind to check whether there was enough fat on it to be used for frying, to make sure it was young and would be tender after cooking. The hen was fortunate. It didn't suit Mother's requirements. With a grimace, she pushed the bird back into the cage. The bird, its life spared for a while longer, stood there, inside, frightened, dazed by the shock. Then it spread its wings and fell upon the tin can of water; it raised and lowered its head like a pious Jew thanking God for a miracle.

Meanwhile Mother's hand was again rummaging about inside the cage, and this time she found what she was looking for. I watched her handing the bird over to the ritual slaughterer. Then she took the slain hen, popped it into her basket, and gave it to me to carry. On the way home with Mother and the dead bird, whose still-warm body I could feel through the thin net of the basket, my heart ached because of the injustice done to the bird. But I was even more hurt by the ugliness of my mother whom I suddenly saw as a voracious animal. Yet I accepted her two-facedness. Her behaviour was normal, human. She had every reason to rejoice in being able to permit herself the luxury of going to the market to buy a chicken for the Sabbath. Because we humans are meat eaters. Eating meat is good for us.

Then came my student days. I dissected corpses and became acquainted with the details of human anatomy. Our similarity to other animals struck me as if I had not known it all along. A question arose by itself: if there is no difference between a dead animal and a dead person, is there one between a live animal and a live person? My conclusion was, of course, obvious: we possess something which animals don't: finer brains. Mind, spirit are a new phenomenon in the development of life on earth. And in this very newness — in the fact that we are a transitional link in the chain of evolution — lies our tragedy.

That is why there is so much restlessness in us, so much contradiction and confusion. We long for peace, yet are the embodiment of aggression. We are hunters of animals and hunters of fame, hunters of possessions and hunters of beauty — murderers and angels at the same time. We are frightened by the new sense we are endowed with: the sense of morality, the desire for justice, the need to be good; and we are stupefied by the discovery that our moral voice is a voice in the wilderness, without an echo; because nature and the universe are indifferent, neither moral nor immoral. In the meantime our confused instinct of self-preservation drives us on, we don't know where to, with increasingly maddening speed, while instead of preserving, we destroy others and ourselves. Who knows when this "state of transition" will be over, when a new man, a higher kind of human being will emerge, when serenity and contentment will dawn for us and we shall be able to live our days to their fullest?

What remains for us to do until then? To be passive, to sit with folded hands, justifying our ugly deeds with the excuse of our "unhappy" situation in the process of evolution? A thousand times no. We must listen to the "newness" within ourselves; it may offer us the only means of self-preservation as a race. We ought to stop murdering God's creatures, whether they are two-legged or four-legged; we must grasp the thin thread of cause and effect, beginning with the murder of a bird and leading to the murder of a human being. Deep within us we know that we could be healthier and happier if we did not lead our lives at the expense of other lives. If we recognized that every creature has the right to live out its days in a natural way, we would acknowledge the same right for ourselves as well. And I think that medicine, science, religion, art, philosophy, and yes, politics too, ought to strive in that direction.

You'll smile reading my "deliberations". You'll think, "My poor Michal doesn't get enough sleep and is chattering away like that because of fatigue." Perhaps it is so. My defences are down because of fatigue and the real "me" is leading my pen without control.

Yesterday I visited my parents. Every time I come home, the apartment looks smaller. Strange, how we become gradually uprooted from the place of our beginning. Father has his mind constantly on party business, and since elections for the City Hall took place recently, we thrashed out the topic ad nauseam. Yes, we have a socialist City Hall; the mayor is a member of the Polish Socialist Party for which Father cannot find enough words of disdain. The Polish Socialists have once again decided to run in the elections by themselves and not together with the Jewish Socialists; aware of the anti-Semitic sentiments of the Polish masses, they refused to take the chance. Father's triumphant conclusion is, of course, Zionism. No one else will protect us or stick his neck out for us, he says; even the best *goyim* are nothing but *goyim*. When I ask him why he cares so much for what is going on here, if all he wants is to transplant the Jews to Palestine, he replies that as long as we are here, we ought to participate actively in life here; this does not exclude, he says, the duty of working for the creation of a National Home over there. His attachment to the dream of Palestine replaces an attachment to religion. When he sits at his tailor's machine, pulling the stitches out of the suits he makes, he thinks not only of himself and his piece of bread, but also about the community, an entity of which he is a part. This makes him less egocentric than you and I are.

How is it that I grew up in this home and everything that Father tried to teach me has fallen away from me so completely that it might have been a strait jacket from which I have freed myself? And although my freedom has become less comfortable than the strait jacket, I know that there is no way back for me. True, I have no religion, nor any particular attachment to the soil and the surroundings in which I grew up; true, I feel suspended in a kind of vacuum, nourishing my soul with naive dreams which I don't know how to translate into reality, yet I don't wish to limit my outlook. It has to embrace the entire firmament. And since I have returned to this topic, let me say once more: I am fully aware of my duty to take a stand now. This is the true reason why I am philosophizing so much in this letter. This is my mind's daily bread, of which I share a crust with you, dearest.

Now I shall conclude with a bit of very good news. My chief, Dr. Harkavi, is going to Italy for two months, and he wants to hand over his practice to me for the whole summer! Besides the fact that this flatters my professional ego, we shall have money as well. During the winter I accumulated some savings from various replacements and house calls. (I have also organized myself so as to be able to take most of my meals at the hospital.) In one word, I have a tiny bit of capital. The only worthwhile thing to spend it on would be to pay your train ticket, if you decide to come home as soon as you get your degree. If, on the other hand, you accept the offer to work there as a physician in a summer camp, you would be able to pay your expenses home, and in September we could rent an apartment with a room for an office for the two of us. (I can hardly believe that our old tired dream has a chance of being realized so soon.) Please, let me know your decision immediately.

One way or the other, Mira, the closer it is to summer, the closer we come to our happiness. Keep well, my love. I kiss your sweet eyes and your wise forehead. Write me just one more letter before your exams and I shall be satisfied.

Yours forever,
Michal.

P.S. Regards from my parents. Mother is proud of having caught a wife for her son, and for herself a daughter-in-law with a medical degree.

P.P.S. *Mazal-tov!* I just had a girl! (My little patient, that is.)

✦ ✦ ✦

Dr. Michal Levine,
City Hospital, Lodz,
April 26, 1939

Dearest Mira,

May has not arrived yet, and here I am writing to you again. As long as you work well, I don't mind your long silences. On the other hand, neither would I mind if, out of the generosity of your heart, you dropped me a card with a few words more often. But your day of judgment will come, don't worry. Just let me see you again.

I had a fine Passover; spent a great deal of time with my parents. My sisters were here from Warsaw and we had a splendid *seder* (conducted in Father's "traditional", not "religious" fashion). Guttman, the new friend I wrote you about, was also present.

Guttman and Father enjoyed each other's company enormously. Father is very much at home in the artistic-Yiddishistic milieu of the city. So they gossiped about the Yiddish theatre, sang some lively stage songs, while Mother wiped the tears from her eyes out of sheer pleasure. Father, of course, asked Guttman's opinion of the painters in town, and they also discussed the local literati in detail, which was very educational for me, who listened to their heated conversation like a Jew listening to Turkish preachers.

In general, thanks to Guttman, whom I saw quite often during the Passover days, I really had a "national and cultural" holiday, as Father would say. Guttman took me along to the house of *Monsieur le Rédacteur*, Mazur, the editor of the local Jewish newspaper. There we discussed Yiddishism and nationalism thoroughly, and once again we talked about the theatre. Mr. Mazur is convinced that the Jewish theatre in Lodz is on a much higher level than the theatre in Warsaw, because here, in Lodz, the influence of three cultures meet: the Polish, the Russian and the German; and this helps to raise the niveau of art in our city. Guttman was not very pleased with the German influence and vigorously questioned Mazur's thesis. Finally, they all arrived at the conclusion that the Jewish theatre created a style of its own, and that the influence of the German culture was not purely German, but European and universal; that Germany was only the gate through which world culture streamed into the Jewish garden.

Mr. Mazur, a sharp speaker who compels you to listen to what he has to say whether you want to or not, gave an example of a poet, a sort of *troubadour*, poor as a church mouse, who writes his poems on cigarette paper. This folk poet, although incapable of reading a word of German, is, in Mazur's opinion, also influenced by the German culture. What does that prove? Mr. Mazur concluded that in cultural life there is a kind of magnetic relationship between individuals as well as between groups and societies, just as in physics there is a relationship between substances. That relationship exists for the better or for the worse, depending on the power of the "giver" and the intuitive discrimination of the "receiver". Mazur thinks that the "Hitler Culture" will also have its impact on other nations. For instance, it is having a tangible influence on the Poles, and even we, Jews, who are the scapegoats, will be, or already are slightly influenced by the *Kultur*. There is a danger, says Mazur, that even Hitler's Jew-hatred might influence us. We might begin hating ourselves. We have learned a little of that already from our previous enemies.

My Yiddishistic education, led by Guttman's experienced hand, did not stop there. He took me along to the literary cafés, the Astoria and Under the Cup, and there I made the acquaintance of a whole group of promising talents, in particular one, a certain Berkovitch, a rising literary light. As soon as this Berkovitch, a quaint young man in traditional clothes, heard that I was a physician, he began nagging me about his tubercular friend, a certain Friede, the greatest talent that has ever risen on the literary sky. And Berkovitch explained to me that it was my national and cultural duty not to finish my cup of coffee, but to get up right away and go with him to save this great star for humanity.

I wanted to go to my room first, to fetch my bag, but Berkovitch categorically forbade me to do so. His sick friend, he said, hates doctors, and I was not allowed under any circumstances to reveal my adherence to that detested tribe. I was supposed to talk to the sick genius about anything in the world, except his illness. Only at the following session, when Friede realized that I mean no harm, could I examine him. This would, of course, have to be done with the greatest delicacy, so that Friede would not suspect any scheming by anyone, since he possesses a very "sensitive intuition".

I let myself be guided by Berkovitch and Guttman, quite pleased by the familiarity into which they included me. Between the two of them there is a sort of neighbourly closeness wrapped in a warmth which reminds me of Friday-night meals at home. As far as sick Friede is concerned, we did not find him at home then, nor the next few times when they took me to see him. But there is no doubt that he will eventually fall into my "criminal" hands. Berkovitch will take care of that.

Why do I write to you about all this? Simply because I find it hard to be without you and I carry you along wherever I go. My impatience to see you is growing from day to day, from hour to hour. Sometimes I feel like leaving everything and running to you. Our separation has made everything seem meaningless. Even spring has begun to pain me. A restlessness has taken hold of me, as if I were hurrying somewhere, afraid of arriving too late. Perhaps it would help if I talked to Guttman about you. But I find it hard to part with my intimate thoughts. And he, on the other hand, is poor in the art of extricating secrets — although we both feel that we are, so to speak, on the same wave length.

We, he and I, are very different in character, yet there is something inexplicably similar in our way of thinking. Like me, he does not mix in politics, yet his whole being, his whole life tends towards action, socially and humanistically, as if he were a member of my ideal non-existent party. As for his painting, I am no judge. As you know, of all the arts only literature, poetry in particular, is attractive to me, although whether I grasp even that properly remains an open question. The strangest thing though is, Mira, that he, the artist, seems more down-to-earth, more realistic than I, the scientist; as though he had the ground under his feet, while I am in the clouds. His strength, a sort of spiritualized prowess, and his knowledge of precisely where he is heading make me feel as if I were nothing but an abstraction.

As for my decision not to remain passive but to join some action group, it remains, for the time being, only a decision. I now see such a step as merely an exercise in futility. What we need is a movement of world proportions and perhaps it's too late even for that.

Mira, I think that you should come home right after your exams. I don't wish to bother you with my longing for you, dearest, but for the last few days, although other people have calmed down with the arrival of spring, I personally feel very troubled; I shiver inwardly. Write me at least a word. I kiss you.

Your Michal.

Chapter Five

THE CHILDREN in the orphanage at Helenovek were dressed festively; the boys wore white shirts and the girls white ribbons in their hair. It was both a Polish national holiday and the anniversary of the founding of Helenovek. The children along with their guardians and teachers were assembled in the gym hall for a celebration.

The stage was decorated with green bows and fresh flowers. On the back wall, the portraits of the late Marshal Pilsudski, President Moscicki and General Rydz-Smigly were displayed underneath a huge white Polish eagle. Garlands of red and white paper chains and silk ribbons framed the portraits, transforming the entire background into a kind of altar towards which the children in the auditorium looked with awed reverence. A little girl, her curly head of cropped hair resembling sheep's wool, stood at the front of the stage and in a quavering voice sang a hymn of praise to Poland's fields and forests.

Mr. Rumkowski, a sentimental Polish patriot and a man who loved children, was unable to divert his attention from the little girl. With adoring eyes he embraced her slender figure, combing her curly feather-like hair with his gaze, unaware that he was shaking his head in delight to the rhythm of the music. As soon as she had finished singing, he got up from the table where the other teachers sat — the table was covered with a green tablecloth and located centre stage — and he hurried towards her. He kissed her on the head, once, twice and then once and twice again. The little singer, bewildered and blinded by the spotlights, made a face which indicated that she was about to cry. She took a few steps and turned in a circle, searching for a way to run off the stage. However, Mr. Rumkowski grabbed her firmly by the hand, pulled her towards his seat and made her sit down on his lap, kissing her head and stroking her cheeks non-stop. The spectators in the hall clapped and shouted with great excitement.

It was time to calm down the youngsters and move on to the next item on the program. Mr. Shafran, the presiding teacher, rose, fixed his tie and faced the public. "Silence, please!" he called out straining the veins on his neck. Usually Mr. Shafran was capable of controlling a large gathering of children; but now, in this rare moment at Helenovek when Mr. Rumkowski was well-disposed and the children happily relaxed, his voice became lost in the clamour like a siren in the roar of a stormy sea.

Mr. Rumkowski raised his hand prophetically and in his hoarse voice exclaimed, "Where is the photographer?" The ensuing silence was loaded with a rising tension and expectation. Meanwhile, two other little girls, one of them holding a huge bouquet of tulips and carnations in her hands, appeared on stage. With the wavering uncertain steps of four-year-olds, they moved more or less in Mr. Rumkowski's direction. Behind them followed a buxom girl of about thirteen, who prodded them lightly ahead. Mr. Shafran sat down. Mr. Rumkowski's voice thundered, "I called for the photographer! Where is the photographer?"

A few hundred eyes had noticed the photographer's shadowy figure between the rows of chairs. Weighed down with his heavy apparatus, he had been battling with a light metal chair, trying to mount it with his cumbersome equipment. None of the children dared open their mouths to call out, or burst into laughter at the funny scene. Finally, the photographer conquered his chair and, shaking on trembling legs, appeared above the heads of the spectators.

"Wait a minute!" Mr. Rumkowski ordered. He fixed the eyeglasses which had slid down to the tip of his nose, and began to push the children holding the flowers, to the front of the stage. He stretched out his hand to them, ready to take the bouquet; then he bent down to the girl closest to him and, planting a kiss on her head, kept his mouth glued to it until the camera light flashed. Once again composed, he straightened up, took the flowers from the children, buried his nose in them, and swinging them in his hand as if he were handling a broom, he deposited them on the green table. He sat down and concentrated his attention on the full-bodied thirteen-year old who came centre stage and unfolded a sheet of paper.

"Dear Mr. Rumkowski," she read in a high-pitched quavering voice which betrayed the rapid hammering of her heart. "We, the children of the Orphanage of Helenovek, offer this modest bouquet of flowers to you, on the occasion of today's celebration, as a token of our gratitude and love. You are, dear Mr. Rumkowski, more than a guardian to us, more than a friend. You are a good and devoted father. We thank you from the bottom of our hearts for everything you have done and are doing for us, and we promise you, dear Mr. Rumkowski, to remember you always and always to be grateful to you for devoting your life to the orphans of Helenovek."

Mr. Rumkowski's eyes, proud and triumphant, were skimming the front rows of the hall where his foes were sitting: the members of the commission that, under the pretext of looking for a means to solve the financial problems of the institution, had undertaken the task of pushing him out of Helenovek. To spite them, he smiled even more radiantly at the children in the auditorium, and they, at the sight of his cheerful face, understood that they were allowed to shout with enthusiasm again. He drew out a creased handkerchief from his pocket. Using it to mop his forehead, he got up, approached the tall girl who had finished reading, and kissed her on the red glistening cheek. The photographer took another picture.

Mr. Rumkowski cleared both his glasses and his throat and with priestly solemnity lifted his hands. As if evoked by a magic wand, deep silence descended upon the crowded hall. And indeed, as Mr. Rumkowski swung his outstretched arms as though prompted by a desire to embrace the entire public, he seemed to the children to be a powerful magician. His gray hair, illuminated by the spotlights, shone like pure silver; his hypnotic eyes pierced the darkness in the hall like daggers, stiffening the body of each child and filling each heart with an awed tremor of both fear and admiration.

"My children!" he raised his hoarse voice. "My children both big and small! Yes, I am your father and I love you and care for you like a father. I want only one thing from you: that you love me too! That you respect me and obey me as children are supposed to respect and obey a father. If you do that, you will be happy in Helenovek. Study well and grow up to be fine people, so that I won't be ashamed of you. Take good care of Helenovek. This is your home. Yes, your own home! The home I have built for you! Because I have only your well-being in mind and my efforts and my work are all for your sake!" He was breathing heavily as he finished his little speech. The children applauded vigorously. He made a sign to the girl who had addressed him, to leave, and shaded his eyebrows with his hand, searching with his eyes for the photographer. "You, photographer!" he exclaimed as he noticed him. "Come here and take a picture of me with the visitors!"

The photographer's sweaty head popped up above the stage border, "Right away, Herr Direktor!" He snapped his fingers and ran for his chair.

Mr. Rumkowski, standing at the very edge of the stage, faced the men sitting in the front rows and addressed them in his hoarse voice, beckoning to them with inviting movements of his hands. The visitors exchanged glances and began whispering among themselves. Mr. Rumkowski, hiding his impatience with an effort, called them, each one by name, and finally exclaimed with an air of artificial cheerfulness, "Come on, the children are waiting!" He wrinkled his nose in time to catch the glasses which had slid down to its tip.

The reluctant guests got up and climbed the side-stairs onto the stage. They greeted the teachers at the green table very awkwardly, nodded or tried to shake their hands. But Mr. Rumkowski cut them short. He assembled them, placed them in a straight line and ordered them to keep quiet and pay attention. He made a sign to the photographer, grabbed the bouquet of tulips and carnations from the table, and placed himself in the very middle of the row of guests. The camera bulb flashed. The gentlemen rushed to the stairs as if threatened by sudden danger. But Mr. Rumkowski blocked their way even more hurriedly. "Wait," he ordered, "we shall go into the next room and have a schnapps." He ran to the green table, quickly whispered something in Mr. Shafran's ear, and put himself at the head of the parade. Waving his hand, he led the distinguished guests down from the stage.

◆   ◆   ◆

In the adjoining room the walls were decorated with photos in brown and black frames. In the middle of the room stood a ping-pong table covered with white paper and on it, plates of assorted cookies and fruits. Small glasses filled with vodka were waiting for the guests.

Mr. Rumkowski walked among the visitors, trying to liven them up. He handed out glasses of vodka, leaving the gentlemen of the commission to look into Helenovek's financial problems until the very end. "Drink *lechaim*, friends!" he laughed, displaying two rows of pearly artificial teeth. The visitors answered him with "*Lechaim!*" and lifted their glasses. Tired and bored with the ceremony they had attended, they rushed to the chairs arranged along the walls and before long they were sitting, jackets unbuttoned, mopping the sweat from their faces, sipping the burning schnapps and sighing with relief.

"So what do you say to my kids?" Mr. Rumkowski asked as he approached Samuel Zuckerman who was wandering along the walls, looking at the pictures, a glass of vodka cupped in his hand. "You were supposed to write a book about my Helenovek, weren't you? So what are you waiting for?" Rumkowski patted him on the shoulder in a fatherly way and moved his mouth closer to Samuel's ear. "And how about a little cheque?"

Samuel turned his head to him in amazement, "Don't you receive my donations?"

"I do, I do. But I have to show these committee wizards ..." He winked furtively in the direction of the committee members who were looking the picture of gloom. "Secondly," he added, "on such an occasion, a celebration ..." Smiling, though ill-at-ease, Samuel reached into his pocket. But Rumkowski stopped him good-naturedly. "No hurry. A word of yours is good enough for me now." He pointed to the pictures on the wall. "Look them over, go ahead. They might be of some help to you." And giving Samuel a light push towards the pictures, he left him and hurried back to the ping-pong table. He took a glass of vodka and turned to Mr. Mazur who was sitting nearby, absorbed in a conversation with a few members of the Jewish Community Council. "*Lechaim*, Mazur!" he lifted the glass to the editor, but did not taste the drink.

"*Lechaim*, Rumkowski! You have nice children, may they be healthy and live in peace!" Mazur replied.

Rumkowski beamed with pride. "So, why don't you write an editorial about them, eh?" The editor, rather than reply, turned back to his companions, ready to continue his conversation with them. Rumkowski felt hurt. "Gossiping already?" he jeered.

Mazur's companions, neatly dressed, dignified gentlemen with skull caps on their heads, laughed. "Don't worry, Mr. Rumkowski," said one of them. "We won't divulge any Council secrets. We're telling him the secrets everyone knows and that way we cover up the real ones."

"In our Council there are no secrets!"

"Very true," another man of the group agreed with him, and winked at Mazur with a pair of sharp twinkling eyes. "But a newspaper man's job is to uncover secrets, even if they are not secret. Right, Mr. Mazur?"

It was obvious that Mazur was waiting for Rumkowski to leave them alone. But Mr. Rumkowski, who well understood that his presence was not wanted, did not move, in order to spite Mazur. "You see," he made a sweeping gesture with his hand towards the room, "No one showed up from my party."

Mazur gave him an ironic glance. "And I don't count?"

"You? You are here as a newspaper man. And you think I didn't send out invitations to them? The big shots! They have excommunicated me! They think they have the power to declare me a non-Zionist, the great politicians!" Unable to conceal his anger, he lashed out vehemently. "They expelled me from the party, me, who ate my teeth up on Zionist work! Breach of discipline they call it. Ask them if they know what discipline means!" He hit his chest with his fist, making it obvious how much his dispute with the party hurt him. "They want to make a soldier out of me, the Generals! Because *they* don't find it suitable to sit with the *Aggudah* Party in the Council, I am supposed to throw the whole business at the *Aggudah's* head too! And who will take care of the community, pray tell me? A bunch of deserters, that's what they are! And I will not dance to their music, oh, no, I'm not a puppet!"

"The problem is not as simple as you make it sound, Rumkowski," Mazur replied gruffly. "And you know it yourself. We refuse to go along with the *Aggudah* Party's craven intercessionist policies. We don't want to support an anti-Jewish government party and try with flattery to wheedle out a softening of the very laws that same party has issued against us." The two Council men he had been chatting with, both devout *Aggudah* members, straightened, ready to defend their party's position. But Mazur would not let them interfere. "I want to tell you one thing, Rumkowski." He looked up at him with open antipathy. "If you belong to a party, you have to submit to the resolutions of the majority, even if you don't like them."

"Is that so?" Rumkowski broke into his speech. "Even if the fate of a people is at stake, eh? Even when it is a crime not to intervene on behalf of a community which is in the hands of such a government? Is doing nothing better than doing whatever there is in our power? Yes, even with flattery, even going in by the back door to intercede! You want me to submit to the resolutions of the majority, even when I see that the majority is a bunch of idiots?"

"Yes, even then!" Mazur grabbed Rumkowski by the lapels. "You have every right to convince the majority that they're a bunch of idiots, but only within the framework of party discipline. Until you have convinced them of that, it is your duty to subordinate yourself to their decisions."

"Not me!" Rumkowski freed his lapels from Mazur's hands with a jerk. "I don't dance to anyone's crazy music. I do what I consider right. I don't abandon a people just like that. I work for my country, for my city, and for my community. They're what's most important, and the rest is worth a rotten egg!" He glanced at Mazur triumphantly and in order to prevent the latter from having the last word, he turned from the group, grabbed a cookie from a plate, stuffed it into his mouth and washed it down with a long gulp of vodka. He drew out the creased handkerchief from his pocket, wiped his eyeglasses and his face with it and glanced stealthily at the young businessmen who belonged to the committee which was supposed to be looking into the problems of Helenovek. He walked by them rapidly and approached a group of Council employees clustered by the open window. All of them belonged to the city's intellectual élite and he liked to call them derisively, the "Shmintelligentia".

Their hands gripped the light-weight iron chairs, as they passionately discussed the White Book recently issued by the English government which halted any legal Jewish immigration to Palestine. The chairs squeaked unpleasantly. As the nervous hands holding onto them pushed them back and forth, left and right, they seemed to be involved in a discussion of their own. Mr. Rumkowski made his way to the very centre of the group and let himself down into one of the dancing chairs. The other chairs halted for a while, as if in surprise, while the people holding on to them continued talking. The discussion of the White Book had arrived at the topic of world politics.

"I am certain that the situation has changed radically," Mr. Moshe Sochar, the Council archivist, raised his hands as if to defend himself against his listeners. "The fact that our Minister of External Affairs, Mr. Beck, had the courage to say that Pomerania, although called the Corridor, is and will remain a Polish province, that Danzig, although it has a German population, is tied to Poland, this fact is a good sign in itself."

Mr. Sochar was interrupted by Mr. Zimmerman, the Council bookkeeper, who could not bear Mr. Sochar's optimism. "Tell me, who attaches any importance to what Beck says? Does Hitler's pact with Mussolini mean nothing to you?"

"It might be only a political manoeuvre," optimistic Mr. Sochar defended his point. "Hitler wants to test the world, to see how much it will let him have without any trouble. Until now this policy has paid off quite handsomely, hasn't it? But don't worry, he knows quite well that when it comes to measuring up against the military might on our side, he won't be such a great hero. Don't forget, my friends, that with all his militarism, he is economically at the point of bankruptcy, nor should you forget that an army marches on its stomach. How could he go to war with soldiers who eat margarine instead of butter, drink *Ersatz* coffee and whose wives cook *eintopf* meals? And then, if Russia were to join us . . . He wouldn't dare. I'm telling you, he wouldn't."

Mr. Rumkowski who had become both a bit tipsy and actively nervous was unable to hold back any longer. "That's what you think!" he exploded, jumping to his feet and facing the disputants. "So I'm telling you that you are talking nonsense! Do you really have any idea who Hitler is? You measure him with your little minds and want the account to come out straight?" He waved his finger in their faces threateningly. "One thing you should know and remember, that whatever Hitler wants, he gets, by hook or by crook, be it with peace, be it with war, and all this blubbering and boiling will help the world like cupping glasses will help a corpse! This big shot said this and that big shot said that! All these politicians and Chamberlains don't reach to his ankles! Hitler laughs up his sleeve at them. He'll crush them, like this!" He stamped his foot emphatically against the floor and kicked the chair he was holding so fiercely with the tip of his shoe, that it toppled over, hitting the floor with a loud bang.

The people around him consulted their watches and blinked meaningfully at each other. As Rumkowski saw them buttoning their jackets, he realized that he had more important things to do now than to indulge in fruitless political discussion. The anger vanished from his face as if at the touch of a magic button. He ran ahead of the weary visitors, placed himself at the exit and shook everyone's hand, thanking the distinguished guests for the honour of their attendance at the celebration. Discreetly, he whispered in their ears that he was expecting a small donation for Helenovek. As for the gentlemen designated to look into the financial affairs of the orphanage, he took leave of them, fixing his eyes on a point somewhere above their shoulders. When Mr. Mazur and Samuel Zuckerman approached him, he grabbed both of them by the sleeves and pulled them towards him. "I am very worried, my friends," he said heatedly, looking into Mazur's eyes with warmth, as if there had never been any misunderstanding between them. "We are at the threshold of a war, do you hear?"

"You are not the only one who is worried," Mazur cut him short.

"So, is that supposed to console me?"

"Whatever happens to the people of Israel, will happen to Mr. Israel as well."

"What do you mean?" Rumkowski stared at him astonished and hurt. "You think I worry about myself? It's the children. The contributions have diminished by thirty percent already." After a moment of silence, he reminded himself, "Wait, I'll give you some lilacs for your wives. Go down to the garden!" They had no time to reply as with a slight limp, he rushed ahead of them along the corridor.

Rumkowski sent the janitor down to cut the lilacs for his visitors and entered his office. He took off his tie, unbuttoned his shirt collar and let himself sink heavily into the chair behind his desk. His limbs sagging with the weight of fatigue, his chin resting on his chest, he shut his eyes and immediately began snoring aloud, immersed in the blessed sleep of old age. He slept no more than five minutes, after which he woke abruptly, combed his damp sweaty hair with the fingers of both his hands and breathing loudly, puffed out and sucked in his cheeks which resembled two parched bladders. He rang the bell leading to the kitchen. A chubby little woman in a white apron, with a white scarf on her head, came in. From under her scarf, two strings of stiff hair curled into two large locks stuck out, looking like two pencil lines traced on her short forehead. She focused a pair of sheepish eyes on Mr. Rumkowski.

"A cold drink!" Rumkowski ordered. She left and returned with a glass of soda water. In her hurry to please the boss, she had left the door open; from the gym hall where the celebration was still going on, could be heard the gay tunes of a military march. "The door!" Rumkowski exclaimed, grabbing the glass from the cook's hand. "How many times do I have to tell you to shut the door behind you?" She ran back to shut the door and returned to the desk. Her round face lit up with satisfaction as she watched him drinking the water. Refreshed and enlivened, he cupped the glass in her hand and smiled at her. "My children look nice today, don't they?"

"Yes, Mr. Rumkowski," she nodded, eager to please him.

"You think I don't remember how you looked when you were a little shrimp, as small as a grain of pepper?" He stroked her arm lightly. "The teachers used to say that you had cabbage in your head, or sawdust, instead of brains. But I protected you."

"You were always good to me, Mr. Rumkowski."

"Sure, I was always good to you. But then, why were you always afraid of me, eh? You used to tremble like a leaf when I as much as looked at you." He played with her fingers and grinned. "That's exactly why I was so good to you, my dear. And now, are you still afraid of me?"

She smiled uneasily, "Yes, Mr. Rumkowski."

"But now you're afraid of me in a different way, aren't you?" he chaffed her, pulling her by a finger. "I always treated you as if you were my own child. And . . . and who married you off, if not I? How is he, by the way, your hubby?"

The woman's face was afire, a vein on her neck swelled, pulsating vigorously; the little goitre under her chin trembled slightly. "He is a good husband," her voice took on a whimpering sound. "He would jump into the fire for me . . ." She fixed a pair of watery eyes on him. From their corners, tears began rolling down her nose and her rounded cheeks.

Ill at ease, he coughed. Female tears filled him with both revulsion and tenderness. "What's wrong?" he lifted her chin with his hand. She did not answer, but wiped her face with the edge of her apron. He grew impatient. "Stop wailing!"

"Yes, Mr. Rumkowski," She looked at him with her red overflowing eyes and burst out, "I want to be a mother! I want to have a child!" Her whole body shook spasmodically. "Five years I've been married," she wailed. "Five years and seven months and . . . The doctor says . . ."

The more she wailed, the stiffer Mr. Rumkowski became. A familiar discomfort attacked him, pressing like a hoop around his heart. He felt a gnawing emptiness within him, something he had not experienced for a long time. At length, he mastered himself and exclaimed, "Go, I have no time!" The woman's chubby figure bent as though it had become smaller and rounder under the impact of the unexpectedly hostile words. To Mr. Rumkowski it seemed that she was about to be transformed into a ball rolling towards the door. He felt like kicking her behind.

Once again alone in the room, he adjusted his glasses and scrutinized the desk. His eyes fell upon two piles of papers arranged in two wooden boxes. In one of them he kept the accounts of Helenovek, and in the other, the accounts of his private business as an insurance agent. The sight of the second box gave him no pleasure. The state of his private additional source of income was even worse than the financial situation of Helenovek. He put two account books into his pocket, buttoned his shirt and passed his head through the loop of his tie, adjusting it tightly around his neck as if he were about to strangle himself with it. He looked out of the window.

Samuel Zuckerman and Mr. Mazur were walking along the garden path towards the gate. They walked arm in arm, both holding bouquets of lilac in their free hands. Rumkowski found the sight of the two men walking arm in arm repulsive. The inner discomfort he had felt before took hold of him again. "I send them off with flowers," he muttered to himself, "for their wives . . . their homes." A wave of envy and resentment swept over him. "I am an old man, while Mazur is still a dandy, Zuckerman's friend, although he is old enough to be his father. May the devil take it!" he cursed and rushed to the door, coming face to face with the mass of children who, the ceremony finished, were streaming out of the gym hall. "What's going on here?" he burst out impatiently.

Mr. Shafran came abreast of him. "We promised them a surprise, Mr. Rumkowski. Ice cream," he whispered in his ear. Mr. Shafran was one of those people who lacking malice, cannot be provoked. He never changed his quiet tone of voice, nor was he ever seen to become heated about anything. Mr. Rumkowski, who disliked the type with all his heart, called Shafran a cold fish. In spite of himself, however, he usually mellowed after only a glance from Shafran's eyes. "Come along, Mr. Rumkowski," Shafran proposed, "and you'll see the kids enjoying themselves."

Rumkowski shook his head, "No time." He watched Shafran tousle the hair of the youngsters passing by them, and unaware that he copied the gesture, he did the same. All of a sudden, he exclaimed, "Do you want to eat ice cream, children?"

"Yes, Mr. Rumkowski!" they replied in chorus, clapping their hands.

He caught the grateful glances beaming up at him from their eyes and in his heart a voice sang out soothingly, as he recalled the buxom girl's speech, "They will always remember me. All their lives they will remember me. Each one of them will. I am their protector, their father." The word "father" echoed sweetly and consolingly in his mind; but the echo of that echo resounded with a remote bitterness and pain somewhere deeper inside him.

✦ ✦ ✦

Mordecai Chaim Rumkowski had a good memory for the important dates in his past. Not that he celebrated their anniversaries, or talked about them, but he marked them in his mind as milestones he had passed on the long road of his life

— a road which was supposed to lead somewhere, but had led him nowhere. However, he did not dwell for too long on his memories, nor on trying to find out where and why his road had gone off course and betrayed its promise. He was not the type of man who indulged in self-pity or bewailed his fate, endlessly chewing the cud of his miseries. He hated digging inside himself. Therefore he would only say to himself on such occasions, "Today is twenty years since . . . Today is thirty years since . . ." and would let his mind jump backwards for a moment, towards that significant day many years ago. He would scrutinize it as one would the page of a book known by heart and with one glance measure the lights or shadows it had cast on the days that followed.

It was the same with the anniversaries of his wives' deaths, in particular the death of the second one, for the first wife he could hardly remember. The memory of the second wife, however, remained with him along with the tender love-name he had used to call her: Shoshana. With a strange clarity he could also recall her voice, particularly on the anniversaries of her death. Then he would hear her speak in her soft lilting tone, so endearing and so alive and clear as if he were possessed by a *dybbuk*. For this reason the anniversaries of her death were not days of mourning to him. On the contrary. Something pleasant and intimate came to visit him on that date. Shoshana's voice was his home.

He would not light any remembrance candles on those days, but he did go to the cemetery sometimes, especially when the weeks before had been difficult and the present days were so tangled that he felt smothered by them in his loneliness. In the cemetery, there was a double grave; one was hers and the other — waited for him. There, in front of the tombstone engraved with his name, the memory of Shoshana's voice made him aware that he had come here, not so much to visit her, as to visit his own living self. He looked at the empty place by her graveside, and saw the twisted road of his life straightening out; but he also saw it becoming worthless — because it was leading to this very spot where it was supposed to end. The meaninglessness of all this was absolutely impossible for him to grasp or to accept. Consequently, coming here revitalized him. Because what was impossible to accept, he simply did not accept. Death was both a truth and a lie. Shoshana's body was in the grave, that was true. But her voice was alive and it denied death. It told him that buried here, in his grave, so close by her side, he would actually be further away from her than he was now. And it called out to him to live on, to start anew, to shake off both his disappointment with his past and his thoughts about the futility of his future. And so it happened that, thanks to his visit to Shoshana's grave, his mind became illuminated by the promise of leaving the cemetery behind and moving onwards — into immortality. At moments like these, he felt that he was to be given the opportunity of putting down great and important milestones on his road which would become a highway leading to undying glory.

Recharged with energy and filled with these lofty thoughts, he would hurry back to the orphanage, to his social and political work and to his private business. Elated and armed with courage, he would throw himself into the daily struggle, a new man.

It was a sunny crisp morning when Mr. Rumkowski left for the cemetery on this particular day. Although he had left very early, he came back late, on account of the distance he had to walk, and of the physical fatigue he had felt that morning. In the orphanage lunch was about to be served, but he did not stay to take his meal. In spite of his fatigue, he felt inspired and ready for action. He ran upstairs, to his office, grabbed his account books and set out for the city.

Despite his slight limp, he passed the garden in front of the orphanage with brisk steps. The sun lay aglow upon the carpet of young grass; with its broom of rays it swept away the patches of shadow hiding beneath the trees, releasing into the air a fragrance of warm soil and baked pollen. As his eyes embraced the clean festive garden, he noticed something white moving underneath a lilac tree. It looked like two pieces of paper suspended in the air, shaking lightly. He adjusted his glasses and realized that what he was seeing was a pair of short white socks belonging to a girl; a pair of bare legs, like two columns of sunshine grew out from the patches of white. He came closer and noticed the brown of a girl's short dress, and two long blond braids. They seemed to be growing out of a branch and resembled lilac boughs with their indeterminate blondness. The tree shook lightly, its clusters of flowers engulfing the head and face of the girl.

He pulled her by the dress and heard a faint shout. The girl detached herself from the tree, together with a large bouquet of lilacs. He saw a glowing agitated face which turned red and twisted at the sudden encounter with him and with the glaring sun. She blinked her eyes; their lids with their long lashes fluttered like two trapped butterflies. Her lips, tiny and round, opened and shut like two cherries unable to tear themselves from each other.

"For whom is this bouquet?" he asked, surprised that his voice was not as sharp and severe as he had intended it to be.

She too was astounded by the mildness of his voice, and after blinking again, mustered the courage to answer him. "For you, Mr. Rumkowski, for your study."

He smiled at her good-humouredly. "Your name is Esther, eh?"

"No, Sabinka, Mr. Rumkowski."

"Yes, of course, Sabinka," he corrected the error, looking at her face which had smoothed out. The face, oval, with a perfectly sculptured nose, and skin as soft as delicate velvet, invited his hand to stroke it. Lightly, he brushed his fingers against her cheek, and let them drum a while under her chin. Her face reminded him of the painting of a beautiful young woman he had seen somewhere. Suddenly he had a great idea. "Come," he said and took her by the arm. "Run upstairs and tell the supervisor that I'm taking you with me to town."

Her face expressed thrill mixed with amazement. Before long, she was running in the direction of the building. From underneath her flying dress her graceful bare legs shone like two columns of sunshine. He followed her with his eyes. Of course this was not Esther. Esther had been a redhead, a beauty who had left the orphanage years ago, he recalled, and smiled to himself. The redheaded Esther continued to lurk in his memory because she had responded to his goodness with hutzpah.

After a while, the girl, her dress aflutter, her braids soaring, the bouquet of lilacs still in her hand, was racing back towards him along the path. He hurried to the gate, letting her follow from behind, until she came abreast of him. She realized that she was still holding the flowers in her hand, and exclaimed, "Oh, I forgot to leave them!"

He laughed, "Take them along. They're yours." Completely confused, she walked beside him, taking tiny steps, as if held back by the sudden good luck that had come her way. The street was covered with the fallen petals of the acacia and chestnut trees which were roofing the sidewalk with the blossoming fans of their branches, and the girl raised a dust of white and yellow petals with every step; a few of the petals stuck to her shoes. He looked back at the tramway rails sparkling in the sun, then remembered that he had taken her away from lunch. He asked, "Are you hungry?"

"No, Mr. Rumkowski," she replied shyly, not taking her eyes off her shoes.

"We shall go to a restaurant. I will order whatever your heart desires. What do you like to eat, eh?" He glanced at her profile. Where did she get her refined traits, he wondered. She looked like a princess, with her aristocratic forehead, her eyes and the marble colouring of her skin.

"I like to eat everything." She lifted her head to him for the first time. The expression of confusion and astonishment disappeared from her face, leaving behind a smile of trustful childlike curiosity which awoke a tenderness within him.

He took her by the hand and her smooth soft fingers cooled the heat of his burning palm. "You don't have to be so afraid of me . . . hm, Sabinka."

"I'm not," she replied hesitantly.

"You're not? Not at all?"

"No, not now."

There was an inexplicable grace in the shake of her head, something endearing and very sweet in the words, "Not now," uttered by her charming cherry lips. Most certainly there was no likeness between her and that redhead Esther, his ex-student. The beauty of the latter was that of Lilith, of a devil, whereas the beauty of the girl walking beside him was that of an angel. Only because they were such opposites could he have paired them in his mind with the illusion of similarity. "You are a nice girl," he said squeezing her fingers lightly as they softly and submissively nestled in his palm. "Oh, will you ever have a ball today, Sabinka!" He laughed contentedly. "Have you ever been to Luna Park?"

"Never, Mr. Rumkowski."

He felt enthusiastic and young. An energy he had rarely felt before surged through his limbs. He could no longer tell whether it had risen in him thanks to his visit to the cemetery that morning, or thanks to the charming young creature with the live fresh body, who moved so gracefully at his side. "Come on, we have to hurry," he pulled her by the hand. His gait quickened and he limped as he usually did when hurrying. From between the trees there issued a buzzing sound. The rails at the side of the road began to vibrate. The streetcar was approaching.

Now it was she who pulled him by the hand. He breathed quickly and heavily; sweat bathed his forehead, but he did not diminish the speed of his steps, delighted with his ability to keep abreast of the girl. She climbed into the tram, pulling him behind her. The tram, having just left the terminus, was empty. "There, sit by the open window." He let her pass in front of him and watched as she made herself comfortable in her seat, cradling the bouquet of lilacs like a baby in her arms. The tram began moving. Mr. Rumkowski watched as Sabinka's profile became wrapped in the wind's breath which combed a delicate mesh of hair over her forehead. One of her braids dangled outside the window and as soon as the tram began to pick up speed, it flew up in the air and fluttered like a pennant with its white untied ribbon. She inhaled the air deeply, as if determined to take in all the wind through her nostrils. Her mouth, shut tightly, was spread in a broad sensuous smile of delight.

As he abandoned himself to watching her, the pounding of his heart subsided. Slowly he wiped the sweat from his face, taking care not to avert his eyes from her for a second, in order not to lose even a glimpse of the freshness she radiated. "You like to look out of the window, don't you?" he asked, contemplating her round chin.

"Yes, Mr. Rumkowski. Everything looks gay out there," she answered without turning her head. "Everything is running, the people, the houses, the sky. And the wind is the best thing of all. Do you like it when the wind blows in your face, Mr. Rumkowski?"

"Yes, I like it when the wind blows in my face."

"If I were a man, I would perhaps become a tram conductor," she giggled.

He looked at her bare round knees which the short dress she was wearing had left uncovered. Then his gaze slid down the shapely legs framed at the ankles by the short white socks. He moved closer to her. "You are a sweet girl," he praised her. His eyes, up to now of a clear grayish blue, were covered by a mist through which his hungry gaze was beaming at her. She sensed the change in him. As she turned her head away from the window, her eyes fell into the flame of his, like two moths trapped in the blades of a fire. She buried her nose in the bouquet. "And do you know why you are such a sweet girl?" he asked, then halted, nibbling on his loose underlip. She felt the unpleasant heat of his breath on her ear, but was afraid to move away from him. "Because, hm . . . Because you like me a little bit," he concluded. "Isn't it true that you like me a little bit?"

"Oh, a lot, Mr. Rumkowski!" she readily admitted.

Gratitude and goodness took hold of his whole being. He reached out for her hand and squeezed it with a desire to let all that filled his soul stream over into her. "Golden child," he whispered. After a long moment of silence, he asked, "How old are you, Sabinka?"

"Don't you know, Mr. Rumkowski?" she wondered. "I am fifteen. Last month was my birthday. You sent me a card with best wishes. I still have it."

"Yes, I remember now," he assured her, his heart full of gratitude to Mr. Shafran for taking care of such things as sending birthday greetings in his name to the children of the orphanage. He broke off a twig of lilac from her bouquet and played with it, plucking off one little lilac bloom after the other. He squeezed the heap of tiny flower cups in his palm, rubbing their softness against his folded fingers. Then he opened his fist and allowed the fine dust of the crushed flowers to fall onto his jacket and into his lap. He lifted his hand to his nose and inhaled the aroma. "This is the way I smell the flowers," he said, grinning. "Their fragrance is stronger when you crush them with your fingers. All the perfume comes out. Try it."

"I don't want to," she pressed the bouquet to her breast with a maternal, protective gesture.

"You're silly. Flowers are there to be smelled."

She looked at him sullenly from behind her brows. "They have their lives too. To squeeze the life out of them like that is almost like killing."

He stared at her with a hazy absent gaze, as if through her he had suddenly seen someone else. "Do you know whom you remind me of?" he whispered. "You remind me of my wife. If I had had a daughter, she would have looked like you."

Anger vanished from the girl's face; instead, she looked at him with compassion. "You don't have a daughter, Mr. Rumkowski?"

"No daughter, no son. Nor do I have a wife."

She sighed, "You are an orphan, just like us."

He felt a closeness to her, as if her heart were one with his. He lifted a heavy blond braid from her shoulder, darted a furtive glance around him, and pressed his mouth to the white ribbon. "I love you as if you were my own daughter."

She smiled sadly, "You are a good man."

"You are a good girl."

"I have no one to be good to."

"Be good to me."

For a long while they continued in silence. As they approached the centre of town, the tramway filled with people. Now Mr. Rumkowski sat at a proper distance from Sabinka, her braid, like a blond sleeping snake, rested on her shoulder. At length, he fixed his tie and combed his dishevelled hair with both hands. "Come, let's go," he said and stood up, letting the dust of the crumpled lilac blossoms fall from his suit.

She turned her head towards him, "Is this Luna Park already, Mr. Rumkowski?

There was still a long way to go to Luna Park. Mr. Rumkowski had a lot of business to settle first. The promise of going to a restaurant and having a good meal was reduced to a bag of sandwiches from Dishkin's delicatessen. He gave her ten groschen to buy herself two ice creams, and another twenty for an illustrated movie magazine, then he left her on a bench in the Allées, while he rushed into town to collect the payments for Helenovek and for his private insurance business.

Sabinka took leave of him cheerfully. She was hungry, impatient to open the bag of delicious sandwiches which tempted her with their spicy aroma. She leafed through the magazine with the photos of movie stars in it, holding it carefully, so as not to spill any crumbs on the pictures of the elegant ladies. She ate heartily while her envious eyes followed the details of the beautiful dresses.

The afternoon wore on. The bouquet of lilacs she had carefully placed on the bench beside her was drying out, twig wilting on twig. When the afternoon sun wandered off, even the cool shadow it left behind had no power to revive them with its freshness. By the time evening came, Sabinka had already walked the Allées several times from one end to the other, and had read the movie magazine over and over again, up to the last advertisement on the last page. The two ice creams had been consumed long before, and nothing remained for her to do, but to wait and ask herself if Mr. Rumkowski would still take her to Luna Park.

At last she saw him coming from afar, limping towards her with his slightly halting gait. She ran to meet him and he handed her a chocolate bar. "Come," he ordered her firmly.

She walked beside him. Then she remembered, "The flowers! I left my bouquet on the bench. I'll be back in a minute!"

He grabbed her hand. "Let it be. What do you need to carry that around for?" She walked obediently by his side, but turned her head back. He noticed her restlessness and asked in a softer tone of voice, "So, why don't you eat your chocolate?"

She unwrapped the chocolate and bit into it. It slid down her throat with difficulty. She had to turn her head around again, in spite of herself. There, on the empty bench, lay a small heap of withered beauty, her first bouquet of flowers, her very own, and she had taken such poor care of it. During the hours she had spent with it, holding it, cheering herself with it while waiting for Mr. Rumkowski, it had become a living presence to her, close and so dear, that now, that she had left it behind, it reminded her of herself and her own mother who had abandoned her in a dark alley never to return.

They took the streetcar again. The ride seemed interminable to Sabinka. Mr. Rumkowski sat beside her, tired and silent. The window in the tram was shut and when she looked through it, she could see her own reflection and that of Mr. Rumkowski's head. His face looked angry; his nose, carrying his eyeglasses on its tip, seemed very long. His chin was resting on his chest and he kept his eyes shut. His lips moved; he was kneading one against the other, emitting dull groans. She was also tired. Her face was smeared with sweat and dust and her tresses hung down from her shoulders, their white ribbons creased and the bows untied. She drummed on her reflection in the glass with the rolled magazine, feeling sleepy and bored.

Suddenly Sabinka saw thousands of colourful lights winking at her from Luna Park. The tram stopped. Her excitement immediately rekindled, she jumped to her feet, hardly able to control her impatience, as she waited for Mr. Rumkowski to stand up. The sound of the music, the gay clamour which reached her ears from the whirling carousels, from the roller coasters, sent a tremor down her spine; it practically lifted her up in the air, transforming her into a bubble of quicksilver. Her face radiant, eyes emitting sparks of joy, she stretched her hands out to the throngs of people, as if pulled towards them by a magnet. "Look, Mr. Rumkowski!" she was unable to contain her excitement as they descended and waded into Luna Park.

He was looking at her. "How young and fresh she is!" he thought. His body and soul were gradually lifted above their heaviness and fatigue by the sight of her youth and beauty. She pulled him by the hand towards a whirling carousel which, like an open umbrella, circled above their heads with its flying seats. She stepped impatiently with one foot upon the other. "Do you want a ride?" he asked.

He read the answer in her eyes. She handed him the magazine. "Don't throw it away, Mr. Rumkowski. I want to keep it as a souvenir." She darted a grateful glance at him.

"Aren't you afraid?" he asked.

She giggled nervously. "What is there to be afraid of? Have you ever ridden on a carousel, Mr. Rumkowski?"

"Oho!" his face lit up. "Have I ever! What do you think, that I was always the old man I am now?"

"Then come, ride with me!" she grabbed him by the hand.

"Ay," he shook his head. "I have ridden enough. You go ahead, child. I'll wait for you on the bench."

The music of the organ grinder at the carousel's centre began to weaken as the two hefty men pushing the huge wooden axles under the umbrella-shaped awning diminished the speed of their steps. The swinging seats descended until they levelled, hanging above the ground. Rumkowski paid for Sabinka's ride, helped her to fasten the safety chains over her lap and to settle comfortably into her seat. The two burly men began trotting, pushing the wooden poles in a circle. From behind the gaily-painted cylindrical centre post, the jarring music of the organ grinder started up again. Sabinka grabbed the side chains with both hands and threw up her head, as if to reassure herself that the chains were strong enough to carry her. She swung lightly in her seat, her face frozen in a stiff uncertain smile of expectation. Rumkowski, himself overcome by youthful exuberance, watched her, a twinkling smile in his eyes.

The girl flashed by in front of him and then gradually began to rise in the air. At first, as she made the initial few circles, she waved her hand at him every time she passed by. But later she kept her head lifted, stretched towards the roofs of the houses, towards the sky. She soared above his head, circling like a bird over it. Her two braids, their waving white ribbons flapping, her ballooning dress, and her dangling naked legs in the white socks — all flashed by him with accelerated speed. She gave off sharp thin laughs, now and then exchanging screams with her riding companions. "Cute *Panienka*, wait for me!" a flying fellow on the seat behind her shouted, stretching his arms out to her. When he came close, he grabbed her seat from the rear, swung it with all his strength, then pushed it away. Her laughter turned into a breathless staccato scream of joy. She rose above all the riders as if about to tear herself from the carousel altogether and zoom away to the stars. The chains holding her seat became tangled. As they untwisted, they turned her in her seat, carrying her along in their winding irregular dance. Her voice became thinner and sharper. It fell upon Rumkowski's turning heart like a gramophone needle, playing a tune on it, which was old and long forgotten and yet strangely new.

He sat down on a bench. "Life is like a carousel," he thought philosophically. Unexpectedly, he saw the cemetery in his mind's eye and he remembered today's date. The cemetery and Luna Park became one. Here again there was a similarity of contrasts. "Life seems to be like a straight road, but it is not. It turns in circles and because of that, it is sometimes hard to make out the sense of it. But also because of that, it is interesting, since it is not entirely like this carousel here which attracts me no longer. This is a child's game, a silly plaything, and my time for being silly has long since passed. This carousel turns and turns, passing by the same vistas, staying in the same place and always coming back to the same. But the carousel of life is different, always new and never boring. You only have to have the courage to ride it, have the strength and the wisdom to give sense to the spiralling intricate maze through which it carries you. You have to transform it into clarity, to give it a purpose. That is called living," he concluded, nodding his head gravely.

While he had the feeling that Shoshana's grave was here, somewhere in Luna Park — as was the empty lot waiting for him — it appeared to him that it was all turning backwards, taking on the semblance of a weaver's spindle unwinding its thread towards its beginning with increasing speed. The unwinding thread of thought led him back to recollections of his hometown which seemed to find itself here as well, somewhere in Luna Park. "How enthusiastically I boarded the carousel of life, how high I was flying!" He sighed as a remote lively scenery flashed by his mind's eye with the speed of a merry-go-round. "I had no patience for the *heder;* I hardly had the patience for any schooling or preaching. And that father of mine, how he wanted me to study, not to waste my good brains, my fiery brilliant mind! But I couldn't. Life, my only real school, was calling me. I had to be out there, where things were happening; I had to join the gang of youths, to become their leader. I became their god. Had Mordecai Chaim asked them to jump into the fire for him, they would have jumped into the fire for him. And who had given them an ideal, if not he? Who had heated them up with fiery speeches, if not he? Small thing Mordecai Chaim! Small thing a word of his! And oh, how good it was to be the uncrowned king of the *shtetl,* to have the world under your feet, like your own estate!" Then Rumkowski's face became overcast. "But on the carousel of life you don't always fly high. Sometimes you fall off it to the ground, breaking head and neck, and then you need the might of a Samson to rise to your feet again. I had that strength, that fortitude to endure all my trials. I've always had it — my only treasure in the worthlessness of my past. I had the stamina to climb up from the bottom of the deepest pit."

He shook his head as he thought of the difficult moments which had filled his days. How hard it had been for him to grow up and find a purpose in his private life. He had searched for it in the world: Germany, Czechoslovakia, England, at one time almost reaching the top of the hill, at another, rolling back down to the point where he had started, losing everything he had gained before. He had built his velours factory with success, but then had come bankruptcy. He had started a new business, which was followed by another fiasco. And it had been the same with his wives: a waltz about with the first one and then — into the grave; a waltz about with the second one and again — into the grave. Life lost its lightness. Days became heavy like rocks suspended from his neck; days he wanted to be rid of, to pass by with a curse. But then something awoke in him again; vitality exploded within him like a volcano. A desire for life, for action overpowered him; and he went on, looking for a new trail, ready to overcome the new difficulties and forge his fate with his own hands. Real action, history-making action — how strongly he felt that this was his calling! But people were reluctant to follow him the way the youths in his home *shtetl* had. People were always blinded to the potential of his personality. An eternal misunderstanding rose like a wall between him and them. No one was ready to follow him through fire again; no one worshipped him like a god any longer. He had become one of the millions — a speck of dust, an ant, a nothing.

But his heart cried out for the times of his youth, for his devoted followers. He had searched for them everywhere, was still searching for them now, ready to serve them and lead them. He had never given up the struggle to give his name some value, to reach the place he had been designated by fate to take up — to become more than a gray nonentity, a mere ant, a speck of dust. Even when his wives had come along and with them his great defeat, even when he realized that not only was he nothing more than a gray nonentity, but that he was still less than other gray nonentities; even during those times when he began feeling the pressing hoop around his heart and the gnawing emptiness inside him, times which had left their imprint on him forever, even then — when he had felt himself to be buried ninety miles deep in the pit — he had not given up the struggle for self-respect. Indeed, this potential for struggle, this strength to stand up straight after every blow, like a punching bag supported by a flexible but unbreakable spring, this was still in him and no misery in the world could destroy it.

In this way had he finally reached the heights of his renewed ideal, Zionism. He lived for the Zionist dream, although he had always been pushed aside by his comrades who would not allow him to spread his wings, nor give him the place in their ranks that he deserved. In this way also he had succeeded in building the orphanage, his orphanage — and having his children. He had become their father in a higher sense than an ordinary father. Here he did have a chance to spread his wings, to bring back the flavour of bygone years when he had been a commander, a god almost. Now he was flying high again, very high. He recalled the heartache he had had only a few hours ago, the unsuccessful tiresome day which had passed, and he smiled to himself. "Just don't give up, Chaim! Hold on to the chain of life and you'll see what great things there are still in store for you."

The music coming from the carousel weakened, and Sabinka's seat began descending. Rumkowski got up from the bench and approached the carousel. Sabinka came down, searching for the ground with the tips of her shoes. He unhooked the chain over her lap and helped her to get out of her seat. Suddenly, she lifted his hand to her mouth and planted a moist loud kiss on it, pressing her face against the parched skin of his fingers.

They edged through the crowd. "You see, Sabinka," he beamed. "When Mr. Rumkowski promises something, he always keeps his word." He laughed loudly, amazed at the youthful sound of his voice, then he drew out a creased paper zloty from his pocket and pushed it into her hand. "Here, change it and go ahead, have a ball! Do you see that patch of field over there?" he pointed to a quiet bushy place near the fence. "I will be waiting for you there."

She looked at him with wide-eyed astonishment. "A whole zloty?" She held it tightly clasped in her fist, and before long she was gone.

He walked over to the plot of ground in front of the fence and let himself sink down to the grass. His head cushioned by the hands which he locked behind it, he gazed up at the starry sky. "How delightful she is," he thought of Sabinka. "Fresh like a juicy apple and beautiful as a painting. And the charm of it is that she is unaware of the power she possesses, the power of a good wine, a sweetness which makes your head turn, makes you light and carefree." Now he was certain that the tide of new strength rushing to his limbs was different from what he usually felt on the anniversaries of Shoshana's death. This time it was all on account of the girl, of Sabinka. "There must still be a spark of youth in me," he thought. "Otherwise she wouldn't be able to do to me what she is doing. There is still energy in your body, Mordecai Chaim! There is still something to fiddle with, ho, ho!" He laughed at the deep sky above his head.

Time was passing. At length he noticed Sabinka approaching rapidly. She stopped in front of him. "Are you mad at me, Mr. Rumkowski?" she asked guiltily.

"Why should I be mad at you, child?" He smiled and stood up.

She relaxed. "And where are we going now?"

"Let's walk a bit further." He took her hand in his. "There, you see, closer to

the fence, there is not as much noise as here. We will sit down for a while."
They walked ahead, closer to the fence and to the bushes, arriving at a place
where the lights of Luna Park did not penetrate. The grass, completely steeped
in shadow, looked almost black. "Here . . ." he made an inviting gesture to her
to sit down. She obeyed, looking around somewhat ill at ease.

"It's dark here," she giggled.

"It is quiet," he replied. "So, did you have a good time?"

Her face lit up in the darkness. "Oh, Mr. Rumkowski, never in my life . . .
Never have I had such a good time."

"So . . ." he breathed heavily. "Don't I deserve something for it?" She was
about to utter words of gratitude, when he put both his hands around her head
and bent the upper part of her body over his lap. He pressed his sagging lips to
her half-open mouth, hungrily kissing the fresh cherry lips. As the screaming
fright in her eyes began to drown in pearly moisture, Rumkowski sucked on
them, the salty taste on his lips kindling a fire inside him.

He was about to reach for the white thighs underneath the short dress, when
he heard the branches of the surrounding bushes break and the grass near him
rustle. An uncanny shriek burst forth from the bushes. "Hep, hep, give it to
her, old Jew boy! Give it!" Suddenly, all the bushes exploded with deafening
laughter and whistles, making Rumkowski scramble to his feet, lashing him like
whips and chasing him and Sabinka down the field and through the crowd —
towards the exit of Luna Park.

✦ ✦ ✦

The building of the orphanage was enveloped in darkness when Rumkowski
arrived back with Sabinka. He ordered her to sneak into the dormitory as
quietly as a mouse. He gave her permission to tell everyone that Mr.
Rumkowski had taken her to Luna Park, and he also remembered to push the
magazine of movie stars that she had wanted to save as a souvenir, into her limp
hand. But he warned her that he would throw her out of Helenovek, into the
street, if she were to so much as whisper to anyone about what had happened in
the field. He promised to take her to Luna Park again some day, if she were as
nice as she had been this time.

When Mr. Rumkowski, before going to bed, emptied his pockets of all the
papers and collection books, many crumpled broken lilac cups fell out with
them onto the table. He mopped them up with his fingers and threw them into
the garbage pail.

Chapter Six

IN THE JEWISH girls' *gymnasium* Wiedza, recess had just finished; the bell had already rung. The girls were in their classrooms and the teachers, class registers under their arms, were heading towards their respective classes with dignity and purpose in their every step.

In front of the fourth year class stood the botany teacher, Professor Hager, animatedly shaking his goatee in Miss Diamand's face. In a voice hoarse with emotion, he was telling her of his experiments in cross pollinating a certain kind of field flower with a particular species of narcissus, experiments which had only recently produced good results, and which brought the Professor into such a state of euphoria that he was unable to talk about anything but his flowers. However, Miss Diamand, although not indifferent to the subject of his discourse, was not paying any attention to him. Her class was waiting for her. So, when she noticed the silhouette of the Directress, Miss Biederman, looming at the far end of the corridor, she interrupted him, and slipped away from him into her classroom.

The light of thirty pairs of eyes, mingled with the luminous glare coming from the window, beamed at Miss Diamand's fragile figure as she appeared in the doorway. There was an air of extreme delicacy, of sheer weightlessness about her. Her body seemed to consist of nothing but bones, but bones possessing the unbone-like qualities of softness and lightness. Her elongated face created the profile of an exotic dream-like bird; her eyes, blue but misty, appeared doubly large and doubly nebulous through her frameless glasses. A few short gray hairs protruded stiffly from where her eyebrows should have been. Similarly, the hair on her head was thin, showing the pink of her skull through the strings of gray fixed at her neck by a few black hairpins. A mauve dress hung limply from her shoulders; yet it gave no appearance of sloppiness but rather seemed to be a perfectly appropriate apparel for her. It resembled a Greek tunic in its cut and harmonized with her bearing, enhancing the spirituality that permeated her being.

Her eyes embraced the classroom. From the warm glow kindled inside them, it was easy to infer that what was about to happen between these walls had a particular meaning to her; that she was here now, not to begin an hour of work, but to initiate a kind of sacred service of which she was the priestess. "Good morning, *Panienki*," she greeted the girls with a soft voice, her pearly words rolling forth to the furthest benches. The girls rose from their seats and remained standing, while she, radiant and solemn, stepped up onto the dais where her desk stood. On it she deposited the pack of exercise books she had been carrying under her arm. She wet her bloodless lips, moved the eye-glasses

103

up onto her forehead, and with her naked eye scrutinized the class, gliding her gaze from bench to bench, from face to face. She put her hand to her ear as if she were listening to a sea shell and bent over her desk. "I sense a disquiet here this morning," she rolled her pearly words through the silence in the room.

"We are nervous about the results of our essays," a student explained in a hushed voice.

A pale smile lit up on her lips. "It is quite healthy to feel a bit restless before you start working, children, to be a bit fearful, a bit apprehensive, but after the work is done, such feelings are futile." However, she had no intention of prolonging their anguish; it seemed to her that she could hear the throbbing of their hearts. Therefore she began her evaluation of their work without any further ado.

"With some of these essays I am quite satisfied," she began, putting her hands on the pile of copy books as if she were blessing them. "But I am sorry to add that there are many which made me sad, which don't suit young ladies about to get their graduation certificates, at all. We have been working on literature for four years. Of course, it is impossible to embrace the entire field ... even in a lifetime. But, after all, we are not dealing here with a question of quantity, but rather with one of quality. What I have tried to teach you was not to make you juggle in later life with the imposing list of masterpieces you had read, or of poems you had learned by heart. What I wished to achieve was to develop your taste for literature, which is the art closest to life and which influences life more than any other art. I wanted to develop in you an ability to discern the value of a work and the goal its author set out to achieve, be it a moral, or a philosophical, or merely an aesthetic one. Because, once you have the ability to enter the world of any one writer, you actually have the key to literature as such. And this was my purpose: to help you find that key. Indeed, girls, I was ready to forgive you all your shortcomings as far as quantity is concerned, as long as you could show me how your hearts and minds reacted during your encounter with the artist and his work. This is the reason why the topic I gave you for your essays sounded so childish and naive: 'The Writer Closest to my Heart.' I chose this title because I wanted you to be subjective, because art can be appreciated only subjectively, and its impact on us is purely subjective as well. And now, what was the result of the test I gave you? Most of you chose a writer about whom you happen accidentally to have studied the most. I mean, about whom you know the most facts. But even in the best of your essays the analysis of your personal point of view, of your reactions, your feelings, your attitude towards all the treasure that the writer of your choice has produced took up the smaller part of your work, although I expected it to be just the opposite. That is all," she concluded.

She was about to open the first writing book on top of the pile, when she reminded herself, "Yes, also a curiosity. A strange essay caught my attention." She lifted the glasses to her forehead and searched among the benches with her eyes. "Miss Eibushitz!" At the other end of the classroom a girl jumped to her feet. "Of all the writers, my child, you chose precisely one ..." Miss Diamand fingered the writing book she had pulled out from the pile and lifting it to her face, flipped it open. "Izchak Leibush Peretz," she syllabled the words.

"He is the writer closest to my heart," came the answer from the far end of the classroom.

"But we have not studied him, Miss Eibushitz."

"You said we didn't have to write only about those we studied."

"Yes, but then I meant a writer well-known in world literature, like Tolstoy, or Goethe, or Romain Roland. But when you write about ..." The teacher lifted the writing book to her nose again. "About Peretz, the question arises ... If the writer is in fact all that you claim him to be, how is it that the world doesn't know about him? Why have I, for instance, never heard of him? You say that he was the founder of modern Yiddish literature. Very nice, but is it not an altogether questionable assumption that a jargon can have a literature and that people living shut up in a Ghetto can be modern, let alone capable of producing modern literature?"

"I think," Rachel Eibushitz's hands made a frantic effort to discipline her stubbornly dishevelled forelocks. "I think ..."

She was ready to tell the teacher what she thought, but Miss Diamand stopped her short, with a gesture. "Here, let me quote one of your sentences." With her glasses still on her forehead, she slowly began to read from Rachel's exercise book. "You write: 'The mysticism and poetry of his Folk Tales made me look into the soul of my people as if through a magic looking glass, and see our past, our present and our future in a crystallized light of beauty and sacrifice.' Even if that sentence were not so bombastic, I for one, would not be able to agree or disagree with you, for the simple reason that I do not know. I, your teacher of literature, confess to you and to the class that I had no idea that a Jewish literature written in a jargonized German existed, and therefore, my child, I am unable to evaluate your work at all." Miss Diamand pointed her thin nose in Rachel's direction and called her, with her finger, to the dais.

The girl, tall, broad-shouldered and broad-hipped, walked with pride and determination between the rows of her classmates who stared at her with curious, amusedly twinkling eyes, and approached the teacher's dais. She darted a glance at the open exercise book on the desk. Its pages were crossed out, from one corner to the other, with a red pencil.

The teacher put her hand on Rachel's shoulder and sang out in her pearly voice, "You suffer, my child, from a Jewish complex, and I advise you to fight it and to come out of your spiritual ghetto. The sooner you do that, the better it will be for you." At this, the girl shook her head vigorously and stepped back, letting Miss Diamand's hand drop from her shoulder. Miss Diamand, sensing the rigidity and resistance in the girl's behaviour, did not change her mild tone and went on talking, partly to Rachel, partly to the whole class. "I am aware that all this is the fault of your environment, but understand, Miss Eibushitz, that the world in which you live is a narrow one and one doomed to vanish. My purpose is to open new horizons to you, to lead you out into the wide open world, where men are brothers, where great minds meet and understand one another. And you, my child, defend yourself against it." The teacher stopped talking for a while as she noticed Rachel pulling out a handkerchief from the pocket of her black school apron. "You need not cry, Miss Eibushitz." Miss Diamand moved over to the edge of her desk, putting her hand again on the girl's shaking shoulder. "Why are you crying, child?" the girl shook off her hand and, with the handkerchief at her eyes, rushed back to her seat.

Miss Diamand's hand remained suspended in the air. For a while she stood there, utterly confused; then she came down from the dais, trotted over to the centre of the classroom, and halted there as if something had abruptly stopped her from approaching Rachel. The teacher's face was sad, overcast;

astonishment and pain flickered in her misty eyes which were framed by a reddish rim along the eyelashes. "You see, children," her voice rustled, quivering with emotion, "there are tears which have the power of healing. I hope that Miss Eibushitz's tears are of that nature." She faced the class. "Your classmate, my children, is defending herself against the new approach to life, against broad-mindedness which is so necessary to the study of art, of literature in particular. One of the classic masters once said, 'I see the right, but I follow the wrong.' There is no doubt in my mind that Miss Eibushitz sees the right way as well, but, hampered by the conditions of her environment, she chooses the wrong, justifying her forced choice by proclaiming it as a right. I am sure you understand me, Miss Eibushitz, don't you?" She cast an apologetic maternal glance at Rachel.

The girl, her face red and smeared with tears, jumped to her feet. "No! I don't understand you! I don't know what you want of me!"

The teacher was shocked. Her face, resembling that of a rare delicate bird, constricted, as if it had just been spattered with mud. "How dare you talk to me in that manner, my child?"'

"It is true!" the girl shouted, beside herself. "This is not a school here!" She threw up her hand, pointing at the window which had a grating of bars on the outside. "It's a prison! A jail with bars on the windows!"

"You know quite well why we have bars on our windows. There used to be a bank once in this building." The teacher fought with all her strength to regain her composure. She forced herself to joke, "And you see, we, your teachers, are trapped in that jail as well."

"That's right!" the girl disregarded the teacher's conciliatory efforts. "It is your jail and all you want is to trap our minds behind your bars, calling them freedom and broad-mindedness. You preach about great minds, about universal spirits, but when a Jew happens to be a great spirit, you shrug him off, you throw him out into the dust bin. And all of them, all the writers you want me to write about, they were all creating amongst their own people, in their own language. Why should the Jews not do the same? Why should I be ashamed to write about Peretz? Perhaps those who don't know who Peretz was should be ashamed of themselves!" This speech was too arrogant even for the taste of Rachel's classmates. Rachel, however, met their disapproving glances with a haughty fling of her head and sat down. Her cheeks were afire, but she was no longer crying.

During the silence that followed, the girls, spell-bound, watched the sad shadow on Miss Diamand's face become increasingly darker. She seemed as baffled as someone who, certain of walking on familiar ground, was suddenly struck by the sight of an alien landscape.

"It saddens me, child," she spoke with difficulty, "that you don't show me the respect due me. But I am making an effort to forgive you. I am convinced that your own words have given you no pleasure either." Now she looked the girl straight in the face. "Your soul is restless. I can judge it by the sight of your dishevelled hair. You are as disordered inside as you are outside . . ."

The class burst out laughing. From which the teacher deduced that she had made a jocular remark, and she smiled faintly, her face brightening. Gradually, she regained her composure. However, she thought it her duty, as well as that of her students, to learn something from the unpleasant incident that had just occurred.

Relaxed and serene again, she continued talking to Rachel, "You are a child of a tragic people, my dear; a people about to disappear from the face of the earth. You and those among whom you live refuse to admit this fact. You battle with the winds of time as Don Quixote battled with the windmills. The Jews were an historic people a very long time ago. They had their land, their language, their religion and their philosophy. But their country and their language disappeared. The ideas of their religion and philosophy impregnated other, newer peoples that had sprung to life during the march of history, the march of that force which is capable of creating and destroying. What had happened to the Persians, to the ancient Greeks, to the Romans, happened to the Jews as well. There is however a physical remainder still left of that old people, of the Hebrews, which, although emptied and drained spiritually, is still endowed with a strong vital drive. They stick to their archaic religious forms; they have created a jargon for themselves which is a mixture of the languages they have encountered in their wanderings, and they refuse, in every way possible, to become a part of the new young nations which have sprung up after them. Here, in Poland, the leftovers of this people live in compact masses, isolated from their surroundings, declaring themselves still to be a people when, in truth, they are only a caricature of one, a live unhappy trace of something which was once great and beautiful, but is no more. The more intelligent ones among them, those aware of reality, have freed themselves of their anachronistic yoke; they have consciously incorporated themselves into the Polish nation and have become a healthy part of our society. And these are whole people; they live a full life. And this, my dear children, is the purpose of a school like ours. We want to make it easier for you, to alleviate the pains of assimilation, to help you in the process of inner and outer liberation. Do you understand, *Panienki?*"

A girl raised her finger and asked flatly. "Then what do we study Hebrew for?"

"Oh," Miss Diamand spread her hands. "For the same reason you study Latin. Hebrew is a wonderful language. The Bible was written in it and, from the point of view of your origin, the language should interest you very much. We don't ask you, children, to deny your origins. No one should do that."

Miss Diamand invited the class to ask more questions. But no more hands were raised. The girls were restlessly stirring in their seats, keeping their eyes glued to the pile of writing books on the teacher's desk. She understood that their worry about the marks on their essays prevented them from concentrating on the discussion. So she trotted back to her desk and began distributing the essays, commenting on each as she handed it back, all the time hoping that a few minutes would remain at the end of the lesson, to come back to the important subject which had come up so spontaneously that day.

After recess came the turn of the Hebrew teacher, Mrs. Karmelman, or *Karmelka*, as the girls called her. They considered her a good sport and their behaviour towards her was even a bit too friendly and familiar, since it lacked any kind of respect. Knowing quite well how little her subject was appreciated in the *Wiedza*, *Karmelka* accepted the situation with cheerful resignation.

To her, Hebrew was certainly not a language to be compared with the dead Latin. And in order to convince her students that the case was just the opposite, she taught them *horas* and sad languorous Hebrew songs. The girls learned the songs and enjoyed singing them, even though they rarely understood more than one or two words of the text. But when it came to the business of homework and the study of grammar, it was a different story altogether. During *Karmelka's* lessons, they prepared their homework for other, more important teachers, and her entreaties delivered in Polish with a Hebrew-Yiddish-Russian accent, were to no avail. The most the girls would do for her, since they genuinely liked her, was to remove the math or history books from their desks and keep them on their laps, or to cover them with the Hebrew exercise book. Consequently, *Karmelka* had to be satisfied with working with those few girls who had an inborn diligence and an innate respect for teachers.

At first, *Karmelka* had considered Rachel Eibushitz her ally. She often chatted with her in Yiddish, and when Rachel paid attention, she was able to grasp the grammar rules easily and to learn many words quickly, words familiar to her from the colloquial Yiddish. She felt a kinship with *Karmelka* who reminded her of her own mother and of the teachers at the Bundist elementary school which she had attended. But on one point Rachel agreed with Miss Diamand: Hebrew was a dead language and had a relationship to life only insofar as it had a relationship to Zionism; and Rachel refused to have anything to do with Zionism. *Karmelka's* Hebrew songs, which carried her away with their liveliness or moved her deeply with their sadness, did not achieve much as far as her opinions were concerned, nor did, for that matter, *Karmelka's* argument that language has nothing to do with politics, that Rachel ought to study Hebrew in order to enrich her own Yiddish. She argued with the teacher during the Hebrew lessons, or like most of the girls, she prepared her other subjects.

Now Rachel was sitting on her bench, oblivious to what was going on around her. Through the grating on the window she stared at the trees in the school garden and felt bitter and dissatisfied. She could not forgive herself for having cried in front of her classmates, for having defended her case so poorly and for not having found the right words to refute Miss Diamand's arguments. She felt hot and longed for a refreshing drink, or for some soothing inner tune which would make her forget the unpleasant incident. She thought of David, her boy friend, and repeated his name in her mind, calling on him to sustain her.

The girls in the class, excited at the thought of the approaching vacation, were making their plans aloud and telling them to the teacher. Their voices rose above each other, interrupted by *Karmelka's* incessant pleading, "Hebrew! Say it in Hebrew!" orders to which no one paid any attention.

Rachel's eyes fell on *Karmelka's* dress which was of a faded blue, with open wrinkled pleats, an old garment, its fabric worn ragged by constant use, its dull appearance made more vivid only by black darned patches and the shiny traces of an iron. Rachel became aware of the exchange of familiarity between herself and the teacher's dress. She felt drawn towards it, craving to exchange a few warm words with the person wearing it. Gradually, the importance of what had happened during Miss Diamand's lesson diminished until it became completely meaningless to her. She, Rachel, knew what she wanted, what road to choose in life. There was a strange beauty to *Karmelka's* worn dress.

After the lesson, she did not approach *Karmelka*, yet she left school in a composed frame of mind and, as usual, surrounded by a bunch of classmates. Intoxicated with the warm summer air, the girls clustered on the sidewalks; jackets unbuttoned, they fanned themselves with their berets, cracking jokes about the heavy school bags of which they would be rid so very soon. Somewhere in the middle of that lazy carefree stroll, Rachel remembered that she had to hurry, since she still had a long afternoon loaded with private lessons to get through. She brought the animated conversation with her friends to an abrupt end, took leave of them and raced home for a quick lunch.

✦ ✦ ✦

The nights always seemed too short to Rachel; it was as if the moment she had shut her eyes, she had to open them again. In the very middle of a most delightful sleep, a voice would penetrate her, "Rachel, it's getting late!" and she would feel her limbs, so cosily abandoned to oblivion, briskly shaken by her mother's hand.

This particular morning she was so deeply submerged in a dream that although she had heard her mother's voice, she did not care what it was telling her, nor did she mind the shaking. She went on sleeping, until she realized that her mother had removed her blanket. "Aren't we going to school today? Get up!" came the order.

Rachel opened her eyes and rubbed them slowly. An unpleasant recollection loomed remotely in her mind. "I dreamed something," she said as if to herself. She leaned on her elbow and glanced at her mother who, dressed in a long housecoat, stood at the table, cutting thick lumps of bread from a soft round loaf. "I think I dreamed that thieves broke into the room and were about to steal something . . ."

Blumka Eibushitz buttered the thick slices of bread energetically. Without turning her head to her daughter, she shrugged her shoulders and said in a hushed voice, "Who would be so stupid as to break in here? A thief steals things worth stealing, things he wouldn't find here. That's why they say that dreams are silly."

"No, this was another sort of stealing." Rachel sat up slowly, letting her feet dangle from the bed. "We, all four of us, were running along some street and they were chasing us, and then . . . Then I was all alone. The thieves caught me by the hair. In the dream I still had my braids. So, in my dream, I thought that if it is my hair they are after, then let them have as much of it as they want. But that other thing I won't give to them. I don't know what that other thing was. Anyway, I was glad they were unable to find it." Rachel went over to the basin of water her mother had prepared for her. While she washed, the dream came back to her with increasing clarity. "Yes," she went on, "the thieves said to me, 'We shall shave your head to make it look like a loaf of bread,' and they laughed. Stupid thieves, I thought in my dream, they forget that hair can grow back. 'But this . . . this important thing, you won't be able to take away from me,' I told them."

Blumka put away the knife, folded her hands over her bosom and looked at her daughter reproachfully, "You are not going to school today?"

Rachel, towel in hand, rushed towards her, embracing her with her arms, "I would gladly not go."

Blumka pushed her away, "Get dressed, this minute!"

Rachel went over to the window and pulled the drapes aside. She turned to Blumka, "Do you know that it's raining? I could go back to bed. It's so pleasant to sleep when it rains outside."

"Starting that again? Next time don't read until dawn. I gave you a new candle last night. I can see what's left of it. And your walks with David don't have to last until midnight either," Blumka chided her.

Resigned to her fate, Rachel trudged to the dresser to consult her father's watch. Then a thought struck her: she was supposed to distribute leaflets at school today! She rushed for her clothes and was dressed in the blink of an eye. Blumka darted amazed but contented glances at her, and called her to the table. But Rachel shook her head, "I can't eat, I'm in a hurry!"

"Sit down!" Blumka commanded.

"Mama, please . . ."

Plate in one hand, spoon in the other, Blumka ran ahead of her daughter, putting herself in front of the door. "Eat!" she ordered, forcing one spoonful of scrambled egg after another into Rachel's mouth. "Nice, isn't it? Spoon feeding a young lady of sixteen. David should see this!" She put a glass of milk in Rachel's hand, and after the latter had gulped it down, she sighed with relief and removed herself from the door. Rachel pecked her hurriedly on the forehead and rushed out, sliding down the four flights of stairs on the bannister, her school bag in hand. The minute she was out on the street, she heard her mother's voice calling from above. Impatiently, she looked up to the window beneath the roof and saw Blumka's head and her outstretched hand from which a jacket dangled. Blumka released the jacket, letting it fly down to the sidewalk where Rachel caught it in mid-air and slung it over her shoulder. "Put it on!" her mother's voice followed her. "Don't run! Be careful!" Rachel pretended not to hear. She was running.

The air was heavy and humid, the sky full of water. The rain, however, was about to stop. The sidewalks shone with mirror-like puddles, reflecting patches of cloudy sky and branches with dangling leaves, haggard from the lashing of the rain.

She did not run for long. The school bag weighed heavily in her sticky palm and she constantly changed it from one hand to the other. It occurred to her that it might be better to come to school a little later, after all. She would be alone in the cloakroom and could slide the proclamations into her schoolmates' coat pockets undisturbed. She slowed down and walked at a more relaxed pace along the Allées in the centre of town. On both sides the sidewalks were crowded with people on their way to work. Somewhere in the midst of the crowd a redhead flashed by. Rachel wondered if it were Red Esther, a young woman whose hair colour was in accordance with her political predilections. Rachel would often meet her in the library and carry on heated political discussions with her. Now, the redhead disappeared around a distant corner and vanished from Rachel's mind as well.

She was approaching the synagogue bordering the very end of the Allées. She liked dome-shaped buildings, and the synagogue, a Polish interpretation of the Byzantine style, caressed her eyes with its rounded roof which fit so harmoniously into the cupola of the sky and the wave-like, softly contoured clouds. She preferred this style to the Gothic which, with its tapering forms and sharp outlines, was supposed to symbolize man's longing for God, but instead brought to her mind the angular sharpness of swords or daggers. The cupola of the synagogue, now wet and glistening, enveloped in the low clouds as in a prayer shawl, seemed submerged in meditation, wrapped up in itself and isolated from the world.

However the world around the synagogue was teeming with the hustle and bustle of a busy weekday. This was the very heart of the city and Rachel waded with effort into the congested streets swarming with people like the corridors of an ant hill swarmed with ants. The cobblestone midways and the asphalt sidewalks seemed to be moving along with the crowd, by-passing the obstructions created by the grocery stalls, by the fruit and cigarette stands, all clustered with shoppers, with traders, with beggars, with cripples and with plain riff-raff. Similarly blocked were the house gates and every inch of space along the walls, against which leaned idle porters and jobless people of all kinds, all waiting for a chance to earn a few groschen. Gossips of both sexes were everywhere, making islands and eddies here and there.

Like other pedestrians who grew impatient with the congestion on the sidewalk, Rachel descended to the middle of the street, diving into the stream of wagons, cars, droshkies and carts until the density of the vehicles forced her to climb back onto the sidewalk. Hurrying in this zigzag manner, she passed the movie house, the Magic, and darted curious glances at the posters in front of it. It had been quite a while since she had seen a movie; her plans to go to summer camp meant that she had to deny herself the luxury and save her earnings. When a little later she passed the concert hall, the torn posters, soaked with rain, waved at her from the entrance. "You have never been to a concert," they seemed to mock her, bringing her classmate, Bella Zuckerman, to her mind. "I've never even heard her play the piano," she pondered, recalling her rare visits to Bella's which always began and ended at the door of the latter's beautiful home. But then the sight of the splendidly decorated window of the imported-food store cheered her up. It reminded her of David who had brought her an orange when she had been sick with diphtheria the previous winter. Not far from there was the very clock under which she and David met every day. Passing it, she looked up. With its black wrought-iron hands it indicated how many long hours separated her still from David and how very late she was for school.

The *gymnasium*, with its large barred windows, was steeped in silence. It seemed empty and, as usual, the sight of it made Rachel's heart freeze. She ran into the school garden by the back gate and quickly descended to the basement, into the cloakroom. On the way, she put her hand into her school bag to make certain that the roll of leaflets was still there. She imagined the faces of her schoolmates as they found the sheets of paper in their coat pockets on their way home. Tomorrow, ominous whispers would be passing through the corridors, while she, Rachel, walked about, lending an "innocent" ear to the murmurs, inwardly proud of herself and her work.

It was not the first time that she had taken an assignment of this nature upon herself. She was an experienced distributor of leaflets and knew the content of this day's batch by heart. They called the students to attend the last meeting before the summer holidays of the Socialist Students' Organization, the SOMS, the purpose of the meeting being to propagate socialist ideas among the students and to stimulate them to think during their vacation of all the urgent problems of social injustice. Another reason for the meeting was to find out where most of the students would spend the summer, so as to organize groups for them at these country places. This was very important, since it was a known fact that youth was more susceptible to revolutionary ideas during the summer than during the winter.

She stepped into the cloakroom, wading among the drying umbrellas, which resembled colourful mushrooms. Hiding behind a stand heavily laden with coats and jackets, she went down on her knees and opened her school bag. At that very moment she heard loud steps approaching, then coming to a sudden halt. Her heart skipped a beat. She tried to conceal herself by burying her face between the coats. But then she thought better of it, closed her school bag quickly, picked it up and straightened herself. Someone was standing in the door. She knew very well who it was. She faced the directress, Miss Biederman, and curtsied.

Miss Biederman did not return Rachel's greeting. She raised one hand to the cameo pinned near the neckline of her severe black dress; the other hand she lifted to consult her watch, as if she had had no previous idea of the time. She shook her head and the flat ringlets tightly pressed to it shook along with it, like a regiment of soldiers jumping to attention at a command. She pursed her unpainted lips which betrayed her middle-aged maidenhood and fixed a pair of cold metallic eyes on Rachel. Their glare sent a chill down the girl's body, from her head down to her toes.

"We allow ourselves a little bit too much, don't we, Miss Eibushitz?" the directress asked, holding her watch up to Rachel's eyes. Rachel searched her mind frantically for an excuse, but before she managed to open her mouth, the directress caught the edge of Rachel's collar. "Is this supposed to be a white collar?" Miss Biederman pulled it with a jerk and the thread which kept it fastened to the apron burst, stitch by stitch, until half of the collar came dangling down the girl's back. "Take if off!" came the order. Rachel ripped off the rest of the collar and pushed it hurriedly into her apron pocket. But Miss Biederman had not finished with her yet. Now she concentrated her attention on the blue crest fastened with a safety pin to the student's sleeve. "So, you wear the insignia of our school on a safety pin? Off with it!" Rachel busied herself unfastening the safety pin, all the while thinking of an officer whose medals and epaulettes were torn from his uniform during a demotion. The directress locked the fingers of both her hands over her flat chest and rubbed the palms against one another, a sure sign of unspeakable anger. "Come to my office right away, please," she ordered, made an about turn and marched off, leaving Rachel to follow behind.

To Rachel, who had never been in the directress' office before, it seemed strange to find bars on the windows there too. Against this background there stood on a window ledge a single potted hyacinth in full bloom. "Sit down," Miss Biederman ordered, as she took her place behind her desk. Rachel sat down opposite her. She put her heavy school bag down between her feet, brushed the dishevelled curls away from her forehead and slowly raised her head.

To her surprise, Miss Biederman's forehead had relaxed, its many furrows dissolved as if pressed flat by an unseen iron. She glanced again at her wrist watch, then moved her eyes back to Rachel. Their metallic coldness seemed to have melted. "Since you have missed the lesson anyway, Miss Eibushitz . . ." she said, interrupting that sentence with a short artificial cough, and commencing on a new one, "It is not just a question of coming late to school, or of having the school crest fastened to your sleeve by a safety pin . . . Such things happen sometimes, although they are not supposed to." The directress added with the hint of a smile, "We are inclined to forgive you for these transgressions of our regulations, once." She gave another little cough. "However we take this opportunity to speak to you of another, more serious problem, of which we have just recently become aware. The problem is, Miss Eibushitz, that you are committing a great sin against your friends, against your teachers and against your school as such, and this, you see, we cannot forgive you." Miss Biederman did not in the least change her mild tone as she said this, but the deep furrows reappeared on her forehead, settling above her eyebrows, one on top of the other. As Rachel noticed this, she pressed the school bag tighter between her legs, making ready to protect it, if necessary. "You are about to graduate from our *gymnasium*, Miss Eibushitz. You have been accorded various stipends and reductions in fees. Have you made an effort to deserve all this? Have you shown the least bit of gratitude to your school? We don't have academic achievement in mind right now. What we have in mind is loyalty and devotion to an institution which spared neither means nor effort to make a good, educated citizen out of you." With a show of controlled emotion, Miss Biederman raised her hand to the cameo on her dress. "We are surprised and saddened by the news which reached our ears, that you belong to a political organization, and moreover, that you propagate your silly theories among your friends. No use denying it, we have witnesses."

Rachel immediately realized who the "witnesses" might be. It was the mother of Inka, her classmate, at whose house her SOMS group had held its last meeting. Inka had assured Rachel, that her parents would not be at home; however, after the meeting, Inka's mother had come out of the adjoining room and said good-bye to the girls in an overly polite manner.

"Don't you know, Miss Eibushitz," Miss Biederman went on, "that as long as you attend *gymnasium* you are forbidden to belong to any political organization? That four years ago an entire graduating class was denied its *matura* diplomas for the same reason, that the students left school with 'wolf tickets' which prevented them from ever continuing their studies?"

"But they were communists! They're illegal!" Rachel burst out, then bit her tongue. Her remark was silly.

"We don't know to what party you belong, nor do we want to know. The fact that you belong to one is sufficient to upset us gravely. You are too young to be mixed up in politics. People your age should study. We give you all the opportunities, all the liberties possible to work socially in the Student Council and in the student clubs. But the curatorium explicitly forbids students to engage in any political activity and if all schools must follow the law, so certainly should a Jewish school. Therefore we think, Miss Eibushitz, that you deserve to be punished most severely." Tears filled Rachel's eyes. Everything was finished and done with, she thought. "And now," Miss Biederman seemed ready to conclude, "after we have explained, sufficiently, I hope, the gravity of your transgression . . . If you want us to . . . to forgive you, of course on the condition that you will promise us solemnly that until you graduate from our institution, your feet will not pass the threshold of any political organization . . . If you promise us this, we will be inclined to give you a chance to rehabilitate yourself."

At this point, the directress changed her royal "we" to the more intimate "I", although she retained the same solemn urgency in her voice. "However, I want one thing from you, Miss Eibushitz. I want you to give me the names of all the students, not only those of your class, but of the entire school, who belong to your organization. All the names . . . now, before you leave this room."

Rachel opened her mouth, sipping in the air quickly, like a fish suddenly thrown upon dry ground. She thought she was choking, suffocating. The bars on the windows danced vertiginously in front of her eyes, drawing closer and closer, like daggers about to pierce her. Her dress and apron were drenched with perspiration and stuck to her skin; the sweat ran down her forehead, trickling behind her ears. She sat motionless, fearing that her throbbing heart was about to jump onto her dry tongue. In a fraction of a second, she saw the dream of the night before in every minute detail; she saw someone chasing her, someone who wanted to take something sacred and dear away from her. Then she thought of famous revolutionaries who were threatened with torture unless they betrayed their accomplices by revealing their identities. Then she thought of her difficult years at the *gymnasium*, of how hard she had worked to pay her tuition by giving countless private lessons. Now all that would come to nothing; her dreams were dead, her plans for the future destroyed.

Then rage began to accumulate within her with increasing intensity, until she could hold it back no longer and she burst out vehemently, "This is a prison, not a school! A jail! a jail!" and she broke into sobs. As she wiped her eyes with her hands, she remembered her morning at home: Father still asleep, Mother preparing breakfast, Shlamek, her younger brother, chopping wood in the backyard, preparing the daily supply for the stove, before running off to school. And she cried still more, while at the same time her anger kept growing. She tore her hands away from her eyes, raised herself, and bent forward toward the stupefied directress. "You give us possibilities?" she lashed out, "You give us liberties? Some liberties! What kind of liberties are they, if you don't let us say what we think, if we have to hide our convictions? You want to make a good citizen out of me? How? By asking me to betray . . ."

"Miss Eibushitz!" the Directress cut her short with a hiss. But to Rachel's surprise, her voice immediately mellowed. "It is not heroism that you are showing with this behaviour. On the contrary, you show me that you are still a child. Your tears . . ." she smirked. "You are not going to betray your friends and deliver them to the Inquisition. I am not an inquisitor. What I ask you to do is for your own good as well as for the good of your friends."

Rachel was burning with both shame and pride. "Yes, directors of schools under the tsar used to say the same!" she shot back.

"Miss Eibushitz!" the directress cut her short with a hiss. But to Rachel's surprise, her voice immediately mellowed. "It is not heroism that you are showing with this behaviour. On the contrary, you show me that you are still a child. Your tears . . ." she smirked. "You are not going to betray your friends and deliver them to the Inquisition. I am not an inquisitor. What I ask you to do is for your own good as well as for the good of your friends."

tears washed her face. She drew from her pocket a crumpled-up wad consisting of her handkerchief and her collar and furiously rubbed her eyes with it.

Miss Biederman, utterly beside herself, jumped to her feet. "Your parents must come to school immediately. I must talk to them!"

Rachel snatched the school bag from between her legs and also jumped to her feet. "My parents know that I belong to the Bund. They belong to it too and they are on my side. Besides, they speak Polish badly and I don't want them to humiliate themselves in front of you. So, they won't come. I am old enough to hear your verdict by myself."

"Your behaviour proves just the opposite. That you have not grown up, that you are irresponsible and arrogant into the bargain." During the momentary silence that followed, the long ringing of the school bell pierced the air like a thick needle. "Go home now, and don't come back without your parents!" came the order.

Rachel dashed out of the directress' office into the stream of girls and teachers pouring into the corridor from the adjacent classrooms. Coming out into the garden, she skirted it quickly, avoiding groups of strolling girls, who were munching on candies and repeating their lessons. In their black aprons and white collars, they seemed like happy nuns inhabiting a remote cloister. She found it difficult to look at their relaxed calm faces. How she envied them! She knew very well what kind of days the near future held in store for her. Already they weighed on her with their anxiety and with the chagrin of her parents. The school garden seemed like a paradise lost.

It was too hot in the street to continue running. She slowed down and as she walked on, she felt a hand touch her shoulder. Bella Zuckerman came around to face her. "What happened?" she panted. "Why did you leave?"

Rachel felt like telling her to mind her own business. She wanted to run away and leave her behind. "Because," she said gruffly, "I am going home." She turned her head away, so that Bella would not see her red eyes.

Bella asked no more questions, but walked mutely at Rachel's side, holding on to her arm. With her sharp features and homely face in which two beautiful grave eyes nestled, she resembled an odd bewildered creature. The fragrance of fine perfume vibrated discreetly in the air about her. After a long while of walking in silence, she sighed and raised her head towards the sky. "Full of rain," she remarked. Rachel was so charged with tension, so impatient to be rid of Bella, that she could barely maintain the latter's quiet pace. "I like days like this," Bella went on, as if she did not sense her friend's rigidity. "When the sky is low, the world seems cozier. When the sky is open, the earth's fragrance dissolves in the blue. But on days like this, the earth allows itself to be savoured . . . For me, the earth has the same depth as the sky. Do you understand what kind of depth I mean? Chopin was very ill on such days, but that was also when he created the most beautiful music, in Nohant, where he lived with Georges Sand. She was his lover, you know. A strange love. But then, perhaps all loves are strange in their own manner. He loved her and then he hated her. It must be the same with all strong emotions; they reverse themselves easily. They flare up, burn, and go out, leaving only ashes smouldering . . . with hatred, which is, I suppose, an expression of sorrow, of regret that the flame has died . . . or a kind of remedy for the wounds of love." Bella smiled shyly as she suddenly awoke from her thoughts. "I'm talking nonsense."

"Go back," Rachel said to her flatly. "You'll be late for the next lesson."

Bella did not loosen her grip on Rachel's arm. For a long time they walked on without exchanging a word. Then she spoke again. "You know, Rachel, I admire you. I really do. You are capable of expressing so well what you feel, of formulating your thoughts so clearly. But I, when I talk . . . it is like now. I stammer. And if you want to know, there is something in you which makes you resemble Georges Sand. Seriously. You are realistic, down to earth, but at the same time you have a sense . . . for the nakedness of veiled things . . . for the soul of things. And she, Georges Sand, also had a strong feeling for the common people, just like you. She hoped for revolutions, but they disappointed her when they occurred. And people never understood her. I don't think they will ever understand you . . . Because at the same time, you are very individualistic."

Rachel, in spite of her worry and anxiety, had begun to pay attention to

Bella's words. She burst out aggressively, "Tell me, how much do you know about me? I rather feel that I frighten you. Whenever I try to get you interested in certain thoughts of mine, you change the subject right away."

Bella smiled faintly. "Yes, that happens when you talk about things which make me feel uneasy; noisy things. I like silence. When you talk out of your silence into mine, I like you."

Rachel stopped short. She turned to Bella and looked coldly into her eyes. "The directress sent me home to bring my parents to school," she said roughly. "You've heard of the SOMS groups, haven't you? Well, I'm a member, and if you want to know, I'm one of the organizers. Now they've found out about it."

Bella brushed her hand against her forehead and mumbled confusedly, "How strange . . ." Then she added, "Last week they threw my sister out of school; she attended a Polish school, you know. She was boycotting the German lessons. They had hired a new teacher, a typical *Gretchen* who brought magazines of the Hitler Youth to the classroom and spread Nazi propaganda among the girls. Junia was the only Jew there. She started protesting, and my sister doesn't mince words. Finally she stopped attending the German lessons. The director called her into his office and told her, 'Zuckerman, we refuse to keep such vermin as you in our school.' Mother got hysterical. She was ashamed, afraid people might think that Junia was thrown out of school for communism." Bella sighed. "The whole world seems to have turned upside down."

They heard the squeak of a cart behind them. "*Lody! Lody!*" A little Jew with a long straw-like beard was pushing an ice cream cart. He called and winked at the girls invitingly.

"Let's have some," Bella proposed.

The little man scrutinized them with his small eyes. "You girls look as if you had lost a boat of sour milk at sea," he said, busying himself with the tin cans fitted into his white cart. "Here are two big delicious *lodies*." He handed them the ice cream cones and shaking his long skimpy beard with satisfaction, moved on.

The girls walked on silently, licking their cones. "Do you see that house across the street?" Rachel asked, pointing at a massive shabby structure. "That's the elementary school I attended. Come, let's have a look inside." They crossed the street and entered the backyard of a tenement house which harboured the Yiddish school supported by the Bund. The backyard, full of noise and cheerful commotion, was teeming with children. "Look at what's going on here!" Rachel exclaimed, not realizing that Bella had released her arm. "Here I spent my happiest years!" she said wistfully, as she watched the unkempt youngsters, intent on their games, who were rushing past in faded tattered clothes and shoes on the verge of falling apart. "I can still remember when Mother brought me here to enroll. Mrs. Rubinov, the teacher of the first grade, asked me what my name was and took me around. For as long as I can remember she has been old and gray. Her hair is cut short like a little girl's, with bangs over the forehead, which also makes her look like a child grown old. Only her smile is not childlike but wise, grandmotherly. She greeted me with such a smile." Rachel moved her head close to Bella's ear. "Do you see that tall man, there, with a cigarette at his mouth? That's the principal. When we were in the classroom, we could sometimes hear him playing the violin in his living quarters. Some living quarters! He lives in a corner of the school corridor, isolated by a divider. From him I heard the first sounds of music. I can still remember the *Zigeunerweisen*. You see, all these teachers would have been better off in other schools, where they wouldn't have to wait for months to be paid their wages. But they all came to work here out of idealism. Come, I'll introduce you."

Bella stepped away from her. "No, I must hurry back . . ."

They took leave of each other quickly and Rachel faced the crowd of children rushing towards the stairs, since the bell had begun to ring. "Was I indeed so happy here?" she suddenly wondered. Unexpectedly, the memory of the loneliness she had experienced in this school came back to her. Her classmates had not liked her; in some way she had been different from them, and neither she nor they had actually known in what way. They would not speak to her for months on end and had a nickname for her. Little Treasure they would call her, meaning of course that she was the teacher's pet, the favoured student of Mr. Holzman with whom she had been "madly in love". He had had a wonderful gift for story telling and would transform every history lesson into a fascinating voyage of the imagination. And beneath her compositions he would write little "love letters" in red ink: "There are many corrections in this composition, but it is for the good of the work and may it also be for the good of its writer." And the most painful experience she had had in this school was also connected with him.

It had happened during the revolt in Austria against the dictator Dolfus. Day in and day out the children and the teachers alike discussed the situation in Vienna. Then, one day, during a lesson, one of the boys in the last grade had overdone his arrogance towards Mr. Holzman who lost his "iron-strong" patience and punished the boy by sending him home. Overcome by the "spirit of Vienna", all the children had joined their "innocent comrade" and expressed their solidarity with him by grabbing their satchels and also leaving school. They had all gathered in the backyard to organize a "spontaneous" mass meeting, and the school went on strike. But she, Rachel, had been unable to understand how one could go on strike against dear Mr. Holzman, against teachers and one's own school. So she had stood in the door of her classroom, bewildered and confused. "Come on, express solidarity!" the children called her as they left the room. Then she was all alone. Her heart ached. She knew well enough that not to express solidarity was one of the greatest sins of a socialist; for the last two years she had been a member of the socialist children's organization, *Skif*.

And then the teacher himself had appeared in front of her, his face overcast, his bearing stiff and tense. Without a trace of friendliness in his voice he had said to her, "Don't stand in the door. Either come in, or get out." She began to cry; she had always been a silly crybaby. And so she had returned to the classroom and sat down on her bench. She was alone in the room with him, as she had often dreamed of being, of having a chance to open her heart — the heart of an eleven-year-old — to him. But it was not at all as she had dreamed. The teacher did not utter a word during the entire long and terrible hour, and she had sobbed the entire time, certain that even the teacher had lost his respect for her. Then, when she had finally left the schoolhouse, she was met by the children who had been waiting for her. They put themselves in two rows, letting her pass between them as they raised their fists at her and attacked her with jeers and laughter. They had shouted after her at the top of their lungs, calling her by the most horrible of all names: Strikebreaker!

She had never reached a final judgment about her behaviour on that day. Had she acted well? Had she acted wrongly? Only one thing was clear to her: she could not have acted differently. And with that clarity, a knowledge grew within her that she was indeed a cat who chose its own path.

As she now walked slowly through the empty schoolyard, she thought of her present life. "Why do the girls at the gymnasium consider me a good sport?" she asked herself. "Why do they follow me like a herd of sheep, whereas here, in the best school in the world, I had so few friends? Why do I go to the party clubs or to summer camp, although I sometimes feel so lonely in the crowd? Why do I miss it, when I run away from it? Am I really an individualist, as Bella thinks, or am I an extrovert and a sociable person? Am I good or bad? What am I? Who am I? Where are my days leading me?" The weight of her confrontation with the directress began to press on her heart again. She had an impulse to see her first grade teacher, Mrs. Rubinov.

She met her in the stairway. "I want to talk to you, Mrs. Rubinov," Rachel said to her with a half smile.

"Then come, walk home with me." Mrs. Rubinov took Rachel's arm, and leaned heavily on it as she put her swollen feet down with an effort. "I have to prepare a lecture for the women of the YAF," she said, breathing heavily. "Will you honour me with your presence and come to listen?"

Rachel who was on the point of unburdening her heavy heart to the teacher, shook her head with forced patience. "You know my opinion, Mrs. Rubinov. If I agree partly with your brand of Bundism, I don't agree with your ideas about the YAF at all."

Mrs. Rubinov's Bundism was slightly different from the Bundism generally accepted by the party members. Mrs. Rubinov thought that the Bund had in reality not been founded in 1897, but that it was an ideology as old as Jewish thought itself; that the two trends in Jewish life, Zionism and Bundism, were two ways of understanding the mission of the Jewish people and, consequently, she was not as much of an anti-Zionist as other Bundists were. She thought that both Zionism and Bundism had acquired too much of a political character and emphasized too little the philosophical ramifications of their respective ideologies. And she tried to convince her comrades that, as a socialist movement fighting for complete freedom of thought, the Bund ought to be more tolerant of other trends in Jewish life, since tolerance was the first step to true democracy, and that one ought not to wait for the creation of a socialist world order, to apply that noble attitude. She wanted the conflict between Bundism and Zionism to be raised to a higher level of discussion and not to remain narrow and limited. And as far as these opinions were concerned, Rachel agreed with her, although she considered them unrealistic, since a struggle was going on between Zionism and Bundism to win the Jewish masses, and in such a struggle it was impossible to be tolerant.

Mrs. Rubinov was also an activist in the Bundist women's organization YAF, and was stubbornly set upon the idea of creating a branch of young women in the organization. But Rachel resisted her fiercely. She was not only opposed to the creation of a branch of young women, but was against the existence of the YAF as such. She had no use for the idea of a separate organization for women, since by creating one, the women themselves emphasized their being different from men, and thus negated the principle of the equality of the sexes.

"But what harm would it do you to come and listen?" Mrs. Rubinov insisted. "I'm not interested," Rachel shook her head.

A soft smile played on the teacher's face. "To listen, to learn never did anyone any harm, you know."

It was about noontime and the air was thick and sticky with heat. The city — its people, streetcars, wagons — moved past them lazily, as if in slow motion. The teacher's face glistened with perspiration. She continued to talk about her upcoming lecture, puffing deep sighs into the air, as if trying to rid herself of the heat inside her. "Come up to my room," she said to Rachel as they neared the house where she lived. Rachel did not wait for her to repeat the invitation. Slowly they climbed the many flights of stairs, and were met by a wave of suffocating heat as soon as they entered the teacher's narrow room which was cluttered with furniture and books. Mrs. Rubinov lived here alone. Her daughters had left for the U.S.S.R. many years before, and her husband had died during the World War.

The minute she entered the room, Mrs. Rubinov sank onto the iron bed and began massaging her swollen feet. She looked at Rachel with tired eyes and with the grandmotherly smile on her lips. Rachel knew that the moment had come to tell the teacher what had happened. She brushed the sticky strings of hair away from her forehead, sat down beside the teacher's bed, on the only uncluttered chair, and came out with her story. When she had finished, Mrs. Rubinov said thoughtfully, "They don't expel a student so easily nowadays." Then her face lit up. "You acted well, Rachel."

Rachel blushed. "I cried . . . in front of her. When she asked me to give her names. You are fortunate Mrs. Rubinov! You cut yourself off from the world which did not suit you. But I live in two worlds."

"You're talking nonsense," the teacher shook her head. "Do you realize what world I cut myself off from: my parents' world. I left them behind. How would you feel ruining your home like that? My generation caused suffering. What do you know of the tears shed by mothers, of the heartbreak of fathers? It was not a joke. We were mourned as though we were dead. And do you think that such things don't weigh heavily on a person's conscience? We burned bridges behind us, true, but those bridges still burn within us like wounds. It is you who are fortunate, Rachel. You have your home to give you support, you have your environment. You live in your world. The *gymnasium* is not your world, and you speak your mind there and stand on your own ground. That you have problems with them, that they take action against you — that cannot be avoided. And if you cried a bit, so what?" she blinked, amused. "You're a girl, after all; secondly, a sensitive girl; thirdly, a slightly spoilt girl. They put stones in your way, and that frustrates you. Didn't you know that the administration would never approve of your activities? But in your heart of hearts you hoped that, like your parents, they would forgive you and let you go on doing whatever you please. Now you have found out that it is not so. At the beginning this hurts, but you will get used to it."

Rachel looked sullenly at the teacher. "I just was not born to be a heroine."

"A heroine?" Mrs. Rubinov shrugged. "There are no heroes, there are only people who can pride themselves with a few heroic moments in their lives." She gathered Rachel's hands in hers. "But you're a beautiful young fighter."

"I can't stand myself!" Rachel cried out.

"Come, come now. You must like yourself. It's healthy. They teach us, 'Love your brother as yourself.' How can you like your brother as yourself, if you don't like yourself, tell me?"

"I am a weakling. I didn't defend myself properly."

"So you didn't. It's not the words that give value to what you are. What's important is what you do for the things you believe in. Take the pious Jews. They fight for their religion every hour of the day. A Jewish socialist has to do the same. Because socialism replaces religion in our lives, because it too expresses a longing for the coming of a Messiah, whatever one may mean by that. We hope that a time will come when we will live according to the prophecy of Isaiah." She looked at Rachel searchingly. "What do I bother you with this for? Such a heat, and you are worried."

"I wouldn't like to give up my studies," Rachel sighed.

"It won't come to that. Send your parents to see the directress. Do you still want to become a teacher?"

"Yes, more than ever."

Rachel stood up. Mrs. Rubinov shook her hand affectionately. "Just keep it up, Rachel. Struggle on."

Rachel walked the street with a brisk hurried gait. Now she too thought that everything might somehow work out. Her mood was considerably improved by the time she came home. Nevertheless, Blumka noticed immediately that something had happened. She was beside herself with worry when she heard Rachel's story, although Rachel recounted it nonchalantly, adding what Mrs. Rubinov had told her. Blumka set Rachel's lunch on the table, wrapped herself in her plaid and rushed down to the barber shop to discuss the issue with her husband. It was soon time for Rachel to hurry back to town. She had to earn her wages, no matter what. She washed, changed into a dress, arranged the tousled mass of hair stubbornly curling around her face and, after she had devoured her lunch, rushed down into the street.

The same afternoon Mr. and Mrs. Eibushitz paid a visit to the directress of the Wiedza, during which they signed a paper which said that Rachel would forgo all political activity until her graduation from *gymnasium*, and that she would be automatically expelled if proven guilty of breaking her parents' promise.

✦ ✦ ✦

The afternoon wore on. Rachel hurried from one private lesson to the next, from one pair of dull children's eyes to another, until evening came and with it — her freedom.

The sky, heavy with clouds all day, at last delivered its torrential rain. A storm swept over the city. Lightning sawed the clouds with fiery blades; thunder rolled down from the heavens, now with the sound of heavy rocks tumbling from mountain tops, now with the staccato noise of gravel falling from an enormous shovel. As she sat in the streetcar, on her way from her final lesson, Rachel had the impression that the houses jumped in the air with every peal of thunder, that the window panes which reflected the lightning would crack at any moment and free themselves from their frames. The air in the tramway was extremely hot. Rachel reached out to open a window, but her neighbour on the right began to curse her thickly, and her neighbour on the left flatly warned her that whoever sits with her back to the draft is actually sitting with her face to the grave. But before long it was time for her to get off.

As soon as she set her foot on the pavement, she fell into the watery arms of the storm. In no time she was soaked through to the marrow of her bones. But she did not mind it. The rain was warm, its taste sweet. It immediately washed away her fatigue. With every flash of lightning, with every roll of thunder, heavy rocks of worry and anxiety rolled off her chest. Now there was nothing and no one else in the world but she and David.

The rain sewed the street with a hasty spray; the threads of water seemed to be stitching themselves into the hard pavements, ejecting streams of pearly buttons into the air. As she ran, Rachel saw herself tearing apart the threads like curtains which opened before her and closed behind, brushing against her body, against her heart, upon which they drummed, announcing the coming of a festive hour. The gutters at her side foamed boisterously, gaily, bubbled as if with cascades of laughter. Here and there they swelled up into waves, running over their shores like rivers; their waters spread over the sidewalks and cobblestone roads. The lights in the windows were misty. The windows mirrored the glistening street and were themselves reflected in it with yellowish blotches, which seemed like patches stitched on by the rain to its floating tapestry.

Rachel's shoes were full of water and with every jump she took, they mewed like hungry kittens. The dress clung to her legs, and as she raced onward, she had to keep peeling it off her skin; but it fell right back, as if its inside were covered with glue. It was not a pleasant sensation, but already she could see the clock from afar. Then she noticed David as well. He was standing, with his arms stretched out to her, under the awning which protected the window of "their" imported-food store. She took another jump, another step and found herself in his arms. "Hold me tight!" she exclaimed, warmth spreading all over her. Smothered by his embrace, she panted, "Don't hold me so tight! I can't breathe!"

He pressed her to him more tightly still. His partly boyish, partly manly face, with the irregularly sprouting stubble of a beard, pricked her cheeks roughly, but pleasantly. "If I really did what I feel like doing now," he laughed, "You wouldn't be able to breathe at all."

She tore herself away from him. "Are you starting that again?"

"What did I say? I said, if I did . . ."

Their eyes locked. She looked into the light of his, discerning a strange little flame, unfamiliar and alluring, lurking in their darkest deepest depth. She pressed her hand against her heart. "It's hammering!" she announced, feeling his eyes all over her body, swallowing her completely, with such voracity that it made her feel weak in the knees. "Why do you stare at me like that?" she shook her head, trying to shake the water from her hair along with the strange mood that had come over her. "Don't you know me?"

"Of course I don't. Twenty-four hours is an eternity. I've almost forgotten what you look like." He pulled her by a string of hair. "I was impatient to see you," he whispered. "I've been waiting here for half an hour."

She was about to tell him how much she too had wanted to see him, how during the day she had counted the hours to their meeting. The events of the past day flooded her mind, ready to flow out through her lips. But the impulse passed and she laughed out loudly, "You did well. You're wise, David. You came half an hour earlier, and that's why you are dry and I am not."

"Of course! And this should teach you a lesson, to miss me from now on at least a little bit." His eyes continued to devour her. "On the other hand, if you only knew how beautiful you look like that. The Maiden of the Foamy Waves . . . the Goddess of the Seas. As far as I am concerned, you could walk around like that forever. It suits you. Your hair looks . . . let's see, yes, like a fire just extinguished, upon which water was poured, like dying coals . . . so brown, so violet, glowing darkly . . ." He turned her around towards the shop window which, with its colourful display of exotic food and fruits, looked like a luscious still life. "Look at the bananas!" he said excitedly. "Do you see their colour?"

"I do. A banana colour."

"And look at their shape, their form . . ."

"Yes, a banana shape."

"No, really. Look how nicely they're stuck together, like a comb. I'm curious how you'd look with such a hat of bananas on your head."

"You're a clown."

"And the apples? Have you ever seen such red apples? Such an apple would suit you, held in your hand. You'd look like Eve from Paradise."

"It would suit me more to have it between my teeth. Come on, let's turn around. My mouth waters at the sight of it."

They faced the street, their eyes looking up at the watery curtain the rain was weaving around the awning. The little square of sidewalk in front of the shop window was dry and belonged to the two of them. It was like a tent, isolated from the world, intimate; the sound of the sweeping drumming rain made them feel sheltered and protected. They stood snuggled up to each other, listening silently to themselves, to each other, to the storm which seemed to play a tune of gratitude beyond words. David was the first to speak again. "Are you cold?" he asked.

Rachel simulated a shiver and made her teeth chatter. "I'm cold and hungry . . ."

With make-believe earnestness, he took her hand in his. "In that case, listen, my friend. Since the rain situation isn't going to change very soon, as we can judge with the fullest objectivity, I propose, oh, Rachel, that we race over to the world-famous cinema, the Magic. But, mind you, not directly. First we must halt at the gate there, where I can see, if my eyes serve me right, a certain bagel vendor with a basket full of fresh, hot and delicious bagels." He winked at her. "I'm a genius, don't you think?"

"Of course, you're a genius, oh, my David!" She tousled his hair which was cropped in a "porcupine" style, meant to make him look a little older and somewhat taller. "There is only one little flaw in your otherwise ingenious idea. Namely, it is for the birds."

"Leave my 'porcupine' alone," he jumped away from her, "and tell me on what you base your criticism."

"On our finances, Comrade Dreamer; they equal zero. I have only fifteen groschen to my name."

"Oh, then the situation is very critical, indeed," he crooned in a Talmudic singsong as he opened her hand, palm up, and counted into it the groschen he drew out of his pocket, one by one.

She looked at him in wide-eyed amazement. "Did you hold up a bank?"

"For you, I wouldn't mind holding up a bank, I swear. But today there is no need for it. I got paid for two lessons. Cash on delivery. Now let me have your fifteen groschen. It would be a crying shame if it weren't enough for the bagels as well as for the movie."

They remained in place a while longer, embracing the tent-like roof over their heads, with their eyes. Then he pulled her by the hand and they dashed out into the street. As the downpour attacked them, they began to scream inarticulately, with wild abandoned shouts, competing with the storm's deafening bellows. The bagel vendor, sheltered in the arched house gate, filled a bag with bagels for them. With loud intoxicated laughter, they counted the money into his palm. As she counted, Rachel heard cart wheels squeaking behind her back and she looked over her shoulder. She recognized the quaint *lody* vendor pushing his cart; his long beard was soaked with rain and stuck to his wet gaberdine. The little white ice cream cart, shiny and dripping with water, seemed like an extension of the man behind it. As he turned his head towards them, she called out to him, "You have good ice cream, Uncle!"

His eyes lit up like tiny bulbs. "Then you should always buy from me," he countered, trudging onward in the rain as if he did not mind it.

David hid the bag of bagels under his shirt and they started out again. Running, he held his arm around her waist, carrying her with him, practically sweeping her off the ground.

The movie house was empty. Rachel and David chose their seats in the very centre of the hall and sat down, snuggling up to each other. They took care of the bagels immediately. "Too bad we didn't see what movie is playing tonight," he whispered in her ear with his mouth full.

"Something you like," she replied, her mouth full too. "The Adventures of Tarzan. I passed by here this morning."

"Then we hit upon the right thing," he beamed. "And we came just in time. The priests won't take long."

The newsreel was showing a Sunday ceremony in a new church in the town of Radom. And sure enough, the priests soon disappeared, and all of a sudden the *Reichskanzler* Hitler exploded with all his fury into the empty theatre. He was followed by an army of heavily booted soldiers on *Parademarsch;* their enormous figures advanced from the depths of the screen and seemed to leave it behind, stepping out of it and heading straight at Rachel and David. But soon they vanished as well. The newsreel finished and the lion of Metro-Goldwyn-Mayer emitted its majestic roar. Immediately thereafter, Tarzan appeared in all his mighty glory, flying downward, suspended from a swinging jungle vine. Rachel and David split the second bagel.

"It's great to sit here, isn't it, Rachel?" David whispered in delight, his cheeks swollen with bagel. "You see, you're actually in Africa now. Look at the horde of elephants coming out. Soon you'll see how Tarzan handles them." The well-baked crust of the bagel cracked pleasantly between his teeth. "And there, look between the trees. His fiancée is coming out . . ."

"Why doesn't he marry her?" Rachel asked. "In every film she is his fiancée."

"What's so bad about being a fiancée?"

"What's so good about it? How long is she supposed to be a fiancée anyway? Do you think it's nice to be an old fiancée?"

"Fiancées are never old."

"Oh, I didn't realize that. But it must be boring anyway, to be a fiancée all the time."

"I don't agree with you, Rachel dear. A fiancée is generally more romantic than just a wife. Tarzan's wife. It sounds ridiculous."

"You are right, David dear. It does sound ridiculous. A wife! We two will never get married, all right?"

David was busy with what was going on on the screen. "What's all right?" he asked.

"That we will never get married. It's not romantic."

"All right. Let's never get married."

"But you told me that you wanted to marry me."

"Sure I do." He put a finger to her mouth. "Shush . . . Look, you see . . . there, in the bushes . . . a snake, a boa constrictor. He'll notice it, I'm sure . . . Look, he's turning around . . ." David tore his eyes away from the screen and looked at Rachel questioningly. "Why don't you watch it? It's fun."

"It doesn't fascinate me. I'd prefer to watch a marvellous drama instead, with a love affair . . . a hot beautiful love."

"Our love affair is the most beautiful of all love affairs and it's for real. Don't you think so?"

"Of course not. I don't even know if we love each other."

"Is that so? Then what do we do, hate each other?" He leaned his head against hers.

She pushed him away. "What kind of love is it, if a silly film is more important to you than I am? You missed me so much, and now you're busy with Tarzan and his fiancée."

His face turned grave. "I feel good with you. When I am with you, I feel as if I were a child again, light, playful. Although in reality . . . in reality, I feel just the opposite: very serious."

It was the same with her. What she felt towards him was serious, grave, yet she felt somehow younger and more childlike in his presence.

Rachel was unable to fall asleep for a long time that night. The worrisome events of the past day, the ambiguous result of her parents' interview with Miss Biederman mingled with the joyful hours she had spent with David. Again her inner voice returned to nag her: "Where am I heading? What is there in store for me?" She felt uneasy with herself. At length, she reached for a match and lit the candle on the chair at her bedside. Shlamek, her brother, sleeping across from her on the sofa, turned towards the wall. Her father lifted his head from his pillow, blinked at her remotely, and went back to sleep. She jumped out of bed to get a pencil and a sheet of paper. For a long time she sat on her bed, her hand and pencil poised over the blank white sheet. Then she put it aside, picked up her library book and lay down. She read on until a delicate veil, woven out of the printed lines, blurred her eyes and curtained her eyelids, pulling them downwards. Gradually, slowly, sleep took the heavy volume out of her hands, letting it fall back on her blanket. The candle light died out with the last piece of wick.

Chapter Seven

SIMCHA BUNIM BERKOVITCH was born in Lynczyce. He was named Simcha after his own grandfather and Bunim, after the great rabbi, Reb Simcha Bunim. Berkovitch's father, the preacher of Lynczyce, felt an affinity between himself and the rabbi whose teachings were full of profound thoughts, of humanity and of a thirst for truth.

When Simcha Bunim, the baby of the family and his parents' only son, was very small, his double name was spoken with endearment: Simcha Buniml, for he was indeed the *simcha*, the joy of the household, the apple of his parents' eyes and the lively laughing toy of his nine sisters. Until the age of three the locks of his hair remained uncut, and his alabaster face with the pink plump cheeks and big blue eyes bespoke such fineness that it reminded one of the beauty of the most delicate angels.

Later on, when at the age of three his father carried him, wrapped in a plaid, to the *heder* and put him down on a bench in front of the open prayer book with a large-lettered alphabet on the first page, it became clear that not only did he deserve his first name, Simcha, but that he would not shame his second name, Bunim, either. Effortlessly, his eyes would glide over the pages of the Bible, and later on, over those of the Talmud, and every year his conversations with his father at the Sabbath table would grow more profound, more heated. And since he remained good-humoured, always smiling and open-hearted, the affection of his father and his "ten mothers" changed very little with the passing of time.

Tears hot with pride and worry washed down their faces when he, a youngster for whom there was no longer a rabbi good enough in Lynczyce, set out on his way to the *yeshiva* in Lublin. They accompanied him to the train, heaping kisses and blessings on his head, begging him time and again to take good care of himself, eat well, and not catch cold. When the train started moving, he could still hear the sound of their tear-soaked voices over the rumbling of the wheels, calling endearments after him.

Then, in the foreign town, a new world revealed itself to him — naked and rough. Up to now it had seemed to him that life was a glorious garden cushioning his steps softly with its soil. The garden seemed glad to have him in it, so he himself was glad to be there. Now, suddenly, it had turned into a desert. There were no smiles for him, no caressing words. Now, cold indifference enveloped him, and he was not prepared to endure it. Night after night he would cry himself to sleep on his alien cot, dreaming of home, yearning for it; and every sunrise which woke him to meet the day would find him more and more altered. Smiles began to shun his boyish lips; his once open and direct words now stopped short upon the threshold of his locked mouth. Like a flower transplanted into unreceptive foreign soil, his soul closed itself up and held back its fragrance in the protective coils of silence. He remained alone with himself.

The world did not notice him, so he, in turn, stopped noticing it. It would be incorrect to say that people were unkind to him. After all, he was a quiet delicate youngster, slightly awkward, withdrawn, shy and given too much to brooding. But he was pleasant to look at and his manners were impeccable. People could not help but be friendly to him. But he did not feel their friendliness. After he had been caressed by the hot sun of his home, other people's kindness seemed like the cold sun of a winter's day. He did not dislike these people and feelings of hatred were still alien to him; actually he even liked some of his acquaintances, but it was a detached liking. In reality, he cared for no one.

There was only one place where he felt at home: the *yeshiva*, or perhaps not so much the *yeshiva*, as the Scripture. The moment he opened the Holy Book, he came back to life. At the *yeshiva*, he was not the only one with erudition and intelligence, as he had used to be at home, but he did not mind that. On the contrary, the challenge excited him. Like a young stallion he galloped over the immense pages of the Talmud, over the luscious fields of thought. All reins fell from him and nothing mattered but the goal which loomed in the distance of hundreds of pages. When night fell and someone would touch his shoulder to tell him that it was enough for today, he would wake up as from a good sleep, fix his frightened astounded eyes on the person who had woken him and murmur, "Already?"

Shrinking inwardly, he would go out again to meet the indifferent world which consisted of the stretch of street from the *yeshiva* to his boarding house, and of the few steps in his alien home that led him to his cot.

But even more than his studies, he loved prayer. Here, in this foreign place, prayer became love itself to him. All his fine feelings, all the delicate threads of tenderness which had begun spinning within him when he had been still a *heder* boy, threads now washed and soaked in tears of loneliness, were woven into his prayer, which became like a carpet that his soul unrolled upwards, so that his devotion to the Almighty might ascend higher and higher. The ceremonial of winding the strap of the phylacteries around his arm and his prayers at sunrise and sunset were his dates, the silent stations where he met peace. Every concluding "Amen" had the power to armour him and send him back to life strengthened and fortified.

As the years wore on, Bunim grew used to his loneliness and it ceased to bother him. His soul ceased to feel uneasy behind the bars of his self-imposed isolation. However, precisely at that time, when he had come to appreciate the comforts of loneliness, he began to look for an opening to the world outside. One day, as he raised his head from the Book, and cast a glance at the young man sitting beside him on the *yeshiva* bench, who was coughing incessantly and spitting into a dirty handkerchief, he realized that his neighbour actually knew about him all those things which he had so carefully hidden from the world. Their long conversations on the subject of their studies abandoned their original course more and more often, imperceptibly sliding into by-ways which led to each other's secret qualms, yearnings and dreams. They could no longer do without one another.

Sender, his friend, was an orphan. When Bunim talked to him about his home and his childhood, it all seemed to Sender like a fairy tale he would never tire of hearing. But rather than feeling envy for Bunim, he loved him still more on account of his good fortune. He thought that love was due to Bunim, that he was born for it, and that it was his destiny; because Sender felt in Bunim the potential for paying it back a thousandfold. Therefore he, the one who had been deprived by life, worried about his friend and cared for him as a beggar would for a suddenly-found treasure.

On frosty mornings, Sender would wait for Bunim at the door of the latter's boarding house, to make sure that his absent-minded friend had not, God forbid, forgotten to take along a scarf. He himself would shudder in his thin gaberdine, coughing and spitting into his handkerchief. And at the *yeshiva*, as they diligently swayed over the Book, Bunim would indeed forget the world around him — but Sender would not. More than once he would raise his eyes from the page, to read his friend's face. And when he noticed that Bunim's forehead furrowed, he would immediately move closer to him and ask warmly, "Something is not clear to you, Simcha Bunim?" Together they would set out to untangle the skein, and when they reached the proper conclusion, they would reward each other with a grateful glance and each would return to his own corner.

All day long they were together, and still found it difficult to part for the night. Every morning their meeting was like getting acquainted anew. They had a strange admiration for one another. Sender admired Bunim's beauty, his capacity for elation, his imagination and his complete abandonment during prayer. While Bunim admired Sender's wisdom, his logic, the facility with which he unsnarled the most entangled problems of *Halacha;* he admired his simplicity and kindliness in daily life. Sender knew people; he knew the aches and worries which filled the life of the man in the street. He would notice the blind man waiting for someone to guide him across the road, or the shy beggar who had not yet mustered the courage to hang on to the coattails of passers-by, but stood in a dark doorway, his outstretched hand trembling. Into that hand Sender would put the last groschen he had; and afterwards, moved by the suffering he had met face to face, he would bite his lips with shame that he had done so little to help.

He thought little of his own troubles. He knew that there was something wrong with him, since his cough was getting worse day by day, but this awareness did not touch him inwardly. Sometimes, especially during the winter, he found it hard to get up in the morning. His body, hot and feeling as if it were not his own, was glued to the bed. So he gave in to it. What use was there, after all, in struggling with the weakness of a dried-out bundle of bones? He would rather submit to its little caprices, so that it would not bother and nag him so stubbornly. He would stay in bed and with the Book in his hands soar away from the pain gnawing at his chest.

On days like that Bunim would go to the *yeshiva* for a few hours and then spend the rest of the day at Sender's bedside. He too was aware that something was wrong with his friend, who was growing increasingly thinner, shrinking from day to day — but he had not the slightest idea what the reason for it was. He was glad that Sender stayed in bed. Let him rest, so that he would become stronger, he thought. He would buy half a dozen tasty bagels, and they would munch on them during their long conversations in Sender's tiny alcove.

The year both of them were to receive their rabbinical ordination, Sender was unable to get out of bed altogether. A strange flame began to burn in his eyes, and when Bunim looked into them, they seemed to be telling him something, revealing a secret impossible to grasp — a truth which made his heart stand still. Their conversations ceased to flow so smoothly. In the middle of his talk, Sender would whisper shyly, "Say the psalms for me, Bunim, please . . . Your voice makes me feel good." So they recited the psalms together. When they parted, Sender would smile with more animation, "You know, I really feel better now."

One day, when Bunim went up as usual to see his friend, he no longer found him in his bed. The thin shrunken body lay on the floor covered with a black plaid. At his head, candles were burning. The friend was no more.

✦ ✦ ✦

Then it all began. Bunim failed to go to the *yeshiva* for weeks in a row. He stood in the synagogue, wrapped in his prayer shawl, talking to the One to whom he had given his love. True, he did not belong to those who set their minds upon deciphering the ways of the Almighty, but this one thing he had to comprehend.

"Ruler of the Universe," he begged, "forgive me for the reproaches I make to You in my heart. You know very well, it is the resentment of a child towards his mother who has punished him; and although she has done so, he runs back to her and clings to her apron. Console me! Let me understand Your ways this one time, so that I can love You more strongly still, and more faithfully than ever. Why have You taken him away? For what sins did You cut the thread of life of the quietest, the most devoted, the best of Your children? Why did You leave me and take him? Help me! Throughout all these years I have filled my head with so many of Your laws, without questioning. Let me know this once which of Your laws You have applied in Your verdict against Sender. Punish me for my arrogance, pour out Your wrath upon my head, but show me the light, give me an account of Your case against Sender!"

Day after day Bunim would come with bitterness to bargain and wrestle with his Maker; sometimes he would beg in humility, at other times roar like a wounded leopard; now and then he would pray with more fervour and devotion than ever. But the wound refused to heal. His impatience mounted; his feelings of frustration and despair grew increasingly deeper. And Sender was not there to help him. On the contrary, his shadow hovered over Bunim, looked over his shoulder and drove him down into bottomless pits of grief. Sender was the one who finally whispered into Bunim's ear, to leave the Books and go outside, into the streets, there to search for the answer to God's ways.

Bunim began to wander the streets of Lublin, to look at the faces of by-passers, to peep through the windows into strange houses and to listen to the conversations in the prayer houses after services. The abstract man in the street took on individual features and became a person with particular surroundings which were his home, the street, the town. And so, on one of those days, Bunim stopped believing in the After Life and in the Other World.

It dawned upon him that even in the beginning, at the cradle of humanity, Paradise was the garden that God had planted, not in the heavens, but on earth — for the joy of Adam. And hell, *Gehenna*, the Valley of Hinnom, was on earth as well: it was the valley where people had sacrificed their children to Moloch. And Paradise was also here in Lublin. Bunim saw it in the sprouting of blossoms at the awakening of spring; he saw it in the smile of a dirty child playing in the gutter; he saw it in the secretive alluring glance of a young woman's eyes as they watched him from behind a window curtain; and he smelled Paradise in a freshly-baked loaf of bread. And here too — was hell. Here lived Mr. Velvel Krant, the fine Jew and rich man, in whose factories young boys and girls spent twelve to fourteen-hour days, working until all the marrow in their bones was sucked dry and they were thrown out onto the street like rags, sick and useless. Here lived all those who were crushed by fate, the shamed and the abandoned; and here was the gentile with a rock in his hand, shouting, "Dirty Jew!" Here was Moloch.

But if there is no other world, God's judgment must take place in this one; and if that is so, then what kind of judgment is it? Could it be His, if He is a God of compassion and justice? And if it is not His, then whose — if He is the Only One? Is it Satan's? Then who is Satan? And how is it that God the Almighty has no power over him? Or perhaps He Himself is Satan? Then how is it that there exists, besides evil, also love and beauty in the world? Could it be possible that they were only the beauty of Lilith, a disguise, an illusion, a terrible joke played on man? Yet there is such holy perfection in the breath of all living things. Who had created them? If not Satan, nor God, then who? Who created life, and being?

Bunim felt lost in the boiling cauldron of his thoughts, turning all the time in the same vertiginous circles. He was ready to look the answer squarely in the face. But there was no answer. Somehow, somewhere, it slipped away from the light of reason and perception and became lost in emptiness. Bunim looked into it with his eyes open — and saw nothing.

Meanwhile, he received his rabbinical diploma. However, he did not return to his home town. His family had moved to the big city of Lodz. His father had aged, his voice had turned hoarse and weak, and he could no longer preach, but Bunim's sisters had found work in a big textile factory. They rented a place in a tenement on Hockel Street, and there tried to live as they lived in Lynczyce. The dwelling even looked the same as in Lynczyce, the furniture was the same, the same curtains hung on the windows, and the same expectation permeated the rooms: the hope of seeing their Symcha Buniml come home a rabbi.

Now he was back — a grown son and brother. They could not take their eyes off him. They would gladly have thrown themselves upon him with open arms, but they controlled themselves. It would not be appropriate; after all, a future *rav*. And besides, they were held back by shyness. Somehow he had come back changed; his eyes avoided theirs, they looked stealthily aside, guiltily, somewhat lost.

He would not leave his father's side. All day long he followed him, eagerly listening to every word he spoke. It seemed to him that only his father could save him; the father who had once so simply brought him to meet God's word, who had carried him wrapped in a plaid to the *heder*, to the open prayer book with the sacred alphabet on its first page; the father who had stood in a corner of the *heder*, watching the rabbi throw candies to the *heder* boys, so that God's word would be sweet to the new student. And how sweet it had been! But now, that he had raced through the Scripture's length and breadth with his eyes — with how much bitterness did he return to it! And his eyes would say to the gray shrunken man, "Thank you, Father, for the sweetness of old times, but somehow I have lost it on my way. Start with me anew." And the wise old man would understand; his old heart would shrivel with sorrow: The hope of his life had come to him looking for hope. His tired mind, alarmed, despairingly and feverishly hurried to save the son, to save the lost one.

They would sit down to the Books together, day after day, night after night. Their double singsong escaped through the closed door, sounding like a cry for help, like an imploring lament from the depth of loneliness. Like the wings of a wounded bird it would hit against the walls of the dwelling, and leave its shadow upon them.

No one in the household had acknowledged it as yet, but they all knew the truth: Simcha Bunim would not become a *rav*. And that was not all. They perceived something even more serious, something terrible, a thing frightening even to think about. The home changed its face; the family walked about as if someone fatally ill were lying in one of the rooms. The sisters did not know for whom their hearts should ache first — for their mother, for their father, or for Simcha Bunim himself. And he, lost in himself, lost among those who meant everything to him, smothered by their silent suffering which was so much like his own, felt that he ought to do something, but he could not find the strength for it.

Then, during a silent moment in his father's room, his mouth opened; the words long since prepared, slid out, cold and brutal, "Father, I went astray."

A heavy groan, "I know, my son."

"Father, don't you think it would be better if I left home?"

"If you feel that way, my son, then go."

Thus Bunim shut the door of his home behind him, aware that he had left it a ruin. But he also knew that he took it along with him on his way. He mourned the loss of his home, longed for it and felt guilty towards it forever. But he came to believe that he had an Almighty Partner to share his guilt with him.

✦   ✦   ✦

A young man in a long traditional gaberdine, a traditional cap on his head and curly brown sidelocks tucked away behind his ears, came to work in one of the great textile factories in Lodz. He was hired as an unskilled hand, to sweep the huge factory halls, to carry the empty spools away and to act as a messenger boy. However, as he busied himself about the factory, walking among the machines, he watched the experienced workers doing their tasks deftly. And if some of the procedures were too difficult for him to grasp, he mastered his shyness and asked for an explanation, repeating his questions until he got the information he wanted.

His handsome face expressed determination and will power. Although he was a mere factory cleaner, there was dignity and nobility in his bearing. The workers poked fun at his long traditional frock covered with strings of thread; they cracked jokes about the sidelocks hidden behind his ears, and mimicked his *yeshiva* boy manner, which was ridiculously out of place in those surroundings — but basically they liked him and taught him the trade.

Before long, Bunim appeared at a machine. He discarded his long uncomfortable frock-coat and along with it, his sidelocks, and made an effort not to single himself out from the others by his appearance. And with each passing day he acquired more knowledge of the art of serving the rumbling monsters. One by one, he was given new machines to attend to, until he became the master of six roaring giants — and with that, his new life began.

He liked the clatter produced by the machines. Like reliable mills they ground out all the hardness, all the bitterness from his heart. Everything became simple and clear. The machines did their work so regularly and surely that they left no room for doubt. When occasionally some cogs broke, or the threads became entangled, a wave of disquiet would sweep over Bunim.

His life, translated into the language of the machines, began to transform itself into rhythms which in turn, imperceptibly, shaped themselves into verses. He would write them down during his lunch hour; at first, just for the fun of it, to kill time, but later on more enthusiastically, more seriously, until it became a passion. He began to devote his evening hours to writing and, later on, long stretches of his nights as well. The secret little pile of papers with his hastily jotted down poems grew, resounding with the echoes of his experiences, with his yearnings and dreams; and it began urging him, demanding to be freed from its paper life to become a living sound. Often he read his poems aloud to himself, but somehow he felt that only by bringing them to the ears of others could he make them come to life completely and help them reach their fullest meaning.

He had heard of a literary coffee house called Under the Cup, and set out to visit it. But he lacked the courage to go in and could only pace the street in front of it. He stopped a few times by the large window and peered through its misty pane. The writers sat close to the window, at two tables pushed together. He could see their lips moving and notice the glow of the cigarettes stuck to the corners of their mouths. He envied them. Never before had he been tempted to savour the pleasure of discussing problems in a group. What he had liked was to converse eye to eye, heart to heart, with Sender, or with his father; he was convinced that such an intimate dialogue had more to offer the soul than talking in a group. But now it occurred to him that during an exchange of ideas in such a group, the mind might become enriched, stimulated by opinions coming from many directions; and perhaps, illuminated from different angles, truth itself would reveal its face more clearly. In any case, he had no doubt that what was being talked about inside, in the café, was of great importance to him.

Early the following evening he returned to the coffee house, overcame his shyness and walked in. Awkwardly, absent-mindedly he navigated between the tables, and found a seat not far from the window where the writers had convened the night before. The two tables were still waiting for their occupants. Bunim ordered a cup of coffee and sipped it through a lump of sugar which he held between his teeth. He was tense, as if he were awaiting a trial of some kind.

He noticed a man sitting close to the two tables, his head turned towards the window, apparently waiting for someone as well. The man's back was rounded, arched in the middle and hunched over at the bony shoulders. Bunim heard him cough and thought of Sender. The waiter put a glass of milk in front of the man. "How do you feel today, Mr. Friede?" he asked.

The man fixed his eyes on him, inquiring, "Where is the gang tonight?"

"They went to the theatre, to see the 'Golem' again. A powerful work," the waiter said authoritatively.

He had no time to elaborate on the subject, since at that moment a boisterous crowd of young men and women came pouring in through the door. The man called Friede, apparently feeling Bunim's insistent eyes staring at him, turned his head to him and pointed to his glass of milk. "They refuse to serve me anything else. What can I do?" he laughed loudly. "Milk is for me what manna was for the Jews in the desert. It acquires whatever taste I wish. Now, for instance, it has the taste of beer." He lifted his glass in Bunim's direction, called out, "*Lechaim!*" and gulped it down with simulated eagerness. His loud words, spoken in a resonantly boyish tone, made Bunim feel ill at ease. He did not know how to reply, and so only spread his mouth in an awkward smile and rearranged the glasses on his nose. The stranger continued looking at him with an open, slightly arrogant curiosity. "I don't think I've ever seen you here before," he said.

"I'm here for the first time," Bunim mumbled.

"You see, I noticed you right away! I've been a steady patron for the last five years. Better not ask about the number of waiters who have passed through my hands. But this one," he winked in the direction of the waiter, "is a fine chap, one of ours."

All of a sudden, Bunim realized that he had a writer before him and he blushed. "Is he a writer?" he asked, pointing his chin in the waiter's direction.

"More than that," Friede replied. "He's a good reader. The best critic we have in town. You think I'm joking? You think that to be a critic you need to be loaded with highbrow wisdom, to have a polished tongue and to specialize in crushing and grinding down every written word until the last breath of life is driven out of it? Do you think so? Well, then you're wrong. All a real critic needs is good taste, a good ear, and an open heart. And this waiter here has all these things." He stopped short and scrutinized Bunim's face. "I'm annoying you," he added with a chuckle.

"Heaven forbid!" Bunim exclaimed.

Friede rocked his chair on its hind legs. "I understand," he nodded. "You want to find out how some people kill time nowadays."

"Some may kill time," Bunim replied heatedly, "but for others it is more than that."

"What more?"

"It is instead of . . . of living."

"Do you mean writing is instead of living?"

"Yes, something like that. What one is unable to live through, one writes about . . . Or sometimes you want to live more than just your own life, or want to see the world through other eyes than your own, or experience passions through other hearts; then you create other selves in addition to your own, and you build another world with words, around these selves."

"And what would you say about someone like this same man sitting in front of you, who never stops writing about his own boring self, who describes, not the life he has never lived, but precisely the nothingness that he has lived through? Fed up with the drudgery of his past, he nonetheless goes back to it again and again, to taste the same poison over and over, without ever getting enough of it. What would you say to such a *meshugas*, tell me?"

After his initial burst of verbosity, which had been prompted by his excitement, Bunim was sorry that he had spoken out so recklessly. "What should I tell you?" he mumbled. "You yourself know best why you do it."

"I haven't the faintest idea. I'm desperately looking for someone who can explain my own riddle to me. Tell me . . ."

"I am no judge. There are probably others who write for different reasons."

"I want to know what you think of me."

Bunim, felt completely at a loss, "I don't know you," he muttered, distressed. "I haven't read . . . your books. I've read very little in general."

"He hasn't read my books!" Friede countered with sarcasm in his voice. "I haven't published any books! But you shouldn't put yourself into a baby carriage. I don't want anything from you but that you continue with what you were saying before."

Bunim had no clear idea of what Friede wanted from him. But from the expression on the latter's face, he could see that there was no way out, but to talk. "I think," he began slowly, "that a person writing in the manner you told me . . . is unable to let his imagination take a large step away from himself, since he has not finished with his personal account yet. There is still a riddle left nagging at him, an ache he has not found a remedy for. So he walks backwards, following his own footprints, looking for what is missing . . . in order to achieve his oneness." Bunim was aware that he was actually talking about himself. "If you repeat the pain, it means that you haven't found a cure for it yet. Hence your dissatisfaction. Everyone wants to free himself from the Self, through words, through confession. But a writer cannot be satisfied only with confessing. He has to . . . How should I say it? He has to knead the blood of his soul into a dough which, although part of him, becomes devoid of him . . . or becomes more than just he alone. That's the cure. Such writing would give me . . ." He groped for words. "I can't bring it out. I talk nonsense."

Friede, sitting on the very edge of his chair, leaned forward towards Bunim. "It is I who should ask your forgiveness," he smiled. "When you sit at these tables, you get into the habit of taking yourself apart, even if you hardly know the person you're talking to; it's a kind of exhibitionism which goes hand in hand with the writing profession, I guess." He rose from his chair abruptly, moved over to Bunim's table, sat down so close to him that their knees met, and introduced himself. "I'm about to publish my first volume of short stories," he added. "You write too, don't you? What? Poetry, no doubt."

"Yes, poetry."

"You see, I guessed right away. And tell me, what kind of 'instead' is that for you?"

"Instead of prayer."

"Cliché! That's what they all say."

"If they all say it, it doesn't necessarily mean that it is not so."

"But I meant something else. I meant to ask whether you're writing, as you said, in order to build new worlds for yourself, or if you only go backwards . . ."

Bunim's face flushed, "Let's not talk about that."

"You don't want to talk about yourself? And I, you see, would talk about myself and my writing all day long. I am ready to read to anyone who has the slightest bit of patience to hear me out. How come you don't want to talk?"

Bunim chuckled. "I would gladly talk . . . about my writing. I came especially . . . But I think it might be better to keep it a secret for a while. I want to warm up a bit first."

Friede patted Bunim's shoulder amiably. "If you prefer it that way, I won't say a word. The gang can be quite brutal to a beginner. But you can come to my place. Tomorrow, let's say. You'll read to me and I'll read you some excerpts from my stories." Bunim nodded gratefully and wrote down Friede's address. With that, he assumed their conversation had come to a close. But he was wrong. "You know what?" Friede said in a whisper. "Let's get acquainted for real, right now. The gang won't show up for a while. I will read you a fragment of the thing I am working on now. You must have something on you too, still warming in your breast pocket." Bunim, won by Friede's cordial tone, agreed. They moved closer to one another, each becoming slightly more self-conscious and ill-at-ease. They both dug into their pockets, and drew out a few folded sheets of paper. However, just at the moment Friede was about to begin, the door opened with a loud bang and a tumultuous crowd poured into the coffee house. These were not only the writers, but the actors and their cronies as well. Friede cleared the table hurriedly, thrusting his sheets of paper back into his pocket.

There was not enough room for them all at their usual place, and the crowd spread out to occupy seats at the other tables, so that unexpectedly Bunim found himself in the very centre of a large vociferous group. One of the newcomers ordered beer and pickles with sauerkraut for the entire company, and the conversation, which had apparently begun on the street, continued to spin, chaotically and noisily around the name Leivik, like a thread around the axle of a spool. Bunim did not dare ask Friede who Leivik was. The others mentioned his name with such familiarity and admiration that it seemed wiser to conceal his ignorance even from Friede.

He was so absorbed in what he saw and heard that he was oblivious to the fact that, one by one, his neighbours were tugging at the smiling Friede's sleeve, inquiring with a whisper and a wink, about the stranger in orthodox attire, with the round orthodox cap on his head, who, cheeks aflame like those of a bridegroom, was sitting at his side without uttering a word. For, in spite of the noise and the animated discussion, Bunim's presence had not gone unnoticed. There was even someone who, seated at the far side of the table, was carefully tracing the outlines of Bunim's profile on a sheet of paper; the painter Guttman was drawing a sketch of him.

Later that night, the crowd, with Bunim in tow, poured out into the street and strolled through the sleeping city. Outside, under the protection of darkness, it was easier for him to speak. He had never been so talkative in his life, nor had he ever felt so well. He felt as though his mind was simultaneously intoxicated and at the peak of sobriety, so sharp were his thoughts and with such ease did he express them. He wished the night would never end.

They already all knew him by name and when they took leave of him, asked him not to forget to bring along his writing next time. Yes, they even knew about that.

The following evening Bunim did not go to Under the Cup, nor did he go to see Friede. He was too busy writing. The experience of the previous evening had opened up a well within him. Stanzas flew out from under his pen, covering sheet after sheet of paper, lightly and effortlessly. Like bees released from a beehive, words soared above his head, buzzed in his ears and dictated their rhythms to him. He spent the whole week with his poems and when the Sabbath came, he went to the library to ask about Leivik. The librarian gave him two volumes, one of plays, the other of poetry. He took them home with him to read, and there was a new joy born within him. He had discovered Leivik and discovered himself through Leivik. He had hardly finished reading the volume of poetry, when he jumped to his feet, found Friede's address in his notebook and rushed out to see him.

Friede, looking the picture of injured pride, received him with reproaches. "What, the blazes, happened to you? I waited for you a day and a night, prepared good things, a celebration. And you didn't even show up!"

"I was writing," Bunim said shyly.

Friede fixed his protruding misty eyes on him. "Writing? The entire week?" His face changed immediately as it lit up with admiration. "What do you know! Just fancy! Really writing the whole week! In that case, I envy you. Because ever since we met, I haven't been able to take the pen into my hand because of you. That's my nature. I go through every new acquaintance like measles or the chickenpox, or a smallpox vaccination, before it takes. Good thing that you came today. If not, who knows? I might never have taken the pen into my hand again. So what are you standing there for? Come over here, to my bed. Let's move the table closer to it." Friede busied himself about the messy narrow room. "We'll have a glass of tea, what do you say?" Bunim handed him the bag of bagels he had brought along. "Good heavens!" Friede exclaimed. "What kind of an idea is that?"

"A tradition of mine," Bunim explained, "from my *yeshiva* years. It helps the conversation." As Friede lit the spirit burner, Bunim looked at his hunched back and could not help thinking of Sender; the resemblance between the two frightened him.

Friede poured the tea into two tin cups and put them on the table along with two spoons and a cone of paper with a few lumps of sugar in it. He took a bagel out of the bag and chewed on it without enthusiasm as he sat down on the bed at Bunim's side. "I drink from tin cups," he explained, "because now and then I get drowned in a thought, or in a daydream, and I forget what I'm in the middle of doing. The cup slips out of my hand and the dream costs me a few groschen. This way, with tin cups, only the tea is wasted, but the cup remains intact. So, go ahead, drink, and read me what you brought along. I am in a great mood to listen."

Bunim looked at him cautiously. "I brought along Leivik's poems. Let's read them together."

"What!" Friede exploded, jumping up from the bed with such violence that the cups shook and spilled half of their contents upon the paper which served as a tablecloth. "Are you playing hide-and-seek with me, or trying to make a fool of me? I won't ask you to read a thing to me again. Who, the blazes, ever heard such a tale! From the minute we met, you've been trying to wriggle out of it. All right. So be it. You want to keep your secret to yourself, do it in good health, but don't you bring any Leiviks to me. Him I can read whenever I want to. There he is, on the window ledge, or look in the closet. Leivik he brought me, how do you like that?"

Bunim realized that it would make no sense to explain to Friede the feelings that had prompted him to grab the volume of Leivik's poems and come running to him with it. "Don't be angry," he said. "If you want me to read my own things to you, I will."

"What do you mean, if I want you to?" Friede was beside himself with indignation. "Don't do me any favours. I wanted it for your sake more than for mine! As long as you don't feel how your words reach my ear, you will have no idea of what you have written down. And don't be such a nincompoop. You think that many people would want to listen to you? Wait and see. Just give it a try."

"Friede," Bunim put in meekly, "I am ready . . ." Friede stopped talking; an unexpected smile brightened his face. Bunim thought that this sudden smile after the outpouring of his anger was the nicest thing about Friede. Again he saw the pallid face before him, looking at him invitingly, eagerly. Bunim drew out the most recent poem from his pocket and began reading — an ode to friendship.

✦   ✦   ✦

Bunim and Friede saw each other every day. For Bunim it was just like the old days with Sender. They found it difficult to take leave of each other. They ran to share with each other every new piece of writing, every new experience. Together they read other writers, together they went to the coffee house and together they walked the streets at night.

The rhythm of Bunim's life accelerated. Like a maturing tree he branched out in all directions. He had his life at the factory, his work at his writing table and had the companionship of his colleagues, the writers. He had a close friend in Friede, and finally, he had a girl friend as well.

He had met Miriam at the factory. She worked in the spinnery, a few flights of stairs above his hall. She was neither pretty nor ugly. Her figure was short, outlined by curves which were not particularly shapely. However she seemed strong and healthy, and it was through this strength that her femininity revealed itself to Bunim. There was a softness to it, a warmth which attracted his attention. He liked to let his eyes linger on her hips, on her bosom, or to follow the lines of her chubby face and short neck. Such a potential for motherhood lay dormant in her small young body!

One day, on his way home from work, she walked up to him. "Excuse me," she caught hold of his arm without great ceremony. "Is this yours by any chance?" She drew a notebook out of her shopping bag, and he recognized it at once as an old notebook he had lost.

He took it from her hand. "How did you get it?" he asked angrily.

"I found it at the exit. I sometimes see you writing during lunch hour, so I thought . . ."

"Did you read anything in it?"

"No, that is, yes."

He thrust the book into his pocket, gave her another severe look and crossed the street. But then he turned around and searched for her with his eyes. A yearning for her small feminine body awoke again in him. He realized how brutal his behaviour towards here had been and he chased after her, until he caught up to her. He walked by her side, distraught, his face afire. "I didn't even thank you," he said.

"Don't mention it," she answered flatly.

Her calm angered him; it was as if she were teasing him with her composure.

"You're probably aware that it is not very nice to read someone else's writing," he remarked sullenly.

"I was curious," she replied, and added, "I didn't understand a word of it anyway."

Bunim, his sensitivity touched, looked straight into her face. "What was so hard to understand?"

"Everything."

He drew the notebook out of his pocket and flipped through it. "These are only bits and pieces," he explained.

"You are a writer, aren't you?"

"Yes, sort of."

The next day, during lunch hour, he wandered through the corridors, looking for her. When he found her, he proposed that she have lunch with him. She showed neither surprise nor any other emotion at his invitation, but agreed, and they sat down on a roll of material, in a corner of the large factory passage. A few loose sheets of paper appeared in his hand. "I brought you the poems you were unable to read by yourself," he said. "With my help, it might be easier." In a quavering whisper, he began reading an epical idyll to her, which described his mother lighting the Sabbath candles; it was a poem written in memory of the lost Friday nights in his parents' home.

As he read, Miriam looked straight at his mouth. She thought the poem sad and beautiful. Her eyes grew big, her cheeks flushed and her thin eyebrows joined together above her nose. By the time he had finished, her face was transformed; it radiated with the very spirit of his poem, as if his stanzas were reflected in her eyes. He himself felt moved and elated. Slowly, he unwrapped his lunch while she, still enraptured, observed his every movement. When she realized that his bread was dry, she pushed one of her sandwiches into his hand. "Eat this," she ordered.

He pushed away the sandwich and stood up. The next minute she saw him run down the stairs. He returned, his hands full of things he had bought at the corner store. He put a bottle of soda water down in front of her. "I have something else," he said, opening a bag of cherries. At the sight of the cherries, she smiled. It was the first time he had seen her smile.

After that, they had their lunch together every day, always sitting in the same corner; they grew more and more intimate as the days and months wore on. She told him her story in a few words. She had come to Lodz to work from a *shtetl* near Warsaw. Apart from the relatives at whose house she was staying, she knew no one in the city. She had learned to read in the *Beth Yacov*, the orthodox school for girls, and she had never read any books, except for the *Tzena Verena*, the women's Bible written in Yiddish. The poem Bunim had read to her was the first Yiddish poem she had ever heard, except for the prayers she had learned to recite. That was all she had to tell him about herself and after she had told him this much, Bunim became the speaker and she his faithful listener.

In general, she accepted everything he said as the only truth possible. Not that she did not have any opinions of her own, but it just so happened that her thoughts would shape themselves in accord with Bunim's way of thinking. It was as if he had cast a spell on her. One day he asked her if she was pious and she conceded shyly, "I haven't said my prayers in a long time. I don't observe the Sabbath as I should." She looked with apprehension at his orthodox cap, at the gaberdine which he discarded while working but wore during lunch and after work. She was afraid of how he might react to her confession.

But to her surprise, he replied, "There is more piety in you than there is in me."

She was astonished. "You are a religious man, aren't you? You wear religious clothing and you say the blessing before touching food."

"I'm accustomed to it," he replied. "As far as clothes are concerned . . . I wear them for my parents' sake. From other things I've freed myself easily — the sidelocks, for instance, and the beard. But the blessing comes to my lips automatically, at the mere sight of food."

She listened to him with a serious concentrated look on her face. Although she was sure that she understood him well, she sensed that there was something in his words that was beyond her comprehension. But this did not really matter to her. What was important was that he was sitting beside her, telling her about his life as if it were an offering he was making to her. And the gratitude and admiration she felt for him turned gradually into devotion; it awakened a sense of belonging in her, to such an extent that she felt her own life mingled with his, until she no longer knew who she was, unless defined through him. She devoured his words and his beauty, the traits of his face, the shape of his body. Taking it all in, she made him so much her own that she could identify with him as she identified with herself and call him "I". She knew that this was how things would be for the rest of her life.

After a time, he took her along with him to visit Friede who, sensitive as he was, sensed immediately how far advanced the pair were in their relationship. He did not make the slightest effort to conceal his dissatisfaction. "What's the meaning of this?" he asked Bunim jokingly, but with bitterness in his voice. "You came to tease me, to introduce me to my replacement in your heart? When will I have the pleasure of wishing you *mazal-tov*?"

"We are not getting married yet," Miriam mumbled disconcertedly.

Friede came towards her with a leap. "And why, my lady? It is perhaps beneath your dignity to marry him, eh?"

Miriam was thunderstruck. Her head hanging, her body bent under the blow of his words, she snatched her coat and dashed out of the room. Bunim followed, running through the street after her, until he caught up with her. She was sobbing, completely at a loss. He stroked her arm awkwardly, "Don't be angry with him," he begged her.

She looked at him through her tears, confusion and silent reproach in her eyes, "Why do you introduce me to people who make fun of me?"

A wave of tenderness swept over him. "Don't talk like that, Miriam, please. You'll see how he will come to like you."

By that time, Friede had caught up with them. He grabbed both of them by their sleeves and jerked their arms vigorously. Shaken and gasping for breath, he was unable to utter a word. "Children," he finally stammered out, "good heavens, what happened?" Still panting, he waited for them to reply. When they failed to, he again began pulling them by the sleeves, slurring his words. "I didn't mean a thing I said, God forbid. I swear to you by the Holiest of Holies." He faced Miriam, letting her look into his hollow-cheeked, tormented face. "I don't know how to explain," he went on. "I think I was afraid to lose him." He turned to Bunim. "Tell her how close we were, tell her, Simcha Bunim. Let her know at least."

Something stirred painfully within Bunim. Humility and guilt overcame him on account of the devotion both Friede and Miriam had revealed to him. He put his hand on Friede's bony shoulder. "Don't worry," he mumbled. "We will always remain close."

Friede sighed, "So help me God, I wish for your happiness, Simcha Bunim."

The three of them stood in the middle of the sidewalk. They spoke no more, but in their forlorn silence an unbreakable current of emotion flowed back and forth between them. Amorphous and undefined as it was, it grew steadily stronger. Until Bunim, overcome by a wish to transform this moment into the most memorable event of his life, turned to Miriam with a wistful light in his eyes, and said, "Let's get married, Miriam."

✦ ✦ ✦

Their marriage was celebrated in accordance with the law and ritual of Israel, in the home of Bunim's parents. It was a modest celebration, but one filled with the spirit of serene joy and forgiveness. The regret and sorrow of Bunim's parents and sisters had grown milder during these days and never returned to their previous acuteness. Miriam pleased Bunim's family greatly. Before long they considered her one of them. And she herself began to change. Love and her recent experiences had pinched her face, leaving dark circles under her eyes, but she had acquired a new charm; there was an alluring, enigmatic air about her — an expression which only the pains of happiness can bring out on a woman's face. She looked beautiful in her white dress, her brown eyes gleaming through her veil, hot and proud. And when Bunim stood with her under the marriage canopy, he realized fully how dear she was to him. One of the gayest guests at the wedding party was a fragile-looking young man, who did not have a skull cap of his own and had to borrow one from the groom. That night, Friede allowed himself to drink wine instead of milk.

Bunim and Miriam rented a room and kitchen close to the factory where they worked. They furnished it with only the most necessary things, but Miriam was a good housewife and her pride at being Bunim's chosen awoke a desire in her to display all the ability which she herself had for creating beauty. She sewed the curtains for the windows, embroidered the tablecloths and towels and she decorated pillow cases with flower designs stitched with silk thread.

They went to work together and spent their lunch hour together, just as they had done before the wedding. But before long, a baby began to knock at the gates of life, forewarning the parents to prepare for its reception. It became increasingly difficult for Miriam to get up in the morning, and Bunim decided not to let her go to the factory any longer. It was time for him to become the family's sole provider.

Returning home from work acquired a new taste for him. Miriam would wait for him at the window, and when he entered the room, he would be greeted by the warmth of her rounded body clinging to him, by the aroma of the delicious meal she had prepared and by the air of expectation permeating the room. Very often Friede would be waiting for him as well. He would lie on the sofa reading a newspaper, or sit at Bunim's desk, working. The three of them would sit down to supper. Miriam prepared the simplest meal as if it were a feast, setting the table upon a well-starched white tablecloth, with the plates, glasses and cutlery, all of the cheapest quality, looking refined, sparkling and glittering with cleanliness. To her and to Bunim, eating together was always more than just a meal; from the first bite they had taken together, it had become a kind of ritual. And when Friede was present, the ritual turned into a celebration.

Miriam would serve at the table silently, rarely interfering in the conversation of the two men. However both of them felt her presence, and if she was gone from the room for too long, they missed her and their conversation ceased to run as smoothly as before, until the moment when she reappeared and sat down beside them, watching them with her quiet maternal eyes.

Then, unexpectedly, during the last weeks of Miriam's pregnancy, a sudden disquiet swept over Bunim. For a while he managed to keep the mood away; he covered it up with talk and superficial gaiety, until the moment arrived when he decided to meet it face to face. He conceded the truth to himself: he was alone again. Again his soul was shut up, suffocating. He had stopped writing, as if all his wells of creativity had become blocked, worse still — as if they had dried out. He felt at a loss, and there was no one to whom he could pour out his heart.

Miriam was his wife, devoted and loving, but he had to admit to himself that he was bored with her, even though he was unable to be alone in the house without her even for a minute. Their conversations had long since descended from their lofty heights and reached the level of small talk and trivialities; a kind of chatter, pleasant and intimate like the skin of one's body, but excluding any involvement of the inner being. Now he realized that even during their former conversations in the factory, he had talked to her out of a wish to find out more about her, to stimulate and waken her, and perhaps also to show off and win her love, rather than out of a need to reveal himself to her. Now he knew her, with her possibilities and limitations — or at least he thought that he knew her — and he was sure of her love.

Now, when he sometimes tried to regain the mood of their past conversations, and made an effort to talk to her the way he had used to, he discovered that it had lost its magic. Set upon reviving their lost intimacy, trying by force and at any cost to make it vibrate between them anew, he would sometimes re-read his poems to her. She would listen to him just as she had before, her eyes moist, her mouth open, devouring every word; but he realized that although the mood of his poems was reflected in her face, she had failed to grasp their essence. A year earlier, he had not minded it, but now it annoyed him. Her admiration for him, her awe of his every word only unnerved him more. He felt a growing need to split his soul in two, to leave one half to Miriam, and keep the other half for himself.

And something was going wrong in his relationship with Friede as well. Friede came to see Bunim practically every day and knew of Bunim's every worry and trouble, but the intimacy was gone. Strange as it now seemed, the sensitive Friede had been right in his premonition that Miriam would take Bunim away from him — she, to whom he no longer belonged. Friede made no more reproaches. He never asked for anything and accepted in good faith the bit of friendship Bunim was capable of offering him. But sometimes a look from Friede would strike him and force him to avert his face, and to avoid any true contact all the more. It was as if they were still capable of knowing what went on in each other's minds, but were unable to reach out to one another's soul.

Bunim reproached himself for his attitude, for his neglect of both Miriam and Friede, which was not so much shown in his behaviour, as in his heart and in his thoughts. In his mind, time and again he went over his life. He had met with so much devotion, had received so much love — and had given so little in return. He thought of his parents, of his family; he thought of Sender, his first true friend. And now there was Friede, devoted, lonely and sick, trying to warm himself at Bunim's hearth. And finally, there was Miriam, the most devoted of all, who still loved him as romantically and passionately as a bride, who served him as if he were a kind of saint. He asked himself where the narrowness of his heart had come from, recalling Sender who had believed that he, Bunim, was blessed with love, because he had the potential to return it a thousandfold. Had Sender been wrong?

He did not know the answer to this question. All he knew was that he had a need to run away from the people most attached to him, to shut himself up behind the bars of his self-built inner cell. But when he asked himself what it was that he was trying to hide behind its seven locks, he was forced to concede that he could find there nothing but this urge to escape.

He renewed his solitary walks. Just as he had done in Lublin after he had lost Sender, he wandered the streets, looking for people, for the city, for the world, searching for the key to the riddles which plagued him. He began attending the meetings of political parties, listening to discussions and speeches which expressed familiar ideas, yet were dressed up in alien phraseology. Again there was food for thought, horizons opened for speculation, a sea of words tempting him to find a grain of truth in them. What he meditated upon now was real and concrete. The struggle for social justice swept him along, or perhaps swept him away from his personal, less tangible struggles. The anger of the masses kindled his excitement, enriching his vocabulary with forceful words with which he tried to outshout and silence the insistent, gnawing inner voice. He began publishing in the literary supplements of the newspapers the poems he had written months before. His words, dressed up in print, acquired a new face, an additional meaning. It was exhilarating to see one's intimate thoughts and feelings presented to the world side by side with the daily bread of headline news. And all in all he found such great pleasure in the active, outgoing life he was leading, that he succeeded in eliminating his other, hidden life which was not at all joyful.

He had still not come to any conclusion in his struggle with himself, nor had he managed to digest completely the truths he heard at meetings and lectures, nor made up his mind about his political predilections — when his daughter, Blimele, came into the world. With one gigantic leap, passing over everything that had happened before, he regained his home, his equilibrium and came to terms with himself.

The world receded into the background. The tiny creature in Miriam's arms, tied by her little mouth to the nipple of her mother's breast, the folded creased little face just awakened to life, yet so reminiscent of old age and death, this helpless little daughter of his — was everything. Everything that vibrated with life within him was drawn towards her with overwhelming force.

He could hardly wait for the workday to be over, so that, like someone afraid to miss his train, he could hurry home in order to be present at the ritual of Miriam nursing Blimele. He would rush into the room like a wind and, still wearing his coat, approach mother and daughter, place himself behind them, and watch. Miriam would grow angry with him for being so reckless in bringing in the cold from the street, and sheepishly, he would take off his coat and warm his hands by the stove before he returned to watch them.

He was just as capable as Miriam of taking care of Blimele. But Miriam, who had acquired a pride of her own since she had had Blimele, rarely allowed him to take her. She thought that he handled her awkwardly, that he hurt the child or frightened her with his glasses. Guiltily, with a meek smile on his face, he would listen to her reproaches and lectures, but as soon as she left the room, he would rush to the crib and take the tiny creature into his arms. He would make faces, wrinkle his nose, smack his lips, or tickle the rosy heels, until Blimele would deign to offer him a smile.

His relationship with Miriam underwent a change. He had more tenderness for her now and expressed it more frequently in words than he had done before. He often kissed and caressed her; he worried when she looked tired or upset. But he no longer desired her. He looked at her with the same adoration as Blimele did from the crib. And he felt good with these feelings. Passion receded deep into the recesses of his being, allowing the pure calm love for the mother of his child to emerge.

As Blimele grew, so did his attachment to her. Her hands stretching out to greet him were the most beautiful poem that ever came his way. Blimele's chatter, her weeping, her eating and sleeping, her coughs and bowel movements set the tone of his days. He began to write again. Every little noise in the house disturbed him at such moments, but Blimele's laughter, or tears, or her constant chatter were necessary for him; he could hardly work otherwise.

With Blimele's arrival, Bunim's tongue unwound as well. He had previously never had the habit of talking to strangers and, as a rule, was poor at any kind of small talk. Blimele taught him to talk about trifles, about everyday things, with the same earnestness he had used to talk about spiritual matters. She acquainted him with the neighbours. Before her arrival, he had had no idea who lived in the apartments around him. But the little female chatterbox of a year and a half knew everyone who lived in the building and paid regular visits to each neighbour. Her father, when he was home from work, would run to look for her, stopping here and there, often staying on for a while to exchange a few words, to listen to what had happened in the backyard that day, or hear out this one's confession or become involved in that one's life for a while. Neighbours would show up in his apartment too. Blimele would bring them in, or they would knock at the door, attracted by her laughter or crying.

Bunim came to realize that no one had opened the window to the world for him as Blimele had. He felt this especially on the Sabbath when he took her for a walk and sat down on a bench in the square. His little teacher, as if aware of the function she was performing, came constantly to her father with new "material for study". Radiant, she would lead the strange "guest" by the hand and point from afar with her little finger at her *Tateshe* sitting on the bench. And her method never failed. After a few introductory remarks about the beautiful child, about children in general and about the weather in particular, the "guests" would sit down beside Bunim and open their hearts to him. There was a certain air about him that made people discard their reserve, or perhaps it was simply the fact that he was a complete stranger whose name they did not know and who did not know theirs, which made them dare to uncover their wounds as before a doctor. Besides, the little girl's father was a good listener. The expression on his face bore ample evidence of his involvement in the story. And then there was the green of the square, the mildness of the sun, which made it so much easier to approach and talk to another human being.

After such a walk with Blimele, Bunim would often sit down at his table and write a short story, which only a few hours before he had not dreamed of writing. He hardly noticed how his own self had moved out of his pages, to make room for the experiences and dreams of his characters who were his neighbours, or the people he had met in the square. He had ceased writing poems, but he felt that his soul was becoming healthier.

There was still another thing for which he had to be grateful to Blimele: the ability to see life in detail. She taught him to notice the obvious, the unimportant trifles which contained the potential of revealing entire worlds. She called his attention to the fly buzzing against the window pane, pointing it out to him with her perpetually searching little finger. And all of a sudden, Bunim saw human fate in the knocking of the fly's wings against the hard transparent pane. There seemed to be such clarity between man and his Creator, such transparent closeness between man and nature, and yet there was between them that impenetrable wall of glass, through which man could see, but through which he could not pass. And just like that fly man buzzed around himself, deluding himself that before long he would emerge into the light, unaware that all he was doing was beating against a glass window; until he fell down from the pane, death in his exhausted wings.

Blimele heard the grains of sand crunch under their steps as they walked in the square, and asked in her childish language why people hurt the tiny grains of sand which, unlike birds, had no wings to fly away. And Bunim would see human fate in the fate of the grains of sand. The ability to soar in the air, to rise in a flight of one's own was given only to the few. The rest of mankind lay close to the ground, only to be lifted and thrown about by storms, stepped and walked on by boots; they knew nothing of the lofty heights. But he also saw the power of the grains of sand. The birds in the blue skies eventually fell into their laps, making their graves among them. But they, the sands themselves, continued forever. Storms might throw them about, but could not destroy them; boots might stamp upon them, but could not crush them.

And the older Blimele grew, the more she taught her father, the more things she noticed, and the more she asked. With his ears open, he would listen to the language of his little teacher. Her every word or expression, the direct name she found for everything led him back to the source of language itself. Bread without butter was "naked bread", eyelids were "the window-shades of the eyes" to her . . .

It had been four years since Bunim married Miriam. They were happy with each other, each in his or her own way. They both had an idea of the course their relationship had taken. They were like two close parallel paths, heading in the same direction, yet leading towards different regions. This did not disturb their feeling of having a common destiny and of being inseparably bound together. Miriam could not imagine her existence without Bunim; he could not imagine himself without her. And the awareness of being together gave them the feeling of fulfilment, of happiness. Each of them was desperately calling: I am alone. But they had already learned from their life together that this was the human course, that no matter how strong a love, no matter how powerful a friendship, two people could not be forged into one. You have to suffer alone, rise to your climax alone, and die alone. They said to themselves: I have a companion, but my torment has no companion. Yet they consoled themselves that without the companion at hand, the torment might have been worse.

✦ ✦ ✦

July of that year was exceptionally humid and hot. The city seemed suspended in a density of smoky dusty air which was baked by the sun from above, and by the boiling asphalt from below. It had not rained for weeks. The soil in the parks and squares was rutted and cracked with dryness; the leaves dangling from the trees were withered and parched, waiting only for a breeze to unhinge them from the boughs. But there was no breeze.

This particular day, Bunim came home late from work. His new boss, Mr. Adam Rosenberg who, after Bunim had gone without work for weeks, had hired him to work in his factory, thanks to the intervention of the painter Guttman, had just cut short his vacation in the woods of Bialowieze. At least this was what the workers whispered among themselves, since Mr. Rosenberg himself had not yet been seen at the factory. Suddenly there were strange orders to be carried out, such as transferring machinery and raw materials from one place to another, and loading the unfinished products onto wagons and trucks. Whoever wanted to work overtime could do so, and Bunim had signed up.

Mr. Zaidenfeld, the general manager, gave his orders in a flat military tone of voice, confiding in no one; and it did not even cross the workers' minds to ask him about the meaning of the work they were doing. However, when the bookkeeper, Mr. Wiseman, came out of his office at seven o'clock and ploughed his way through the rolls of material strewn about the backyard, en route to the wagons blocking the exit, one of the more courageous workers approached him to inquire. Mr. Wiseman shook his head and waved his hands like someone who knew but could not tell. The workers watched his twisted face and mousey eyes peering about him in all directions. They saw him force his way through the gate, then look back over his shoulder, then shake his head and run off.

This foretold no good. The workers speculated that even if all this upheaval did not indicate the total liquidation of the factory, it certainly meant that there would be layoffs. Moreover, there had been ominous rumours among the workers that their boss had interrupted his vacation because of the war scare, and that he was hurriedly transferring his fortune abroad where he and his family would follow it in the near future.

Bunim came home late. He was greeted at the door by Miriam and the child. Blimele threw her arms around his neck, hoping he would carry her around the room for a while. But he disengaged her hands and put her hurriedly down on the floor. Avoiding Miriam's eyes, he took off his work clothes and washed up. He was nervous and had to suppress an impulse to run out of the room. It was something more than just the heat that was suffocating him here. He sat down at the table which was covered with a spotless tablecloth, all set and waiting for him. Blimele came over and asked him to build a bridge out of the forks for her. He built a bridge, although he could scarcely remain sitting in his chair. Miriam prepared to warm up his food.

"You're not going to light the stove!" he burst out in spite of himself. "Isn't it hot enough as it is?"

She sensed his nervousness acutely, becoming nervous herself. She stood undecidedly at the stove for a moment, then grabbed a pile of old newspapers and lit them, pushing them in through the burner. Thin wisps of smoke issued from the cracks around the stove rings; they rose lazily above the pots and spread throughout the room. They remained suspended in its very middle, as though too weak to climb towards the ceiling.

Blimele's plump little fingers stroked Bunim's cheeks and brushed against his forehead and neck. Dressed only in a pair of panties, she stood between his knees. She put a finger to his nose. "Do you know that you have hair growing in your nose, *Tateshe?*" she asked seriously, pushing a finger into one of his nostrils.

Miriam carried a steaming bowl over to the table. Bunim pushed the child away and picked up the spoon. "Can't you prepare something else in this heat?" he groaned. Miriam sat down opposite him, taking Blimele onto her lap. The two of them had already eaten their meal and could now devote all their attention to him. He lowered his face over the steaming bowl in order to avoid their eyes, and forced himself to eat the boiling dish.

The window stood open, the white curtain hung immobile as though its fringes were pulled down by heavy weights. The dark, dusty-looking sun shone through the motionless curtain, covering Bunim's desk with a dark splotch of red. It seemed as though the sun itself were tired of its own heat.

Cautiously, Miriam inquired, "If there is so much work, that must mean that there is no danger of war coming, don't you think, Bunim?" She added with a sigh, "And here, if you pay attention to the jabbering of the neighbours, you would turn gray and sick with fear."

"Do you know, *Mameshe*," Blimele interrupted with her melodious voice, "that *Tateshe* has maybe twenty or a hundred hairs growing in his nose?" Bunim got up from the table and she jumped down from Miriam's lap to grab him around the knees. "Now you will go with me for a walk in the square, won't you?"

He freed himself from her hands and rushed out of the room.

He was in the street, carried forward by a feverish impetus. There was something boiling and bursting within him, and he knew that it was caused by his anxiety. For the last few days he had been unable to rid himself of it. Something inexplicably frightening was hovering in the air, permeating the city. Yet it seemed to him that no one felt it as clearly as he did. The street, its air still thick and humid, was thronged with passers-by and with boisterous children at play. Trade and commerce went on as usual; buyers clustered around store entrances or besieged the stalls and bins laden with goods. Salesmen stood in the shop entrances and called out their wares. In the middle of the street the clanking streetcars jammed with people crept slowly ahead, surrounded by carts, horses, buggies and cars. Wheels crunched upon cobblestones, horses' hooves clopped, cars honked their horns, and interspersed amid the street noise were the shouts and cries of barefoot children. The sun was beginning to set behind the rooftops. It was still daylight, still hot, but the air was turning gray.

Bunim quickened his steps. Ever since his days at the *yeshiva* in Lublin, walking had been his way of releasing tension, of eluding the feeling of suffocation which sometimes menaced him. Walking brought clarity to his thoughts and relaxed his heart; it led him away from one thing and brought him closer to another. But this time his walking led him away from one thing and brought him back to the same — from fear to fear. He tried to face up to it, to take it apart, to analyze it. "Is it the fear of getting drafted into the army?" he asked himself, "the worry about Miriam and Blimele? About my parents and sisters?" It was that, but something more on top of that, something gruesome, unthinkable and incomprehensible.

On Freedom Plaza where the statue of Kosciuszko looked majestically down upon the first evening strollers, a few *gymnasium* students were marching, whistling a tune together. Girls walked by arm in arm, laughing their carefree girlish laughter. Bunim tried to find his calm by watching the older strollers. "They know as much as I do," he tried to convince himself, but the fact did not quiet his mind. They knew as much as he did, yet he knew something more.

He came to the house where Friede lived. He had not seen Friede that whole summer and had not visited him in his room for years. Ever since Bunim's wedding, it was Friede who would come to see him, never the other way around. Bunim's place was more of a home than Friede's, and Friede needed Miriam's and Blimele's presence sometimes more than he needed Bunim's. Miriam's wise silence was the best background for conversation, while Blimele's presence was the refreshment, the relief after the discussion. Her smile, her questioning blue eyes brought the sky down into the room. She called him Uncle Friede and was forever grateful to him for the doll, Lily, he had given her on her birthday.

Bunim had hardly noticed that Friede had not shown up during all the hot summer weeks, but Miriam would ask about him and wonder what had happened to him. She nagged at Bunim to go over to Friede's apartment and find out. Bunim would promise to go, but never got around to it. Was it because of his fatigue after work, or because of the heat, or because of his restlessness and impatience; or perhaps it was his fear of finding out that something bad had happened to his friend? He wanted peace. He wanted to be left alone. Even Miriam and Blimele had become too talkative to suit him lately.

He stood in front of Friede's door, listening. On the other side he could hear a woman talking and laughing in a thick unpleasant voice. When he finally entered the room, he saw Friede lying in bed and a woman sitting by his side, her back turned. She held a bowl on her lap and was feeding the sick man. The air in the room was sticky; it filled Bunim's nose with an acrid unpleasant smell. The woman turned her head to smile at him, with lips thickly smeared with lipstick which extended beyond their outlines, so that her mouth looked unnaturally large. The woman did not look old, yet her face seemed old. The powder and rouge covering it like a mask brought out a network of deep wrinkles, pierced by a pair of big eyes, both moist and glowing. Bunim noticed that two of her front teeth were missing.

"What do you want?" she asked in a thick masculine voice. The eyes she fixed on Bunim seemed to have no relation to her face, or to her voice. Like two young birds that had strayed into a strange nest they peered out from under her black pencilled eyebrows. He stared at her sleeveless beet-red dress, at the hand which she used to feed Friede. Her arms were shapely, rosy and fresh. They too seemed to have nothing in common with the rutted worn face.

"This is the Simcha Bunim I told you about," Friede introduced the visitor. Pointing to a chair, he added, "Take my clothes off of there." The woman put the bowl down on the floor and rose to clean off the chair. Her smile was gone. From beneath her puckered pencilled eyebrows she shot a resentful look at Bunim. "Every day she prepares my clothes for me," Friede explained, "and every day they remain lying on the chair. I've gotten very lazy, Bunim." Bunim sat down on the edge of the chair. The woman picked the bowl up from the floor, ready to go on feeding the sick man, but he pushed her hand away. "Go now, Sheindle, I've had enough."

She stood up, motioning at Friede. "He doesn't stop talking about you."

"Really?" Bunim stammered.

"Yeah, really." She took a step towards him with the bowl in her hand, as if she were about to empty it over his head. "He says you're his best friend. May the cholera take such friends as the like of you, Mister. May such friends sink into the ground! Why didn't you come to find out what was the matter with him? For two months now he has been lying abed boiling like a baking oven!"

"Shut your mouth, Sheindle!" Friede tried to cut her off.

Sheindle decided to put the bowl down on the table. She cleared an edge of it, shoving away some books, tin cups and pieces of clothing. "Why are you so afraid that I should give him a piece of my mind, idiot?" she shot back at Friede. "Let him at least know that he's a pig."

"Get out!" Friede pointed to the door with a bony yellow finger. His eyes locked with Bunim's; a glance flashed between them like lightning. All of a sudden, Bunim remembered that he had already sat like this somewhere before; that he had once before met with just such a gaze. He felt himself sinking into deep darkness.

The woman returned to Friede's bed, fixed his pillow, brushed crumbs of food off his blanket and put her hand on Friede's forehead. She turned to Bunim, the expression of anger on her face transformed into one of worry. "He's boiling like a baking oven," she whispered hoarsely to him as she headed for the door. With her hand on the doorknob, she showed Friede a cheerful face. "I'll be back later."

"Don't you dare!" Friede shook his finger warningly. "Your Rudolf Valentino will tear all the hair out of your head. Go now!" She guffawed, exposing the holes in her mouth left by her two missing front teeth, and blew him a kiss with her hand.

Left alone in the room, Friede and Bunim tried to avoid each other's eyes. Both felt uneasy; words refused to come and link the broken thread between them. They waited thus mutely for a long time, until Bunim, unable to bear the silence any longer, asked, "Who is she?"

The smile reappeared on Friede's face. "Well, she is a prostitute from the brothel downstairs. She's fond of me, mind you, has attached herself to me and refuses to leave me alone. The blazes! Here you have the old cliché of a sinful body combined with a heart of gold. I really don't know what I would do without her. She feeds me, washes me and my sweaty underwear; she changes my sheets and whatnot. There is nothing in the world that disgusts her; used to the muck, I suppose. And that suits me fine. I don't have to be shy with her. Eh, Bunim, literature is swarming with generous little whores, but here you have one in real life, my Sheindle, the jewel in my crown, the apple of my eye. I would gladly marry her if I were well. I really would. But on the other hand, if I were well, she wouldn't so much as want to look at me. Now, as long as we are both buried ninety miles deep in the pit, we are a pair. What am I saying? We are not a pair even now. She has a husband; for two thousand zlotys he bought her from her previous beau. And he is not just anybody, mind you. He is His Majesty, the Prince of the Baluty Underworld, Rudolf Valentino they call him." Friede's bead-like eyes were fixed on Bunim, but seemed not to see him. He continued talking as if in a trance. "I would buy her from him. With the royalty money from my book I would buy her from him. My book is coming out any day now, my first one. Not a bad idea to buy a wife with the income it brings, don't you think?"

Friede was on fire. Only his pointed nose was pale, the nostrils fluttering, spreading and collapsing in an effort to inhale more air. His chest expanded and contracted with a wheezing sound. A shudder went down Bunim's spine every time he looked into Friede's eyes. They were goggled and glassy, like the eyes of a drunkard, but in their depth, there burned fear, sober and sharp, giving the impression that Friede was two people at the same time: one, who was lost in a high fever, entangled in a web of feverish delirium, and another who watched over the first and knew everything. Bunim had to turn his head away.

"You don't have to apologize to me," Friede said suddenly in a completely different tone of voice.

His remark took Bunim by surprise. "And if I apologized?" he muttered. He picked up his chair and brought it closer to Friede's bed. "I am worried, Friede," he said loudly, as if he were trying to reach not Friede's visible ears, but another pair, concealed behind them. "Something terrible is hovering over our heads. I have no peace of mind. I don't write, I don't live. Everything around me seems to be hanging suspended over a precipice. I have no patience for the child. I don't know what's come over me. I take a newspaper in my hand, and I feel that every word strikes me on the head like a hammer. I can't stay in the house for a minute. I go to the party clubs, thinking the people there might know some facts that I don't. But the clubs are empty. Everyone is taking it easy. The young people have left the city, or they go for walks in the parks. Everything is as usual. So perhaps it's only my sick imagination running riot? Maybe I'm hallucinating?" His words were slurred, as if they too had been burned by the heat. He himself felt feverish and ill as he watched Friede stare at him with his double gaze, which seemed at once both very close and very distant. "Where are our leaders, I ask you?" Bunim shouted. "The leaders of the parties, of the movements? Why don't they wake the people from their lethargy? Why don't they warn them? Why don't they sound the alarm? Because if there is nothing to warn or alarm people about, then why is my boss cleaning out his factory? Why are we loading trucks with unfinished merchandise?"

Friede smiled crookedly; his voice sounded mockingly boisterous and disdainful. "I am fortunate!" he hit his chest with his fist. "I care about your worries like I care about last year's snow."

"You are just like the others."

"No, it's the others who had better care! But I don't give a damn."

"Tell me why."

"Because I'm an egoist. Because when bad comes to worse, comrade, I'll have finished my account with the world at large." He contemplated Bunim for a while, then raised his head from the pillow. "I have written a new story," he said, and pulled a few creased sheets of paper from under his mattress. "Do you want to hear it?"

Before Bunim had time to recover from the shock of Friede's words, he heard the latter's hoarse voice, struggling against his heavy breath. He was reading his story to Bunim, a story about two children in a tiny *shtetl*. Friede's tongue got tangled between his teeth, he garbled his words and left out entire sentences. Bunim could not understand a word. He was back in the darkness, sinking deeper and deeper into it. He had a wish to stretch out beside his sick friend and perish along with him. He had a desire to jump to his feet and run out of the room, hurry home to kiss Blimele and to embrace Miriam in their cool soft bed; but he remained glued to his chair, feeling suddenly guilty, not because he had not seen Friede for two months, but because he was not listening to him now, not paying attention to the story. The story, he thought, was there to give them support. It was something beyond fear. He took the sheets of paper from Friede's hand. "Let me read it myself." He turned to the table, made room among its clutter, spread his hands on the paper and began reading.

Silence fell on the hot room. Bunim forgot where he was and did not feel Friede's eyes watching him. He read quickly, his eyes sweeping over the crooked, almost illegible handwriting, swallowing the lines speedily, feverishly. He felt the story's living breath penetrate him deeply, image after image, event after event. He saw young Friede in his home *shtetl*, saw him falling in love with spring, with beauty. The story had a sad ending, not so much sad as banal — like life itself. Love drained out of the children's hearts, its charm faded and vanished. Dreams woke up to reality and everything became ordinary and gray; everything, except nature. The trees and the grass withered to drabness in fall, but were restored to their health in spring. Human hearts, craving to copy nature, once wakened from their dreams, tried to return to them time and again. But the older they grew, the more reality entered their dreams; the more fall encroached on their summer, the more the weekday penetrated their holiday. The older the hearts grew, the less were they hurt by their awakening, but there was also a dullness and impoverishment in that lack of pain.

Bunim raised his head from the last page and turned to Friede who had been lying immobile, lest by some movement he waken Bunim from the spell; now he raised himself onto his elbow. "Good. Very good," Bunim grew enthusiastic. "Really. I'm not saying it just to please you. Your prose is excellent."

Friede fell back on the pillow. His forehead relaxed as if smoothed by an invisible hand. "From you I like to hear such words," he whispered gratefully and checked his pulse. "You know . . . I can feel the fever coming down."

"I would get rid of all the minor characters though," Bunim remarked, "and leave only the two children. The boy is you, isn't it?"

"Yes, the boy . . . I haven't thought about it for ages and I don't know why it came back to me. But ever since I've been stuck in bed, my childhood returns to me again and again, performing its dance for me in all the most minute details. It seems better and sweeter now than it ever was in reality. Who knows? Perhaps this is the way things are supposed to happen. Before the end, you must return to the beginning. The circle must be closed." He watched Bunim mutely for a while, as he nibbled on his red cracked lips; then he looked straight into Bunim's eyes. "With you I can be frank, don't you think? I know where I am . . . Of late, this thought never leaves me. A great thing for me . . . the greatest. With you I can talk about it, not so? With you . . . It pains you . . . But perhaps if we speak about it, it might bring some relief. And it has to do with my writing. Somewhere it is tied with it. Did you say my writing is of value?"

"Yes, your prose is excellent," Bunim groaned.

"My prose is excellent, you say. I don't know why I still care about my prose, but the fact is that I do. They say that a woman cares about her looks even on her deathbed. I care about my looks as a writer. Friede will remain a writer of excellent prose . . . You see, it is not so much the leaving itself, as it is the fear of going into nothingness. Do you understand me? I have every reason to bewail my life, Bunim. But since things are as they are, I am resolved to be satisfied with it. Because I was writing; because I am writing. It was worthwhile, if only for that alone. People like you and me, Bunim, live a life that other people don't even know exists. For us moments can equal eternities, not so? And . . . I may still get better, after all. My book will appear. I'll take a trip to the mountains, to a good TB sanatorium, and there I may get cured, let's say not completely, but I shall live . . . and write. Writing can put me back on my feet. Yes, writing." He licked his lips. The haze in his eyes grew thinner. He did indeed seem to have less temperature. "And you, Bunim," he asked with curiosity. "What's been happening to you? Are you writing?"

"I told you. I haven't taken the pen into my hand the entire summer."

"Why don't you force yourself?"

"There's no point," Bunim waved his hand. But as soon as he uttered the words, he felt that it was a lie — because of Friede and thanks to Friede. It was not pointless. The moment he realized this, something began to melt away within him. He felt the blood stirring in his veins, as if this very word "pointless" were a password which opened up all the dams obstructing the inner musical current. Sounds began to stream through his limbs towards his heart in gigantic waves. In his mind, a thought was born, fragile and trembling, touching upon strings of feelings, so as to make them vibrate and sing. A sentence, a line of words cut through his imagination. His hands felt clammy and uneasy. He bent over to Friede. "I think now that I could jot down a few lines," he said.

Friede stirred in his bed. "So what are you waiting for? Throw off your shirt. It's hot in here. And make yourself comfortable at the table. Put all that junk down on the floor. There is a pencil in the drawer, paper too. What else do you need?"

Bunim looked at him. Friede's excitement was contagious. This time their eyes met without fear. Bunim took off his sweaty shirt and cleared the table of the things strewn about on it. The room seemed to have become airier, roomier than it had been just a moment ago. He took some sheets of paper out of the drawer, pages from an accountant's book, typed on one side, clean on the other. He drew his pencil out of his pocket and sat down. His anxiety vanished behind the proverbial seven mountains as he tightened his fingers around the pencil and held on to the sheet of paper.

"I'll correct my story, as long as you're busy," he heard Friede's eager voice behind his back. "But first come over here for a minute." Bunim rushed to his bed. "Move my pillow up and raise me a bit. Now give me the cigarettes, yes, the cigarettes; they are near the spirit burner. Light one for me, go ahead, and give me the kneading board. Sheindle provided me with it, to serve me as a table. Take out a pencil from the drawer and a few sheets of clean paper. I'm going to rewrite the whole thing."

There was silence in the room, as both men were working. The night covered the window with its cool soft curtain. It separated Bunim and Friede from the world outside, watched over them and fanned them with a navy blue star-lit fan.

Just as he had done years ago, after their first encounter, Bunim now wrote an ode to friendship. However, this time it was a poem of a completely different nature. The first one had been rather a premonition of friendship, a looking forward to it, an awaiting it. It had been a light and airy poem. The one he was writing now was dark, heavy, and wrought in grief. The first poem had had the wind at its core, this one had fire; a fire produced by the rubbing of hard rough rocks of loneliness against each other, a fire emerging from the clash of black clouds of despair. Yet it possessed the power to smoke out all the anguish and fear from the mind and to forge solitude into pride, making the heart so defiant and unbendable that neither time, nor life or death had any power over it.

In a sense, this poem of Bunim's was written in response to the first one, as an epilogue to it. Bunim felt that with this poem a circle was coming to its close as well — the circle of his friendship with Friede.

Chapter Eight

ESTHER'S UNCLE, CHAIM the Hosiery-Maker lived in the second entrance of the large noisy yard on Hockel Street. The entrance, like all the other entrances in the yard was dim, with a winding dilapidated wooden staircase leading up to a murky hallway. Many doors gave off it. Chaim's door was located at its very end.

The first thing greeting the eye of the visitor upon entering the apartment was the large tiled oven situated in its centre. A cardboard wall met the oven on both sides, dividing the space into a "kitchen" and a "room" which served as a parlour, dining room and bedroom. Although both the "room" and the "kitchen" were quite large, it was not easy to find room to move about in them. Beds, cupboards, merchandise and machinery occupied all the available space, so that it was almost impossible to take a big step or move one's arms to the side, without hitting against an object of one kind or another.

The hand machines which produced the hosiery were screwed on to both window ledges, two machines to a ledge; and at each machine sat one of Chaim's daughters. The remaining two daughters sat at the table and repaired the faulty stockings, fixed the runs, sewed the heels together and pulled the finished products onto wooden forms of various sizes. The piles of socks lay on the table in a medley of bright colours, infusing some liveliness into the monotony of the surroundings, created by the faded shabby wallpaper and the dark furniture. Even the girls' flaxen hair seemed brighter as it dangled from above their ears in thin tight braids like the sidelocks of *yeshiva* boys, and complemented the multi-coloured heaps of socks on the table.

In the "kitchen" sat Aunt Rivka turning the spinning wheel. The heat from the tile oven attacked her squarely in the face, so that she was constantly forced to mop the sweat from her forehead with an edge of her apron, or with the border of one of her underskirts. The clay pots on the stove sizzled and heaved with steam, obliging her ever so often to rise from the spinning wheel, stir the stew, taste it and ascertain whether the household meal had cooked enough.

All day long the house was full of the noise of the hosiery machines, with the murmur of the spinning wheel, the sizzling of the pots on the stove, and with the singing of Uncle Chaim's daughters. It might have seemed that the house was not standing in one place, but was moving, like a ship afloat, heading for distant ports; the singing girls at the windows, turning the cranks of the machine wheels, looked like the ship's navigators at the helm.

In general, Chaim had been lucky with his offspring which also included two sons who worked as hosiery-machine mechanics. The children were devoted and obedient, never asking for anything impossible. True, once in a while they bothered a little, said an unpleasant word to their parents or to each other, but they meant no harm and were not out to pick a serious fight. After all, the days ran so fast that before one had time to look around, Friday had come, and the holiday announced its arrival. The children were as grateful to their parents for the Sabbath as though it were a gift from them, and the rooms would begin to buzz with happy commotion and excitement.

After the Friday lunch, the girls would cover the machines with white sheets, bring buckets full of water and scrub the floors clean, covering them afterwards with rags of sacks to protect them from the dirt. The Sabbath meal had already been placed in the oven of Blind Henech's bakery, and the festive Friday evening meal, cooked and ready to be served, was being kept warm on the oven burners. The girls would delight in the aroma released into the air by the steaming pots, in particular the one with the fish, cooked, according to the custom of Lodz, with a lot of sugar and a drop of lemon, to make them taste more sweet than sour.

Rivka and her daughters would set the table. They put the brass candlesticks on the white tablecloth, prepared the *halah*, filled the decanter with cherry wine, and then, when everything was ready, they would turn their attention to themselves, scrubbing themselves and washing their hair. They strained the water from the pot of beans and poured it into the wash bowl, preparing a rinse that would hold their hair stiff and keep their hairdos in place, since the hair could not be combed on the Holy Day. The girls braided each other's hair, arranging it in a style more elaborate than what they wore during the week, by setting the strands on their foreheads into ringlets which they called "love hooks". Then they eagerly slipped into clean undergarments which were as white as snow and smelled of lavender leaves, and put on their Sabbath dresses. They drew some colourful ribbons and strings of beads out of a drawer to adorn themselves, and felt as if they had been reborn.

Every once in a while at such moments, Rivka would come up with a surprise, such as a blouse which she had bought at the bazaar. The girls rejoiced as if it were a gift meant for all of them, although it was most often offered to Baltche, the eldest, since she was the saddest among them and the time when she should have found a groom for herself was almost past. The girls wanted her to be cheerful and to look pretty for the Sabbath when the young men of the neighbourhood came by to pay them a visit.

The young men who visited Chaim's daughters every Sabbath evening were not politically minded nor completely free-thinking. Usually they would gather in front of the bakery, close to Itche Mayer the Carpenter's cellar window. They would listen to the noise coming from the cellar, to Shalom playing the mandolin, and to the songs and laughter of the gathering inside. The more daring among them would peer in through the dirty pane, but none had the courage to enter the "nest" of the leftists. Sooner or later Yossi, Itche Mayer's happy-go-lucky son and the best dancer in Baluty, would emerge to greet them and would invite them in his jovial clowning way to join his party. Invariably, he would wind up accompanying them to Chaim's house instead, where he could show off his fancy footwork by dancing for a while with Chaim's daughters, before running back to his own social assemblage.

In Chaim's household it was still said that the young men were coming to see Baltche, although for some time now they had shown a preference for dancing a rhumba or a foxtrot with her sisters, leaving her to sing along rather than dance. There was, however, a silent agreement among the girls to keep the young men interested, for Baltche's sake, so that they would not stop coming to the house before their parents had saved up enough money to marry her off.

When all the Friday preparations were finally finished, the girls would surround the festive table, while Rivka lit the candles and blessed them. She kept her face covered with her hands and the girls searched for her eyes through her slightly spread fingers. Afterwards, Sarah, one of the sisters, would take down from the top of the wardrobe a tattered volume by the popular romances writer, Czarska. She would stretch herself out on a bed and let herself be carried away by a gripping melodrama of eternal love and bottomless sorrow. Urged on by her sisters, she would read excerpts aloud to them, or tell them about the latest developments in the plot. But most often the girls did not hear her out to the end, since very soon the footsteps of Chaim and his sons returning from the prayer house would be heard in the hallway.

Chaim, his face radiant, would kiss the *mezuzah* on the doorpost and greet his family with a serene "Good Sabbath". When his steps fell softly on the rags of sacking spread on the freshly scrubbed floor, the whole household would feel that walking with Chaim on the rags like on an exquisite carpet Queen Sabbath herself had entered the house. The family would stand around the table, the gleam of the candles reflecting in their faces, as they all quietly intoned, "Welcome, ye angels of the heavenly chariot". The old grandfather clock leaning crookedly against the wall would begin counting the minutes of festivity in Chaim's house, with a solemn ticking, which seemed louder but also slower than on ordinary days. Then Rivka, her face aglow, would begin serving the fish.

There was something of a Sabbath air about Rivka on weekdays as well. A faint smile would play on her dry wrinkled mouth, a smile rarely extinguished when any of her family were around, and which she would also offer to a stranger. Her door was always open; a hungry person never left it without a chunk of bread, or a thirsty one, without a drink of water. And although most of the time her wallet was practically empty, and Chaim was forever running to his employers to borrow some money, to be subtracted from his next week's account, to help him make it through the current week — she always prepared her meals more lavishly than she could afford, so that she would not have to let a beggar leave her threshold without a bite of hot food. Often Chaim himself would bring a visitor from the prayer house home to dinner. She always received the guest graciously, placed him at the table, and from the first mouthful he ate, the stranger felt at home.

And Chaim appreciated his wife. "Your mother is a holy woman," he would say to the children. "God's *shechina* is reflected in her face." And in trying moments, he would put his hand on her shoulder and console himself, saying with a sigh, "As long as I have you, Rivka, I don't worry. God the Almighty won't fail us, I trust." From a man like Chaim, these words were more than a compliment.

✦ ✦ ✦

Esther well remembered the day she had come to live with Uncle Chaim's family, although at the time she had been a very small girl. She was born in a shingle-roofed cottage a few blocks away from Hockel Street. She could not recall her father's face, since he had left for Argentina when she was still a toddler. At first, he had sent money and letters with solemn promises to send papers and, with God's help, bring over to Argentina not only Esther and her mother, but also Uncle Chaim's entire family. But as time went on, his promises weakened and his letters arrived after increasingly longer intervals of silence, until they ceased coming altogether. Esther's mother took ill and died and Esther became an orphan.

The first night at her uncle's remained indelibly fixed in Esther's memory, and she remembered the following morning too, when Aunt Rivka, wearing a black dress and a black scarf over her matron's wig, had spoon-fed her a soft boiled egg, with a remarkably white hand. They were standing by the window and the sunlight coming through it seemed to dissolve in the egg yolk on the spoon. Tears had run down the aunt's face, dripping onto the slice of buttered bread she had given Esther to eat. Esther thought that it was the tears which had made the bread so soft and tasty.

At first, Rivka would weep a lot while taking care of Esther. In the morning, when she combed her hair, her tears would fall on the girl's red curls; in the evening, when she put her to bed, they fell on her face; Friday, when she gave her a bath and washed her hair, they fell into the wash bowl of bean water; Saturday, when it was a sin to cry and to be sad, she would let them run down to her mouth and swallow them, her lips smiling. But with time the tears vanished, and the usual smile came back to brighten her face. Little by little the face of Esther's own mother and that of Aunt Rivka became one and the aunt became Mother.

Now Esther had a big family with six sisters and two brothers. To them she was both something more and something less than a sister. They had to be good to her and to love her, although she was petted by their parents more than any of them were. If ever a child forgot itself and treated Esther as an equal, grabbing a tasty slice of bread out of her hand, or taking a better place in the bed, and Esther began to cry, Rivka, usually so even-tempered, would be beside herself with anger. Esther's tears made her frantic.

Esther was enrolled at school along with the two other girls who were about the same age as she. But when the time came for them to quit, so that Chaim could put them to work at a machine, or initiate them into the skills of finishing off the stockings, Rivka and Chaim were faced with a dilemma: they were forced to put their own children to work, but it did not seem right to take a helpless orphan out of school and at such a tender age require her to earn her own bread. Consequently, they took first one girl and then the other out of school, while Esther remained to continue her education for one more year, and then for another.

By then she was already fully aware of not being treated like the other children, and the privileges became burdensome to her. They gradually made her feel like an outsider, a visitor who had to be accommodated. She wanted to leave school like the other girls and begin working, so as to earn her keep and thus feel more secure in the family constellation. But all her complaints and outbursts of anger were good-humouredly brushed aside. No one in the family understood her, least of all Aunt Rivka.

But then, bitter times came to harass Uncle Chaim's household: a sudden drop-off in business. There was no work and only the two eldest girls still sat at the machines, while the others were idle. They played in the backyard, or sat in the Garden under the cherry tree all day long, but they had hardly a thing to eat. Every morning Rivka cooked a big pot of sorrel *borscht* that they drank three times a day, accompanied by a slice of bread and a piece of herring.

It was on one of those days that Uncle Chaim took Esther to the streetcar and set out to enroll her in the orphanage of Helenovek. Upon their return, he ordered Rivka to make a bundle of Esther's things. Frightened and bewildered, Esther fluttered between her aunt and uncle, imploring them to have pity on her and not chase her out of their home. The cousins stood by the side, sobbing dolefully, and a sadness reminiscent of the Day of Atonement permeated the entire house.

Uncle Chaim asked Esther to sit down with him at the table. "You're old enough now to understand," he said, nervously plucking the hair of his abundant beard. "I can't help it that my own children suffer, but I don't want to have you on my conscience as well. Even if there was enough work, I would finally have to put you to a machine. So, what kind of future would that be for you?" But his reasonable words convinced Esther only of one thing: that she was not wanted. Aghast at this discovery, she huddled against her aunt and cousins, frantically trying to make them realize how abandoned and lost she felt. The aunt wrung her hands until her knuckles turned white; tears the size of peas rolled down her rutted cheeks. She looked just as she had on the day Esther had come to live with them.

In the orphanage Esther was rebellious. She missed her aunt, her cousins, the backyard with the stables and the cherry tree, although now she had a real garden, large and beautiful. She quarrelled with her teachers and guardians whom she hated fiercely, and who in turn repaid her with little sympathy. Every day she ran to Mr. Romkowski to ask for permission to visit her relatives. He would grant it to her only occasionally, most often on Saturdays. Then she would run through the streets hardly able to master her impatience. As soon as she passed through the gate and rushed into the backyard on Hockel Street, she flung her head high towards the familiar windows, calling her cousins and aunt in a voice thick with excitement, to let them know that she had arrived. She was received with shrieks of enthusiasm. The girls rushed to meet her with open arms, smothering her with kisses. Arm in arm, they would go down to Blind Henech's bakery to fetch the *cholent*. The *cholent*, which Rivka and most of the women of Lodz prepared as a *Yapzok* — with mashed potatoes and beans and with fat meat and bones when they could afford them — tasted heavenly. Rivka took delight in watching Esther sit beside her and devour her portion. A full ladle of *Yapzok* in her hand, Rivka would wait, ready to refill her niece's plate.

After the meal, the family would bombard Esther with questions about the orphanage, and she did not mince words, painting life there in the darkest colours possible, with the most negative adjectives her vocabulary could muster. She never stopped pulling at Uncle Chaim's sleeve, asking him imploringly, "Uncle, when will you finally let me come home? The bad times are over already, aren't they?" But she never received a direct answer to this question. At such moments, Uncle Chaim would suddenly grow very sleepy. He would rise from the table, give Esther an affectionate pinch on the cheek and, an embarrassed smile hidden behind his beautiful beard, would lie down on his bed to have a look at the paper and take his after-*cholent* nap. Then the girls would sit down to play bingo. Time went quickly and before Esther had managed to forget herself in the game, she had to take leave of her family and hurry back to the orphanage.

And so she stayed on at the orphanage. She finished school there and gradually adjusted to her new way of life, finding moments of satisfaction and pleasure in it. As time passed, the ice that had formed between her and her tutors melted away. The latter came to realize that the redhead "porcupine", as they had nicknamed her, had stopped pricking so fiercely and was turning into quite a charming creature, after all. Esther grew to fear Mr. Rumkowski just as the other children did. She had hardly noticed when and how this had come about, but it had. If Mr. Rumkowski displayed a smiling face somewhere in the building, the news spread with the speed of lightning, and the children would sigh with relief, Esther included. On such days it was permitted to sing and talk in a loud voice and to play all the usually-forbidden games. But if Mr. Rumkowski's face were overcast, there was no need to transmit the news from mouth to mouth. His hoarse bellows and snarls were heard all over the orphanage and the children, quiet as mice, waited for the storm to pass — Esther among them.

As soon as she had turned into a docile ward of the institution, the teachers began to discover Esther's talents. She had a good ear for music and quite a pleasant voice, and they singled her out to participate in all kinds of official functions, as well as in the children's performances. In particular, she found favour with Mr. Rumkowski, perhaps due to his pride in the pedagogical advances he had made with her, or perhaps for the simple reason that it was impossible not to take notice of her suddenly blossoming beauty. He often called her to his office, to give her important duties to perform. He liked to stroke her cheeks and to put his fingers into the ringlets of her red curls. At such moments Esther's body would stiffen, her heart would fill with dread and she would feel dizzy and nauseous.

She tried to avoid him as much as she could and discovered that the safest place to hide from him was the library, located in a little side room of the building and directed by Mr. Shafran whom Esther did not feel like avoiding at all; in fact, he was her "real great friend". She would stand in front of the open closet laden with books, wishing she could swallow them all at a gulp. The fact that the closet revealed its secrets to her gradually, volume by volume, prompted her to speed up her reading, so that before long the attraction of the library weakened for her, as it lost part of its mystery with every book she read. Then Mr. Shafran, the embodiment of all the heroes she had come across in the novels she read, in order to keep her interest in books alive, began to provide her with books he borrowed for her from a library in town.

A new world revealed itself to her. The poems and novels she now read seemed to pull a heavy curtain apart within her, exposing another self to her. It was at this time that she read "Victoria" by Knut Hamsun, "Jean Cristophe" by Romain Roland and "Thais" by Anatole France. She was visited by strange visions and disquieting dreams during her restless nights; and her days were filled with yearnings and with a feeling of bottomless inexplicable sadness, both pleasant and painful. This was also the time when she read books of a different nature, which touched not only upon her feelings, but upon her thoughts as well. As she read "The Weavers", "Hunger", or "Fontamara", she realized that the craving for bread, known to her from her childhood, was a craving known to millions of people. And the thought that she was familiar with the experiences of masses of strangers, that she could feel what they felt, fascinated her. The world suddenly became wide-open — strange and yet intimately close. Life was both good and sweet, bitter and cruel. She would soak her pillow with tears at night, weeping over the fate of "The Insulted and the Injured", as waves of helplessness and frustration swept over her. The characters in the books were her neighbours, her relatives, her brothers. They were her own flesh and blood and she loved them.

Her disquiet increased, gradually transforming itself into a compelling curiosity about life as it was lived outside the orphanage. She wanted to reach out to it, to participate in it. So it happened once she had a free day, that she failed to visit Uncle Chaim and his family. She ran to the unions instead, looking for work; and before long, she found a job at a knitting factory.

She stood in front of Mr. Rumkowski for the last time. He released her gladly from under his care. For the last few years he had been unable to keep cool when he saw her; her red hair and her graceful body kindled desires in him which he was hardly able to master. At the same time, her arrogance had reappeared, not so much in words, as in her attitude towards him, in her wordless shrug of the shoulders when he innocently touched them, or in the expression of disgust on her face as he stroked her cheek. He sensed the devil dwelling in her, and feared for her as well as for himself. Thus he only offered her a paternal smile and some wise advice when she came to beg for a discharge. He asked her meekly whether she would remember him. "Always, Mr. Rumkowski," she replied, burning him with the green flame of her eyes. He believed her, but was not sure in what way she would remember him.

She packed her belongings and took leave of her friends and teachers. The only one she was sorry to part with was Mr. Shafran who had helped her discover the world she was about to enter. She was in love with him; and he knew that he had unwittingly put a spell on her. But he also knew that at her age one loves love itself rather than the object one bestows one's love upon. Therefore he took leave of her as his heart dictated. "Well, Esther," he said, "let's not be shy. I am going to kiss you." They embraced and kissed. That was the first kiss she had received from a man. For a long time she remembered the exact spot on her cheek where Mr. Shafran had planted his kiss.

✦ ✦ ✦

She rented a garret room in a four storey tenement in the centre of town, and very soon she transformed it into a neat pleasant corner which she could with pride call her home. She liked her room and in particular her roof window. Through it she could see a vast expanse of sky, and beneath it, the roofs of Lodz and the countless factory chimneys. The columns of smoke rising from the chimneys seemed to be leading a life of their own; suspended between sky and earth, they embraced and parted, collided and devoured each other, while engaged in a never-ending contest with the blue of the sky. Often they succeeded in creating an enormous blanket of gray and black, smothering the city beneath it. Even the sun lost out to the smoke which let the rays pass through the density of its nets only at the expense of their lustre and clarity.

Esther was now seventeen years old and she was independent. Her life acquired a new taste, a new rhythm. She had her work during the day, and the business of getting acquainted with the city, at night. She walked streets of whose existence she had never heard before. Suddenly she realized that she was the inhabitant of a city of a half a million people. It seemed to her that she had arrived here only now, from some remote village at the end of the world. Now she also had new friends and, most important of all, she had the party. She became a member of the K.Z.M., the communist organization of Polish youth.

Her heart throbbing, she would rush to her first illegal meetings. The atmosphere of these secret assemblies with the heated whispered discussions filled her with such awe, that sometimes, sitting huddled in a chair, she would become short of breath. At every noise coming from outside, a cold shudder would run down her spine, a feeling both morbidly stifling and pleasantly exciting. But as time wore on, her tension subsided, while her interest in the topics discussed grew. She read different books now, studying them with the diligence of a student about to pass an important examination. Her room was full of illegal publications, of history books, of books on the Russian Revolution, of the biographies of great revolutionaries and leaders of the working class.

She considered her joining the revolutionary movement an obvious and normal part of the process of growing up and maturing, and did not view it as a drastic change or a break with her former life. The piety and religious beliefs of Uncle Chaim's home collided in no way with her new faith; she thought of them as actually being one and the same. After all, Uncle Chaim and his family were poor hard-working people, sharing their crust of bread with others, and they dreamed, just as she did, of better times to come. What was new was the form in which her new friends described that dream, a question only of words and arguments. And at first she found it difficult to understand why her comrades attacked the "religionists" so vehemently. This had bothered her slightly when she was still "green" and soft, before she had managed to remake herself into the iron mould of the revolutionary. It had taken some time before her comrades succeeded in shaping her into that mould by convincing her that religion was the opiate of the masses, a means of keeping them ignorant, that religion is a power tool in the hands of the capitalists and the bourgeoisie. They began storming God's fortress in her heart and in time they succeeded in levelling it; while life itself lent a hand to its destruction. On the Sabbath she worked in the factory, and she no longer had any Friday nights with lighted candles; she had also ceased to say the daily prayer. Certainly the Sabbaths she had spent in Uncle Chaim's house lived on in her memory — but like framed pictures cut off and divorced from the life around them. These pictures were eternally fresh, eternally beautiful, but they had nothing to do with Esther's everyday experiences.

Trustingly, she let herself be guided by her comrades. They were strong in their wisdom, cheerful in their outlook on the future, and their attitude towards the present was reflected in positive action. They saved her from brooding, from becoming entangled in complicated thoughts. They offered her simple, ready-made solutions, formulated by minds more clever than hers, and all she had to do was to accept them. She did so, not blindly, but with conviction.

And then, apart from the questions of ideology, there were the excursions, the walks together and the singing of rousing meaningful songs. Of what importance then were the little faults she now and then perceived in her new friends? She loved them and thought that the little things which displeased her were things she did not as yet understand. She was grateful to them for having delivered her from her loneliness. She had an enormous family now, consisting of millions of members, and she had a fatherland — the Land of Socialism. The phrases she had repeated only mechanically at the start became the language of her soul; they coursed with the blood in her veins. At the same time, her spirit hardened. The sentimentality and softness of disposition, nurtured in Uncle Chaim's house and by Mr. Shafran and his books, retreated, freezing in the hidden depths beyond awareness, to come forth and melt her only in rare moments — in her moments of weakness. Now she had become hard as steel, clear in purpose, determined, and the possessor of an unbendable will. Now she also gave vent to her bitterness; the bitterness of an orphan who had never had a real home, the bitterness against Uncle Chaim who had enrolled her in the orphanage, the bitterness against Mr. Rumkowski who had taught her to fear and hate the strong, those who considered themselves masters over the lives of others. This resentment, freed from the locked prison of her heart, surfaced, and was now called indignation at the existing order of the world. Esther was ready to fight that order. She had become an accomplished revolutionary.

She was sent out to do party work, to distribute leaflets and to carefully carry out propaganda activities among the women workers in the factory. She was assigned to a cell of the "Pioneers", to conduct programs with the children. What she liked most, however, was to set out with one of her comrades at night and cover the walls and fences with revolutionary slogans in white or red paint, or to sling little red flags over streetcar wires, monuments and treetops. It gave her great pleasure to pass the same places on the following day and watch her flags flutter in the air and her slogans call from everywhere. "I have done this! This is my work!" she would boast in her mind, and proudly looking at the passers-by, she would feel like singing, like laughing. Of course, it did not always go smoothly with that kind of night work. More than once she had to run away before her task was finished. But even as she ran, her revolutionary zeal burned on. "I am running away," she would say to herself and to the empty street witnessing her flight, "but tomorrow I will be back!" And tomorrow she was back.

When she had Saturdays off, she would not go to visit Uncle Chaim and his family. It was a pity to miss out on a meeting, on a cell gathering, on an "action" or even just on a walk. And even when she could no longer bear her pangs of conscience and set out on a Sabbath afternoon for Baluty to visit them, it was no longer the same as it had used to be. Her cousins were now grown into pretty young women. They wore their long flaxen braids wound in a crown around their heads; but, in honour of the Sabbath each of them still had the usual firm lock of hair, the "love hook", dangling over her forehead. Nor had they changed much in any other way. They were still working from dawn to dusk at the hosiery machines or at finishing the stockings, waiting and longing for the Sabbath as before. And what pleasure could she, Esther, find now in lying on the bed, reading Czarska's love stories, or in playing bingo?

Bored, she would sit with them, listening indifferently to the same stories which had once fascinated her, to the gossip about events in the backyard or on the street. She would crack pumpkin seeds with her teeth and ask herself whether or not it would be rude to leave so soon. The cousins would look at her, smiling embarrassed, wondering how it happened that Esther had become so estranged from them. And if she tried to talk the girls into accompanying her into town, to meet her friends, or to go to a lecture or to a movie, they would complain that it was too far, that their parents would not like it, that all six of them had only two good pairs of shoes, that they would come home too late and be too tired for their own Saturday night party.

These little parties, still attended by the same young men of Baluty, had finally brought results. True, Baltche, the oldest of the sisters, tired of tearing the gray hairs out of her tresses, was actually an old maid by now, as were the two other girls who came after her in age. But the second of the middle ones, Sarah, was engaged. Too impatient to wait for her parents to save up enough money to marry off the older girls, she had made up her mind and chosen the finest young man among the visitors for herself. He had fallen so much in love with her, that he was ready to marry her without a groschen to her dowry. Nonetheless, there could be no talk of marriage yet, for the celebration alone was an expense Chaim could not afford. Still, the girls rejoiced in their sister's bridehood as if it meant the happiness of each of them, and there was practically no other subject of conversation in Chaim's household than the forthcoming wedding. As a rule, however, this topic was avoided in Esther's presence. Because on the day that they had enthusiastically announced the good news to her, she had told Sarah that if she really loved her fiancé, she would go off and live with him, and not wait for a superstitious ceremony to sanction her union with the man.

Esther reproached herself for not being able to kindle any enthusiasm for her beliefs, in her cousins, for not introducing her own optimism for the future into their lives. Whenever she tried to lead the conversation in that direction, carefully avoiding such words as "socialism" or "revolution", so as not to frighten them, but using instead their own language, the girls would sink into silence. If she were too persistent in her efforts, they would look at her in an annoyed, almost hostile way, and Sarah, the most outspoken of them, would ask coldly, "What good does your Union do, after all?"

"It organizes the workers against exploitation," she would reply cautiously. "It fights for a shorter work day."

"Against whom do you want us to fight? Who are our exploiters, our own parents? And if we worked eight hours a day, who would feed us? You?"

All afire and quite nervous, Esther would explain the meaning of such terms as "proletariat" and "capitalism", in her excitement forgetting not to call the "dangerous" things by their proper names. She spoke of small workshops like Uncle Chaim's, as promoting slavery and exploitation; and she would bite her tongue when she realized that her cousins had stopped listening to her, obviously deeply hurt by her words. Then Aunt Rivka would interfere. She would fill the plate with some more pumpkin seeds and try to cheer up both her children and Esther. "What good will come out of so much talking?" she would ask. "Sing something instead, children." But the children, embittered, did not feel like singing.

Nor was Esther's relationship with Uncle Chaim what it had once been. Of late he had grown more pious than ever, having come to the conclusion that all the worldly issues that had interested him were actually insignificant and that the only truth constant and eternal was the truth of the Talmud. His worries about making a living had diminished considerably, and his children now took more care of him than he of them. His one worry was to marry off Baltche and the rest of his brood, and he trusted to God that with the latter's help he would, in a blessed hour, be able to lead them, one after the other, to the marriage canopy. Consequently, he took less interest in Esther as well. As he relied on his own children to manage somehow, so he relied on her too. He was glad to see her looking well and healthy. Although the things she said irritated and annoyed him greatly, he tried, like Rivka, not to take them too seriously.

Only Aunt Rivka remained the same. She would still greet Esther with open arms, her eyes lighting up with delight at seeing her "blooming and shining as bright as the sun in the sky". She would notice every new dress Esther wore and would inquire who had made it and how much it cost, not out of jealousy, heaven forbid, but out of her motherly interest. And for her birthday, she gave Esther an umbrella as a gift, since she thought it an absolute must for a young lady living downtown to possess this accessory which was the highest expression of feminine elegance. (Of course, Esther would not think of going out with this gift into the street, for it was not at all becoming for a revolutionary to parade about with an umbrella.) Aunt Rivka listened to Esther's inflammatory tirades, as she had listened when Esther was small and chatted charming nonsense. She was still very curious about Esther's life and eager to know every detail of it. And Esther would gladly have opened her heart to her. But Aunt Rivka belonged to another world; it was as if she were speaking a different language. Esther knew that if she told her aunt what she wanted to tell her, the chasm between them would widen instead of closing.

◆ ◆ ◆

When Esther became intimate with Hersh, she stopped visiting Uncle Chaim's house altogether.

Esther and Hersh had known of each other's existence for a long time. Esther had often caught sight of the husky young man who looked as if he had been cut out of a poster on a factory wall somewhere in Moscow. She came to recognize his erect figure with the long hairy neck protruding from his open shirt collar which was spread out on the lapels of his jacket, in the fashion introduced by the poet Slowacki. She knew his blond hair, his bony jaw, his strong eagle nose and the powerful chin which gave his muscular face an expression of unswerving will power.

And he had come to recognize her, the shapely redhead, light and nimble in her gazelle-like walk. He even knew the greenish-blue colour of her eyes, which brought to mind not the greenish-blue of the sky, but rather that of a flame of fire.

Every once in a while they would run into each other accidentally, at a meeting or on the "bourse", the street corner where the comrades met to exchange information, or in a corridor of a workers' club, or in a coffee house. She knew that he was a communist, and he knew that she was one too. So when they met, they would exchange meaningful smiles, sometimes looking at each other longer and with more curiosity than usual, but soon forgetting the encounter, until they met again.

That year the First of May was a wet day; it was drizzling a thin watery snow and the sun, hidden behind the "seven skies", seemed to have no intention of leaving its hideaway. Esther dressed festively. She put on a new dress and clean underwear, as was her habit before going to a demonstration, in case a bullet hit her and her body were exposed to strangers' eyes. She put on her new shoes and pinned to her blouse the red carnation which she had kept fresh through the night in a glass of water.

She hesitated for a while, trying to decide whether she should put on her new hat as well, but then decided against it. She would look more like a revolutionary without it, she thought, and it would be a pity on May Day to hide the personal red flag nature had provided her with: her flaming red hair.

And so, coatless and hatless, she dashed down into the dreary city, heading for the illegal demonstration scheduled to start in a narrow side street, near Piotrkowska where the legal demonstrations of the Polish Socialist Party, the P.P.S. and the Bund usually passed by. She was late, having lost too much time on her festive preparations, and she arrived at the exact moment when the people stepped down from the sidewalks into the middle of the street. Panting, she plunged into the ranks as the march began and the "Internationale" was struck up, the red flags flashing by somewhere at the front of the demonstration. But before Esther had time to catch her breath, the crowd began to sway back and forth and people started to scatter in all directions. Police on horseback appeared at all the street corners; deafening whistles pierced the air. Police clubs swung over the heads of the demonstrators and the screams of those hit or caught were heard all around.

"Why don't you run?" a hoarse voice buzzed in Esther's ear. Someone grabbed her by the arm. She let herself be carried onward, dizzy and numb with fright, keeping her eyes lowered to her new shoes which were pinching her toes pitilessly. Limping hurriedly, she darted a glance at the man who was dragging her along with him, and she recognized him immediately. They made it to the street corner, but had to turn back. All the accesses to other streets were cut off by the police; all the house gates were bolted shut. Esther and the man were trapped. The only thing they could do was to hide in the doorway of a closed store. He pushed her into a corner, pressing himself against her. "No sense running," he hissed through his teeth. "I hope you know what to say at the police station." Nervously, he patted his pockets and drew out a pack of cigarettes. He had hardly managed to light one, when two policemen, swinging their clubs threateningly, dashed towards them. A hand like an iron plier manacled Esther's wrist tightly. Hobbling, she let herself be dragged off, feeling fully the cold air and the whipping of the wind through her blouse.

The paddy wagon was crammed. Esther stood glued to her companion who seemed not to see her. The muscles in his face tightened, the veins in his neck protruded; he stared through the barred grating of the tiny window, his eyes following the cobblestones which created oblique lines as they drove by in the opposite direction. Only once, when the wagon made a sharp turn at a curve and she fell against him, did he offer her a glance. She tried to smile, to show him how calm and courageous she was; however it aroused no response in him.

During her imprisonment, she thought of him incessantly, going over the sequence of the May Day events in her mind. She remembered the warm firmness of his grip around her arm, and she killed time by trying to recall his face with the blond forelocks full of snarls covering his severe rippled forehead, the deep arched wrinkles at both corners of his mouth, and his lips, broad, thick and full. Only the colour of his eyes was beyond her recall and she could not forgive herself for having overlooked such an important detail of his physiognomy.

Her stay in prison did not last long. Questioned repeatedly, she was consistent in her statement that she had just happened to be passing by the street in question when she was prevented from continuing on her way. And she had, of course, no idea of the identity of the man with whom she had been caught. Although the interrogators did not believe a word she said, they had no proof to the contrary, and since she had not as yet been registered in any of their books, they let her go, warning her that if she should again happen to be passing by those places where she was not supposed to be, and if she should again be forced to pay a visit to the police station as a result, she would be kept there somewhat longer than this time.

Free again, her first thought was to find out what had happened to the "stranger"; however, she did not know his name, and it was forbidden to inquire too much into the lives of comrades. She haunted the places where they had used to meet accidentally, looking for him; but he was nowhere to be found. Months passed. She returned to her routine existence and forgot about him. Again she went with other comrades to do night work; she attended illegal meetings, or strolled about with friends in the parks. She sang, frolicked, flirted. Once in a while, when a young man held her around the waist a little tighter, or looked into her eyes a little longer than usual, she would enjoy it, and take pleasure in her success; and with the limited means of coquetry permitted a proletarian girl, she would abandon herself to innocent pleasures through which she both calmed and awakened the woman within her.

One cool summer evening she was on her way home from work. Tired and hungry, she dragged herself through the streets, her gaze dull, hooked on to a distant point on the horizon where the night clouds were assembling. Someone blocked her way. Before she had time to come to herself, the "stranger" was holding her firmly by the shoulders. "How are you? Do you remember me?" she heard his voice coming from somewhere above her head. She was so stupefied by this unexpected encounter, that she was unable to utter a word in reply to his countless questions. She squinted. The memory of the cold May Day flashed through her mind, and she remembered the grip of his hand around her arm. Everything within her cried out to reach forward and embrace him; everything within her cried out to run off immediately. Beneath her lowered eyelids, her eyes were fixed on the creases of her slovenly working blouse. She knew that her hair was uncombed, that kinky threads of wool were still in its snarls; she was not even sure that her face was clean. She hardly heard what he was saying. At length he removed his hands from her shoulders. "I see you're in a hurry. Nice to have met you anyway," he shook her hand firmly and marched off.

She roused herself and began to run. The moment she reached her room, she fell upon the pail of water, filled the scoop and gulped the water down with big noisy gulps. The encounter with the "stranger" had set her on fire. She did not know what to do with herself and the surge of jubilation that came over her. Her room became too narrow to hold her swelling excitement. She washed, changed, fixed her hair and dashed down into the street. She wanted to see him again, although she knew that fate would hardly be so generous as to bring him to her for a second time the same day. Indeed, the city hid him from her eyes, but at the same time it was full of him. Her exultation did not subside.

She met him in the library the next evening. He was sitting at a table, flipping through the pages of a catalogue. She approached him. "*Servus*," she greeted him with a slight tremor in her voice. He reached out his large sinewy hand, all five fingers spread apart, to shake hers. "Today I'm not in a hurry," she said ill-at-ease.

He pulled the book she was carrying out from under her arm and thumbed through it. "You read poetry, I see," he grimaced. "If you absolutely have to read that stuff, then why not Mayakowski? He is a poet who knows what he wants at least. In general, my dear, there are more important things to do than to read poetry, don't you think?" He waited for her to nod agreement.

"Of course," she readily agreed. "But petit bourgeois weaknesses awaken in me sometimes, especially during the summer." She suddenly laughed a carefree, enticing laughter. The redness receded from her face, leaving a few blotches on her cheekbones which seemed to reflect the heat of her blue-green eyes. She took her book back from him and approached the librarian. "Give me something by Ehrenburg, anything by Ehrenburg," she whispered to him.

He gave her "Thirteen Pipes" which she had already read. She thanked him and returned to the table where the "stranger" still sat. He pulled the book out from under her arm again and opened it, glancing at the title page. "And tell me, comrade," he looked at her, giving her a chance finally to see the colour of his eyes; they were of severe but watery brown. "You don't read serious stuff at all? I mean Marxist literature? You don't study at all?" A shadow swept over his face; the furrows at the sides of his mouth deepened. "How is it that you find time for things like this?"

"I like good literature," she answered. "So I manage to find time."

He gave her back the book, stood up and took her arm into his strong grip. "Let's go for a walk," he proposed. It was an evening in late summer. The air was permeated with the sweet fragrance of fruits and wilting flowers. The "stranger" and Esther walked along the Allées. She felt the aroma of the air as acutely as if she herself were a garden releasing the exquisite scents into the evening breeze. She felt dreamlike, intoxicated. The husky man marching at her side, hands in his pockets, moved away and came close to her as they walked on. He seemed to be weighing something in his mind. At length he spoke as though through clenched teeth. "We Polish communists, still have a lot to learn. We've erred somewhere on our way, perhaps precisely because we have read too much of that so-called 'good literature'."

She knew very well what he meant. This was the painful misunderstanding which had bothered her lately, filling her heart with sorrow and shame — a problem she wanted so badly to understand and could not: the dissolution by the Comintern of the Polish Communist Party. This blow had confused her completely, as it had all her comrades. They felt shocked, lost, like children whose mother had no more use for them, who had thrown them out of the home and left them alone in the cold. Of course the comrades went on meeting illegally, doing their work and sticking together, because they could not go on living without each other, without the great ideals and hopes. But they were ashamed to look each other in the face. For how could they, if their most important leaders, the great party heroes of Poland had turned out to be spies and traitors? It was hard, almost impossible to believe it, but finally one had to, since otherwise these dangerous men would not have been condemned and annihilated in Moscow. But what was really beyond comprehension was the suspicion the Comintern had of the party membership itself, of each of the members individually. How could it be that they, the avant-garde of the Polish proletariat, the daring painters of slogans, the organizers of strikes, the devout agitators for socialism, they who were ready at any minute to lay down their lives on the altar of the sacred ideal — that they too had been branded by the Land of Revolution as provocateurs and servants of the Polish Secret Service?

"Perhaps we have no right to call ourselves communists any longer," she remarked in a whisper.

"Then we have to work to earn that name back again," he bent towards her as if to underline the importance of his words.

She wanted to say something but refrained. She had imagined their first walk together differently. He kept silent as well, pacing by her side, hands in pockets, moving away and coming closer to her. Now and then he would turn his head to glance at her, as if to make certain that she was still beside him. In that manner they reached the end of the Allées and took leave of each other.

Their accidental encounters began to occur more often, and the walks they took grew longer with every meeting. The silence which had crept in between them during their first walk, remained. One of the reasons for this might have been that they had met in bitter, unfortunate times when words were about to lose their meaning.

To Esther, Hersh seemed like a wounded lion carrying a poisonous arrow sunk deep into his flesh, who walked around himself and chased his own tail, looking for the shaft and unable to find it. Only once had she met him when he was relaxed, even cheerful. That evening he had recalled the days of his imprisonment, "I fell asleep and had a pleasant dream. A redhead came to visit me. She had a white face which glowed in the midst of a burning forest of hair. Her face looked like a lake, transparent, mirror-like. In it I saw two slivers of eye revealing a bluish green suggesting the colours of fire. Very dangerous slivers, or rather deep chasms." He came close to her, burying his nose in her hair. "Into these abysses a tired wanderer happened to fall . . ."

His words poured down on her like a sudden torrential rain on a hot summer's day. She mustered the courage to take his hand. "And you say that you dislike poetry."

"Should I tell you what you probably know already?" he asked and squeezed her hand with his large hard fingers, moving his face closer to hers. But then he stopped short. "No, I don't dislike poetry, but there is no time for it. The time hasn't yet come." He thrust his hands into his pockets and resumed his habitual manner of walking.

The silence during their walks continued. However, it did not weigh heavily between them. Esther felt quite at ease with it, since she had no clear notion of what he expected or wanted of her, and she considered herself utterly devoid of any talent for intellectual coquetry. It seemed to her that what he felt towards her was nothing but a vague sensual attraction of no deeper meaning. Sometimes she thought that this was good enough for her, at other times, she felt hurt. She asked herself why he never inquired about her life, or her work. But then she shrugged off all these questions as nonsense, convinced that he knew much more about her than she could tell him in words. The silence between them was filled with looks, with a touching of bodies, of fingers — and perhaps this was the most non-deceptive and the only exact language possible.

In very rare moments, he would put his heavy arm around her shoulder and stare at her as if he were seeing her for the first time. "Who are you?" he would ask.

"Who am I?" she repeated his question in the same tone of voice.

"You are Esther." This apparently sufficed him.

Weeks, sometimes months would pass when they did not see each other. He would disappear from town, and she, running to look for him, would find him nowhere. She felt that she had fallen into a void. Lodz was like a ghost town, dead and empty without him. She would run to cinemas, to kill one evening after another, quite often leaving in the middle of a film, impatient, indifferent to the fate of the characters appearing on the screen. Nor was she able to talk with her comrades, or read a book. She wanted to sleep, to sleep through the time of his absence. But she could not sleep. She would lie awake on her bed entire nights and go over in her mind all their walks, all their short conversations. She counted all the looks he had given her, all the smiles, and she longed for the touch of his lips on her hair.

By then she knew his family name. She also knew that he was on the editorial staff of an illegal publication, and she was frightened. Every time he disappeared, she was sure that he had been imprisoned. She had visions of him in the detention camp at Kartuz Bereza. She indulged in self-torture by recalling the accounts of comrades who had come back from that "paradise" for political criminals. There was no doubt in her mind that Hersh deserved a long "vacation" in that infamous "health resort" for his sins. And when, her mind full of these dreadful fears, she met him suddenly, her surprise and delight were so great, so sharp and painful, that they became almost unbearable. Then, instead of questioning him, of talking or laughing, she would resume her mute walks by his side as if nothing had happened.

There were also long tiresome days when, after she had filled her evening hours with party duties, she would be too weak to face the disappointment of not finding him, since they never made any appointment, but left their meetings to chance. On such days she would feel like a roulette player who had no courage to lose. She stayed in her room, mended her stockings, washed her hair or cleaned up, or she forced herself to concentrate on a theoretical work he had given her to read. At the same time, her thoughts would run their way, beginning pleasantly and cheerfully, but most often ending in anguish and despair. Her acquaintance with Hersh gave her an acute tormented feeling of happiness paired with a premonition of loss. At the same time, she could not help but see him as a figure in a muddled dream, enigmatic, incomprehensible. He was still the "stranger" to her, and she felt lost in him as on an enormous stormy sea whose shores she was unable to reach. Often, in order to shake off the insistent repetitious notions obsessing her, she tried to hang on to the thought that she was only imagining that something unusual was happening between them. She tried to convince herself that he was a comrade just like all the others. But she could not fool herself.

When Esther and Hersh met again, tired of their loneliness and of their need for each other, they would ask themselves again, "Is it love?" They would wonder about their past longing and know that tomorrow they would long again.

✦ ✦ ✦

Eventually, he had to find the way to her little room and to her everyday life. Esther feared his coming, but without reason. He felt at home right away, as if he sensed that he had actually lived there for a long time; that the walls and every corner of the room had recognized him the moment he confronted them physically.

During those days in January, Esther and Hersh ceased wondering and asking themselves questions, forgetting that they had ever done so. Nothing between them had been clarified and yet everything was clear — as clear as the curtain of ice and snow which separated them from the world. They were like mountain climbers who had reached the top of the mountain, with no road left to lead them higher up. They prayed that they might remain on the peak forever and not be punished by the descent downhill. They wished time would stop.

It did not. The snow heaped on Esther's window sill turned darker and darker. Transformed into mud, it gradually slid down into the street and allowed reality to pierce the naked panes. The turbulence of the city outside climbed up to the garret and dragged it down to earth. The world was approaching trying days, so was Lodz, and so was — love. In Hersh's caressing hands, the pulse of those anxious days began to hammer again. Calm vanished from his eyes, guilt and confusion quivered in them. Every kiss he gave was the kiss of a sinner, almost of a criminal. He grew restless and took her into his arms less often. He did not say so, there was no need for him to tell her, but the time for "weaknesses" was past. The armour had to be put on again. Hard matter-of-fact strength was the order of the day.

This time Hersh did not keep silent as he would have done before. He paced the narrow room for hours, exploding with vehemence, "Swallowed Austria! Devoured the Sudeten! While here the national flags fluttered in the air. What jubilation! Just fancy, the long-enslaved town of Szczecin is ours again! The dog-catcher has tricked the dog into the net with a little bone! Do you remember how the papers praised healthy Polish diplomacy? Woe and shame to us! And how long ago was it that Göring went hunting in our forests of Bialowieze? Meanwhile Mr. Hacha delivered the Czech people into the hands of the devil. And now it's our turn. The suffering of the German people in Eastern Prussia must come to an end, and Danzig and the Corridor must return home as well!"

Sometimes his tone of violent despair changed into one of exaggerated optimism. He spoke of the Soviet Union; never before had the liberation of the people of the world seemed as near as now. "You will see," he would grab Esther by the shoulders, "one bright morning, the Red Army will move past this town. The great march towards the liberation of the world will begin with a breathtaking sweep, just as it says in our songs. The Bastion of Revolution is on guard, don't you worry! That's why there is no news from there. The silence before a storm, that's what it is! Just think, they will march on and on; a red avalanche, carrying the entire international proletariat with them on their way. Armies of liberation will spring up in every country. Even the Germans, yes, especially the Germans will muster their courage and overthrow Hitler and his gang of bastards!"

Often, when he began pacing in this way and talking, Esther would cling to him and try to shut his mouth with kisses. She wanted to protect their love. She caressed him more daringly than ever before, and when she noticed that his thoughts were elsewhere, she would try to call him back with jests and laughter.

She figured that he probably thought her stupid not to take note of what was going on around her. But she had stubbornly set her mind on avoiding subjects which had no direct bearing on their life together; and she so badly wished that all the things he spoke about would have no such bearing. Eventually, she achieved what she wanted, at least as far as his talking was concerned. Silence set in between them again, but not the kind of silence they had once known. Their previous silence had been loaded with intimacy, this time a void divided them.

Spring arrived. The air carried the promise of bright days and of soft nights, of blooming trees and sprouting grass. The city opened up, unlocking its doors and windows to make itself familiar again with the outdoors. And although the newspapers fluttered like black crows from hand to hand, people immediately forgot their warnings. It was May after all, and it was impossible to pair the sunny re-awakening of nature with the morbidity of the alarming tidings. The outdoors calmed people's nerves and alleviated the burden of premonition in their hearts. They refused to believe in anything but the resplendent sky. That was the only truth — and they let themselves be cheated by it.

Esther was pregnant, but she had no opportunity to tell Hersh about it. She rarely saw him, and when she did, he no longer had ears or eyes for her. He would make love to her with something akin to hostility and run off with his nerves taut, his mind distracted. Often, when she was expecting him, a message would arrive with a few words and an address where she could write to him. She waited for a moment of peace and calm between them, so that she might embrace him, or at least look at him with a smile. But there no longer were any such moments, and it was becoming increasingly difficult to keep the secret to herself.

She would come home from work when the day was still bright. She would eat her meal, change, take a book and go down to the Allées. But she could not read. Waves of oppressive thought swept over her. The longer she carried her secret, the more she feared to reveal it to Hersh, afraid of what he might ask her to do. She knew that she would not be able to obey him — ever. As she sat there, enveloped in thought, the sky turned ink-dark and the first stars appeared. She heard snatches of conversation as people strolled by her, heard the rustle of light summer dresses and the sound of the breeze in the tree branches. The surrounding air of carefree abandonment made her feel the burden of her worries all the more heavily.

Finally, she could no longer restrain herself and told Hersh about her pregnancy. The result was not as beautiful and romantic as she had hoped, but neither was it as bad as she had feared. After she had told him, he sat down at the table and drummed on it mutely with his fingers for a long while. Then, averting his eyes, he said, "*Mazal tov*," rose, and left the room.

They were still estranged, but he came more often to see how she was. He would say a few nervous sentences to her and run off. On the slightest pretext he would quarrel with her, or heap reproaches on her for not having seen a doctor, for running around too much, for not waiting for him but bringing up the pails of water herself. Every trifle made him lose his patience — and Esther felt good about it. She smoothed his creased forehead with her fingers and kissed his full broad lips. But her calm would enrage him even more. He would chase her away from him, avoid her caresses and leave without saying goodbye.

The summer days chased one another with amazing speed, and every day drove Esther further away from her surroundings, from the life in the street. She built a fence between herself and the world, hearing everything, fully aware of what was going on — but not letting it reach her. True, she could not become like Hersh, hard and armoured with determination to face whatever may come. But she was strong in her own way. She had her "secret" and she had Hersh. She felt his presence everywhere. His heart throbbed in the rhythm of the city; his smile greeted her from children's faces and the sun in the window brought her a message from him every morning. She was so completely full of him, that she did not mind his impatience with her, or his absence. She was sorry that he was so nervous and worried, but she could not share those moods with him. She thought that if she were only able to talk to him from the depths of her heart, from the source of her hope, she would be able to convince him that everything would turn out well. But she could not talk to him.

It was precisely at that time that he moved in with her. Along with his books, he brought a bundle of clothing, and a suitcase with his most important documents and writings. Esther was radiant. Now, when she opened her closet, she could see his suit in it. From the shelves, his books looked at her. From the walls, his few pictures greeted her, and outside, in the shed, lay his hidden treasure: the suitcase with the important papers. She did not ask for more. At night he came home, restless and irritable — but hers. He began to talk her into leaving the city and spending some time in the country. "Do it, not for yourself, but for the . . . thing," he would say in a rough tone of voice.

Enchanted by the care she sensed under his harsh tone, she obeyed him, packed a knapsack and left for the workers' colony. There, she celebrated her incipient motherhood. She opened up completely, laughed a lot and sang. Somewhere at the end of distant roads lay sultry Lodz with its nightmares, while here, between the enormous sky and the luscious earth, was real life. The half-naked members of the colony took their collective meals at crooked rough-planked tables. The intoxicating fragrant air reverberated with their shouts and laughter; the plates and cutlery participated noisily in the general outpouring of exuberance. It might have seemed as though heathen orgies were carried on here.

Esther came to like the sound of her own voice and she would sing all day long, surprised at the clarity of tone issuing from her throat. She walked the open green pastures, not knowing what to do with herself and with her overwhelming joy. Her "secret" reigned over her powerfully, triumphantly. Now she knew that her loneliness had come to an end forever. As she lay stretched out on the grass, her face buried in the blades, she inhaled the intimate smell of the soil, along with the smell of the new life sprouting within her — making the unknown the most familiar part of her being. And Hersh was nearby. As the sun burned her arms and fried her back, she felt him close by her, as if he were lying beside her in the pasture and she had only to let her hand wander over the grass to reach his cropped hair. She had only to prick up her ears and she would hear his voice coming from the murmuring forest beyond the river, telling her with whispered words of his yearning for her. But what did she need words for? She knew everything.

On bright nights, when the campers set out, arm in arm, for a walk; when one languorous song extended into another, with Esther lending her voice to the chorus, she refused to think of how good it would be to have Hersh holding her arm instead of someone else. She felt that it was he who held her arm, and no one else. On her return from the walk, she would stretch out on the soft straw in the barn where she slept with the other girls, unable to close her eyes for a long time. She would look up at the slanted roof and listen to what was going on in her body, until the morning twitter of the birds nestling between the beams under the roof rocked her to sleep.

The four weeks in the country passed by like a dream. Too soon the moment came when everything had to be left behind and a return made to the turbulent stuffy city which was choking with the anguish of a queer incomprehensible August.

The sultry streets, the snarled traffic, all seemed at first glance to be the same as usual, but they were not. The city shuddered in the heat like a sick person running a high fever. Apprehension hovered over Lodz. On the walls at every street corner, were pasted posters and bulletins; restless sweating crowds clustered in front of them. While still at camp, fragments of the news had reached Esther's ears, but then it had all seemed foreign and remote, so that now, as she walked the streets, reality hit her in the face with a shock. She did not stop in front of the placards, but hurried home, impatiently climbing the stairs leading to her room. Her body seemed enormously heavy, as if it were being propelled upward only by the loud throbbing of her heart.

The room was a mess, the bed unmade, piles of newspapers lay strewn about on the pillows and blankets. The cupboard doors stood open; the drawers were pulled out. The table was cluttered with glasses and cups of unfinished tea and with dirty pots. Esther felt faint; her head spun, but she tried to pull herself together to receive Hersh. Soon a neat tablecloth covered the table and on it stood a glass holding the bouquet of wild flowers she had brought along from the country. The drawers and the cupboard doors were shut, the bed was made and the papers were put away. However, despite the order in the room, peace of mind failed to return to her. Her eyes were still full of the light of the countryside, she still carried the fragrance of the fields in her nostrils, and her skin, baked brown by the sun, still burnt on her back — but fear engulfed her. She lay down on her bed and shut her eyes. Something moved inside her, and she had to respond to it with a smile. Tenderness relaxed her heart and limbs. The world began to retreat. She drifted off to sleep.

A draft tore the curtains apart and swung the window wings on their hinges. She opened her eyes and saw Hersh. There was not a trace of summer in his appearance. Through the unbuttoned shirt collar his muscular neck and a part of his hairy chest shone with an unhealthy autumnal yellow. His brown eyes were covered by a shadow and looked almost black; around them the skin was loose, bluish and creased. Esther shrank, preparing herself to fight against his looks, against his words.

He sat down on the bed and put her head on his lap. "How are you?" he asked, burying his large hands in her hair. To feel him so close was happiness. It was as if, by lifting up her head and putting it on his lap, he had pulled her out of the swamp of anguish. He showered her with questions. For the first time since they had been together, he wanted to know everything about her, down to the smallest detail. "And the place itself?" he inquired. "Is it close to a forest or to a river?"

His questions intoxicated her and she replied tipsily, "Very close to a forest and to a river. I had my own little corner there, a place where the river loses itself in the grass and the water almost stops running. There I stretched out, close to the shore, face towards the sky. I spread my arms as if I were swimming, and . . ." She was about to say more, but the rumbling of airplane engines could be heard overhead. There was probably a large number of them, for as the planes neared the house, the window panes began to clink with the echo of their heavy roaring and the building shook. Esther realized how silly it was to talk about all these things now. But Hersh stretched out his hand and pulling the casements partly shut, asked her to go on. She noticed a kind of imploring undertone in his voice, which disarmed her. She cuddled still closer to him and resumed talking. "Every morning I took a long walk. On both sides of the road were fields of rye, with a sand path between them, on which I walked. The rye reached above my head when I sat down and shut my eyes. I heard the sheaves pass over me like the waves of the sea. I called my baby, and it answered me with the push of a hand, or the kick of a foot against the wall of my belly, as if it were telling me, 'Mother, I'm on my way.' But then I gave up my walks. Harvest came." Her voice broke, tears appeared in her eyes and streamed profusely down her face. She pressed herself against Hersh as if trying to bury herself in him. His lap shook with the spasms of her chest. "What's going to happen now?" she asked in a quaver.

He lifted her with an abrupt gesture and made her sit up. Looking her straight in the face, he said, "A directive has arrived. I'm going east. Tomorrow. Early in the morning. I was supposed to leave yesterday, but I was waiting for you."

She felt the bed falling away beneath her. "And I?" she screamed with the panic of someone overlooked in a rescue operation. Frenzied, she clung to his neck with her hands.

"You're staying." He slowly freed himself from her arms and looked at her severely. "What happened to your self-discipline?"

She fell back on the pillow, all the strength drained out of her. But then, in her weakness, her heart began drumming against her bosom: she must not remain in Hersh's memory looking like this! She needed her strength to be courageous now. "I am not such a weakling as you think," she whispered, letting the tears wash her face freely for a little while longer. "I'm only nervous. Give me your hand." She took his hand and placed it on her protruding abdomen.

He leaned over her. "What shall we call the child?" he asked.

She wiped her face. "I've been thinking about it a lot," she whispered. "Both of us have no parents; why then choose the name of one and not the other? I've thought of the name of a hero of the revolution, of the movement, but again, why favour one over the other? A name just happened to cross my mind. It sounds nice, a bit unusual. How about Emmanuel? How do you like Emmanuel for a name? I mean . . . In my mind I've been calling him by that name. What do you think?"

"I think it's fine . . . the way you pronounce it. It sounds powerful, a name that would suit a son of ours." His eyes smiled both tenderly and proudly, suggesting the way that he would one day look at their child. "And what if it's a girl?"

"In that case we'll sugar it a bit. We'll call her Emmanuela, or Mania . . . or Ella." She roused herself, wiped her face once more and climbed out of bed. She pulled out the assorted items of a hand-sewn layette from her knapsack and spread them out on the blanket. "I didn't go idle in the country, as you can see," she said, ironing out the frills and folds of the baby clothes with her fingers. "Don't you think they're cute?"

✦ ✦ ✦

The following day they tried to retain the calm and composure they had forced upon themselves the day before; but it was difficult. Words became stuck in their throats and every remark intended to be cheerful came out from their mouths like a groan. It was almost time for Hersh to leave for the train station and he still had many things to do. Although his clothes were packed in no time, he could not make up his mind about the contents of the suitcase he had kept hidden in the shed. He fingered the piles of paper, unable to decide which to take along, which to burn, and which to leave with Esther.

Esther helped him as best she could; she stood at the stove and fed it the manuscripts, documents and pamphlets which he had finally decided to burn. At last there was only a small bundle of papers left at the bottom of the suitcase. "Listen," he said to her hurriedly, pointing to the suitcase. "Take care of this for as long as you can . . . but no longer."

She forced herself into her Sabbath dress which was much too tight on her; but she wanted to look nice for him. She threw a jacket over her shoulders and took him by the arm. Down in the street, she leaned her head against his chest and felt him touching her hair with his mouth. She wanted to say something to fortify him as well as herself, and she raised her eyes to him. "You'll see, Hersh," she said, "this trip will turn out to be even shorter than all your previous ones."

"Why?" he smiled faintly.

"Because the Soviet Union . . ."

He cut her short, looking her up and down with a pair of ice-cold eyes. "The Soviet Union has more important things to do than return your lover to you."

"I don't mean . . ." she stammered, dumb-founded. "I mean the liberation of the peoples of the world . . ."

"For the liberation of the peoples of the world you have to make sacrifices. It won't come as easily as you want it to. In a world of double-dealing and falsehood, revolutionary zeal and a desire to free the nations of the world isn't enough. You have to fight the enemy with his own weapons. Don't you understand?" Indeed, she did not. She had not the vaguest idea of what he was trying to tell her. She bit her lips. Stumbling over her own feet and leaning heavily on his arm, she let him drag her along. "Politics, Esther," he went on in a strangely unpleasant tone, "has become a part of our revolutionary tactics. Times have changed. It is no longer a question of ethics to walk a certain distance hand in hand with the enemy. You cannot conquer a world of swindle and brutality with purely ethical principles."

She puckered her eyebrows. "What are you talking about, Hersh?"

He realized that she was not aware of the latest turn of events, and he informed her flatly, "A pact of non-aggression was signed in Moscow between the Soviet Union and Germany."

They had arrived at the railroad station. From all directions mobilized soldiers and their relatives were flocking to the platform which swayed with clamorous feverish crowds. Trains packed with soldiers were pulling out, just as others were making ready to leave. Hersh's train, designated for departure in the opposite direction, to the east, was practically empty. Esther and Hersh climbed the steps of his car, not knowing what to do or what to say. Esther's mind was still working, trying to digest the news he had announced to her just a while ago. But she did not want to waste their last precious minutes on questioning him about it. The clamour around them was unbearable. An orchestra played sprightly military marches over and over again. People were running to and fro in all directions, screaming and wailing. Handkerchiefs fluttered in the air. Hundreds of pairs of eyes, misty, tearful were hanging on to the windows of the departing traincars.

The locomotive of Hersh's train began to heave. The sound of a whistle pierced the air. It was time to part. Hersh put his arms around Esther and kissed her tear-washed face. She could hardly keep herself on her feet. "Emmanuel is his name," he said, helping her to climb down the steps. "I will call him by that name." Before she had time to utter a word in reply, he let go of her, jumped into the wagon and vanished from her sight.

The train began to move. She searched the passing windows with her eyes, hoping to see Hersh in one of them; but he was nowhere in sight. Then, the train was gone, revealing the glistening tracks in the pit. She stared at them as she trudged along the platform, jostled and pushed about like a rag doll. A young soldier, late for his train, came rushing straight at her, pulling his preoccupied mother along by the arm. Neither of them noticed Esther, nor did she notice them. They lurched into her, pushing her to the side. She fell down, the upper part of her body hanging off the platform, dangling over the pit and the tracks as over a precipice. Someone's hands grabbed her by the tight Sabbath dress. She had no idea of how she found herself on the street again.

The same afternoon her labour pains began. It was four weeks before her time. It seemed to her that she had known all along that something would go wrong. Yet she was calm and composed. She was on her way to the city hospital. It drizzled unpleasantly and a wind swept through the streets, lashing the passers-by with early-withered leaves and grains of dust. She staggered slowly ahead, her heart unable to free itself from a sudden longing for Aunt Rivka.

She had to wait a long time for her registration in the hospital. She was given a chair and was left sitting there. While she waited, she did not think of Hersh, nor of herself. Everything within her was concentrated on her ballooned belly and on the pain taking hold of her now and then. When she was free of it, she watched the nurses hurrying busily past her. There was something dainty and soft in their energetic movements, in their serious faces, calm and reassuring like those of nuns. She caught the sound of someone's warm laughter. Behind a door bleated the voice of a newborn baby. From behind another, issued the talk of women who had just become mothers. The small wheels of the medicine cart squeaked intimately on the mirror-like floor. A telephone rang somewhere. And from still further away, in the delivery room, a sharp shriek pierced the silence. This was all there was. This was the whole world. There was nothing beyond it.

The figure of a doctor clad in white loomed from afar, coming closer. He approached Esther and they scrutinized each other. He was young, with a pale face and a pair of serious expressive eyes. He exchanged a few words with the receptionist and then turned to Esther. "I am Dr. Levine," he introduced himself and took her by the arm, helping her to get up. "I will be taking care of your delivery." He led her off with him.

Later on, when she was lying in bed and the cramps had momentarily ceased, she thought of the young doctor. The outside world with its pettiness, its hatred and struggles, with its moods which came and went like the seasons of the year must appear strange to him, she mused. Because here, in the doctor's "workshop" there was no doubt about the meaning of life. And in her mind she smiled to the pale young man who would help her bring her child into the world. She was involved with him, united with him in a sacred union, as though in a certain way he too had fathered her child. And as she thought about him, she recalled some lines of a poem about Prometheus which Hersh had remembered from his *gymnasium* years and would quote on entirely different, more prosaic occasions. "Here I sit and form man after my own image . . . a race which resembles me . . ." She felt as though the poem had been created in Dr. Levine's honour; that he was indeed like a young god.

But then, suddenly, the verse and Dr. Levine vanished along with the entire world. The light of the day turned into darkness; the darkness lit up with sparks of a breathtaking pain which refused to let go of her.

When she opened her eyes again, it was all over. It was morning, but she had no idea of what day. She felt the emptiness of her torn body, but the ache was different from what she had felt during the long hours of darkness. Her thoughts were clear, yet she was aware that their clarity was strange and unreal. She knew that the tree outside, which peered in through the window, washed by the rain, was not white, nor green, but gray and naked, and that it was one tree, not many — but it nevertheless seemed to be a green forest, then a white one, covered with snow. And the dream she was still dreaming although wide awake smelled at one moment of the fragrance of sunbaked fields, and at another of the January air in her garret room. A frightened enormous clock pounded in her heart, in her veins, in her entire body and she did not know whether it indicated the dawn of life or its dusk.

She felt Hersh's face against her swelling breasts. With broad eager lips he reached out for the nipples from which a white life-sustaining light was supposed to shine forth. Her fingers began to tremble, moving nervously about the blanket. It seemed that all the discomfort of her empty body was concentrated in her own fingertips which searched and were unable to find what they were looking for. "Emmanuel!" she called through the forest at the window. Her face, her skin longed to touch him. Her arms stretched out to embrace him. The large bed became increasingly narrow in its emptiness.

For a moment she regained consciousness and noticed the other beds in the room. Around each of them people were assembled. Someone bent over the neighbouring bed, stroking the wet worn face of the woman in it. "Why is she crying?" Esther wondered. A tall, skinny fellow waved a newspaper over a bed across the room, saying something about men of his age being mobilized.

She heard everything, but understood nothing. She kept on searching with her hands around her body. She was feverish. The entire room seemed covered with snow. But then it took on an air of festivity. She looked at the man who had grown out of her and heard his full wise mouth whispering, "Mother." She saw Hersh's handsome body; but then she saw tiny hands and legs growing out of it, his head becoming small and bald. Then it grew again; the tiny arms became Hersh's arms and his voice came back to whisper, "Mother."

By the time she had completely recovered from the narcosis, it was late in the evening. The windows were blinded with dark patches of sky. In front of her stood Dr. Levine, his face looking much older than it had looked the day before, as if he had skipped over many years in that short fraction of time. He looked upset as he sat down on the edge of her bed and took her hand in his. "Courage!" he said, and it seemed to her that someone had said it to her not so long ago; she strained, collecting all her strength to remember who it was.

"I'm not such a weakling," she whispered. "I'm only nervous."

"I would have waited for another day or two . . ." Dr. Levine stroked her arm. "But because of the situation at hand . . . and we need the bed. You probably have someone to take care of you for a while, don't you?"

"My baby!" she screamed. He looked her straight in the face. His mild eyes were like two stilettos piercing her through to the marrow of her bones. "Mother!" another shriek issued from her insides. This was her own call for help; it was Hersh's call; it was the call of a dying baby.

She was sent home by ambulance, carried up to her room on a stretcher and placed in her bed. Realizing that she had no one to take care of her, the kindhearted orderly who had come with the ambulance provided her with a few apples and a quarter of a loaf of bread. He also set a glass and a pot of water at her bedside. He inquired if she had a husband or any other relatives and, unable to get any answer out of her, left the room.

Days and nights passed by, timeless, hourless, empty. She knew that she had come to the end of her road and did not mind it. All the threads which had kept her tied to this world were cut; she was tired of her twenty-two years of life and longed for peace. However, one morning, as she was staring in front of her, the door of her room acquired the shape of some important familiar object, and the suitcase with Hersh's papers came to her mind. From that moment on, it would not let go of her. She remembered her promise. She had to keep it.

Now her hours were filled with schemes of how to save the treasure. All her mental faculties were at work, and when her alertness faltered and her thoughts fell into the black circles turning in front of her eyes, she sustained herself with a bite of apple or of bread, or with a sip of water. "I am not such a weakling," she whispered to herself. Finally, of all her plans, one appeared realizable, and of all the familiar faces one remained that she had to see immediately: the face of the *gymnasium* student, Rachel Eibushitz, whom she had used to meet in the library while waiting for Hersh. She recalled the conversations they had had, how they had talked about books, recommending this or that book to each other. When it had become clear that Rachel was a Bundist, they would indulge in heated discussions, each of them thinking of what a gain it would be for her party to win the other to its cause. With this in mind, they had shown a kind of sisterly concern for each other, as if each had had nothing but the other's good in mind. They even exchanged addresses, but never made use of them. The library had been the only place where they ever existed for one another.

Esther congratulated herself on her clever idea. Her own comrades were under suspicion, unsafe at all times, since they were communists. But Rachel's party was beyond danger and there would never be a search in her home. Esther also knew that the girl had respect for literature and for the written word in general. Who could take better care of a person's manuscripts than she?

Esther dragged herself out of bed, jotted down a few words on a piece of paper and called in a boy who had come up to play in the attic. She begged him to deliver the note to Rachel's address and, that chore finished, she went back to bed, relieved that she had freed herself of the great burden. All she had had to accomplish was done.

When Rachel arrived, she found Esther listless, hardly breathing. She bent over her and shook her frantically. Aghast at the sight of Esther's limbs falling back like blocks of wood, she stared at her, then she rushed towards the window, opened it wide, and let the cold air enter; then she dipped a towel in the water pail and dabbed and patted Esther's face and arms, until the latter gave a sign of life. Finally, she rushed down into the street to look for a doctor. She found a barber-surgeon who promised to come.

She waited for him for many hours. At dusk, he appeared, a short fattish man wearing spectacles. Sighing and panting after his climb of four flights of stairs, he had to sit down and catch his breath before he was able to attend to the patient. The examination took him quite a while. Then he moved the spectacles up to his forehead and turned to Rachel with reproach in his voice, "She has just had a delivery. Why didn't you tell me right away?" Blood rushed to the girl's face, she stared at him, her eyes and mouth wide open. He asked, "What is she to you, a sister?"

"No, nothing. An acquaintance," she mumbled, utterly at a loss.

He grew impatient, ordered her to shut the window, sat down to catch his breath once more, and drummed his fingers against the table top, as if expecting something from her. "She needs to eat well and to have a lot of rest," he said and then burst out, "And what about paying me for the trouble?"

Stupefied, Rachel blinked at him. "I don't know," she mumbled. "I have no money."

"And what do you know, silly goat?" He jumped to his feet, grabbed his shabby instrument bag and, grunting madly, left the room.

"Did Hersh come in?" a faint whisper issued from Esther's mouth.

Rachel could not make out the name Esther had uttered and she asked her to repeat it. "Say, Esther," she shook her, "who is it you mentioned? Do you have anyone, relatives, or someone you want to see?"

Esther whispered in a far-off voice, "I have no one."

Rachel lit the stove. She found some food in the cupboard and prepared a soup which Esther devoured eagerly, keeping her eyes on the girl. She could not recall who the girl was.

Rachel left in a hurry, knowing that her parents would worry about her.

When she returned the following day, Esther recognized her immediately. Before Rachel had time to take off her coat, Esther said to her, "I sent for you . . ." She stopped short, unable to remember why she had sent for Rachel.

"You did well," Rachel busied herself, lighting the stove. "I brought you a quart of milk and Mother sent you some pancakes." Rachel was amazed at how greedily Esther devoured the food. Never in her life had she seen anyone eating so eagerly, so savagely. Esther gulped down a large part of the milk almost at one swallow. But then she stared at the remaining milk in the bottle. An expression of pain appeared on her face. Although she still drank eagerly, it seemed as if every gulp hurt her.

The sight of the milk brought Esther back to reality. Suddenly, she knew everything. She was aware of the food spreading warmth throughout her body; she felt it colouring her cheeks, strengthening her heart, and she wanted to keep on eating and drinking. But a brutally clear voice sitting like a demon within her, ordered, "Stop eating! Stop drinking!" All her limbs called back to the voice, "But I want to!" The voice inside her denied it, "No, you don't! There is only one thing that you want." And she knew what it was. She raised her eyes to Rachel. "I sent for you. I have a suitcase that I want you to keep safe. I want you to take it home . . . Important manuscripts. A comrade, a communist . . . Remember the library? I used to meet him there. You'll recognize him, find him . . . when all is over. I beg of you."

"I don't understand," Rachel stared at her. "Where is he? And why are you giving the suitcase to me?"

"He's gone . . . had to leave. " Esther stirred abruptly, roused herself, and leaning on her elbow, grabbed Rachel by the hand. "What's new? Where is the Red Army now?" Then she went back to her pleading. "You'll take the suitcase, won't you?"

Rachel straightened herself. "I don't understand a thing you're trying to tell me," she said resolutely. "Why can't the suitcase stay with you?" But then the truth dawned upon her. "Oh, I see," she exclaimed. "You think you're dying, that's why." Esther shut her eyes. Tears appeared on her eyelashes. Rachel grew impatient with her. "You've made up your mind already, haven't you? You give your heirloom away and good-bye, sweet world. Is this what you have learned throughout all these years, my great revolutionary?"

Esther fell back on the pillow, moving her head from side to side. "You don't understand. I can see you're afraid . . . You don't want the risk. Go in good health."

Rachel put on her coat. "All right, I'm going," she said drily. "But I'll be back later. I won't leave you alone."

"It's true, isn't it? You don't want to take it?"

"Of course, it's true!" Rachel, nervous, stooped over her. "I'm afraid for my life, for my family's lives. You have no idea what's going on in town. All the men are being mobilized. Any day now they might call my father. And we . . . we burn books and documents all day long; the whole town is shivering with fear. And here you ask me to take your suitcase full of manuscripts. No one will take it from you, believe me, not even your comrades, that is, if any of them are still around." The expression on Rachel's face softened. She stretched her hand out to shake Esther's, adding with a superior, wise smile, "If the papers are so important to you, you have to go on living, so that you can take care of them yourself."

Tears were streaming down Esther's face. "And what about the pact between the Soviets and Germany?" she asked.

Rachel's smile became wiser still, "We'll talk about it some other time."

Esther pulled her by the hand down closer to her face. "You know," she whispered, "I was supposed to have a little boy. His name was going to be Emmanuel."

"Emmanuel?"

"That's what it was supposed to be."

"Do you know what that name means? If my Hebrew is correct, Emmanuel means 'God is with us'."

Chapter Nine

(David's notebook)

Friday the first of September, at six o'clock in the morning, the Germans crossed the Polish border. Between Friday and Wednesday, life turned upside down. The Germans advanced, taking one town after another. Against seventy German infantry divisions and fifteen armoured divisions, we put up a pitiful army. We lacked armoured troops, motorized units and adequate air defence, so that shielding a border of more than two thousand kilometres was a ludicrous proposition.

It was not long before we saw hordes of our beaten soldiers and caravans of wagons overloaded with injured men dragging through the streets of Lodz. Crowds of people clustered around them and followed behind in funeral-like processions. The people handed out water, food and candy to the tired soldiers and questioned them about the battle front and the fighting. But the soldiers were reluctant to answer. Women wept, men shook their heads and sighed. In the houses, relatives were mourning for those who had left to fight and had not returned. Supplies of food were prepared and stored for the hard days to come. Hardly anyone went to work. People gathered in the streets, to discuss the situation. Neglected children ran astray and got lost in the crowds. It seemed like a long holiday, unpleasant, nevertheless exciting. Then the news hit the city like a thunderclap: The Germans were heading for Lodz!

Halina and I had been burning books. They were Father's treasure, and with them a world of wisdom went up in smoke, with us lending a hand to its destruction. It was already dark outside when our parents came in. Nervous and absent-minded, they wandered about the apartment. Father came up to us. "People are leaving town," he said as if asking for advice. Father, a union leader and a Bundist councillor, had to avoid falling into German hands at all costs.

"Then you must leave too," I said to him.

Abraham came in, his arms loaded with toys. "You see," he said to me. "I found all this in an empty room. Many things are lying around. Whatever you want, you can take."

We sat down to eat. No one said a word except Abraham who could not stop talking about the wonders happening in the street. Before long, we rushed down into the street again. The street lamps were not lit and the windows of the houses were covered for the blackout. It was pitch dark and difficult to discern people; everyone blended into the darkness; only the faces shone like pale moons. Although I saw many people and listened to much talk, it seemed to me

179

that the town was eerily silent, holding its breath. On my way back, I met Father and Halina. They told me that Leon, Halina's fiancé, had left for a conference with the leadership of the P.P.S., and that he would come back with some concrete facts about the situation. We would decide what to do then.

That is how that night started. Except for Abraham, no one went to bed. As for myself, I dozed off at the table. I wouldn't call it sleep, since what I remember, although seen through a haze, is clearly imprinted in my memory.

I can see Father as he stands at the window, looking out into the night. The city is both asleep and awake, just as I am. Lodz is having a nightmare. I hear steps, many steps on the sidewalk. Running. Voices calling. A car rushing noisily by. Doors banging open, thumping shut. Father sits down at the table opposite me. I feel the book that my arm is leaning on slipping away. My copy of *Horace*. Father is thumbing through it. I hear him ask in a whisper, "Halina, what does this mean?" He pronounces the words in such a funny way that they sound like Turkish.

"You have to scan it. It's Latin poetry," I hear Halina answer.

Father gets up, paces the room. "What did Horace mean by that?" I hear him asking again. He does it just to say something, to kill time. He drums lightly on the window pane with his fingers. "Why don't you answer me, Halina?"

I hear mother saying, "Look, Isaac, a bedbug under the picture." Of late we have had few bedbugs in the apartment. Before we left for the country, Mother had smoked them out of their holes and they had not come back until now. I dream of our summer cottage. We are fooling around. Halina and Leon take their long romantic walks with Lord, the farmer's dog, following them. Sometimes they come home without him and Abraham and I race off to the forest to find him. At night we sit with Mother on the bench in front of the house, singing. Or I wrestle with Leon while Abraham rides on our backs. As I see all this, sitting with my head buried in my arms, I am quite aware that all this belongs to the irretrievable past; yet it seems more real to me than anything happening right now. The present seems a muddled dream.

Then I hear Halina exclaiming, "It's the landlord and his whole family! They're leaving!" I hear the sound of a car engine; a car door slams shut. Somewhere a clock is chiming. Three o'clock. I hear Father's voice above my ear, "*Exegi . . . monumentum . . . ere . . .* Perhaps you'll enlighten me, Halina? You see, the word *monumentum* I understand. But the rest is Chinese to me."

"What's happening to you, Father? What do you bother me with that for?" Halina says impatiently. Indeed, what's happening to him, I ask myself. Why is it so urgent that he knows this now? Poor Father. I hear Halina burst out, "It means, 'I have built a monument for myself, stronger than bronze and iron, than palaces and pyramids. No storm will destroy it, nor years, nor generations of time. I have not died completely. A major part of me will live on into eternity . . .' Garbage!" she exclaims. I hear her thrust the volume onto the heap of books which are ready to be burned tomorrow.

I hear father say, "What are you so mad at the book for? Don't you think that the words are quite appropriate for the occasion?" The nagging devil within him speaks through his mouth, I think.

Then we rouse ourselves. The stairs squeak. As we come to the door, Leon pushes in against us, his eyes darting frantically over our faces. "We have to leave immediately," he says with urgency in his voice. "The city administration has left already, the police too. Start packing, quickly!" He continues pàcing the room and talking. "The army is retreating. The Germans will enter Lodz tomorrow or the day after. There is not a minute to lose. All the men have to run. Everyone is heading for Warsaw." Does he mean me, too, I ask myself, watching Mother and Halina rush about the room, opening cupboard doors, pulling out drawers. Leon continues his monologue, "I don't envy the men they find left in the city. (My heart gives a jump.) Warsaw is still defending itself. Going strong. We can all make ourselves useful there." Halina, with Leon's bundle in her hand, approaches him as if ready to embrace him, but he pushes her away, saying, "Hurry up, pack some bread or whatever you have. It's getting late."

Mother hands Father a bulging bag. Two elongated shadows merge on the floor. Halina and Leon take leave of each other in the kitchen. I sit on the sofa; my heart is pounding. Father embraces me, then he walks over to the bed and kisses Abraham. I jump to my feet, but stop short in the corridor. My parents say good-bye to each other. The door opens, then thumps shut — behind Father and Leon. I lie down beside Abraham. In my mind I accompany Father and Leon. I run along with them. I run and I run . . . Then I hear Mother's tear-soaked voice, "Am I going to deliver my child to them with my own hands?" I have no idea whom she has in mind. But then I feel her shaking my shoulder. "David, get up! You have to run!" She doesn't stop shaking me. I get up. She pushes a parcel into my hand along with a five zloty bill and shoves me into the kitchen where Halina sugars a glass of tea for me. Both of them stand close to me, following my every gulp with their eyes. Mother's eyes are the colour of the tea I am drinking. I feel as if I were swallowing her gaze; it burns inside me and makes my heart feel hot. But then, as if a curtain were drawn apart in Mother's eyes, I see Rachel's eyes inside them.

"I have to say good-bye to Rachel!" I call out and before they can say a word, I am out of the house.

The backyard is in an uproar. Neighbours, loaded down with packs and valises, emerge from the stairways. The streets are turbulent, the people in them look hypnotized, like lunatics with burning eyes. Laden with luggage and dressed in their best clothes, they look like travellers on their way to a wedding, who are afraid of missing their train. I race ahead, thinking of what to say to Rachel. I ask myself what will happen to her, to Mother, to Halina and Abraham if the Germans enter Lodz. I arrive at Rachel's house and start to call her down by whistling our usual tune (the first bars of *Avanti Populo*), but it seems somehow out of place.

I find Rachel's door locked. She has probably left during the night with her family, I think, and race home again. Lost in thought, I don't notice the fellow coming towards me and run into him full force. He pushes me down onto the pavement. "May the cholera take you, dirty Jew!" he offers me his blessing. I scramble to my feet and run on. For the first time such words don't impress me. I rush into our backyard and up the stairs. Rachel comes out of our apartment, wearing her blue suit and new shoes. She falls into my arms. "You have to hurry," she says.

I look at her closely and see a sad misty cloud in her eyes. "And you?" I ask.

"We are staying," she answers. I feel like sitting down beside her on the steps and resting for a minute, like putting my hand on her shoulder and saying something to cheer us both up. But she pulls me by the hand, "Come on. Your mother is coming down. You'll say good-bye downstairs." I am about to tell her that I don't want to run away, that I would rather stay with her, with Mother, with Halina and Abraham, and let come what may. But I don't say it. Downstairs, in the entrance, I pull her towards me, to kiss her, but I hear a noise on the stairs. Mother and Halina are coming down. Mother gives me the parcel she has prepared for me, and takes me into her arms. From the other side, Halina embraces me, kissing me on the cheek. Rachel watches us from a distance. Now I will kiss her, I decide. I free myself from all the arms holding me and approach her. She shakes my hand. "So long," she whispers as if we were to see each other tomorrow. Her face is wet and I have no strength to take her in my arms. I turn around and run off.

◆ ◆ ◆

The street resembles a restless river. Masses of people sway like waves between the banks of the houses. Now and then the "river" splits in half, letting through a wagon or a rumbling car. New streams of people pour in from the sidestreets, and the further we go, the denser the crowd becomes.

At first, the clamour, the groans and wailing deafen me, but after a while I no longer hear them. I let myself be carried onward, feeling that I am still asleep at home. At the same time my eyes take in everything around me. The sky, clear and deep, seems more distant than ever. A poetic description of a sunrise comes to my mind (or to my dream), and I begin writing a composition in my thoughts, about what I see. I choose nice literary expressions, but soon I run out of them. How can one describe such ugliness with pretty words? My vocabulary is too poor to sketch such a sight. Which brings me to the conclusion that only great writers are capable of finding the right words to describe not only the sky, but also the earth. The earth can be as beautiful and poetic as the sky, but when it is not, it is a thousand times uglier.

Meanwhile the people around me begin to undress, gradually peeling off articles of clothing and discarding them. All the elegant outfits look like rags on the ground; they make walking harder still.

The sack of my neighbour on the left is comfortably propped against my shoulder. At my back, the situation is even worse. The woman behind me holds a clothes wringer in one hand, a little girl clutching on to the other. The clothes wringer prods me in the back as if it had made up its mind to cut me exactly in two. Finally, I decide to get acquainted with her. Poor soul, I think of the woman, she is probably a washer woman, a proletarian. How she presses the heavy wringer, her work tool, to her bosom! If I were a true socialist, I reflect, I would help her carry it. I turn my head and say, "If the lady wishes, I will help her . . ."

She jumps at my unexpected words; her forehead ripples like a washboard as she presses the wringer tighter to her bosom. "Never mind," she groans.

But I am obsessed by the urge to help her and don't give up. "Then, please, let me take care of the child."

An ugly grimace disfigures her face as she heaps a torrent of curses upon my head. "Will you leave me alone, you snotty Jew! If not for you and the likes of you, it would never have come to this, thieves that you are! May the earth swallow you forever! Jesus Maria! Wherever one goes, the scabby lot of them follows like rats, pfui!" And she spits.

Her words strike me like a whip. I am on the verge of throwing myself at her, when a head in front of me turns and I see a face with a pair of Jewish eyes. "Button up your mouth and don't say a word," comes the friendly advice.

I am glad to find myself in the company of Jews. "You are right," I say to the man, ready to strike up a conversation with him. But he has turned his head back and is walking on with his two companions. "Mister," I touch his shoulder. "Do you know what time it is?"

The Jewish eyes look at me again. "Perhaps you'll take your dirty paws off me, eh?" he says, and I realize that I am doomed to pass along this road in loneliness.

Meanwhile the houses at the roadside disappear. The air is fresher. The stream of people flows out onto the highway and into the fields on both sides. From a side road rumbling wagons come abreast of us, raising the dust. On the wagons sit soldiers in unbuttoned dirty uniforms. Their hands and faces are black. They look like scarecrows, strange, spooky. Staring at them, I imagine the lost battles; I hear the blast of cannons, the buzzing of grenades, the roar of airplanes. They, the soldiers, are coming from there; they have experienced it all.

The sun burns with increasing intensity. I walk through the field. At the beginning I turn my head back to look at the disappearing houses, but later I no longer do so. I know there is nothing. In front of me, a forest comes into sight, fringing the black and green rectangles of field which look like a spread-out quilt. In the middle of the fields are scattered trees. How picturesque! Everything looks so calm, so idyllic. The entire business of escaping seems foolish, an act of sheer idiocy. The clear sky appears to be looking down at us in amazement, the trampled fields gaze in wonder; and the sun seems to mock us.

The past summer comes back to my mind: the cottage, the little river, the dog Lord. I remember the two days when Rachel came to visit me. We went to fetch the milk and watched the farmer's wife milk the cow. A few days later Father came out with the order to pack everything, and the fun was over. Now I walk through the fields and ask myself if things will ever be as they were then. But then I wonder whether what was past had indeed been so wonderful. How many times had I wished for a change? What happiness did my parents have in their lives? Money was always hard to come by, and how hard it had always been to save the few zlotys rent for a summer cottage in the country. And were it not for our good brains and our ability to support ourselves, Halina and I would never have set foot in a *gymnasium*. Moreover, at the university, Jewish students were harassed, while the *Falanga* and their like, who borrowed their "ideology" from Hitler, marched boisterously through the streets.

"Do you really want to go back to that life?" I ask myself. "Didn't you ever dream of new times? With how much longing did you utter the word 'revolution'!" In times of peace, every revolution is doomed, I think. Against the enthusiasm of barricades, there are bombs and tanks nowadays, and they are in the hands of the mighty who have the power. A revolution can be victorious only in times like these, when the masses are armed. Then they can aim these arms against those who have put them into their hands. The German people have probably waited secretly for this very moment. They might arise any day, overthrow their tyrant and form a socialist republic. Other nations may follow suit. Then the "Last and Decisive Fight" for a better world will begin. The people will discover one another in brotherhood. Poles and Jews will fight side by side and build a new life together. I will study at the university and so will Rachel. We will go for excursions during vacation, to the mountains, or to the sea. Maybe we will own bicycles and go for long rides like Maria and Pierre Curie.

These thoughts intoxicate me. I forget where I am and feel neither fatigue nor loneliness. And when I wake up from my daydream, I see the crowd of which I am a part, and it no longer seems strange and unfriendly. After all, these are the people with whom I shall be dancing and celebrating in the streets any day now.

Then, suddenly, the earth quivers. A heavy crashing roar splits my ears as if entire mountains had moved against us. The highway twitches and jerks, as if seized by convulsions; then it becomes paralyzed. A black forest of airplanes covers the sky, heading straight for us. The shadows of their wings cover the wash of sunlight like black shrouds. I hear a crash, then another and another. The people, petrified, fall, then scramble to their feet. They dash from the highway down to the fields, from the fields to the highway. One stumbles over the other as they crumple in heaps, their mouths torn open in shrieks of anguish; soundless shrieks you cannot hear, like the grimaces of actors in a silent movie. The roaring of the planes swallows everything. The highway is strewn with corpses, the crazed horses gallop over them, pulling the wagons along. Small groups of people huddle in the fields which look as they do at the end of the harvest, full of living sheaves. The planes, with their drunken cha-cha-cha, mock us, the helpless little animals who cling to the earth, seeking its protection, while lying on it in the sunlight like bull's eyes on a target.

I have never seen airplanes flying so low. I lie stretched out on the ground and when I raise my eyes, I can see every scratch on their wings, every line of their swastikas. My teeth chatter. I want the roaring to stop. I block my ears with both hands. Then I see one of the airplanes speeding at me. I cover my head with my blazer. A thunderclap makes me jump to my feet. I run into a curtain of smoke. The ground sways under my feet; it pulls me down into deep pits. It lifts me up to newly risen mountains.

Then there is silence. The last airplanes sink behind the forest. Stillness. Slowly the people dispersed about the field begin moving among the corpses of horses and men. Someone dances along the highway, raising two fists in the direction of the forest. A madman? "You'll get what you deserve, you bastards!" he yells. Others join him, "God will repay you, you bloody dogs! You will run from here like poisoned rats, you murderers!" Actually, these are screams of joy at having saved one's life and not having lost any dear ones. Those who have lost someone don't scream. They lie in the field over the warm ripped bodies, aghast at the work of black magic they have witnessed, unable to move from the spot. Somewhere a child howls and gasps.

The marching resumes. I think of Father and Leon who have to be somewhere on this highway. What happened to them? Where were they during the bombardment? I must run after them and find them. I quicken my steps. Now and then my feet get caught in the clothes of a corpse lying near the ditch. I disentangle myself matter-of-factly and walk on, wondering at my indifference. I have never seen a corpse so close before. Now I am so much in death's company that it will suffice me for a lifetime. One thing becomes clear to me: there is still the fear of death in me, but I have learned to look cold-bloodedly at death's finished product. Is this a sign of having matured?

I pass the town of Bzezin. Strange to enter a town deserted at midday. On a porch I see an old woman; she whimpers, crossing herself, "Dear people, look at what happened to us." I march on, leaving the town behind me. The sun is setting, the air turns gray. In the half-darkness the wailing of children who have lost their parents and of mothers who have lost their children sounds uncanny. Long shadows spread over the fields as the air turns cool. Evening approaches. Now we can clearly see the results of the bombardment. The red light on the horizon, which I thought was a nice sunset, stays on to fringe the pitch dark sky and encircle us with a flaming hoop. I feel a dull heaviness in my legs. My head sinks towards the ground. My lips are swollen, grains of sand crunch between my teeth. I am thirsty and dream of open faucets, of wells running with water . . .

I notice something growing in the field. Beets. I take off my blazer and fill it with as many beets as I can. I bite into one. Dirt cracks between my teeth. My mouth becomes rough, but I keep on chewing. Having lost my food package during the bombardment, I am glad to have at least this supply with me. I think about how to spend the night. Home seems very far away, and with it, the good times when I slept in a bed, with a pillow, a slice of sky peeking in through the window and sometimes winking with a star or two. Now I have an enormous sky above my head and there is no place to hide.

A pair of eyes stare at me out of a young fellow's round face. He looks funny, wearing a large loose overcoat with a fur collar, probably picked up somewhere on the road. "Give me one," he says and puts his hand on my blazer. I give him a beet. "Why do you walk around half-dressed?" he asks me, starting to kick the rags strewn under our feet. At length he picks up a fur coat, shakes it out and opens it up for me. "Put your delicate little hands in this," he says. I wrap myself in the coat. In the dark, I see his red moustache painted on by the beets and I burst out laughing. He looks at me and does the same. "With that beet-red lipstick and the fur coat you look like Greta Garbo," he says.

"And you look like a Cossack chieftain with your majestic coat," I shoot back.

He takes my empty blazer and pushes it into one of his enormous pockets. "Like that," he beams, taking me by the arm. "Like bride and groom, so that we don't lose each other." We continue arm in arm and arrive at another little town with empty streets; patches of darkness are framed in windows of the dead houses. We, the thousands of black shadows, proceed along the dead streets, mirrored in the black window panes like ghosts. It all looks like a spooky backdrop for a mystery play. I feel as if I were not myself, but someone else, someone lost in a dream. I can't hear my own steps nor those of my companion. He says, "Let's go in somewhere and get a drink of water." He motions to a house. We enter it and move along the walls. We stand over a pail and drink from a scoop. I put the scoop back in its place and chide myself for doing so. What sense does it make to put the scoop back in its proper place, or to close the door carefully behind us? It's no more than a habit belonging to another era. "Perhaps we ought to go into one of these houses and sleep in a bed?" I hear my companion asking.

"No good," I reply. "If it were safe to sleep in these houses, the people wouldn't have left them in the first place."

We are back in the fields and stop near a hole between two heaps of dirt. "It looks like a grave," he says.

"No, like a bed," I say and let myself down into the pit. He follows me. We sit, our knees drawn up to our chins, not having the wits to lie down. I put up the soft collar of my fur coat and bury my face in it. My eyes burn as if I have been crying for a long time. I shut them with delight and think of nothing.

In my slumber, I hear someone speaking Yiddish: It's the voice of a child and sounds familiar. I open my eyes a crack and see two silhouettes, one big and one small, passing by our "grave". I recognize Yossele, Abraham's friend. I jump to my feet and call him. The child comes towards me with a howl, "Have you seen my father?" The tall man accompanying him moves hurriedly away. The boy clings to me. "Oh, David," he wails. "I lost my father in the field, when the bombs came down."

"Who were you walking with before?" I ask him.

"I don't know. He saw me crying and took me along to Warsaw. He said I will find Father there." I take him down into our "grave". "Who is that!" the boy burst out, feeling a body under his feet.

"My name is Bronek," my companion introduces himself. We wrap the boy up in the tails of our coats while he tells us his story in a whining voice. A wind sweeps over the field. The boy shakes like a leaf. "It would be nice if we had a scarf or something for his head," Bronek says to me.

The boy reminds himself that he has a scarf, and pulls one out of his pocket, saying in a whimper, "Mother said I must take it. She wanted to come too. 'What happens to you, will happen to me,' she said to Father. But Father said that someone has to take care of the furniture or else the Germans will take it all away. And Father said that the Germans shoot only the men, but the girls they leave alone. Father wanted me to stay too, but Mother shouted that I had to go."

I wind the scarf around his head and neck, listening to his story with only one ear. I think of my mother. I am glad she is not here, nor Rachel, nor Halina and Abraham. What madness, all these thousands of women and children scattered around us on the road and fields! I can understand the men escaping the enemy, they will make themselves useful in Warsaw by fighting for the city. But women and children, what for?

We begin to feel the dampness of the ground. We get up, take the boy by the hand and run to the nearest house. We find some bedding and take as much as we can carry back to the field. We find another "grave" and bury ourselves in it upon a heap of pillows and eiderdown covers. We are settled for the night.

It is quiet in the field; practically no one is moving. On the horizon the fires are still burning, a pageant of red and black on the sky. A night bird warbles, crickets sing stubbornly in the grass. Toads croak. A dog barks. The boy lying between me and Bronek is asleep. And I? I think of what I did a while ago: I entered someone's house and took someone's bedding. In the old life it would be called theft. Now it did not look like theft at all. So should we take it all back tomorrow morning, or should we leave it with the many abandoned things lying around? I laugh at myself for these "ethical" thoughts and realize that actually I am already asleep. But then I hear Bronek asking me what my name is. I tell him. Then he says, "I cannot sleep. I keep thinking of my mother. My father died two years ago. He was an invalid, lost his leg in the war with the Bolsheviks. We had a newspaper stand, Mother and I. I'm her only son." I hardly listen to him. The wind blowing through the field makes my thoughts scatter. It occurs to me that all the people lying here are probably thinking of their homes, of their mothers, just like Bronek and I, just like homeless children.

Bronek keeps on talking. I answer him, but am not sure if I do so in reality or in my dream, in which I am thirteen or fourteen years old. A rare evening with Father at home. I am back from my private lessons. Father is playing chess with me. Leon is kibbitzing. It's easy for me to mate Father. He doesn't seem to mind it. He is proud of me. I play another game with him, trying to mate him even faster, so that it will hurt him. Mother sits at the table mending socks. Abraham scribbles in his smudged exercise book. Halina is lying on the sofa, repeating her Latin grammar in a whisper. I mate Father again and Leon takes my place. I pull out Mayer's Encyclopedia with the help of which I study German. I sit over it for a while, until I become impatient and grab my cap. "Oh," I hear Halina's little laugh. "Where are we going at this hour of the night?" I see her winking at Leon. Our parents have a smile hidden in their eyes as well. I don't mind. I rush down to meet Rachel, ready to reproach her for being late. I see her coming from afar and forget to get mad at her. We walk the Allées holding hands.

It's painful to think of Rachel here, on this distant cold field. I cannot forgive myself for not having kissed her before I left. I would have felt better if I had. A desire to see her grips me. Tears run down my cheeks. I am really crying. "Rachel," I call her, "I love you very much." I whisper her name over and over again, and the more I do so, the closer she seems to be, until I have her at my side. She smiles a twinkling smile. We are in a huge park. The trees whisper overhead, flowers smell sweetly, crickets are singing and little dogs bark.

✦ ✦ ✦

Suddenly — I am deaf, I am blind. Have I gone mad? An extraordinary force lifts me to my feet. I run over the field. The sky blinks on and off with fire. A wild sequence of blasts breaks the world apart. Black wings rattle. The earth shudders, spitting up dark soil and columns of smoke. I hear the screams of people as if they were coming from my own insides. Bombs explode one after another. I am swept forward like a piece of paper by the wind. I fall and jump to my feet. Around me fires lock with one another, the field blossoming in the darkness with monstrous burning plants. They loop around me; no chance of getting out. I constantly stumble over soft slimy heaps. In the reddish light the open protruding eyes of corpses stare at me; they bare their teeth. I scream and don't hear my own voice. My legs don't belong to me, nor do my outstretched hands. A completely alien heart hammers inside me, about to crush me to pieces. "Now your end has come!" it drums.

I see a few trees which don't seem to be on fire and dart towards them. Magnificent flaming rockets like multicoloured Christmas trees illuminate the way for me, making my blood curdle. I run up against a tree and embrace it as though it were a dear friend. But then I am met by a sea of eyes. Face after face shining in the reddish darkness. I plunge into the middle of the cluster of bodies. What a pleasure to feel surrounded by so many live people! But I am no longer able to move and begin to doubt my safety. Can these few trees protect us? And as if in answer to my thoughts, I hear a dry roar above our heads. A blast rips my eardrums apart. Again I am deaf. Nonetheless, I hear a scream, "Machine guns!"

"Machine guns! Machine guns!" An echo reverberates in my intestines which are in the throes of unbearable cramps.

"Tick-tick-tick," the clock of death counts time. Around me people fall into one mass of bodies, of limbs. "Jesus Maria!" I hear voices. "God of Israel, oh, listen! Mother! Mother!" People call their mothers and I call mine — with my intestines. I am pressed to the ground and cannot move. But all I feel are the cramps in my stomach. "Run, people, run! the bullets are coming straight at us!" someone bellows.

"Don't run, people! Don't move!" someone else shouts.

The people have gone wild and along with them — I and my rumbling belly. The most important thing in the world is to free myself of that discomfort, no matter what. But I am paralyzed; and so, paralyzed, I relieve myself on the spot, saying good-bye to life and to all my dear ones. I begin thinking that the worst of all fears is that of someone who is part of a panicky crowd. You are like a helpless worm, aware that you are about to be trampled and are unable to do a thing about it. And so, urged on by a violent impulse, I begin kicking, yelling, "Let me out!" I shove with my elbows, shaking off one body after the other as I raise myself, biting, scratching, kicking. I climb up, stepping upon limbs, bellies and backs, until I am free and able to run.

As I run, fear leaves me. I stop short and lift my head. Airplanes like huge silver ducks drop a rain of gigantic eggs. "This is my last night," I say to myself. I am amazed at my sudden unconcern, having just a while before frantically extricated myself from the crowd, to save myself. I stretch out on the ground. "Here I am, you strong ones!" I call to the silver birds up in the air. "Come and enjoy your victim, you fearless ones!" I have agonizing visions of becoming one with the earth, my flesh and blood fertilizing it, making it fat and rich. I see a farmer during peace time coming with a plough to plough the soil. Rye and wheat will sprout from me. Isn't that a worthwhile purpose for my mother to have brought me into this world? But then a furor ignites within me. "May you burn! May you perish!" I lift my fist to the shadowy bird heading straight at me.

I cannot look. I turn and bury my face in the ground. With my hands I cover my ears which are bursting with pain. But the roar goes through my hands, piercing holes in my brains. Smoke winds around me, thick and heavy. It penetrates me, weaving me into its web. I am entangled by a thousand thick cords which wind themselves from one ear to the other, through my eyes and nostrils, through my hands and legs, unreeling through my belly, knotting around my chest, tightening around my heart. "Mother, help me! Mother, I'm dying!" I scream — and then I see her coming, a glass of tea in her hand. She hurries towards me, but the airplanes block her way. She climbs over them. "Where are you, David?" she calls. "I am here, on the ground, tied down!" I yell. But I see her disappearing with the glass of tea in her hand. "So everything is over already," I say to myself, and feel that there is nothing keeping me tied any longer. "I am dead." I state the fact. But then I see Mother again, pouring hot tea into my mouth. "Get up, David," she says to me. "Drink up your tea and run!" The glass slips from her hand, tea spilling on my face. It feels pleasant on my cheeks. "Thank you, Mother," I say, "but please, let me sleep. There is no school today."

When I wake it is full day. The sun burns my cheek; the fur coat is wet with sweat. Slowly, I sift out the facts from the net of my dreams. Yes, there was a bombardment in the middle of the night; and Bronek and the boy — what happened to them? Then I remember the few trees where I hid. There they are. Among the trees — a hill of corpses. The field looks like a huge messed-up bed. On heaps of soil, like on black pillows, the dead lie asleep.

From the highway lively sounds reach me. The multitude flows by swiftly, almost cheerfully. How come, so many are still alive, I wonder, and scramble to my feet. Every limb aches. My feet are swollen, covered with bloated flesh. "Alive, nevertheless," I say to myself, "which means that all is not over yet." This thought gives me little joy. Anyway, something has died in me during the night; something has left me never to come back. What? I don't know and don't feel like breaking my head over it. I am exhausted, hardly able to stagger on. I glance at every corpse, looking for Bronek and Yossele. I remind myself of Father and Leon. Perhaps they too are lying somewhere in the same field? I don't think about them for too long. My sole purpose is to find something suitable to change into. I kick the rags of clothing strewn about the field. I am lucky. I find a pair of pants, even ironed, looking brand new but soiled. I jump into a pit and change. Then I totter towards the highway. The noise there seems almost gay. What happened? And why are they all going in the opposite direction? I hear someone saying, "At least now we will be safe from the bombings."

I hear another voice answering, "But whether they will allow us to reach home remains to be seen."

Everything is clear. We are going back. The man walking beside me puts his dirty hairy face close to mine. "Don't worry," he says. "If we are allowed to make it, we can sleep in our own beds tomorrow night."

"But why?" I ask.

"Why? Because the Germans, may the devil take them, have blocked our approach to Warsaw. A shameful provocation the entire business of leaving Lodz, that's what it was. The Germans spread the panic themselves, so that the civilian population would drag along with the soldiers and prevent them from reaching Warsaw."

"Poland is done to death," I hear someone sigh.

My heart is light. Right now, I don't care about the fate of Poland. I am happy to be going home. But as I drag on, cheerfully and hurriedly, I hear a dull subterranean roaring, a muffled rumbling. The highway begins to shake and the crowd turns jittery. "They're here!" someone screams and the throng quivers. "The Germans!" a frantic scream issues from all the mouths. The mass of people rushes down into the fields. Clouds of dust come into sight, and close behind them a black snake stretches its coils with great speed along the road, sliding in our direction. Countless wheels are rolling, turning fast, hurrying straight at us. The first two motorcycles appear. Green uniforms, green helmets, and then: swastikas flashing, piercing the eyes as they scream down from the passing tanks, the armoured trucks, from the motorcycles, the uniforms, the helmets. An erect forest of pointed guns moves on and on.

"May you burn! May you perish!" a voice shrieks inside me and my eyes become moist. I pray for a miracle, I beg for other airplanes to come, for other bombs — ours — to hit upon the victorious green snake on the highway. What a magnificent sight that would be, to see with one's own eyes these tanks, these engines of war, these stiff figures in green uniforms bursting into flame, exploding and soaring up into the air!

Gradually the crowd begins to move onward (which means backward). I think of a boy who became a Jewish king and who was called David, like me. How easily he had killed Goliath and won the war with the help of his sling shot! Yes, the meek like to invent such stories and thus strengthen their self-esteem. And what would little David have done if he were here, in my place, his heart as full of hate as mine? What would he have achieved? He would tell me that a few thousand years ago, God had helped him in his heroism. Then I would ask him where the eyes of his God are now. Why does He not see the field full of corpses where so many innocent defenceless people have perished? Why doesn't He perform any miracles now? "No, dear David," I call out to him in my heart through the thousands of years dividing us. "I don't believe your childish story. To conquer power you must have power. What use can I make of my rage if I am hardly able to remain on my feet, if with one bang of a green arm I collapse? And all that mass of people marching here, what can they accomplish against one barrage of machine guns?" But then I begin thinking not of God, but of man, of the English and French armies. And I become hopeful again. They will come to help us. We are not completely alone and all is not yet lost.

In the meantime, the people marching through the fields become increasingly daring; they climb onto the highway, edging along its border like a crowd lining up to watch a parade. Everything gradually begins to look peaceful again. The people seem to lose their memory, forgetting that last night's fire from the sky had come from the same source. Some even exchange smiles with the green uniforms, others wave their hands. From a truck, a green arm throws candies and the hordes fall upon them like packs of dogs. (Forgive me, you dog species, your memory is certainly not so short.)

I too walk on the highway, observing the march of the two peoples, one victorious, the other conquered. I think. I philosophize. I see Europe as if it were a chess board. I plan strategies. I lead armies, scheme attacks, celebrate victories. But my thoughts are interrupted; the crowd around me becomes fidgety. And before I have time to realize what's going on, I see single German soldiers darting into the mass of people, stopping one man here, there another, inquiring, questioning. Suddenly — a hand on my shoulder, a green uniform blinding my eyes, "*Jude?*"

"*Was?*" I raise my head, make a friendly face as if I were dealing with a stranger in town asking for information. I strain my memory and mobilize all the bits and pieces of the German language I have learned from Mayer's Encyclopedia. It is unnecessary. The hand gives me a vigorous shove into the ditch where I do a few somersaults before scrambling to my feet.

"*Kommen Sie! Kommen Sie!*" Another green uniform is waiting for me in the field where a guarded group of Jews is assembled. A German guard laughs at me; he even calls his comrade to join him in the fun. "*Sieh mahl diese hübsche Dame im Pelz!*"

His comrade refuses to join him in his laughter. He grabs me by the collar, almost lifting me up in the air. "*Ab damit, Judensohn! Das stinkt doch. Wahre Seuchengefahr!*" I take off the coat. Both soldiers wipe their hands with their handkerchiefs. I hear a few shots. Someone runs through the field, arms outstretched, then falls down.

They line us up five in a row and we begin walking along the field, darting stealthy glances at each other. "Where are they taking us?" someone asks in a whisper.

"To shoot us," another answers shortly.

Eyes look at eyes with dread. "Nonsense," someone else says consolingly. "If they intended to shoot us, they would have done it on the spot and gotten it over with."

We come to a village and find out soon enough the purpose of our assemblage. *"Die Scheisse wegbringen"*, a green uniform drops a word. What *Scheisse?* We climb over the rubble of a demolished church. Along a white fence the corpses of ten Polish soldiers in torn uniforms are spread out, one next to the other. "These imbeciles put up a resistance in a barn," a friendly explanation is given us. "Them we shall leave for display." We come out onto a pasture where heaps of dead people and horses are piled up. We are given shovels and ordered to dig holes and bury all the carcasses. The guards who watch us move to the side, keeping the butts of their guns pointed at us. A conversation in low voices starts up amongst us.

"You see," one says, "they have moved away. Can't stand to look at the disgusting sight they themselves have made."

"Don't talk idiocies," another replies. "They're running away from the stench."

"What do you think, people, are they all really such vermin, all of them?" a third one asks.

"All of them! May they vanish from the face of the earth!" a hairy thick-set fellow whispers hoarsely.

"I don't put them all into the same pot yet," another puts in. "In every nation there are all kinds of people. The Germans are a cultured nation. If a band of ruffians has usurped the power in their country, it doesn't mean that we have to blacken the faces of all of them."

"If you can still defend them, after such a night, you're not worth much in my eyes either," a young man puts in heatedly.

The "defender" of the Germans does not give up. "I am convinced that the average soldier is not responsible for the things going on here," he says courageously.

"There you have your average soldier," someone says with a glance in the direction of the guards who are pointing their rifle butts at us. "Did you hear how they talked to us? Did you see how they looked at us? Is that only obeying orders?"

We continue with the heated discussion in order to blot out the disgusting sight in front of us; until a new group of guarded Jews arrive. *"Los! Aber schnell!"* we hear an order.

Back on the highway, I stagger on, hiding myself behind the blond gentiles' backs as much as I can. I am very tired. My bloated feet have swelled even more from stepping on the shovel. As I begin to wonder if I will ever reach home, a hand pins me by the shoulder again. This time I am led to a troop of Jews walking parallel to the highway. We stop nowhere. A fearful murmur passes through our ranks. Now and then someone tries to escape. A "Halt!" follows, then a shot. I am already half asleep as I walk, when I hear a command, "Those under the age of eighteen are free!" I push myself through to the green uniform guarding us. He measures me with his eyes and shouts, *"Los!"* I think I said *"Danke schön."* *Kultur ist Kultur.* I walk the whole night without stopping. I have to be on guard. Even in the darkness I can occasionally hear: *"Jude? Jude?"*

✦ ✦ ✦

The sky is graying with a new day when I enter Bzezin. I wash myself at a well and drink some water. I feel no hunger, although I have not eaten for two days. I am cheerful. Today I will be home.

"*Komm, Jude, komm!*" A *gemütlich* voice wakes me from my daydream and a uniform beckons to me with a finger. The hand pinning me by the arm is white, with yellowish hairs and short clean nails. I feel like biting into it.

The German leads me to the church in the little town, offers me a kick in the behind and pushes me inside. The door shuts immediately behind me. Night again. I lift up my eyes to the stained glass windows through which skimpy rays of dusty light beam at the figure of the Crucified One on the cross, who seems to be suspended high in the air. I try to take a step but am pushed back by a tight mass of people. The church is packed with Jews. I begin to discern the outlines of heads and bodies half-naked and tangled one in the other. Groans and pent-up screams sound from all sides. I think of Dante's "Hell". The Crucified One, naked, tortured, hanging far above with his arms spread apart and his bent folded legs looks like one of us. And indeed, when did he ever have such an opportunity to be among so many of his own kin? What a fateful encounter!

Someone steps on my foot. I hiss with pain. He has got me at the worst point of the swelling. With my back against the wall I sink down until I touch the floor. My head sinks between my knees, my eyelids close. I hear a quiet voice, "How far is the day advanced outside?" I shrug my shoulders. My neighbour says as if to himself, "I haven't said my prayers for almost two days. Yesterday morning I got trapped in here."

"Yesterday?" I exclaim with disbelief and raise my head to him, looking at him in the dark. A shrunken little Jew; his chin is leaning against his knees; his long beard sticks out like a clump of dried grass. He looks familiar. "Is that how long they have kept you here?" I ask.

"An eternity, young man. First they put us in front of the church, face to the wall, hands raised. But they were only playing with us. Then they herded us in here and that was that. The sorrow is still greater because you're not supposed to bring a sacred word to your lips here. Then again, perhaps we should recite the psalms, shut our eyes and pray?"

"If there is a God and He is unwilling to help, your prayers won't achieve much anyway," I say.

"Be quiet, young man, don't say that," he cuts me short.

"You look familiar," I say, to change the subject.

He shakes his beard. "Many people know me. I sell ice cream during the summer." He licks his cracked lips with his tongue. "You can burn up with thirst," he says. "They put in a bucket of water. People jumped over the dead and over the living to get to it. Those who managed to take a sip let out a scream; the water was full of worms. Better to sit like this and wait. At least this way you don't lose your bit of strength, nor your bit of dignity. Right, young man?" He turns his small face to me. "My goodness!" he exclaims. "You're so very young! And tell me," he looks at me with pity, "who has already managed to knock into your head a doubt about the existence of God?"

"If I had not doubted up to now, I would have started to, here, on this road. And tell me, Mister, what did you think about when the bombs came down? You had no doubts at all?"

"Heaven forbid! I prayed, I recited psalms. Do you know what it means to pray fervently? You become one with the things you recite and not only do you have no other thoughts, but you feel that no matter how much heart and mind you put into it, it is still not enough. Did you ever attend a *heder*?"

"I attended a Jewish socialist school."

"You mean a goyish one. Never mind, there are many Jews who are goyim."

"I am quite a good Jew."

"Mercy upon you! But it is not your fault. A child lost among strangers, that's what you are. Father and Mother are estranged Jews perhaps. And perhaps it's not their fault either. Who knows? A Jewish generation soaked in sin, immersed in it so far that you cannot even find the guilty any more. But let's leave it alone. The main thing at this moment is to retain your strength, not to surrender. If it is God's will, He will in any case let you feel His hand upon you, and if it is His will to keep you alive, you have to help Him by not letting yourself grow weak. Go ahead, sleep a bit. I'll watch you."

"And you?" I ask, feeling somewhat guilty for my previous hostility towards him. I find him even likeable.

"An older person doesn't need so much sleep," he replies. "Besides, I have thoughts which are more important to me than sleep."

"What kind of thoughts do you have?"

"Do you want me to open my whole heart to you on the spot?"

"I'm sorry."

"Sorry-shmorry, never mind. Young people want to know everything. But on the other hand, perhaps you are right. Do we have any idea what is about to happen to us? Perhaps we will be lying in the same grave, and you'll be closer to me than my own wife, closer than a brother, than a father?" A freezing shudder runs down my spine. He catches himself right away. "Believe me, my son, I hope that the Almighty will guard and protect us. But you see, in my own self there is no real fear. That's why I talk with such ease. My only worry is about the nine sparrows I left behind in Lodz. But if this is His Holy Name's will, I am ready. I have had time here to prepare myself. Perhaps you think that it comes easy to me because I am no longer young? So you should know that even the grayest oldest grandfather wants to go on living. No matter how long he has lived, it still seems too little to him. But the readiness to surrender to God's will, to receive death from His hand in the same way as one received life, that, you see, only a pious person can achieve. That's why my heart aches for you. If I could share with you all that I feel inside me, it would be much easier for you to sit here. But I can see that I'm too weak for that."

"I don't need your pity," I answer him.

"Hush, hush," he shakes my knee. "Don't say a thing. Do me a favour and sleep a bit." I notice that he is trembling and cannot understand his excitement. He is sorry for me and I am sorry for him. I am ready to do him the favour and sleep for a while. I curl up, shut my eyes, and in a minute I am asleep. But then, in my sleep, I feel someone pulling me by the sleeve. "Young man," my neighbour shakes me. "Quickly! Get up and go!"

I jump to my feet and look around. The door is open. "Only those under eighteen years of age!" I hear a voice calling in German.

"I! I!" I howl in a voice not my own, pushing myself towards the door.

My tiny neighbour shoves me, helping me to get through. "Good luck to you!" he calls after me.

I want to wish him the same, but I have no time. I fall into the arms of the guard. He gives me a smack and I find myself in the churchyard. My head swims. The fresh air intoxicates me. How come it is night again, I wonder. At the gate, a soldier, flashlight in hand, checks the papers of the many boys lined up in a long row along the fence. I remember that my blazer was left in the pocket of Bronek's coat; in it I had my identification papers. Now I am lost. But no, I won't go back to the church. I approach the line-up. I see the boy in front of me holding a few pieces of indentification, fingering them as if he were unable to make up his mind which to choose to present to the guard. I snatch the edge of one of his papers and, ready for anything, I look into his frightened eyes as if trying to hypnotize him. "You have to give me one," I say. He lets go of the paper. Without even glancing at it, I ask the boy for his name. "I am your brother," I tell him. We press forward. The boy in front of me is free already. The soldier directs his flashlight onto my slip of paper. I am free.

I am cutting through a field in order to avoid the constant danger on the main paths. Walking, I feel a sandal loosening on my foot. The swelling has caused the straps to tear. I pull the sandal off, throw it away and begin running on the wet swampy ground. But soon I am tired. "Save your strength, young man!" I hear the voice of the little man in the church coming back to me. I obey him. But I remember that the night is my protector and I have to make full use of it.

An hour, two hours, go by. I march on and on. A thin streak of light appears in the sky to the east. The grayness of the air turns brighter as the fog rises slowly above the field as if elevated by an unseen hand. Suddenly the contours of Lodz loom into sight. Houses begin growing before my eyes; dark factory chimneys poke up into the sky; the cupola of a church shimmers with the rays of the rising sun. After a while, I begin to pass by the first cottages. It is full day. I enter the first narrow streets. I am half-barefoot and limping, but my steps are measured, sure. I ward off the thought of home, saving my joy for later.

I prick up my ears. Singing voices and marching steps echo on the pavement. As I turn back and enter a side street, a troop of marching boys wearing shorts with brown shirts and black ties comes straight towards me. They march in the middle of the street like soldiers and look with arrogant boastful glances up to the windows, searching for at least a trace of public in the empty street. They see me, their only spectator, and stride on with still more bravura and self-importance. I edge along the walls, looking stiffly in front of me, until I have the "army" behind me. I sigh with relief. Then I notice that the singing behind my back sounds fainter than before. I am about to rouse myself and run, when I feel a dull pain in my head. A rock rolls away from me into the gutter. I grab my head between both hands. My fingers are wet, smeared with blood. Ahead of me I see the shimmering streetcar tracks. I sit down on a doorstep and try to put myself in order while waiting for the streetcar. I tear off a piece of my shirt, wipe the blood away with spittle, cover my head with the same rag and clean the dirt and dust off my pants. I decide to rid myself of the other sandal as well. Going completely barefoot I feel better dressed than walking with one shoe on and the other off. I realize suddenly how tired I am. The wound itself doesn't hurt, although the rag becomes increasingly softer and wetter with blood. Nor do the swollen feet bother me too much without the sandals on. The fatigue is inside me.

I raise my back to stretch it and see someone standing in front of me: a blond boy of about twelve or thirteen. He scrutinizes me and puts his hand on my shoulder. "Are you *Jude*?" he asks me half in Polish, half in German. "Come with me. I am *Folksdeutsche*!" He pulls me by the collar.

He is dressed in the same uniform as the boys in the group I had the honour of meeting previously. I can escape from him easily, but am ashamed to show the stinker that I am afraid of him. I give him a smack on the chest, "Bugger off!"

He puts a small whistle to his mouth, blows on it, and grabs me with both hands. I try to get up; he pushes down on me with the weight of his entire body. I free myself and jump to my feet. I am about to dash off, when two strapping fellows appear in front of me, wearing the same brown shirts and black ties. They grab me by the arms and drag me off, bringing me to a square full of dug-out trenches. Half-naked men, shovels in their hands, are working at filling the pits. The fellows hand me over to a German civilian who gives me a shovel and pushes me towards the trenches. "*Arbeiten!*"

I try to put my foot on the edge of the shovel and emit a hiss of pain. Escape, I decide. I wait until the German turns around and I let the shovel fall to the ground. I vanish, turning behind a house and running past a yard. I see a streetcar halting at the stop. I hang on to it as it begins moving. I huddle up inside, in a corner, keeping the wound on my head covered with both hands. I want no one to see me. Nonsense. Curious eyes stare at me from all sides. The only one who pretends not to have noticed me is the conductor. He does not come over to me. At one of the stops a soldier's helmet appears in the door. "*Alle Juden runter!*" he commands.

I don't move. The streetcar continues. I am downtown. The people in the street seem to be going normally about their business. I jump out of the streetcar and mingle with the passers-by. I am on my street. With the last bit of strength, I set out at a run. As I run, I notice a group of German boys at the corner, stopping every man who passes by. Among the boys — how is it possible? — I see the same little German who bothered me before. I can hardly believe my eyes. Already he has caught sight of me; he reaches me, pushing himself against me. "You'd better work, or we'll shoot you!" he yells in broken German. He turns to call his comrades who are chasing after someone else, deafening the street with their screams and whistles. He grabs me by the shirt from the back and hangs on to me. "*Judisches Schwein!*" he screams as I drag him along with me. I feel the remainder of my shirt tearing off my back. The passers-by avoid us. Some stop at a distance and watch. I see my house already, but I don't want to drag the brat to it. I pull him into a gateway instead and get ready to give him a licking. A husky fellow follows us. He tears the boy away from me. The boy puckers his mouth, about to put his whistle to it. The man hits it out of his hand and lifts his fist threateningly. The little German shouts at him. "You will go to labour too!" The next moment he is gone. I exchange looks with my protector. A few people who stood at a distance watching the scene, come close. Someone gives me a handkerchief to wipe the blood off.

"Let's vanish," the stranger says to me. I want to thank him, but no word comes out of my constricted throat. One of the onlookers goes out of the gateway to check if the way is clear. He gives us a signal with his hand and we dash out. The stranger crosses the street, disappearing into a house. I find it hard to take a step. The eyes of the people who saw my helplessness follow me. I burn with shame. The closer I come to home, the weaker and more depressed I feel.

The familiar colour of our gate. The backyard. Neighbours on the thresholds. Children romping around. Heads poking out of the open windows.

"David! David!" voices call me from all sides. Women run up to me, heaping questions on me: have I seen this man or that man? Someone calls in the direction of our window, "Your son is back!" With the last bit of strength I climb the stairs. Mother rushes out, her arms open.

At last there is a bed and long restful sleep. Mother and Halina put cold compresses on my wound. Around me everyone walks on tiptoe. Warm whispering voices sound like the soft rustle of leaves in an autumnal park. Pleasant. It caresses the ear. Near the window, Rachel is standing, shy and sad. She looks at me, her eyes wide open. Doesn't she recognize me? I call her with my eyes, but she doesn't move.

Instead, Abraham slips over to me on his tiptoes. When he sees that my eyes are open, he nags me, "David, tell me how it was." His eyes burn with curiosity; his respect for me has increased tremendously. I remember how I myself felt at the beginning of my escapade, when I saw the soldiers returning from the battlefields. It is difficult to refuse him, but it is even more difficult to tell him. I know that not now, not tomorrow, nor the day after tomorrow will I be able to tell him. Perhaps never. (Just as I try and am unable to really tell it here, on these sheets of paper.) I am grateful to Mother for calling him away, and even more to him for obeying her.

I look at Rachel and finally bring myself to utter her name. She comes over, sits down on the bed and scrutinizes me as if she really had doubts about my identity. Is she the only one who feels that a different David has come home? "I was worried about you," she whispers.

"There was reason for it," I am about to say, but I know it isn't necessary. "Any news about Father and Leon?" I ask her.

She squeezes my fingers and shakes her head. There is nothing else to add.

Chapter Ten

NATURE CONTINUED on its natural course. The calendar indicated October and, as befits a month in early fall, time playfully dyed the city's attire, changing its vivid late-summer colours into the monotony of a cobwebby gray. Like burned dry rolls of paper, the leaves fell profusely from the trees, rustling and cracking under the feet of the passers-by like the bones of a disintegrating skeleton. The air, frosty and foggy in the morning, would perhaps have warmed up somewhat during the day, had it not been for the homeless wind which blew in from the distant fields, scouring the streets as if it were looking for a place to lay down its head. With prickly fingers it swept the sidewalks, raked the leaves together and heaped them into mounds, padding pillows for itself, which it carried from place to place, then left behind, in order to nose about in the overloaded garbage boxes and pull odours out of them. The sun became a stranger. Like an offended mother-in-law it looked down on the city to see how it was fairing on its own. It was easy to read in the sun's face that all that was happening to Lodz was no longer any of her business.

The building of Jaszunski *Gymnasium* was enveloped in the windy sadness of such an afternoon in fall; the windows of all the storeys were curtained by a dull dreary gray. The open entrance led up to a long empty corridor where a dusty bulb shed a meagre light. Whispy snarls of dust like kinky balls of wool lay in all the corners; the woodwork, covered with an even film of powder, showed no sign of having been touched by any hand.

Miss Diamand climbed the stairs slowly. Once she reached the landing, she walked from door to door, looking for the teachers' room. She listened to the sound of her own steps bouncing back from the walls with a loud double echo and strained her ears to hear human voices; but none could be heard. A large clock on the wall looked her straight in the face, its hands still pointing to twelve o'clock. She thought of the day when the clock had stopped. It belonged to the end of another chronological system, another era.

The teachers' room, spacious and newly furnished, was full of dust, the table covered with pieces of paper and with overflowing ashtrays. The floor was littered with books, boxes, broken pencils and crayons. From the glass-doored cupboards packed with files and registers, cobwebs like thin curtains climbed up the wall towards the ceiling. The odour in the room made Miss Diamand feel faint. She opened the window and unbuttoned her coat in front of the dusty matted mirror.

Wisps of her thin white hair had escaped from the pins meant to hold them in place. The furrows between her eyebrows were deeper, the red circles around her eyes redder than usual. However her eyes expressed satisfaction. In her purse lay the letter inviting her to participate in the newly-organized *gymnasium*. Her days of hopelessness were over. Was it any wonder that she had shown up so early for the meeting of the newly-formed teachers' committee? She could hardly wait for her first encounter with her students.

Hurriedly, she arranged her hair and looked around, trying to decide how to tidy up the room a bit. She noticed a rag on a shelf and began dusting the furniture slowly, systematically. She approached the map hanging on the wall and with light stroking movements went over it with the rag, bringing the freshness back to its colours which had seemed faded under the layer of dust. "Republic of Poland" the inscription read. She sighed. Suddenly she felt very tired and sunk down into a chair near the map, keeping her eyes glued to it.

Her gaze halted at the small patch of blue to the north on the map. She blinked her blood-shot near-sighted eyes — and saw the sea, the fishermen's boats swaying on the blue waves and the sea breeze, frivolous and free, dancing on sandy beaches. She saw the crowds of children from the summer camps, heard the water bubbling in their laughter as the sun washed their tanned faces, shoulders and backs with showers of light. She saw her friend Wanda and herself, both of them barefoot, wading along the shore in the soft, slippery sand. The breeze licked their faces, combed their hair and with mischievous freshness lifted their dresses, flapping them against one another. Sea gulls circled dreamily, noiselessly overhead, the morning sun edging their white wings with delicate streaks of gold. How huge the world had seemed to her then, and how intimate and dear! She loved the sea. She liked water in general, its rustle, its splashing, the whispery music of its flowing. She liked to let it run over her hands and slip through her fingers.

She moved her chair closer to the map and allowed her eyes to descend southwards, towards the brown splotches, the dark brown — to the mountains. She touched them with the tips of her fingers, halting at the black dot which represented the town of Zakopane in the Tatras. There, tall green walls climbed up to the Sleeping Knight on the peak of the Gevont Mountain. She saw herself climbing up to him, Wanda beside her. Rocks slid down from under their hiking shoes. Soaked in sweat, they exchanged exultant glances; it seemed that they heard each other's hearts pounding. Each step upward opened new vistas before their eyes. How was it possible to take in so much beauty? Then, when they reached the peak, they saw the Sleeping Knight encircled by the lower mountains and hills like children holding hands around a giant. Everywhere the roofs of tiny huts poked out like the heads of flowers from the green. And she picked a real flower too, an edelweis, a flower in love with the heights. And there, across from them, hovered the other giants, the neighbouring peaks, their snow-covered heads wearing diadems of cloud. They enticed and called, beckoning alluringly to her, the old teacher, and to her friend, promising splendid new rewards. Then they were in the valleys between the mountains. They marched along swiftly flowing rivulets and mountain springs. They rode the cable car across the valley; above them a blue abyss, beneath them a green one — and they were suspended between them both.

Miss Diamand wiped her tired eyes. There was something she had to do. She would do it soon. But first she must follow the line of the Vistula with her finger — the thick black line of Poland's mother river. It seemed to her that it had sprung from her heart and was flowing back to it, passing through her whole being, through her life. She rested her fingertip on the dot marking Cracow. Had she not been there just recently, on an excursion with the girls of the Wiedza? How wonderfully the children had expressed their delight! A girl had handed her a photo album with wooden handcarved covers. "This is for you, Miss Diamand, a gift from all of us." They had watched her, their eyes full of kindness. Youth was so devoted.

"Vistula, my Vistula . . ." she hummed, as the line of the river carried her along. She saw herself on a rowboat, not far from old Kazimierz, the town of a thousand legends. Crooked narrow streets, old churches, synagogues, enormous orchards and the ruins of the old castle passed by her — Poland's ancient history, illuminated in the sunlight, spread out along the shores of the river. The Vistula was now wide and spacious. Like a rich farmer's wife she opened her arms towards the abundant fields of grain. Warsaw came into sight. There, the sky was dark, enveloped by the hot breath of asphalt and stone. Old Warsaw, dear Warsaw. The heart of Poland throbbed in the rhythm of its streets. A swarm of reminiscences flocked to Miss Diamand's mind. But she would not give in to them. Warsaw was dear, but caused pain. With him, with her beloved, she had lived there at the very beginning.

Someone entered the teachers' room. It was a while before Miss Diamand came back to herself. She smiled, ill-at-ease, as someone greeted her with a handshake. "I've just come back from Warsaw." She pointed absent-mindedly at the map. Then she recognized Mrs. Feiner who had been assigned to the post of directress of the new *gymnasium*.

Mrs. Feiner glanced sullenly at the map, then, with a brutal sweeping gesture of her hand, made a cross over its entire length. "Our Poland cut into pieces for the fifth time in history," she said, turning away from the wall. She took off her mannish raincoat, straightened her forelocks with the comb which she kept tucked in her hair at the back and scrutinized the room with a sharp critical gaze. "This room is a garbage dump," she declared, taking the rag out of Miss Diamand's hand. She rolled up her sleeves and washed the rag over the sink.

The teachers began to gather; the room filled with their talk. Mrs. Feiner's voice rose above all the other voices. "My friends," she addressed the teachers, "I hope we won't remain sitting around in this dirt. Miss Luba," she prodded the young Latin teacher who was busy repainting her lips. "Who will admire your beauty in such a mess?" Miss Luba snapped shut her compact, straightened her skirt on her narrow hips and ran out to find some more rags. Other teachers also made themselves helpful. "Tomorrow we shall have a janitor," Mrs. Feiner announced. "The building has to look decent before we let the children in." Professor Hager, who had been busy making room on the shelves for the stray heaps of paper, wiped his hands and combed the dust out of his goatee with his fingers. He drew out a cigar butt from his pocket. As he lit it, he apparently felt the cold air coming from the open window, for he went over to shut it. But Mrs. Feiner was on guard. "My dear colleague," she exclaimed, "have you decided to suffocate us by adding the smoke of your cigar to the stench? Leave the window alone, please!"

The Professor left the window, buttoned his jacket over his protruding patriarchal paunch and smiled at her like a shamefaced school boy. "We have to take care of our health, Feinerova, now that our lives are about to acquire some value again."

Miss Diamand agreed with him whole-heartedly. She stepped up to him. "How are your flowers doing, Professor?" she inquired.

He bowed to her. "The flowers? Thanks, they are in the best of health. I don't ration their food as yet, nor do the Nuremberg Laws impair their psychological well-being. They don't wear yellow armbands, mind you."

Unhappy with his joke, which did not seem at all funny to her, she whispered, "The new experiment, the cross-pollination . . . the new flower you created?"

He stooped down to her, speaking with less sarcasm and with more sadness in his voice, "The flower of my dreams! Do you know what I call it? Felicia, I call it. My wife's name." His eyes met with those of Mrs. Feiner who was listening to him as she busily sharpened some pencils which lay gathered in a heap. "Do you remember, Feinerova, how we both danced at Zuckerman's ball last New Year's Eve?" He grinned. "Who could have imagined, tell me . . . And who could have imagined that Mr. Rumkowski, the bore with the coiffure of a prophet would become the head of the Jewry of Lodz, the *Älteste der Juden?*"

Mrs. Feiner exclaimed sternly, "Professor, not another word!" He immediately blocked his mouth with the butt of the cigar, puffing the smoke into his goatee.

"Oh, these smokers!" exclaimed the German teacher, Mrs. Braude, a stocky matron with a bloated face and water bags under her eyes. She sat at the table waving away the smoke drifting around her. "I would make smoking illegal once and for all." She shook her goitre.

The Professor of physics and chemistry, Mr. Lustikman, a devout chain smoker, felt deeply hurt. "We can expect that too, without your intervention, dear colleague," he snapped out peevishly, and to spite her, drew a pack of cigarettes from his pocket. "You women have nerves of iron and steel!" He lit a cigarette and blew the smoke straight into Mrs. Braude's face. Then he made an about turn, to face a group of chatting lady teachers. "You women are incapable of grasping situations in their entirety." He spread his arms over the ladies' heads like a bird of prey would its wings. "You are only capable of perceiving aspects of things, elements, but not the whole. That's why you're strong enough to endure everything."

"You mean to say, Professor, that we women are not overly smart, don't you?" Miss Luba said, as she searched for a clean spot to deposit her hat and bag.

"I wouldn't go as far as that," Professor Hager put in. "Their feminine intuition does help them. From the fraction that they manage to grasp, they can sense quite well the entirety of things; it is only that the entirety usually reveals itself to them in a milder form than it is in fact."

"Very true!" Professor Lustikman gave Professor Hager a condescending pat on the shoulder, as if the latter were a student who had come up with the right answer to a question. "We men," he proceeded, "when we deal with a phenomenon, we see it in its completeness as it is, and we respond to it with all our senses, giving priority to our reason, of course. And since some situations are very sad, we need a narcotic to help us stomach them."

Miss Luba stood in front of him, waving her small finger in his face. "You men are nothing but colossal egotists!"

Professor Hager guffawed, "The lady knows what she's talking about!"

Miss Luba looked up at the tall Professor Lustikman with the pride of a young peacock. "And we women will have more endurance than you men, during the hard times to come. We have a stronger life instinct than you do."

Professor Hager was amused. "And perhaps the reverse is true? Perhaps our very egotism is an expression of our powerful life instinct?"

Miss Luba shook her graceful little head. "No, an egotism like yours is self-destructive, it weakens your character and unbalances your actions. Because you think only of yourselves, you men. Female egotism is the egotism of the species, it embraces her husband and her children, and this makes her strong."

"Have you heard?" a woman teacher sitting at the table interrupted. "Jewish bakers won't get any more flour to bake bread with."

The argument about male versus female superiority was over. Miss Luba sat down beside the woman teacher. "This morning," she said to her, "I saw a Jew wrapped in a prayer shawl, riding in a droshky with two Gestapo men at his side."

Although she had spoken in a whisper, all the others heard her. Mr. Berger, the history teacher, a young man with the pallid face of a *yeshiva* boy, shook his head grimly. "It was Rabbi Segal. I heard a rumour that the Germans led him into the synagogue and ordered him to spit on the Torah Scrolls. When he refused, they paraded him through the city. And did you hear about the Jew whose beard they set on fire?"

"Enough!" Mrs. Feiner exclaimed, pounding on the table with her fist. "We are not gathered here to tell each other horror stories!" She buttoned all the buttons of her sports jacket. "Time to begin," she said, waiting for everyone to settle into a seat. "My friends," she started in an official tone of voice. "Soon the Presess, Mr. Rumkowski, will arrive. As you know, the first thing he, as the *Älteste der Juden*, decided to undertake was to persuade the police authorities to give permission for our children to return to school. Today the Presess will disclose his plan for the reorganization of the school system and will discuss with us the problems of the *gymnasium* in particular. I appeal to you not to ask too many questions, in fact to refrain from any discussion whatsoever. Don't forget that whatever the Presess tells us has already been decided. It remains for us to do our best in the framework of the possibilities offered to us." She stopped. She abhorred superfluous talk. Consulting her large wrist watch, she added, "For the time being, let's discuss the division of work among ourselves."

But before they could begin, they heard a tumult outside. Mrs. Feiner marched out of the room. Soon she returned, followed by the Presess, Mordecai Chaim Rumkowski. An awed murmur swept over the teachers' room. The Presess' head was dressed in large white bandages, like a crown; strings of silver hair stuck out from beneath it as if they were an integral part of his strange headgear. The part of his forehead not covered by the bandages was swollen, marked with violet and brown blotches, as was the rest of his face. His eyes burned with dark-blue flames under the thick gray eyebrows. For a moment he stood in the doorway, majestic and solemn, as if waiting for all the eyes staring at him to register his magnificence. Then, leaning heavily against his walking stick and limping considerably, he hurried towards the table. Mrs. Feiner put a chair behind him, but he shoved it away. "No time to sit," he growled and nibbled on his lips nervously, screwing up his nose in an effort to readjust the glasses which had slid down to its tip.

Mrs. Feiner, assuming an official air, adorned her face with a grimace meant to be a smile. "Mr. Presess, dear colleagues," she gave a short nod to the Presess and another one to the teachers. "The Presess, Mr. Rumkowski, is well known to all of us for his love of children and youth. He is determined to make it possible for our young people to continue with their education in the present difficult times. And it is thanks to the effort and perseverence of the Presess, that the establishment of the *gymnasium* is about to become a fact. And dear Mr. Presess," she turned to Rumkowski, "we fully appreciate your coming here, in such trying days when you are sick and troubled with so many worries, when you risk your life day in and day out to save people from torture and death."

Mr. Rumkowski's eyes sparkled proudly, but his face twisted and he knocked his stick against the floor. "This is beside the point! I have no time!"

The subsequent sentence became stuck in Mrs. Feiner's throat. She, the most to-the-point speaker that ever was, was not used to being called to order. But she checked herself immediately, pulled down the tails of her jacket and blinked wisely and meaningfully at her colleagues. She knew quite well that despite Rumkowski's remark, she had touched upon the right chord, and she would not allow herself to be diverted from her initial course. "Our Presess," she continued in a resonant voice, "has just risked his life in the Astoria Restaurant where he tried, alas in vain, to save a hundred people from a terrible fate. We all know this and we bend our heads before you with the utmost respect." She bent her head in his direction. As she did so, the Presess pounded his walking stick still more loudly against the floor. Nonetheless, there was no doubt in Mrs. Feiner's mind concerning the expression in his eyes. She read gratitude in them and was glad that she had not been mistaken. Her words were for the good of the school, of the Presess, as well as of her relationship with him. "And now," she renewed the official smile on her face, "the floor is yours, Mr. Presess." She did not find it necessary to stand any longer and with a sweeping gesture, she pulled the chair towards her and sat down.

"My dear teachers," the Presess knocked his walking stick against the floor, no longer in anger but rather to insure that he would be listened to attentively. He nibbled on his underlip, fixed his glasses and pressed his fist down on the table top. "A school system must exist in Lodz and a school system will exist in Lodz! As long as I am here, no child will roam the streets idle and uncared for!" His voice was rusty. He had to cough a few times and clasp his bandaged head between his hands. "Just as I am a father to a whole town of Jews, so am I a father to their children, and I shall take care of them and do everything possible for them, so that they can lead a normal life and not turn into riff-raff. We are starting our project with the *gymnasium*. All Jewish youths who wish to continue with their studies must find a place here. We have to manage, and you, dear teachers, must help me. I give you a building, I give you wood for heating, and perhaps in time there will also be a warm meal for the children. You yourselves will get paid, when and how much I can't tell you as yet. And this is all that concerns you. Leave all the rest to me. If you need me," he turned to the directress, "hm . . . Feinerova, you know where to find me. But bear in mind that you are not my only worry, so don't bother me too much. I carry the burden of an entire city on my shoulders, don't you forget that, and good luck to all of you." His speech was over. He drew a creased handkerchief out of his pocket, wiped his mouth and chin with it, groaned and stooped over Mrs. Feiner, giving her a friendly poke in the shoulder, "You see, Feinerova, I haven't forgotten you. I gave you this job."

The directress' face splotched a deep red. Ashamed, her head hanging, she muttered, "Yes, Mr. Presess, thank you very much."

Miss Diamand had been sitting in her chair dumbfounded, unable to digest all that was going on in front of her. The sight of the Presess made her think of what Professor Hager had recalled only a while ago. Now there were four people in the room who had attended the New Year's ball at the Zuckermans. But looking at Rumkowski, she could hardly believe that this was the same man she had met there for the first time. She could not make out much of what he had said to the teachers. The singsong Yiddish in which he had delivered his speech was repulsive to her in its strangeness and disgusting because it so monstrously crippled the German words which she had been able to under- stand. Yet for the first time in her life she deeply regretted that she could not understand the jargon of this tribe. Awe-struck, transported, she looked at Rumkowski. What an imposing figure he made! How majestic was the sight of his bandaged head with the proud eagle eyebrows and the silvery gray hair! He was an old man, but there was none of the weakness of old age in him — only its strength. The light of eternity emanated from his face, as if in that crown of white bandages he were carrying all the suffering and stubborn endurance of that stiff-necked people which refused to disappear. For the first time in her life she felt respect for the tragic heroism of the Jews. The Jew who stood before her, a hand's reach away, looked like a patriarch who had emerged directly from the Bible — like a prophet. It seemed to her that he was not flesh and blood, but sheer vision and legend, a miracle wrought by the dreams of Jewish hearts and those of her own heart, in this hour of utmost despair and helplessness.

Mrs. Feiner, pro forma, asked the teachers whether they had any questions they wished to ask the Presess. But he had already turned around and, leaning heavily on his stick, was heading towards the door. Mrs. Feiner followed him, waited until he had left and returned to her colleagues. Now she began to conduct the actual business of the meeting, planning the details of their forthcoming work.

✦   ✦   ✦

It was near the curfew hour when Miss Diamand made her way home. She felt wonderful. The possibility of work meant salvation. It seemed to her at that moment that the war was over. Besides, her encounter with the Presess contributed its share to her elation. "Oh, Wanda," she whispered in her mind to her friend. "If you had seen him, you would have had to agree that there is still pride and beauty in old Jewry." It seemed strange that she should think like that, but she could not help it. Something was happening to her. She wondered, "What is this strange closeness I suddenly feel with this old man, Rumkowski? Why am I so sentimental about him? And why is it that my feelings about the Jews and about myself, which never had anything to do with each other before and were always expressed in terms of 'I' and 'they', have suddenly fused into an awkward 'we'?"

Indeed, some of her judgments had become confused, although her previous convictions remained untouched, and she had not the slightest doubt of their correctness. The remainder of the historical Jewish people represented nothing positive; they vegetated in their mouldy conditions, isolated from the world. They were doomed by history to perish, to assimilate with other peoples and join the mainstream of life — thereby fulfilling the only positive function left to them. No, it was not in her mind that she conceded to feeling bound to them, but rather in her heart. In it, the word "Jew" had grown to extraordinary proportions. "Is it the Germans who are giving me this feeling of involvement?" she asked herself. "Is it possible that the enemy is capable of influencing my innermost convictions?" She could not bear this question and, instead of trying to answer it, she chose to suppress it. She had lived her life with her truths, and she would not now, in her old age, begin to doubt them, especially not under the pressure of the strange present times — in spite of the enemy who was out to break her spirit.

In order to regain her inner strength, she relived the moments she had spent before the map of Poland in the teachers' room. One feeling was clear and not subject to any doubt: her feeling for the Fatherland. There was no other love to rival it. A voice sang out within her: how good it was that she was starting to work again! In her mind's eye, she saw a classroom full of young people, their eyes fixed on her, their teacher. How should she begin the course? How should she set their minds afire with curiosity? But then, her enthusiasm became overshadowed with worry. What if these harrowing times were affecting the students as well? Perhaps they too were changing? How then could she talk to them, what should she say? Again she felt at a loss, torn by conflicting thoughts and emotions.

She hardly knew when and how she had made it to her room. She looked around it. This place was reassuring. Everything looked ordered and neat. The furniture glistened. The floor, painted red and polished, reflected its sheen in her eye-glasses. On the desk, near the lamp, books and exercise sheets lay in neat piles, on one side hers, on the other, Wanda's. But then her eyes fell on the wall above the wash basin. Wanda's towel was missing; the hook stuck out from the wall, bare. She put on her warm slippers, took off her coat and approached the basin to wash her hands. Her eyes were drawn to the empty hook. Where was Wanda's towel?

She was unable to think about anything but Wanda. Would Wanda sense the strange things going on in her? Would this have a bearing on their relationship in any way? A chill went through her. How could such an absurd thought enter her mind? Did friendship take into account such external matters, in particular a friendship like hers and Wanda's, the friendship of a lifetime? There were ties in the bond between the two of them that nothing could destroy. For apart from the devotion to their work which they both shared, apart from the companionship and intellectual stimulation they provided for each other, there was above all a profound understanding between them. They knew each other as well as one human being could know another. Did the fact that Wanda was Catholic by birth, and she, Miss Diamand, Jewish, ever have any significance for them? And if this detail had come up in conversation, weren't they both detached and truly objective in dealing with it? After all, neither of them was religious in the traditional sense of the word. Throughout the years they had together managed to create a kind of abstract godhead for themselves. How often had they speculated about Him and how similar was their concept of Him, of His world and the life which emanated from Him! And besides that, there was the other "religion" which they had in common: Poland. Many years ago the two of them had sacrificed their most precious treasures on its altar.

Miss Diamand approached the window, wiped the fogged-up pane with a bony finger and looked out into the street. It was dark outside, with only a circle of light cut out in the darkness of the pavement by the gas lantern. As she stood there, staring at the bright circle, images from years past emerged from her memory with unusual precision, as if time had had no power to efface them. She thought of her first years with Wanda, of her illegal school work under the tsar; years when she had given herself to life completely and had received something complete in return. She had had a full beautiful youth. She had loved and been loved, and she had had an ideal in which she believed. But the storm had broken out, cutting her personal life off from its continuity. The day her beloved was shot on Ogrodova Street, a chapter in her life was finished, and a new one had begun. She was incapable of ever again giving or receiving love as a woman; instead there was a giving and receiving love of a different, more sublimated nature.

Once a year, every year, Miss Diamand would go to Ogrodova Street on the day which marked the anniversary of her fiancé's death. She had not missed the occasion even this year, and, as usual, had taken along a few flowers. As she walked up the street, she would drop flower after flower to the ground. An approaching wagon or car might trample them right away, or people might step on them; now and then someone would pick one up and walk off, holding the flower to his nose. To her, these things did not matter. All the flowers she had strewn on the street throughout the years had created for her a sacred cemetery where her beloved and her womanhood had been put to rest.

Wanda's fate resembled hers. But Wanda did not even have an anniversary or a place where she could drop a flower, or a tear. For many long years she had nourished hopes that her beloved might return from Siberia. The revolution broke out, the tsar fell, and with it came the bitter sobering up. There was no one to wait for, and there was nothing more to expect from one's youth. Miss Diamand could barely remember the taste of those critical years of ripe femininity which followed, when their bodies and souls had yearned for the touch of a man's hand, or for the joy of having a child. Somehow those years were harder to remember than the ones that preceded them.

But now the souls of the two women were like quiet ponds, transparent and clear. Their bodies, never given the chance to produce fruit, shrank and closed themselves up like flowers withered while in full bloom. Because within themselves, they could still feel life's nectar untouched, their dreams still young and their inner beauty untarnished. Their gray hair, their wrinkled skin and their sagging dried-out breasts were only the shell, the veneer, behind which, unchanged, a bride, delicate and wistful, was still waiting on the threshold of things to come. Neither she nor Wanda considered themselves entitled to bewail their fate. They still possessed such richness. And what charity had life extended to them, by bringing the two of them together!

It was good to march with Wanda through the streets of the city, then part at a corner, each of them heading towards her own school, to fulfil her mission on this earth. Both dressed alike, in shawls and coats of their favourite mauve colour, they would walk erect and carry their heads proudly on their shoulders, fully aware that their frail delicate figures, graceful yet strong, would single them out in the street by their particular beauty. They would smile at the students passing by, and would answer their greetings with a nod of the heads. Quite often they would notice a glint of irony in the eyes of the young, fully aware that it was their age that was being laughed at. They would respond warmly just the same, look bravely into the mocking eyes and their gazes would say "Happy ignorance, we forgive you."

In the teachers' rooms, each at her own school would notice the same ironic looks in the eyes of their colleagues, who often did not refrain from ridiculing the old maids openly, albeit under the pretence that it was not the old ladies themselves they were scoffing at, but their "idealistic, romantic" attitudes, their "living on the moon". For they, the younger teachers, were people with positions in society, heads of families, mothers, fathers, possessing the treasure called a future. It meant that they were modern progressive individuals with a sense of reality and purpose, who felt at home in the twentieth century and believed that it belonged to them and to their offspring. And they, the old maids, forgave their colleagues as well. After all, the latter were also nothing but children, older children, who deserved to be pitied since they had lost the charm and freshness of childhood. In reality, Miss Diamand and Wanda considered themselves younger than all their colleagues, since the essence of youth had remained within them. They had the courage to fight for their "outdated theories". The élan of their stormy youth, their elation and enthusiasm were qualities which they both tried to keep alive. They stuck to their convictions, argued, explained, and never compromised. They rarely succeeded in their struggles, but they never lost their zeal.

Miss Diamand heard steps on the stairs and rushed to the door to meet Wanda. The latter came in with a smile on her face. She stretched out to her friend a hand which carried a bulky briefcase. "Be careful," she shook her gray head, undoing the mauve shawl from around her neck. "There's something inside, Dora dear, a treasure." Childlike, radiant, she freed a part of the briefcase's handle for Miss Diamand to hold on to, and together they carried the briefcase to the table. "I brought a dozen eggs and a whole loaf of bread," Wanda whispered solemnly, opening the briefcase and taking out the bag of eggs. Then she lifted the round loaf up in the air, beaming, "A loaf of gold! I passed a bakery this morning, I joined the line and had luck." Wanda was slightly taller than Miss Diamand, stockier and more raw-boned. Her skin was not as pale as Miss Diamand's; it shone with two dark red splotches at the very height of her cheekbones. But her eyes, like those of Miss Diamand, were of a watery blue.

Miss Diamand took the loaf out of Wanda's hand. "Next time I will go," she said.

"Out of the question!" Wanda laughed, changing into her soft slippers. "From now on I provide the food for this family." Unaware that her friend's face had changed, she went on, "You know very well that it is easier for me . . ." Her eyes investigated the inside of the briefcase. "I saw people with yellow armbands being thrown out of the line . . . Look what else I have!" She showed Miss Diamand a package of butter wrapped in parchment paper.

Miss Diamand had to sit down on her bed. However, she gathered her strength to ask, "Where is your towel, Wanda?"

Wanda turned her head to her. "I packed it. I still want to go to the country today. Our mathematician got hold of a four-wheeler. Nice of him to take me along. I'll bring back some potatoes, lettuce, beets, whatever possible." She shook her briefcase out over the waste basket. "This little briefcase will come back full of treasures, Dora. We'll have a supply of food 'to kiss your hands', as my students would say."

Miss Diamand wrinkled her forehead. Suddenly it became painfully clear to her that something was happening to Wanda as well, something odd. To her dismay, she sensed it even in Wanda's manner of speaking. "Since when have we become such voracious creatures?" she asked.

Wanda approached her and stroked her arm lightly. "It is not a question of voracity. We have to be more practical nowadays. You never know what might happen, and do we have anyone to take care of us? So, since there is an opportunity . . . And you should see my colleagues. They talk of nothing but potatoes and cabbage, bread and sugar. After all, we are a household too, aren't we?" She waited in vain for her friend's face to clear. Finally, she sat down beside her. "Will you feel lonesome all alone, Dora?"

Miss Diamand roused herself and put her wrinkled hand on Wanda's bony fingers. "Come back soon," she smiled faintly.

That evening the four-wheeler did not come to fetch Wanda. The two women spent the time cosily beside the little "cannon" oven while Miss Diamand enthusiastically made plans for the forthcoming school term. She decided that it would be best to start it with "The Tempest" by William Shakespeare.

In the afternoon of the next day, Wanda left for the country. Miss Diamand sat down at her desk, to work on her notes and program outlines. The hours wore on, until finally she completed her task, took off her glasses and faced the empty room. She felt Wanda's absence acutely. A long lonely night awaited her and she barely had the courage to endure it. It was not that she feared being alone in the room; she was too old to be disturbed by that kind of fear. It was rather the fear of staying alone in a room which had lost its soul. Up to now she had always felt the presence of something very intimate in her home. There was an air about it which had enveloped her, making her feel comfortable, as if its walls were a protective cape; beneath it she could walk about with her soul bared, just as she was. This atmosphere had vanished from the room, as if Wanda, by leaving it, had ripped the cape apart, and taken along its warmth, leaving nothing but the cold behind.

"Wanda has gone for only one night," she tried to defend herself against the cold invading her heart. "Tomorrow she will be back and everything will be the same as before." She recalled how it had been almost a year ago when Wanda had not slept at home. She had left to visit her family, while Miss Diamand had been invited by the Zuckerman family to the New Year's ball where she had met the Presess for the first time. How well that night had passed! And how grateful she was to her student Bella for remembering her!

Miss Diamand stood at the window, thinking of Bella Zuckerman. It seemed to her that she saw the girl's face in the hazy flickering light of the lantern in the dark street. How much sensitivity and beauty there was in that ugly face with its irregular features! What depth in those sad velvety eyes! Miss Diamand liked to talk to those eyes. They seemed to be looking directly into one's soul, drawing out of it not only what one had to say, but also what one was unable to say.

The next moment Miss Diamand was at the closet, taking out her coat; her hands shook as she hastened to put it on. She thought it discourteous to invade someone's privacy uninvited and unexpected, especially in the evening. She would never have done such a thing before. But now she did not care. She told herself that nowadays people did a lot of things which were unsuitable and were all right nevertheless. She left the room without offering it as much as a glance.

She shuffled alongside the walls of the street, the wet wind lashing against her. Wet drops, ice-cold and prickling, fell from the roofs down onto her forehead. The Zuckerman house, white in the surrounding darkness, seemed magnificient to her. In the sombre foggy mist it seemed to be built of a rare and expensive stone. There was no light behind the delicate fine tulle curtains covering the windows, except downstairs where she caught sight of a warm shimmer penetrating the blackout paper on one window. It was quite a while after she had rung the bell, that she heard a "Who is it?" on the other side of the door. She tried to pronounce her name as loudly and as clearly as she could. The door inched open and a face appeared above a chain. A pair of wide-open eyes scrutinized her for a long time before the chain vanished.

Samuel Zuckerman stood in front of her. He was in his shirt, the sleeves rolled up, his unknotted tie dangling over his chest. He held a little glass and a lit cigarette in the same hand. He was dishevelled and hardly resembled the elegant imposing Mr. Zuckerman whom she had known as the father of her student. "What is it you want, Madam?" he asked politely, puckering his eyebrows in an effort to recall where he had seen the old lady before.

"I would like to see your daughter, Bella," she said with difficulty.

He was taken aback, "Bella? And . . . and who are you?" He bent down to her, pricking up his ears as if he were deaf and did not want to miss a word of what she had to say. She smelled alcohol on his breath.

"I am Dora Diamand, Bella's teacher."

"Forgive me a million times," he whispered, pulling her into the vestibule.

"Where is Bella?"

He pulled her by the sleeve into his study, pointed to an armchair and let himself down into another. "Bella, you see," he spoke, slurring his words, "is already asleep." He grimaced as if he had seen something odious on the wall above Miss Diamand's head. "She is tired, so are they all, my wife, my other daughter and the cook. They were caught in front of the house and dragged off to forced labour. Therefore . . . I decided to toast the occasion." He lifted the glass and emptied it into his mouth. "My wife has some acquaintances among the officers from her home town, Leipzig, so we lack nothing. *Wódka Wyborowa!*" He looked at Miss Diamand. "And you . . . You've come so late in the evening. Has something happened?"

She stirred uncomfortably, moving to the very edge of the armchair. "No," she whispered. "I only wanted . . . to chat with Bella for a while. I did not think that I would cause you so much trouble."

"No trouble at all." He stood up and walked over to his desk, letting his fist down heavily on a dusty pile of papers. "Bella is lucky," he shook his head drunkenly, chuckling. "At her age, I had no teacher who felt like talking to me, not even one to whom I could talk." He reached for the bottle on the table, refilled his glass, took a sip and looked at Miss Diamand intensely. Her birdlike delicate face was pale, almost transparent. It seemed to him that she was only the reflection of an apparition he was seeing on the wall. "I have a lot of work, Madam . . ." he said, then caught himself, realizing that it would be tactless to send the old lady off in that manner. He added, "You see, hm . . . I am getting ready to write a book." He bit his underlip, not knowing why he had said this to an old woman he hardly knew. "Do you see all these papers?" he chattered on in spite of himself. "These are our family archives, just part of them, mind you. You should see what I still have in the basement." It occurred to him that the old lady might want to leave, but now he felt that she could not leave before he told her more. He sat down in his armchair and moved closer to her. "Oh, those years, those fabulous young years, Miss . . . Diamand. Such peace here, inside . . ." The next moment he was completely submerged in a flow of melancholic reminiscences about his childhood and youth.

Miss Diamand looked straight at his mouth. She forgot what had initially brought her here, forgot where she was, or even who she was. In front of her sat a child with an adult's heavy heart, confused, lost in his inner turmoil. With all the tenderness she possessed she wanted to reach out to him, to help him, at least by hearing him out most attentively, and thus partly alleviate the weight of his burden. Her hands, which he absent-mindedly touched now and then, felt a compulsion to stroke his dishevelled dark head; she felt a need to encourage him by saying, "Talk . . . go on. I am here to listen to you." She was not surprised at the sudden familiarity that set in between them and gave her the feeling that she had known him all her life.

Finally, Samuel came to the conclusion of his reminiscences. "You know, Miss Diamand, lately I've been having trouble falling asleep and," he chuckled, "when you lie in the dark for a long time, in a horizontal position, something happens to you. Images I never remembered before come back to me, as if they were coming from the prehistoric times in my life. Prehistoric times, a good expression, isn't it? I mean the times when your memory is still a fluttering page from which the writing falls off . . . But its traces remain . . . elsewhere." He grew thoughtful. Was he really drunk, he asked himself, consulting his watch. It was after curfew. How could he have forgotten about it? Perhaps she was too polite and too kind-hearted to interrupt and embarrass him? He stood up and touched her shoulder, "Please, sleep over, Miss Diamand, will you? It's after curfew, you know?"

"Thank you. I'll gladly stay," she eagerly responded.

He had a strange impulse to kiss her hand, but instead he turned away from her and walked around the table a few times. He threw the butt of his cigarette away and lit another one. "I drank too much anyway, to be able to work. I will tell you about . . . my life, let's say . . . about my work. I've never tried to do it before. And actually, how does one go about it? I mean . . . a life reduced to words?" As soon as he said this, his talk stopped flowing. It was silly — this sudden compulsion. It was absurd. He was not the kind of person who talked about his own life or his past. Yet he told her about his grandfathers and of the eternal question which haunted him, whether or not some of the strength of his forefathers had been passed on to him. The hours wore on. Miss Diamand listened to Samuel, looking at him with an unfaltering, tender curiosity. Her eyelids did not close for a minute, although the hour was late and she was usually asleep by this time.

In the very middle of his monologue, long after midnight, Samuel saw the old woman in front of him in the full light of reality, and he also became aware of his own presence in his study. The flow of his words was cut off. Shyly, he stammered a few conventional phrases and, completely sober, he led Miss Diamand to the guest room.

◆ ◆ ◆

The corridors of Jaszunski *Gymnasium* were empty. On the hooks along the walls hung an assortment of coats, scarves and hats. The big clock on the wall, at the end of the main corridor, ticked monotonously, counting the hours, its rhythm joining with the quiet buzzing of voices issuing from behind the closed classroom doors.

In the gym hall boys and girls sat shoulder to shoulder on the benches which were placed close together. Those who could find nowhere to sit stood along the walls. Writing books were open; those students who were forced to stand, leaned their pads against the back of a neighbour, or propped them up on their raised knees, or against the wall.

The air in the room was sticky, warm and heavy with the breath of over a hundred people huddled together. The window panes were wet and gray, as if it were raining outside. A quiet rustling sound passed through the room, and above it, pearly and soft — the voice of the teacher who stood in front of the benches wrapped in her mauve shawl. Miss Diamand was speaking about Shakespeare. Her misty blue eyes wandered from bench to bench, from face to face. As she spoke, she listened to the murmur in the room. How she had longed for it! To her, it was the most glorious music on earth! Yes, only among the black school desks covered with papers and books, only at the head of the classroom, illuminated by the light of young eyes, did she live her real life. Just like that of an actress who only came alive on the stage, Miss Diamand's daily existence was nothing but a preparation for the moments spent here.

Now, as she spoke, she thought with a certain pride that she was practically indestructible, invulnerable to time. For so many years she had stood like this, in her dark tunic-like dress embellished with the mauve shawl. Her white hair was always combed the same way, her eyes always aimed at the same target: the children's faces and a point slightly above them, as if she could see them simultaneously in the present and in the future. The sound of her thin silken voice was always the same and she herself, altogether unchanged, stood at her post of duty. It seemed that her hair could not grow any whiter, nor her shoulders more stooped; her mouth could not be criss-crossed by more wrinkles, nor the red circles around her eyes grow redder than they already were.

However now, in spite of the solemnity of the moment, there was something in the air which disturbed her. The murmur in the classroom may have been music to her ears, but this time it was a music to which she was not yet completely attuned. There was a wall of glass between herself and her students that was impossible to penetrate. They all seemed to be paying the utmost attention to her, their pencils running swiftly over their notebooks — and yet, there was strain in the atmosphere. It was so vague, so barely perceptible, that only she, with her trained sensitive ear, could detect it. And this obstacle had to be removed, because it was destructive; it made her breathe with difficulty. So, summoning up all her courage, she started the struggle immediately.

She wanted the reality of the street outside to become as meaningless to her students as it was to her. She wanted them to hold on, as she did, to eternal indestructible values. She knew that this was not easy. She was aware of what was going on around them, in their homes and in town. But here at least, all that must be made to fade out of their minds; for only in this manner, she felt, could they acquire the strength and dignity to deal with the storm raging outside. She had therefore begun the first literature lesson by choosing the giant Shakespeare to assist her in her task. She spoke of Caliban and Prospero; she discussed Prospero's dialogue with Ariel. The students listened to her, but their faces told her that she had not achieved what she desired.

Then she spoke about Miranda and Ferdinand. She talked for a long time, reading, explaining, trying to convince her listeners, she was not sure exactly of what, until, suddenly, she noticed that the students' heads had lifted, their eyes shyly began to search each other out among the benches. The colours of the girls' skirts and blouses seemed to have brightened, the messy forelocks on the boys' foreheads suddenly seemed to express a kind of masculine prowess. Mouths flashed smiles, and in no time the glass wall was gone. It had melted away. Miss Diamand was so stupefied by the unexpected change of mood in the room, that the book in her hands began to tremble. "The very instant that I saw you, did my heart fly to your service; there resides, to make me slave to it; and for your sake I am this patient log man," said Ferdinand to Miranda, in Miss Diamand's quivering voice. Her delight danced about the room along with the lines she recited. All the faces in front of her seemed aglow with excitement. "Do you love me?" Miranda asked. In Miss Diamand's heart all the lights were on. She had found the answer. Love was the only power that could measure up to the hatred running amuck in the streets of Lodz.

The sound of the bell cut through the air of harmony in the classroom, grating unpleasantly on Miss Diamand's ear. The spell was broken. Ferdinand and Miranda had retreated into the printed page. The young people stirred impatiently in their seats. She closed the book as the students rushed to the door. She waited, in no hurry to leave. No one noticed her or paid any attention to her.

She entered the teachers' room and took her lunch out of a paper bag. She chewed slowly, without tasting the food. Eating had always been a routine for her, a mechanical activity which just had to be done. Her misty eyes wandered over the faces of those of her colleagues who had not been assigned enough classes and were now fighting for a few more hours of work. The food stuck in her throat; she lost all desire to finish her meal and decided to go down into the schoolyard to get a breath of fresh air.

The yard was teeming with hundreds of adolescents. They bustled about, laughing, talking, getting acquainted and flirting. Around the yard, near the walls, pairs of boys and girls hid from the general hubbub. Miss Diamand noticed Rachel Eibushitz, her student from before the war, standing on a doorstep and looking for someone. Miss Diamand waded slowly in her direction. The "glass wall" between herself and that girl had existed even in the other life, a misunderstanding impossible to clear up, which had used to disturb her. Now she approached Rachel with an open heart. Perhaps the time had come, she thought, to break through the "wall" and reach out to the girl.

A youth with a narrow elongated face, his dark hair cut in a "porcupine" style which made his pallid face look doubly long, approached Rachel. For a while the pair stood there mutely, watching the cloud of soot which descended into the yard in a snow of black flakes. The youth said, "The Germans have started an offensive against France. And I've heard that Jews won't be allowed to walk on Piotrkowska."

Miss Diamand stood there in utter confusion. This was not a good moment, after all, to break through to her student's heart. In her mind she asked the pair sadly, "What do you still remember of Shakespeare, children?"

Then she heard the boy again, "Do you see the soot? All the prayer houses and synagogues in town are on fire." Miss Diamand remembered that in the morning, on her way to school, she had been haunted by a smell of smoke. She saw the two young people move closer to each other; broken words, the meaning of which she was unable to make out, reached her ears. Then she noticed that the two were about to part. She heard the youth ask, "Do you have anything to eat by any chance?" Miss Diamand thought of the lunch she had not finished and felt ashamed. Then it occurred to her that it was bad form to be listening in on someone's private conversation. She would never have done such a thing before. She immediately calmed herself however. Nowadays people did many things which were bad form and were all right just the same. Slowly she edged away from the doorstep and made her way through the crowd in the direction of the staircase.

The bell had not yet rung, but a wild scramble broke out at the staircase. A throng of people arriving from the yard pressed at Miss Diamand; they were all frighteningly silent. She saw a sea of pale, twisted faces around her. As she reached the landing, she saw Mrs. Feiner directing the students to the classrooms. No one waited for her to repeat the order. Before long, the corridor was empty. Miss Diamand pulled the directress by the sleeve. "What happened?" she inquired with a quivering voice.

"They're taking the men for labour," the directress explained hurriedly and rushed towards the teachers' room. A deathly stillness lay behind the classroom doors, as if the school had suddenly been completely emptied. Now Miss Diamand could clearly hear the thick bellowing voices, the shouts and yells issuing from the yard. Mrs. Feiner reappeared in the corridor, rushing towards the washroom with a key in her hand. She was followed by a long row of male teachers whom she let into the washroom, locking the door behind them with the key. The women teachers dashed out of the teachers' room and scattered in all directions towards the classrooms.

The students of Miss Diamand's class clustered in front of the windows. She had an impulse to walk over to them, but instead, she halted in front of the empty benches and whispered distraughtly, "We will start the lesson." No one responded or turned to her. She approached them slowly; noticing Rachel Eibushitz standing with her nose flattened against the window pane, she pushed herself through to her. She wanted to put her hand on the girl's shoulder, but somehow could not do it. She was ashamed of herself without knowing why. As if through a fog she saw below her a huge truck idling near the gate, packed with a load of youths, among whose backs she could discern the goatee of Professor Hager. She shivered with cold, as if she too were standing in the wind outside. She saw the youths in the truck pull up the collars of their blazers. They were looking up at the windows, making signs with their hands, calling aloud and asking their classmates to let their families know what had happened. She noticed Rachel's boyfriend. His "porcupine" stood up stiffly. He waved his hand as the motor began to rumble and the truck moved away.

Miss Diamand, unable to control the shudders running through her body, finally mastered her voice and called out, "We are now going to start the lesson." Her teeth were chattering loudly. She wrapped her arms around the shoulders of two young people standing close to her.

Bella Zuckerman approached her with a coat over her arm. "I saw you were cold, Miss Diamand," Bella said shyly, handing her the coat. Miss Diamand wanted to thank her, but could not utter a word. She wrapped herself in the coat, draping the mauve shawl around her neck. She dragged herself to her place in front of the benches. The students moved silently away from the windows and took their seats. The room was spacious now; there was no one standing along the walls.

Miss Diamand took the book into her hands: Shakespeare. She was set upon opening it at the proper page and going back to Prospero's island. But it was extremely difficult to do so; the young people sitting in front of her were expecting something from her. As if in an effort to shield herself from their cold expectant gazes, she wrapped the coat tighter around her body. "The lesson has begun," she repeated again, and then let the book fall from her hand, determined to pick it up again in a moment. "When there is a strong wind blowing outside," she raised her voice, but frightened by its unusual force, brought it back to normal, "and you must go somewhere, don't you still go, in spite of the wind holding you back?" The question remained suspended in the air. She waited, not for an answer, but to let them absorb what she had said; then she snatched up the book and began to read resolutely, "'Spirit', said Prospero. 'We must prepare to meet with Caliban'." Heavy silence hovered over the class. It could not mislead Miss Diamand's ear. No one was listening to her; her words were falling into a void. A hundred pairs of eyes looked at her icily. The book closed in her hands as if by itself. "Well," she whispered forlornly. "In that case, you are free to go home."

✦ ✦ ✦

It was a day full of unfortunate experiences. For the first time in her teaching career, Miss Diamand felt like going home early, to be with Wanda. The burden in her heart had become too heavy to be carried alone.

The streets were full of preoccupied people, rushing about, almost knocking the book and the bag with her unfinished lunch out from under her arm, almost pushing her over. The closer she came to Piotrkowska, the harder it became to walk. Thick clouds of smoke appeared above the roofs and settled down on the street. Miss Diamand's glasses became blurred. The black snow of soot danced in the air, covered her coat, penetrated her nostrils and made her cough. She saw the clouds of smoke from very close now, thick black tongues sticking out towards the sky. "The synagogue is on fire!" The news swept through the throng like a subterranean murmur.

She let herself be carried forward by the mass of people. As she approached the Allées, blades of fire lashed out from around the corner, and the air became thick and suffocating. Her head turned; black circles whirled in front of her eyes. She heard a heavy blast and the street rang out with the sound of broken glass falling from the windows of the surrounding houses. The crowd turned and began to disperse in all directions. Miss Diamand dragged herself home through a side street, shaking off the soot and dust from her coat and shawl as she walked; her head was swimming.

Wanda was not at home.

As Miss Diamand washed, the floor shook beneath her feet and she heard repeated explosions. The window panes clinked as clouds of smoke rushed swiftly past them. Somewhere stones and bricks were falling with a heavy rumble. Miss Diamand kindled a fire in the little "cannon" oven. As soon as the wood caught fire, she put her arms around the stove, huddling up close to it.

She thought of the synagogue. Before the war, she had often walked past the Allées and the little garden surrounding the temple. On sunny days, its cupola was covered with a wash of golden light and it emitted shimmering sparks. Old chestnut trees encircled the structure with a wreath of green leaves, and the path leading up to it stopped in front of a magnificent entrance door. She recalled the holidays when the students from the Jewish *gymnasiums* streamed towards the temple, carrying their school flags. For a while they would stand in the garden, one school beside the other, waiting for the door to open. The students, festively-dressed, would laugh and jest, calling to each other gaily. The teachers too greeted each other, chatted in whispers, solemn and composed. Then they went inside, to behold the awe-inspiring beauty. The cantor, in white-satin ceremonial dress, wrapped in a white prayer shawl, with a white skull cap on his head, appeared at the pulpit. A choir of children sang out with their pure angelic voices. Miss Diamand would sit blinking her misty eyes. A cleanliness, a transparent clarity permeated her soul.

Indeed, there had been a quaint exotic attraction for her in the religious ceremonies of the temple — a beauty against which she was unable to defend herself. She had liked the atmosphere of the synagogue, although it was more foreign to her than the smell of incense in the churches she often visited with Wanda. The charm of the synagogue, she told herself, had been precisely in its strangeness, in its remoteness, in the detached aesthetic pleasure it had given her. But at this moment, Miss Diamand could not understand why she lived through the burning of the synagogue so personally, so thoroughly, as if the flames were forging a new intimacy between the temple and herself.

When Wanda entered the room, Miss Diamand was still standing with her arms around the stove. Wanda, worried, immediately came up to her. "What happened?" she looked searchingly into Miss Diamand's pale face. Recently she had developed an acute sense for Miss Diamand's moods and she dealt with them as if they were the moods of a person stricken by a grave illness.

"Nothing," Miss Diamand whispered, pressing heself still more tightly against the stove. "I am only a bit nervous, my dear." Then she took Wanda's hand in hers, adding, "They took my children for forced labour. Practically out of the classroom they took them. And . . . Have you seen the synagogue?"

Wanda nodded. "I heard that they set all the synagogues on fire, the vandals. And the monument of Kosciuszko has also been demolished, gone. Do you know what idiocies they are talking in my school? Imagine, they whisper among themselves that it's the Jews who destroyed the monument and that all the synagogues are being burned today as a punishment."

"You don't know what you are talking about!" Miss Diamand, beside herself, burst out with unexpected anger.

"Dora dear," Wanda was dumbfounded. "It is war, and not our first one. The masses are like cattle."

"And you believe that the Jews did such an outrageous thing?"

"No, dear, I am telling you . . ." Wanda patted her friend's shoulder affectionately. "Let's not allow all this to enter . . ." She did not finish the sentence, but gave Miss Diamand a hug and went to prepare their meal.

They ate in silence. Miss Diamand kept her face buried in her plate; the steam rising from it moistened her skin. She could not control the shaking of the spoon in her hand. Wanda kept her eyes on her friend all the time, but was afraid to speak. They washed the dishes together. The air in the room was gray; a smoky dark vapor covered the window. The fire in the stove seemed to shine threateningly from between the rings of the burner. In the red glowing pipe, pieces of coal cracked; the wind which blew through them made an eerie noise. Wanda turned on the light, although it was only around noon; but she thought that the light would infuse some cheerfulness into the grayness of the room. She kept her eyes fixed on her friend's face. Was there a misunderstanding between them? No, impossible; it was only a mood which would soon pass. She just had to be patient. She filled two glasses with tea and moved the table closer to the stove. "Come here, Dora dear, drink your tea." Miss Diamand obeyed her and sat down at the table. "Why don't you drink?" Wanda's voice betrayed her sense of helplessness.

"I'm not thirsty, Wanda."

"You're mad at me," Wanda touched her hand. "I want to know why."

Miss Diamand shook her head, "It has nothing to do with you."

"Not with me, just with you?"

"With me alone, Wanda. We are nervous today."

"Who is 'we'?"

"We Jews."

Wanda's eyes opened wide; her hand slid slowly away from Miss Diamand's. The wrinkles in her forehead turned into a maze of deep furrows. "You talk as if the war were only against the Jews. And we Poles are not nervous, you think?" Her eyes lit up with dread. "Listen to us talk, the two of us! Dora, my angel, it must not go on like this, not between us two."

"No, it mustn't." Miss Diamand's trembling hands, like two mortally wounded birds, fell into her lap. "I can't help it. Something . . . I . . . If you want to know, the Germans have managed to make a Jew out of me. I should be grateful to them for that. My children were dragged away from their desks today because they are Jews. I don't know. It seems to me that it is an honour to be a Jew now." She let out a pathetic whimper.

Wanda's head began to shake, quickly, desperately. "This, Dora, this . . ." she stammered, "I did not expect this from you. And all . . . all that you have thought before . . ."

Miss Diamand spoke with difficulty. "All that I thought before . . . has nothing to do with being a Jew now. Why can't you understand that?"

"Because I can't. All I can see is that you are mad at me, as if I were the one who set the synagogue on fire. Dora, what has happened to us?" A tremor took hold of both of them, as though their bodies were mutually infected by fever. They caught hold of each other's hands, and wept. They wept for a long time, until a current of devotion flowed through their knotted fingers and quieted their trembling. "We are both the same, after all," Wanda attempted a smile through her tears. "Aren't we? If you want me to, I will put on a yellow armband as well. I don't mind it. But let's . . . let's hold on to each other."

"You're right. Yes," Miss Diamond sighed with relief. "They must not divide us."

Wanda sugared Miss Diamond's cup of tea. "Tell me," she said softly, "does it make sense that this story about the synagogue should destroy our moods to such an extent?"

The sip of tea gagged Miss Diamond. She felt as if something had burned her. She jumped to her feet with an energy unusual to her, rushed for her coat and left the room.

The wind whipped against her face, shrinking the skin of her cheeks which were still wet with tears. She dragged herself aimlessly through the streets. Everything was finished for her. This time there was no wall of glass. Between Wanda and herself there stood a wall of darkness. "Wanda is no more, she is gone," she whispered to herself, her heart a burning wound. She tried to think of what would happen now, how she would go on, but her thoughts broke and scattered. "This story about the synagogue . . ." Wanda's words hammered in her head. "No, my good old Wanda, to me it is no longer just a story about a synagogue." A horde of people dashed by her, running. Someone pushed her into a gateway.

"Madam, you'd better not go out!" A man in a crumpled coat, wearing a cap with a visor pushed far back on his head, advised her as he shoved her forward from behind. "They're beating up Jews!" he whispered in her ear, and after he got her into the gateway, he moved around in front of her, his face close to hers. "Perhaps you need candles for the Sabbath, Madam . . . to light tonight's table? Have you forgotten that the holy Sabbath is approaching?" Seeing her confusion, he reassured her, "Don't worry, in the worst case, we can run up the stairs . . . Perhaps you need shoelaces, buttons? I have good soap, from before the war, best quality. Perhaps a quarter of a loaf of bread, still warm, just out of the oven? Or a piece of butter? I'll let the price down especially for you, cheap, almost for nothing." She took a step towards the exit, but he blocked her way. "Don't go out! They're beating up Jews!" He stood with his coattails spread open as if ready to protect her against any attack. "Perhaps a sheet of bobby pins? Cord? Thread? Anything?"

She realized that she would not be rid of him unless she bought something, and she let him pull her up a flight of stairs to where a half-filled sack was leaning against the wall. A dirty little boy sat doubled up beside it, his bluish bare legs shaking. Miss Diamond asked for a sheet of hairpins. She put a few groschen into the man's dirty palm, and another one into the child's. She looked into the latter's big black eyes and found herself completely lost in their depths, immersed in a gaze which was beyond sadness or pain, so stunningly wise and knowing was it. It was as if she had emerged from those eyes naked and so deeply shamed that her face began to burn and a cold sweat broke out on her forehead.

She was back in the street. People were still running confusedly in all directions. She edged along the walls and in another moment had forgotten what was going on around her. She felt the child's eyes embedded in hers, and she thought of Wanda. Her anger melted away. All she felt was guilt — a guilt which had to do with this child, with her students, with Wanda and with much more. "How could I?" she asked herself over and over again. Burning with shame, she chided herself, not knowing clearly against what or whom she had sinned. She wept and wailed inwardly, as she suddenly felt engulfed by a yearning for the only pair of hands capable of consoling her in the emptiness of that windy incomprehensible world. "Home! Home!" an inner voice carried her forward. A young fellow greeted her hurriedly as he passed her. She recognized him as one of the students she had seen being taken off in the truck this morning, and she called him back. "They only just freed you?" she asked.

"Yes, Miss Diamand," the exhausted boy took off his cap, running his eyes impatiently over her face. "It wasn't too bad, I only got beaten up twice. I've got to go," he waved his hand at her. "There is a line-up for potatoes at the stores."

"Be careful, they're harassing Jews!" she warned him, but he was already gone. She quickened her step, still thinking of the boy. "Dear beautiful youth," she murmured. "Youth is kind and generous, and old age makes one mean and bitter." She had never felt as old and tired as she did today. As she climbed the stairs, her heart pounded loudly. She had to stop for a while to give it a rest. She had hardly touched the door knob when the door opened from inside and she fell into Wanda's arms. "Forgive me," she sobbed.

"Forgive me," Wanda sobbed.

The same evening the old ladies had a visitor. Mr. Samuel Zuckerman staggered in with a basketful of vegetables. He was exuberant with a hilarity which made the old ladies feel ill at ease. Miss Diamand knew that he had come to talk to her, and she was bothered by the strange notion that Wanda was in their way. A smell of alcohol reeked from Mr. Zuckerman's mouth.

Chapter Eleven

Michal Levine,
Lodz-Litzmanstadt,
November 7, 1939.

Dear Mira,

This time I am trying to reach you through the Red Cross. The important thing I have to tell you is that I was wounded in the left leg during the last day of fighting at the front, and that I will probably be lame for the rest of my life. The other news that might be of some interest to you is that Father has been imprisoned. I now live at home with Mother. My friend, the painter Guttman lives with us.

It is cold here, and the town is dressed up not only in its between-fall-and-winter dress, but also in a new name. Nature has made up the new face of the city gradually, but the new name and everything that goes with it happened overnight, which makes me think of someone just gone mad, who wakes up from a nightmarish sleep to discover that he is no longer himself, but someone else, and that his name is not what he had thought it was. In the same manner, one nice bright morning, our Lodz discovered that its name was not Lodz at all, but Litzmanstadt (to keep alive the memory and name of the German general who conquered and possessed the city during the First World War), and that it did not belong to Poland anymore, but was a town in the *Warthegau* and thus a part of the mighty Third Reich.

You can imagine how overjoyed we were with this discovery. An historical moment, an epoch-making transformation! And in order to mark the occasion properly, the town adorned itself with metres-long blood-red banners with swastikas. The Prophet of the Third Reich, the Minister of Propaganda, Herr Goebbels himself came up from Berlin to greet us. He rode in his limousine along the Piotrkowska, which was packed with the *Folksdeutsche* citizens of our town. Children waved pennants, women threw flowers and the men lifted their arms with a jubilant *"Zieg Heil!"*, drowning out the music of machine guns which celebrated the day with spectacles of their own, in other parts of the town. (How do I know about that? Guttman, who serves as my eyes and legs, provides me with detailed information.)

Indeed, just as someone who has lost his mind is not taken aback by the strange things happening to him, so our Lodz is not at all surprised by its new name. And it seemed only natural to us that the street signs should disappear from the corners and be replaced by brand new signs, carrying the proper German names for each street in Gothic letters. Somehow we have managed to decipher the hieroglyphs and discovered that Piotrkowska Street, as befits a main street of Litzmanstadt, has been rechristened Adolf Hitler Strasse, and that, accordingly, the Allées are called Hermann Göring Strasse; and that in like manner we now have a Ludendorff Strasse, a Berliner Strasse, a Krupp Strasse, a Zeppelin Strasse, and a Minken Weg, a Glocken Weg, a Bush Linie, a Böhmische Linie and many more Linien and Wegen and Gassen and Strassen.

From this, I hope, you will realize that Lodz is in fact gravely ill. Needless to say, the German Police Administration looks after it like a skilled and conscientious nurse who, with minutely-ordered regularity, gives it bitter but healing pills to swallow, pills which are meant to help the poor town forget its previous identity and put it on its new German feet as soon as possible. Now, as far as the city's Jewish limb is concerned, the Police Administration has probably doomed it to amputation. But until the operation can be successfully performed, they have wisely decided to paralyze it instead, and for that purpose, they make use of the surest and most modern methods. And everything ticks like a German clock.

The German Police Administration came to help us organize ourselves, in order to make their own relationship with us easier. They badly need a central address to which they could send their evil decrees. Consequently, they called into being a representative body of the Jews themselves, and have assigned a president to it, whom they call *Der Älteste der Juden* and whom we call the Presess. In order that our "collaboration" with our "saviours" might go along even more smoothly, we all, including the apostates, had to register at the Council office. We have to wear yellow armbands, and of late we are forbidden to leave our houses from five o'clock in the afternoon until eight in the morning, so that if they need us, they know where to find us. During those times when we are allowed to move about the town, we are forbidden to use the street car. If we have a few Polish zlotys, we are not allowed to exchange them for German marks. We are not permitted to buy coal for the winter and our food rations are much smaller than those of the Poles.

But you would be amazed, dear Mira, at the normalcy our lives have acquired. A crazy normalcy, says Guttman. People have learned not to run through the streets, not to hustle and bustle in the market places; and no one gathers in the corners or in the gates any longer. We have learned to slink along the walls and be afraid of our own shadows.

Most of the Jews have lost their previous occupations. The owners of the little stores have sold out their merchandise, and the Jewish firms have been taken over by German directors. Many factories in town have stopped working and those still active can do without Jewish workmen. Nonetheless the Jews manage to go on; they have changed their skin overnight, everyone helping himself as best he can. Some peddle their private belongings, others secretly produce articles of primary necessity in their homes, knapsacks, for instance, or yellow armbands. Others go idle, busying themselves with splitting their saved-up groschens, to make them last longer, and those who have started to go hungry, run to the Council to replace, for a few marks, the rich Jews who want to free themselves from their turn at forced labour. Everyone's main occupation is standing in line for bread, the acquisition of which depends as much on luck as does winning a lottery, since people with yellow armbands are not looked upon with friendly eyes in these lines. Or we sit trapped at home in the long evenings and argue with the neighbours about how long the Germans will hold out.

Dear Mira, I wanted to write you a "diplomatic" letter, avoiding personal things, and not give in to the weakness which overcomes me whenever I think of you. But what I have written is impossible to send off for the time being. Yet I do want you to have news from me, so I shall start another one.

Dear Mira,

Many months have passed without news from you. Your last postcard was dated the first of July, and I don't even know whether you receive the letters I am constantly sending to you. I am trying to send this one through the Red Cross. Sometimes I am sure that you receive nothing anyway. But it has become my illness to write to you, and I don't know if I will ever cure myself of it. Perhaps I do it more for myself than for you.

What I urgently want you to know is that I was wounded in my left leg during the war operations. I will be lame for the rest of my life. I have been out of the hospital a week now. I am at home with Mother. A few times a day I take a walk around the table if someone holds me by the arms. It is very difficult nowadays to come by a pair of crutches.

Father is not at home of late. He was, as you know, an excellent football player. Mother goes every day to take him food, but he is so busy, that she comes home with the pots full. People say that the Blond One has scored a goal against all of them.

Guttman, the friend about whom I wrote you, lives with us now. He has travelled extensively in Southern Europe and tells me a lot of interesting things. I talk to him too — about my philosophies. As you know, loquacity helps in resisting pain. As far as my philosophies themselves are concerned, they are still popular with me, which should prove to you that only my leg is disabled, not my optimism. I am stubborn. A major part of my optimism I owe to the fact that you are there and not here.

As far as food is concerned, we don't go hungry. Guttman scours the town, haunting all the food lines. When I "grow up", which means, when I start walking, it will be easier. Many of my colleagues have left town, among them my chief, Dr. Harkavi. For those who remain behind, it is, my friends tell me, forbidden to heal the Jans and Anteks, but there are, "thank heaven", a lot of sick Moseses and Solomons left. I don't want to burden my letter with too many pages. Perhaps if it is lighter it has a better chance of reaching you.

I love you, my dearest,

Your
Michal.

✦ ✦ ✦

Blizzards penetrated every nook and cranny of the city. Clumps of mud like black slimy reptiles crawled between people's feet and under the wheels of wagons; like snails they stuck to the walls and like snakes slid down from the roofs and fences. The foggy air enveloped the city in veils of gray which pulled the sky down very low, making it sag between the rooftops. Beneath that sky the naked city shivered in its wintry shirt.

Morning. With the first light of day, the houses woke up to their hidden life behind the drawn curtains. The silent empty streets became watchful, attentive. The long lines of people who had stood since the middle of the night along the walls, waiting for the bakery doors to open, stirred. The throngs, huddled close to each other, encircled the houses like dark swaying fences. They listened as the first boot steps were heard approaching from the distance. A few armbands emblazoned with swastikas flashed by at a corner, followed by hoarse shouts punctuated by the sound of spurs. Out of the fog, the first shiny limousines appeared, and behind them, open trucks loaded with rows of soldiers and guns, with guns and with soldiers. The limousines glided by gracefully, arrogantly, splashing the mud onto the sidewalks. Their chauffeurs had exact addresses and knew their destinations. They stopped in front of a house. The sound of thuds coming from the upper storeys reached the street, along with the sound of rifle butts and boots hammering against bolted doors: *"Aufmachen!"* In the upper storey windows, dishevelled heads appeared, desperate eyes searched the street for help. The stairs groaned; a needle-sharp shriek pierced the cold misty air. Then the giants in green uniforms dragged a heavy body, head hidden between hunched shoulders, through the gate. The limousine doors thumped shut; the car set out for another address.

The open truckloads of soldiers moved more slowly along the street. They had no defined addresses and only haphazardly picked their victims among the houses. They would stop in front of a gate and before long, the inhabitants would appear carrying beds and tables, wardrobes and sofas, bedding and clothing, merchandise and machines. Piled up in multicoloured heaps, the things would be scattered around the trucks, while the frightened women and children continued to bring their possessions out from their homes. The men, the heads of the families, would climb onto the platforms of the trucks and arrange the products of their life's work with their own hands. From nearby the green uniforms watched them with pointed guns. Eyes darted furtively at them, as if to inquire, "How much longer must this go on?" The green uniforms did not stir, and this meant, "Carry on and bring more!"

The street watched and listened mutely. From far-off corners, steps would be heard approaching, wavering, staggering. A huddled horde of men appeared, their heads and sleepy bodies swaying drunkenly. Dragged out from their beds, or caught somewhere at a gate, or in front of a bakery, the men, with the eyes of frightened animals, looked around with bewilderment. A green uniform walked behind them, and lashing them with words which cracked like whips, commanded them to hurry onward. So the men hurried on, one with a jacket hanging over his shoulders, another dressed only in his pants, with a scarf wound about his neck probably by a wife's hands at the last moment, still another in his slippers, wearing his pyjamas. As they walked, their yellow armbands swayed back and forth. This was the day's first group of Jews to be caught for labour.

Rachel rose at three o'clock in the morning along with the rest of her family, except for her father who had gotten up earlier and was already gone when the rest of them woke up. They dressed without putting on their yellow armbands and left to join the queues for bread. The gate of the house was still locked and they jumped out into the street through the window of a neighbour's apartment downstairs. They set up a vigil at different bakeries, and Rachel got in line at the bakery nearest her house. The family had split apart in this manner, in the hope that if one of them were thrown out of line, another might be more fortunate.

In front of Rachel there was a huge line of people. She was cold and huddled up to her closest neighbours: in front of her, there stood an old man, and against her back leaned a woman wrapped in a plaid shawl. But the bit of warmth these two provided her with was not enough to keep her stiff limbs from freezing. She exhaled into her turned-up coat collar, warming her pinched nose and chin with her own breath. Her head was full of fantastic visions as she watched the shadows move from one sidewalk to another, as if rocked back and forth by the wind.

When the darkness thinned out, the shadows scattered. A deafening racket struck up along the coils of the snake-like human mass. Rachel poked her head out from between the lapels of her coat. She recognized her janitor's daughter in the woman behind her. She felt reassured, and began thinking about the bread she might get. Up to now the bread had not entered her mind. In her previous paralysis she had had the notion of serving a sentence, condemned to stand here until the moment of her release. Now she looked ahead, searching for the bakery door with her eyes. The road leading up to it was long. True, in actual distance it consisted of a fence and a couple of houses, but this short distance stretched through hundreds of minute steps, through hundreds of single bodies and through the multitude gathered in front of the entrance to the bakery. And for Rachel, the end of this road was even more remote than for the others, because it was uncertain.

Before long, she realized that she could not expect much from the woman standing behind her. Since daybreak, the latter had not stopped chatting with her other neighbours, and Rachel had heard her repeat the words "scabby thieves" which could only mean one thing. The janitor's daughter was a nice honest woman. In the past, she had come up to the apartment every few weeks to help with the big washing, and had brought along her little boy with whom Rachel and her brother liked to play. The two would have supper with the family and at parting, the woman would ask her boy to kiss Blumka's hand. Now the woman's voice grated against Rachel's ear with increasing volume. "They've taken off the yellow armbands and think that no one will recognize them. Wait till a German sees them and they'll catch it good and proper, the cankers!"

As if the woman had charmed them out, the gendarmes appeared. The crowd sank into silence. To Rachel it seemed that everyone could hear the loud pounding of her heart in her stiff body. The gendarmes began to make order, passing a few times along the line and straightening it with their pointing fingers, until it turned into an almost aesthetically-ordered row of people. Now they set about cleaning out the undesirable elements.

The first fortunate people were already leaving the bakery with fresh loaves of bread. Hundreds of greedy wide-opened pairs of eyes stared at the shiny round loaves in their hands; each loaf seemed as bright and radiant as the sun appearing on a gray morning. The onlookers licked the bright bread-suns with their eyes, they tasted them with their nostrils, they chewed them in their imagination, and weighed and measured them with the craving of their empty stomachs.

The gendarmes continued their leisurely pace along the line, their pointing fingers in front of them. "Raus! Raus!" Rachel heard their cheerful voices, and she hung on to the man in front of her. The boots came closer. Her ears were deafened by the hammering of her pulse, and as if through a thick wall she heard, "Jude?"

She heard a sound of wrestling, then a woman left the line, sobbing. Right after, Rachel heard the voice of the janitor's daughter behind her. "I am Polish, *Herr Offizier*, real Polish!" Rachel felt a finger touching her own shoulder. The gendarme, a strapping fellow, looked her over with a pair of playfully twinkling eyes. The finger removed itself from her shoulder and a feeling of gratitude to the green uniform with the handsome face was about to settle in her heart, when she heard the woman behind her back burst out, "She is *Jude, Herr Offizier, Jude!*"

A hand came down on Rachel's shoulder with unbearable weight. "*Raus!*"

The dear place paid for with so many hours of waiting was no more. Rachel's hands reached out to take it back. She snatched the plaid of the woman who was already pressing herself against the old man. A fist jabbed at her from behind the plaid. Rachel's hands reached up to the woman's face, tore at her hair and with pent-up shrieks, she hurled the woman against the wall, hitting her in the hip with her knee. She had a wild urge to squeeze the woman into the wall, to hammer her into the place she had robbed. "Let go of me, Jewish bitch!" the woman yelled, trying to free herself from the girl's hands.

The gendarme who had watched their fight in amusement, as if they were hens plucking the feathers from each other's necks, decided to put an end to the spectacle. He tore Rachel away from the woman. But the girl had gone wild and did not stop throwing her arms and feet about, pulling towards the wall. The gendarme's eyes were gay. Holding the squirming girl with one hand, he thrust her to the ground.

The mud splashed around Rachel; clots of dirt slapped her in the face. Someone was kicking her in the thigh; a pain spread through her limbs. There was an explosion of hilarity around her, as the people in the line joined in the gendarme's contagious laughter. The sound of the guffaws revived her. She raised her head. The bakery door seemed to be close now. Someone came out, carrying a loaf of bread right above her head. Its aroma made her scramble to her feet. A man handed her the shopping bag she had dropped and so, doubled up, she dragged herself home. The moment she entered the room, she shook off her wet coat and dropped onto the bed.

Her mother and Shlamek came in; they too were empty-handed. Blumka took off her plaid and scrambled into her bed. Shlamek paced the room with his hands in his pockets. His face, sprinkled with pimples, looked bluish, raw. He stopped in front of Rachel and noticed the mud smeared all over her face. "Did you fall?" he crowed in his mutating adolescent voice. She turned her head away, listening as he got undressed. In a moment she heard his rhythmic calm breathing. He lay on the sofa with his mouth half open; his two large front teeth reflected the light of the day crowding into the room. She looked at him, looked at the walls, the furniture, at the pieces of clothing strewn about, her limbs longing for sleep.

Then, her father entered. Rachel immediately noticed his empty hands. She heard him approach the bread box, open then close it. She saw him kindle a fire in the stove. Then he was standing in front of her. "You fell?" he asked, trying to rub the dirt off her forehead. "We have to get used to these things," he whispered. "But I can assure you that before we manage to get used to them, the boil will burst. I give them three months, do you hear me?"

"Three months, but in the meantime they'll bleed us to death," said Blumka who had apparently been lying awake. "In the meantime they'll chase us out of our home. It's not for nothing, people are talking. Lodz will be free of Jews."

Moshe Eibushitz cracked his knuckles. "I can bet you that they'll be gone from here with the winter. . ." He turned to Blumka, "Get out of bed." He shook Shlamek vigorously by the shoulder to wake him. "I wouldn't pay any attention to all that," he continued, "but at the slightest mishap, you all fall apart. Here you have Rachel, the heroine, the revolutionary. As soon as something goes wrong, her eyes begin to sweat."

Rachel's eyes now began to "sweat" in earnest. Her parents and Shlamek surrounded her bed, insisting that she tell them what happened. After she had recounted her story between sobs, Blumka gave her husband an angry glance, "What do you say now?"

"They are a blind mob, the Poles, that's what I say," Moshe replied. "But fate will open their eyes, don't you worry."

"I can't stand them!" Blumka threw her head up in rage. "At least the Germans declare openly who they are. But they, our dear neighbours, are false—nothing but a band of jackals lying in wait!" Moshe lifted his hand to stop the flow of her words. She burst out "What's the matter? Are you going to lecture me now about socialist morality and all the other niceties? Thank you very much. You think the janitor's daughter is the only one, that nice sweet little woman who never stopped kisssing my hand? They're all the same, all of them. I hate them and I'm not ashamed of it." She shook her finger threateningly in her husband's face, "I hope with all my heart that they never climb to their feet again, that they never have a country of their own again, because they don't deserve it!"

"There, there. A discussion on an empty stomach!" Shlamek said with a yawn.

Blumka mastered herself, glanced at the clock and ordered her men to move away from Rachel's bed. She pulled up Rachel's dress and scrutinised the bruises on her thigh and hip. But Rachel refused to let her apply a wet towel to them. "It's getting late," she said, adding with a hurt smile, "Father is right, I pamper myself too much."

Before long, all four of them were sitting at the table eating cabbage soup. The hot soup calmed their nerves and their mood grew lighter. A distant memory of the good old times flashed about the room for a moment. Rachel and Shlamek made themselves ready for school. But they did not go there together. Rachel left to meet David.

The street was practically empty. The bread sold out, the bakery door was bolted. The only people visible were far away, where there still stood a German truck which men were loading with their belongings. A thick wet snow began to fall. Rachel was tired and sleepy, her wounds hurt with every step she took. The street danced in the snowy whirl before her eyes like a picture in an old fuzzy film. Then, as if on a screen, the outlines of a figure appeared in the distance — and the powdered street was transformed into a bridge thrown over a cold reality. The trees skirting the sidewalk with their black trunks and white boughs took on the appearance of a guard standing at attention, in honour of the young pair. The bridge between them gradually shrank, until of all the trees, only one was left, beside which they met.

David immediately noticed Rachel's changed face. "Have you been crying?" he asked taking her arm. His touch was new. This was how it had been lately between them, ever since the day of David's return home: a shy, uncertain feeling at the start of their meetings. She did not answer his question. Her back still hurt, but now there was also something pleasant in the pain.

She smiled, "I feel good."

The shyness between them gradually faded; they walked on huddled against each other. "You know," he said, "this is actually the best time to meet. Right in the morning, before school, before everything. You remember nothing, and that's that."

She nodded in agreement. She noticed a warm light playing in the sky behind the mass of cloud and predicted, "There will still be some sunshine today." She pinched him in the arm. "Say, aren't we really breathing the air of a story book?" She pinched him harder. "Did you feel that? No? That proves that we are really story-book characters."

He pulled his gloves off his hands. "Take off your gloves too," he proposed. "I want to feel your fingers. Take off your beret too." He lifted his hand to take the beret off her head.

She would not let him. "I'll freeze!"

"Only for a minute. I want to see your hair, to feel it," he insisted. She gave in and slowly and uncertainly took off the beret. He held her waist with one hand and buried his face in her short hair. "It smells like the forest near our country cottage. Remember when you came to visit me in the country?"

"May I put my beret back on?"

"Ey, you're not romantic at all."

"I am so!" She jumped up and pulled his cap off his head. Twirling it on one finger, she moved away from him. "Do you still want to be romantic?" she stuck the tip of her tongue out at him.

"Give me back my hat, or else I'll give you a going over!"

"All right!" she exclaimed, setting out at a run along the empty sidewalk. Her back hurt badly, but again she felt a kind of pleasure in the pain. She laughed aloud.

He ran after her laughter. "I didn't know you were such a good runner," he panted for breath and stopped. She stopped as well, a metre in front of him. He saw her bosom moving up and down with the fur on the lapels of her coat. Her face was flushed, radiant; the locks of hair fallen over her forehead were tracing lines in the shape of alluring question marks. Her ears were as pink as two sea shells, inviting a warm palm to cover them. Her mouth was moist and shiny. It was as if he were noticing its shape for the first time, and for the first time it awoke in him a completely new kind of desire to kiss it. Was this really the same Rachel? Was he himself really the same? He grabbed her waist and held her tightly in his arms, her breath was warm against his face. He squeezed her so hard that the school bag almost slipped out of her hand.

"Let me catch my breath!" She wrestled with him. "You'll choke me. Here . . . Here is your cap and now let go of me."

"Thank you. I want something more."

Their eyes locked. "What for instance?" she muttered, the pink shells of her ears turning purple.

All of a sudden, he was furious with her, overcome by an anger he had never experienced before. "What's wrong?" he asked, letting go of her.

"You make me serious," she replied.

"Yeah, whenever I ask you for a real kiss, not the idiotic pecks you have been giving me, you become serious."

"A real kiss is a serious thing."

"Sure! With you it's a world-shaking event. We have never kissed for real, do you think that's normal?" They paced along the sidewalk at a distance from each other. His heart pounded madly, weirdly. He admonished himself for his weakness, for his wanting her to offer him her willing ready mouth.

Her hand slipped into the crook of his arm. "Why are you so angry?" she asked.

He shook her hand off. "Because I feel bad when I am with you, bad, as a man."

"That's a bitter reproach."

"That's what it is! You should know the truth once and for all. I let you lead me around by the nose, constantly waiting for you to condescend to do me the great favour. I'm an idiot, that's what I am, a stupid idiot! Yeah, who are you, some saint, an untouchable Holy Mary, or what?" he raged, while at the same time a voice cooed inside him that that was exactly what she was to him: a saint, a Madonna. He did not feel her at his side and turned his head back. "What are you stopping for?" he shouted.

"I'll go to school through another street," she replied shyly.

He approached her. "Do you think you'll solve our problem by running off?"

There was confusion in her eyes. "I love you, David," she said. "I know very well that it's stupid. I would gladly . . . really . . ." Her face was afire.

"Then why do you defend yourself against it so much?"

She spoke with difficulty, "Something holds me back. We wouldn't stop at kissing, not the two of us. I know that what you want is right. It would be good to be able . . . to be free . . . I don't mean only because of the present times, but I mean that too."

"Eh, you're looking for excuses," he waved his hand impatiently. "Yes, in the present times, precisely because of them . . . If you only knew how I felt about us on the way to Warsaw. Never mind. But one thing you had better remember. We're not children any longer."

He stopped short. There was silence between them. Then Rachel paused; her face acquired a strange expression. Her eyes were tearful but she smiled a full smile. The strong sharp gaze burning through her tears took him completely apart. His heart stirred violently. Suddenly, he felt helpless, unprotected, and at the same time opened up, unravelled and overwhelmed by a sensation of triumph, of freedom. Her cool soft hand was around his neck. Her lips were dry and puckered, like two slices of a purple orange. There was thirst on his tongue and hunger between his teeth to bite into their cracks, to reach the juice beneath them and suck it. He pressed his mouth against hers. The houses around them swayed and vanished. The world turned into two pairs of lips, one mouth, knotted both in delight and in anguish. Somewhere high above their heads, both their hearts pounded with one beat.

When they opened their eyes and tore their mouths away from each other, it seemed that everything had changed, that all which had been the same and looked alike would never be the same again. They began to walk, holding hands loosely, trying not to look at one another. It was difficult to find the previous ease of talk, impossible to go back to what had been before their mouths had met. Mutely, they arrived at the *gymnasium*.

It was a morning to remember. Rachel had made an important discovery about herself. She had hurt her back when she fell on the pavement near the bakery, her every step caused her pain, but later she was able to race happily through the street, to feel a burning ache — and laugh. This discovery had allowed her to enjoy her first real kiss with David. She was sure that fate could not be cruel to their love, that some higher justice would protect it.

She began to pay attention to her appearance. She found time to knit a sweater for herself and coaxed Blumka into lending her her scarves, blouses and pins; and she wheedled out of her her only pair of sheer stockings. She enjoyed standing in front of the mirror for hours, to look at herself, scrutinizing her figure, her face, her bosom, her legs — with strict objectivity, and yet with uncritical self-adulation. She also changed her hairdo, wearing her hair loose and wavy, combed away from her forehead. She remembered the remark Miss Diamand had once made, that her hair reflected the dishevelled state of her soul. She liked the state of her hair much better now, and even more so the state of her soul. She felt a constant urge to run somewhere, to fly, to soar.

She was happy. However her interest in the events taking place around her, in the worries of her parents and friends had not diminished. Moreover, she now felt herself capable of consoling others, as if she had become a vessel filled to the brim with light, eager to pour it out and brighten the faces of everyone around her. And most of all she wanted to help her father.

Until recently, Moshe Eibushitz had "held himself in his hands". But of late the armour of his courage had worn thin, betraying his nervousness and despair. In his manner of talking, in the "conclusions" at which he was constantly arriving, this did not show. He continued to encourage his family, to feed them hopeful promises that "It won't last much longer." But the hope was fading from his eyes.

Business had gone on as usual in his barber shop, until the Germans began paying him visits, pulling his clients away from under the shaving knife and taking him along for labour as well. Unable to continue working in such a state of constant tension and uncertainly, he had closed up his shop altogether and now practised his trade only among his neighbours in the backyard. But his main occupation was taking up vigils in the food lines, an activity from which nothing could drive him away; here the fear of being caught for labour did not count. As for his evenings, he spent them at the neighbours', going from one apartment to the other. He hunted for snatches of news, for hints that would help him endure at least one more night. His nights were sleepless. He lay in bed, his ears like seismographs attuned to the noises penetrating the windows, sensitive to the faintest rustle coming from the street. As soon as he heard a suspicious sound, he would rush to the window. Perhaps the Germans had gone? Perhaps something vitally important, which should not be missed, was going on? He looked for a sign, for the slightest good omen. And since the nights were so stubbornly uneventful, he looked for his omen in the windows of the houses across the street; they became his oracle. He knew that this was a silly superstitious game that he had invented. However, the power of auto-suggestion was so strong in him, that he had succeeded in dragging the rest of his family into it.

The windows across the street belong to homebred Germans, a *Folksdeutsche* family. Ever since the occupation of the city, little red flags with swastikas would appear in these windows, one flag behind each pane. But these flags had a habit of vanishing occasionally for some mysterious reason and then reappearing. Moshe fancied that this was related to world events, and every time he noticed the flags missing from the windows, he abandoned himself to a kind of hysterical drunkenness which he was incapable of overcoming. He would rush from one window to another, first to make sure that he was not mistaken, then, unable to bear it all by himself, he would wake his wife, "Blumka, look, they're running off. No flags in the windows!"

Blumka would jump out of her bed, snuggle up to him in her flannel nightgown, and half-asleep and fuzzy-minded, would allow herself to be carried away by his passionate words, as she gazed at the windows across the street. They would exchange their remarks in heated hurried whispers, so as not to wake the children, who nonetheless would wake up and seeing their parents at the windows, would jump out of bed — and they too would see that the flags were gone. After a while, shivering with tension and cold, all of them would rush back to bed to wait for dawn. The children would go back to sleep immediately, but not Moshe and Blumka. They would whisper until the wee hours of the morning and daydream about what would happen after the Germans had suffered their final defeat.

In the morning there were queues in front of the food stores as usual. In front of the houses the German trucks would still be sitting, the loot being loaded into them. People were still being caught in the street for forced labour, and the little red flags with the swastikas were back in the windows. In spite of that, a few nights later, Moshe and his family would let themselves be cheated again by the same trick.

But Moshe had really changed after the last two times he was caught for labour. The first time, dragged off to unload coal from a freight car, he had received a gash in his back from a German boot. The second time, next morning, he had gone down in his slippers to get a few cigarettes. Through the window, Shlamek saw him being led off. Blumka, grabbed Moshe's shoes and coat and followed the troop of Jews. She begged the guard to let her give the shoes and coat to her husband. In reply, the gendarme gave Moshe a bang on the head with his gun, as a punishment for being such a dummy that women had to nurse him. After that, Moshe was no longer the same. His bloodshot clouded eyes half-closed and dull, his forehead rutted as if he were in constant pain, a dried unlit remainder of a homemade cigarette glued to the corner of his mouth, he would pace the room for hours, cracking his knuckles. He felt most at ease when Blumka and the children left the room and put the lock on the door, locking him up inside.

On this particular evening Moshe was more nervous than usual. He paced the room between the beds, puffing on his dead cigarette. Twice this day he had had an argument with Blumka; the second one actually turned into a real quarrel. It had started with the news that Mrs. Rubinov, Rachel's elementary-school teacher, had left Lodz all alone to try and make it to the U.S.S.R., to join her daughters who were living there. Moshe could not make up his mind: should they try to do the same, or should they stay put. Blumka was of little help in reaching a decision. "Whatever you decide, that's what we'll do," she said to him.

"Why not decide together?" he asked.

"All right, let's decide together."

"So what do you say?"

"What do *you* say?"

"I am asking you for advice. What do you think we should do?"

"Do you want me to take all the responsibility upon myself, so that later you can say, 'I told you so'?" That was when the storm broke loose.

They lay in their beds with the light turned off. The room was lit only by the fire crackling and hissing in the oven. Rachel lay tucked under her cover, her gaze following the reflection of the light escaping through the cracks in the oven onto the floor; the lights played with the shadows like a horde of golden kittens frisking with a horde of black ones. She thought of her parents. Lately the question had more than once come to her mind, whether they were really as happy with each other as she had always thought them to be. In her mind's eye she saw her mother's face with the high Mongolian cheekbones and the generous mouth which was capable of producing the most radiant smile. She saw Blumka's body, full and warm, her skin so smooth and delicate that nothing in the world could compare with its softness. She asked herself if Blumka was pretty and tried to appraise her as if she were not her mother — to look at her rather with her father's eyes. How did he love her? How did she love him? Were the feelings they had for each other as powerful and sacred as David's and hers?

Then she recalled her father's face as it had looked before the war, in the good times. She saw his high forehead with the few wrinkles which added an air of maturity and distinction to his face, yet did not make him look old. She saw his hazel eyes, wistful, dreamily blinking, often with the eyelids half-lowered, resembling the eyes of a newborn baby. She saw his chin, rounded, jovial, saw his straight strong nose, his full mouth with the expression of dreaminess on it. She saw his figure. He was slightly taller than average, with shoulders somewhat stooped, but his movements were solid and smooth, never rigid or abrupt but measured, steady and graceful. Above all, she loved his hands which she considered the finest part of him. They seemed to lead a life of their own, they practically had a soul of their own. There was an air of elegance about them. The slender shapely fingers were gentle, although there was not a trace of softness in them. And the strained bulging veins on their backs, blue beneath the hairy skin, added a special expression of strength which seemed more than merely physical. Often she watched these hands as they flipped through the pages of a book, or chopped wood, or polished the floor. A princely ease accompanied their every gesture. No, by no means could she see her father through her mother's eyes. Him she could see only through her own eyes.

She knew that her parents were not asleep. It was still quite early and the family went to bed so as not to add coal to the fire in the oven, and because there was nothing else to do. She leaned on her elbow, gazing at their beds. They were quiet. She knew that they were lying in each other's arms, however she felt that right now Moshe would be glad to hear some encouraging words. "Father," she said in a cheerful resonant voice. "Do you know, I think that you are a man of lost talents." She laughed artificially. "Father?" she listened, waiting for an answer.

"Perhaps I will find them in you," he replied after a long silence.

She did not give in, but let herself be carried away by her rhetoric. "I feel it in you, seriously. You're different from all the people I know. And the great

Yonatan Eibushitz from whom we are descended, why don't you ever tell me about him? Aren't you proud of him?"

"His accumulated merits won't be added to my account," Moshe's voice became particularly unfriendly. "Everyone has his own account-book to take care of." He stopped talking. Was he still nervous because of his quarrel with Blumka, or because he was unable to make up his mind? Was there something else besides that? Or was it just that her, Rachel's way of going about boosting his morale was so silly? She pulled the cover over her head, and lay there, wondering. Gradually, she arrived at the conclusion that her father had never been a happy person; with his family, with Blumka and his children he had perhaps been happy, but not with himself. The sadness which he could no longer disguise had been with him for many years. The times had only brought it to the surface. And she felt ashamed of herself for hurting him instead of cheering him up. He was right, she thought. Everyone had to map out his own road and follow it.

It occurred to her that her father's fears, which he was unable to control, and which — she had to admit to herself — lessened her pride in him, were also rooted in his past. She felt that she knew their cause. They derived from his dissatisfaction with himself, from his feeling of worthlessness; as if he expected to be punished by the Germans for not having achieved what he had meant to; just as if the Germans were the hand of God. Then she asked herself if those people who had lived a rich life were less afraid of death than those who had made no good use of it. Her heart contracted with regret and compassion for Moshe. At the same time, her pride in herself soothed her mind. She had no fears. She knew that hard as it might be, she would climb on, striving to live her own life fully. Indeed she would finish what Moshe had never started. And while aware of this, she felt more than ever like his daughter. Her achievements would be sure to boost his pride in himself, because she was a part of him; then, in a certain way, justice would be done and the account would balance.

When she later asked herself what it was that she hoped to achieve, she could not find the precise answer.

◆   ◆   ◆

(David's notebook)

Three months have passed since my return home. Father came back as well, and he was with us for three days. Three days after the Germans entered Lodz, the Gestapo came to arrest him. He is in prison along with other Jewish councillors and party leaders. We used to bring him food parcels, but lately the guards won't accept them. One thing is now clear to me: Father did not want to escape, or wanted it only half-heartedly. It was not only a question of money, as I thought at the time. During the night of September 6th, when we ran towards Warsaw, he let himself be dragged along by Leon. But after his return, he didn't even want to hide. Didn't he realize the danger? Did he think that his duty was to remain with the people, with us? This riddle bothers me. Will I ever know the answer? When they came for him, he rose from the table and marched off with them, just like that.

Halina and Leon have left for Warsaw. Probably our intellectuals and political leaders consider it more important to be active there. I try to convince myself that I don't resent Halina for having left us, but in vain, although she could probably not have acted otherwise. When we were saying good-bye, she whispered in my ear that if I found out something about Father, I should let her know. Will I ever find out?

There are only the three of us now. Home is no longer what it used to be. It makes one want to run away, and at the slightest excuse, I do so. Mother doesn't talk much, and when she does, it is to rage at me. I am a good-for-nothing, she says. Whatever I do displeases her and gives her an opportunity to criticize me.

In spite of Mother's "good" opinion about me, I am quite a hotshot. I run to all the lines possible, find connections to get in through back doors, and push myself in to all those places where I can find something to take home. I may get thrown out of ten lines, but in the eleventh I sometimes have luck. The thing is only that as much as I achieve, I am still no match for Abraham who has stopped playing his former games, now that he has discovered a new,˙far more interesting one: to play at being grown up, which he realizes is easier now than being a child. Consequently, he does not consider that the grown-ups deserve much respect. After all, they do the job worse than he. No wonder that he behaves like the despot of the family. Not only does he give Mother advice, but he also orders her around. And more often than not, when you think about what he orders you to do, you realize that it makes sense, and you obey him. At night he drops onto his bed dead tired and immediately falls asleep. Then he is a child again.

I sleep badly of late. Every creak of Mother's bed wakes me. Often, when I open my eyes, I see her standing at the window, looking out. Sometimes I am unable to get back to sleep and everything in the room takes on strange forms. I recall my escapade and see bellies of corpses ripped open, I hear Yossele whimpering, "I have lost my father," and the word "father" gnaws away at my heart. I stir in my bed which groans under me; then I hear Mother asking, "Why don't you sleep, David?"

My razor broke and for a while I was rid of the headache of shaving. But this morning, as I went to the sink to wash, Mother, who was sitting at the machine, (lately, she earns some money by sewing knapsacks for the neighbours,) said to me as I passed her, "Aren't you ashamed to walk around with such a beard?" and she stood up and arranged Father's shaving things for me on the window ledge.

It took me perhaps an hour to shave. I had completely forgotten how to hold this tool in my hand and my fingers tangled in each other. Soon red dots popped out all over my skin, and on top of it all, dear Abraham would not stop cruising around me, giving me advice. Then he saw me in the mirror and exclaimed, "You look exactly like Father!" My hand stopped moving, but he burst out laughing, "What are you standing there like a telegraph pole for, the soap is running down your pants! You know, Mother," he rushed to the sewing machine, "I would have done it much better than he!" In the mirror I saw Mother's shoulders sinking. She stopped sewing and rested her forehead on the top of the machine. Abraham exclaimed, "What's the matter, Mother, something got into your eye?" and he gave her all sorts of advice on how to take it out.

To get back to more personal things, I would like to note that a new chapter has begun between Rachel and myself. We don't see much of each other apart from walking to school together, since both of us are too busy with worries at home; and then there is also the early curfew hour. However when we do meet, we forget about everything. It seems as though nothing is happening in the world, and that the only thing that has happened is our renewed love. We talk less, but if we do, it is mostly about our feelings for each other. They seem more important than the most important facts in history, and that they can fill ages of time. Rachel makes plans. She dreams about the room where we will live together. The walls will be covered with books from the floor to the ceiling, all around, she says. On the window sill there will be a lot of flowerpots and a white curtain will sway over them. Her words sound like music, like a symphony to my ears. As she talks, I think of my future, and it seems bright and rosy, within reach. I see laboratories, huge telescopes and an enormous sky filled with stars and planets.

Last time, we were in snow-covered Poniatowski Park. I was telling Rachel about my definite decision to become an astronomer. We walked on the white path, our heads flung up to the starry sky. In its navy blue depths, the outlines of the constellations were traced very clearly. I pointed them out to her. It was breathtaking. But then we heard steps in the snow. A few German soldiers were approaching. One of them shone a flashlight on us (also a star, of human production). "Look here!" he exclaimed "*Eine jüdische Hure mit einem jüdischen Hurensohn!*"

"*Der hat eine Nase wie ein Horn,*" another one laughed. They did nothing to us, removed the glare of the flashlight from our eyes and moved on. For us, all the stars in the sky went out.

◆　◆　◆

Adam Rosenberg remained in Lodz even though he had begun his preparations to escape the fire long before any one else had smelled smoke. He had been on the vacation which he had planned and looked forward to so impatiently. At last he had gone hunting with his dog Sutchka; he had shot rabbits and deer and chased after wild ducks and partridges. But his pleasure had been short lived. Just as Sutchka became wild and impatient when her sensitive nostrils detected an approaching animal, so Adam, with canine sensitivity, smelled that somewhere behind his back, a monster was lurking, an animal whom he could not fight, but from whom he must escape as soon as possible. He was beset by anxiety for the safety of his factory, of his capital and of all his possessions.

Consequently, he put away his hunter's outfit and returned to Lodz with his devoted Sutchka. The summer was at its hellish peak as Adam began his feverish existence. He had no time to file his nails or to play chess with himself, nor did his correspondence consist of any more letters to charitable organizations. Now, he was endlessly writing long confusing letters to all kinds of banks in Switzerland where he intended to transfer all his moveable capital, as well as himself and his family.

Adam lived with such intensity during those hot weeks, that he had no idea where his days went; he did not remember the dates, nor did he ever know what time it was; every hour seemed decisive, every minute — the last. He was grateful that he was all alone with Sutchka. Yadwiga was still at the sea resort, unaware of what was going on, and Mietek — about whom Adam had correctly predicted that he would fail his matura examinations, but who had nonetheless received a new motorcycle from his father — was driving around somewhere on Poland's roads and was not there to ask questions. Adam pursued his activities unobtrusively, not showing up at his factory where he was sure everyone thought him to be in the Forests of Bialowieze; everyone, that is, except the general manager, Zaidenfeld, without whose help Adam could do nothing.

Before long, Adam had secured all his moveable capital and entrusted it to a bank of the utmost discretion in Switzerland. His account was marked with a coded number, which Adam knew by heart; it was tattooed on his memory; the rhythm of his pulse beat it out. The Number and Adam became one — and he allowed himself to breathe a sigh of relief. As a matter of fact, he felt as light, as if he had become only a shadow of himself; a shadow wandering the hot streets of Lodz, while his real self was on the other side of the border, protected and safe. In his imagination, he saw himself taking promenades in Switzerland, along Lake Lugano, at the foot of the Alps, or in the parks of Bern or Geneva. He smelled the good Swiss food with his refined nostrils and saw himself sitting at the spotless white restaurant tables, near picture windows which served as frames for the most beautiful landscapes in the world.

But the hour was apparently later than he had thought. Adam could not flee to Switzerland just like that and leave behind his enormous factory, his pride and glory which was worth a fortune. Nor could he just abandon his little palace which was among the most luxurious modern structures in town. He was ready to sell everything at a loss, but the problem was that there were no customers. Polish businessmen were not interested in acquiring new possessions, and the German merchants and capitalists who lived in town had shut themselves up like rats in their holes during those pre-war days. Meanwhile, Mietek came home with his motorcycle and Yadwiga returned from the sea resort. Both were suntanned and in high spirits, and both looked forward to the forthcoming trip abroad. Then Mietek came up with a senseless idea that rather than leave for Switzerland, he would prefer to go to Paris, which tempted him more with its charming easy life. Yadwiga, on the other hand, accepted Adam's choice cheerfully and did not mind leaving the beautiful house behind, knowing that she would have comfort wherever she went. But she insisted on taking all her crystal and porcelain along, since they were her major weaknesses, apart from her fondness for clothes.

Mietek did not cease quarrelling with his father, determined to go his own way no matter what; and Yadwiga did not stop curling the last hairs left on Adam's head, with her red-nailed fingers, telling him that if her treasures stayed behind, she would stay behind as well. She giggled, talked in her kittenish tone of voice, and refused to understand the difficulties her capricious decision would create if he gave in to her.

Then came the first of September and Adam woke up to a different world. Yadwiga had her crystals and porcelains and Mietek had what he wanted, namely, that they did not go to Switzerland. Mother and son, without being overly shocked, passed the threshold into their new life quite matter-of-factly. But Adam felt cut off from his own self as if by an axe. Torn away from the most valuable part of his treasure, he considered himself a beggar, a mere miserable worm worthy of being trampled. He did not know what to do with himself, everything in his life having become both loose and tangled at the same time. His daily number of cigars grew from four to ten, and the more difficult it became to obtain them, the more he needed them. It seemed to him that he was losing his reason. He often buried his head in Sutchka's soft furry neck and cried hot tears.

Then, to all his troubles, another was added: suddenly there were hordes of customers ready to buy his factory and his house. No sooner had the city been occupied, than the rich German citizens, for whom he had been so desperately waiting only a short time before, dashed out of their holes like rats and besieged miserable Mr. Rosenberg, thereby robbing him of what was left of his peace of mind. They would rarely come alone; each of them brought along an escort of German officers, or of civilians with high posts "in Berlin"; and each of them had documents where it was written in "black upon white" that he had the exclusive right to buy the factory as well as the house from *Herr* Adam Rosenberg. The sums they offered were a mockery and they threw them in Adam's face, pricking him with them like pins in an open wound. Quite often the Germans quarrelled among themselves over his head, as if he had nothing to do with the bargaining, or as if he were not even there.

Every time the customers came into the house, they first rummaged about as though it were already theirs, and when they left, they usually took along an object or two which had pleased them very much, as a token — a kind of reverse deposit. At first, the coquettishly smiling Yadwiga would sweetly and kittenishly try to take the objects out of their hands, but once she was honoured with such a "caress" of five spread-out fingers across her smiling face, that she became completely indifferent to their carrying things out of her home. The expensive crystals and rare porcelain pieces lost all their value in her eyes.

The negotiations about the house were at the peak of indecision when, one crisp morning, a huge truck appeared in the carefully kept garden. Adam, Yadwiga, Mietek and all the servants were invited to empty the house of all moveable objects and load them onto the truck. The house was left with only the beds to sleep in, with a heap of clothing which the guards had overlooked in the process of loading, and with the jewellery and money the Rosenbergs had managed to hide at the last moment. Apart from that, as punishment for not having left his factory in operating condition, which was considered sabotage, Adam received an invitation to the *Polzeicommissariat*, from which he was immediately transferred to the city prison. He spent two long weeks there, then he was freed — after the intervention of Matilda Zuckerman's friends, a few influential officers from Leipzig, and after he had paid the round sum of ten thousand reichsmark. The factory was *beschlagnahmed*, and the problem of the house was definitely solved as well. The day he returned from prison, Adam received the order to clear out of his home within twenty-four hours.

Although the Rosenberg family and the Zuckerman family were never overly close and had met only when business or social occasions required it, Adam, at this tragic hour thought immediately of Samuel. Adam, who had never known any people whom he could call friends, realized now that he did have one, and a good one at that: Samuel, whose wife had helped to get him out of prison and by doing so had perhaps saved his life. Now, that the Rosenbergs were thrown out into the street, it was the most natural and obvious thing to knock at the door of the Zuckermans, since friendship obligated one to certain things. Adam did not doubt that he would be received with open arms. The Zuckermans' home was, after all, the only place where the Rosenbergs could feel safe and secure.

The Zuckermans received them, not with open arms, but with the hospitality characteristic of the times. The only problem was the dog, Sutchka, who was not received too cordially by Barbara, the cat, who had an atavistic dislike for dogs, much the same as Sutchka had for cats. The wild scuffles of these two arch-enemies, their mewing and barking, got on everyone's nerves, and Matilda, who had so graciously agreed to accept the guests, decided to put her foot down. She decreed that the dog should be sent down to the basement and forbade it to trespass on other territories. Adam interceded on Sutchka's behalf with great dignity, defending her rights and protesting against the inhumane limitations put on her freedom of movement, but Matilda, with still greater dignity, shook her head adamantly and, in this way, the sphere of influence of the domestic animals was definitely decided.

On top of that, the first week they moved in with the Zuckermans, Adam became angry with his host for still another reason. He refused to contribute money to the Jewish Council, even though all the other rich Jews who had stayed in the city did. First, he did not want Presess Rumkowski or the Germans to know that he was in town; second, he considered himself a near-beggar, who was himself in need of support. Samuel nagged him, insisting in a very categorical and arrogant manner, until Adam gave in, on the condition that Samuel would hand over the money without mentioning Adam's name. Adam himself considered this to be an expense paid, not to the community, but to Samuel for providing him with shelter. And with that, the friendship of the two men was over.

Since the moment that Sutchka had been sent down into the basement and forbidden to show her face on the upper floors, Adam too had begun to spend the major part of his empty days in the basement. There, amid the boxes and other objects brought over from Zuckerman's old house, he felt best. Sutchka, the only consolation he had, would lie at his feet and share her warmth with him. She was closer to him now than his wife or his son, both of whom had become total strangers, as had Samuel and all the rest of the people in the house, as had the entire world upstairs, above the cellar.

He would rarely exchange a word with anyone and during meals, he kept his face buried in his plate. As soon as he finished eating, he would leave his seat and go downstairs, the cellar having also become his shelter from the danger threatening him upstairs. From the time he had spent those two nightmarish weeks in prison, he had acquired such a fear of the Germans, that the mere sight of the colour green, of a piece of green material, or of a leaf in a flower pot reminded him of the colour of a German uniform. Now he truly acquired Sutchka's sensitivity, an alertness of the ear for the slightest noise coming from outside. Every visit of Matilda's officer friends brought on one of his attacks of dread. All the people in the house would come down to the basement then, and while sitting among them, he would suffocate with fright. It seemed to him that he heard boots approaching, that soon they would climb down, break into the cellar and pull him out of his hideout. He wanted to be left alone by everybody; by the Germans, by his wife and son, by the people in the house, by the entire world.

He tried to kill the endless hours of the day by reading his once favourite detective stories. But this did him no good. Every story seemed to be about him, about Adam. He was the criminal, the persecuted robber. The law of the world was after him, the hand of justice was reaching out to strangle him. He felt guilty, sinful, and these feelings appeared self-evident and logical to him. There was a kind of reverse reasoning behind them. If he were not sinful and guilty, he would not have to hide in this cellar, but could walk the streets free as a lark, without fear of punishment. This notion filled him with disgust at his own self, disgust with his clan, with the entire Jewish progeny — and he feared still more for his life.

✦ ✦ ✦

The first weeks of the war were critical for Samuel Zuckerman as well. As soon as he had returned home from the front, the glass of vodka had become the only means by which he could strengthen himself. But after a while, he regained self-control and even managed, at least superficially, to live without fear. After all, his philosophy of life had always been that all situations, no matter how black and gruesome they might be, would end well, so long as death did not interfere; for he belonged to that brand of people who are ready to accept the dramatic aspects of human fate, but not the tragic ones. The few weeks he had spent as an officer on the battlefront later appeared to him as a nightmare which had perhaps never taken place. He gradually forgot the details of these experiences and scarcely remembered where and when he and his soldiers had rushed into battle, thrusting themselves into fiery darknesses torn apart by animal-like howls, by deafening grenade and bomb explosions, by cannon shots and by the roar of airplanes. Having avoided capture, he returned home unharmed; this only strengthened his belief in his lucky star and nourished his optimism.

At home, once the great shock of transition was over, he slowly adjusted himself to the rhythm of the strange days. As time wore on, he would listen to the depressing news, to all the horror stories that people repeated, in a detached manner, as if they had no bearing on his own life. He considered himself and his family to be beyond any danger. Even the fact that the Germans had begun to liquidate Jewish bank accounts, that his own money was frozen and that a German manager had been assigned to his factory and to his business did not bother him much. Before the repressions and chicaneries had started, he had, thanks to tips received from German friends, provided himself with enough cash to live comfortably for an entire year, and he did not care about the rest, since he was sure that the war would be over in no time. The harassment and looting, the forced labour and all the other discomforts imposed on the Jews he considered to be very sad indeed, but as long as they did not represent a real danger to life, in particular his own and that of his family, he felt them to be more or less bearable.

He and Matilda had many friends among the Germans in town and these friendships they now put to good use. Samuel had obtained an "iron letter" assuring his personal immunity, and no Star of David was fastened to the door of his house as was required on all the doors behind which Jews lived. When German hooligans knocked at the door, shouting the question, "*Jude?*" The answer from inside was a quiet "No". Samuel had a *Passierschein* which allowed him to move about the city freely, without an armband, even after the curfew hour. Nothing was touched in his house, and when the many German and Polish friends offered to hide some of the Zuckermans' valuable objects until "the storm blows over", the latter obliged, sending over objects of secondary importance, but keeping those which were most precious and closest to their hearts with them. At this time, Matilda acquired a characteristic that Samuel had always had: an attachment to objects which had become woven into her memory of bygone years. And their mutual devotion to the house and to everything in it created a new bond between them.

The atmosphere in the Zuckerman house was almost the same as before the war. Matilda actually became more even-tempered and good-humoured, although she still seemed to float in the lofty realms of her dream world, as estranged from any contact with reality as before. The one time she and her daughters had been caught for forced labour seemed to her an accident which would never be repeated, and she refused to dwell on the thought. Nevertheless, there had been a sort of awakening; an alertness had sprung to life within her, that made her more than ever conscious of her responsibilities towards her home. She also felt that, of all the people dearest to her, Samuel was the one who was most endangered, not so much physically, as mentally. She knew his nature, his "masculine childishness", and she thought that he, no more than herself, was not made for times of upheaval. But she was a woman, sure of her instinct, of her inborn strength; she sensed the hazards of reality clearly, in spite of her "blindness" to it. She often asked herself if Samuel also had something within him to equal the power of her intuition, to make him alert and ready to protect his family when it was threatened by perilous circumstances.

Thus Samuel and Matilda came to new terms with each other during these uncertain days, and there developed a kind of comradeship between them. It was not expressed in words, in conversations or confidences; rather it permeated the air around them.

Matilda had no difficulty obtaining food for the family. If Renia the nanny could not get a certain product, Matilda would get it through her Leipzig officer friends, who were stationed in Lodz, and with whom she had gotten in touch through some acquaintances among the *Folksdeutsche* who lived in town. When these officers came to visit, they would bring bottles of vodka, bread and sausage, and Matilda would sit down at the piano, which was lately uncovered only on these occasions, and play for them. She would offer them familiar pieces, popular half-classical works, favouring particularly the Leipzig songs which she, like the officers, had used to sing in her youth. After her concerts, the guests would become melancholy and give vent to their *Sehnsucht nach der Heimat*. Matilda would exploit these moments in a delicately refined manner. She would complain of her bitter situation, and the visitors, by now thoroughly mellowed and feeling their own *Wunde am Herzen*, would console her compassionately. They liked her. She represented a part of their *Heimat* to them and they would assure her, as if she were one of them, that the Führer had no idea of the tactless acts committed in his name. Of course, they shared the Führer's opinion that world Jewry was responsible for this war and they did not hesitate to say so to *Gnädige Frau* Matilda, since she was, of course, the exception that proved the rule. At such moments, *Gnädige Frau* Matilda did not blink an eye, nor did she make the slightest effort to defend world Jewry against their criticism. She would just listen amiably. But as she served the coffee, she would complain with a sigh that she had to sweeten it with saccharine, since sugar was so impossible to come by. Then the *Herren Offizieren* would shake their heads sadly, mumble "*So was!*" and make a mental note to bring along a few kilograms of sugar on their next visit, to sweeten, at least slightly, the bitter lot of Gnädige Frau Matilda. They would take their leave, kissing her hand gallantly, and after they left, Matilda would feel supplied with protection for another few weeks.

Samuel and the daughters would never show up in front of the German visitors. Matilda saw to that. Without them around, she could more freely play on her Gnädige Frau coquetry, without exposing herself to the critical eyes of the members of her family. Indeed, the visitors had asked a few times where Der Herr Gemahl and the daughters were, and Matilda had informed them each time that the daughters were with friends and that her Herr Gemahl was a Polish Jew who did not understand any German. This information killed completely their desire to make his acquaintance.

Samuel was satisfied with things as they were. Satisfied with the visitors, because their coming meant protection and security, and satisfied that he did not have to see their faces, which made him almost feel as if the visits had never taken place. The story was slightly different with the daughters. They would protest, ashamed that their family was singled out for all the privileges; and while they ate the good meals Reisel, the cook, was able to prepare thanks to the unwanted guests, they would let their parents know how low they had fallen in their children's eyes. In truth, the girls were rarely home during the Germans' visits. Whenever Matilda expected a visit, she would get rid of the girls by sending them to sleep over with friends or relatives, not so much to avoid the children's protest as to protect her daughters from male eyes, since she had an inborn distrust of members of the opposite sex, German officers included. She had always valiantly protected the girls against this danger and now her watchfulness was doubled. After all, these were unbridled times.

According to Samuel's prognosis, the war was supposed to last no longer than through the winter and for that stretch of time he had to arm himself with patience. He walked around doing nothing and made an effort not to be bothered by it. He counted the days — a slow count. They moved as if congealed, gray and eternally long, filled with emptiness, without perspective. He was unable to look beyond these days, as if beyond each of them stood a thick wall which prevented him from seeing the following morning. His head was without plans, his imagination without visions, life became a stagnant swamp in which the hours crawled like slugs, purposeless, aimless. Were it not for his reluctance to give in to depressing thoughts, he would finally have fallen a victim, not to fear, but to that emptiness. But he pushed it away from him, just as he pushed away his fear, not letting himself be overpowered by it. Initially, he spent a lot of time with Matilda and the girls, and passed his often-sleepless nights which lengthened his days even more, by going over the material for his history of the Jews of Lodz. His notes were all in order and prepared, and he was only waiting for the proper moment to start the writing. That moment, however, was slow in coming.

There were nonetheless a few good moments in the daily emptiness: the moments of the news broadcasts. The nine-tube Telefunken, which the Zuckermans had gotten as a gift from Professor Hager and his wife, was no longer fitted into the elegant mahogany box. Now it was placed in a rough fruit box and hidden in a hole behind a painting in the bedroom. This box became the centre of Samuel's life, his only reminder that time was not congealed and motionless. With its waves of talk, it pierced the black wall in front of every day, carrying a thread of light through it — a link to the other side. Samuel had made the hole in his bedroom wall the day the order came that all radios must be delivered to the police. He had looked up an acquaintance who was a radio technician and diligently learned from him the art of setting up radios and of taking them apart, since he refused to part with his treasure.

Every evening, around seven-thirty, the room would fill with all those who were present in the house, as well as with friends and with neighbours. People would sit on the beds, on the floor, or lean against the walls. The front door would be locked, Wojciech with his broom standing on guard outside. The windows were covered with the blackout curtains as the room, crowded and hot, would grow loaded with tension, electrified with anticipation. They all held their breaths, their eyes searching like projectors for Samuel's slim figure in the dark as he approached the painting on the wall. He would work with a small flashlight; his hands were like two odd fireflies prying into the secret hole of darkness.

Suddenly, the room would sway with an awed tremor as a voice proclaimed, "This is the BBC, London". The sacred service had begun. A brother from the outside world was talking — the mighty, the Almighty. Hearts would cease their throbbing, for fear of losing a word, so dear was the voice which filled the darkness. Then, after the broadcast, they would sit for a long time in silence, motionless, each with his own thoughts, listening to the echo of the stilled voice, to the forecast of his own fate hidden, as in a murky incomprehensible oracle, in the words just heard. The mood in the room became permeated with anguish and the darkness became unbearable.

Samuel would remove all traces of the "visitor" and turn on the light. Then would begin a heated discussion about the news they had just heard. Everyone gave his own interpretation. They took every sentence apart, analyzed it and tried to deduce the hidden meaning of every nuance of the broadcaster's voice; they would look for the deepest significance of the voice's tone and inflection; most of all, they searched for a hint, a promise that the war would not continue much longer. Slowly, the people in the room would work themselves into a frenzy, a kind of trance; logic was left behind, reason was shut up behind ten locks. Imagination ran wild. Freedom seemed so close that it was enough to take a step to the window, to tear the curtains down — and it would be day instead of night, a bright sky instead of darkness; and over that sky, like dragonflies in the spring, the airplanes of General Sikorski would come buzzing, and salvation would be at hand.

More than anything else, these broadcasts inspired Samuel to become actively interested in the affairs of the community. It was a time of brotherhood in the world. The foreign brother had promised his help and one could be worthy of it only by becoming a brother oneself. Samuel had always had hundreds of friends, but now their number doubled and tripled. Whenever the German guests were not present in the house, Wojciech, the servant, had orders to let in everyone, stranger or acquaintance, who asked for Samuel. People would come to beg for advice or for charity. It began to look as if Samuel were some great lord who was unaffected by the laws of Jewish tragedy, who was capable of performing miracles. For him, these interviews became a wonderful means of filling the emptiness of his days and of sustaining his equilibrium. He had always hated to be alone, and in the present times — even more so.

At first he received everyone in his study; later, he received them in his bedroom where he had begun to spend most of his days. Matilda was not very happy about the constant traffic in and out of that most intimate corner of the house; the sight of mud stains leading to and from it pained her. It seemed to her that the restlessness of the street had swept over her privacy; that the family fortress, of which she was the queen and which she made such an heroic effort to protect, was being taken apart by the cold coming in from outside. But she bit her lips and kept silent, for Samuel's sake. Besides, she, like Samuel, felt that a price had to be paid for their privileged position in order to justify it in some way. But before long, Samuel's activities for the community lost their private character and became more official.

As soon as the Eldest of the Jews in Litzmanstadt, the Presess Mordecai Chaim Rumkowski, set out, seriously and responsibly, to organize his administrative body, he started to gather around him people whom he more or less liked, like Samuel, for whom he had a paternal feeling, as well as people whom he considered socially important, even if he found them personally displeasing, like the editor, Mr. Mazur. And so the two old friends became members of the Community Council and Samuel's life was finally filled with content.

However, despite the removal of Samuel's "office" from his home, the house did not go back to the privacy of former times. With the arrival of winter, the Zuckermans acquired permanent tenants. Samuel could not watch the helplessness of Professor Hager and his wife, and invited them to move into his home, turning over his study to them. A few weeks later, it was the turn of the Rosenbergs, who took over the guest room; from there Adam's morbid silence and his anxieties permeated the entire house.

However, Adam had no monopoly on fear. This particular day was the day not of his, but of his host's attack of anxiety.

Samuel stood at the bedroom window looking out into the street through an opening in the blackout curtains. It was early afternoon, gray and foggy, with bursts of needle-sharp hail piercing the fog, storming the pane, as if it were trying to cut its way through to Samuel's face. He was pale; his lips were sucked in between his teeth, giving his face the appearance of a white mask. A chill went through him. Fear had come over him like a disease, like an attack of high temperature, ready to burn every nerve. He let the curtain fall and pressed his face and the rest of his body against the oven; but the cold inside him refused to subside. The notes for his book, strewn about the table, caught his attention. He realized what a burden this work had become to him and had an impulse to throw all the accumulated piles of papers into the oven and be rid of the enormous task he had taken upon himself. But instead of doing what he felt like doing, he let himself drop onto the bed and allowed the fear to puncture his entire being. His pullover moved up and down with the heaving motions of his chest, as if a struggling bird were trapped in it. His thoughts fluttered in his head also like birds.

He thought of Matilda, of his daughters. He imagined how the house would look without him. But at the same time, he was unable to grasp that his not being here would also mean his not being at all. Not to be was inconceivable — only a speculation of the mind. Yet he went on thinking how painful it would be for Matilda to lose him, and he took a secret pleasure in the thought of her grief, as he used to do when, as a child, he would dream of avenging himself on his mother, saying to himself, "I'll get sick and die and then what will she do?" It was just that kind of desire for vengeance that he felt now, and he knew full well its reason. Matilda's newly acquired strength, her composure, her refined way of assuring the safety of the house and of himself — all that was well and good, and yet it was not good at all. The scales between the two of them were only superficially balanced. In reality, the higher she rose, the lower he fell. The stronger she became, the weaker he felt, and the more childish. If he died, she would bewail him and bemoan him, he thought, but not forever. She would not lie down at his side and die too. Rather, she would step over his grave and go on without him, as if he had never existed. Even that trace of himself, along with that of his forefathers, which he longed to leave behind, even that would be crossed out, razed by the storm.

His thoughts wandered to his daughters, to Junia. The resentment he had felt towards her during the weeks of the last summer, when she had brought about her expulsion from the *gymnasium*, had long since vanished. Now he saw the mark of courage in her behaviour towards her German teacher. Who knows, he thought, perhaps she was the only true heir of his grandfather, Shmuel Ichaskel Zuckerman? She had matured, but lost none of her sense of humour. Were it not for Junia, he thought, there would be no laughter in the house at all. Her mischief-making and her wisecracks, repulsive to him in the past, now seemed full of charm. Actually, he had always loved her. Perhaps he had been so resentful and dissatisfied with everything she did because she resembled him so much. Perhaps he could not accept her as she was, because he could not accept himself as he was. Now, however, he did not want her to change, what he wanted was to change himself, to become stronger, more manly. The bird hidden in his chest, beneath his pullover, continued to flap its wings of fear.

But if the thoughts of Matilda and Junia circled around his fear, the thought of Bella was at its very core. Thinking of her reinforced his worry about himself. Bella was defenceless. Every brutality she witnessed or heard about drained the blood from her face, making her look uglier and more forlorn. She was so quiet these days; and she looked at him, her father, as if she had grown aware that he was not capable of protecting her. Nor was there any help for her. She was one of those unhappy souls who come into life unarmoured and can be wounded by anything ugly or brutal. At the same time she was as stubborn as Junia. She would not hide in the shelter of her home. Every day she went to school, and returned poisoned by the horrible sights in the street. Then he would see her in the salon, pacing about listlessly like a shadow and he would know that she was listening to the silenced music of bygone days. Sometimes, in a surge of tenderness, he would forget the orders of the police authorities which forbade Jews to play musical instruments. He would rush to the piano, pull off the dark plaid which covered the instrument, and ask her to play. She would dash out of the room. Sometimes he wished to take this child, this seventeen-year-old daughter of his and rock her in his lap and kiss that painful sadness out of her eyes. If he were no longer here, what would become of her?

He could not stay on the bed any longer. And as soon as he got up, he realized that everything he had thought while lying down was strange, crooked — true and false at the same time. Yes, lately he had discovered that what he thought while stretched out in a horizontal position made everything appear as if seen through a distorting mirror. The truth of the matter was, he now admitted to himself, pacing with large steps about the room, that he had no one on his mind but himself, that the dread he felt in all his bones was the fear of losing his own life, and nothing else. Disgusted with himself, he decided to go downstairs and join Matilda and the girls. But he had to master his nerves completely before he could show himself to them. He tried to reason with himself. It was impossible that anything should happen to him. He had always had his lucky star to protect him and everything suggested that it would save him this time as well.

He had scarcely managed to regain his composure when he noticed through the wet window pane the huddled figure of the editor, Mr. Mazur, approaching the gate. Obviously those in the other rooms were also standing at the windows, since everyone came out into the corridor to meet the visitor; everyone, meaning Matilda and Yadwiga Rosenberg, both with their knitting in their hands, Mrs. Hager leaning on the arm of the professor, Bella with a book under her arm, Junia with a piece of hot baked potato at her mouth, and Reisel, with a wooden ladle between the hands which she held folded over her bosom. From the washroom door poked out the small gray head of Renia, the nanny, and from the cellar door, the head of Wojciech, the servant. Only Mr. Rosenberg did not show up, nor did his son Mietek who lay on his bed all day long.

Junia, a bite of hot potato in her mouth, kissed Mr. Mazur on the cheek. All the others approached him and helped him to take off his coat, while they bombarded him with questions. "How dare you run about the city on such a day?" Matilda exclaimed, putting away her knitting and taking the editor's ice-cold fingers in her soft hands.

"Is it true that they've taken everything out of your apartment?" Mrs. Hager asked, shaking the neatly combed curls of her gray hair.

Reisel waved the wooden ladle. "They certainly make us all equal, the Germans, may a black year come on them! Soon there won't be any difference between the rich and the poor." There was an undertone of satisfaction in her voice, but she sighed sadly.

Junia and Bella hung on to Mazur's arm. "Come with us into the kitchen," Bella begged him.

"Yes, we will analyze the situation," Junia winked at him mischievously.

"And why didn't you bring your wife along?" Yadwiga smiled a kittenish remote smile, which did not seem meant for Mazur, but rather for someone behind his back. The knitting needles continued to clink between her red-nailed fingers.

The editor neither saw nor heard them. He stared at Samuel who was standing on the landing. Matilda was the first to notice the tension between the two men; she pulled her daughters away from Mazur, thereby freeing the passage to the stairs for him.

As soon as he was alone with Samuel in the bedroom, Mazur rushed toward the stove, slapped the tiles with his hands and pressed his paunch against it. "What did I tell you?" he made an abrupt about-turn and nervously hit his back against the stove. "All have been arrested, all of them! Now you understand what premonition means, don't you?" He rubbed himself against the tiles like a bear against the trunk of a tree. "Something kept me from going. I've acquired that much sensitivity. I can smell danger from miles away."

Samuel, his face white as chalk, stopped in front of him. "You saved me," he mumbled.

"Sure, I saved you! You were as eager to go there as a child insisting on going to a wedding."

"Whenever I'm called, I go. I haven't missed a meeting of the Council yet. Secondly, I was afraid not to go."

"Now you'll be rid of all the meetings."

"They'll create a new Council."

"And Rumkowski will trip up its members again. That's how he will eventually free himself of all the people who might get in his way."

Samuel grimaced, "You are overdoing it, honestly."

"Why? Do you think he's incapable of doing that? Bear in mind, Zuckerman, that the handle for the axe is made from the same tree that the axe will one day cut down. It wasn't for nothing . . ."

"Leave me alone! You're blinded by your hatred for him; you're incapable of seeing the man as he really is. A man who sticks his neck out for us. Did he go to save the people in the Astoria Restaurant, or didn't he? How much would it have taken, do you think, to shoot him down along with the other hundred men? Had the Police Chief not come on time, there would be no more Chaim Rumkowski, are you aware of that at least?"

"Yeah, I'm aware of that. But whether it was a conscious act of courage on his part, I don't know. Maybe he had only deluded himself that the S.S. would listen to him, to the *Älteste der Juden*, as if he were a field marshal, and not treat him like a dog from the rabble. But I, you see, Zuckerman, don't belong to those who are absolutely set upon diminishing someone else's bravery. He went, he stuck his neck out, he got a good beating for it, all right — a good deed, a great act. Satisfied? Now what else do you want of me?"

"I don't know why you hate him so much."

"I? Hate him? God forbid. How can you accuse me of hating a Jew, in particular nowadays? But I fear people who have no sentiments."

"On the contrary. He is a sentimental man."

Mazur smirked, "Well said. He's a sentimental man, but he has no sentiments. Listen to what I'm saying. He is like a dog. As long as he has a leash around his neck he's not dangerous, is even useful sometimes, but the moment you take the leash off, you will never know whom he'll lick and whom he'll kick." He waved his hand, "Ey, we have more important things to discuss. What are we going to do now?"

"What are we going to do now?" Samuel echoed.

Mazur stopped rubbing himself against the oven. "Either we hide somewhere, or we leave town. I personally would like to leave. The waters have risen to my neck; my apartment is finished anyway. Besides, now I see quite well that I can contribute nothing. And a man wants to keep on living. Yes, you're old, you suffer, but you want to protect your bundle of bones; the stupid bundle of bones looks for all kinds of ways to save itself; it refuses to know any morality, or duty, or obligations towards others. If I at least had the feeling that my torment serves a purpose, I would perhaps try to overcome my instincts. But as it is . . . Aye, Zuckerman, I'm incapable of bringing out a word of hope." The editor, who with his bearing and manners had once been an imposing figure, now looked shrunken. Only in his eyes did there remain something of the Mazur of old. His gaze was neither defiant, nor determined; it was a knowing gaze, one that had looked into the open cards and had seen the truth. This knowledge produced such a powerful expression of despair in his eyes that Samuel felt it removing the floor from under his feet.

"Perhaps we should go to the Presess?" Samuel muttered. "He could clarify the situation for us. We would find out what really happened to the Council members."

"I can tell you what happened to them. You'll never see them again."

"Then what should we do?"

"Perhaps you, Zuckerman, should do nothing. First of all, you have your 'iron letter' and the protection of the officers from Leipzig. Secondly, the Old Man might indeed intervene on your behalf. He needs to surround himself with people who look up to him as if he were the Messiah himself." A mocking grimace disfigured Mazur's face. "But better make sure that you don't have to count on his help. Say, have you ever thought of fleeing across the border, to the Reds?"

Samuel smiled bitterly. "And there, you think I'd be safe? You forget I'm a bloodsucker, a capitalist?"

"And yet it is more dangerous to stay here, even for you. Anyway, we'll have to leave. Lodz will become *Judenrein*, not only Lodz, but all the territories incorporated into the Third Reich." Mazur sank into a deep silence, then he spoke again. "I talk . . . talk of escaping, don't I? And you think I don't know that I'll sit in this mire and not budge an inch? Yeah, there are cursed creatures like you and me who have lead in their feet, who are so frozen into the familiar dirt that the most bitter truth cannot pull them out of it."

With one jump, Samuel was at his side. "Listen," he grabbed Mazur by the lapels. "Why shouldn't we hide here, in the garret, for instance? From the windows you can see a large stretch of the street, and if someone comes, we could run up the ladder, pull it in, and that would be that. Besides, the Germans might overlook us."

"Sure, sure, and don't they have a list of all the Council members? And don't you know that if they do anything, they do it thoroughly?"

"All right, but first move in here with your wife. Our heads will cool off. We'll have some more information. Your wife will feel better, and so will you." Samuel was aware that above all he had himself in mind. He would feel better having Mazur at his side. There was something unbearable in Mazur's gaze, true, and yet Mazur meant support. Samuel put his hand on the latter's sunken shoulders. "Don't be so pessimistic," he implored him.

Mazur jerked his shoulders, "Who says I'm pessimistic? I know that they'll have a bitter end, the dogs, that the Jews will outlive them and will still dance on their graves, but for me and for many like me, I can't foresee any good . . ." He buttoned his jacket.

Samuel blocked his way, "So, it is decided?"

Mazur raised his head to him slowly. "When do you want us to come?"

"Right away!" Samuel caught Mazur's hand and pressed it in his. "I'm glad, honestly."

At the sound of their steps, the people downstairs came out to meet them once more. "Now you have to come and drink something," Junia exclaimed to Mazur, pulling him into Samuel's study where the Hagers now lived. "This is our chatter corner," she informed him.

Samuel's study was completely changed. The desk had been placed against the wall, covered with a white oilcloth on which there now stood many cups and glasses and a teapot whose spout emitted a steam of vapor. The sofa and a bed were placed along the walls. There was hardly any room left to move about. However, they all crammed in somehow, sitting down on the sofa, the bed and the floor.

"How are you Professor?" Mazur smiled with his bloodshot eyes, raising the glass of tea he had been given, to his lips.

Professor Hager wiped the hot tea drops which escaped his lips off his goatee. "My wife thinks," he said, "that the state of my liver has improved, but now I'm having trouble with my bile."

Everyone laughed, without Mrs. Hager realizing that the joke was on her. She had a habit of fearing all kinds of diseases that might beset her husband, taking them as fact even before they occurred. "They catch him constantly for labour," she complained to Mazur. "I beg him not to go out of the house, I don't want him to teach in such times, but he doesn't listen. He even refuses to shave off his beard. I can understand a religious Jew insisting on keeping his beard, but he . . ."

"Believe me," the Professor turned to Mazur, "I don't mind their catching me for labour. The only thing which really hurts me is their disdain."

Mazur's knees jerked and he caught the glass of tea which he supported on them, just in time. "That's what bothers you? Their disdain?" he lashed out passionately. "May they do nothing else but offer us their disdain! It is your life you have to protect, Professor, the skin on your body. That is our dignity. With words, you understand, they are not big enough to hurt us!"

Samuel, who was standing in the doorway, drinking his tea, emptied the last drop into his mouth. He found the moment suitable for announcing the news, and he said in a resonant voice, "Mr. Mazur and his wife are moving in with us, my friends."

After the brief silence that followed, Yadwiga burst out with a kittenish absentminded giggle, "The more people, the gayer the party!" Her glass clinked against the saucer, producing a sound of chattering teeth.

✦ ✦ ✦

Mordecai Chaim Rumkowski sat in the waiting room in front of the office of S.S. *Brigadeführer*, Herr von Strafer, waiting for an interview. He felt bitter. The arrest of the Jewish Council members that morning had hurt him personally. Who could have imagined that a meeting of a representative body of the community could be invaded without any warning and all its members arrested without ceremony and carted off to prison? It had not even looked like an arrest, but rather like an onslaught of pirates.

Mr. Rumkowski's blood was boiling. True, the members of his Council were of little help to him; however, they were the most dignified citizens in town. And if such a thing could happen to them, where was the guarantee of the *Älteste der Juden's* own security? Certainly, this was only a theoretical question, because he had no reason to worry about his own safety — if he could only resist the temptation to stick his head out voluntarily, trying to protect his endangered brothers. Had he only behaved more wisely, not so impulsively at such moments, it would certainly be better for him. But anyway, everything pointed to the fact that the authorities could not do without him. Herr von Strafer was satisfied with him and he, Chaim Rumkowski, could not help but exploit the police chief's satisfaction for the good of his own people. He, Chaim Rumkowski, was there to protect them. That was what history wanted, that was what his own fate decreed. So he decided to speak to Herr von Strafer without mincing words, flatly and clearly, either-or: If they wanted to have order, they had to respect the Jewish representatives, otherwise he, Chaim Rumkowski, would refuse to take any responsibility upon himself. He would ask that the detainees be freed, and if not, yes, if not, he would ask to be freed from his post. That was the ultimatum that he would give them. There must be an end to this wantonness immediately.

He stirred restlessly in his chair. He had no patience; that was his nature. Waiting here in the hall was a true ordeal. Before he had even entered the place, he had had a desire to escape. The gloom of a spotless elegant funeral parlour pervaded the air, each enormous closed door looked like the cover of a coffin. The leather-covered armchairs along the walls glistened as if occupied by ghosts. They blinked at him, the only living creature present. And the white face of the clock — a ghost with a large black moustache — indicated five o'clock, which meant that he had been sitting here for fifty minutes — and all the doors were still shut; doors he wanted to enter, doors from which he wanted to escape. He lifted his hand to his head. The wound no longer hurt him. He thought that he should have taken off the bandage in spite of his doctor's warnings. He had walked around in this headgear long enough. But perhaps it was for the better that he had not taken if off. Let Herr von Strafer see it, let him be ashamed of himself, and let him have respect.

Mr. Rumkowski felt like jumping to his feet and rushing forward to knock on Herr von Strafer's door. He imagined himself doing so, but remained put. The arms of the chair held him trapped in their patient embrace. They knew him well. The very chair he was now sitting on could have carried his name. And it seemed to him that the ghosts on the empty chairs in front of him were blinking at him familiarly, asking him, "Do you remember when you met us for the first time? No more than a month ago, and you think that an eternity has gone by, don't you?" And as if to tease him, they brought back images to him of those recent and yet far-off days.

The critical days between the outbreak of the war and the German occupation of the city had taken the ground away from under Mordecai Chaim's feet. The orphanage in Helenovek which he had directed slipped out of his hands; another power, independent of his will, began to reign there. Gradually, he felt overcome by the burden of old age. There was nothing to hold on to anymore. No one cared for him. A city of people lived its feverish life, without him; the world boiled in a fateful kettle, without him, without Mordecai Chaim. Consequently, it seemed to him that he had ceased to exist altogether, life having stopped for him the moment he had stopped being active in it.

Then came Poland's defeat. The city was in the grip of the German fist. As much as he, Rumkowski, had been numbed by his depression, it was a shock nonetheless, a shock which had eventually awakened him. As evil decrees were heaping upon Jewish heads, he had all of a sudden remembered that he was a member of the Jewish Community Council. Then, an idea had flashed through his mind with overpowering light; a vague formless idea, which did not yet know what it wanted, but would not let go of him, spinning and weaving in his mind, mistily, intangibly — and yet stubbornly sure of itself.

It was not in Mr. Rumkowski's nature to sit down with a thought, take it apart and listen carefully to what it had to say. He had no patience for that kind of mental digging. For him, the smell of a thought, its taste was enough, and he immediately set out to act on it. In fact, there had never been a great distance between what he thought and what he did; both came together, thought and deed. He sincerely believed that the more time a man devoted to analyzing an idea, the weaker he became in realizing it, as if half of his energy got lost in the process of weighing and measuring, while his enthusiasm wore out in between. For every analysis, in Mr. Rumkowski's opinion, meant doubt, and only by engaging oneself quickly, on impulse, could a person's entire potential be exploited to support his idea and assure its success. In one word: Mr. Rumkowski was a man of action.

And he acted right away. For him, it was beyond any doubt that all the dreadful things happening to the Jews were happening because there was no one to take their fate in his hands. He felt the finger of destiny pointing at him. The Jewry of Lodz was waiting for him, the Jewish people needed him — and he was ready.

Although not rested, he would get up briskly every morning, impatient to begin his work for the good of the community. He would dress and eat in the blink of an eye, always remembering to glance at himself in the mirror before leaving and to carefully comb the gray silken hair that was his pride. Then he would grab his threadbare coat and his creased hat and run to the office of the Jewish Community Council. There, everything was in a state of chaos. Practically none of the Council members were to be found, all having vanished with the rest of the community leaders. "Cowards!" Mr. Rumkowski would rage, running from one room into the other, slamming doors. "Here you have your spokesmen!" he would shout to the crowds of frightened Jews who besieged the building. Angry and jittery, opening filing cabinets, drawers and cupboards, he would order about the confused Council officials, and command them to make order everywhere. They obeyed him. It was obvious that everything was waiting for him.

Everything was waiting for him — this was the shape his formless idea had come to acquire. A distant echo of an ambition of his youth, of a green dream that had lain dormant through his worthless bygone years, survived to burst out within him now with a Messianic echo. He had come into this world to fulfil a mission: to become a Moses. He had always felt that he had been called upon and chosen, just like the other leader of the Jews. And now Mordecai Chaim Rumkowski knew that he would not leave this world before his mission was accomplished. For he had been created not in order to direct an orphanage, but to direct an entire people. His time as head of the orphanage had fulfilled the same function as leading Jethro's sheep had for Moses. Because, after all, what difference was there between his orphans and the Jewish people? Were not all the Jews abandoned sheep now, without a father, without a leader? He, Mordecai Chaim Rumkowski, would become their father. He would console and protect them, arrange their lives for them, caring for them all together and for each one separately. And they would listen to him. One had to listen to people like Mordecai Chaim, since just as he felt that his calling was to lead them, so they must feel that only he knew the way. He would lay down the foundations for a normal social organism of which he would become not only the head but also the heart. Yes, the heart. The gratitude of his people would centre upon him like rays of light centre upon a prism. And as a prism reflects the light, he would reflect their gratitude, repaying them with his love.

This was the idea which he set out to marry to his actions, and which he desired to free from its fantasy wings and base in a tangible reality. And since the tangible reality was German, and the gigantic shadow of Adolf Hitler hovered over it, so his train of thought began to chart its way towards the German Führer.

Mr. Rumkowski had a kind of weird respect for Adolf Hitler. He admired his magnetic power, his ability to hypnotize millions of people and make them do his bidding, make them worship him like a god. In a way, he felt related to this man of action and he thought that basically they were both kneaded out of the same clay. Now, that the Führer's armies had occupied Poland with such amazing speed and were prepared to overrun all of Europe, Mr. Rumkowski's admiration for him grew to a still greater degree; an admiration about which he had, of course, told no one, and which he was reluctant to admit even to himself, but which was there. On it, he set out to build the structure leading to the realization of his dream.

Now he also felt closer to the Führer because he had become one of the latter's subjects. And it did not seem completely impossible that one bright day they would come together and meet somewhere in a quiet study, to talk like two equals who understood each other and who understood life. Then Mr. Rumkowski would come out with his plan. He, the Führer, disliked the Jews, (although in Mr. Rumkowski's opinion, Hitler had nothing to do with the ugly games the Germans were playing with the Jews in Lodz). He, the Führer, thought that the Jews had had a hand in all the wars, in all the cataclysms and tragedies which had afflicted the world. True, his was a naive and false approach, but after all, Hitler had the right to hate Jews. He, Chaim Rumkowski, despite the fact that he paraded his Polish patriotism, hated the Poles. The American whites hated the Negroes. The Turks hated the Armenians. Evidently, hatred was a normal feeling — why then should Hitler be free of it? And the truth of the matter was that the Jews were strangers everywhere; they lived among peoples with whom they had nothing in common and in countries to which they had no historical right. They behaved differently from the rest of the population, yet at the same time demanded equal rights and privileges for themselves. Why did they deserve them? Which Jew would like to have a goy in his house, with the goy demanding an equal seat at the Sabbath table? Why then should the goyim tolerate the Jews moving about so freely in their countries, grabbing the best positions for themselves, pushing the goyim out of the professions, of the businesses, while raising a hue and cry that they were mistreated? Rumkowski would explain all this to the Führer, and the latter would agree with him. They would sign a contract that after Germany had taken over the entire world, the Führer would give Palestine back to the Jewish people and make him, Chaim Rumkowski, the Head of State. In this manner, the two of them, Adolf Hitler and Mordecai Chaim Rumkowski would save the Jews from the Diaspora for all eternity.

This was the peak of his idea, yet the realization of that part of it was still remote, wrapped in the secrecy of an unclear future, and would have to remain in the realm of a dream for quite a while. Chaim Rumkowski rarely allowed it to play on his imagination. He was only just beginning, and it was not in his nature to give himself to thoughts which could not be realized immediately. Although the mood of his dream accompanied him in each of his present actions, urging him on, he was still in the dark about many things. He was like someone wandering in a dark forest who has seen a light shining in the distance. The exact path by which he reached the light was, after all, unimportant.

Then came the day which had to come. Mordecai Chaim happened to be away from the Council office that morning. The previous night he had been overcome by a high fever, was harassed by nightmares and had slept late into the morning. A knock on the door woke him and a man clad in a heavy winter coat came in, approached his bed slowly and showed him a face which seemed to belong to none other than the angel of death itself. It was quite a while before Rumkowski recognized the engineer, Mr. Fefer, who had been a member of the pre-war Community Council. Rumkowski leaned on his elbow, and instead of a greeting, exclaiming shrilly, "Fefer, what do you want?"

Mr. Fefer, undoubtedly used to Mr. Rumkowski's "politeness", stretched his hand out to him and said, "There was a German officer in the Council again today, Mr. Rumkowski. He asked for the names of the members of the pre-war Council and mentioned something about a Jewish representative group, a delegation of some sort. I met with Moshe Sochar, and we decided to go to the Chief of Police. It cannot go on like this anyway. We have to create an administrative body. So I thought you'd come along. After all, we are the only people left from the Council."

Rumkowski's face went off and on with red fever blotches. "What do you mean?" he groaned, momentarily unable to bring out another word. "What do you mean, you thought I would come along? Thanks for the invitation. Who else is there doing something in the Council besides me?"

"That's why we think you should be in the delegation," Mr. Fefer lit a cigarette.

With one jump, Rumkowski was out of bed. Unembarrassed, he dressed in front of the visitor, shaking on his spindly legs. In a few minutes he was ready. Hurrying on his winter coat, he took a step towards Mr. Fefer, waving his finger before the latter's eyes, "I won't permit any scheming, you hear, Mr. Fefer? Nothing will be done behind my back! This is not Poland and you won't lead me around by the nose here!" This time too, he did not forget to stop in front of the mirror on his way out and dart a glance at himself. He reached for his hat, then turned to his visitor with a pair of burning feverish eyes, "So what are you standing like that for? Come on!" He had no patience for Mr. Fefer's calm and in spite of his shaking knees, he rushed down the stairs ahead of his companion.

Outside the gate, a gust of cool fresh air lashed his face, making his head swim. Suddenly it occurred to him that he was not dressed properly, that he should have put on a clean shirt and that his hair was in disorder. "Come in to the barber's with me," he ordered, pulling Fefer by the sleeve. However, Fefer did not let himself be pulled. He stopped short and fixed his clever gaze on the old man. "What are you staring at me like that for?" Rumkowski exclaimed. "I can't show myself to people in this condition, straight out of bed and into the office of the Chief of Police."

"It doesn't have to be on the spot." Mr. Fefer puffed on his cigarette. "We have to prepare ourselves."

Rumkowski shook his head, "We're going right now!"

"Mr. Rumkowski," Mr. Fefer said icily, "You don't go just like that. We have to call a conference of responsible people, work out a platform, render an account as to what and how."

"What do you need people for?" Rumkowski panted. "What is it, a fair or what? Conferences-shmonferences, what is there to talk about so much? You better hurry and get Moshe Sochar. I'll wait for you at the barber's. But remember, if you don't come in half an hour, I'm going by myself!"

A couple of hours later the three of them arrived in a newly-washed droshky at the Security Department which was located in one of the nicest buildings on the Allées, now called Hermann Göring Strasse. The shiny droshky pushed itself in among the sparkling limousines at the curb, acquiring the appearance of a poor relative among rich guests at a wedding. The nag had probably sensed its inferiority right away, since it turned its head back toward the raised hood of the droshky, as if it too asked to be covered. And as the horse felt, so felt the driver. As soon as the three distinguished Jews climbed down from his droshky, he himself jumped down and scrambled up onto the back seat to hide under the hood, snuggling up in a corner to cover his yellow armband. And as the driver felt, so felt the three distinguished Jews. Even Rumkowski, the bravest of them, felt slightly less brave. The sight of the enormous red flags with the swastikas hanging down from all the windows and covering the entire facade of the building, filled his heart with dread. He suddenly realized how sick he was. Yet he regained his composure, straightened up and put himself at the head of the delegation.

At that time, they had waited for only half an hour in the room where Mr. Rumkowski was now sitting and waiting, after which a uniformed giant appeared in front of them, and invited them in with a gesture of his green arm, so politely, that it could have implied nothing but mockery.

The Police Chief, Herr von Strafer himself, sat in a broad leather-covered armchair in front of a huge glass-topped desk. On the wall above his head hung a large portrait of the Führer in one of his favourite poses: one hand between the buttons of his green uniform, à la Napoleon, the other hand clenched in a fist, resting on a table. Mr. Rumkowski saw both at the same time: the Führer in the portrait and the Police Chief beneath it. He bent his gray head and waving the creased hat in his hand, made an effort to cover the distance between the door and the desk with the lightest steps he could manage, although his effort was unnecessary since the floor was thickly carpeted. He was amazed that his stride was so soundless, and he turned his head worriedly to see if his companions were following behind. Yes, they were there; the massive heavy door shut soundlessly behind them.

The S.S. *Brigadeführer* Herr von Strafer continued to study the papers on his desk, as if he had not noticed the delegation which had entered the room. Then he raised his head very slowly. Rumkowski saw a pair of small green eyes framed by stiff blond eyelashes; a stiff, smoothly combed crop of hair with short blond bangs fringed the Chief's narrow forehead. His moustache was rectangular and bristling above an invisible upper lip; a moustache like Hitler's, but of a faded, yellow pighair colour. He could have as easily been thirty as fifty years old; there was something in his appearance which made the assessment of his age impossible. Willy-nilly, Rumkowski had to compare the two Germans whom he saw simultaneously: the one in the portrait and the one in the armchair. The pure Aryan race had a better representative here, in the armchair, than on the wall. And another comparison imposed itself on him. He had never seen Hitler from so close and with such clarity, and at this very moment he had to admit to his own satisfaction that he, Mordecai Chaim Rumkowski, was firstly, taller than the Führer, and secondly, a handsomer man. The Führer's small stiff bangs looked like the hair of a wig and the famous black moustache, as well as his entire pose reminded one of a cheap little actor in a vaudeville theatre, or of someone who was acting out a caricature of Napoleon. Only the eyes in the portrait seemed authentic and unpleasant. Although they were only painted, only copied, they projected such an icy coldness and hypnotic heat that it was impossible to look at them for longer than a second without averting one's gaze.

The thin lips beneath Herr von Strafer's moustache parted, emitting one word and then another, "*Meine Herren.*"

Mr. Rumkowski's two companions moved closer to the table and he hurried to block their way. Before either of them had managed to open his mouth, he roused himself, shook his silvery head, and valiantly began his speech. He spoke about the order and discipline which had to be introduced into Jewish life, about the necessity for an understanding between the German authorities and a Jewish representative body which would help to regulate all administrative activities. His German was garbled and incorrect, but somehow he managed to clearly bring out his plan for the reorganization of the Jewish community. Mr. Fefer and Mr. Moshe Sochar tried to put in some words of their own, to correct Rumkowski's errors and to point out some problems which he had forgotten to mention. But Chaim Rumkowski would not let them cut into the thread of his thoughts, which revealed clearly how up to date and how competent he was as far as Jewish community problems were concerned. And since he felt that Herr von Strafer's small green eyes were indeed concentrated solely on him, and that he alone had the Police Chief's full attention, he spoke with increasing courage and freedom, feeling stronger and more sure of himself with every moment.

It was obvious that Mr. Rumkowski was to the liking of Herr von Strafer, that the latter was intrigued by this excitedly chattering Jew. There was something imposing in this Jew's appearance, in his gray patriarchal head, in his remote hot gaze, in the shape of his stubborn sharply-traced mouth which emitted a flow of submissive words. The old man added a certain air of distinction to that submissiveness, making it rather more valuable and more flattering to the heart of a conqueror.

As Mr. Rumkowski talked on, the Police Chief did not remove his cat-like eyes from him, eyes that shone curiously, perfidiously. He studied every trait of the old man's face, every wrinkle, every movement and line of his mouth, around his eyes, on his forehead, as if he were busy reading a page in a fascinating book. Before long it became clear to Herr von Strafer that the man standing before him knew what he wanted. And Herr von Strafer badly wanted to know what this Jew wanted; how one could reconcile the stubborn determined gaze with the servile words that came out of his withered but still strong mouth. Whose good did he have in mind, this Jew? His eyes said that it was the Jewish good that he wanted; from his words, it almost seemed that it was the German. But according to Herr von Strafer's reasoning, one excluded the other — the German good being based on the very destruction of the Jewish. If so, then what was that old patriarchal-looking beggar driving at? Was he so crazy as to try and bridge the impossible — the deepest chasm that had ever existed between two human races, of which one was the negation of the other? However he did not appear to be such an idiot. There had to be an opening somewhere, a missing piece in the puzzle. There had to be something supporting the will power of this grandfather who was aiming for a goal which was somewhere between the German and the Jewish good. What was it?

Herr von Strafer wrinkled his forehead; intrigued, he mobilized his entire knowledge of human nature. Then a thought struck him and he knew the answer: personal ambition. From now on, everything went smoothly. As long as Mr. Rumkowski talked, fold after fold of his soul unravelled itself in front of Herr von Strafer. Ever so slowly, the Police Chief put the traits of the old man's face together, realizing the secret desires it revealed. He, Herr von Strafer, the refined connoisseur of human nature, had found the key to the code: the language of the stubborn eyes and that of the submissive lips created one harmonious entity. And Herr von Strafer congratulated himself for having discovered the mechanism of a character which had enough positive qualities to be exploited for the good of the fatherland and of the Führer. Herr von Strafer grinned with mock amiability. He too had been inspired with a great idea. He made a decision. As if further explanations were unnecessary, he interrupted the stream of Rumkowski's words with the same kindly, ironical smile. "Herr?" he said, questioningly.

It was a moment before Rumkowski could stop the bubbling outpouring of his words. Finally he cut them short, "Rumkowski *ist mein Nahme.*"

Herr von Strafer took a pencil, opened a notebook, and casually jotted down a few words. "*Meine Herren,*" he said, "please come back in three days."

Rumkowski bowed deeply, respectfully, lowering his silver-gray head to his waist; a bow expressing pride and humility at the same time.

Downstairs, in front of the entrance, stood the droshky, but the driver was missing. All three members of the delegation sat down beneath the hood to wait for him. Rumkowski cursed him, impatient, boiling with irritation. But before long, he forgot about the driver, no longer caring whether the droshky was moving or standing still. With an inner shudder, he relived the past hour in his mind. This time it was not a shudder of fear that he felt, or of fever. It was a shudder of excitement, the stage fright experienced only by great actors before they appear on stage. He nibbled quickly and nervously on his lips, shaking his head at his companions who looked worriedly out from beneath the hood and talked to him in rustling staccato voices. He had no idea what they were saying.

At last the driver appeared, coming out of the same entrance which they themselves had used only a while ago. He held his coat over his arm; streams of sweat ran down his dirty face. He clambered onto his seat and the horse shambled forward. When they left the Hermann Göring Strasse, he turned to his passengers, informing them, "I've cleaned ten toilets for them."

Mr. Rumkowski's flu vanished as if by magic. He did not wait three days as Herr von Strafer had ordered, but the very next morning rushed to Hermann Göring Strasse and went up the marble stairs which were meant to help him climb to greatness. He asked to be announced to the Chief of Police and did not have to wait long before the door to Herr von Strafer's office opened before him. Again there was the soundless walk towards the desk behind which sat Herr von Strafer, and there above him — the portrait of Adolf Hitler whose gaze it was better to avoid at this moment. Approaching the desk, Chaim Rumkowski bowed and excused himself for having come uninvited. The strings of his white hair shook over his forehead, creeping behind his glasses which in his extreme excitement had slid down to the tip of his nose and which he forgot to push up.

Herr von Strafer raised his green penetrating eyes to him. He seemed neither surprised nor angry. On the contrary. It looked as if the S.S. *Brigadeführer* had been sitting here since yesterday, waiting for him, for Mordecai Chaim. "*Tach* . . . Herr . . . Rumkowski, sit down please," he greeted him, his thin mouth barely opening. Rumkowski did not wait for the invitation to be repeated a second time. Already he was sitting, grateful, in his solemn confusion, to Herr von Strafer for his culture and good manners. Sitting, he could disguise the unpleasant shaking of his knees from Herr von Strafer's eyes. He was about to explain the purpose of his visit, to talk about the order and discipline he wanted to introduce into Jewish life, taking an example from the great German culture, but before he had time to open his mouth, Herr von Strafer opened a file, took out a sheet of paper and handed it to Mr. Rumkowski, announcing, "From now on you are the *Älteste der Juden* in Litzmanstadt, Herr Rumkowski."

Chaim Rumkowski let Herr von Strafer hold the paper in his hand for quite a while before he took it from his fingers. The nomination lay in his old wrinkled hand, shaking along with it. His misty eyes blinked at the fine print from behind his glasses; the long sentences, the foreign expressions danced a vertiginous dance before his eyes. He knew what they meant, and yet could not believe it. How gladly would he now hear them again from Herr von Strafer's mouth! He wanted to make sure that he had made no mistake, that he was really and truly assigned to be the head of the entire Jewish community.

But it was not in Herr von Strafer's nature to repeat the same thing twice. He watched Rumkowski with the satisfaction of a puppet maker who sees that the puppet he has made moves with the previously calculated precision. He opened his thin lips, revealing the tip of his tongue pressed between his yellow teeth, then he added slowly, "Detailed orders as to your duties will follow."

Rumkowski bowed lower than his belt, "*Danke schön, Herr Polizei-präsident.*" That was all he could manage to say.

Now here he was sitting in the same waiting room again. The clock indicated twenty past five and the door to Herr von Strafer's office was still shut. The recollection of the day he had received his nomination and the recollection of the disappointments which had followed as he began to act as the *Älteste der Juden*, of all the abuses he had had to suffer came back to him now to fill his heart with still more bitterness and self-pity. He had had a false idea about the Germans. Those Germans he had known so well from the First World War and from his trips to Berlin, no longer existed. Instead, he had to deal with a horde of wild Huns who only spoke the language of what had once been the most civilized nation in the world. How could he forgive them for what they had done to him in the Astoria Restaurant, where he had rushed to save a hundred people from death? Or for the slaps he had received there and, worse than that, for the mock spectacle they had made of him, calling him the Jewish King? At the very thought of that day, Rumkowski was overcome by the fury of a circus lion teased by its trainer. Shame boiled within him. He embraced the entire waiting room with his wild eyes, and suddenly could bear it no longer. He jumped to his feet. Hastily, he walked over to the side door behind which Herr von Strafer's secretary was working and knocked on it firmly. He heard a resonant, "*Ja wohl!*"

The secretary's office was not much different from Herr von Strafer's. Like the latter's it was padded with carpets. Near the wall stood a similar desk, but here the portrait above it represented Hitler at full length, his feet spread apart, his arms crossed over his chest as if he were reviewing a parade. Also beneath the portrait, sitting in the armchair, was a different figure, a different face: oval, young and arrogant. A pair of sky-blue eyes looked provokingly up at the world and down at Mr. Rumkowski. "What do you want again?" The secretary pointed his rounded chin at the intruder.

"Please, *Herr Offizier*," Rumkowski did not lose his courage. "Have you announced me to the *Herr Polizeipräsident?*"

The sky-blue eyes turned stern, dark, "Herr von Strafer is busy! What is the purpose of your visit, Herr . . . Herr . . .?"

"My name is Rumkowski, *mein Herr*. I would like to talk to Herr von Strafer."

The expression on the arrogant face grew sharper, "Answer my question, please!"

Rumkowski nibbled on his underlip but did not give in, "It is very personal, *Herr Offizier*, very personal."

Suddenly, the young mouth opened and a cascade of laughter poured out from between two rows of sharp strong teeth. "That is very nice! Ve-ry nice!" The amused secretary stood up, walked around the desk and halted in front of Mordecai Chaim who was two heads shorter than he. He bent down to him like a giant bending down to observe a strange dwarf. "You make me curious, old man. What kind of personal business could Herr von Strafer have with you? Come, come now, *los damit!*" The young lips were still pulled apart in a smile, but the eyes were threatening.

Rumkowski felt the blood boiling within him. He gagged, coughed, and gave in, "I would like to beg Herr von Strafer to free the arrested members of the Jewish Community Council, *mein Herr*."

The light vanished from the secretary's face completely. A cold metallic mask faced Mr. Rumkowski with two sky-blue eyes looking daggers, "Next time you come, you will submit a plea for an interview in writing first, old man. And don't forget to put down the reason for your demand." He turned from Rumkowski and moved strangely silently across the carpet with his heavy shiny boots, in the direction of the side door leading to Herr von Strafer's office. Rumkowski remained alone, face to face with the man who looked down at him from the portrait on the wall. Again Rumkowski had the impression that he was looking at a second-rate actor. It was incomprehensible. All these portraits did not at all agree with his own mental portrait of Hitler. Only the gaze, now aiming straight at Rumkowski's eyes, had a demonic power, forcing him to turn away from the wall. As he did so, the secretary reappeared. He took up his place behind his desk and remained standing in front of his armchair, pounding his clenched fist on the table, Hitler-like, "All those who were arrested are criminals and will be punished as such!"

Rumkowski doubled up, as if the young fist had not fallen on the table top, but on his gray bandaged head. "May I speak to Herr von Strafer anyway?" he mumbled, bowing deeply. "Please, *Herr Offizier*."

The fist hammered once more against the table, "Nein!"

Rumkowski knew that such a "Nein!" could not be bent. He raised his hand, touching the bandage around his head. For some reason, the wound had begun to hurt again. Exhausted, he made an about turn and dragged himself towards the door. Then he remembered, turned his bandaged head and said, "*Auf Wiedersehen, Herr Offizier*."

Herr Offizier did not answer.

Chapter Twelve

Michal Levine,
Lodz-Litzmanstadt,
December 5, 1939.

Dear Mira,

There has been some ominous whispering among the members of our family that we will have to move in with Uncle Jan who lives in the Protectorate, since our landlord, *Herr Yeke*, has given us notice. One thing we know for certain: one quarter of our membership has to leave immediately. Many don't wait for an invitation and set out on their own. If I could, I would rather leave to visit with Uncle Vania as my sisters did. But the problem is that Mother absolutely refuses to budge without Father. (As I wrote you before, he has been absent from home recently.) And there are also some difficulties because my leg is not fit for extensive marching as yet. So if they don't come for us and see us off in state, we won't leave our place.

We don't lack food for the time being. It is high season for vegetarians and our ranks are swelling with new followers. My most recent news is that an old colleague, an "eternal" psychology student who was working at the orphanage in Helenovek has looked me up. His name is Shafran. He is a bachelor and it was not difficult for him to bring his meagre belongings over to our apartment. Guttman is very efficient as far as standing in lines is concerned, so Mother is spared from freezing in the streets in this weather.

The fact that I have found two friends here, and that you, my dear, are there, fills my heart with gratitude to Him who reigns over the world so justly. Don't worry about me, Mira. There is something within me which has saved itself up throughout all these years, preparing me for the present. When I am well-disposed, I call it strength, when I am bitter, I call it "diabolic nerve". If you write to me, address the letter to my colleague Stanislaw who is still working at the City Hospital. His address is surer than mine. With all my love,

Yours always,
Michal.

P.S. The doctor has forbidden me to walk on Piotrkowska Street as well as in the Allées. Nor am I allowed to ride in a car, a tramway, a droshky, or use any other means of transportation. Yes, and I have to "tattoo" my chest and my back with a six-cornered yellow star, the symbol of the magnificent sun, the source of life.

Love,
The same.

✦ ✦ ✦

The season of heavy snows arrived, bringing with it the promise of a long and cold winter. Day and night frosty gales came down to cover the city, whirling and spinning over sidewalks and curbs. Like swiftly dancing brushes, they painted over all the houses and every nook and cranny with thick layers of white. They wound the snow around the electric wires, telephone poles, trees and slipped it onto the black bars of the iron fences, like white gloves onto black fingers. Heaps of snow gathered on the sidewalks. At first they were carried from one place to another by the wind, but soon they hardened, to look like a glassy icing on top of old crumbling cakes. The city froze. The branched network of streets lay blank like a body from which all blood has been drained. Odd passers-by slinked along the walls with swift soundless steps, as if afraid of the footprints they might leave in the snow. Raw sharp silence hovered in the air, ripped apart every now and again by a scream issuing from a distant house. Somewhere, someone was being led off . . .

There were a few arteries off the main streets however which did pulsate with a kind of life, although without rhythm or regularity. Like by huge blood clots, they were blocked by crowds of people who flowed slowly away from the frozen city. Starting at dawn, day after day, caravans of wagons, large and small, loaded with suitcases and sacks, with furniture and bedding moved on and on along these streets. The caravans swelled with dark new streams of wagons that poured into them at every corner, and so, they proceeded towards the distant snow-covered highways, towards the wide open roads, into the unknown.

Children sat on top of the loaded wagons, tucked in among the furniture and bedding — trembling bundles of life, with running noses and cheeks exposed to the icy wind, to the cruelty of homelessness. Their parents, dark shrunken figures, walked behind and held on to the wagons, shivering with cold, despite an armour of heavy clothes, as if they were walking naked. However their eyes looked as if they had been set on fire by the frosty blaze. They burned like pieces of coal, with fear, with disquiet, with despair. They darted hurried glances back and forth, impatient to escape the frozen city. They did not even offer it a last affectionate glance, as if they had erased its existence from their memories even before they left it. With their shaking bodies and the columns of warm breath released into the air through their mouths and nostrils, they looked like small lost locomotives following the light of their eyes, in the direction of unknown stations which were supposed to harbour and shelter them against the raging blizzard sweeping over the world.

Simcha Bunim Berkovitch woke up at dawn. He was unable to make up his mind what to do: to stay in town and wait until he received an "invitation" to leave, or to set out immediately on the road, joining the thousands who passed daily by his window. In the meantime, he had to burn his library. This would, in any case, have to be done. If he left the city, he would not be able to take the books along, and the thought that German hands might desecrate them was unbearable to him; he preferred to sacrifice them on the altar of the kitchen stove. On the other hand, if he remained in town, keeping the books was dangerous. German eyes exploded with fury at the sight of the Hebrew alphabet; that was what people were saying. All his neighbours and acquaintances had burned their books and Miriam had nagged him with increasing bitterness to do the same.

He stood at the stove tearing the covers off the books and watching their pages become fringed with black smoke, then kindle and roll up, acquiring the shape of flowers bursting into sudden bloom at the same time as they quivered in agony — flowers of destruction. He watched them shrivel up soundlessly and transform thenselves into a heap of ashes. Each book he threw into the fire represented a fragment of his life. He remembered vividly when and where he had acquired each volume, what the attraction had been that had prompted him to save up the few zlotys and purchase it for himself; now he tried not to look at the books' titles. Down in the street, the wheels of the countless wagons squeaked in the mud. He thought of the people leaving town and both envied and pitied them.

Blimele was asleep in her bed, covered with an eiderdown and Miriam's warm plaid on top of it. Only the blond silk of her hair could be seen spread over her pillow. Miriam was dressing. Bunim watched her pulling on her dress, her sweater, fastening her stockings and slipping a pair of his socks on top of them. He saw her only with his eyes. His heart was locked up, indifferent. An icy estrangement hung between the two of them every morning, as if they had just returned from far-off separate worlds and did not recognize each other, or were afraid to do so in the light of the day. This freezing mood between them would often persist throughout the day, sometimes carrying over into the night. Dishevelled and shivering with cold, she approached the stove and warmed her hands over the burner. Then she snatched a book from the heap and ripped off its covers. She crumpled the pages, tore them out of the sticky backs and shredded them, pushing them through the burner. Soon another book was in her hands; she tore it too to pieces, stuffing it into the belly of the stove before the smothered flames had time to catch hold of it.

He gave a jerk, as if she were brutally tearing apart, not the books, but him. "What are you doing?" he asked angrily.

"You can see what I'm doing, can't you?" Without turning to him, she went on ripping off the covers and breaking the books in half with her swift strong hands.

He knew very well that she was right in what she was doing, that he had to get the job done as quickly as possible, since the sparks coming from the chimney might be noticed outside. But as she continued to hurry on with the work without paying any attention to him, he tried to shove her away with his shoulder, "I want to do it by myself . . ."

She stayed where she was, bent over the stove, blowing at the smoldering fire until the flame burst out against her face. She seemed to be a monster devouring his very soul. "It's time you stopped bewailing your books," she said finally. "As long as there are people, there will be books too. Imagine the great tragedy! A world is being turned upside down, you can't even be sure that you'll survive the day, and you have books on your mind!" She bit her lips, wrecking one volume after another with increasing ferocity. She knew that he hated her at this moment, but she could not help it. "You want me to become a hard person, don't you, Simcha Bunim? Don't you keep telling me to knead my heart into a different shape, to make it ice-cold?" He was already at the door, hurrying into his coat. He dashed out of the room. She remained with her sentence unfinished, a lone figure over the blazing stove. She had chased him away and now he would punish her by leaving her alone. She stirred the fire with the iron rod and sighed, whispering, "Never mind, take it out on me if you want to."

As he passed through the gate, a neighbour stopped Bunim to warn him, "Don't go out, the hunt is on!" He paid her no attention and stumbled out into the street. The caravan of wagons had thinned out; many of them were standing in the middle of the street, while crying children mewled on top of the heaps of bedding. By the side of those wagons which still moved ahead, only women were walking. The men skittered like hunted rabbits from gate to gate, from nook to nook. Whoever came near Bunim spat out the same warning, "Don't go!" He rushed onward, at first not knowing where he was headed, but then turning in the direction of the Community Council building. He decided to register for labour, to replace some rich Jew for a few marks and be rid of the empty maddening days.

The Community Council building looked desolate. He entered an empty corridor. At the sound of his steps, a head poked out from a distant door. A short man came running out on shaky legs, looking him over anxiously. "The door was unlocked?" he asked, locking it hastily with bolt and chain.

"Are you taking care of the volunteers? I want to replace someone on the labour detail," Bunim said.

It took the little man a while before he understood the meaning of Bunim's words. "Oh, they've left already," he said and came closer to Bunim. "The devils were here no more than ten minutes ago!" Bunim heard the man's teeth chattering. "One of our employees is lying downstairs, in the archives. He went out with his *Passierschein*. Much good it did him. They almost thrashed the life out of him." He gave a sudden jerk as they heard the sound of distant gunshots. "Come," he pulled Bunim by the sleeve. "Let's go downstairs."

Bunim's nostrils caught the smell of mouldy paper as he descended into the cellar. At first he could see nothing through his fogged eyeglasses, but as he walked carefully down the steps, he heard the rustling sound of many voices. Then he was confronted with a room so crowded that he found it hard to wade into it. People were sitting on benches, on tables, or crouched on the floor. As soon as they noticed Bunim, their whispers centred upon him, questioningly, "How did you manage to get here? Where are they now?" In utter bewilderment, he declared that he had had no idea of anything, that no one had stopped him on his way, and saying this, he felt his knees give way under him.

"You jeopardized your life!" someone said to him. The others gave him accounts of their trials during the past few hours. He listened to their garbled words, feeling his heart jerking in his chest with increasing anguish. He remembered making his way through those streets where danger had been lurking so close, and only now, here, where everyone felt safe, did he meet it eye to eye. On one of the tables he noticed the prostrate form of the employee who had been beaten up. A group of people were bent over the man dabbing at his face and winding bandages around his wounds. Bunim saw the soles of the unconscious man's shoes; melting clumps of snow dripped from them.

He recognized a few familiar faces in a corner and ploughed his way through to them. He was greeted with looks which said, "So you are here too." The editor, Mr. Mazur, was crouched on the floor, surrounded by a group of people who were listening to a story he was in the middle of telling. Bunim squeezed himself into the group.

"It was about midnight," Mazur picked at the lapels of his winter coat, as he talked. "We heard the rapping of gun butts against the door and six Storm

Troopers burst in like tigers; they pushed me against the wall as if I were some stinking rag. They scattered into all the rooms, putting on all the lights as if they were about to begin a great celebration. And as if the lights of the chandeliers were not enough, they turned to me and blinded my eyes with six flashlights, screaming out, 'Who lives here?' I answered them, as composedly as a man could answer in such a confusion, 'Mazur,' I said, ''Raphael Mazur.' And as I said it, they offered me a bang on the head. So I thought that they had not understood my name, although what is there to a name that needs to be understood? However, I repeated, 'Gentlemen, I, Raphael Mazur, live in this apartment.' The next bang almost knocked me out and I fell to the floor. They waited patiently until I came to and got to my feet. Then again the same question, again the same blows on my head. I must have a skull made of iron because it didn't break and I could still hear my wife's sobs as if through a wall, and to understand that she was begging them to give her permission to bring me a glass of water. They gave her permission, but took the glass of water out of her hand, and emptied it in her face. She wiped it and repeated the plea, and the same scene was re-enacted; all in all, her face was showered with six glasses of water. At length they told her that they would resuscitate me themselves, which they did; they gave it to me good and proper. My legs and stomach no longer seemed to be mine. Luckily, I fainted." Mazure smirked. "Otherwise, I wouldn't have survived it. But since there are many degrees of fainting and I have, as I told you, a head made of iron, I was able, in all my numbness, to hear my wife's screams. 'Why do you hit him?' the poor soul refused to understand. So they let go of me to teach her a lesson in morality. 'We don't hit him, Madam,' they explained to her. 'We only teach him to tell the truth.' 'Has my husband lied to you?' the silly woman argued with them. 'Of course he lied to us,' they guffawed. 'And from now on if a German citizen asks your husband who lives here, we assure you, Madam, that he'll know what to reply. He'll say, 'Here lives the dirty swine, the Jew so and so, who has brought about this war and infected the human race with his putrified blood.' Then they grabbed me, lifting me up in the air as if I were a puppet. 'Who lives here?' they yelped, and I replied, as if not with my own mouth, 'Here lives the dirty swine Raphael Mazur who has brought this war about and has infected the human race with his putrified blood.' Then they forced my wife and me to carry everything out of the apartment; everything, which means whatever was left over from the previous onslaught. How many times we rushed up and down the stairs perhaps even He, up there, would be unable to count. But it was really beyond my strength to carry down the heavy armchairs. So my stupid wife ran to beg the *Herren Offizieren* again, to let her help me carry the load. Of course they let her, taking the armchair out of my hands and pushing it between her trembling arms. I thought she would break in two under the load, but I had, as it seems, misjudged the strength of my woman. She stumbled down the stairs, shaking and quaking, and then, as soon as she arrived at the bottom, they sent her back up again with the same load. And so she struggled up and down until her legs gave out underneath her; the armchair slipped out of her hands and fell down the stairs, my wife rolling down after it. She remained still, stretched out on the landing, and I did not know whether she was dead or alive. I passed by her with the pieces of furniture as if she were a heap of garbage. They warned me that they'd shoot me on the spot if I so much as looked at her. And so I loaded my home, so to speak, onto their truck. Afterwards, they ordered me to beg their forgiveness for having robbed them of their sleep and wished me an amiable *Auf Wiedersehen*". Mazur grabbed himself by the lapels, pulling them down with the weight of his hands. "Yes, my friends," he shook as if in a trance, "the lion is come up from his thicket and the destroyer of the peoples is on his way; he is gone forth from his place to make thy land desolate; and thy cities shall be laid waste, without an inhabitant. For this, gird you with sackcloth, lament and howl; for the fierce anger of the Lord is not turned back from us."

Bunim shuddered. A voice deep within him repeated the words like an echo. At first he had been furious at Mazur for telling his horror tale as if he were deriving a secret pleasure from digging at his own wounds, but now he felt that the heart-broken Mazur, who had such power in his despair, had roared out the unalterable verdict. Bunim had the feeling that the end of the world had arrived, that night had engulfed the globe, and that if this were not true for others, it certainly was true for the Jewish people. But he, Bunim, refused to accept this judgment. Everything within him called desperately for help, searched for a ray of light, a trace of promise — an escape. So, in this darkest pit of gloom, he tried to swing his soul upwards with his will, to force it to ring out with its old devotion to the Creator — as one tries to set a long silenced bell in motion. His young body, the living blood pulsating in his veins called back his piety, trying to cling to it. No, this judgment could not be true. What sense was there in suffering without a reward? The One who was pure Meaning and Purpose would crown such suffering with gratification. And if there were no reward for the suffering as such, perhaps it was inherent in it. Perhaps the Jews were granted an honour in being the offended, and not the offender, the murdered, and not the murderer? Then perhaps they should go out dancing and singing, rejoicing that they had been chosen as the innocents? But instead of bringing him the ray of light he was searching for, this thought plunged him into deeper darkness, more dense, more blinding. Was this the only compensation awaiting the people after two thousand years of wandering, he thought, after two thousand years of stiff-necked devotion to the Almighty — to be trampled now and erased from the face of the earth by the boots of the Devil?

However, it was precisely this unbearable darkness in which he was submerged that forced Bunim to lift his head and focus his near-sighted eyes on the people surrounding him: a cellar-full of shrivelled Jeremiahs. They rocked back and forth bleakly, yet seemed far from having completely surrendered to fate. Bunim sensed this, as he had sensed it a while ago in Mazur. It was a despondency which had strength. And precisely the sight of these hanging heads and stooped shoulders began to swing the bell within him anew — with prayer, with demand, with rage — until it rang out in his mouth with power, as if the Almighty Himself had whispered the curse into his ear, "All the devourers shall be devoured, calamity shall come upon them!" It was as if the crouching people had been waiting for these words. Backs straightened up slowly, heads lifted like plants sensing a drop of fresh water. There was something in Bunim's voice which said more than the words themselves.

Mazur's eyes covered with a warm mist, "Bless you, Berkovitch, for the bit of hope you're trying to give us."

"I don't know if it is hope," Bunim muttered. "Anyway, both hope and despair are no more than signs of our helplessness. We have no say in our fate. But just like Jeremiah, who both bewailed our destruction and hoped for salvation, we can do the same . . ."

"Which is the same as doing nothing," someone put in wisely. Bunim bit his lips. How poor was the solace which had burst out of him so violently.

Someone else spoke, "What kind of action could be expected from us? Not to put on the Stars of David? To go to the stake for that piece of rag? Refuse to be abused and get a bullet on the spot?"

"The only thing is to survive," a third man agreed. "Whoever has the opportunity to escape and thinks that by doing so he will save himself, then let him. But the majority of the people are unable to escape. The only thing left for them to do is to wait and hope."

"Right. Passive resistance is also a form of action," another voice put in.

Before long, there flared up a heated discussion between the optimists and pessimists.

Faces flashed, eyes sparkled. They became involved in discussing the news from the battle fronts; they indulged in political speculations, each one displaying his expertise in the field of strategy. Until suddenly, a sharp shriek was heard, "Escape, people! They're coming back!"

Someone broke the glass in the little window of the cellar; the crowd made a wild scramble towards it. The next thing Bunim knew, he was running, bruised and bleeding, through the snow-covered backyard of the Council building, along with other dark confused figures who skittered like hunted animals in search of a place to hide from the approaching danger.

In the early evening of the day when the Jews definitely had to take off their yellow armbands and put on Stars of David, Miriam found a piece of old drapery which she had put away with the rags of used clothing. She unfolded the piece of yellow material and cut out six squares, ten centimeters to a side, trying to shape a precise Star of David out of each of them. She reached out for her coat, put it on and approached the mirror.

She stared at herself in the mirror with cold strange eyes. The woman she saw in front of her was a different Miriam, ugly and old. Her round face, which had used to conceal whatever was going on in her heart, betrayed her now. Along the entire width of her forehead there lay a deep furrow, resembling the cut of a knife. Her first serious wrinkle. It descended to the sides of her eyes, making her gaze seem severe and angry. This was not like her normal gaze at all, these were not the eyes into which Bunim had liked to look long and silently. And her mouth, to which Bunim had used to press his, was nothing but another deep cut, curved downward, bloodless, the lips disappearing into a gash. Her hair, which had used to be heavy but silky and soft, and which Bunim had liked to slide his hand through tenderly, was unkempt and dull, with kinky snarls sticking out all around her head; it fell in tangled knots down her shoulders. She lifted her hands to comb the hair through with her fingers. They became entangled in the knots. She clenched them in her fists tightly, pulling them with a jerk, as if she wanted to tear the snarls out by their very roots. Her eyes became misty.

She put a Star of David against her bosom. As she fastened it on with a pin, she had an urge to push the pin in much deeper than only through the coat material. She took another star and measured a place for it on her back, more or less at the same level as the star on her bosom. However, as soon as she sat down to sew the stars on, something tore open in her heart, as if her bleak mood were a boil lanced by the needle. Every time she pulled the thread, she had the feeling of pulling threads of anxiety out from within her. She sighed heavily, with relief. Peace gradually entered her mind; determination welded her confused thoughts together. The present moment was unusually meaningful. And she welcomed her calm, taking it for a sign that she would be strong enough to endure the hardships, stronger than she had thought. She threw her coat on the bed and approached the window. Gusts of snow flew against it. She put up the blackout curtains, turned on the light, added some wood to the stove and spread slices of bread on its hot surface. The coffee pot began to infuse a refreshing aroma into the air. It was time to cover the table with the white tablecloth.

She thought of Bunim. Again he had been away from home for the entire day. In her mind, she saw him rushing through the streets, the snow sprinkling on his face, on his eyeglasses. She saw him at Friede's bedside, or in Baluty at his parents' home. In her mind, she called him back to the peace and quiet of their room, to the white table. She felt no bitterness towards him. She imagined him coming in and saw herself talking mildly to him. She washed her face, combed her hair, and put on a clean apron. It was getting too late for Blimele to wait for her father with supper, and she placed the child's meal on the table. She opened the door; the light from the room made the darkness of the long corridor recede. "Blimele!" she called.

A door opened, a streak of light fell on the other side of the corridor. In it, Blimele appeared, approaching her mother with swift tiny hops. She fell into Miriam's arms and locked her hands behind Miriam's neck, whispering solemnly, "*Mameshe*, make yourself smaller than Blimele." That meant that an important secret was about to be revealed. Miriam knelt down and Blimele put her mouth to her cheek. "I want to tell you . . ." She clucked her tongue. "In Minda's house they're making stars, not like in the sky, but to put on." She took a deep breath, then added joyfully, "Yellow stars to wear on coats, for the children and for their father and mother too!" Miriam stood up and led her over to the wash basin. Blimele lifted her eyes to her, "They really look like stars. Minda says it's called Jewish Stars of David, but I think it looks like a golden flower too. One you put on here," she pointed to her chest with a wet finger. "You see, here on your heart, and the other in the back, on your heart." They sat down at the table. Blimele took a piece of toast and bit into it thoughtfully.

"What are you thinking about, Blimele?" Miriam asked.

"I think," Blimele bent her head sideways, "I think, if Minda has many zlotys. Does she? I have to know, tell me!"

"No, not many."

"And you don't have many either. So it doesn't cost much, I think, and I want to have some too."

"You will."

"Just as nice ones as Minda's?"

"Yes, just as nice."

Blimele began to eat with her usual good appetite. Miriam kept her eyes on her, delighting in the sight of her sharp little teeth cracking the crust of the slice of toast with obvious pleasure. She could not help thinking how much Blimele resembled her, not only in her delight in eating, but also in the build of her body, in the shape of her face, of her hands; even her movements and the tone of her voice were like hers. How much of her, of Miriam, there was in the way Blimele would play with Lily, the doll she had received as a gift from "Uncle"

Friede. However, Miriam also saw other traits in Blimele which did not resemble hers at all, traits which would sometimes make her wonder how it could have happened that such an unfamiliar being had come out of her own body. It was not a question of the colour of Blimele's hair which was unlike Miriam's, dark blond, curly and thin; nor of the colour of her eyes which were also unlike Miriam's, bright, grayish-blue, like Bunim's, with an expression of astonishment ever present in them. It was something which she could not see, but rather sensed — an inner resemblance to Bunim. The way Blimele's mind worked was his; her moods, her sensitivity, the way every trifle provoked a storm, an immediate explosion were his. His was that exaggeration in joy as well as in sadness; his was the sudden change from one mood to another — between laughter and tears, only a cat's leap; as if the seeds of tears were planted in her laughter; as if in her crying the promise of laughter was seeded, the sounds quite often difficult to distinguish from one another. This difference between Blimele and herself was like a thin demarcation line, setting her, the mother, apart from the one who had come out of her body. It separated them, yet united them even more.

The ticking of the clock reached Miriam's ears. She followed its hands with her eyes, frowning each time they marked a minute and moved ahead. It was close to the curfew hour.

"All children will have such stars, won't they, *Mameshe?*" Blimele concluded. Miriam nodded absent-mindedly. "And little Stasio too?"

"Stasio? No, not Stasio. Stasio is a Polish boy."

"And I'm not a Polish girl?"

"You're a Jewish girl." Miriam stepped up to the window and pulled away an edge of the blackout curtain. She blew a little "eye" in the frost on the pane and looked out.

Blimele pulled her by the dress, "It's good to be a Jewish girl, isn't it, *Mameshe?* If Stasio will obey everything his mother says, he will also be a Jewish child like me, won't he?" There was something in her mother's face which cast a shadow on the blue of Blimele's eyes. "Do you have a tummy ache, *Mameshe?*" she asked.

Miriam paced the room, her arms folded over her bosom, her eyes on the clock. Blimele followed her like a swaying shadow. The air in the room began to vibrate loudly with the beat of the clock's pendulum, but it was soon stopped by Blimele's soft whimper. Miriam took the child's head between her hands. Blimele's blue eyes floated in a sea of tears. Shiny wet bubbles popped out of her nose; saliva streamed down from her lips. "What happened, Blimele?" Miriam asked, pressing the child's head against her belly.

"I'm scared. . ." Blimele sobbed dolefully.

"Of what, daughter?"

"Of the witchman. He took *Tateshe* away in his sack."

"Oh, you're such a silly little girl," Miriam tried to make her voice sound cheerful. "*Tateshe* will be home soon."

Blimele lifted her wet face to her mother. After a moment, as if she had found a consoling thought, she said trustfully, "*Tateshe* is not afraid of the witchman, right, *Mameshe?*" She calmed down immediately. Her face was still wet and she kept on sniffling, but she turned away from Miriam, and looked about the room. She exclaimed enthusiastically, "*Mameshe*, your coat has the Jewish Stars of David on already!" Miriam peered through the "eye" in the frost-covered pane. The street was desolate. It was still snowing. Again she heard Blimele's voice behind her, "Mameshe, sew me on my stars too!"

Fearing a new outburst of tears, Miriam gave in to her; she took Blimele's coat and got the Stars of David ready. "Lets try it on," she said.

Solemnly, Blimele put her hands into the sleeves of her coat. "Here, on the heart, Mameshe," she pointed with her finger. Miriam fastened the star onto the coat with a pin. "And now in the back on my heart." Blimele turned with her face to the mirror, folding her arms over her chest. She scrutinized herself with serious eyes and shook her head appreciatively in a grown-up manner. Miriam cast a glance at Blimele's serious face and a tide of tenderness surged into her heart. She grabbed the child in her arms and covered her cheeks, eyes, brows and hair with kisses. Nothing had happened to Bunim, she was sure; soon she would see him come in, unharmed. Blimele wriggled impatiently in her arms, sliding down to the floor. "Come on, hurry up, sew it on!" she commanded. "You have to use some very nice thread," she decided, pulling the box of sewing accessories towards her. She noticed a little ball of blue wool, "Here, this is very nice!" The Stars of David sewn on to Blimele's coat came out fringed with a light blue thread. It seemed to Miriam that they really did look cheerful.

Blimele rummaged about on the floor, picking up triangular pieces of the yellow material. She arranged them on the table, working at them with two fingers as with a pair of scissors. Then she jumped down from her chair, approached her doll carriage and took her doll out from under the cover carefully, cuddling her in her arms. "Now come, my child," she said solemnly, "I will sew on your Stars of David." She arranged the piece of yellow material on the doll's chest, moving her hand as though she held a needle between her fingers. Now it seemed to Blimele that streams of tears were pouring out from beneath Lily's bushy eyelashes. "Why are you crying, child?" she chided the doll good-humouredly. "It doesn't hurt, does it?" But Lily apparently refused to be comforted and Blimele scolded her, "Be quiet, silly little girl. How many times must I tell you that the witchman won't come here with his sack. And if you cry for another hour, I won't sew the Star of David on you. Because a Jewish girl isn't supposed to cry. A Jewish girl must behave . . ."

It was after curfew. Miriam paced the room between the clock and the window, biting her lips. At length, she wrapped herself in her plaid. "I am going down for a minute, Blimele," she said, leaving the room before Blimele had time to comment. She halted in the gateway. The snow whirling on the spindle of a vertiginous wind slapped her face with icy blasts. The sidewalk was thickly covered with snow; on both sides lay white heaps, silvery, fresh and fluffy; the wind climbed above them, peeling off the fuzzy top layers. The middle of the street was smooth, the traces of the wagon caravans which had been passing through all day were wiped out; no sign of life anywhere. It seemed to Miriam that she did see a shadow very far off, but after a while, the whirling snow carried it away and it vanished. She wanted to run aimlessly ahead through the streets; anything would be better than just standing there waiting. But the thought that she had left the child alone held her back. She paced back and forth beside the gate, peering through the snowy darkness, her eyes turning tearful, blind. Her heart hammered. She felt as if she had been standing by the gate for eternities that could not be measured by the normal measure of time; eternities during which her hair had had time to turn snow white.

Again it seemed to her that she saw a shadow looming around a distant corner. Quickly, madly, she rubbed her eyes with the edge of her plaid. The shadow swayed in the snowy fog. She could no longer hold herself back and ran out, edging along the fences and walls. The wind attacked her with fistfuls of snow, filling the folds of her plaid. Icy streams ran down her face from the strings of hair which escaped from behind the plaid covering her head. She sensed rather than saw that the shadow in the distance was still there, that it was sliding along the walls, just as she was, that it was coming closer. Her heart jumped. She recognized Bunim. She wanted to run forward faster, to greet him with open arms, but instead she stopped and turned back to the gate.

As her tension melted away, the tears dried on her face, freezing to her skin. The thought of the worry that had taken her apart throughout the time she had waited for him stiffened her back. She had been in the deepest abyss of fear, and here he was, coming towards her, safe and sound, as if nothing had happened. He passed by her in the gate without noticing her. She called his name. "Why so late?" she asked, making an effort to betray no reproach in her voice. He did not answer. She sensed that some bad experience was hidden in his silence, yet she could not disguise her bitterness. "I didn't know what happened to you."

This time he answered, "If you worry every time I . . ."

"I'll lose my mind!" she burst out vehemently. In the murky stairway she saw him take off his glasses, heard his heavy breathing, and knew that everything was boiling within him. She felt like touching his arm, stroking his shoulder and calming him with a warm word. But she could not. In her confusion, she realised that she had really changed; that the mildness of her disposition, the softness of her being had frozen, and that instead, something ugly and bitter had come forth within her: the acrimony she had read in her face in the mirror a while ago.

When they entered the room, Blimele was sitting, her head against the table, asleep. Bunim ran over to her; she quivered, wakened by the cold surrounding him. "Where were you all night, *Tateshe?*" She raised her head to him. With sudden vigor, he shook off his coat and came back to her, rubbing his hands together.

As she made the beds, Miriam watched the father and daughter. She saw that Blimele, sitting in his lap, had brought him the peace which she herself had been unable to offer him. Her heart sung out joyfully, although with a twinge of jealousy.

The snowstorm raging outside swept past the window; the gusts of snow pounded against the pane. The four walls of the room were like snugly sheltering arms.

Blimele jumped down from Bumin's lap, rushed to the closet and opened its doors wide. "Look, *Tateshe,*" she exclaimed, "my coat already has the Jewish Stars of David on!" She pulled him by the hand. Silently, he came with her, shut the door of the closet and led her to her bed, where he undressed her. "You have to tell me a story," she yawned, rubbing her eyes with her fists. He tucked her in under the covers and stooped over her; she gave him a peck on the cheek, seizing him by the hand. "Tomorrow morning, will you tell me a story?"

"Not tomorrow morning. Tomorrow morning I'm going to work, Blimele."

She frowned, blinking her eyes, "Where are you going to work?"

"To the Germans."

"You'll have zlotys again, won't you, *Tateshe?*" she pulled him down closer to her face. "The Germans are good, aren't they? Minda says that they're the ones who gave us the yellow Jewish Stars of David."

His rage came back to ferment within him. He burst out in spite of himself, "Because they are bad. Because they don't like us."

"Me, neither?"

"You neither, nor me, nor *Mameshe*, nor Grandma and Grandpa, nor Minda . . ." It poured out of his mouth as if all the tensions of the day had forced themselves upon him, to be released, so brutally, in his frankness with the child.

"Why?" Blimele's eyes opened wide, looking at him with the innocence of two bright skies.

"Because we're Jews."

"But it is good to be Jews," she mumbled, pulling out her lower lip and rolling it against her chin which had begun to tremble slightly. "The Germans are just like the witchman with the sack, *Tateshe?*" She let out a long sob, "Why do you make me cry?" He lay down beside her on the bed, putting his mouth to her wet cheek. She fell asleep in his arms.

Miriam, warming herself at the stove, her hands held out over the burners, looked at Bunim with icy eyes. He waited for her to burst out with reproaches, to quarrel and heap bitter words on him. He wanted her to do so. Her anger would relieve him, would help him explode with the storm raging within him. Her controlled cold silence made him suffocate. She left the stove and undressed. The next moment, she was in her bed, shivering and still looking at him with the same icy eyes. He rushed towards her and faced her provokingly. He growled, "You didn't like the way I talked to the child, did you?"

"No, I didn't," she said shortly.

"You want to shut her up in a glass box, don't you?"

"She's still so small."

"Not for the Yellow Star!" he spluttered. "She is big enough for that, can't you see?" His voice was hoarse, each word as if it were squeezed out and strangled. With hurried uneven steps he paced the room. A cord was tied around his neck and he absolutely had to cut it loose. "Wherever I go," he went on, "people are sewing on Yellow Stars; sewing and thinking of nothing, not even looking in front of their noses. They sew because they're ordered to, they'll go because they'll be ordered to. They'll bury their fathers and mothers because they'll be ordered to." Suddenly he stopped in front of her. "Miriam," he groaned, "the editor . . . Mr. Mazur is dead." He pushed out his lower lip, making a grimace like Blimele would before starting to cry. "They shot him a few hours ago, after forcing him to dig his own grave in his own backyard." Bunim let himself down by Miriam's side, took her hand in his, and pressed it as if he wanted to knead their hands together. "Listen," he choked on his words, "we don't know what's awaiting us. Miriam . . . let's run away. The city will be cleared of Jews anyway . . . The evil decree has not been called off as you can see. This home is not ours any more. Any minute they may break in, and we'll be in their hands. Perhaps you should get up right away? Let's pack and leave first thing in the morning. All the writers I know are getting ready to leave tomorrow . . . Here we'll suffocate. I beg you." She was crying; her entire body convulsed with sobs. She felt as if the bed was falling apart beneath her and she was afraid of falling out. She grabbed him by the arm, while he went on groaning, "Do you know what they made me do all day? Scrub floors. Then, after that, I went to see my parents. Everyone looks at me there as if I could bring them salvation. What do I know about advising those two old people? I left them and dropped in to see Friede and watched him for a while as he roamed his feverish worlds. Perhaps he is to be envied. Yes, imagine, the withering Friede inside, the snowstorm outside. I ran out into it with my heart wrecked and crushed, and met Guttman racing like a madman through the street. He told me about Mazur. It took us no longer than the blink of an eye, as we stood and looked at each other, and from somewhere the dogcatchers appeared. They led us off to the barracks and only let us go a little while ago. I planned to go to the Community Council again tomorrow and register for labour, but I don't want to, Miriam . . ."

"Get undressed," she mumbled, her hand falling limply from his arm. "Do you know how much money we have? There are only two marks left in my wallet. Not even enough to hire a wagon. Do you want to go on foot in such weather? And what will we live on in a foreign place? Here someone might still help during the darkest hour. And the child? What will happen if she should, heaven forbid, catch a cold? Here she has a bit of warm soup, a bed of her own. And you think the Germans are only in Lodz?" Her teeth chattered. She shivered with cold beneath the eiderdown cover. Strange thoughts began to weave in her mind; suspicion began pricking at it. It occurred to her that he was sorry that he had a wife and child, that he was not a free man. She knew that it was a silly thought, born in her feverish head, but it nagged at her. She sputtered in a quavering voice, "I'll stay with the child. I'll take care of her with . . . my everything. Perhaps that will be enough. But you . . . you go with your friends, go to Russia. You don't have to worry about us at all."

Now, at long last, he could let his scream come out. "Shut up!" he lashed out, heaping bitter, uncontrolled accusations on her. Then he scrambled to his feet, threw off his clothes, turned the light off and jumped into bed. The heat of her body burned through to him. He clasped her in his arms. "She is sick!" the thought flashed through his mind. Frightened, he caressed her as if trying to ward her sickness off with his touch. He slurred uncontrolled, incoherent, affectionate words in her ear. Through the convulsions that racked her entire body, only one word reached her consciousness: "Together".

✦ ✦ ✦

The main reason why Itche Mayer the Carpenter had trouble sleeping was the proximity of Uncle Henech's bakery. The bread-lines which sprang up around midnight passed by the window of the cellar, and although the people in line kept quiet until dawn, they stamped their feet; and this stamping of so many feet in the snow penetrated Itche Mayer's mind so deeply that it seemed to have become an anvil hammered upon by a thousand muffled hammers. At dawn, the clamour became unbearable as screams and scuffles were added to it; it split his head into a million pieces. Yet this hubbub came from outside, from the street, and somehow the frozen window gave some protection against it. But at dawn there was another deafening racket added to the first which exploded in the gateway proper, at the back door of the bakery: the noise of his own neighbours whom Uncle Henech granted privileges by giving them bread separately, before the police arrived.

Everyone in the cellar became used to these "white" nights. Sheyne Pessele would lie in bed with her eyes open, as if all the hullabaloo were none of her business, and a thousand times during the night she would praise the Lord for having sent down an Uncle Henech, thanks to whom they had their daily piece of bread. And Shalom, the youngest son, would jump down from the worktable at the first sounds from outside, dress and rush out to help Uncle Henech distribute the bread, and not even a trace of fatigue would show on him later in the day.

Not so Itche Mayer. For him, sleep had lately become his only escape from the mad world, and he refused to give it up. He struggled for it, heaping the most obnoxious curses he knew on the heads of all the scoundrels outside, Uncle Henech included. And so he squirmed and wriggled in his bed until morning came and the bread was distributed. Then, peace and blessed sleep descended upon him and wrapped him in an eiderdown of forgetfulness, freeing him from all the worries which had made his heart heavy.

It was late in the morning when Itche Mayer stirred in his tumbled iron bed. A rustle had wakened him and before he could even muster the courage to lift his head to see what it was, he felt a bitterness enter his soul; and before he even had time to shake off the state of oblivion that had enveloped him, a pack of devastating thoughts fell upon his mind like a flock of voracious birds of prey, each more bloodthirsty than the next. In that one half second, many things became clear to him. To begin with, he had no reason to get up because he had no work to do anyway, since no one needed his "golden" hands anymore, nor the furniture they were capable of producing. Secondly, there was an evil decree hovering overhead and he could at any moment be dragged out of bed and be deprived of even that bit of miserable sleep which he had been able to enjoy. Thirdly, his son Mottle had left for the border "belt" to try and smuggle himself into his ideological fatherland, and his son Yossi had left for Warsaw for no good reason at all. Fourthly, Shalom, the youngest son, was not at home, but was probably running around, trying to sell the few loaves of bread he got from Blind Henech as payment for his work in the bakery, and was risking his young life every moment that he, Itche Mayer, spent rotting away in his bed. Finally, still another thing became clear to him: that the sound which had awakened him was produced by the candies which Sheyne Pessele had brought home from a candy factory to roll in cellophane paper — a job in which she was helped by Flora, Shalom's bride, and by Faigie, the wife of his oldest son, Israel.

The inescapable conclusion of all these thoughts was that everyone had a reason to get up in the morning, everyone knew what to do with himself, except he, Itche Mayer, the head of the family. This was a galling conclusion to come to, and Itche Mayer tried to disregard it and go on sleeping. Nevertheless, he lifted his head and looked at the walls which, particularly "fruitful" this winter, were almost completely covered with mildew. Then he looked at Sheyne Pessele who, in her threadbare dress which had lost any recognizable colour, was standing at the small table, wrapping candies. The table looked quite gay. The candies were red, orange, yellow and green. A sweet juice watered Itche Mayer's mouth, bringing to his mind the taste of merriment, of children's mouths and little red tongues. And it seemed strangely ridiculous to him, almost like a crazy mockery, that she, his Sheyne Pessele who had become old, whose colourless dress hung crookedly down from her rounded back, whose bent head carried a gray kinky bun knotted messily on her neck, that she — who probably had black thoughts spinning in her mind about the children who had left the nest for the unknown — should stand in front of a brightly-coloured table strewn with brightly-coloured candies and wrap them in shiny cellophane paper, and that they should dance their sweet light dance through her worn crooked fingers.

Itche Mayer's short freckled hand snatched the edge of the eiderdown and with a movement of resignation, he pulled it up over his head. However, precisely at this moment the bubbling of a pot on the stove reached him, not so much through his ears as through his stomach. Moreover, a smell to which he had paid no mind just a little while before, now hit his nostrils, teasing him more than he could bear: the smell of freshly baked bread. In no time, he found himself in the throes of a wild hunger from which, he knew, there was no escape.

"Come and eat," he heard Sheyne Pessele say, as if she had seen what was going on in his insides.

He sat up with a groan, letting his feet down to the cold floor. He leaned both elbows against his knees, dug his fingers into his stiff graying hair and scratched his skull. "What day is it today?" He turned his twisted wrinkled face to Sheyne Pessele. She did not reply and he did not know whether she had not heard him, or whether she just refused to interrupt her train of thought. He dressed slowly, his eyes on the gay table of candies, and on his wife's shapeless fingers moving among them. He could not understand how she managed to handle them so deftly and easily. His nerves taut, he dragged himself to the wooden workshop table and put both hands on its top boards, overcome by a yearning for hammer and saw, a longing as strong as the hunger he felt in his stomach. As he bent down to glance at his work tools tucked away beneath the table, he saw instead three bulging knapsacks which resembled three big-bellied creatures without arms or legs. He turned sharply and in his untied disintegrating shoes shuffled over toward the cupboard. He knew that he had only to open the upper cupboard door and he would see the loaves of bread: well-baked, shiny, with cracked brown crusts; the loaves which Shalom had stored and which he replaced every day with fresh ones, selling off the old. However, Itche Mayer did not open the upper cupboard door, he opened the lower one instead, and took out a bowl and a spoon. He trudged to the stove, bent over the bubbling pot, lifted the cover and grimaced, "Kasha again."

Now Sheyne Pessele deigned to offer him a stern look, frowning as she spoke, "Better not sin with your words, Itche Mayer."

Her tone of voice was such that one might use when talking to a child, or to a milksop. That was the kind of people they were, the womenfolk, Itche Mayer mused, overcome by self-pity: as long as a man was the provider, they had some respect for him . . . more or less, but as soon as things changed . . . "The sight of it makes me retch," he pointed his chin at the soup in his bowl, waiting for her to remove some candy from the side of the table, so that he could put the bowl down. He caught her eye and felt that she was not looking down on him as much as he had thought. Her gaze told him clearly that her heart was breaking into pieces from pain at the sight of him. The soup and her look warmed him somewhat. "You know," he spoke again, "in one of Shalom Asch's books there is a story about a Jew who has forgotten the day of the week. May happier stories than that one come true. Perhaps you'd do me a favour after all, Sheyne Pessele, and enlighten me. What day is it today in this world?"

"Thursday," she did him the favor of enlightening him.

"Thursday, what date?"

"This you want me to know, too?"

He sighed, "We don't even know the date when the boys left." He pushed the bowl away and put his hands on the table, sliding them forward, until his fingers were immersed in the heap of candy. His hands and arms, freckled and hairy, looked like two caterpillars burying themselves in a mountain of sweetness. The candies wrapped in cellophane paper rustled against his skin as they fell into his hands. He rolled them between his palms, listening to them chatter. Images of long ago awoke in his memory: the children young, each one smaller than the other. He saw their faces: four little boys chewing candy and laughing. He saw their sticky red lips, their tongues shining with colourful streaks. Itche Mayer looked about the room. Here and there pebbles of colour were scattered about the floor, candy which had fallen off the table and rolled away behind the beds, into corners. He rose from the chair and got down on his hands and knees to pick them up. He felt as if he were searching for the last twenty-eight years of his life which lay strewn about on the floor of the cellar. And it seemed to him that all those twenty-eight years looked as bleak and crooked as the floor, with only here and there a speck of colour, a small candy, the smile of a child.

"What are you looking for?" Sheyne Pessele asked.

"For my lost yesterdays," he tried to make it into a joke.

Sheyne Pessele sensed immediately that something was wrong with him. "Go upstairs for a bit, to Uncle Henech's, or go to a neighbour's," she advised him.

"Right now? In the morning?" he grimaced, then straightened himself and buttoned his shirt sleeves. "I'll go into town."

"Can't you think of a better idea?"

"I can't dawdle around like this, Sheyne Pessele, can't you understand?"

"Never mind, you can allow yourself to dawdle a bit, it won't hurt your health in the least, believe me."

"I'm going out of my mind."

"No one goes out of his mind so easily."

"Everybody has found something to do. Why should I be an exception?"

"Because there is nothing for you to do." She seemed to be speaking more to the candy in her hands than to him. But she stopped working and turned to him with her eyebrows puckered, a deep furrow above her nose. "I don't want you to go into town, Itche Mayer," she groaned. "I want to have a quiet head about you at least."

"And you don't mind if the children go out?"

"Of course, I don't mind. Am I their mother, or what?" She divided the heap of candies with her hand, pushing the smaller part over to him. "Here, help me roll them."

He took a candy in one hand and a piece of cellophane paper in the other. He watched Sheyne Pessele's deft movements and tried to copy her, until he came up with some more or less properly wrapped candies. He felt slightly better. "He's a good boy, isn't he?" he smiled faintly.

"You mean Shalom?" She agreed with a nod, but added, "And what's wrong with the others?"

"Who says that anything is wrong with them? But he's devoted. Remember the other Wednesday, when the whole town was running to Warsaw, before the Germans came? He had his knapsack on already, but his heart wouldn't let him leave us alone."

"But his heart didn't stop him from volunteering for the army, when all his brothers were already on the battlefield. Luckily there was no one he could talk to any more. The Germans were already knocking at the door."

"Luckily, you said?" he asked. She did not reply. He stopped rolling the candies and rubbed his face with his sticky hands. "I'm suffocating, Sheyne Pessele."

"Who's not?" She bent her head lower as if her eyes had stopped serving her. "Go and shave," she said. "How many days is it since you last shaved, tell me?"

"I don't give a hang."

"You walk around looking like a tramp. Go and shave, then go to a neighbour's for a little while."

"Leave me alone!" he burst out, standing up. "You won't let me go into town, and here you chase me out of the house." He shuffled over to the little window which was half-covered with a dark-gray dirty snow. With the blunt nail of a finger he scratched away a part of the frost from the upper pane and put his eye to it. As usual, he saw nothing through it but the feet of the passers-by, feet without bodies. They seldom passed by, appearing only occasionally on the snow-covered sidewalk, like actors on an empty stage; some feet sure and strong in their stride, others shaky and undecided, still others light and nimble, or heavy and tired.

A pair of shoes halted in front of the window. Although they were splashed with mud and snow, the leather underneath looked new and of good quality. Itche Mayer, who had for years used to imagine the face of the owner by the "face" of the shoe, was stupefied at the sight of this pair of shoes. He saw their "faces", but was unable to conceive of the man who wore them; they were just a pair of new shoes. He thought of the tattered shoes he himself had on, and of Sheyne Pessele's chopped heels, and of the holes in Shalom's soles, and also of Masha's, his grandchild's loafers. And a yearning for nice healthy footwear for his family and for himself came over him; a yearning which brought back his feeling of guilt at going idle. A storm was raging in the world, and his family was walking around practically barefoot. He definitely decided to resist Sheyne Pessele and go out into the street right after lunch to find himself an occupation.

The shoes in front of the window stirred. They took a few steps to one side, then a few steps to the other, as if they were at a fashion show, displaying their qualities to Itche Mayer, or perhaps only trying to tease him. Then, suddenly, they vanished. Itche Mayer was about to take up his place at the table near Sheyne Pessele, to discuss the shoe situation of his family with her, as well as his definite decision to go into town, when the door of the cellar opened and the handsome beard of Chaim the Hosiery-Maker poked itself in, and behind it came Chaim himself, and with him — his feet, and on them — the new shoes which had paraded before Itche Mayer in front of the window.

"May I come in, neighbour?" Chaim the Hosiery-Maker asked shyly.

Chaim the Hosiery-Maker was a rare visitor in the cellar. In fact, before the war he had never set foot over its threshold at all, since, in Chaim's eyes, Itche Mayer was a goy, a traitor to Israel, who was friendly with the left-wing neighbours in the backyard, both those in left-wing politics and those doing "left-wing" business, which to Chaim was one and the same. On top of that, Itche Mayer had four sons who were infected by the same sinful ideas as their parents, and for a man who had daughters of marriageable age, it was best to shun a neighbourliness of that sort as one would shun fire.

But in the present disordered times, when the ground was falling away from under people's feet, the entire backyard on Hockel Street seemed like a lost ship thrown about by stormy waves, and its passengers, the neighbours, turned into one crowd facing the same danger. They ceased to pry into one another's pedigrees and moral "passports" as inquisitively as before. To this Chaim was no exception. Of course it was not easy for him to become better disposed to the godless faction of the backyard's population; but could he help it if Itche Mayer's cellar was the only place where one could hear a piece of news which was not a "duck" hatched in someone's imagination; where one could discuss politics and be cheered by consolations which had some logical basis? So, when it seemed to Chaim that his heart was about to burst with worry and despair, he would knock at Itche Mayer's door.

As a rule, he was received as a welcome guest in the cellar, and it did not enter anyone's mind to hold his pre-war "coldness" against him. After all, this was the way all the religionist neighbours have behaved. They despised the free-thinkers. But the same was true for the free-thinkers. They abused the religionists, teased them and blamed them for keeping the masses in darkness. All this was no more than natural, and it was no more than natural that in the present most tragic of all tragedies, the differences between the two groups should vanish by themselves, although, in his heart, everyone remained the same as before.

"Come in, neighbour. We haven't seen you for ages," Sheyne Pessele cast a satisfied glance at her husband, like a mother happy to receive a visitor for her sick child.

Itche Mayer was flabbergasted by the sight of Chaim wearing the expensive shoes. It would never have occurred to him to pair the two together. And more incomprehensible still was the fact that Chaim, who had always worn the same faded light coat with a reddish scarf tied around his neck, in summer as well as in winter, now had a fine winter coat on, also brand new, and a good quality wool shawl wrapped around his neck. It seemed to Itche Mayer that Chaim's handsome beard had acquired an aristocratic dignity with his attire, that the entire face and bearing of his neighbour had changed, had become imposing and awe-inspiring — which went to prove once more that clothes really did make the man.

"Congratulations, neighbour!" Itche Mayer exclaimed, in spite of himself, as he roused himself to greet the visitor. "You look like a real aristocrat!"

Chaim, ill-at-ease, brushed his hand against his coat. "You mean the outfit? I've had it for weeks. The children insisted. 'Father,' they said, 'you have a new coat. You'd better wear it, it you don't want the Germans to take it away from you during a house search.' Don't you know? Children now have more say than their parents. They've grown up and we've turned into children. So I obeyed them."

"And your shoes look quite decent too," Itche Mayer was not able to overcome his envy. He felt like asking Chaim to take off one shoe and let him, Itche Mayer, hold it in his hand, so that he might pat the leather and perhaps put a foot into the shoe as well, out of curiosity, to see how a foot might feel in such a good shoe. But he controlled himself. He noticed a parcel sticking out from under Chaim's arm and realized that the man's prayer shawl was hidden in it. "You're coming from the prayer house, neighbour?" he asked, "jeopardizing your life like that?"

"A Jew has to pray, neighbour, especially nowadays. We meet in a private room."

"And your beard? Forgive me, it's none of my business, but don't you know that they pull beards?"

Chaim chuckled with open haughtiness, "A Jew has to wear a beard, neighbour."

It was not a proper way of striking up a conversation and from the table Sheyne Pessele interrupted. "Why do you let the man stand at the door, Itche Mayer? Give him a chair," she ordered, talking to her busy fingers.

Chaim sat down on the edge of the chair Itche Mayer had offered him. "I just popped in for a moment, to hear a bit of news from you, to strengthen myself before I go home."

Itche Mayer scratched his head. "Perhaps you can give me some news. I've just gotten out of bed."

"I don't mean local news, neighbour," said Chaim.

"You mean world news?"

"Yes, world news, to help us endure the local news." Chaim noticed the bulky, stuffed knapsacks under the workshop. "I see you're getting ready for the road," he pointed to the table with the tip of his shoe.

The muddy but shiny shoe flashed by in front of Itche Mayer's eyes. "And you, neighbour," he asked, "you don't pack at all? If business is good, the fear is not as great, is it?"

"We still hope that our sons will come back home, with God's help," Chaim said meekly.

"They might have set out for Russia," Sheyne Pessele put in encouragingly.

"They would have come home from the battlefront first, as your sons did."

Itche Mayer's envy subsided. He realized that the nicest pair of shoes might hurt a person sometimes. As a matter of fact, he was more fortunate than Chaim. At least he knew that his sons were alive. He tried to change the subject. "And as far as business is concerned, you have no reason to complain, do you?" He felt compelled to return to the same topic in spite of himself.

"Thank heaven," Chaim replied, somewhat annoyed. "People need stockings, war or no war. Some want to put in a supply for the winter, others are afraid that their money might completely lose its value, and clothing never does. For the same reason, I acquired some clothes and footwear for my family and myself; my girls used to have only two pairs of shoes for all six of them. But I don't enjoy it, neighbour, believe me," Chaim said as if he were consoling Itche Mayer. "Had I my boys at least . . . And in general, somehow it seems wrong for a man to become prosperous when the luck of others falls with the butter-side down."

Sheyne Pessele turned in his direction. "I presume you can allow yourself to buy an additional loaf of bread as well, can't you neighbour?" Chaim stirred in his chair, dismayed by the tactlessness of the hosts. "My Shalom is dealing in bread," she went on emphatically. "So why don't you buy your loaf of bread from us, instead of running to strangers? Are you afraid my boy will skin you, or what?"

"Heaven forbid, of course not!" Chaim moved his eyes between Sheyne Pessele and Itche Mayer, back and forth, as if both of them were two carnivorous animals who had attacked him when he was least expecting it. In a last desperate effort to free himself from the couple's aggression, he turned to Itche Mayer and asked in an imploring tone, "So what is the latest news you've heard, neighbour?"

Itche Mayer let himself down onto his tumbled bed. "The story about Finland you've probably heard. You haven't heard?" Itche Mayer's voice acquired a slightly contemptuous ring. "Something is going on there. But on the other hand, no help for us can be expected to come from that quarter. You should know, neighbour, that what we need is something concrete, tangible and radical."

"For heaven's sake, Itche Mayer," Sheyne Pessele put in impatiently. "Don't make a man wait from now until doomsday for the facts. You have something to tell, then tell it, and let's get it over with."

Itche Mayer offered her one of his hard glances, which was meant to tell her not to butt in where she was not supposed to. Struggling to regain his feeling of self-importance, he concentrated on Chaim. "Let's say this is Russia." He traced a line with his short blunt finger along one side of his lap. "And here, let's say, is Finland." He gave another stroke with the same finger on the other side of his lap. "And here is the border between the two countries." He drove his hand along the groove between his legs. "In one word, they are neighbours; but mind you, not of the same kind as you and I. So they, the Reds, want to tear away that slice of territory," he made a circle on his knee. "Why exactly that slice and not another, you may ask. Well, they say it belongs to them since the six days of the creation of the world." Itche Mayer raised his eyes from his pants. He heard steps outside.

Shalom burst into the cellar. "The evil decree is called off! No one will have to leave Lodz!" he cried out before he had time to shut the door and catch his breath. His face was afire from the frost and shone moistly and merrily.

Itche Mayer and Chaim jumped to their feet. Sheyne Pessele let the candies fall out of her hands. "Called off?" all three of them exclaimed.

Shalom was already at the stove. "I'm starved!" he announced light-heartedly.

Sheyne Pessele licked her sticky fingers. Wiping them on her dress, she rushed for a bowl and a spoon, turning her unclouded face to Chaim with pride as if Shalom had not only brought the good news into the house, but was the one who, personally, had relieved them from the evil decree. She pushed her son away from the stove and filled a bowl with kasha for him. He attacked the food, almost dipping his black dishevelled hair and his entire face into the bowl. His eager lips could hardly wait for his impatient fingers to bring the spoon up to his mouth. Before long, the bowl was empty and spotlessly clean and his hot face emerged from its depths.

"How do you know it's been called off? Perhaps it's only a 'duck' hatched in people's minds, nothing but wishful thinking?" Itche Mayer asked, feeling the heavy stones of worry rolling off his chest.

"All of Lodz is talking about it," Shalom informed him. "The *rav* is driving around in a droshky, telling everyone the good news. It seems there are no trains, not enough wagons, no other means. What's important is, we don't have to leave."

"If it is so," Chaim briskly fixed the new woollen shawl around his neck, "I must rush home to announce the good news to my family."

Shalom followed him to the door with his eyes, wishing that he had the courage to run after him and inquire about Esther. He had been seeing her in the backyard lately. She looked completely changed. Except for her flaming red hair, there was scarcely a trace left of the Esther in whom he had been so interested for so many years. She looked exhausted, sickly. As if to chase away the thought of her, he turned to Sheyne Pessele and inquired, "How come Flora isn't here yet?"

"She's in no hurry, your Flora," Sheyne Pessele said almost without reproach.

For some reason her words irritated Shalom. Hungry again, he approached the cupboard. "I'm going to take myself a piece of bread," he announced.

"Not on my life, you won't!" Sheyne Pessele retorted.

"Let him have a piece of bread," Itche Mayer intervened. "He has earned it, if only for the good news he brought home."

Sheyne Pessele shook her head emphatically, "We decided to eat bread for lunch, and that's when we are going to eat it, not before."

Instead of taking a slice of bread, Shalom filled another bowl of soup. Today was a lucky day and there was no sense in spoiling it. As he sipped the kasha, he pulled a roll of paper bills out of his pocket and threw it on the table with an expansive, nonchalant gesture. "Count it, Father!" he commanded.

Itche Mayer did not wait for him to repeat the order. With one clumsy leap he was at the table; he licked his thumb and counted the money over and over again. Then he rolled it up and approached the "coffin", that is the rough-planked wardrobe where the family kept its clothing. He pulled a sock out of its depths, patted the toe which was bulging slightly at the tip, and pushed Shalom's earnings into it. In his imagination, he saw a pair of shiny shoes for himself, a pair of shoes with straight heels for Sheyne Pessele, a pair of shoes without holes in their soles for Shalom, and a pair of strong little loafers for his grandchild, Masha, even though he knew quite well that the entire sockful of money would go for half a sack of potatoes, if they were lucky enough to get it. When he had finished hiding the money, he stepped over to the workshop and kicked the swollen bellies of the knapsacks. "Time to get rid of these scarecrows," he said.

"And what do you care if they remain packed?" Sheyne Pessele asked.

"What for? Do you absolutely have to call the wolf out of the woods?"

"Now, now, dear husband," she argued cheerfully. "You consider yourself an enlightened man, don't you? Then why are you so supernatural?"

Shalom laughed, "You mean superstitious, Mother." He rubbed his hands together, "All right. What do we have on the agenda now?"

"Make the beds!" Sheyne Pessele ordered. "It's a crying shame with people entering this place. Wash the dishes, and you, Shalom, take out the slop pail!"

Itche Mayer blinked at his son, "Did you hear what the General ordered?" He faced Sheyne Pessele, "You know, my wife, you could lead an entire battalion of infantry to battle."

"You said you had nothing to do, didn't you?" she shot back.

"And this is the profession you thought up for me? After lunch I'm going into town anyway," he announced, taking the broom and sweeping the dust out from under the beds. "There may be lightning and thunder and you may stand on your head, Sheyne Pessele, but you won't turn me into a henpecked husband, not on your life!" He avenged himself on the boards of the floor, fiercely scratching together the dirt with the broom, in a sudden attack of anger.

"Believe me, Father," Shalom put in, "It's better to stay home, take my word for it."

"So!" Itche Mayer exploded. "You're supporting her verdict, I see! You're scheming to bury me alive here, both of you!"

"On the contrary. We want you to survive. How many fathers do I have, after all?"

"You insist, the two of you, in making a coward out of me!"

"Who could make a coward out of you? That's absolutely ridiculous. My father a coward?" Shalom took the broom from Itche Mayer's hand and swung it as if it were a bandleader's baton. "Is it possible that such a hero as I should have a coward for a father? Look at me!" He marched around Itche Mayer with his chest thrust out, saluting him like a soldier. "Tell me, Father," he beamed, "are you really in want of anything? You have enough potatoes to fill the holes in all your teeth. You have enough bread to fill your nostrils with its smell. You have enough meat to chew on all day long, so what else do you want?" And more seriously he added, "People would consider themselves lucky to be in your place."

"Oho!" Itche Mayer grabbed himself by his prickly chin. "That's what you mean! All this luxury is thanks to you!"

"I wouldn't say that." Shalom lifted both hands to the ceiling, crooning a tune with mock piety. "It's thanks to Uncle Henech's loaves of bread, may the Almighty bless them!"

At that moment the door opened slowly, noiselessly, as if by itself, and a head appeared in it. A pair of frightened eyes looked around the cellar, halting at Shalom. "Mister," a hand poked out with a crooked frost-bitten finger, "may I have a word with you?" Shalom remained glued to his place, motionless; then, as if hypnotized, he followed the finger, the face, and the wild-looking eyes into the corridor, closing the door behind him. The stranger had the look of a hollow-cheeked corpse, his skin was so yellow that even the frost had not managed to redden it. Only his stiffly bent hands were purple. He grabbed Shalom by the lapels, hopping up and down and knocking his feet together. "Are you taking me for a partner?" The bloodless mouth clicked its teeth. "I'm asking you for the last time, yes or no?"

A surge of rage swept over Shalom, waking him from his stupor. "I'm telling you, you'd better lay off, I'm warning you!" He waved his finger in front of the man's long dripping nose.

"I won't lay off, my dear Sir!" The stranger continued in a feverish singsong. "I'm ready for anything. A Jew should have a little humanity in his heart."

"I gave you twice already."

"I always want, every day, dear Sir. I have a wife and two small children. Why should one Jew have all the luxury and another none? Oy, the tragedy is equally ours, dear Sir."

His whimpering singsong penetrated Shalom's bones to the marrow. He shuddered. "Go and find yourself a better occupation, you *shnorrer!*"

"I won't go! I have a wife and two small children. Give me a quarter of a loaf!"

"Get up at night, put yourself in line, and you'll have your loaf."

"I don't have the money to buy it, Mister, not a groschen to my name. Oy, the tragedy is so great!" Shalom thrust his hand into his pocket and scooped out a few groschen. He handed them to the stranger who locked them in his red hand, while continuing to hop up and down in front of Shalom. "I still want the quarter of a loaf, Mister!"

"I have no bread!" Shalom felt sick at the pit of his stomach.

"You do, you do! I have a good nose for the smell of bread. Your whole room smells of bread. With the smell of bread you can't fool me, oy, not with the smell of bread, Mister."

Shalom's patience ran out. He grabbed the stranger, lifted him as if he were a block of wood and pulling him to the gate, threw him to the ground. He wanted to re-enter the cellar and bolt the door, but the stranger jumped to his feet, snatched him by the jacket and hung on to him, dancing up and down and stamping his feet. Shalom freed himself from him, hardly able to control the urge to really make use of his fists. Once again he pushed the stranger down, dashed into the cellar and locked the door behind him.

No sooner had he stepped over the threshold than Sheyne Pessele was beside him. "Who was it? What did he want of you?" She followed him, insisting, "Was it a 'leech'?"

He nodded. All three looked at each other. "Someone like that is liable to denounce us," said Itche Mayer.

"We have to get rid of the loaves right away!" Sheyne Pessele decided. They went over to the cupboard. Sheyne Pessele opened it. A few smiling brown loaves confronted them. For a moment they looked at them with tenderness and adoration, then Shalom took a sack and tossed the bread into it. "Take it upstairs to Chaim's," Sheyne Pessele ordered. "He's an honest man."

Shalom slung the sack over his shoulder. "Father, go out and see if he's gone," he told Itche Mayer.

A few hours later, having just finished their lunch, they were sitting at the workshop table which was covered with a threadbare oilcloth. On it were empty plates shining as if they had been newly washed, so neatly had the food been scraped and wiped from them. Only the glasses were dirty, half full of bitter chicory coffee. There was an air of dullness and laziness about the room.

Itche Mayer lay on his iron bed, stretched out in his clothes, ready to take a nap. His tiny tired eyes blinked at the dusty electric bulb. He was immersed in his pre-sleep thoughts which had no exact shape or content. At the table, Sheyne Pessele sat struggling with the last bit of coffee in her glass, as if she considered it her duty to drink it down to the last drop. Opposite her, their eldest son, Israel, was drawing on the oilcloth with the tip of his fork.

Israel was a hefty man. Although he had inherited his short stature from

Itche Mayer, there was something in him which made him appear more imposing than the other members of the family, not only physically, but also in his bearing, in his character; something which made the others, his parents included, look up to him with respect. His face was round and broad; it was not flabby, but rather muscular and hard. Sheyne Pessele's stubbornness and down-to-earth wisdom were in the expression of his eyes, in the firmness of his chin and in the shape of his strong mouth. His hands were like those of Itche Mayer, hard, veined and short; the broad fingers with their slanted blunt nails and rough bruised skin spoke of hammer and saw, of the work that they had produced and were capable of producing. His short blond hair revealed a broad forehead already deeply rutted, with inlets of baldness to both sides.

At his side sat his wife Faigie, petite, shapely, with a young girlish face fringed with straight brown bangs. She had a pair of warm cherry eyes which looked at the world with mild feminine submissiveness. Close to her, her daughter Masha, a miniature copy of her mother, was playing with some shiny cellophane papers which were used for wrapping the candy.

Across from them sat Shalom and his fiancée Flora. In a way, Flora was a dissonant chord in the harmony of the family picture — someone who neither fitted in, nor could be completely considered an intruder. It would be difficult to say how her foreignness expressed itself, but all of them felt it, Flora included, not that it mattered to her. Her head, its long dark hair reaching her shoulders, was leaning against Shalom's arm. Her face, charmingly alive, smooth and alabaster-like, ready to smile at the slightest provocation, was turned towards him. Her sultry eyes shamelessly teased him; they lured and spoke of the feminine restlessness vibrating in all her limbs. Her full breasts rising under her knit blouse were like two kittens lying in wait, ready to leap out. Motionless as she was now, she still seemed to be the embodiment of movement which had halted only momentarily.

Faigie was making signs, to let Flora know that it was time to go back to work. But Flora saw only Shalom. She pushed her hand behind his arm and whispered in his ear, giggling quietly, her eyes hanging on to his lips. Sheyne Pessele, however, did catch Faigie's glance. She pushed her empty glass away, got up from the table heavily, and assembled the dishes. The next moment, mother and daughter-in-law were standing at the water bench washing the dishes. "She cares as much for her work as I care to go dancing," Sheyne Pessele whispered to Faigie.

Faigie cast a furtive glance in Flora's direction. "What do you want, Mother, isn't looking at Shalom more interesting than rolling candy?" She smiled confidentially at Sheyne Pessele, "Were it not for the war, we would have had a wedding in the family by now. Not so, Mother?"

"Yeah, they're quite advanced, don't worry. But I don't foresee great harmony between them. Shalom needs another kind of a girl, a homey one, someone like you, for instance."

Faigie flashed a shy smile, "You're paying me compliments, Mother."

"You know that it isn't my nature to pay compliments. But 'what's on my lung, that's on my tongue'. Firstly, her German upbringing shows in every step; secondly, she doesn't understand life as we do. Because you should know," Sheyne Pessele became philosophical, "that there are two categories of women in this world. One category was created for pleasure and the other for bringing up children. One category is made up of coquettes who wiggle their behinds all the time, always ready to display the merchandise; and the other category is our kind, who live a bitter life and put all their sweat and blood at the service of their families; women who don't think about themselves in the slightest, who are mothers to their children and to their husbands too. And she, Flora, does not belong to that category. Oh, no!"

"Don't say that, Mother," Faigie put in. "You can see that she has eyes for no one in the world besides Shalom. Such a pretty girl, with a temperament like hers, with the language and education she has, could easily have found a rich boy from Piotrkowska Street. But she's in love with Shalom."

"Of course she's in love with him. And don't you dare think that my Shalom can't compare with the dandies of Piotrkowska Street. They aren't worthy to step into his shoes."

Faigie's face flushed at her inept remark. She hurried to cover her embarrassment with a question. "Does Shalom at least know, Mother, that you're not overjoyed with their relationship?"

"Sure he knows. With me 'what's on my lung, that's on my tongue'. But do I tell him what to do? Not on your life. I have brought up my children, true, but they have to build their lives by themselves. That doesn't belong to me any more."

"And perhaps it will end well, Mother. Shalom is not a boy to take a girl with his eyes shut. He has had time to find out about her."

"Come, come now. A man doesn't fall in love through the assistance of his reason, but through the assistance of what they call the 'minstincts'. And she knows how to play on them, rely on her."

They heard a subdued laughter. Shalom had finally submitted to Flora's whispered wisecracks. He caught himself immediately and covered his mouth with his hand, so as not to wake Itche Mayer. "What do you need them to get cross at you for? Go, start working." He pushed her away from him, and got to his feet.

She hung onto his arm. "We don't see each other all day long," she said coaxingly in German.

He chucked her on the nose, "Don't exaggerate, we see each other almost all day."

"Like this . . . with everybody around?" she pouted. "*Ich möchte dich nur für mich haben.*"

"*Haben-shmaben,*" Shalom chuckled. "If you speak that language to me again, I won't answer you." Gently he freed himself from her arms. She spread them lazily, then stretched them as if trying to reach the ceiling, pushing forward her big bosom which swayed under her blouse. Shalom felt like putting his arms around her snake-like waist. But instead, he only kissed her on the cheek. Flora's face lit up with kittenish delight. She threw herself at him again, knotting her hands behind his neck, her body glued to his. He felt her moist mouth on his lips, but dared not abandon himself to the pleasure. He looked about him ill-at-ease, pushed her vigorously away and went to sit down beside Israel who was still bent over the design on the oilcloth. "Israel," he said, "what's new in the party? When will it begin doing some work?"

Israel made a long stroke with his fork on the oilcloth, "It will take some time."

"How long? Don't you think a party should do more than just give support to its members? And tell me, is it true that the party gives financial assistance to the families of German socialists?"

"True. They're in a hell of a mess."

"Really?"

Israel noticed the irony in Shalom's voice. "You think solidarity is only a word that we use in our phraseology?"

"And how about Jewish solidarity? Have all the Jewish ills already been attended to? Are there no more Jews in need of support?"

Israel stood up and reached for his coat. "We'll talk about it later," he said, stroking little Masha on the head. He waved to his wife and left.

In little more than a second, he was back — and the green of a German uniform loomed into sight behind him. The soldier shoved Israel to the wall, pushing his way into the cellar.

With one jump, Itche Mayer got out of bed. Still half asleep, he was unable at first to grasp what was going on around him. Before his drowsy eyes, the face of the soldier changed places with that of Israel. The soldier was much taller than Israel, also more broad-shouldered and massive, but he had a freckled face, a broad nose and hard jaws with a stubborn, protruding chin, just like Itche Mayer's son. Itche Mayer's eyes jumped between the two men, seeing one in the skin of the other, each in the other's clothes. But then a pair of cold eyes pierced right through him. The chill going through his sleepy body descended to his legs, making them shake. He was, however, freed from his awkward comparison. The difference between the two men was slight, hardly noticeable, and yet so essential, that it obliterated all resemblance. The difference was in their eyes. Israel's eyes would never fit the green uniform with the swastika on its arm. And when the soldier began to rummage around the cellar, Itche Mayer, in his confusion, realized that besides the eyes, the gait of the two men was different as well. Israel would never have stamped and strutted about another man's home in such a manner.

The soldier kept both his hands in his belt and marched with such thunderous steps that the boards of the floor shook beneath him, while from between the cracks, black streaks of mud sprouted under his every step, squeaking like cats whose tails were being stepped on. Now and then he took one or another of his freckled hands out of his belt and opened doors, cupboards, throwing everything down from the shelves with one sweeping gesture. His boots kicked the knapsacks under the workshop, turning them over. Then he tipped the little mahogany table, spilling all the pictures and albums onto the floor. He approached the table full of candy, and with one push of his green arm, lifted it sideways, making it rain with gay colourful splotches which scattered all over the cellar. Then the soldier stopped short, as if trying to recall what else he had to do. At length he went to the door and beckoned to someone outside with his finger, "*Komm!*"

The shrivelled figure of the "leech" appeared on the threshold.

On his trembling feet, Itche Mayer walked over to Israel and so did Sheyne Pessele. She placed herself behind her eldest son, her head and her entire body swaying like the upside-down pendulum of a clock, appearing now to the left, now to the right of Israel's arms. Little Masha dashed toward her mother, clutching at a fold of her dress. Both of them joined Israel, each grabbing him frantically by the hand.

Shalom stayed in the middle of the room. His body stiff, paralyzed; he heard the blood roaring in his ears. Only Flora seemed undisturbed by what was going on. She put her hands on her hips, curiously watching the action.

"*Das ist er!*" The "leech" indicated Shalom with his crooked finger.

The expression of curiosity vanished from Flora's face. She dashed over to her fiancé, ready to protect him and put herself between him and the German, smiling a coaxing uncomfortable smile. The German put his stiff finger against her bosom, pushed her aside and placed himself in front of Shalom with his feet spread apart, his hands on the clasp of his belt. "*Wo ist das Brot?*" His voice was so thunderous that all those present jerked backwards.

Shalom cast a nervous glance at Israel and immediately composed himself. "*Herr Offizier*," he took a mouthful of air and spread his arms, searching in his mind for all the necessary German words which he had learned from Flora. "We have nothing but the bread of our ration."

"Don't believe him! Don't believe him, *Herr Offizier*," the "leech" hopped up and down, shaking, his teeth chattering. "He has stolen bread from the bakery!"

"Where is the bread?" the German thundered, edging closer to Shalom.

Shalom felt the unpleasant breath of the stranger's mouth in his face. "Please, search for it, *mein Herr*," he spread his arms.

Sheyne Pessele rushed to the cupboards, opening the doors which the soldier had failed to open. Inside one of them there was half a loaf of bread cut into three equal parts.

"This is from their ration, *Herr Offizier*," Flora put in protectively, swinging her hand gracefully in the direction of the cupboard. "*Ja, wirklich!*"

The German looked her over from head to toe, his eyes creeping over her face, her bosom and her rounded hips. He moved his feet wider apart. "*Kommst du vom Reich?*" he leaned over to her.

"*Ja wohl, Herr Offizier, von Hamburg.*"

"Then you should know that no one is ever supposed to lie to a German." As if unwillingly, his freckled hand with its five spread fingers flew out of his belt, fluttered in the air like a bird, and landed on her smooth alabaster cheek with a loud slap.

Shalom's head swam. He suddenly found himself close to the German. "*Sie sollen . . .*" he stuttered.

Flora's hand covered his mouth. She pushed him away. She acted as though the slap had not hurt her in the least. She did not even touch the cheek which displayed the imprint of the German's five fingers, like white grooves in the pink of her skin. Her eyes, misty and so deep and dark that they seemed to consist only of their pupils, glared at Shalom imploringly. She pulled him to the corner of the cellar.

Israel let go of little Masha's hand and approached the "leech", grabbing him by the collar of his thin coat. "Let him show where the bread is hidden," he said drily to the German.

"I can show! I can show!" The "leech" shrank back into his coat behind the raised collar. Wagging his head, he danced about the cellar sniffing with his long snotty nose like a bloodhound. "The smell of bread! The smell of bread!" he quavered, crooning in an eerie pitch, finally getting down on all fours and nosing with dog-like impatience under the beds, the tables and in the depths of the "coffin".

They followed him with their eyes. Itche Mayer recalled that he had crawled about like that on the floor that very morning, collecting candies, looking for his "lost yesterdays". His revulsion at the "leech" was a thousandfold stronger than his hatred for the German in the green uniform. He felt capable of tearing the odd skeletal Jew to pieces — while at the same time, he was overcome by a pity both for himself and for the miserable stooped creature on the floor who was searching for what was not there, just like he, Itche Mayer, had done that morning.

The German looked up from the crawling figure on the floor, riveting his gaze on Flora and Shalom. It seemed as if the sight of the pair in each other's arms both amused and enraged him. Slowly he put his hand to the leather holster on his hip, unbuttoned it lazily, and in a moment, the raw metal of a revolver flashed in the light of the dirty electric bulb.

At the sight of the gun, Itche Mayer forgot his thoughts, as if the revolver had shot through them. He squirmed, taking a step forward toward the soldier, as did Israel. Between them, like a wind, Sheyne Pessele swept by in her flying colourless dress and hung onto the German's arm. "Bitte, bitte schön, Herr Offizier!" she sputtered.

The Herr Offizier shook her off, as though she were a disgusting piece of rag, and paced to the corner where Flora and Shalom stood. He tore the young man out of the girl's arms, thrusting him into the middle of the cellar. Shalom swayed, but found his equilibrium without falling. As he straightened up, he felt the hard cold touch of metal on his temple. "Now, you'll speak!" the soldier bellowed.

The cold metal froze the fear in Shalom. "I have no bread," he said calmly.

A silence which rang and rumbled in everyone's ears descended upon the room. They all stood motionless, breathless; even the "leech" stopped nosing about the cellar. Leaning on his elbows, he pointed the tip of his running nose toward the revolver, saliva dripping from his mouth.

Nor did the German move. His eyes darted from one face to the other — until the dagger-sharp strength of his gaze began to falter. He removed the gun from Shalom's temple and carried it slowly back to the holster on his hip. As if he had suddenly become bored with his own performance, he adjusted the tails of his uniform jacket and marched over to the "leech". With all his strength he kicked him in the behind. The "leech" let out a shriek, and fell to the floor. The German chuckled. One last time he looked around the cellar with bright cheerful eyes, waved his hand and, whistling loudly, left, leaving the door open.

The sound of his whistling floated in from outside carried by the gusts of cold air which enveloped the inhabitants of the cellar, awakening them from their stupor. They looked at the "leech" as he lay motionless on the floor, unable to take a step towards him. Finally, Israel approached him, shaking him by the shoulder.

"Water!" the slavering mouth whimpered.

As Israel went over to the water bench to fetch a scoop of water, Flora jumped forward at him, snatching the scoop from his hand. She poured the water back into the bucket. Israel, smiling faintly, took the scoop from her hand, filling it with water once more. "Shame! Shame!" she burst out sobbing. Her tears were the signal for the other women to release their tension. Sheyne Pessele blinked her eyes and began crying dry tears, as was her habit. Faigie and little Masha sobbed freely and with great relish, letting their flowing tears wash down their faces.

Israel lifted the "leech's" head and poured water into his mouth. The "leech" swallowed with loud gulps, followed by hiccups. Then he hung onto Israel's arm with one hand and with the other grabbed himself at the spot where the soldier's boot had jabbed him, exclaiming, "Oy, God Almighty!" Swaying like a drunkard, he finally managed to scramble to his feet. "Thank you people," he said and headed in the approximate direction of the door, holding himself from behind with both hands and moving on his legs as though they were stilts attached to his body.

"Thank you, too!" Sheyne Pessele called after him, sniffling angrily.

The "leech" looked back, embracing them all with a desperate foggy glance. Then his eyes goggled and he fell to the floor. "I'm hungry!" he squealed, throwing his head back like a slaughtered hen.

Once more it was Israel who stepped over to the stove, uncovering one of the pots. "Mother, give him some food," he said.

"A disease I'll give him, not food!" Sheyne Pessele rushed towards him with a scream, as if her son had burned her with his words. But since Israel stood calmly waiting, she gave in, brought a bowl and a spoon and emptied the pot into the bowl. The next moment, she was standing over the "leech", pushing the spoon into his limp fingers. As if the touch of the spoon had the power to revive him, the "leech" opened one eye, then the other, and tried to grip the spoon firmly in his hand, while they all watched him. As he began eating, the soup spilled over his face, running down his chin onto his coat.

"Shame . . . Shame . . ." Flora sobbed.

The "leech" made an effort to sit up. He lifted the bowl to his mouth with both his shaking hands and gulped the soup down. He tried to scramble to his feet, but could not, and had to lean against Israel's arm. As they stepped out of the cellar, Itche Mayer took the "leech" by the other arm. "You're ready to help everyone, isn't that so, son?" Itche Mayer said to Israel cheerily, "The one who deserves it, as well as the one who doesn't, even this louse here!"

"I hadn't thought about it, Father," Israel answered quietly, freeing himself from the "leech's" hand. But before he let go of him completely, Israel suddenly delivered a fiery slap to the "leech's" hollow cheek. "That's for being a stool pigeon!" he said.

When they returned to the cellar, Itche Mayer badly felt the need to strike up a serious conversation with his eldest son, to relieve himself of some anxious thoughts. But Israel was in a hurry. He took leave of his family, then stopped for a moment in front of Shalom, realizing that his youngest brother saw nothing and no one but the imprint of the soldier's five fingers on Flora's cheek. He patted Shalom's shoulder. "We'll talk later," he said and left.

It was indeed so. Shalom saw nothing but the soldier's five fingers on Flora's cheek and felt nothing but the ice cold touch of the revolver against his own temple. "Come, Father," he said. "Let's go out and chop some wood." Itche Mayer did not wait for him to repeat the suggestion. He had to talk to one of his sons. Quickly he wrapped his long scarf around his neck and followed Shalom.

Meanwhile, the women made order in the cellar, picking up the candy from the floor and putting everything back in place. Sheyne Pessele kept her eyes on the door. She thought that during the time Itche Mayer and Shalom had been gone, a man could have chopped not only a few blocks of wood, but an entire wagonload. Finally they came in. She read on their faces that something had gone wrong once again.

Itche Mayer, his eyes avoiding hers, announced, "Shalom is leaving for Russia."

Shalom was about to snatch his knapsack from under the workshop when he felt Flora's arms around his neck. "I'm coming with you," she said.

Sheyne Pessele raised both hands to her mouth; unaware of what she was doing, she licked her fingers as if they were still sweet and sticky. Then she wiped them on her threadbare dress and approached the cupboard, taking out all three portions of bread. She cut them into slices. With a nod of her head, she sent Itche Mayer to the "coffin". He pulled out the knotted sock of money and pushed most of it into Shalom's hand. "Faigie, sew the money into his jacket," Sheyne Pessele ordered.

When Shalom and Flora had been gone for quite a while, Itche Mayer remembered that he had not asked his son to tell him what date it was.

Two weeks later, Shalom and Flora were still on the border "belt", at Malkin Train Station, with seven thousand other people who were also trying to escape the Germans by going to Russia.

This particular night was beautiful and white, a real storybook night. Around Flora and Shalom the world was enveloped in a kind of festive innocence: a night of white fairies and silver bells. The frost shimmered not only on the fluffy snow in the field, not only on the glistening sleeves of the boughs, but also in the very air: a thin transparent veil with blinking diamonds in it. Above their heads, the sky was starry and the moon hung from it, white and round — and seemingly angry and brutal. Like a reflector, it beamed at the huge black shadow of people spread out over the whiteness of the earth and disturbing the harmony of nature. As though determined to scare this huge shadow away with its cold light, it illuminated the cadaverous faces, the half-frozen bodies of those who had been waiting for weeks for the Gates of Freedom to open before them.

"Shalom, look," Flora whispered. She was cuddled up in Shalom's arms, as both of them sat squeezed into the middle of the crowd. "The peasants are coming with pails of soup. Come," she pulled at his sleeve, "Get up!" A part of the crowd which lay on the ground rose. The more hefty among the men threw themselves on the peasants, counting out money and pulling the pails of hot soup out of their hands. They scuffled and fought for the food among themselves — while the moon flooded them with its light, as though it were staging an extraordinary show of convening demons.

Flora, limping stiffly, dragged Shalom towards the moving mass of people. The smell of the hot soup tickled their nostrils, their mouths watered. The next moment they were in the very centre of the scuffle, jostled and pushed in all directions. It was impossible to find out where the pails were or what was going on. Flora and Shalom became part of the multi-faced monster which, with hundreds of mouths, emitted one raw howl.

"Stop, I tell you!" Shalom pulled Flora backward with all his strength. He pressed his mouth to her cheek, whispering heatedly, "Come, let's try instead to cross the 'belt' by ourselves." He led her out of the crowd and they slipped away, walking quickly, relishing the renewed lightness of their limbs. They held hands, increasingly enjoying the march. Free, carrying no load, they felt a kind of bitter gratitude to the Polish hooligans who had cut the knapsacks off their backs a few days before. They had nothing else to take care of but each other.

And there was no one else now in the world, except the two of them and this white beautiful night.

The snow yielded softly under their soundless steps. Yet it seemed to them that they were making a great noise. They walked along the train tracks and entered a little forest through which they continued to march further away from the station. They walked on and on, feet into the snow, feet out of the snow. But as time wore on, it became increasingly difficult for them to lift their legs. The snow was sometimes hard and frozen, at other times it was like a deep swamp. They came out onto a spacious field — a white desert — the two of them alone, with the moon, the cruel reflector, above their heads. Time ran backwards with the footprints they had left in the snow. Finally, neither Flora nor Shalom could take another step.

As they stopped, they noticed something protruding from the snow in the distance. A piece of fence? A roof? They dragged themselves towards it. It was a piece of fence all right; and the roof? A stiff rag of canvas — as if sent down by a charitable hand. "Let's rest here," Shalom suggested, pulling the canvas out of the snow. He shook it out, straightened it and attached it to the boards and wires of the broken piece of fence. It made a kind of tent. He ordered Flora to crawl inside. She was about to take her shoes off and shake the snow out, but he stopped her. It would be harder to put them back on over her wet stockings; as it was, her feet at least were warm from their march — wet and warm. Perspiration made their clothes stick pleasantly to their bodies. Flora and Shalom clung cozily to each other, to the ground beneath them and to the piece of canvas. He held her hands in his; she held her face against his cheek. They peeked out through a hole in the fabric. As though it were a cut-off slice of the moon, a white form was coming down towards them, taking on strange shapes, until it was transformed into a rider on a white horse, who flashed by soundlessly, dreamily. "This is freedom," Shalom whispered before he dropped off to sleep.

As he slept, he felt that he was being lifted into the air, was being rocked back and forth, as if he were hanging from a branch of a tree. He opened his eyes wide, letting himself be rocked and swung. A scream brought him to his senses. He saw everything lopsided, askew, close by, but sideways. He saw the screaming Flora at a slant, practically upside down. Then he became aware of himself, hanging by the collar from the jaws of a white horse that held him up in the air, swinging him back and forth. The rider said something calmly to the horse, and the next thing Shalom knew, he was lying in the soft snow. His heart twitched with joy. He jumped to his feet. "Comrade!" he exclaimed, raising his clenched fist in a socialist salute.

"Back!" came the voice of the rider.

Flora stood beside Shalom. She was no longer screaming but was nagging the rider, imploring him to allow them into his fatherland. She took off her watch and Shalom took off his. She took off her earrings and Shalom snipped a hole in his coat where his money was sewn in. The rider bent down from the horse, took everything he was offered, then sat up straight again and pulled at the reins lightly. The horse trotted slowly against Flora and Shalom, pushing them backwards, chasing them like sheep that had strayed from the flock — back . . . back . . . back.

The same night, a few other groups of Jews who had been waiting at the "belt" tried their luck, crossing by way of the train tracks. Shalom and Flora joined them, determined to get through to the Russian side that night, no matter what. Time and again they crossed the tracks, dragging themselves through the snow. The first blue of dawn lit up the horizon with a pale golden fringe of light. A new day was beginning with the promise of sunshine. Shalom whispered encouraging words in Flora's ear, about another life, about a new future in the Soviet Union. Flora was too tired to listen. Holding on to his sleeve, she staggered on with her eyes shut, letting him pull her ahead. They arrived at a little town along with the last group of people they had joined. There, the riders were already waiting for them on their white horses — many riders, many horses, guns ready in gloved hands. Once more they chased the intruders away, galloping against them and hitting them over the heads with the butts of their guns, because the horde of Jews refused to obey. Like nagging flies they swarmed around the riders and their horses, begging for pity.

Suddenly Shalom realized that Flora was no longer holding on to him. He wanted to race forward, but a horse galloped against him. He turned back, skittering across the field with the rest of the crowd — but without Flora. Back at the "belt", he plunged into the mass of people spread out along the train tracks. He thought that she had perhaps arrived earlier and was waiting for him. He waded through the snarls of bodies, roaring Flora's name at the top of his voice; he looked at faces, climbed over bags, sacks and human limbs; he fell, jumped to his feet and continued to call her more hoarsely as time wore on, and more despondently.

The crowd on the "belt" woke from the night-time stupor. People moved their stiff limbs, they rewound the rags around the bodies of their children, warming their frozen fingers with their breath. Some speculated, made plans, quarrelled and dreamed aloud about warm food to revive them. Others cried. At times it sounded like the crying of sick children; at other times, like the cawing of crows — the dry sobs of women whose tears had frozen; the short desperate sobs of men unable to look on the suffering of their women and children, not knowing what to do: whether to drag themselves back to the Germans or to keep on waiting for a miracle here.

Flora was nowhere to be found. Shalom kept looking for her, but he no longer called her name. As he wandered about, he could hardly believe that she was not at his side. He felt her presence as if she were there, but had become invisible. Like a bloodhound, he tried in his confusion to smell out her scent. A voice whispered in his ear that she had probably had luck in the little town, and had succeeded in getting herself across to the other side.

He saw himself all alone in the forest. Under a tree, he noticed two stooped dark figures. Perhaps one of them was Flora? He dashed ahead breathlessly, but then he stopped. In front of the two people, on the ground, lay a motionless bundle. Parents were digging a grave for their child. He raced on, without knowing where he was. All he saw was snow and trees, trees and snow. He was lost and did not mind. He felt Flora's presence; he smelled her invisible footprints and hoped that in his erratic wandering, he would somehow come out on the other side and find her.

He was neither tired nor hungry. He raced among the trees, retracing his own footprints. The first light of the day penetrated the forest — what beauty in the play of the first sunrays against the white boughs! The snow under his steps seemed warm, fresh and fluffy; it invited him to rest. It seemed to him that he was still running, when in fact he was merely trudging along, step by step.

His eyes burned; black circles turned in front of them. As he moved on, he dreamed of dropping down into the snow, of burying himself in it and forgetting about everything. But Flora would not let him. Everything within him was asleep, except her voice. She was calling to him from the surrounding emptiness. He had to find her.

He found himself at the edge of the forest, on a path to a village. The first hut some metres away looked inviting. He made for it, but before he could reach it, a telegraph pole came forward to meet him. On it, a warning in German: "For hiding Jews — the penalty of death." He crouched, passing under the windows of the first hut, so that he would not be noticed from inside, and entered the yard. A barn door gave in to his touch. As he entered, he met with the eyes of a shaggy dog. He had a way with dogs. Before it had time to bark, Shalom stooped down and patted it. The dog wagged its tail. Shalom put his face against its warm fur and embraced it, leaning his whole body against that friendly live little oven. The dog growled with delight and licked his face, pressing itself tighter against him, as though it knew what its warmth meant to the man, and was eager to share it with him.

Shalom was ready to continue his search for Flora. But he noticed a heap of dirty straw in the corner of the barn. His head turning, the black circles in front of his eyes blinding him, he dragged himself to it and dropped down on it like a block of wood. The dog was beside him, snuggling its shaggy warm body next to his. The last thing Shalom saw before he fell asleep were the animal's brown eyes, close to his face, devoted and watchful — or were they Flora's eyes?

✦ ✦ ✦

In the beginning, Esther would lie in bed for days in a row. There was nothing else left to do, she would tell herself, allowing her physical weakness to support her apathy. She liked the night and sleep, liked the frequent dreams that carried her back to the past or created another reality for her, one in which all did not seem lost. She would dream about her child and see herself carrying it in her arms, so clearly, that the illusion would not disappear even after she woke up. Her eyes open, she would hug her pillow as if it were alive.

During the day it was harder to retreat into such dreams, awake or asleep. Often, it was the silence outside, contrasting so strangely with the light of the day, that would bother her. Now and then the silence was shattered by the squeak of a door, by a sound in the street or on the stairway. She would hear broken sentences, unfinished screams, and their incompleteness would screw itself into her mind with sharp question marks. So she stayed in bed with her nose buried under the cover, inhaling the smell of her body, until pangs of hunger would make her restless and force her to get up. They lighted her mind with sparks of curiosity: perhaps something had happened? Perhaps the war was over and Hersh was back? A need to see people, to listen to them would overcome her then, making her rush to the cupboard, grab a chunk of bread and bite into it. But at the first bite, both the frost in the room and her own apathy would overwhelm her. Again she would ask herself, "Where do you have to run? What do you care about the world? Hersh is not here. If he were here, you would know. And it is cold everywhere." She would climb back into bed, pull the covers over her head and suck on the chunk of bread for a long time.

But when the bread was gone and the cupboard was empty, she was no longer able to go back to bed. She feared the moment when her hunger would go wild and she would have nothing to calm it with. Then she would dress and go to Baluty, to Uncle Chaim's house. She went there with revulsion and bitterness in her heart, disgusted with herself in her humiliation and resentful of Uncle Chaim and his family. It was her good fortune that Uncle Chaim could afford to offer her a piece of bread, she thought, but it was also unjust that he should have the bread and that she should have to go begging for it. And she was, in a way, angry with the rest of the family too, for the heartiness with which they received her. She could not bear the silent questions that she read in their faces, as their eyes creeped over her wasted figure. But the worst was Aunt Rivka's tenderness. When Esther had been on her way to the hospital, her body quivering with pain, she had badly wished to have her aunt by her side. Then, it had seemed to her that Aunt Rivka was her only support in this world. Then, all she had wanted was Rivka's arms, a chance to free herself from her own anguish, from feeling so alone in the world, suspended in its emptiness without a thread to bind her to it. But now, that she had Rivka's tenderness, it became once more unbearably clear to her that what she had wished would never happen; that there would always be an abyss between her aunt and herself, that her heart would always remain locked behind seven locks, and that she would always be alone.

During her visits, she would sit, talking, heaping lie upon lie, waiting for her aunt or for one of her cousins to come in from the kitchen, with a bag in their hands, and shyly implore her to take it, since they "hardly knew what to do with so much food". She would thank them, blushing, cringing with shame; then take the gift and run off.

Although Uncle Chaim's household was far from being so opulent that they did not know what to do with the food, it was nonetheless true that they suffered from no lack of work. The girls toiled feverishly at the machines and before the finished stockings even left their hands, they were already sold. Aunt Rivka stood at the window all day, on guard, in case Germans should appear in the backyard, and then the machines as well as the merchandise would have to be stashed away in the blink of an eye. Indeed, they now had not only enough to eat, but also enough to wear, although they were unable to enjoy their good clothes; firstly, because the two sons and brothers had not come back from the battlefront; secondly, because the girls were too exhausted and sleepy to care about dressing up; thirdly, because it simply would not do in such times, to show off, to look pretty and well-dressed and thus hurt people's feelings. Consequently, the beautiful hats and handbags were kept hidden in the closet, the new dresses were rarely worn even on the Sabbath, and the new shoes were used only for standing in line for food. The only satisfaction the family had was the sight of Chaim. The girls, who worried about him, insisted that he wear his new things instead of the old torn shoes and the light faded coat. They took great pleasure in watching their father wearing all these genteel-looking clothes which shielded him from the cold and frost at the same time.

The bags of food that Esther received at Uncle Chaim's increased in size with every visit. The truth was that Aunt Rivka did not need Esther to tell her about herself. She saw for herself that there was something wrong with the girl and a determination grew within her, as strong as Esther's stubborn gloominess, to infuse new life into her, to fill out Esther's skinny body with flesh, to make her cheeks bloom again and to kindle the light in her eyes. Rivka considered it an omen from heaven that Esther had come to them for help during this era of "luxury" in their lives. It was in order to give them a chance to make up for the "sin" of having enough to eat when others went hungry, for going on with their lives after the loss of their two children in the war.

And indeed, after a time, Aunt Rivka's persistence began to bring results. Esther grew stronger; she stayed out of her bed for longer periods of time and began to feel a kind of revulsion towards it. At length, there were days when she would dress right in the morning and later on, go out. But the stronger she became, the more reluctant was she to visit Uncle Chaim's. Instead, she began to visit her comrades.

Before long, she found herself surrounded by all those who were left of her pre-war party friends. It seemed to her that only they, who in a certain way had brought about her acquaintance with Hersh, they, with whom she had demonstrated on May Days, with whom she had slung red flags over wires and painted revolutionary slogans on walls — that it was they who infused her with new life. With them, everything was simple; she had no need to tell them any tall tales. They understood her and helped her to loosen her tongue and speak. Of course, she would not reveal all that was within her even to them — the intimate woe, the intangible complicated thoughts, the torment that remained locked in her soul. Yet this matter-of-fact, superficial way of relating her experiences signified health to her. It also helped her to hide from herself her deeper feelings, the tender and confusing ones. She considered them a weakness of which she had to rid herself.

Her comrades freed her from her loneliness; they made her tragedy seem less unique and more a part of human fate which depended on economic conditions and political circumstances. Such suffering, no longer exclusively her own, was easier to bear. She no longer saw herself suspended in an emptiness, nor did her life seem purposeless. She could sacrifice it on the altar of her ideal, and for this reason it became dear to her again. She began to pay attention to the news, to discuss the political situation and talk about the Soviet Union. She could still remember how shocked she had been when Hersh told her about the pact of the U.S.S.R. with Germany. Now she understood him. There was no question of friendship between the two countries, or between fascism and communism. It was a question of gaining time, of diplomacy. Hersh was right: a world of lies could not be conquered with truth. One had to fight it by using the enemy's own weapons. All means were justified in the achievement of communism, the highest of all goals. Yes, communism was the only truth, and she believed in it firmly. It was as clear as day that the times for which she and her comrades had so valiantly lived and fought were approaching with gigantic steps. She was enthusiastic, and she grew more courageous and stronger with every day. Her past experiences, all she had gone through, had not been wasted. They had helped her cement her will power; they had made her more stubborn and determined. This both revived the former self within her and created a new one — one that had been forged in the flames of suffering and feared it no longer.

Moreover, she felt that she was still tied to Hersh through her ties with the Movement; that each time she served her ideal, she was giving herself to her vanished lover — a giving of herself which was more complete and elating than when she had actually been with him. This awareness helped her later on in making the most fateful decision in her life. When she felt ready to set out for the land of her dreams, to find Hersh, she was disciplined enough to calmly accept the directive of her leaders, that she stay on in town and assist in organizing the work which had to be done, even without the recognition of the Comintern and with so many comrades missing. She accepted this duty, fully aware of the beauty of her sacrifice. The next time she went to visit Uncle Chaim, it was not to beg for food, but to ask him to give her work.

The day she went to work for the first time, she got up early and prepared breakfast for herself more cheerfully than usual. She put on her clothes with the good feeling of a productive useful person, taking care to dress warmly, and she ran down the stairs crooning a tune from the good old times. The frost enveloped her, pinched her cheeks and sent snow dust into her eyes. She felt good and indulged her impulse to smile coquettishly at the rare passers-by in the street. Her heart was full of hope for herself and for the world. She thought of Uncle Chaim's household, reflecting that it was actually her mission to infuse some fresh air into the narrowness of their lives, to at least kindle some sparks in the hearts of her cousins, whom she had been unable to win over before. Now times were different. She herself was different, more experienced; and most probably her cousins had changed as well. In their present confusion they were probably seeking a new faith.

The red brick church surrounded by a white fence at the corner of Hockel Street came into view. Snow, like clumps of cotton was heaped between the slanted roofs of its turrets. High above the church, circled a flock of crows, their black wings like black sails against the background of the sky. She glanced at the clock in the tower. It was still early. She would not be late for her first day of work. The blue Madonna in the niche of the church wall held her hands pressed together in a blessing aimed in the direction of Hockel Street. The snow, stacked in the corners of her arms, seemed to form a diaper wrapped around a tiny frozen baby. Her painted pink face looked frostbitten, alive, expressing infinite sorrow over the fate of all tiny naked and abandoned Jesuses who shrivelled all over the ice-covered world.

As soon as she turned into Hockel Street, Esther stopped, aghast at the sight that greeted her. In front of all the gates, crowds of people stood in knots, talking, screaming, wailing. In the middle of the snow-covered street, colourful pieces of clothing, of mud-smeared bedding were strewn about. Sheets of paper, letters, photographs poked out of the snow or danced about on the pavement, carried off by the cold wind. In front of the house where Uncle Chaim lived, a crowd of people blocked Esther's way. She pushed herself through; the black letters of a placard stuck to the boards of the gate caught her eyes. The placard was still fresh and wet with glue. She tried to read it but was unable to understand a word.

"Oh, Esther," a woman burst out with an hysterical sob, recognizing her. "They were all led off, taken away!" The woman squirmed, embracing her; the convulsive spasms of her body made Esther shake as well.

"They took them all out of their beds in the middle of the night," someone informed her. "The entire street is empty and a few of the other streets as well."

Esther freed herself from the woman's arms and looked into the backyard through a crack in the locked gate. Rags of clothing, packs of bedding, baby carriages and utensils were spread about the huge empty yard. Deep inside, she saw the cherry tree buried in snow to the middle of its trunk. It looked shrunken and desolate. She stared, unable to grasp that what she was seeing was true and what she had just heard had really happened. Her eyes remained dry as she recalled the cherry tree in full bloom, herself frolicking around it with her cousins. Not far from there, near the stables, was the place where the boys would kick around their rag ball. Old women would lie stretched out in the grass under the tree's shade. The smell of horses and straw would issue from the stables. There, the strong men, the load carriers, the fish-and-meat merchants would display their athletic prowess, while the handsome dark-haired Valentino bossed them around, guffawing loudly as he introduced them into the sports of weight-lifting and boxing. Blind Henech, the baker, would sit on the well, surrounded by a circle of his neighbours, to whom he recounted stories of thefts and thieves. Nearby, Itche Mayer the Carpenter, standing amidst a group of the weavers who lived in the yard, would philosophize about life. She heard the heated words of young men, communists, Zionists, Bundists, discussing politics, raising their fists in passionate quarrels about whose party was right and which of them would bring salvation to their own people and to the entire world. Indeed, it was inconceivable that all that life by the cherry tree could be cut down during one single hour of the night.

The crowd near the gate grew; the news about the evacuation of the inhabitants of Baluty had reached the centre of town. People came running along the streets from all directions, towards houses where they had had relatives, friends, acquaintances. They pushed themselves through to the white placards, reading them without understanding what they read.

Esther stepped back to let someone else look through the crack in the gate. She noticed a man with a crumpled but young face and hunched shoulders, sitting on the steps of Blind Henech's bakery. His body was still, motionless, as if it were a stone sculpture. He seemed familiar and she pushed herself through to him. She sat down beside him on the stair. "You are the son of Itche Mayer the carpenter, aren't you?" she asked and introduced herself, "I am Chaim the Hosiery-Maker's niece."

"I remember you," he muttered.

"What could have happened to them do you think?" she asked.

"I know as much as you." He did not turn his head to her, his eyes were riveted on a deathly pale man standing at the edge of the sidewalk, wrapped in an old-fashioned winter coat with a fur collar. Tears were streaming from behind the man's heavily-rimmed glasses, washing his face and dripping down into his heavy collar. "Berkovitch, the son of the Preacher from Lynczyce," Israel said, as if to himself. "Lucky man, unashamed to cry in the middle of the street."

Esther's throat constricted with dread; a sudden ache pierced through her. The tear-drenched face of the man at the curb made her realize more than anything else that the house on Hockel Street was no more. "What do you think it all means?" she again asked Israel, her voice breaking.

"Why do you ask me?" He looked at her now, her question peering out of his own eyes. He stood up and climbed down the steps. However, he did not leave, but pushed himself through to the gate, putting his eye against the crack. She stood up as well, and, as if to shake off the unbearable gloom, she walked along the street, passing the crowds of talking and weeping people. Familiar faces were brought back to her mind by the houses she passed. Here her childhood friends had lived; there, comrades from the party; here, a vendor of pumpkin seeds who had liked her; there, a girl friend from the factory.

Then she came back to the gate of Uncle Chaim's house, unable to move too far away from it. Israel was still there, standing against the wall, hands in pockets, eyes staring straight ahead, but seeming to see nothing. She went up to him and leaned against the wall beside him. "I am left all alone now," she said to him, without knowing why. Then she asked, "And you, are you married?"

"I've a wife and child, a girl."

"So you are not alone."

"Whoever has no parents is alone."

"I never had any parents."

"Then you should know how it feels."

"My aunt and uncle replaced my parents for me."

"To tell the truth, we are all alone; alone, and in the hands of damned scoundrels." He tore himself abruptly away from the wall, put his hands in his pockets and walked off, leaving her behind.

She followed him, as though compelled, and came abreast of him. "I think that they'll manage somehow, wherever they are," she tried to console him as well as herself.

"I see you've calmed down. Good for you," he said without looking at her. "You're right. We have to protect ourselves against fear as well as we can." He pushed himself through the throng and she followed him. What did she want from the stranger? Why could she not let him go, she asked herself, amazed at her own behaviour. There was something in his bearing, in his way of walking, of talking that made her feel safe at his side. He stopped at the curb, lifting his serious, lined face to her, "You probably have friends, don't you?" he asked.

"Yes, I do."

"Then stick with them," he shook her hand firmly, made an about turn and crossed the street. She wanted to run after him, to exchange another few words with him, but she controlled herself and went back to the gate of Uncle Chaim's house.

Chapter Thirteen

Michal Levine,
Lodz-Litzmanstadt,
December 31, 1939.

New Year's Eve.

Dearest Mira,

My friends look at me as though I were a fool, sending these letters off into the world. Making serious faces, they take the letters from me and go to the Red Cross with them. Behind my back I am sure that they shrug their shoulders, thinking that I have become not only a physical but also a mental invalid. What if I stopped this insanity and no longer sent you these scribblings? It would be very bad, believe me. This crazy "contact" I have with you keeps me calm. It actually makes me feel superior to my friends. I pity them. Both of them have sunk deeply into the swamp, and they have nothing to lift them out of it.

Guttman has stopped painting. He says that he has more important things to do. All he does is supply us with food and coal and get caught for labour a few times a week. In the evening, after curfew, he still has enough time to continue with the work which could help him keep his equilibrium, but he has packed away his paint brushes so that they will not "prick his eyes". We are furious with each other. I nag him constantly and he yells at me to leave him alone. Which I cannot do. I cannot watch the artist in him committing suicide, while the man in him is left with the humiliation. He says that this is none of my business, while at the same time he takes care of my business completely, constantly bringing, giving. Yet he refuses to take the only thing I am capable of offering him in return, or what I am willing to share with him: my equilibrium. I am sure that if he found the courage to work for a few hours a day, it would help us both. But he keeps on screaming that an artist is not a clock one can turn on to make it work; that an artist has to have his creative impulses. I ask him, the realist, the one who used to boast, that through his faithful reproduction of the minute details of factual life he was revealing the most tragic aspects of human existence — I ask him why the present reality does not boost these impulses sufficiently. So he replies that painting means contact between the artist's soul and reality, and that he has lost that contact. "Well," I say, "then leave reality alone. Allow yourself to escape it for a while and paint from your imagination." Then he answers me that his imagination needs reality as a springboard in order to soar up into the air. And since, as far as arguments about painting are concerned, he is the specialist and not I, he triumphs over my ignorance with a mocking smirk and a look of disdain in his wild eyes.

Be that as it may, Guttman at least screams and rages, which might be a sign that, after all, he has not given up. But Shafran, the other friend who lives with us, has become numb. During the day he busies himself with his orphans, keeping in touch with the former director of the orphanage, Mr. Rumkowski, who is the "Eldest of the Jews" now and gives substantial support to the institution. But at night Shafran comes home, sits down at the table and keeps his mouth shut for hours, which I cannot stand. I begin nagging him, as I nag Guttman, and he looks at me and offers me his meek smile which is worse than tears.

One day, I insisted for so long, that I forced a reply out of him. "Look, Shafran," I said. "You're a psychologist after all. The human soul is now bared, free of any make-up; it's in the best condition to be studied." At that, Shafran asked, "Yes, but by whom? You can't study monkeys when you yourself are a monkey in the same cage, can you?" So I said, "Man is not a monkey. Man has the ability to raise himself above his conditions and observe them objectively." At that, he whispered, "Perhaps you're right, but I've lost the talent for it. I'm no longer capable of seeing man from a distance. I'm unable to think logically. I'm too engaged with my object. Perhaps that is my undoing as a psychologist, and perhaps all of psychology is undone now." Realizing that despair was taking hold of him, I said, "Shafran, all you have to do as a scientific man, you are able to do. Your duty is not to draw conclusions, but to observe human behaviour as it is and write down your observations. Conclusions will be drawn later, in the proper perspective." So he answered me that even observing and note-taking cannot be done objectively, since all the phenomena one chooses as significant and worthy of being studied depend on one's way of looking at things; and this, in turn, is influenced by the conditions in which the observer finds himself, and which he shares with the objects of his observation. And that, he said, is a far cry from being scientific. So I insisted that he put down bare facts, at which point he told me that he had come to the conclusion that there is no such thing as a bare fact. I asked him if he believed in objective truth. He answered me that indeed he did not believe in it. And with that, he sank once more into his numbness.

However, occasionally, we enjoy some good moments too, when friendship becomes a pleasure, fitting as comfortably as a pair of faithful slippers. On such evenings we three bachelors jump around Mother like baby cocks around a hen. She doesn't talk about cheerful things, yet there is an air of cheerfulness about her. The boys cuddle up to her as affectionately as if she had brought them into the world, fretful Guttman as well. You should see how he woos her, how he begs for compliments and kind words.

About me personally, there is nothing special to report. My foot is healed, but I am limping and I am doomed to do so for the rest of my life. However, in another week or two I shall have forgotten about my foot and, hopefully, about the rest of me as well. I will start working in earnest, because up to now I have only been able to practise on our neighbours.

It is New Year's Eve, dear Mira. What are you doing now? Are you thinking of me at this very minute? I speak to Shafran about objective truth, about logic and bare facts, while at the same time I would like very much to believe in telepathy. This letter will probably share the fate of the previous ones, whatever that may be. However, I want you to read it, to feel it. Is that possible? Should I wish you a happy New Year? What sense is there in wishing, if you know that your wishes will not come true? Our New Year will begin when I hold you in my arms. Meanwhile, it is still the old year. I love you. Good night.

Your Michal.

✦ ✦ ✦

New Year's Eve.

Miss Diamand and her friend Wanda sit in their room, close to one another, warming themselves at their little "cannon" stove. Usually they are asleep at this late an hour. But not tonight. Tonight they will stay up until twelve and wish each other a happy New Year. With few exceptions, this has been their tradition throughout all the years of their friendship, and whenever the two old ladies are able, they stick to their traditions.

They did not especially dress up for the occasion. They had never done so. But they baked a small cake. Wanda had brought home a basket of apples from her last trip to the country and they have cooked some apple sauce with a lot of sugar to make it really sweet. They have also brewed a fresh pot of tea, a feat they allow themselves only once a week.

They sit by the stove, listening to the pot sizzle. Soon it will boil. They will sit down at the table where the perfect little cake and the bowl of apple sauce is waiting for them. Meanwhile, they read together; that is what they have usually done on past New Year's Eves. For hours they sit with a de luxe edition of Slowacki's poems. The volume itself is an objet d'art, bound in soft brown leather, the corners of the pages as well as the title letters on the back edged with gold. On the first page of the volume, there is an impressive picture of the young poet in his black cape with the broad white collar laid out. Like a column of marble, his white neck with its manly Adam's apple rises from the collar, gracefully supporting his shapely head with the pale face. His sad eyes reflect the romantic longing of his poems.

They love Slowacki and it gives them a particular pleasure to hold this volume in their hands. They had bought it together as a gift to themselves, many years before. Every time they take it down from the shelf and remove it from its gray protective covers, their room becomes transformed into a kind of temple; a different air begins to vibrate between the walls. It seems to them that they can feel the very breath of the young poet, their intimate friend, their son almost, who understands and consoles them like a father. It seems to them that he pours out his soul to no one in the world as fully as he does to them — and deeply moved, proudly, they absorb his sadness, are intoxicated by its beauty, until they no longer know which tears are his and which their own.

Miss Diamand flips the pages of the volume dreamily, letting their gold-edged corners brush against her bony fingers. Her eyes are caught by a word on a page. She shuts the book and a wistful light kindles in her watery blue eyes. Words drip down from her lips like drops of sweet wine, "I am sad, my God. For me you paint a rainbow of glittering rays in the west; before me you extinguish a fiery star in the azure water; and although you spread a wash of gold for me upon sky and sea, I am sad, my God . . ."

A melancholy smile lights up Wanda's face. "How beautiful his sadness is," she whispers.

Miss Diamand remains silent, thoughtful. A sigh escapes her lips, "Yes, his sadness is rather soothing."

Wanda pats her on the knee, "And the two of us, Dora dear, we prefer that kind of sadness to gaiety, don't we?"

Miss Diamand nods sorrowfully, "That's how our sadness used to be. What a happy sadness that was!" She shuts her eyes and again the words pour down from her lips, "Like a hollow stalk, with head uplifted, I stand emptied of ecstasies, yet satiated. To strangers my face seems always the same: sky-blue silence. But before you I shall open the depths of my heart: I am sad, my God." Behind the red rims of Miss Diamand's eyelids, a glittering tear trembles. Somehow the sweet wine of words has turned bitter.

This alerts Wanda. "Give me the book," she says, carefully taking the volume out of Miss Diamand's hands. "It affects you the wrong way. I can see it."

Miss Diamand smiles ill-at-ease, rubbing her wet eyes, "You have no idea how much good it does me."

"I don't want you to cry."

"What's wrong with crying a bit, silly girl?" Miss Diamand struggles to keep her voice calm. "What are tears after all, if not poems too, bubbles released from an overflowing heart?"

"Please," Wanda says imploringly as she closes the book. "I don't want your heart to be heavy tonight."

"On the contrary, my dear. He does . . . He gives me relief." She puts her hand on the cover of the volume. "Then *you* read, if you want to."

Wanda is no longer sure if she wants to. "No," she decides, "We're going to the table now. The pot is boiling."

They sit down at the table, cut the cake and divide the apple sauce which smells of cinnamon, putting it onto small plates. Silence hovers over their gray heads. Wanda looks at the clock. "It's precisely twelve," she says.

Miss Diamand cups the glass of tea in her bony fingers, clinking it against the glass in Wanda's hand. "Happy New Year," she says.

"Happy New Year," Wanda replies, adding in a low voice, "May we never be parted."

They sip the strong burning tea with little sips. In Miss Diamand's heart, a tearful harp strums, "I am sad, my God . . ."

✦ ✦ ✦

New Year's Eve.

They sit in the kitchen and play poker. Matilda has learned the game from Yadwiga Rosenberg. Lately, she has become completely obsessed by it. Yesterday, the piano was taken out of the house. One of her devoted Leipzig officers came with a truck and "borrowed" the instrument for his girl friend, a German lady from Lodz, who needed it badly for her New Year's ball. Matilda is unable to enter the salon, nor is she able to talk about the piano. She wants to play poker.

At her side sits Mr. Adam Rosenberg. It was quite a job to make him come up from the basement to spend New Year's Eve with his family and friends. He gave in only after they warned him that if he did not come up, they would come down, which he could not allow to happen for anything in the world. The basement was his. He even had a lock and a key to lock himself in downstairs, in case he considered himself in danger. Those upstairs knew nothing about it, of course, except for the servant Wojciech who had also assisted Adam in another job, the traces of which were still difficult to disguise. So he decided to go upstairs and play poker. But he bungles, playing absent-mindedly, worse than Matilda. He, the ex-master-gambler, the clever bluffer, has to borrow some pfennigs every now and then from his wife.

On his other side sits his son Mietek. With his big shoulders and torso, he hovers above the entire table. His mother chides him sweetly and amiably, asking him to take his big arms off the tabletop because they disturb the other players. He obeys, pulling his arms in towards his chest, but then he stretches them out again. He has changed a great deal. He resembles a young caged animal who has been given a drug to tame his wildness and stun him. His eyes are dull, extinguished. His constant guffaws sound false, weird. He is pale after the weeks of staying indoors, since, like Adam, he refuses to set foot out of the house. Father and son have not been caught for labour even once; this is the only thing they can boast about lately. Mietek spends all his days in bed, leaving it only to take his meals. Now he sits at the table fiddling with his cards. He does not shut his mouth for a moment, babbling an uncontrolled nonsensical chatter which is supposed to be full of wisecracks and jokes and which he interrupts with explosions of weird laughter.

Junia, Matilda's younger daughter, sits close by. She has Mietek's silly chatter on her mind more than the game, and is the only one who laughs at his jokes. In constant motion, she fidgets in her chair, poking Mietek with her elbow. Throwing back her head of short dishevelled hair, she abandons herself to cascades of hearty laughter. Her black eyes sparkle mischievously. Sometimes her gaiety becomes so contagious that it forces everyone, Adam included, to laugh with her.

At her side sits Yadwiga. She has the proper amount of powder and rouge on, her fingernails are painted a screaming red and, as usual, she resembles a mannequin in a shop window. Holding the cards in her hands with the air of a professional, she deals them out deftly. She makes fun of her husband in her old kittenish way, which entertains Junia enormously. Yadwiga is actually the soul of the game and in front of her is gathered the largest heap of pfennigs.

Bella, Matilda's older daughter, does not participate in the game. She hates poker. She sits with her back against the stove, pretending to read a book. The chit-chat and laughter at the table grate on her ears and hurt her with an almost physical pain. The piano that is no longer in the house wails within her with sobbing legato chords. She feels that all the beauty which had used to fortify and enrich her soul has been transformed into a tool to destroy her. From the moment the piano was carried out of the house, she carries its vibrating chords inside her. Favourite pieces of music linger on in her memory, painfully, as if they had come to avenge themselves on her for having loved them. And the presence of her other love — Mietek, the boy of her dreams — has also turned into a cup of bitterness which fate has forced her to swallow to the last drop. He lives in her home now, she can see him all day long from very close, as if fate had decided on purpose not to let her forget her disappointment for a moment. She is forced to watch her sister disappear behind Mietek's door, to listen to their laughter and screams, or to sit with the two of them at the table. Yes, he had sat down beside her a few times too, trying to excuse himself for his offence of a year ago, when she had waited for him in Stashitz Park and he had not shown up. He had not forgotten about it as she thought. "You are too good for me," he had told her a few days ago. She did not react. She could find no words to lift her above the storm raging within her. Now she sits, book in hand, listening both to the noise inside her heart and to the noise at the table.

Suddenly she hears Matilda saying, "Good heavens, only five more minutes!"

In the silence that follows, the last New Year's ball enters everyone's mind with the remote pale remembrance of another life. This brings the poker game to a halt; the cards fall from their hands, as if both the thoughts of those present and the sound of Samuel's footsteps, upstairs in the bedroom, have knocked them out, one by one.

Upstairs, Samuel, racked by memories of Editor Mazur, is pacing the bedroom, up and down. A year ago, Mazur had been here, to participate in the celebration. A question nags Samuel: why had Mazur not come to hide in the house as they had planned? When they had met two weeks after the decision, and Samuel had asked him about it, Mazur waved his hand, "Ey, the Devil won't take us." But the Devil did take them, just as Mazur had previously foreseen. Then why? Samuel thinks of Mazur's frequent insinuations about the "iron letter"; he thinks of Mazur's ironic comments about Matilda's compatriots, the officers from Leipzig. Were they the reason? Did he refuse to be protected by the same dogcatchers who were lurking in the corners, chasing him and all the Jews? Was he right in doing so? Was it better to choose danger and death? Could that be called victory, to put oneself in front of the dogcatchers — he, Mazur, who wanted so much to live — and say to them, "Here I am, take me!" Samuel is unable to forgive his dead friend and this deepens his sorrow.

It is almost twelve o'clock. Soon he will have to go down to wish his family a happy New Year. He thinks of Professor Hager and his wife, his permanent guests, who went to bed, refusing to wait until twelve. That was also a childish senseless form of protest. He, Samuel, is against making his life harder than it already is, against refusing willingly the quiet moments he can enjoy. He thinks of the gift he received from the Hagers exactly a year ago — the radio. A few hours ago he heard the broadcast from London. It fortified him like a good glass of vodka. How strange that this gift has become his greatest treasure! He thinks of what he will do with the radio if he is forced to move into a ghetto. His body twitches, as though a swarm of ants were crawling up his back. Was it possible that this evil decree would go through? Had wise Mazur prophesized correctly during those Saturday Nights of by-gone days, in calling the present times the Modern Middle Ages? But perhaps the news about a ghetto is only an ugly "duckling" hatched in people's imaginations? And if it is true that the Jews will have to move into a ghetto, then are they, Samuel and his family, not protected against the danger? Does he not have an "iron letter"? And what a blessing it is to have it! No, his conscience does not bother him. It is not true that he is being devoured by guilt. He will not go into a ghetto. And if the question arises as to what he will do in a city without Jews, he knows the answer. Just like Josephus Flavius at the time of the Romans, he will write the history of the Jews: "The Jewish Wars". And he knows two other things for certain: he will not part with the radio, nor with his grandfather's Passover Haggadah.

Stealthily, he glances at the bottle of vodka under the table. It has scarcely been touched. He is proud of his will power. He no longer needs the help of alcohol to assist him in keeping his composure. But now, he will take a sip, before going down with his wishes to his family.

✦ ✦ ✦

New Year's Eve.

Chaim Rumkowski is alone in his room; alone with a bottle of champagne which he has received from the Gestapo officer who officiates at the Community Council and delivers the orders of the Chief of Police. Mordecai Chaim is supposed to drink the champagne to the health of the Führer and for the victory of the Third Reich. That was what the officer said with a knavish smirk when he handed him the bottle. But as far as Chaim Rumkowski is concerned, the Third Reich and its Führer can go to hell. He is utterly disgusted with Hitler. What kind of greatness is there in bullying and harassing a defenceless people? And if Hitler is ignorant of these facts and all this is the handiwork of a band of hooligans — then what kind of greatness is that again, when the right hand does not know what the left is doing? No, if he is to drink "*lechaim*", he, Rumkowski, will drink to his own victory and to the victory of the Jewish people.

But he does not belong to that type of drinkers who can enjoy a drink all alone, especially when not in the mood to celebrate. He thinks of what kind of day he will have tomorrow. The Germans are carousing and the Jews will perhaps be left in peace for a few hours, without being caught in the streets or attacked in their homes. The Germans will sleep. But he, Chaim Rumkowski, will have no peace tomorrow either. He has not received any concrete orders yet, but he knows for certain that the Jews will not be allowed to go on living as they are now. A new decree is on its way. The clearing up of some streets in Baluty has something to do with it perhaps. But what? It is ludicrous to imagine that even with those emptied streets, the entire Jewry of Lodz, all two hundred and fifty thousand souls, could be squeezed and fenced into Baluty. On the other hand, it does not seem such a tragic thing for the Jews to be gathered into one place. Their life might become easier, and it might also be easier for him, for Rumkowski, to regulate it, by having his people close under his wings. He could protect them better.

Thus Rumkowski does not know exactly what he will do tomorrow. Only one thing is certain: he will not go idle. He does not mind. He needs no rest. To sit around like this, doing nothing, is torture. And he cannot bear being alone in this room. He hates the room. It always brings the home he had to his mind. It makes him think of his second wife, Shoshana, who visits him in his dreams so often. He thinks with envy of the town full of Jews spending this evening with their families and dear ones. He has no family. His only brother is a complete stranger to him. He cannot bear his gentility, his intellectual veneer, his exaggerated politeness. Nor does he, Chaim, have any friends; he never had any, except during his golden youth when each of his friends was ready to follow him through fire. In later life, he had no need for friends. In any case, no one had ever understood him and everyone who had called himself a friend was false, with nothing but his own good in mind. He did, however, have his orphanage and the love for the children to whom he was like a father; and also, a girl to spend the night with was always at hand. Only now things are bad for him. Now he has no one. So he prefers to hustle and bustle, to be ceaselessly active, to rush about, to have a head full of worries, so that even the remotest nook of his soul should not be confronted by his unbearable loneliness.

Chaim Rumkowski stares at the bottle of champagne, dissatisfied. He abhors thoughts which lead nowhere. He hates to philosophize about himself. He definitely does not belong to those milksops who keep all their sensitivity attuned to every murmur in their own souls — a weakness uglier than that of hypochondriacs who keep themselves alert to the slightest happenings in their organisms. Nevertheless, they have come to attack him tonight — these insights, the bitter feelings of his complete loneliness, as if they had been waiting for this moment. He knows that in order to ward them off, he must think of action, of planning out strategies. But what sense does any new project make today, if tomorrow everything may fall apart like a house of cards? Is not the next day which seems so near, right over the border of the night, just as vague and unsure as the remote future wrapped in the secrecy of fate?

His mind moves in circles, away from himself and back to himself. All of a sudden, he feels exhausted and casts a sideways glance at his bed. The best thing would be to go to sleep and put an end to the boredom. But it is still quite a while until his bedtime. How much sleep does he need, after all? And he knows that his exhaustion is only a result of inactivity, of not knowing what to do with himself. Usually, at this hour, he is still immersed in work, preoccupied with Council business, surrounded by people, and so involved in all the problems that he does not even have the time to consult his watch. And now he regrets that he gave in to his subordinates so easily tonight, letting them go home earlier, to spend New Year's Eve with their families. Just fancy, New Year's Eve! What business do they have to celebrate a goyish New Year nowadays? And it occurred to none of them to invite him, the Presess, the father of a town full of Jews, to his home. He knows that they don't celebrate the occasion with parties or balls, and he would not have accepted their invitation in any case. However he resents his close advisers, his so-called friends who flatter him so shamelessly. He resents all those surrounded by a bit of warmth, of devotion. Ah, he knows very well how they tremble not to lose this happiness — and a weird feeling of satisfaction secretly cools his embittered heart.

He decides to go to bed after all. From a remote corner of his mind, like a little demon, the thought of a passion pops out, charming him, cajoling him. Yes, even if he is unable to fall asleep immediately, he will have a chance to play with his dreams for a while. A man, as long as he is dressed and walking around on his two feet, has no right to follow his fantasies; but in bed, the demonic charmer whispers in Rumkowski's ear, before falling asleep, he has the right to set free the caged pigeons: his secret wishes. Yes, even his reason can be harnessed to the breathtaking game and precisely with its assistance, through it, as through sharp field glasses, he can look at the tempting images. His reasoning in these pre-sleep hours makes them appear more true, more realizable than ever. He, Mordecai Chaim, will go to bed now, and in honour of the New Year, take off on the wings of his fancy towards the very peak of his desires — to become a second Moses. He will let himself be carried off to the time when it will be given to him to lead the Jews out of the diaspora and bring them to the land of Israel. And he, unlike Moses, will be allowed to set foot upon the soil of the Promised Land. He will be permitted to reign over his people like a benign father.

He marches over to the sink to wash himself. He looks in the mirror. Whenever he is alone in the room he likes to look at himself in the mirror, so that he can see a human face at least, he jokes to himself. He scrutinizes himself carefully, proud of his patriarchal looks. No, he is not an average man, he has to admit it to himself. Is not his imposing leonine head with the tufts of silvery hair, proof? Or the majestic dignity expressed in his face? Or the prophetic light in his eyes? The only problem is that his age shows so much in his appearance. It occurs to him that all the majesty he is projecting could actually be the costume in which His Majesty, Death itself, has decked him out in, before leading him off to His Kingdom. Mordecai Chaim grimaces. How could such a thought enter his mind all of a sudden? He hates to think of death and if he does, he thinks of it as the fate to which others succumb, not he. For him personally, there is no death. He does not delude himself, heaven forbid, that he is physically immortal, but as long as he is alive, physical death does not exist for him, therefore he permits it no place in his mind.

As he begins to undress, the bottle of champagne meets his eye again, as if it were waiting for something — reminding him of its presence, as though it were not a sealed bottle full of untasted wine, but a sealed mouth full of unpronounced words. And in it, Chaim Rumkowski now sees the mouth of the liaison officer who gave him the gift. He sees the mouth of Herr von Strafer, the Chief of Police. And he sees the mouth of Adolf Hitler. To drink to the health of the Führer and for the victory of the Third Reich — this is what the bottle wants, what it says with its sealed mouth. It does not merely say it, it commands it. Chaim Rumkowski sees himself involved in a kind of duel with the bottle. No, by no means will he fulfil its wish. Chaim Rumkowski hates those who order him around. He will do something to spite it. He will open it, drink it, but to his own health and to the health of the Jewish people! However, he cannot open it. Something does not let him, as if he were afraid that it could play a trick on him; that as soon as he opens it, its wish will come true, not his; that its mission will be fulfilled, and not his, Chaim's dream.

He grabs the bottle, hastily tearing off the label from around its neck. He takes a corkscrew and screws it into the cork of the bottle with all his strength. Holding it tightly between his knees, flushed with strain, he pulls at the cork, pulls and pulls, until the cork gives up, pops out, releasing a breath of liberated air — and right after, unwarranted, a foaming streaming fountain shoots out straight into his face, like the spittle from someone's mouth. He wipes himself quickly with his sleeve and, bottle in hand, approaches the sink. He pours the champagne out into it, scarcely having the patience to watch the bottle emptying. He washes the wine down with a stream of clear water from the tap. For a while he stands with the empty bottle in his hand, looking into its hollow mouth. It no longer talks; it is the mouth of a dead fish. He feels like destroying it, like smashing it to splinters. And vengefully, furiously, he throws it into the wastebasket with a violent swing of his arm. At the sound of breaking glass, he sighs deeply, with relief.

He takes out a half-full bottle of Carmel Wine from the closet and fills a glass with it. He drinks it down in one gulp. Right after, a light goes on in his mind while an inner voice tells him that no, it was not a curse that his homes did not last, that he was unable to warm a corner for himself anywhere in the world, that his wives died, that he had no children. It was an omen sent down from the heavens — a sign that he was the chosen. He fills another glass of Carmel Wine and gulps it down. A wonderful feeling of might sweeps over him. Yes, just as he has crushed the disgusting bottle of champagne, so will he crush all the enemies who rise against him and his people. Not in vain is his name Chaim; Chaim means life in Hebrew — and life is victory. He sees himself in the mirror from a distance and straightens up, ceremoniously raising his hand with the glass, to the majestic face across the room, to the leonine head with the silvery wisps of dishevelled hair. He exclaims, "Lechaim! To Chaim! To Life!"

✦ ✦ ✦

New Year's Eve.

Esther reads Hersh's papers. For the first time since their parting, she has mustered the courage to open his suitcase. She spreads the written pages over the table, making a kind of tablecloth out of them. Some pages are hand-written on thin tissue paper clipped with a pin, others are hectographed on single long sheets; but most of them are written in pencil, in cheap notebooks with black covers, almost illegible, full of crossed-out lines, paragraphs, or entire pages. She begins with these notebooks first, for in them she feels Hersh best.

She deciphers word after word, line after line, not even omitting those lines which are crossed-out. She feels Hersh's closeness, the freshness of his thoughts, as if they had only now, in this half-ripe form, come out of his mind. Here is Hersh, here are engraved his visions and hopes. She feels that Hersh is now hers in such a manner as he has never been before. The time and space which divide them do not exist. And how fortunate she is, she reflects, that in the moment of her weakness, when she lay in bed thinking that all was over, that spoilt egotistical Rachel Eibushitz had refused to take the suitcase for safekeeping. She should be grateful to the girl who had been right in saying that if the suitcase was so dear to her, to Esther, she had to find the strength to live for it. No, she harbours no resentful feelings against her, just indifference, such as one feels for a weakling endowed both with petit bourgeoise sentimentality and cowardice, an indifference such as a true communist feels towards someone who has grown up in social-democratic circles. After all, how could she condemn Rachel? Had the latter gone through the school of communist upbringing, she would be just like any of Esther's friends, ready for self-sacrifice, for self-denial. A feeling of pride engulfs Esther; a powerful wave of devotion and love for Hersh, for the party, for the sacred ideal sweeps over her.

The hours wear on without her realizing that it has become increasingly harder to decipher Hersh's handwriting, that she has begun to skip words or entire lines. She ceases to understand what she is reading. But she does not stop flipping through the pages. The breath of life permeating the notebooks pours into her through the touch of her hands against the paper. Now her fingers, like those of a blind person, are reading.

A light tapping on the door sends a shudder down her spine. She covers the treasure strewn about on the table, with both palms, not knowing what else to do. A voice reaches her, "Esther, a friend." She calms down, fixes her hair and unlocks the door. It seems quite natural that Comrade Baruch, who has never before passed the threshold of her room, should appear in it now. She takes his hand and presses it in hers with warmth and familiarity, as if Comrade Baruch were a friend from whom she had parted only yesterday.

Comrade Baruch is a middle-aged man who, in his rimless glasses with their thin golden nose piece, looks more like a middle-class professor than a leading figure of the revolutionary movement. He is a thickset man, his back is slightly stooped, his walk resembles that of a *yeshiva* boy. He unwraps his light trench coat and responds once more to Esther's greeting with a firm grip on her hands; she feels as though her hands are clasped between two bricks of ice. "Please, come over to the stove," she invites him, without removing her eyes from his face. In fact, she is seeing him from so close for the first time; and she asks herself if he has ever seen her before. Comrade Baruch's eyes are already buried in the pages spread out on the table. She offers him a chair, remarking proudly, "I'm organizing Hersh's papers . . . Hersh, my husband."

"You forgot to lock the door," he says without lifting his eyes from the table.

She locks the door and remains standing at it thoughtfully; she takes in the man's stooped back with her eyes and sees the neglected hair on his neck crookedly trimmed with scissors. "He has brought news!" the thought flashes through her mind as she approaches him. "You have perhaps received news about Hersh?" she stammers.

Comrade Baruch, without turning his head to her, shrugs his shoulders, "How, comrade?" She lights the spirit burner, putting on the kettle. Comrade Baruch, bent over the table, thumbs the tissue sheets. All of a sudden, she has become completely indifferent to him. She has nothing to talk to him about, nor does she mind his awkward silence. It seems as if he has come only in order to do what he is doing now. Only after she hands him the glass of hot water coloured with chicory, does he tell her, between gulps, the purpose of his visit. "We're trying to rebuild the organization. You are co-opted to the committee, comrade, and I want to inform you of the situation, so that you will be able to participate fully in the meeting tomorrow." Unexpectedly, he smiles at her, friendly, affectionately, "Congratulations." He leaves after midnight, telling her not to worry about him, that there is someone living in the same building who will let him in for the night.

She lies in her bed; sleep refuses to come. All the cells in her body are awake. A car passes by in the street with a muffled thud. The wind rings on the window pane like a glass bell. A locomotive rolls by with heavy wheels over rails. A prolonged whistle pierces the night with the sharpness of pointed blades, tearing it open. Into its void, Esther whispers soundlessly, "Hersh, where are you?" She is aghast at her feelings. She felt so determined and strong a few hours ago. And how has it happened that Hersh's suitcase and his works are not sufficient for her any longer? Is it because Comrade Baruch, who was wearing such a thin coat on this frosty New Year's night, has made her room doubly empty after his departure? Could he, who brought her proof of recognition for her party work, have caused her to become so weak just because he doggedly avoided talking about Hersh?

The hardened frost on the window panes blinks at her with a thousand cold eyes, above each eye a white icy brow of snow. Again a car passes outside in the street. The snow squashed by its wheels lets out an almost inaudible suffocated squeak. It penetrates the room; every cell in Esther's body hears it. Then, nothing. The street is mute. The world is mute. But other sounds intrude upon the silence: words. People are talking. Someone is climbing up the stairs. The stairs are quiet. No, they creak. Someone is coming. "Hersh," she mutters to her pillow.

She clearly hears someone talking, not on the street, nor on the stairs, but through the wall. Someone is sobbing. A man is talking. She is unable to understand his words. They are calm, warm — the blessed sound of a man's voice. Woman, on the other side of the wall, why are you crying? Your man is with you. Let him embrace you, let him caress you and you will fear nothing. Someone sobs throughout the night.

✦ ✦ ✦

New Year's Eve.

Shalom lies in a bed all by himself and his legs do not move, yet it seems to him that he is still walking. Before his eyes snow-covered fields flash by, cut through by gray streaks: the icy muddy roads. He wades through them, slips and falls, scrambles to his feet and walks on and on — back home.

He sees himself walking alone or with a group of Jews. A frozen peasant with a dripping moustache comes forth to meet him. He leads Shalom through side roads towards the river; a blown-up bridge lies submerged in it. Instead of the bridge, a single, endlessly long board leads from one shore to the other. Shalom walks it like a tightrope walker. On both sides of him, the water is black, with ice floes gliding over its surface like white pieces of laundry. They make his head swim. He stops in the very middle of the board, raises his eyes and sees another board over the water further away, then another and another. Over the boards many black shadows creep like rows of black ants along thin straws: the multitude of Jews from the "belt" are walking back into the mouth of the beast, to be devoured.

He sees the peasant again. Frozen, but vivacious and cheerful, he leads those who have reached the other shore to an empty hut which is waiting for them. He kindles a fire in the oven and continues to wipe his long melting moustache. He smirks good-humouredly. "The kids and the woman sent away ... Made room especially for you, little Jews — a hotel." He points to the floor covered with dry straw.

They lie down on the straw. The fire in the oven crackles. It is nice and warm in the room. In the pale reflection of the flames, blinking eyes shine in the dark like wandering stars on a pitch black sky. Then the first gray of dawn crowds in through the window. The peasant busies himself by running to the railroad station to ferret out the easiest way to get onto the train without being noticed.

The wagon rocks and sways with the illegal travellers spread out on the floor, so that they will not be seen through the windows. But then someone struggles with the door. A wind breaks in and with it, a German officer. Thunderstruck at the sight of the passengers lying on the floor, his eyes stare, his mouth opens, his body in its green uniform becomes frozen, motionless. He seems like a figure in a film reel which has suddenly stopped. At length, he stirs. On his face an enormous question mark is written, "What are you doing here?"

Shalom sees himself standing in front of the officer, and in his correct German which he has learned from Flora he tries to explain to him, to tell him about the weeks that they, the travellers, had waited on the "belt"; that now they want to return to Lodz-Litzmanstadt. But the officer is still dumbfounded. He shakes his head violently, finally breaking out in a stutter. Don't they know that for trespassing on German territory they deserve the penalty of death?

At this, Shalom feels like laughing, "If not to Germany, nor to Russia, then where should we go, *Herr Offizier?*"

The officer points his finger towards the sky and guffaws, "*Nach oben!*"

Again they walk. They enter the town of Sedletz. A Jew wrapped in a heavy coat with a tall collar of brown fur comes forth to meet them with the expression of someone who expected his relatives and is glad to see them arrive. "Jews from Lodz?" he asks. "You must be looking for a place to spend the night." They follow him, seeing in their mind's eye a bed, a basin of warm water, a plate of potatoes. Suddenly, the man's words reach their ears, "They say that thousands of Jews have been evacuated from Lodz. Baluty is supposed to have been cleaned out."

In front of the man's house, his wife, wrapped in a few shawls, with a woollen turban on her head, is waiting for them. "A cot for the night costs three zlotys," she informs them, "A cold basin of water, a zloty; a hot one, two; a cup of coffee with sugar, a zloty and fifty; tea without sugar, one zloty." The wanderers neither see nor hear her. Already they are lying down on the cots in twos and threes. Shalom looks up at the ceiling. Now he is really homeless.

Again he sees himself walking on and on. He has heard it said that the majority of the evacuated Jews from Baluty have found shelter in a village called Glovno. So he goes to Glovno. How awfully far Glovno is! It seems that he will never get there. Sometimes he hangs on to a wagon, other times he steps up onto the runners of a peasant's sleigh. Children with their dogs jump out of the huts at the roadsides and watch him; or they follow him in gangs way out of the villages; they run after him as if he were the country fool, screaming, "A Jew! A Jew!" He sneaks into barns or stables to sleep.

Then he sees himself entering Glovno, feeling no fatigue, no longer sleepy. He is a mechanical doll which has only one thing to do: move its legs. Past the first empty cottages, he suddenly finds himself at a fair; a multitude of people. Familiar faces. So many acquaintances! All of Hockel Street comes forth to embrace him. Yes, they will all show him the way. Itche Mayer? Sure he is here. And Sheyne Pessele? Sheyne Pessele as well. And Blind Henech and Chaim the Hosiery-Maker? What a question! Even Lame King is here and Valentino with his wife, practically everyone!

Shalom lies in a bed by himself, without company. His feet don't move but he is still walking. "With the New Year coming, the devils will be smoked out of here and done to death," he hears a familiar voice. Too lazy to open his eyes, he knows and yet does not know whose voice it is. Sheyne Pessele holds him by the hand. She leads him on, walking with him. It is easy to walk like that; he hardly feels it. No, he is lying in a bed, not moving. He pulls Sheyne Pessele by the hand. "Mother," he says with an effort, opening one eye a slit to let through a mischievous twinkle. "Mother, you see, we have lived to lead a 'ristocratic life too, only instead of a summer cottage, we have a winter cottage."

He opens his eyes wider to find Itche Mayer and Blind Henech. He knows that many heads are bent over his bed. But out of the corner of his eye, he catches sight of a face he would rather not see. Her mother's face. He shuts his eyelids tight. But he sees the face, even with his eyes shut. "Where is Flora?" it asks him. He is on the road again, walking on and on. Flora, where are you?

✦ ✦ ✦

New Year's Eve.

The windows are covered with blackout curtains, yet it is not completely dark in the room. The windows across the street, where the *Folksdeutsche* live, are badly protected and rays of light coming from there beam through the curtains, thinning the darkness in the room. Across the street, a gramophone is playing. Scattered snatches of music break into the room and flutter in the air, hitting against the walls like birds which have strayed and became trapped under a foreign roof. Rachel stirs in her bed. When she opens her eyes she does not know at first where she is. The room seems like a boat carried off by a turbulent sea. Waves of screams and laughter coming and going lift her mind up and down, shaking it, making it swim. She turns around and sees Shlamek sleeping on the sofa across from her. In the dark, his large white front teeth revealed by his parted lips look like two tiny light bulbs.

Then the ship stops rocking. The beds of her parents creak quietly. She sees her father climb out of bed, approach the window and move away the heavy curtain. A big beam of light shoots into the room, hitting against the wall where the portraits of her grandparents hang. Grandfather's cap and his long black beard appear sharp and clear. But his face is invisible. Between the cap and the beard, only two black dots: Grandfather's eyes. Nearby: Grandmother's matron wig, and the black of her dress. Her face is also invisible. It gives one a spooky feeling, to look at a wig and a beard, at a cap and a dress and at two pairs of eyes — without bodies.

Moshe lets go of the curtain and goes back to bed. "In every single window you can see the flags tonight," Rachel hears him whisper. "Yesterday they were gone, today they're back again."

"It's time you stopped watching the damn windows," Blumka says.

He sighs, "I know it's silly."

"You'd better go to sleep. Tomorrow you'll be nervous again. Oh God, how you've changed during these last few weeks."

"I can't help it. It eats at me."

The bed creaks. Blumka slips into Moshe's bed. "Hush," she whispers, "You'll wake up the children."

Rachel pulls the cover up over her head. She thinks of David and imagines him at her side, kissing her mouth. His hand is on her face, caressing it, sliding down under her low-necked nightie; his hand covers her breast like a cup. What would she feel with his hand on her breast? She lifts her hand slowly, feeling the softness of her breasts with her fingers. They pulsate and flutter like frightened little creatures with a life of their own. It would be sweet. Then she removes her hand quickly. A stream of laughter penetrates the room. Orchestra cymbals clash, drums thunder, trumpets bellow. The room turns into a boat again, swaying, rocking.

The next moment, the boat tips over. Rachel and her family, holding hands, battle the waves. They do not know how to swim and try frantically to keep themselves afloat. But they are drowning. A huge fish is after them, a gigantic black shark with enormous jaws and an open mouth full of sharp pointed teeth. The fish talks with a human voice, calling after them, "Give it to me! Give it to me!"

Moshe drags his family along with him. His bald head resembles a rubber ball thrown about on the waves, going up and down, up and down. He urges them to repeat after him, "We won't let them have it! We won't!"

"Hush, Moshe, calm down," says Blumka. "We have hidden it so well that they will never find it."

They swim on, fighting the waves. Where have they learned to swim so well, Rachel wonders, clutching Moshe's hand on one side and Blumka's on the other. But what is that? She does not feel their fingers between hers. Where are they? She is alone on the stormy sea and the huge shark is after her. "Give it to me! Give it to me!" it shrieks with a gruesome human voice.

She feels its teeth combing her hair, trying to tear it off her head. She does not mind it hurting her. "You may tear as much as you like," she screams, "but I won't let you have this." She feels like laughing at the gigantic beast. "This is mine! Even if you chew me up and swallow me, you won't be able to take it from me."

It swallows her. She is inside the shark's enormous mouth. Its arched palate is a black night sky; its tongue is a long red street; its teeth are rows of ash-white burned-down houses. And she herself is a little girl in a short thin undershirt. She wanders barefoot, all alone, along the middle of the long red street. She is lost and frightened, so frightened that she is unable to cry, so frightened that she cannot even run. But then she hears a little clock beneath her cotton undershirt, beneath the skin of her body, ticking, "It-it-it," like a little hammer against an anvil. And the little clock, which is a little hammer, starts to grow into a drum that thunders in front of her, leading her onward; and although she has already been devoured by the black shark, she comes out from between its jaws.

✦ ✦ ✦

New Year's Eve.

(David's notebook)

Lately, we go to bed early, to save coal. Tonight, right after curfew, we ate and crawled into our beds. For me, falling asleep is no problem. I have become like my brother Abraham. As soon as my head hits the pillow, I am off. But my sleep has become light and the problem is that Mother wakes me sometimes without knowing it. Tonight, for example, we had the following conversation which we often repeat with slight variations. I was half asleep already when I heard her voice, "David, why don't you sleep?"

"I am asleep," I tell her.

Says she, "You're unable to fall asleep, I see. And what a sleepyhead you used to be!"

"I'm still a sleepyhead," I say irritably. "And why don't *you* sleep?"

She immediately senses my irritability. "Why are you mad at me?" she asks.

I want to tell her that I am angry at her because she does not let me sleep, but I don't want to hurt her feelings. I try to chase away my sleepiness. "What do you think, Mother, will we have a nice day tomorrow?" I ask, completely awake. I want to tell her that in the morning when I meet Rachel, I like the sun to shine; I especially want it for tomorrow, the first day of the new year. But I don't tell her that.

Mother asks more cheerfully, "What do you need to know that for?"

"For nothing," I reply.

She lifts herself up on her elbow and changes the subject. "What do you think, if the Russians declared war on Germany, how long would the war last? What is the latest news? You don't read the German newspapers anymore?"

"I do, but when you read them, you think that victory is in their pocket already."

"But what do they write about?"

"I told you what they write about."

"I don't let you sleep," she whispers guiltily.

I feel guilty too. "I can't sleep anyway."

"And what news have you heard in the street, from friends?"

"The same as usual, Mother."

"Always the same? Alright, go ahead, sleep, my son."

"Say it again: 'My son'. I like it when you say that."

When she calls me 'my son', I am ready to forgive her for all the bitter words she says to me throughout the day. Lately, she never stops criticizing me and whatever I do displeases her. A few hours ago, I broke a glass accidentally, and she called me all kinds of names. "Silly boy," I hear her whisper. "What else should I call you? Aren't you my son?"

There is nothing left to talk about. All topics are exhausted, except for the one which we avoid touching: Father. I can't sleep any more. I lie in silence, and she lies in silence. Finally I cannot stand it any longer and sit up, "I'll go down and read something," I tell her.

She sits up as well, "Are you out of your mind? Go to sleep, right away!"

I am already in the kitchen, the bundle of clothes in my hand. I hurry into my pants, sweater, jacket; I put on my winter coat and my gloves. It is silent in the other room. Good. But instead of a book, I take this writing pad, and now I sit here in the cold kitchen with it. I wrote down my conversation with mother. What else should I write? I feel so thick-headed; my mind a blank. Beneath today's date, I should make some hopeful impressive notes, or list all my wishes and good intentions for the year to come. My wishes? Do I have to spell them out? Let me mention only one which has to do with me personally: I would like to get away from the chaos within me, to rid myself of the repetitious nightmares. I would like to regain my self-respect. But it makes no sense to indulge in all these things today. Where are we heading? That is the most important of all questions. I don't understand the Germans' intentions in regard to us. Do they want to clear Lodz of all the Jews? What meaning is there in the evacuations they begin and don't finish? Why did they clear only a few streets of Baluty and not the rest? Evil decrees come and are called off. However, as a rule, the Germans are orderly and systematic. What is their system for dealing with us? There is some talk going around about the establishment of a ghetto for us. What would that mean? Will I ever see Father again? No, I don't want to indulge in thoughts about him; it makes me cry and I feel like a little boy. I am cold. My fingers are stiff under the gloves and the pencil is slipping out of my hand. Are you asleep, Rachel? Soon it will be day and we shall see each other.

✦   ✦   ✦

New Year's Eve.

This is how Miriam likes Bunim most: when he sits at his desk. Then the old good feeling comes back to her; it seems that nothing has changed and that he is the same as he used to be. She does not tire of watching him; there is so much to read in his face. It seems to her that she can see his thoughts speeding by in the furrows of his creased forehead, that she can see the words being born on his full agitated lips, even before he puts them down on paper. His lowered eyes are curtained by his eyelids. The reflection of the candle beside him plays on his eyeglasses, intimately, warmly, as if it were reflecting a light beaming from within him.

The candle's stub is shrinking. It is almost at an end, the wick bending its neck to the side as if tired of carrying the flame. Heavy drops of tallow like drops of sweat drip down the short stub. The flame flickers. Bunim pulls the candle closer to his sheet of paper. He wipes his glasses to see better. It is dark in the room; only Bunim's head, or rather his face is illuminated. His hand hurries over the sheet of paper, as though intent on catching up with both his speeding thoughts and the dying light.

Miriam, from her bed, is unable to see the sheet of paper he is writing on. Yet it seems to her that she can see it filling with his familiar handwriting. She can see the rounded letters, hooked together, locked into words which run ahead like wheels. She can see them rolling one against the other, climbing, jumping one on top of the other, as if in a hurry to reach the end of a line at any cost, then of another line and another, to cover the entire white of the paper, so that there would remain not the tiniest spot for one more word or letter, which he will anyway manage to squeeze in before he reaches out for another white sheet. How well she senses this passionate way of writing which is his! She participates in it although she often understands it so badly.

The candle light is fading. A seal of melted tallow on the tiny saucer beneath it is all that remains. There is nothing left of the candle but the shrunken wick curled up on the bottom of the saucer, trembling. Bunim's strained eyes are blinking hurriedly. Miriam whispers, "Bunim, the candle is gone."

He pulls himself up with a quick jerk, as if she has called him back from very far. Suddenly, he seizes the sheets covered with his handwriting and rushes over to her bed, "Do you want to listen? Only the last two pages . . ."

"Light another candle first."

With the newly-lit candle in his hand, he sits on the edge of her bed, reading:

"Jesus of Nazareth, I call you, I invite you today. Come, open the door of my home and face me in your naked greatness. What message will you bring me tonight? What good news? Will you come to announce to me that your blood which we, Miriam, Blimele and I, and others like us, have spilled, will finally be avenged to the last drop? Or will you come to ask us forgiveness?"

Poor, thoughtless, little Jesus. Look what they have done to you. Look at what you have done to them, Sinner. You took the crystal-clear longing of the Prophets, the transparent word of faith, and offered it to children. But children know nothing of a love that sprouts out of pain. They have played with the sacred Word, dragged it through sand heaps of ignorance and crushed it into the dust. Oh, Jesus, aren't those other peoples like children, compared to us in our experience? First they should have tasted, with their bodies and souls, the bitter taste of craving for salvation. But you . . . You wanted to press them to the warm bosom of your faith, to help them to jump over the stage of crawling towards it on all fours through labyrinths of longing. With your love you wanted to spare them the pain of yearning, to shorten and lighten their road to maturity. But the hardship of this road cannot be lightened, if it is the right road. Haven't you realized this, Jesus? You offered them truths, cleansed and forged in all the fires of torment — as food ready to consume. Thus they never discovered, were never able to savour its true taste. They remained the same children that they were before, while you became their waxen doll. They put words into your mouth, words created in their childish minds, not in yours. To them the crystalline tear of your sacrifice is no more than a glass ball. They play with it, kick it, crush it, then put it together again, only to break it and crush it again and again.

"You must feel cold in this strange world, Jesus, my little son. They have nailed you to your cross, inflicted bleeding wounds on your hands and feet and so they carry you before their eyes, lest they forget that they are allowed to sin, for you have paid for that right of theirs with your sacrifice. They say that you have risen from the dead, that you wander about amongst them. Then where are you? Perhaps they do not recognize you because you are flesh and blood? Perhaps they refuse to see your wounds, because these wounds are not painted on, but real? Perhaps they do not recognize you because you deny the false words they utter in your name — and so they deny you too. They dress you up in the Star of David. They kick you in the behind, mocking your stooped shoulders. They spit in your face, despising you for turning the other cheek. To them your wreath of thorns is the fur-edged hat of a rabbi, and they molest you in him. How great is their delight in mocking your living shudders of pain! What ecstasy in their dancing on your wriggling body, as they trample you with their spiked boots!

"Ignorant Jesus, foolish little boy — have you really learned the meaning of love? Is there a way of loving that begins with the Great, the Almighty, the All-Embracing, and reaches down to the tiny, the minute? Have you indeed managed to love that which is tiny and unobtrusive? Has your desire to love as a God not stood in the way of your loving as a man? Did it hurt you to take leave of your mother? Have you ever poured your soul into the open beaker of a woman's body? Were you ever a father?

"Look at my tiny nest, my home, my scarcely visible little flame of love. This is my road. Through the insignificant, through my own — towards the Endless, towards the heart of the world. Look, there is Miriam, my wife, lying in her bed, her heart aflutter with anguish at the thought of the sacrifice awaiting her child, Blimele (You?). Miriam has big brown Jewish eyes — your mother's eyes, filled with the dread of tomorrow — tomorrow of nineteen hundred and forty years after your birth.

"Blimele is asleep in her bed. In the cupboard hangs her little coat with the yellow Star of David sewn on to it. The world which you have raised has already burdened her thin shoulders with your fate, the fate of being a Jew. Soon, she will cleanse herself in pain, become sanctified by the flames of the stake. She is our hope.

"And here am I, Jesus, Simcha Bunim Berkovitch. Am I not like Joseph, your father? Here, I saw my own heart with my pen, I plane the rough raw words of my salute to the world which hates me, the world which you have failed to teach how to love.

"Thus I call you today. We all call you, Jesus, just as we call the souls of all generations — past, present and future — to come and bear witness to our trial — your trial."

Glossary

Ab damit!	Take it off! (Ger.)
Achtung!	Attention! (Ger.)
afikomen	Piece of matzo hidden during Passover feast, for children to find.
Aguda	Political party seeking to preserve orthodoxy in Jewish life.
ahava	love (Hebr.)
Alle Juden raus!	All the Jews out! (Ger.)
Älteste der Juden	Eldest of the Jews (Ger.)
Am Israel chai!	Long live the people of Israel! (Hebr.)
angst	fear (Ger.)
apikores	heretic (Gr.)
arbeiten	to work (Ger.)
Aufmachen!	Open up! (Ger.)
Aufschnitt	cold cuts of meat (Ger.)
baba	a kind of pastry (Slav.)
bellote	a card game (Fr.)
brodyage	riff-raff (Yidd.)
beschlagnahmt	confiscated, requisitioned (Ger.)
Bund	Jewish socialist party
chalom	dream (Hebr.)
cholent	dish served on the Sabbath (Yidd.)
chutzpah (or hutzpah)	impertinence, nerve
Das ist er!	That's him! (Ger.)
Das stinkt doch!	This stinks! (Ger.)
Der hat eine Nase wie ein Horn	He has a nose like a horn. (Ger.)
Du sollst arbeiten, jüdisches Schwein!	You must work, Jewish pig! (Ger.)
dybbuk	soul of dead person residing in the body of a living one. (Hebr.)
dzialka	plot of land (Pol.)
Eifersucht ist eine Leidenschaft die mit eifer sucht was Leiden schaft.	Jealousy is a passion which with passion seeks to inflict suffering. (Ger.)
Einkunftstelle	In the ghetto: post for turning in forbidden items, in exchange for some ghetto money (rumkis). (Ger.)
eintreten	line up (Ger.)

311

Eine jüdische Hure mit einem jüdischen Hurensohn	A Jewish whore with the son of a Jewish whore. (Ger.)
Eintopfgericht	stew, all the courses in one. (Ger.)
Ersatz	substitute (Ger.)
Familienandenken	family souvenirs (Ger.)
farbrokechts	vegetables for a soup (Yidd.)
Folks-Zeitung	the people's newspaper. Name of Yiddish socialist daily in Poland. (Yidd.)
Gemahl	husband (Ger.)
Gemara	the Talmud
gemütlich	cosy (Ger.)
Gettoverwaltung	German ghetto administration (Ger.)
golem	dummy, artificial man (Hebr.)
goy, pl: goyim	non-Jew(s) (Hebr.)
grober yung	person with no manners (Yidd.)
hachshara	preparatory training farm for Zionist youth.
Haggadah	text recited on Passover night (Hebr.)
Halacha	legislative part of the Talmud (Hebr.)
halah	white bread eaten on the Sabbath (Hebr.)
har . . . nar	master . . . idiot (Yidd.)
Hasid	follower, member of Jewish religious movement (Hebr.)
Halutza	female pioneer settler in Palestine (Hebr.)
hosen-kala	groom and bride (Hebr.)
Hashana habaa birushalayim!	Next year in Jerusalem! (Hebr.)
heder	Jewish religious school (Hebr.)
Himmelkommando	commando of the heavens (ghetto expression)
Holzschuhe	clogs (Ger.)
Hutzpah (or chutzpah)	nerve, arrogance (Hebr.)
Ich liebe dich, mich reizt deine schöne Gestalt.	I love you, I am tempted by your beautiful form. (Goethe: "Erlkönig")
Ich möchte dich nur für mich haben.	I want to have you only to myself. (Ger.)
Ich werde krepieren.	I will kick the bucket. (Ger.)
infolgedessen	consequently (Ger.)
Ja, ich hasse dich, kratziger Jude, mach das du fortkommst.	Yes, I hate you, mangy Jew, get lost! (Ger.)
Jude	Jew (Ger.)
Judenrein	clean of Jews (Ger.)
Junker	Prussian aristocrat, member of reactionary militaristic political party (Ger.)
Junkerheimat	Junker homeland (Ger.)

kaddish	prayer for a dead parent (Hebr.)
kalinka	Barberry tree (Slav.)
kibbitz	watch a game, offering unasked-for advice to players (Yidd.)
kiddush	the benediction over wine (Hebr.)
Kiddush-Hashem	to be martyred for being a Jew (Hebr.)
klepsidra	announcement of death, ghetto expression re someone's face
Kohelet	Book of Ecclesiastes
Kommst du vom Reich?	Are you from Germany? (Ger.)
kosher, kashrut	Jewish dietary law (kosherness. Hebr.)
Kripo (Kriminalpolizei)	Criminal Police (Ger.)
lody	ice cream (Pol.)
Los aber schnell!	Vanish, but quickly! (Ger.)
Lechaim	To life! (Hebr.)
Lech-lecho	Go forth ("The Lord said to Abraham, 'Go forth . . .'" Genesis. Hebr.)
mameshe	endearment for mother (Yidd.)
matzo, matzos	unleavened bread eaten during Passover (Hebr.)
mazal-tov	good luck (Hebr.)
menorah	a candelabrum (Hebr.)
mentch	a person, a decent human being (Yidd.)
meshuga, meshugas	mad, madness (Hebr.)
mezuzah	small tube, containing blessing, attached to doorpost (Hebr.)
Mishna	part of the Talmud (Hebr.)
mitzva	good deed (Hebr.)
Morgen . . . nächste Woche	Tomorrow . . . next week (Ger.)
Nach oben!	Up there! (Ger.)
Napoleonkis	a kind of French pastry (Pol.)
panienka, panienki	young lady, young ladies (Pol.)
Pardes	pleasure garden, paradise, according to esoteric philosophy (Hebr.)
Passierschein	a pass, a permit (Ger.)
pintele Yid	the dot of Jewishness
Poale-Zion	Zionist workers' party
Polizei	police (Ger.)
Presess	chairman
pshat, remez, drash	three methods of interpretation (Hebr.)
Rabiner	non-orthodox rabbi
Rashi	commentator on the Bible and the Talmud
Ressort (Arbeitsressort)	name for factories in the ghetto (Ger.)
Sehnsucht nach der Heimat	longing for the homeland (Ger.)

sheigetz	non-Jewish boy, Jewish boy who misbehaves (Yidd.)
Shalom-aleichem	greeting: Peace be with you.
Sejm	Polish parliament (Pol.)
servus	students' greeting
Simchat-Torah	A holiday celebrating the completion of the year's reading of the Torah.
Shishka	privileged person in the ghetto
Sitra-achra	the forces of evil
Seuchengefahr	epidemic, danger of infection
Sonderkommando (Sonder)	special unit of the Jewish police in the ghetto
Sperre	ban, house arrest or curfew
shlimazl, shlimiel	unlucky person (Yidd.)
shnorrer	beggar (Yidd.)
shochat	ritual slaughterer (Hebr.)
shtetl	small town (Yidd.)
Siehe mal diese hübsche Dame im Pelzmantel!	Look at this pretty lady in the fur coat! (Ger.)
Sie sollen . . .	You should . . . (Ger.)
So was!	such a thing! (Ger.)
Sperrkonto	blocked bank account (Ger.)
tateshe	endearment for father (Yidd.)
Torah	the Pentateuch (Hebr.)
Totenkopf	death's-head (Ger.)
treyfa	unkosher food (Hebr.)
tzimmes	vegetable or fruit dessert (Yidd.)
Überfallkommando	raid commando (Ger.)
Übersiedlung	resettlement (Ger.)
Vertrauungsmann der Kripo	confidence man of the criminal police (Ger.)
Volksdeutsche	a German born in Poland (Ger.)
Warthegau	Polish territory incorporated into the Third Reich
wirklich	really (Ger.)
Wissenschaftliche Abteilung	Scientific Department (Ger.)
Wohngebiet	place of residence (Ger.)
Wo ist das Brot?	Where is the bread? (Ger.)
wydzielaczka	woman distributing soup in the ghetto (Pol.)
Yeke	a German, (derisive) (Yidd.)
Yid	a Jew (Yidd.)
yeshiva	institution of higher Talmudic learning (Hebr.)
Yom-Kippur	the Day of Atonement
yomtov, or yom-tov	holiday
Zukunft	the future (Ger. Yidd.)

Library of World Fiction

S. Y. Agnon
A Guest for the Night: A Novel

S. Y. Agnon
In the Heart of the Seas

S. Y. Agnon
Two Tales: Betrothed & Edo and Enam

Karin Boye
Kallocain

Chava Rosenfarb
The Tree of Life: A Trilogy of Life in the Lodz Ghetto
Book I: On the Brink of the Precipice, 1939

Aksel Sandemose
The Werewolf

Isaac Bashevis Singer
The Manor and the Estate